W9-BHP-078

STONE'S FALL

A Novel

IAIN PEARS

ALFRED A. KNOPF CANADA

PUBLISHED BY ALFRED A. KNOPF CANADA

Copyright © 2009 Iain Pears

www.randomhouse.ca

Library and Archives Canada Cataloguing in Publication

Pears, Iain
Stone's fall/ Iain Pears

ISBN 978-0-676-97984-8

1. Title.

PR6066.E175S76 2009   823'.914   C2008-905683-3

First Edition

Printed and bound in the United States of America

1 3 5 7 9 8 6 4 2

To my mother

PART ONE

Paris, March 1953

The Church of St.-Germain des Prés, at the start of what was supposed to be spring, was a miserable place, made worse by the drabness of a city still in a state of shock, worse still by the little coffin in front of the altar which was my reason for being there, worse again by the aches and pains of my body as I kneeled.

She'd died a week before I arrived. I hadn't even realised she was still alive; she must have been well into her eighties, and the hardships of the past few years had weakened many a younger person. She would not have been impressed, but something approaching a real prayer for her did come into my mind just before I struggled back onto the pew. Age has few compensations; the indignity of discomfort, the effort to conceal constant nagging pain, is most certainly not one of them.

Until I read the *Figaro* that morning and saw the announcement, I had been enjoying myself. I was on a farewell tour; the powers that be had scraped together enough foreign currency to allow me to travel. My last visit to the foreign bureaux before I retired. Not many people could do that sort of thing these days—and would not until foreign exchange restrictions were lifted. It was a little mark of respect, and one that I appreciated.

It was a fine enough service, I thought, although I was not an expert. The priests took their time, the choir sang prettily, the prayers were said, and it was all over. A short eulogy paid tribute to her tireless, selfless work for the unfortunate but said nothing of her character. The congregation was mainly freshly scrubbed and intense-looking children, who were clipped around the ear by teachers if they made any untoward noise. I looked around, to see who would take charge of the next round, but no one seemed to know what to do. Eventually the undertaker took over. The body, he said, would be interred in Père Lachaise that afternoon, at two o'clock, at 15 Chemin du Dragon. All who wished to attend were welcome. Then the pallbearers picked up the coffin and marched out, leaving the mourners feeling lost and cold.

"Excuse me, but is your name Braddock? Matthew Braddock?"

A quiet voice of a young man, neatly dressed, with a black band around his arm. I nodded, and he held out his hand. "My name is Whitely," he said. "Harold Whitely, of Henderson, Lansbury, Fenton. I recognised you from newsreels."

"Oh?"

"Solicitors, you know. We dealt with Madame Robillard's residual legal business in England. Not that there was much of it. I am so glad to meet you; I was planning to write in any case, once I got back."

"Really? She didn't leave me any money, did she?"

He smiled. "I'm afraid not. By the time she died she was really quite poor."

"Goodness gracious me," I said, with a smile.

"Why the surprise?"

"She was very wealthy when I knew her."

"I'd heard that. I knew her only as a sweet old lady with a weakness for worthy causes. But I found her charming on the few occasions we met. Quite captivating, in fact."

"Yes, that's her," I replied. "Why did you come to the funeral?"

"A tradition of the firm," he said with a grimace. "We bury all our clients. A last service. But, you know—it's a trip to Paris, and there's not much opportunity for that these days. Unfortunately, I could get hold of so little currency I have to go straight back this evening."

"I have a little more than that, so would you care for a drink?"

He nodded, and we walked down the Boulevard St.-Germain to a café, past grim buildings blackened with the filth of a century or more of smoke and fumes. Whitely—formerly Captain Whitely, so he told me— had an annoying tendency to grip my elbow at the difficult bits to make sure I did not trip and fall. It was thoughtful, although the assumption of decrepitude was irritating.

A good brandy: she deserved no less, and we drank her health by the plate-glass window as we sat on our rickety wooden chairs. "Madame

Robillard," we intoned several times over, becoming more garrulous as we drank. He told me of life in Intelligence during the war—the time of his life, he said wistfully, now gone for good and replaced with daily toil as a London solicitor. I told him stories of reporting for the BBC; of D-Day, of telling the world about the Blitz. All yesterday, and another age.

"Who was her husband?" I asked. "I assume he is long dead."

"Robillard died about a decade ago. He ran the orphanages and schools with her."

"Is that why all those children were in the church?"

"I imagine so. She started her first home after the war—the first war. There were so many orphans and abandoned children, and she somehow got involved with them. By the end there were about ten or twelve schools and orphanages, I gather, all run on the very latest humanitarian principles. They consumed her entire fortune, in fact, so much so that I imagine they will all be taken over by the State now."

"A good enough use for it. When I knew her she was married to Lord Ravenscliff. That was more than forty years ago, though."

I paused. Whitely looked blank. "Have you heard of Ravenscliff?" I enquired.

"No," he said. "Should I have?"

I thought, then shook my head. "Maybe not. He was an industrialist, but most of his companies disappeared in the Depression. Some closed, others were bought up. Vickers took over a few, I remember. The lone and level sands stretch far away, you know."

"Pardon?"

"Nothing." I breathed in the thick air of cigarette smoke and damp, then attracted the waiter's eye and called for more drinks. It seemed a good idea. Whitely was not cheering me up at all. It was quiet; not many people around, and the waiters were prepared to work hard for the few customers they had. One of them almost smiled, but managed to restrain himself.

"Tell me about her," I said when our glasses were refilled once more. "I hadn't seen her for many years. I only discovered she was dead by chance."

"Not much to say. She lived in an apartment just up the road here, went to church, did good works, and outlived her friends. She read a great deal, and loved going to the cinema. I understand she had a weakness for Humphrey Bogart films. Her English was excellent, for a Frenchwoman."

"She lived in England when I knew her. Hungarian by birth, though."

"Apart from that there's nothing to say, is there?"

"I suppose not. A quiet and blameless life. What were you going to write to me about?"

"Hmm? Oh, that. Well, Mr. Henderson, you know, our senior partner. He died a year ago and we've been clearing out his papers. There was a package for you."

"For me? What is it? Gold? Jewels? Dollar bills? Swiss watches? I could use some of those. We prospective old-age pensioners . . ."

"I couldn't say what's in it. It's sealed. It was part of the estate of Mr. Henry Cort . . ."

"Good heavens."

"You knew him, I assume?"

"We met many years ago."

"As I say, part of the Cort estate. Curious thing is that it carried instructions that you were to be given it only on Madame Robillard's death. Which was very exciting for us. There isn't much excitement in a solicitor's office, let me tell you. Hence my intention to write to you. Do you know what is in it?"

"I have absolutely no idea. I scarcely knew Cort at all, and certainly haven't even cast eyes on him for more than thirty years. I came across him when I was writing a biography of Madame Robillard's first husband. That's how I knew her as well."

"I hope it was a great success."

"Unfortunately not. I never even finished it. The reaction of most publishers was about as enthusiastic as your own was when I mentioned his name."

"My apologies."

"It was a long time ago. I went back to being a journalist, then joined the BBC when it started up. When did Cort die?" Curious how, the older you get, the more important other people's deaths become.

"Nineteen forty-four."

"When I get back, send me your package. If it's valuable, I'll be glad to get it. But I doubt it will be. As far as I remember, Cort didn't like me very much. I certainly didn't like him."

And then we ran out of things to say to each other, as strangers of different generations do. I paid and began my old man's routine of wrapping myself up, coat, hat, scarf, gloves, pulling everything tight to keep out the bitterness of the weather. Whitely pulled on a thin, threadbare coat. Army demob, by the look of it. But he didn't seem half as cold as I was at the thought of going outside.

"Are you going to the cemetery?"

"That would be the death of me. She would not have expected it and probably would have thought me sentimental. And I have a train at four. When I get back I will dig out my old notes to see how much I actually remember, and how much I merely think I remember."

I took my train from the Gare de Lyon that afternoon, and the cold of Paris faded, along with thoughts of Madame Robillard, formerly Elizabeth, Lady Ravenscliff, as I went south to the greater warmth of a Mediterranean spring.

She remained in the back of my mind wherever I went, whatever I saw, until I returned to my little house in Hampstead to dig out my old notes. Then I went to visit Mr. Whitely.

London, 1909

CHAPTER 1

When I became involved in the life and death of John William Stone, First (and last) Baron Ravenscliff, I was working as a journalist. You note I do not say I *was* a journalist. Merely working as one. It is one of the better-kept secrets of the trade that you have to be quite serious if you wish to have any success. You spend long hours hanging around in pubs, waiting for something to happen, and when it does, it is often of no great interest. I specialised in court cases, and so lived my life around the Old Bailey, eating with my fellows, dozing with them during boring testimony, drinking with them as we awaited a verdict, then running back to the office to knock out some deathless prose.

Murders were the best: "Railway Trunk Murderer to Hang." "Ealing Strangler Begs for Mercy." They all had nicknames, the good ones, anyway. I made up many of them myself; I had a sort of facility for a snappy phrase. I even did what no other reporter did, which was occasionally to investigate a case myself; I spent a portion of my paper's money on policemen, who were as susceptible then to a small inducement—a drink, a meal, a present for their children—as they are now. I became adept at understanding how the police and murderers worked. Far too good at it, in the eyes of my grander colleagues, who thought me squalid. In my defence I can say that it was an interest shared with much of the newspaper-buying public, who loved nothing more than a good garrotting to read about. The best thing was a beautiful young woman, done to death in a particularly horrible way. Always a crowd pleaser, that.

And it was because of this small expertise of mine that I came across

Lord Ravenscliff. Or his widow, from whom I received a letter one fine April morning, asking me to come and see her. This was about a fortnight after he died, although that event had rather passed me by at the time.

"Anyone know anything about Lady Elizabeth Ravenscliff?" I asked in the Duck, where I was breakfasting on a pint of beer and a sausage roll. It was fairly empty that morning; there had not been a decent trial for weeks and none in the offing either. Even the judges were complaining that the criminal classes seemed to have lost their appetite for work.

My enquiry was met with a communal grunt that signified a total lack of interest.

"Elizabeth, Lady Ravenscliff. Do get it right." It was George Short who replied, an old man who was the very definition of a hack. He could turn his hand to anything, and was a better reporter blind drunk than any of his fellows—including me—sober. Give him some information and he would write it up. And if you didn't give him some information, he would make it up so perfectly the result was better than the truth. Which is, in fact, another rule of journalism. Fiction is generally better than reality, is usually more trustworthy, and always more believable.

George, who dressed so appallingly that he was once arrested for vagrancy, put down his pint—his fourth that morning, and it was only ten o'clock—and wiped his stubbly chin. Like the aristocracy, you can tell a reporter's status by his clothes and manners. The worse they are, the higher up they are, as only the lowly have to make a good impression. George had to impress no one. Everyone knew him, from judges down to the criminals themselves, and all called him George, and most would stand him a drink. At that stage I was more than a beginner, but less than an old hand—I had abandoned my dark suit and was now affecting tweeds and a pipe, aiming at the literary, raffish look which, I thought, quite suited me. Few agreed with my opinion, but I felt rather splendid when I looked at myself in the mirror of a morning.

"Very well. Elizabeth, Lady Ravenscliff, then. Who is she?" I replied.

"The wife of Lord Ravenscliff. Widow, rather."

"And he was?"

"A baron," said George, who sometimes took the rule about giving all relevant information a little too far. "Given a peerage in 1902, as I recall. I don't know why, he probably bought it like they all do. John Stone was his name. Moneyman of some sort. Fell out of a window a couple of weeks back. Only an accident, unfortunately."

"What sort of moneyman?"

"How should I know? He had money. What's it to you, anyway?"

I handed him the letter.

George tapped his pipe on the heel of his shoe and sniffed loudly. "Not very informative," he replied, handing it back. "Can't be for your looks, or your talent, or your dress sense. Or your wit and charm. Maybe she needs a gardener?"

I made a face at him.

"Are you going to go?"

"Of course."

"Don't expect much. And be on your guard. These people take a lot, and give nothing back." It was the nearest I ever heard him come to a political opinion.

CHAPTER 2

I presented myself the next day at the address in St. James's Square—an impressive town house of the sort occupied by the wealthy merchant and financial classes, although these were gradually moving out to leafier parts of town. I had found out all but nothing about Lady Ravenscliff herself, so filled the gap with imaginings. A dowager in her late sixties, dressed in the high fashion of thirty years ago when she was young and (I was prepared to bet) tolerably pretty. An air of geraniums about her—my grandmother used to grow them, and the particular heavy smell of the plant has always been associated in my mind with respectable old age. Or perhaps not; perhaps a little blowsy and crude, North Country made good, still socially insecure, a chip on her shoulder from having wealth but little position to go with it.

My thoughts were interrupted when I was ushered in to meet a woman I took to be a daughter or a companion. I guessed her age to be about forty or so, while Ravenscliff had been nearly seventy when he died.

"Good afternoon," I said. "My name is Matthew Braddock. I have an appointment with your—mother? Perhaps . . . ?"

She smiled in a vaguely perplexed way. "I very much hope not, Mr.

Braddock," she replied. "Unless you are in contact with the spirit world, you can have no rendezvous with her."

"I received a letter from Lady Ravenscliff . . ." I began.

"I am she," she said in a soft voice, "and I will take your confusion as a compliment. A slightly fumbled one, perhaps, but appreciated, nonetheless."

She had enjoyed the little exchange; I could see her eyes dancing in her otherwise expressionless face, as though she was grateful for the first amusement she had had for many days. She was dressed in mourning, but made the black attire seem alluring; she was wearing what was then called a lampshade dress, with a jacket that fitted close around the neck, and a simple necklace of very large grey pearls which stood out against the black velvet of the clothes. I knew next to nothing of such things, only enough to realise that the clothes were the latest in what women considered fashionable. Certainly, even to an amateur like me, the general impression was all very striking. And only the colour suggested anything like mourning.

I sat down. Nobody likes appearing to be a fool, and I had not made a very good start. The fact that she was quite pleased with the way things were going did not help. Only later—very much later—did I consider that my inept beginnings might have had something to do with the lady herself, for she was beautiful, although if you considered her face there was no obvious reason to think so. It was not what you might call conventionally handsome; in fact, you might have almost concluded she was slightly odd looking. There was a distinct asymmetry to her features: her nose and mouth too big; her eyebrows too dark. But she was beautiful because she thought she was so, and so dressed and sat and moved in a fashion which elicited the appropriate response from those who saw her. I did not consciously notice this at the time, but it must have had some effect on me.

The best thing to do, I decided, was nothing. She had summoned me, so it was for her to begin. This allowed her to take control of the meeting, but that was no more than recognising reality. So I arranged myself as best I could and tried hard to conceal my discomfiture.

"I have spent much time recently reading the newspapers, Mr. Braddock," she began. "What I am told are your innumerable contributions."

"I am gratified, Your Ladyship."

"It was not for your literary talent—although I have no doubt you are skilled in your chosen occupation. It is because I have need of someone with an ability to amass information and study it dispassionately. You seem to be just such a person."

"Thank you."

"Unfortunately, I also need someone who can be discreet, which I believe is not normally a characteristic of reporters."

"We are professional gossips," I said, cheerful again now I was on to a topic I knew about. "I am paid to be indiscreet."

"And if you are paid to be discreet?"

"Oh, in that case the sphinx will seem like a chatterbox in comparison."

She waved her hand and thought awhile. I had been offered no refreshment of any sort. "I have a proposition for you. How much do you earn at the moment?"

This was an impolite question. By the standards of journalism I was paid adequately, although I knew that by the standards of Lady Ravenscliff it was probably a pitiful sum. Masculine pride does not like to be so easily damaged.

"Why do you want to know that?" I asked cautiously.

"Because in order to secure your services I will no doubt have to pay you somewhat more than you receive already. I wish to know how much more."

I grunted. "Well, if you must know, I am paid £125 a year."

"Yes," she said sweetly, "you are."

"I beg your pardon?"

"Naturally, I discovered this for myself. I wanted to see whether you would give me an accurate figure, or inflate it in the hope of getting more out of me. You have made a good start as an honest man."

"And you have made a very poor start as a worthy employer."

She acknowledged the reproof, although without any sign of remorse. "That is true. But you will see in a moment why I am so cautious."

"I am waiting."

She frowned, which did not suit her naturally even complexion, and thought for a moment. "Well," she said eventually, "I would like to offer you a job. It will pay £350 a year, plus any expenses you might incur, and continue for seven years, no matter how long you take to fulfil the task I will give you. This will be an inducement for you to accept the offer, and be discreet. Should you fail in the latter, then all payment will be suspended immediately."

It took a few moments to absorb this. It was a phenomenal sum. I would easily be able to save a hundred a year, and so could look forward to perhaps another four years afterwards without having to worry about money. Eleven years of blessed security, in all. What could she possibly want that would justify that sum? Whatever it was, I intended to do it. As long as it didn't involve too long a gaol sentence.

"You are aware, perhaps, that my husband, Lord Ravenscliff, died a fortnight ago?"

I nodded.

"It was a terrible accident—I still cannot believe it. However, it happened. And I must now live as a widow."

Not for long, though, I bet, I thought to myself as I composed my face into an expression of suitable sympathy.

"Please accept my condolences for your loss," I said piously.

She treated the conventional remark with the solemnity it deserved, which is to say that she ignored it totally.

"As you no doubt know, death is not merely an emotional matter for those who are bereaved. The law demands attention as well."

"The police are involved?"

She looked very queerly at me. "Of course not," she replied. "I mean that there is a will to be read, estates to be settled, bequests to be made."

"Oh. Yes. I'm sorry."

She paused for a long while after that little exchange; perhaps the calm presentation was more difficult for her than it appeared.

"We were married for nearly twenty years, Mr. Braddock. In that time we were as happy and content as a couple can be. I hope you can appreciate that."

"I'm sure of it . . ." I replied, wondering what this was all about.

"So you can realise that when I was read his will, which gave a substantial legacy to his child, I was surprised."

"Were you?" I asked cautiously.

"We had no children."

"Ah."

"And so I wish you to discover the identity of this child, so that the terms of his will can—"

"Just a moment," I said in a rush, holding up my hand. The small amount of information she'd given me had already generated so many questions that I was having difficulties holding all of them in my head at the same time.

"Just a moment," I repeated more calmly. "Can we go through this a little more slowly? First of all, why are you telling me this? I mean, why me? You know nothing about me."

"Oh, I do. You come recommended."

"Really? By whom?"

"By your editor. We have known him for some time. He said you were a fine ferreter out of other people's secrets. He also told me you could be discreet and, incidentally, told me how much you are paid."

"There must be someone better than me."

"That is modest of you. And do not think I have not considered the matter carefully. In fact, there are few people capable of performing such a task. Lawyers occasionally employ such people, but none I know of. There are investigative agencies, but I do not feel inclined to trust someone who does not come personally recommended. Besides, they might well require more information than I can provide. I do not know whether this child is alive, when he or she was born, who the mother was. I do not even know in which country it might have been born. There is just one sentence in his will."

"And that's it? Nothing else at all?"

"Nothing at all."

"What did the will say, exactly?"

She paused for a moment, and then recited. " 'Conscious of my failings in so many matters, and wishing to make amends for past ills, I direct that the sum of £250,000 be left to my child, whom I have never previously acknowledged.' So you see, it is not a small matter." She looked at me evenly as she spoke.

I gaped. Money wasn't my speciality, but I knew a gigantic fortune when I lost track of the noughts dancing in my head.

"That's some failing," I commented. She replied with a frosty look. "Sorry."

"I wish to honour my husband's will to the letter, if it is possible. I need to inform this person of the bequest. I cannot do that until I know who he, or she, is."

"You really have no more information?"

She shook her head. "The will referred to some papers in his safe.

There were none there. At least, nothing of any relevance. I have looked several times."

"But if your husband conducted an—ah—"

I really did not know at all how to manage this conversation. Even with women of my own social class it would have been impossible to ask directly—your husband had a mistress? When? Where? Who? With a lady in the first flush of mourning it was completely beyond my capabilities.

Luckily, she decided to help me out. I rather wished she hadn't, as it made me even more uncomfortable. "I do not believe my husband was in the habit of taking lovers," she said calmly. "Certainly not in the last decade or so. Before then I know of no one, and there is no reason why I should not have known had any such person existed."

"Why is that?"

She smiled at me, again with a slightly mocking twinkle in her eye. "You are trying to contain your shock, but not doing it very well. Let me simply say that I never doubted his love for me, nor he mine, even though he made it perfectly clear to me that I was free to do as I chose. Do you understand?"

"I think so."

"He knew perfectly well that I would accept anything he wished to tell me about and so had no reason to conceal anything from me."

"I see."

I didn't, of course; I didn't see at all. My morals were—and still are—those of my class and background, that is to say far more strict than those of people like the Ravenscliffs. It was an early lesson: the rich are a good deal tougher than most people. I suppose it is why they are rich.

"If you will excuse me for saying so, why did he make life so complicated for people? He must have known that it was going to be difficult to find this child."

"It may be you will find an answer to that in your enquiries."

She would never have made much of a living as a saleswoman in a department store, so it was perhaps as well that she was wealthy. Still, it would be an intriguing problem and, best of all, I got paid whatever the result: £350 a year was a powerful incentive. I was getting increasingly ill-humoured about the succession of bachelor lodging houses I had lived in for the past few years. I wasn't entirely certain whether I wanted domesticity and stability—wife, dog, house in the country. Or whether I wanted to flee abroad, and ride Arabian stallions across the desert, and sleep by flickering campfires at night. Either would do, as long as I could get away from the smell of boiled vegetables and furniture polish that hit me full in the face every time I returned home at night.

I was bored, and the presence of this beautiful woman with her extraordinary request and air of unfathomable wealth stirred up feelings I had long ignored. I wanted to do something different from hanging around the law courts and the pubs. This task she was offering me, and the money that went with it, were the only things likely to show up that could change my circumstances.

"You have become very thoughtful, Mr. Braddock."

"I was wondering how I would go about this task, if I decide to accept your offer."

"You have decided to accept it," she said gravely. From many people, there would have been a tone of contempt in the statement. She, on the other hand, managed to say it in a serene, almost friendly tone that was quite disarming.

"I suppose I have. Not without misgivings, though."

"I'm sure those will pass."

"I need, first of all, to discover everything I can about your husband's life. I will need to talk to his lawyer about the will. I don't know. Have you looked through his correspondence?"

She shook her head, tears suddenly welling up into her eyes. "I can't face it yet," she said. "I'm sorry."

I thought she was apologising for her laziness, then realised it was for the display of weakness she was showing me. Quite right. People like her weren't supposed to get emotional about a little thing like a husband dying. Should I have taken out a handkerchief and helped to dab her eyes? I would have enjoyed it; it would have required me to go and sit by her on the sofa, bring strength to her frailty. I changed the subject instead, and pretended I hadn't noticed.

"I imagine I will have to ensure that no one knows why I am asking these questions," I said in a louder voice than necessary. "I do not wish to cause you embarrassment."

"It would cause me no embarrassment," she replied, the absurdity of the idea bringing her back to her senses. "But I suppose a general knowledge of your task might generate false claimants. I have already told a few people—your editor included—that I am thinking of commissioning a biography. It is the sentimental thing that a woman with much grief and money might do."

"And as I am a reporter," I said, cheerful once more to find myself back on home territory, "I can ask indiscreet questions and seem merely as though I am fired by a love of the squalid and vulgar."

"Precisely. You will fit the part very well, I'm sure. Now, I have made an appointment for you with Mr. Joseph Bartoli, my husband's general manager. He has drawn up a contract for you."

"And you?"

"I think you should come and see me every week to report progress. All Lord Ravenscliff's private correspondence is here, and you will have to read it as well, I imagine. You may ask any questions you have then. Although I do intend to travel to France in the near future. Much as I loved my husband and miss him, the conventions on mourning in this country I find very oppressive. But I know I would shock and scandalise if I acted inappropriately, so I must seek a little relief elsewhere."

"You are not English."

Another smile. "My goodness, if that is how quick you are, we are not going to make much progress. No, I am not English. I am Hungarian by origin, although I lived in France until I married."

"You have not the slightest trace of any foreign accent," I said, feeling a little ruffled.

"Thank you. I have been in England for a long time. And I have never found languages difficult. Manners are a different matter, though. Those are more difficult to learn."

She stood and shook my hand as I prepared to leave; she wore a soft, utterly feminine perfume which complemented perfectly the black clothes she wore. Her large grey eyes held mine as she said goodbye.

A drink. Either to celebrate or to recover, I wasn't sure, but I certainly needed assistance to think about the wave of change that had just swept over my life. In about forty-five minutes I had changed from being a jobbing reporter on £125 a year to someone earning nearly three times as much and able to do pretty much as I pleased. If that did not call for a celebration, I do not know what would, and there is a decent pub in Apple Tree Yard, just round the corner from St. James's Square, which caters for the servants who work in the big houses, and the suppliers who keep those inhabitants in the style they require. Two drinks later, I was beginning to feel fairly grand. I would take a house, buy some new clothes. A decent pair of shoes. A new hat. Eat in hotel restaurants. Take a cab every now and then. Life would be very fine.

And I could do my appointed task with as much diligence as I chose. Lady Ravenscliff, it appeared, was still in shock over the loss of her husband and the discovery of his secret life. She had depended on him and looked up to him. Not surprising that she was now throwing his money around.

Why investigate at all? I wouldn't have done. If her husband hadn't troubled to find out who his wretched child was, why should his widow? It seemed to me like inflicting quite unnecessary self-punishment, but what did I know about the mentality of widows? Maybe it was just curiosity, being childless herself, to discover what a child of her husband would be like. Maybe she wanted to find out something about the woman who had succeeded where she had failed.

CHAPTER 3

The offices of Ravenscliff's general manager were in the City, at 15 Moorgate, an anonymous street of five- and six-storey buildings, all erected for commercial use in the past half century. There was nothing remarkable about the street or the people in it; the usual bustle of traders and agents, of young men with spotty faces, top hats, ill-fitting suits and shirts with stiff collars. It was a street of insurance brokers and stockbrokers and grain traders and metal dealers, those who imported and exported, sold before they bought and contrived to keep themselves and the Empire at whose centre they were in liquid funds. I had never liked it very much, this part of town; the City absorbs bright youths and knocks the spirit out of them. It has to; it is the inevitable result of poring over figures eleven hours a day, six days a week, in chilly offices where no talking is allowed and frivolity is punishable by dismissal.

The Stock Exchange is different; I was passing through once when some jobbers decided to set fire to the coattails of a grandee, who was billowing plumes of smoke for several minutes before he noticed. Fights with bread rolls arcing over the trading floor are a daily event, American Funds assaulting Foreign Railways. They work hideous hours for low pay, and lose their jobs easily even though they make their masters much money. It is not surprising that they have a tendency towards the infantile, for that is how they are treated. In the pubs and taverns of the City I had made many good friends amongst the jobbers and brokers, but amongst the bankers few, if any. They are different; they see themselves as gentlemen—not an accusation that could ever be hurled at a stockbroker.

I did not know what to expect of Mr. Joseph Bartoli. This is not surprising, as he filled an unusual position, although the evolution of capitalism will throw up more of his type as industry becomes more complex. Ravenscliff (I later learned) had so many fingers in so many pies that it was difficult for him to keep track of them; nor could he involve himself in day-to-day operations as a mine owner or steel founder might be expected to do. For this he had managers in each enterprise. Mr. Bartoli oversaw the managers, and informed Ravenscliff how each business was developing.

The offices he occupied, above a ships' chandler, were modest enough—one room for himself, one for clerks, of whom there were about a dozen, and one room for ranks of files and records, but he was so large that the room he had taken as his own was nearly filled by his presence. The little space left over was inhabited by a strange pixie-like character with bright eyes and a pointed goatee beard. Somewhere in his forties, medium height, slender, wearing a brown suit and carrying a pair of bright yellow leather gloves in one hand. He said almost nothing all the time I was there, and we were not introduced; rather, he sat on a seat in a corner reading a file, only occasionally looking up and smiling sympathetically at me. I wished I had been dealing with him, rather than with Bartoli. He seemed a much more agreeable fellow.

In contrast, Bartoli wore an orthodox black suit, but kept on scratching himself and running his finger around his collar as though it irked him. His vast belly fitted behind the desk with difficulty, and his red face and whiskers reminded me greatly of many of the regulars I often saw ranged alongside the bars of nearby pubs. His voice was loud and heavily accented, although it took me some time to realise what the accent was. Manchester-Italian, I decided after a while.

"Sit down," he said, gesturing at an uncomfortable chair on the other side of the desk. "You'll be Burdock."

"Braddock," I replied. "Mr."

"Yes, yes. Sit down." He had the gestures of the foreigner; extravagant, and excessive, the sort of mannerisms which an Englishman distrusts. I took against Bartoli instantly. And (I must admit) against Ravenscliff, for putting such a man in a position to give orders. I was a great patriot then. I do not know whether I say so in pride or in sorrow.

He looked at me piercingly, as though sizing me up for some appointment and finding me wanting. "I do not approve of what Lady Ravenscliff has decided to do," he said eventually. "I should tell you this frankly, as you might as well know now that you will get little encouragement from me."

"What do you think she has asked me to do?" I asked, wondering whether he knew of the will.

"The biography of Lord Ravenscliff," he said.

"Yes. Well, as you please. But I cannot see what your objection is."

He snorted. "You are a journalist."

"Yes."

"What do you know of business?"

"All but nothing."

"That's what I thought. Ravenscliff was a businessman. Perhaps the greatest this country has ever known. To understand him, you have to understand business, industry, finance. Do you?"

"No. And until yesterday morning I'd never even heard of him. All I can say is that Lady Ravenscliff has asked me to do this job. I did not solicit it. If you want to know why she chose me, you must ask her. Like you, I could think of many people better able to do justice to the subject. But that was her decision and she offered such terms that I would have been mad to refuse. Perhaps I will do poorly; certainly I will unless I have the co-operation of those who knew him."

He grunted and pulled a folder from his desk. At least I had not puffed myself up and claimed an expertise I did not possess.

"The payment is absurd," he commented.

"I quite agree. But if someone offers you a higher price than you anticipated for one of your products do you bargain them down?"

He tossed it over. "Sign, then," he said.

"I think I should read it first."

"You won't find anything unexpected. You are to write a biography of Lord Ravenscliff and will submit the finished manuscript to Her Ladyship for approval. You are forbidden to discuss anything which might be relevant to any of the companies listed in the appendix. Expenses will be paid at my discretion."

I had never come across a contract with an appendix before, nor one so big, but then I had never been paid so much either.

"How do I get paid?" I asked as I read—more for form's sake than anything else. He had summed the contents up admirably.

"I will send a cheque to your address every week."

"I do not have a bank account."

"Then you'd better get one."

I felt like asking him—where do I start? But knew that his already low opinion of me would fall even further. The paper paid me weekly in a brown envelope. By the time I had paid bed and board, what was left over usually remained—although only for a short while—in my pocket until it was handed over to publicans or music hall owners.

I had thought when I arrived at the office that Bartoli would give me all the information I needed on Ravenscliff's business, but in fact he told me nothing. He would answer questions, but first of all I would have to know what to ask. I would need to make specific requests before he would let me see any papers and even then—such was the hint—he might prove unco-operative.

"In that case," I said cheerfully, "I would like to know—if it is possible—everywhere he went."

"When?"

"Throughout his career."

"Are you mad?"

"No. I also want a list of everybody he knew, or met."

Bartoli looked at me. "Lord Ravenscliff must have encountered tens of thousands of people. He travelled incessantly, throughout Europe, the Empire and to the Americas."

"Look," I said patiently. "I am meant to write a biography which people will want to read. I am going to need personal details. How did he start? Who were his friends and family? What is it like travelling around the world? This is the sort of thing people are interested in. Not how much money he made in one year or the next. No one cares about that."

He annoyed me; he treated me with neither seriousness nor consideration. I have never liked being treated like that. My colleagues believe I am overly sensitive to slights, real or imagined. Perhaps so, but it is a tendency which has served me well over the years. Dislike and resentment are great stimulants. Bartoli had converted me from someone who thought solely about the amount of money he was paid into someone who would have been determined to do the job properly even if he hadn't been paid at all.

CHAPTER 4

I emerged from the office thinking it was time to start work, and there was one obvious place to begin. Seyd & Co. was, by the standards of the City of London, a venerable institution. It had begun near half a century before to report on the credit-worthiness of traders wishing to borrow money from banks, and its investigations had gradually come to cover all aspects of finance. The more complex business became, the more obscure the origins of merchants, the greater the possibilities for duplicity and deception. And the more opportunities for companies like Seyd's to make money by shining light into the murkier recesses of man's greed.

For the most part—and officially—their business was to produce guides. The *Birmingham Commercial List. California and Its Resources.* All of which had to be bought by importers and exporters, dealers and merchants to avoid imposition by scoundrels. But very quietly and discreetly they did much more than that. By its nature, the City was full of rogues and thieves. But thieves have their codes of honour, and Seyd's winkled out those who did not follow the rules. Those who claimed financial backers who did not exist, who forgot to mention convictions for fraud in far-off countries. Who mentioned their assets, but not their debts. Whose word, in other words, was not their bond.

Once upon a time a company like Seyd's was not necessary, for the city of money was a small place, and everyone knew their clients. Life was simple when bankers only accepted people they had dined with. They dealt with gentlemen, and there was nothing easier to know about than the extent of a gentleman's estate, or the solvency of his family. Now it is a gibbering Babel of unknowns. Is a man a penniless scoundrel or really one of the richest men in the Habsburg Empire? Does he really have a lucrative contract in Buenos Aires, or in reality should he be in gaol for having run from his creditors? How can one tell? Dissimulation is the first trick of banker and conman alike.

Seyd's discovered the truth. Not always, and not perfectly, but better than anyone else. I knew because I had on occasion done some work for them. I had been approached a few years previously to discover something of a man who was setting up as a company promoter in the north of England. He claimed to be able to bring seven cotton producers together to combine into one larger unit that could then be offered for sale. All he needed was some capital . . .

I had to take a day off work to travel north, but I got the truth out soon enough. Ernest Mason left the country a day before he could be arrested for fraud, but only because I tipped him off. He offered me money in return, but my conscience rebelled at being paid thrice for the same work. Once by my newspaper, as I wrote up the story of the fraudulent promotions, once by Seyd's, who paid me for my report, and once by Mason. But undoubtedly many in the company's employ do so profit from their knowledge, and do worse. There is good money to be had in the City of London for those who really want it.

Wilf Cornford was too lazy ever to become rich. Had he possessed easy wealth by inheritance he would have been a scientist working out the various species and subspecies of the insect world. Instead, he catalogued the character and follies of *homo economicus;* it was his duty and his pleasure, and he was one of the few men I have ever met who could be considered truly happy. He could have been a power in the land, for all would have been afraid of him had they truly appreciated how much he knew. But he could not be bothered and, so he told me once, it would spoil his observations. All those people who gave him such an interesting time with their activities would begin to behave differently if they knew they were being watched.

It was he who first had the idea of hiring me for the occasional bit of investigation down in the police courts, and payment was occasionally some money, and more often a useful tip about a forthcoming arrest or scandal which his network of blabbermouths had passed on to him. On several occasions he had suggested I come to work for Seyd's properly, but I had never taken him up. I liked a more varied diet.

"Matthew," he said in his even fashion when I knocked on his door and was admitted. "Nice to see you again. We haven't seen you here for a long time."

Wilf's way of speaking was as anonymous as his appearance. He was a portly fellow in his fifties, but not excessively so. He spoke with a measured neutrality, neither sounding like a toff nor yet betraying any trace of his West Country origins, for his father had been a labourer in Dorset, and he had been sent as a child to serve in the house of the local gentry. There he had somehow learned to read and write, and when the family had brought him to London for the season some thirty-five years ago he had walked out one morning and never gone back. He found a job at a tallow chandler's writing up the books, for he had a fine script. Then he moved on to a corn broker, then a discount house, and finally to Seyd's.

"I was busy with the Mornington Crescent trial."

He wrinkled his nose in disapproval. As well he might. This had not been a classic in the annals of British crime, and the only interesting aspect of the case had been the sheer stupidity of William Goulding, the murderer, who had kept the head of his unfortunate victim in a box under his bed, so when the police came calling—as they were bound to do, for the woman had lived in his house—even they could not have failed to notice the smell and the pool of dried blood which had dripped through the floorboards from the bedroom above and stained the parlour carpet. Goulding had not read the penny press, and so was possibly the only person left in England who did not know about the wonders of fingerprints for identifying even headless corpses. It was an open-and-shut case, but the trial took place in an otherwise quiet period, and the public does love its gore.

"I really don't know how you do your job," he said. "I would find it very dull."

"In comparison to the account books you like to read?"

"Oh, yes. They are fascinating. If you know how to read them."

"Which I don't. And that is one of the reasons I am here."

"I was rather hoping you had come to give me information, not ask for it."

"Do you know of a man called Ravenscliff?"

He stared at me for a minute, then very uncharacteristically leaned back and laughed out loud. "Well," he said indulgently, "yes. Yes, I think I can say I have heard of him."

"I need to find out about him."

"How many years do you have at your disposal?" He paused, and looked rather patronisingly at me. "You could spend the rest of your life learning about him, and still never find out everything. Where are you starting from? How much do you know already?"

"Very little. I know he was rich, was some sort of financier and is dead. And that his wife wants me to write a biography of him."

That got his attention. "Really? Why you?"

I summarised my interview—leaving out the truly important bit—and threw in for good measure my brief interview with Bartoli.

"What a strange choice," he said when I'd finished, staring up at the ceiling with a dreamy look in his eye, a bit like a cat that had just finished a particularly large bowl of cream.

"I'm glad you find it so," I said, rather nettled. "And if you could tell me what in particular . . ."

He let out a long sigh. "It's difficult to know where to begin, really," he said after a while. "Are you really as ignorant as you say?"

"Pretty much."

"You reporters never cease to amaze me. Do you never read your own newspaper?"

"Not if I can help it."

"You should. You'd find it invaluable. And fascinating. But I forgot. You are a socialist. Dedicated to eradicating the ruling class and bringing in the New Jerusalem."

I scowled. "Most people live in poverty while the rich—"

"Grind the faces of the poor. Yes, indeed they do. How they grind them, though, is of great importance and interest. Know thine enemy, young man. If you insist on thinking of them as your enemy. Although as you are now a fully paid-up servant of the worst of the grinders—or at least his widow—I have no doubt your views will have to undergo a certain modification. Had you been better informed you might have refused the money, and thus kept the purity of your soul intact."

"What do you mean, the worst of them?"

"John Stone, First Baron Ravenscliff. Chairman of the Rialto Investment Trust, with holdings in the Gosport Torpedo Company, Gleeson's Steel, Beswick Shipyards, Northcote Rifle and Machine Gun. Chemical works. Explosives. Mines. Now even an aircraft company, although I doubt those will ever amount to much. You name it. Very secretive man. When he travelled on the Orient Express he had his own private coach that no one but he used. No one really knows what he owned or controlled."

"Not even you?"

"Not even me. We did begin an investigation on behalf of a foreign client about a year ago, but stopped."

"Why?"

"Ah, well. Why indeed? All I know is that one day I was called in by young Seyd—the son, that is, and you know how rarely he ever comes near the place—and asked if we were looking at Rialto. He took the papers and told us not to continue."

"Does that often happen?"

"Never. Mr. Seyd junior is not like his father, and is not known for his backbone. He prefers life in the country, saving souls and living off his dividends. But he's an amiable enough man, and never interferes. This was the first and last time."

"So what caused this?"

Wilf shrugged. "I cannot say. I don't know that a biography would interest many people, except me," he went on with a slight sniff of disapproval. "Ravenscliff was money. It's all he did. All he ever did. From the standpoint of someone like you, obsessed with the tawdry details of humanity's failings, he was an utter bore. You couldn't even justify a paragraph on him. Which was why his death was so little reported, I suppose. He got up in the morning. He worked. He went to bed. As far as I am aware, he was a faithful husband—"

"Was he?" I asked quickly, hoping that my interest wouldn't seem suspicious. Wilf, however, put it down to natural squalor.

"Yes, I fear so. He might have owned a brothel and have patronised it on a regular basis, of course, but it never came to my attention. What I mean is that he never had any notable alliances, if you get my meaning. With People."

Now, by "People" Wilf meant the sort of folk he was interested in. The rich and the powerful—and, in this case, their wives and daughters. Shopgirls and women of that sort never came to his attention. "People" had money. Everyone else was merely scenery.

"He had no time, and no interest in anything so frivolous, I believe. As far as I could discern, the companies were collectively highly profitable. Do you know anything about his companies?"

I shook my head.

"Very well then. One thing you should keep in the back of your mind is this: why were you asked to write about a subject for which you are perfectly unsuited? Even if you were presented with a full set of accounts for a company, you wouldn't even be able to understand them. So why you? Why not someone who stands a chance of doing a decent job?"

That irritated me. "Perhaps Lady Ravenscliff has a high opinion of my intelligence and ability to learn. But for £350 a year, why should I care?"

"Oh, you should. You should. These are tricky people, young man. The rich believe they are allowed anything, and they are right. Be careful of what you are getting involved in."

He sounded just like George Short. Normally, Wilf spoke with the detachment of the scientific observer; now he was in earnest.

"You like me," I said in astonishment. "I am touched."

"I see you as a little mouse trying to steal an egg from an eagle's nest, thinking it is so lucky to have found such a feast," he said severely.

I thought about this for a second, then shrugged his warning aside. "You still haven't told me where I might begin."

"That depends," he replied.

"On?"

"On what I get in return. I don't want to be too commercial here, but we deal in information and information has a price. You know that."

"I thought you liked me."

"Not that much."

"I have promised to be absolutely discreet on the matter of Ravenscliff's companies. It's in my contract."

"Good for you. But since when has discretion involved not telling me things? I will make sure nothing is ever traced back to you."

"I can't break my word so swiftly."

"You could promise to break it after a decent interval, then."

"You know perfectly well what I mean."

"I do. I don't want tittle-tattle. Mistresses, wild parties, Lady Ravenscliff's lovers . . ."

"She has lovers?"

"I would imagine so. Ravenscliff was hardly a romantic figure, and she, so I understand, is foreign. But I have no idea. I was merely saying that I am not interested in such things. I am interested in money, that is all."

"I've noticed that. You must tell me why one day."

"If you don't understand it will be pointless to try and explain. A bit like trying to explain Mozart to someone who is tone deaf."

"But you are so poor yourself."

"I am paid a perfectly decent salary. More than enough for my needs. That is not the point. Just because I cannot paint doesn't mean I do not like paintings. And before you draw obvious parallels, you do not have to admire a painter to admire his works. Ravenscliff, for example, was a magician with money; I admired his skill and invention. That does not mean I admired him personally."

"So? Tell me."

Wilf shook his head. "We must have an agreement."

I hesitated, then nodded. "Very well. Anything that might interest Seyd & Co. I might pass onto you. But I decide."

"Fair enough. You wouldn't be able to keep it to yourself anyway. You are a reporter. And I strongly doubt that you will find out anything."

"Thank you for your confidence. Now, tell me about Ravenscliff."

"Certainly not. I'm very busy today. I will provide you with information. Some information. The rest is up to you. Besides, I already told you that our own labours were confiscated."

"Then what's the point . . ."

"I prepared a summary of his career and current businesses—current as of about a year ago, that is. I must have forgotten to hand it over to young Seyd. Very forgetful of me. I will provide you with names. I will listen to your speculations and offer advice and tell you if I think you are going wrong. Which you will undoubtedly do."

He levered himself out of his chair and opened a filing cabinet behind him. Pulled out a file and gave it to me.

It was only about five pages long. "Is that it?" I asked incredulously.

Wilf looked offended. "What did you expect? A novel? Every word counts. It is a distillation of years of knowledge. Our clients are financiers, not gentlemen of leisure with nothing better to do than settle down for a good long read. How many words do you need to describe one of your trials, in any case?"

I sniffed. "I was expecting a bit more."

"You'll survive the disappointment. Go and read it. Then, if you want my recommendation, go and read your own newspaper."

CHAPTER 5

It was past five when I emerged, and a day of glorious weather. Not the
sort of day to be working. Do not misunderstand me; I am a conscientious
man. I work hard and have no trouble staying up all night or hanging
around in the rain for hours when necessary. But sometimes the allure of
life is irresistible. London, in all its glory on a spring evening, was
everything that made work, however honest, seem very much a second-
best option.

I loved London, and still do. I have now travelled to many cities,
although at that stage in my life I had seen little, but have never come
across anywhere which even remotely compares with it. Just looking up
and down the street in which Seyd & Co. was located provided enough
material for a dozen novels. The beggar sitting, as he always did, by the
jeweller's opposite, singing a song which was so execrable people gave
him money to keep quiet. The delivery boys giggling to themselves over
some joke. The bearded man in strange clothes walking quietly on the
other side, keeping close to the wall. Perhaps he was the richest person in
the street? Perhaps the poorest? The old man with a military cast to him,
dignified and correct; a doorman or porter, whose best days passed some
forty years previously when he breathed the air of India or Africa. But
punctilious, with shoes shined and trouser creases pressed like razors.

The merchants and brokers and agencies and manufactories which
could be found down the grimy little alleys and in the courtyards had not
yet disgorged their occupants; they would stay as the light faded or until
the work was done. Contracts were being drawn up, shipments prepared,
cargoes checked over. Auctions of goods were under way in the hall over
the road, which had drawn merchants in furs, just as earlier in the day the
room had thronged with traders in wax or whale blubber or pig iron. The
food stalls to feed the office boys and clerks were setting up; the smell of
sausages and fish was just a faint tang in the air, although it would get
stronger as the evening wore on. The odd pair walking together in
conversation, one a huge African, dark as night, the other a pale-skinned,
weedy-looking man with blond hair, Scandinavian, at a guess. Sailors
probably, their ship docked a mile or so up river after a journey of

thousands of miles to deliver its cargo of—what? Tea? Coffee? Animals? Guano? Ore? Precious jewels or dirty minerals?

Just one street. Multiply it by thousands and you have London, sprawling over the landscape, containing every vice and virtue, every language, every kindness and cruelty. It is incomprehensible, unpredictable and strange. Huge wealth and greater poverty, every disease you could imagine, and every pleasure. It had frightened me when I first arrived; it frightens me now. It is an unnatural place, as far from the Garden of Eden as you could imagine.

I had several things to do, and most of them needed the Duck. I had not eaten all day; I wanted to read Wilf's words of wisdom and I needed to resign from my job. The Duck offered food, a quiet table and sooner or later it would offer the sight of my editor propped up against the bar, as he always was before he went in to oversee the production of the next morning's paper. Robert McEwen was a man of predictable habits. At five-thirty in the evening he would travel from Camden to the newspaper's offices. He would walk to the pub and stay for half an hour, rarely saying a word to a soul; under his arm would be a copy of that morning's paper. If he was in a good mood, it would remain there, untouched. If he felt we had been beaten in some particular he would pull the paper out impatiently, look at it, put it back, or rap it on the counter. The office kept a boy in the pub especially to watch him. "He's rapping," would come the report, and a collective groan would go up. He would stump in, glowering, and sooner or later would lose his temper. Someone would be shouted at. An office boy would be cuffed around the ear. A pile of paper would be thrown at someone's head.

Then the storm would pass and we could get down to business, and McEwen would become as he usually was: concentrated, moderate, reasonable and sensible. He could not be one without occasionally being the other, and the evening would pass until near three in the morning when he, and the paper, could be put to bed, duty done, the world informed, the presses rolling.

The *Chronicle,* to Robert McEwen, was not so much a newspaper, it was a mission. He considered it a moral force in the world. Most people—including the majority of those who wrote for it—thought it was just a newspaper. McEwen disagreed. He brought all the fervour of the lapsed Presbyterian to his task, and set about educating the public, and damning the powerful in error, with all the intensity of John Knox castigating sinners. The newspaper, it should be said, was a good one, but not noted for its sense of humour. Not for the *Chronicle* so much as a photograph, let alone the nonsense dreamed up by the *Daily Mail*, the cartoons, the competitions, or any of the other tricks devised to squeeze a halfpenny from the hands of the reading masses. My line of business he considered to verge on the frivolous, but crime is essentially a moral tale. Evil defeated, sin punished. Frequently, neither of these events happened and for the most part evil did very nicely indeed. But that too could point up a lesson.

Besides, McEwen had a weakness for a story, and the annals of the Bow Street Magistrates Court or the Old Bailey generated many a good one. I had even won his favour, or believed I had, for he was notorious for never encouraging anyone. His emotional range went from towering rage to silence, and silence was as near as he got to praise. My work generally passed without comment, but I had of late been asked to write editorials on the Liberal Government's policy towards the poor and on its latest measures to combat crime.

I thus existed in two worlds, for journalism is as class-conscious as any other part of society. Reporters are the manual labourers; most begin as clerks or office boys, or work on provincial papers before coming to London. They are trusted with facts, but not with their interpretation, which is the prerogative of the middle classes, the editorial writers, whose facility at opinion is assisted by their perfect ignorance of events. These grand fellows, who like to lard their editorials with quotations from Cicero, are paid very much more for doing very much less. Few even consider the idea of spending hours outside a courtroom waiting for a verdict, or camping out by a brazier at the dockyard gates to report on a strike.

It was like a betrayal to go into the leader office—they do not even share the same room with us, for fear of contamination—and sit with pen and paper to enlighten the nation on the deficiencies of the criminal justice bill, or complain about rampant drunkenness due to the efforts of brewers to profit by driving the poor ever deeper into despair. I enjoyed it, though, and thought I was quite adept as well, although as often as not McEwen would rewrite my efforts so that my words advocated the exact opposite of my real opinions.

"Not the policy of the paper," he said gruffly when I looked upset.

"The paper supports public drunkenness?"

"It assumes that people are sensible enough to look after their own interests. You, although an advocate of the working classes, seem to think they are too stupid to run their own lives. Write me the same opinion without being condescending to the entire population and I will print it. Otherwise you will maintain the supremacy of free choice . . ."

"But you don't like choice when it comes to trade . . ."

He scowled at me. "That is a matter of the Empire," he replied.

And it was. This was the paper's Pole Star, the one consideration to which all other matters referred, which determined all the newspaper's policies. McEwen was an Imperialist, a man for whom the defence of Empire was the first, only and greatest duty. He held strongly that we faced two great challenges, the envy of Germany and the greed of America. Both would bring the world to ruin rather than permit the continued supremacy of Britain across the globe. Piece by piece his editorials had constructed a coherent policy with which to educate the public and berate the politicians. Imperial preference in trade, to construct a trading block around the world which would develop the dominions—Canada, Australia, New Zealand, South Africa—into equal partners. A naval policy which would construct fleets of battleships able to take on Germany and any other nation simultaneously. A policy to encourage the production of children. Outright opposition to all welfare for the British population on the grounds that it would diminish the appeal of emigration, and divert money from imperial defence. This, of course, brought him into collision with the current government.

But central to all was Germany, and particularly Kaiser Wilhelm, whom McEwen saw as a madman, determined to foment a war. Once restrained by loyalty to his great-aunt, Queen Victoria, since her death this had been replaced by bitter rivalry with King Edward. Great Britain must prepare for war, and hope we would not be too weakened by the contest to meet the subsequent challenge from the United States.

The last election had been a severe disappointment—all the firepower of the *Chronicle* had been brought to bear on the task of ensuring that the Empire was handed over to the wise guidance of the Conservatives. To no avail. They had been decimated in 1906, and three years on they had been outmanoeuvred again. The Liberals had announced a shipbuilding programme for the Royal Navy, without actually placing any orders, announced a rise in the old-age pension without actually increasing it, announced education reform and so many measures costing so much that no one knew how they would be paid for. They had even put up income tax, to 5 per cent. The Prime Minister, Asquith, and his chancellor, Lloyd George, could reduce the editorial pages of the *Chronicle* to virtual incoherence as McEwen contemplated the full range of their folly. In my opinion the newspaper had become so obsessed that it risked boring its readership to death. Not that anyone consulted me on the matter.

Curiously, my failure to please on the subject of public drunkenness did not mean I was sent back to the reporting room; I kept on writing my opinions, and McEwen kept on changing them, although less and less as I learned how to sneak a radical opinion into an orthodox mould. My finest moment, perhaps, was to convert the paper into a supporter of votes for women, which McEwen held to be against the will of the God he no longer believed in. In sheer irritation I wrote an intemperate, and somewhat frivolous, editorial pointing out that it was contradictory to suppose women were going to produce the next generation of imperialists without their having an interest in the Empire itself. It appeared the next day, word for word, not so much as a comma changed.

I was certain that some terrible error had occurred, that my piece of paper had somehow been accidentally taken down to the printers and published by mistake. People had lost their jobs for much less than that. But no; the next evening, he nodded at me. And almost smiled.

"Why did you run that?" I asked.

"Because you were right," he replied. "And I thank you for correcting me on the matter." He never mentioned the subject again. Except that any trial or demonstration by the suffragists I was now sent to deal with, and after a few weeks I realised I would rather spend my time with murderers, who were very much more interesting conversationalists. Besides, many of the women had read my editorial, considered my arguments unsound, and liked to explain, at length, where I had gone wrong. Moreover, their reputation for moral laxity and free love was entirely undeserved.

I bought myself a drink and a pie and waited for McEwen to show up, largely unable to concentrate on the papers Wilf had lent me. I was halfway through both when my editor walked in. He was the sort of person who was not noticed in a crowd, except when he wished to be. And yet he was invited everywhere, had an entrée into the houses of the great. How was this so? He never struck me as a fine talker, was not notably handsome, not well connected through his family. It took me years to grasp that McEwen listened. When someone talked to him, whoever they were, they felt he was giving them his full attention. It is a rare gift, and one I do not possess myself; I have a tendency to judge others before they have even opened their mouths. McEwen could ferret out the good and the interesting amongst dowagers and dockers alike, and persuade them to take him into their confidence.

And there he was, propped up against the bar, looking not at all like a man able to exchange witticisms with debutantes or discuss tariff reform with cabinet ministers. Rather, he looked like a newspaperman about to go into battle once again. Slightly wary, preoccupied, preparing for the struggle that attended the daily rebirth of a newspaper as it began its great cycle from formless idea to wrapping for fish and chips.

"Good evening, sir," I said. He was always referred to in this manner; in the world of the newspaper he was lord of us all. The fact that he was a mere employee himself, answerable to the owners, never occurred to any of us. In fact, no one knew—or particularly cared—who the owners were, as their presence was never felt.

"Braddock." It was a greeting, no more or less friendly than his usual salutation.

"I was wondering if I could have a word with you, sir . . ."

He took the watch out of his waistcoat and looked at it, then nodded.

"I was asked to go and meet a Lady Ravenscliff today, sir . . ."

"Taking it?"

"I beg your pardon?"

"The job. Commission, whatever. Are you taking it?"

"It's a very good offer she has made. Extraordinary. I think I have to thank you . . ."

"Yes, you do. Good. I thought you'd go for it."

"Might I ask why you suggested me?"

"Because it is a bit of a waste having you do crime stories. Good though they are, no doubt. But I think you need to spread your wings. You need to spend some time in the company of those people you dislike so much."

"Why do you say that?" I tried to keep the hurt out of my voice, but did not succeed very well.

"You sympathise far too much with the people and lose sight of the facts. You write about a murder trial and are so caught up in the circumstances that you are quite capable of omitting the verdict."

"I didn't realise I was so inadequate," I said stiffly.

"Yes, you did," he replied simply. "You know it perfectly well. And please don't think I have a low opinion of you. You'd be a good leader writer. Will be, once you lose the rough edges."

"You mean I didn't go to the right school, like those people you do give jobs to," I said, more loudly than I intended.

"I did not recommend someone like that to Lady Ravenscliff," he said evenly, "so don't get resentful. I imagine she is paying you a fortune and you will gain inestimably from the experience as well. On top of that, there was something strange about Ravenscliff's death, and I want to know what. You were the best person I could think of to discover it."

"I thought he fell out of a window."

"So he did. Open window of his study on the second floor. He was working alone and his wife was out. Pacing up and down, tripped on a carpet."

"So?"

"He hated heights. He was terrified of them, and deeply embarrassed by the fact. He never went near an open window if it was anywhere but on the ground floor, and used to insist that all windows were tightly shut."

"And does Lady Ravenscliff share your worries? She never mentioned anything to me."

He gave me a sidelong look, and I realised what he meant.

"You think . . . ?"

"All I know, Braddock, is that this is a matter of the utmost importance."

He said it with such intensity that I didn't quite grasp his meaning. "Why?"

"Because," he said quietly, "Ravenscliff owned the *Chronicle*. And I don't want it falling into the wrong hands. Find out for me, please, what his will said, where his assets go. Who is our new master."

CHAPTER 6

I walked back to my lodgings, something I often did when I needed to think. It was more than six miles, from the city to Chelsea, and it took me well over an hour even though I walked at a fast pace all the way. The sight of the black-painted front door gave me none of the pleasure that the prospect of home should give a man. It was all that separated me from the boiled cabbage and wax polish, the smells that gather in an overoccupied house whose windows have not been opened for a quarter century. It was a dingy house, in a dingy street, in a dingy part of town. Nearly every second house, I believed, was occupied by widows who let out rooms to people like me. Opposite was one that functioned as a school for young ladies, turning them into operators of the typewriter, so they could push men out of their jobs as copyists and clerks. A few houses were owned by shopkeepers or clerks desperately clinging to respectability by their fingertips. All of human life, from a particular stratum of society, could be found in Paradise Walk, behind the grubby windows and cracking stucco. Paradise Walk! Never was a street more badly misnamed. I can only assume that the speculative builder who threw up the ill-built, utterly anonymous houses some half century previously had possessed a strange sense of humour.

Even worse was that my window, second floor at the back, looked over the grand gardens and opulence of bohemian London. Successful artists had congregated in Tite Street, parallel to my own, but lived in a very different fashion. One garden in particular I could see, and used to gaze at the two children—a boy and a girl, dressed in white as they played in the sunshine—the lovely woman who was their mother, the portly father who was a member of the Academy. And dream of such an idyllic existence, so unlike my own childhood, which had contained no sunlight at all.

Not all journalists are editors, not all artists are members of the Academy. John Praxiteles Brock, my fellow lodger, was not then a success; his torment at having to look out every morning at the proof of unattainable glory in the next street was balanced by his desire to rub shoulders with the famous, who might assist him in his career. He would come home occasionally bubbling with excitement and pride: "I said good morning to Sargent this morning!" or "Henry MacAlpine was buying a pint of milk in front of me today!" Alas, it was rare that either said good morning in return. Perhaps his desperation frightened them; perhaps the fact that his father was a sculptor (hence his unfortunate middle name) of retrograde opinions and unpleasant temper put them off; perhaps they felt that youth has to fight on its own. Now he is more successful, Brock gives little encouragement to others, either.

I awoke the next morning with a formidable hunger, as I had eaten little, and walked much, the previous evening. So I dressed swiftly and went down to the eating room, where Mrs. Morrison prepared breakfast for her boys every morning. She was the only reason I stayed in the house and I believe it was the same for the others who lodged with her. As a housekeeper she verged on the hopeless, as a cook she was very much worse. Her breakfasts tended towards the obscene, and she boiled her vegetables in the evening with such vigour that we were lucky if they were merely yellow when poured onto the plate in a pool of steaming water, there to mix with the grey, tough meat that she cooked in a fashion so personal that no one could ever really figure out how, exactly, she had reduced a once-living animal to such a sorry wreck. Philip Mulready, a man who wished to win fame through poetry (he later settled for a wealthy heiress instead) used on occasion to declaim verses in honour of the poor animal sacrificed on Mrs. Morrison's altar. "There thou liest, unhappy pig, so grey, so pale and wan . . ."; although, sensitive to our landlady's feelings, he made sure that she was in the kitchen when Calliope touched his forehead with inspiration.

She might well have missed the irony in any case. Mrs. Morrison was a good woman, a widow doing her best to survive in a hard world, and if the food was vile and the mantelpiece thick with dust, she created a jolly, warm atmosphere. Not only that, she was prepared to mend our clothes, do our washing and leave us alone. All she required in return was a moderate rent and a little company now and again. A pound a week and some chat was little enough to pay.

Though a journalist (now, I remembered, a former journalist) I was not much of a gossip, alas; unlike Brock, who delighted in any excuse that kept him away from work. Mulready was also a conversationalist, although he liked to amuse himself by talking in a way so convoluted, and on subjects so obscure, that the poor woman rarely understood what he was going on about. Harry Franklin was her favourite; he worked in the

City in some lowly capacity, but it was obvious he would not remain in servitude for long. He was a serious man, the sort any respectable mother would like to call her own. Every evening he retired to his room to study the mysteries of money; he intended to learn his business so thoroughly that no one could deny him the promotion he craved. He often returned late, working for his employers without charge and all alone, so that he could be on top of his job at all times.

He was an admirable fellow but (dare I say it) a little dull. He was easily shocked by Brock and Mulready, went to church every Sunday and spoke rarely at dinner. He missed little, though, and there was more to him than was obvious. I could occasionally see a faint shine in his eye as he listened to the exuberance of his fellow lodgers; sometimes see the effort that lay behind all that mortification of the soul and discipline of the body. And he lived with us, in Chelsea, not in Holloway or Hackney, where most of his sort congregated. Franklin considered himself a man apart; different, superior perhaps to his colleagues, and was desperate to match reality with his dreams.

It was not for me to decry his ambition; not for me to say that being the general manager of a provincial bank (presumably the sort of thing he aimed at—I seriously underestimated his ambition there) was a poor sort of thing to dream of at night, when those in the rooms above and below saw themselves as Michelangelo or Milton. His dream was as powerful as theirs and he pursued it with more determination and ability.

"I need your help," I told him as he prepared to leave for work. He paused as he put on his bicycle clips. It was typical of his general approach to life that he pedalled right across London twice a day, because he would not pay the twopence for the omnibus. Besides, an omnibus meant depending on others and risking being late. Franklin did not like being dependent on others.

He looked at me cautiously and didn't answer.

"I'm being serious," I assured him. "I need to learn about money."

He remained silent.

"Can I walk with you a little?"

He nodded and we went out together. He was a curious sight. Mrs. Morrison had stitched him a large, stiff canvas bag to contain his top hat, which might have been blown off or become soiled as he cycled, and this he tied carefully to the back of his machine. Then he began to pull on two cloth leggings, which he tied around ankle and thigh to protect his trousers, and a form of scarf which went around his neck to defend his stiff white collar against the filth of the London streets.

"You do know that you look ridiculous in all that?"

"Yes," he said equably, speaking for the first time. "But my employers are sticklers for appearance. Many a lad has been sent home without pay for not being properly turned out. What do you want to know about money for? I thought you disapproved of it."

Franklin had once heard me discoursing on the evils of capitalism, but had not seen fit to defend his god against the heresies I spoke.

"Have you heard of someone called Lord Ravenscliff?"

Instantly I could see a look of mingled surprise and curiosity pass over his face.

"I have been asked to write his biography. But I've been told that his life was money. Or that money was his life. One or the other."

"Why on earth would anybody ask you . . . ?"

I was getting heartily sick of that question. "I have no idea," I said testily, "but his widow decided I was the right person and is paying me for the job. I will happily pass some of my good fortune on to you if you will allow me to use you as a sort of reference dictionary for anything I do not understand. Which is nearly everything."

He considered this. "Very well," he said briefly. "I will happily oblige, when I have time. I will be free this evening after dinner, if you wish to begin then. What sort of thing do you want to know?"

"Everything. I mean, I know what a share is, more or less. But that's about it. It's not as if I have any money myself, so it's never been of much interest to me. Just a moment."

I ran back inside and up to my room, grabbed the file from Seyd's and went back outside to the pavement. "Here," I said, thrusting it into Franklin's hand. "This is meant to be a summary of Ravenscliff's business. Could you tell me what it's all about this evening?"

He stuffed it into the bag, along with his top hat and his white gloves, and pedalled off.

I went in to confront Mrs. Morrison's bacon and open the post. I rarely got letters of any sort, so the envelope which awaited me, propped up against the toast rack, held an obvious interest, as it was thick, made of heavy cream paper and addressed in a flowery hand. London W was the postmark, and it evidently fascinated Mrs. Morrison as well as she referred to it as she poured my tea, made mention again as she brought me my plate and hovered with excitement as she waited for me to open it.

I could see no reason to deny her the pleasure, so opened it with a flourish using the butter knife as a letter opener. It was from a Mr. Theodore Xanthos, of the Ritz Hotel, who referred to having met me the previous day. Careful thought suggested this must be the little elf I had encountered in Bartoli's office. He said that, as he had known Lord Ravenscliff for many years, he might be of assistance in my work, and would be glad to help if he could. As he travelled a great deal on business, he was not often in London, but if I wished to come to his hotel before next Friday, then he would be most pleased to talk to me.

That was useful. It was pleasant to think that someone wanted to help. I tucked the letter in my coat pocket, finished my breakfast, thanked Mrs. Morrison fervently for the excellent repast, and walked out into the cool morning sun.

CHAPTER 7

Until that evening the day passed uneventfully. I went to Sloane Square, where I knew there was a bank, and asked to open an account. The Midland and County (a joint stock bank, I learned, as opposed to a private bank—these things become important when you study them) seemed quite enthusiastic when I mentioned the regular payments of £6 14s 8d that would be credited to my account every week. They were not so enthusiastic when I informed them that in fact I had absolutely nothing to give them at that moment, but dealt with the disappointment in a manly fashion. They gave me a book of cheques, with strict instructions not even to think of using one until I had deposited some money.

I went then to the Chelsea library to plunge into the world of money. Banking—joint stock, private, discount. Bills of exchange. Bills on London for forward delivery. Consols. Debentures. Issue at, below or above par. Yield. Dividend. First preference (or second preference) shares. Bonds, international, domestic, government or commercial.

Clearly this capitalism was a more sophisticated beast than I had thought. I had considered it to be a means of theft that was more or less magical in its operation, but slowly realised it had its rules. Arcane and incomprehensible they might be, but rules nonetheless. Some people, at least, understood how it all worked. And what they could understand I could understand as well.

This determination was the sole result of my morning in the library. That and a headache, and the information that Mr. Theodore Xanthos was, alas, only a salesman working for Ravenscliff's shipbuilding company. A pity. I had hoped he would have been more important than that, but it seemed he was only a minor figure whose enthusiasm to assist came from a desire for a mention in a book which would never get written anyway.

I walked down to the World's End for a sandwich and a pint, and returned to easier, more familiar matters in the afternoon. The death of Lord Ravenscliff. The obituaries. Journalism. Things I could grasp standing on my head. McEwen said start at the end and work back, and it was good advice, even without his own particular interest. I needed to know and understand the man; and a man's death is often very illuminating.

I summoned the papers—*The Times* and the *Telegraph,* as well as the financial papers, as they always report on their own more fully—and read until my eyes popped out of my head and the library closed. I learned a little, but very far from enough.

The death first. Here the newspapers were singularly uninformative. Lord Ravenscliff had been discovered by a passerby lying on the ground outside his house at two in the morning of 27 March 1909. He was still alive, but had died soon after. Death was due to head injuries sustained from a fall from a second-floor window. It was believed he had tripped on a carpet. He was sixty-eight years old.

The details were much as his wife and McEwen had related, and gave little else besides. The similarity between the various reports was striking. Evidently not a single one of the reporters had written the account himself. They all had a common source, who must have more or less dictated the report. More than that, the brief summary of events appeared in all the papers some three days after the death—that is on 30 March, an unusual delay in reporting the sudden and violent death of a peer, even if one of recent creation. Ordinarily events would have proceeded thus: Ravenscliff found, police summoned. Police go back to their station to report, man on desk informs journalist, who comes in for routine enquiries, as one does every morning. If it is not the stuff of which great scoops are made (and this would not have been considered such), he informs his colleagues in the pub at about eleven. All make whatever enquiries they see fit, and the first account appears in the evening, the rest the next morning.

In this case matters went along differently. The enquiring journalist was not told of Ravenscliff's death, either that day, or the day after. Why not? I decided that this would be my first enquiry. I had to start somewhere, and it piqued my interest. Besides, I had seven years; I was in no hurry.

It would give me something to do, and would place no great strain on my patience or intellect. I looked forward to it, for the rest of my time in the library was passed in much less interesting reading. Only the *Financial Times* gave Ravenscliff much of an obituary, and even there the details were sparse. Ravenscliff was born John William Stone in 1841, the son of a vicar in Shropshire. School, university. In 1868 he had set up the Gosport Torpedo Company. Then followed a blizzard of complicated dealings that made my head spin. Gosport Torpedo had been bought by Beswick Shipyard in Newcastle, which was listed on the Stock Exchange, in 1878. Beswick then combined with the Gleeson's steelworks in 1885, then bought out the Yarnton chemical works, then the Salford railway factory, iron-ore mines in Yorkshire, and coal mines near Edinburgh. Then in 1890 he had put all his holdings into the Rialto Investment Trust and sold that on the Stock Exchange as well. The result, the obituarist told me, was an extraordinary construction which could begin by taking dust out of the earth and change it, bit by bit, into a fully operational and equipped battleship, without ever having to purchase a single object from an outside company. The entire combine was run with a legendary efficiency, so much so that it boasted that it could go from mine to battle on the high seas in less than twelve months.

Even more curious was the phrase "amongst his business interests." The obituary dropped a similar hint later on: "the most publicly known of his financial concerns . . ." What was the author leaving out? What was he not saying? What more was there? McEwen had said he owned the *Chronicle;* Wilf Cornford had mentioned hotels and banks. Is that what they meant?

As in most obituaries, the author said little about the man; they rarely do. But the reticence here was greater than usual. It mentioned that Ravenscliff left a wife, but did not say when they married. It said nothing at all about his life, nor where he lived. There were not even any of the usual phrases to give a slight hint: "a natural raconteur" (loved the sound of his own voice); "Noted for his generosity to friends" (profligate); "a formidable enemy . . ." (a brute); "a severe but fair employer . . ." (a slave-driver); "devoted to the turf" (never read a book in his life); "a life-long bachelor" (vice); "a collector of flowers." (This meant a great womaniser. Why it came to mean such a thing I do not know.)

More browsing through *The Times* Annual Index produced other articles of a general sort, but I could not face reading them that day. I had enough in my notebook at least to present a tolerably intelligent face to Franklin that evening, and I found the bombardment of names and share prices and capital ratios too bewildering to be contemplated on an empty stomach. So I took the bus back down to Fleet Street, where I went into the King and Keys for a pickled egg and a drink.

This was the *Telegraph's* pub, and a dingy little hole it was, with smelly gas lighting needed even on the brightest day as there were few windows to let in either light or fresh air. It stank of sweat, tobacco and sour beer. Why the *Telegraph* liked it I do not know, but there is no accounting for the loyalties and tastes of reporters. It just happens like that. On the positive side, Ma Bell, the landlady, was fat and amiable, always ready to extend credit or even lend money to regulars, and kept the place open all day and all night. It was for the *Telegraph* what a university common room was for dons, or the Reform Club for Liberal grandees. A place to call home. Also, I suspect that the squalor of the place was its main attraction, rather as some people form an affection for a mangy old cat because it is so revolting and unlovable.

Hozwicki was there, as I had hoped. Not an easy fellow, Stefan Hozwicki, but his appeal was his diligence. He was unpopular amongst his fellows, with a reputation for being somewhat superior. This was unwarranted; he was merely very antipathetic. It was near impossible to like him and few had tried. I had made some efforts—thinking when he had begun about eighteen months previously that I could show him the ropes, as others had done for me. Hozwicki did not want instruction, which he considered patronising, and in truth he was a good reporter. Alas, he had never realised that writing good stories is only a small part of the job. Standing around, complaining about editors, moaning about this, that and the next thing is far more important. Cameraderie is all.

By all means keep a scoop to yourself; that is expected. But do not hoard the unimportant. Most stories are picked up because a colleague tips you off, and expects to be tipped off in turn. Hozwicki saw all of life as a competition. He would never tell anyone anything. Instead of relying on, and contributing to, the pool of information offered up in the bar every morning, he went round all the police stations on his own. If he discovered something others had missed, however trivial, then he would keep it quiet. He was ambitious and was determined to make something of himself, no matter what others might think.

I do not know whether he would ever have achieved his ambitions; he died at the Front in 1915, the victim of his own diligence. When others became war reporters, he joined up, determined to show himself a true Englishman, despite his name and place of birth—which was, I believe, Poland. And while his fellows kept their heads down in their trenches, he volunteered for nighttime scouting. His body was never found.

He greeted me with little warmth, but at least he didn't sidle off down the bar as I approached. "I've been doing the Hill End murder all day," he said. Conversation did not come naturally to him. He either spoke to communicate information, or he was silent. At least it spared me the burden of having to make light conversation in return. Hozwicki was the only reporter in London who would not be offended by directness.

"Did you write about Ravenscliff when he died?"

He grunted. Was I about to point out a mistake? Offer some supplementary information? Was an answer to his advantage or disadvantage? He could not yet tell.

"Yes," he said.

"Tell me. It's an old dead story. You lose nothing. And might gain something in the future."

His eyes narrowed. "What?"

"Whatever I discover. Have you heard that I've resigned?"

He hadn't. I felt a little offended. As I say, we are a gossipy bunch. I didn't flatter myself that my departure would have been high on the list of interesting anecdotes, mind, but I had expected word to have gone around a little more quickly.

"I have. So anything I find which might make a decent story will not be written up by me. Do you understand?"

He nodded.

"Good. I want to know why it took three days for Ravenscliff's death to appear in the papers."

"Because the police didn't tell anyone before then."

I frowned. "But why not?"

"I imagine the family wanted it that way. They do that, these people. They ask the police, the police obey."

Something to ask Ravenscliff's widow on our next meeting. "How do you know this?"

Simple, in his account. He had gone to Bow Street police station, as he always did, at half-past nine in the morning. It was his last call of the day; he lived in the deepest East End and started with the City police stations at about five, working his way west on his bicycle round about the same time as I was heading east to work.

"Normally, they just turn the duty book round and let me look at the entries. Then I ask about anything which interests me, and they give me a summary. Simple enough. You know the routine."

I nodded.

"Not that morning. It was the hairy beetroot on duty."

It was a good enough description. Sergeant Wilkins weighed considerably over twenty stone, and had a complexion that ranged from deep red on his cheeks to purple at the end of his nose. Even standing up made him wheeze with effort, and going out on the beat was so far beyond his abilities that he had long since been confined to the desk by sympathetic colleagues. According to the regulations he should have been dismissed as unfit for duty, but the police always look after their own. Wilkins was a sort of saint, universally liked even by the criminals whose cases he processed day after day. The sort who looked as though each crime was a personal disappointment. Normally a more helpful and accommodating person could not be found.

But that day Wilkins had refused to let him see the book and merely read off a couple of entries. "Nothing else today," he said heartily. When a very loud, violent, singing drunk was dragged in by the feet a few minutes later, Wilkins had wheezed over to the door to see what was going on, and Hozwicki had quickly spun the book round to have a look. He only had a few seconds, but it was enough: "2.45: 379 to St. James's Square. Body found. Refer to Mr. Henry Cort FO."

"Refer what?"

Hozwicki shrugged.

"Henry Cort?"

Another shrug.

"FO?"

He shrugged again. Annoying habit.

"So why no story?"

"I was curious, so I went to the morgue, and they confirmed it. A body had been brought from the Charing Cross Hospital, identified as Ravenscliff. I went back to the office, and started to write it up. Just a holding story, as I was going to get it to the desk then go out and get some more information. I also told the editor, so he could get the obituary ready."

"And?"

"And nothing. I went back to St. James's Square to start knocking on doors"—I wrinkled my nose here; Hozwicki was fond of this sort of vulgarity in reporting his stories—"but before I could get anywhere one of the runners found me, and told me I was wanted back in the office."

It happens; it had happened to me often. All newspapers then had their runners, a collection of lads who congregated in the main entrance waiting to earn a penny or two carrying messages. They were often remarkable boys, dirty and cheeky, but the best were exceptional and knew London like the backs of their hands. They would cross town at amazing speed, hanging on to the backs of buses, running; I even saw one going down Oxford Street on the roof of a taxi once, waving insolently to bystanders.

"So back I went," Hozwicki continued, "and was given a dressing down by the day editor. I was not to waste my time on the death of someone so stupid that he had fallen out of a window."

He paused and looked at me. I didn't respond, so he went on. "How did he know he had fallen out of a window, eh? Someone had talked to him about it."

"Do you know who?"

"All I could find out was that a very proper-looking man had arrived in the office a couple of hours previously, and talked to him for about half an hour. Even my short account of Ravenscliff's death was then removed from the paper, and ten minutes after he left, the runner was sent off. The story was squashed, and when it did appear, it wasn't written by me."

"Who did write it?"

He shook his head. "Not someone who works for the *Telegraph*," he said. "I did ask the editor later, but he brushed it aside. 'Sometimes you just do as you are told,' he said. But I think he was referring to himself, as much as to me."

I finished my beer and thought about that. I was sure that Hozwicki was telling me the truth; he seemed positively pleased to share his indignation. Obviously editors are wayward people; everyone knows that. They drop stories on a whim, or to do personal favours, or because of the owners. It happens all the time. But normally you can see why, even if you don't approve. Why sit on a fairly straightforward story?

"Wait a minute," Hozwicki said. "What do I get in return for this?"

"Nothing yet," I said cheerfully. "Except my thanks."

He scowled.

"And my promise that when I have something to give in return, you will have it. Think of it as an investment," I said. "It may diminish to nothing; it may pay rich rewards in due course."

I saluted him, and left, walking up the fug-filled steps into the open air of Fleet Street, so fresh after that dingy basement it made me feel dizzy for a few moments.

CHAPTER 8

I would have liked to have hopped onto an omnibus and gone straight to St. James's Square to ask questions of Lady Ravenscliff. I had quite a few to put to her. But it was six o'clock and I had an appointment with Franklin. I was back in Chelsea by seven, and ready to go. Franklin, unfortunately, was a slow and methodical eater. Normally this did not bother me, but that evening the habit drove me to distraction.

Our evening routine was invariable. At around seven-thirty all four of Mrs. Morrison's boys would assemble in the little dining room, dark and gloomy, lit only by spluttering gaslight, and waited while the clank of pans rose to the climax that heralded the arrival of our evening feast. Conversation varied at these meals, sometimes animated, sometimes nonexistent. Occasionally we would dine *en grand seigneur,* and dally over our tea afterwards. I could always win an audience by describing the latest murder; Brock would compete for attention with an account of a meeting with the artists he didn't really know. Mulready could clear the table by reciting some verse of an experimental hue. Only Franklin said little, for no one was really interested in the movements of the markets or the reception of a South American bond issue, even though the coupon might have been set substantially below par. He spoke a language far more foreign than criminals or artists or poets, one which few cared to learn.

Dinner that evening was a mutton chop apiece, potatoes and (a particular treat) Brussels sprouts rather than cabbage, although it was difficult to tell the difference by the time they were served. Next there was tapioca pudding, which produced a chorus of applause from the artistic types, whose childish tastes were, perhaps, an essential part of their lives. The conversation was not animated. Brock wished to begin a discussion on whether there was going to be a war with Germany or not, and seemed to think that I, as a newspaper man, would have a special insight into the thinking of the Foreign Office on the subject.

His was not an abstract concern in the fate of nations, although as it turned out he was right to be interested. For the war was the making of him when it came. He became a war artist, and what he saw so changed the way he painted that it thrust him to the forefront of the new generation which came to prominence when it ended. The bleakness which made him unpalatable in those sunny days before the conflict started was perfectly attuned to the mood that prevailed during it, and gave him a clarity that eluded him when he lived with us in Chelsea.

No, he had come up with this project for a gigantic portrait of the crowned heads of Europe, a scheme for which he was so totally unsuited that I did not know whether to wonder at his impudence or at his lack of reality. He wished—he, John Praxiteles Brock—to summon every monarch, from Tsar Nicholas to the Kaiser, from King Edward to the Emperor of Austria, and every last kinglet of Scandinavia and the Balkans, to sit together to be painted by him. Presumably not in the dining room of 17 Paradise Walk, Chelsea.

It was a scheme so lunatic in conception that, naturally, we all encouraged him enthusiastically and he spent days doing little sketches, using photographs from newspapers in lieu of the real thing. It kept him busy and happy, and I still don't know whether there was really any grain of seriousness about it. I think not, for although he was unrealistic, he was not totally insane. But the project took on a life of its own, and everything that happened in the world would be related back to it. He became a great supporter of the French monarchists, as he did not see how he could fit a republican president into a portrait of kings. He profoundly disapproved of Russian revolutionaries, and was outraged when the King of Portugal was assassinated, thus robbing him of a subject who had been noted (until his unfortunate death) for his handsome figure.

The dream of glory swept over Brock like a wave as he contemplated his forthcoming knighthood when the project was shown at the Royal Academy. Then he came back to earth as Mulready collapsed into gales of giggles. The dinner came to its end on rather a poor note. Brock stumped off, Mulready began to feel a little guilty and Franklin watched impassively. Eventually we went upstairs to the little sitting room, kept for special occasions only. It was dark, chilly and thoroughly uncomfortable, but Franklin never allowed anyone into his room. He tossed the file from Seyd's back towards me.

"Did you read it?"

"Of course I did. An accomplished summary, but little detail."

"So? Can you explain it all to me?"

While Brock and Mulready were all gaiety even when discussing weighty matters, Franklin was all seriousness, even in his frivolity. He had no sense of humour whatsoever; it made him a good employee and a dull, though kindly, companion. At the dinner table he kept strictly to pronouncements of fact, on which he could be highly pedantic. Was the Battle of Waterloo in June or July of 1815? Mulready did not even care what year it was in; to Franklin it became a matter of the utmost importance, and if he could not pin it down he would become restless. Sooner or later he would disappear upstairs to check, and reassure himself that the world was still capable of being reduced to numerical order.

The file of Seyd's triggered an almighty outburst of this peculiar form of madness; in many cases, Franklin explained, it hinted but did not elaborate. It asserted but provided no evidence. It sketched out, but gave no background detail.

"It is incomplete, I know," I said, sorry that I had introduced the poor man to such a source of annoyance, but feeling at the same time that if his bloodhound-like desire to hunt down the detail could be properly harnessed it might prove highly useful. "Could you tell me what it's all about?"

I will not set it down word for word. That would be intolerable, and do little except highlight how little, even with his expert tutelage, I really understood at that stage. Ravenscliff, he said, was a new breed. Not an industrialist, not a banker, but a capitalist of the most modern sort . . .

Here he had lost me. He began again. In the last few decades companies have sold themselves on the Stock Exchange. People buy shares in them; if a company is successful, its profits increase, more people want the shares, so the price rises.

Easy. I nodded.

In the day-to-day, he went on, settling into his stride now, the managers of a company—let us say a steel factory—run the business. There is also a board of directors which keeps an eye on the managers on behalf of the shareholders. As they own the business, the shareholders can tell the management what to do, if enough of them agree. Often there are so many shareholders and they are so scattered they can never agree on anything. And this is where Ravenscliff saw his opportunity.

Back in the 1870s he realised that you do not have to own a company to control it. So, in 1878, he sold his torpedo company to Beswick, but, rather than being paid in cash, Beswick gave him shares instead. In fact, he ended up with nearly a third of the total. Armed with this, he called a meeting which voted that he should become chairman.

And so it went on. Through careful experimentation, Ravenscliff discovered that really he needed no more than about 25 per cent of its shares in order to control an entire company. And why should the other shareholders object? The companies he ended up controlling performed well; they paid their dividends, the value of the shares constantly rose. And so Ravenscliff's power extended.

"Well, that's very fine. Everyone is happy, then," I said. "Not much for me to go on there. And, although I can see you find all this fascinating, it is difficult to see how it is going to be made so for the reader of his biography. Is that all the report contains? I must say I find it all a little disappointing."

Franklin scowled. "Personally I find it remarkable. But, as you say, few are interested. Fortunately, there is a little more for you.

"When he established the Gosport Torpedo Company in 1868, he had a great deal of difficulty persuading the Royal Navy to buy. Either it would not work, which made it useless, or it would work all too well, which meant that a small dinghy, in theory, could sink a battleship. Naturally this made the navy reluctant to support him. So he gave the machines to them."

"I thought the idea was to make a profit."

"It is. But Ravenscliff realised that an order from the Royal Navy was the best advertisement in the world. What it had, every other navy wanted. Before he had delivered a single machine, he had gone around the world, talking of the British Admiralty's confidence in him. Naturally, everyone else determined to have them as well, even though the cost was formidable. Within five years, he had armed every enemy and potential enemy we had with the weaponry to sink our fleets.

"What could he do? That was his argument. He claimed he had been more than happy to give the navy an exclusive right to purchase his machines, but they had refused. And, by the time the navies of the world realised that their ships needed more protection, Ravenscliff had taken control of Gleeson Steel, which made some of the best armour plating in the world, and the Beswick Shipyard, which could turn out brand-new warships. And so it went on. By 1902 every aspect of the production of ships and weapons was under Ravenscliff's control. His factories produced the engines, the ships, the guns, the shells. Earlier than most he saw the potential of steam turbines, so bought control of a company that explored for and extracted oil in Mesopotamia."

"That was very clever of him."

Franklin did not reply. "Do you know what a trust is?"

I considered replying that whatever it was, in the world of finance it was likely to be a contradiction in terms. But I rested content with shaking my head instead.

"These were invented by the Scots, some twenty years ago. It is a company, quoted on the Stock Exchange, except that it doesn't do anything except own shares in other companies. Now what Ravenscliff did was put all his holdings—in Gleeson's, Gosport, Beswick and so on, into the Rialto Investment Trust, and sold shares in it, keeping only a controlling stake. Do you understand the implications of that?"

"No."

"I am truly glad that in your daily life you have no contact with money whatsoever," he said vehemently. "You clearly have no instincts for it at all."

"I am quite prepared to admit it," I said.

"It is nothing to be proud of. Very well. Think of this. A quarter stake in the Trust means Ravenscliff controls it, correct?"

"If you say so."

"I do. And the quarter stake the Trust holds in Beswick means it controls that. Correct?"

I nodded.

"So Ravenscliff controls Beswick with a quarter stake of a quarter stake. That is, six and one-quarter per cent. The same goes for another dozen or so companies which make up the main holdings of the Trust. To put it another way, he controls companies capitalised at nearly seventy million pounds with a holding of a little more than four and a quarter million."

Finally I understood, although the size of the figures astonished me. Four and a quarter million was such a vast amount of money it made my head spin. Seventy million was almost beyond comprehension. My landlady's house, I knew, had cost her two hundred pounds.

"So," Franklin continued, "your characterisation of Ravenscliff as 'some sort of moneyman' needs to be revised a little. He was, in fact, the most powerful armaments manufacturer in the world. And also perhaps the most ingenious financier in the world as well.

"And," Franklin went on, "there is the founding mystery of his life, which might entertain your readers if you can solve it."

I brightened up.

"Where did the Gosport Torpedo Company come from?"

"What do you mean?"

"Torpedoes are complicated things. Ravenscliff was a financier, not an engineer. But all of a sudden he pops up out of nowhere with a fully operational torpedo. Where did it come from?"

"Are you going to tell me?"

"I haven't a clue; nor, it seems, does your man at Seyd's. It's a cunning document, this. It goes on at great length about what it does know—which is little; and artfully buries what it doesn't, which is a great deal. It's only when you think about it that you realise this document is a confession of ignorance."

That was the essence of my long conversation with Mr. Franklin who, bless him, presented all his information in a way which was almost understandable. Even better, he clearly enjoyed it, and ended by saying that if I had any more questions, I should not hesitate . . .

I wouldn't. I now had some inkling of how little I knew, and how little everyone else knew. I wasn't alone, but no one else but me had the problem of finding anything out. Ravenscliff's way of life was intricate and veiled, almost deliberately so. He had successfully hidden the vastness of his wealth from the world, to the point where he scarcely figured in the public mind.

The thought also occurred to me that, if he could do that, how easy it would have been for him to hide a child where no one could find it.

CHAPTER 9

I wasn't really sure why it was, considering the task at hand, that I devoted myself to trying to understand Ravenscliff's manner of business. I reckoned it was important to know the sort of man I was dealing with, and so far I had learned little. Only his wife had referred to his character, and I assumed her testimony was unreliable. He must have had some friends, surely? Someone who knew and understood him. While the doings of the Rialto Investment Trust would offer little insight into his passions and emotions, they might at least lead to someone who had known him. So I hoped, anyway.

The following day I had a quick lunch with a friend who worked as a jobber at the Exchange; not a grand figure in that world, but one who was around all the time, and the jobber's bread and cheese depends on knowing even the least wisp of gossip. Fortunes are made, companies rise and fall on catching a muttered comment in a pub or club or tavern before anyone else hears of it. The firm which employed Leighton was moderately prosperous, so I understood, and so must do tolerably well in listening.

Not that Leighton looked like a man who spent his time closeted in dark rooms, listening to idle gossip. If there was anyone less obviously suited to the life he led, then I have never met him. Leighton gave the impression of one born to rule an empire, or at least explore it. It would have been more fitting to come across him a few miles from the source of the Nile than the Stock Exchange.

He was huge, and at one time had been a useful rugger player. He had a booming voice incapable of speaking quietly and was inevitably overheard in all that he said. He had prodigious energy, and once took a bet that he could leave the exchange at six in the evening, walk all the way to Brighton and back, and be at his post (in foreign railways) at nine the next morning. Ninety miles in fifteen hours. Naturally, the betting was intense; some thousand pounds was wagered on the outcome, with Anderson's, Leighton's firm, making the book. More or less the whole of the City was there to see him off, and a large number cycled alongside him to make sure that there was no cheating. Even many of these gave up through tiredness or hunger, but Leighton marched on, large, red in the face and sweating profusely until the day cooled enough for him to become chilled. Through the night he walked, never stopping for a moment, even eating his dinner—two bottles of burgundy, three pheasant, and four dozen oysters—as he marched, a member of his firm driving an automobile alongside him laden with food, which was passed to him as required.

His return the next morning was rather like a Roman triumph. No work was done because of the excitement; the finances of the Empire were neglected until all was over. Even the Rothschild's men emerged from their great palace in New Court to be present at the conclusion, a frivolity never witnessed before or since.

He walked up the steps of the Exchange with fifteen minutes to spare, and was carried shoulder high by his comrades to his place on the floor with firecrackers being let off, bottles of champagne popping and the bread rolls flying. He had become a legend with a job for life, for who could ever dispense with the services of such a fine fellow? Of such things are careers and reputations made in the City of London.

Such was Leighton and, as I could be certain that anything I told him would be all around the Exchange within five minutes of our conversation finishing, I had to be careful about what I said. So I told him simply that I had been commissioned to write a biography, and that I was completely lost.

"Grieving wife, wanting a memorial, eh?" he boomed cheerfully. "Why not? She's got the money, or will have soon enough. I can't say that it will be a book I'll buy, though."

"Why not?"

"I've never heard an interesting story about the man. He came, he amassed money, he died. There! I've written it for you."

"I think Lady Ravenscliff wants a little more than that. Did you ever meet him?"

"Once, but not to speak to. Not a very sociable man, you understand. But even he had to show up to the occasional reception and ball. Very handsome wife, I must say. Charming woman."

"Do you know anything about her?"

"Hungarian countess, I think. Who knows anything about Hungarian countesses? I would guess she had not a penny to her name, but the name was something. Run-down old *schloss* somewhere in the Transylvanian mountains . . ."

"Are they in Hungary?"

"Who knows? Who cares? You get the picture though."

"What about Ravenscliff?"

He pursed his lips. "Perfectly polite, but a bit frightening. Didn't say much. Always had a look about him as if he wished he wasn't there. He rarely showed up to anything at all, and would often enough leave as soon as he could. His wife has little time for City society either, so I gather."

"Not much of a figure, then?"

"Oh, Lord, yes. He was immensely powerful. That was why there was such a panic when he died."

"Was there a panic? I didn't notice anything."

"Well, you wouldn't, would you, because you don't pay attention to these things. But there was. Obviously there was."

"Why obviously?"

"Because the instant reaction when someone like that drops out of a window is to think that maybe he jumped. And then you worry that his investments have gone all wobbly. So people start selling shares, just in case."

"The Rialto Investment Trust," I said proudly.

Leighton nodded. "And the underlying investments. What if he had topped himself because Rialto was in Queer Street? It has happened before, it'll happen again. So the moment the rumour started spreading—"

"People started selling."

"Right again. But, and this is the curious thing, they didn't fall much. Even before the stories were in circulation, buyers were coming into the market, picking up every share on offer and supporting the price. We did a roaring trade on behalf of the Consolidated Bank in Manchester. Don't know who they were buying for, though."

"So?"

"If you offer something for sale, and no one wants it, then you drop the price until you find a taker, correct? No one will buy shares in a company which might be insolvent, so the quoted price can fall through the floor. If, on the other hand, there is a buyer, then the price stabilises. No panic, the owners of the shares are reassured, and stop trying to unload them. Understand?"

I nodded.

"With Rialto, of course, the price has been very low lately."

"Why of course?"

"Same with all the armaments companies," he said reflectively. "No orders. The government isn't buying. They've been going through hard times. Anyway, the point is, all of a sudden, there were buyers all over the place. The shares went up, can you credit it? The question is, who was buying? Somebody knew something, but I'm damned if I could find out what. And later Cazenove came into the market, acting for Barings. And the funny thing was, Barings seemed to be trading on their own account."

"What does that mean?"

"Buying for themselves, not for a client. So I'm told. The thing is they weren't trying to make money. They were buying at full price. Whoever heard of a bank not trying to make money? Unless they were doing someone a favour."

"This was when, exactly?"

"When Ravenscliff died."

"No, I mean what day *exactly*? The day he died, or the day the news appeared in the papers?"

"There was nothing in the papers. That came two days later."

"What would have happened if the news had come out immediately? A few hours after he died?"

"Heavy selling, with, presumably, no buyers primed to intervene. Collapse in the share price. Possibly forcing the Trust to sell off the shares it owned in other companies, leading to a general drop of the market."

"Which is not good?"

Leighton sighed. "Not really."

I thought about this. It more or less explained the delay in reporting Ravenscliff's death; gave one possible explanation, at any rate. Keeping the news quiet meant that Ravenscliff's friends had time to prepare. All very well.

"Have you ever heard of a man called Henry Cort?"

Leighton looked puzzled for a moment, then shook his head. "City man?"

"I don't know. Just a name I heard. Not important."

I left him ordering another drink and a pork pie, and went to think. I was accumulating information, but so far it didn't add up to much. Ravenscliff died, assorted people of some considerable authority delayed the news becoming generally known; stockbrokers intervened to stop a run on Ravenscliff's company; the Foreign Office was, maybe, involved. Of all the information I had, this was the most curious. At least, that was the only thing I thought FO might mean. Everything else was the usual sort of thing (I believed) one might expect from the City.

I didn't sleep as well as usual that night; I felt that I was proceeding in an amateurish, haphazard fashion—a bit of information here, a bit there, without having any real sense of what I was doing. I was annoyed with myself, even though I had only been at work for a few days. I felt I should be more organised. More businesslike, in honour of my subject. By the time I finally fell asleep, I had resolved to start again, at the beginning, and go back to question Lady Ravenscliff more thoroughly. She must have known him better than anyone.

I was aware that I was trying to do several things at once. I was, officially, meant to be writing a biography of a financier; I was supposed, unofficially, to be finding a child; and I was also meant, even more unofficially, to be examining Ravenscliff's death to find out what it meant for the *Chronicle*. I had to remember to keep in mind which one of these I was meant to be doing at any particular moment.

The next morning, I sent a note to Lady Ravenscliff requesting an interview, another to Mr. Xanthos asking for the same, and then took myself off to visit the family solicitor.

I should have known that Ravenscliff would not have had a solicitor of the Dickensian type, who still existed in those days. Old clerk, brown wooden desks, glasses of sherry or port, and reassuring conversation surrounded by piles of carefully docketed folders and archival boxes. No; Ravenscliff liked efficiency and dynamism; his solicitor matched his tastes. Mr. Henderson was a young man for his job, perhaps in his mid-thirties, and, in my opinion, somewhat bumptious. The sort who had done well at school, never broken any rules, been a favourite with his teachers. Someone who was going to do well in life, and who, as a result, never questioned whether it was worth doing. I didn't like him much, and he treated me with scant respect in return. The sherry decanter was not disturbed in its rest by my presence.

Still, I was the representative of his most valuable client, trying to do something which he was incapable of doing on his own. He formed trusts and conveyed things. Finding illegitimate children was quite outside his range. As our conversation progressed, I occasionally even felt a slight sense of unseemly interest, as though some long dormant imp buried deep in his well-run life was stirring a little. Perhaps he had really wanted to flick an ink pellet at a teacher, but had never dared.

"You know that for public purposes I am supposed to be writing a biography?"

He nodded.

"And you are also aware of the real reason for my presence?"

He nodded again.

"In that case, I can dispense with all the subtleties. What do you know of this business?"

He sighed in the manner of a man who prefers questions that require a yes or no answer. "Very little more than is contained in the will. That there existed a child, that money was to be left to it, and that material identifying that child was to be found in his safe at home."

"Which is not, in fact, to be found."

"So it would seem. It makes the life of the executors of the will very difficult."

"Why?"

"Because the estate cannot be easily settled until all claims on it are resolved. And that cannot be done while the matter of this child is extant. So the estate will remain in limbo until it is cleared up, one way or the other."

"Do you know what it was, this material? Wouldn't it have been wise to leave it with you?"

"As it turned out, it would have been very much wiser," he said evenly.

"I can only surmise that Lord Ravenscliff had a good reason for his decision."

"What sort of good reason?"

"The obvious one would be that, when he made the will, he had not yet finished accumulating the material, and wished to add to it."

"Tell me how the will was made. He came here . . ."

"He came here and said that he thought it best to make his will. He had realised he was not going to live forever. Although, to be truthful, that was difficult to believe. He was in exceptional health, or appeared to be. His father lived until he was ninety."

"He had not made a will before then? Is that usual for men of fortune?"

"Quite unusual, yes. But men like Lord Ravenscliff do not like to contemplate their mortality. He had given us a rudimentary testament, just enough to ensure he did not die intestate in case of an accident. In that all his possessions passed to his wife. This was a more complicated and complete version."

"The details?"

"The bulk of his estate passed to his wife, there were legacies to other family members, servants and to his old college. Generous bequests, I might say. A legacy to a Mrs. Esther Vincotti of Venice. Six months later he returned to add a codicil concerning this child."

"And when he mentioned that, you didn't ask for details?"

"That is hardly my role."

"Did he say anything about it?"

"No. He simply dictated his wishes."

"You weren't curious?"

Henderson looked vaguely affronted at the suggestion. "Many of my clients are wealthy men, and many have discreditable secrets in their lives. It is my job to look after their legal affairs, not their spiritual well-being."

"So you are no wiser than anyone else?"

He inclined his head to indicate that, incredible though it might seem, that was the case.

"And he said nothing about this material identifying the child?"

"No."

"What is your opinion? Are you allowed one?"

It didn't even make him cross. "Yes, I think I can have an opinion on that," he replied. "I believe that whatever it is, it was to be found in his desk. And that someone removed it shortly after his surprising and unforeseen death. But I will make no further comment."

He didn't need to, of course.

"The other legacies? What about them?"

"I know nothing of either of them, although naturally I have corresponded with the executor, a Michael Cardano, since the death."

"Who's he?"

"He used to work for Rothschild's, I believe. More than that I do not know."

"And he is capable of running a company?"

"I do not know. But he doesn't have to; the duties of an executor are very different. He is the son of an old associate of Lord Ravenscliff's. The father was ruined in 1894 and died in gaol."

"I see. Tell me about this Italian woman."

"We have sent Mrs. Vincotti a telegram. She is due to arrive in London on Wednesday. At least, I hope she is."

"Why? Does it matter?"

"Oh, good heavens yes. Especially with such sums as are involved in this case. Naturally we have to make sure that this is the woman that Lord Ravenscliff intended. Otherwise we would not be able to make the settlement; that would introduce another complication and we would have to look for two people, rather than only one."

"How so?"

"His affairs cannot be settled until all the beneficiaries are contacted, so we can ensure that it contains enough for each to receive their proper due. For example, suppose someone dies and leaves £100 to one person, and the same to another, but there is only £120 in the estate. What do we do? Obviously, if one of those people is dead, there is enough for the other person to receive the full amount. If both are alive, then there is not. That is when matters become complicated."

"So this child . . ."

"Must be found, if the estate is to be wound up swiftly. Lord Ravenscliff left his wife a fixed amount, and a life interest in the residue, which devolves on various others on her death. Whether the legacy to the child is paid out is consequently a matter which affects all the other bequests."

"So what is Lady Ravenscliff's financial position at the moment?"

"She is dependent on the goodwill of the executor and his willingness to make her an allowance out of the estate, which he in effect controls."

"Did Lord Ravenscliff realise this?"

"I'm afraid I don't understand."

"What I mean is, why would Ravenscliff have made his will in such a way that there was a possibility his wife would be left in such a situation? Did you tell him that there was such a possibility?"

"I advised him of all the consequences, yes."

"And he went ahead. What conclusions do you draw from that?"

"That he considered it the best way of organising his affairs."

"No. I mean, why did he consider—"

"I know what you mean. But while Lord Ravenscliff communicated his wishes, he did not tell me the reasoning that lay behind them."

"And did you ever try to guess?"

"The obvious conclusion is that he thought that there would be no loose ends."

"And do you think this Mrs. Vincotti might be the child's mother?"

"That I could not say."

"Did Lord Ravenscliff make any regular payments to people when he was alive? Not employees, or anyone like that, of course. To individuals with no known connection to his business?"

Henderson considered. "Not using my services. He may have made separate arrangements, of course."

"I see. Now, the Rialto Investment Trust. What is the state of that at the moment? And of his companies."

"As you may know, Ravenscliff controlled a large number of companies through Rialto. And his holding in Rialto has passed for the time being into the hands of the executor."

"Michael Cardano."

"Precisely."

"So what happens there? I mean, if the estate is not wound up?"

"In the day-to-day, the companies are run by expert management, and need no external guidance. But I imagine that the other shareholders will get together to protect their interests. Specifically, they may decide to reassure themselves that it is healthy. Naturally, the circumstances of His Lordship's death . . ."

"Produces questions. Quite. Is there any suggestion of that?"

"I am a family solicitor, Mr. Braddock. You would have to ask others.

However, from my limited experience of such matters, I would find it remarkable if there was not a move on the part of shareholders to do precisely that."

"I see. But they would find nothing untoward, would they? I mean, there is no suggestion . . ."

" 'Seek and ye shall find,' " he said with the faintest glimmer of a smile. "No individual I have ever dealt with has been devoid of secrets. I doubt there is any company unencumbered by them either. But I know of nothing specific, if that is your meaning."

"One more question. All of Ravenscliff's businesses are in a sort of limbo, is that right?"

"Yes."

"Including the *Chronicle*?"

"Of course. The executor will decide whether it goes to Lady Ravenscliff, or whether it needs to be sold to raise the cash necessary for the bequests. Naturally, that will not be clear until we know how many bequests are to be made."

McEwen would not be happy to hear that, I thought.

"So, let me get this clear. Lord Ravenscliff made his will about eighteen months ago, and there was no mention of a child. That bit was added six months later. Yes?"

Henderson nodded.

"Why? He must have known this child existed. Why not put it in when he made his will originally?"

"I do not know."

And that was that with Mr. Henderson. I took the paltry gleanings he had given me and went for lunch. I needed a beer and a steak pie before visiting Lady Ravenscliff once more.

CHAPTER 10

I was apprehensive as I was conducted into a little sitting room in St. James's Square. A different room, more cosy and intimate than the grand salon where we had met last time. A fire burned in the grate, making it pleasantly warm and suffused with a smell of apple wood. On the mantelpiece there were trinkets of all sorts—mirrors, pieces of framed needlework, little statues in bronze. A handsome blue porcelain bowl. The walls were lined with books. Evidently Ravenscliff was a great reader. And an accomplished one. These were not there for decorative purposes, as you see sometimes in great houses. These books were to be read. Had been read, in fact. Novels in French and English and German and Italian. Works of history and philosophy; medical journals, books of travel. The classics—in translation and the original languages. Dictionaries and reference books. I knew many of the English titles, and had heard of some of the others. Zola, Tolstoy, Darwin, Mill. Marx, I noted with curiosity. Know thine enemy. Books on sociology and psychology. Even a few on criminology. It was an impressive range. Lucky the man with the leisure and energy to read them all. Ravenscliff, of course was not a man of leisure. Curious. It made me feel a little self-conscious about how much time I spent in pubs.

And on the far wall two paintings, the larger a portrait of Lady Ravenscliff, painted some twenty years ago, I guessed. I could see the appeal. She was one of those people painters must love; her left shoulder was facing the viewer and her head was turned so it faced out of the canvas. She wore a golden red dress, which showed off her long, elegant neck. There was no jewellery of any sort; she did not need any; her face and hair were quite enough. She had been, and still was, a lovely woman.

"Henner," came a soft voice behind me.

I turned. Lady Ravenscliff was standing at the door with a faint smile on her face.

"Pardon?"

"Jean-Jacques Henner. He died a few years ago and I suppose his fame has faded, but he was one of the finest portraitists of his generation. That's me in 1890 before I grew old and wrinkled."

"You are hardly that," I muttered. I really didn't feel like paying compliments. In fact I never did, and I had had little practise.

"And this is John." She pointed to the smaller portrait, tucked away in a corner of the room. "He hated having his portrait taken. He only consented because I demanded it as a birthday present. He grumbled incessantly, and would only have this little thing done. It's so tiny you can barely see him."

I looked. So that was Lord Ravenscliff. I looked intently, but it gave me no clues. He seemed nothing remarkable; there was no look of bestriding arrogance or pride; no hint of cruelty or kindness. It was just a face, that of a perfectly prosperous gentleman, looking calmly out with only a hint of weariness about having to waste his time to placate a demanding wife. He looked almost agreeable.

"May I say I'm surprised he found the time to read so much?" I said as I gestured at the shelves. "I thought these men of business worked all the time."

"He liked reading," she said with a smile at my condescension. "But this is my room. John's is upstairs. He preferred less well-upholstered surroundings. He did not like to get too comfortable when he was working."

"Ah."

"That's right. I can read."

"I didn't mean—"

"Yes you did," she said brightly.

I blushed.

"It doesn't matter. In this country it is quite usual for women of my position to regard reading a book as somehow inelegant. However, you must remember that I used to live in France, where it is not considered wholly inappropriate. But I have loved reading all my life. We must talk more about this some time. I always think it important to know what a man reads. Tell me, what do you think of this?"

She picked up the blue bowl and handed it to me casually. What was I to say? It was a blue bowl. With patterns on. Blue ones. I shrugged. She put it back.

"Well?" I said, I hope a little coldly. "You wished to take your revenge by revealing my ignorance and you have succeeded. You might as well enlighten me."

"Oh, it is nothing of importance," she replied. "And you are right. That was offensive. I apologise. Shall we begin again?"

"Very well."

"So. Tell me, have you made any progress since we last met?"

"A little. I have talked to a few people and done some background reading. But I have to say that I have questions which must be answered before I proceed any further." I did not like this. The meeting had not got off to a good start.

"Dear me," she said with a smile. "That does sound serious."

"It is."

"Well? Go on," she prompted as I lapsed into silence. I had never done anything like this before, and I wasn't quite sure how I should phrase the questions. Thinking of what to say, and actually saying it now she was standing in front of me, were very different.

"Mr. Braddock? Are you going to say something, or just stare at me all afternoon?"

"It's difficult to know where to begin . . ."

"At the beginning?"

"Don't make fun of me. What I need to know is whether you are being honest with me. All the evidence suggests you are not."

"And what," she said, definitely cooler now, "have I said or done to make you think such a thing?"

"Were I a reporter once more, I would leap to one obvious conclusion," I said, feeling better now that I had got under way. "Your husband dies and you instantly go to his desk, remove whatever evidence there is about the identity of this child, and hide or destroy it. Then you call me in to look for something you know cannot be found, so that you can appear to be a dutiful and obedient widow, carrying out her husband's wishes. In due course, all the money which should have gone to this child comes to you."

She looked evenly at me. "In that case you are a very bad reporter. Someone with a flair for a story would also have considered the possibility that I discovered, one way or another, something about the provision in his will. That I was so overcome with jealousy that I not only did as you say, I also pushed my husband out of the window."

Was she angry, or distressed? She held her jaw so tightly that I knew it was one or the other, but her self-control was so great it defeated any attempt to penetrate further.

"I have considered that possibility," I replied.

"I see. So are you here to tell me you do not wish to continue in my employ? Or are you trying to discover a way of keeping the money, even though it comes from a murderess?"

She was quite calm as she spoke, which convinced me that she was furious with me; so furious that I doubted whether it was going to be my choice.

"I am trying to discover what happened. Which is the job you gave me. Part of it, anyway. I must say that I do not really think you are a murderess. But I need to get circumstances clear in my mind. You ask me to find this child, and the task would be easily accomplished if the evidence was where your husband said it was. Someone moved it. It might help considerably if I knew who."

"So? Ask." She had not forgiven me, nor entirely resumed her pose of calm, but I could see my remarks had mollified her a little.

"Did you move it?"

"No. Do you believe me?"

"Who did move it?"

"I don't know."

"Who could have moved it?"

"I don't know that either. Or rather, I could give you a list of people who have been in the house long enough to occupy you for months. I imagine it would have been in the large drawer which contains a strongbox. It would have been locked. Only my husband had a key."

"Forgive me for asking, but could I see this desk?"

"By all means." She stood up and walked to the door. She was not the sort of woman whose clothes needed smoothing down, however long she had been sitting; they simply fell into place. That was expensive couture, I guessed. Or maybe she was simply one of those people who was like that. My own clothes looked rumpled even when they were fresh back from the laundry.

"Was your husband disturbed or preoccupied at all in his last few weeks or months?" I asked as we walked up the stairs. I walked beside her out of modesty, as the sight of her from behind was too enticing to be polite.

"Perhaps. He had been different, more distant for some time before his death. And in the last few days he was very preoccupied."

"In what way?"

"I could see something in his eyes. Worry. I think it was a premonition."

"About his death?"

"Yes. The human mind is a strange and complex thing, Mr. Braddock. Sometimes it can see the future without realising it."

"Did you ask what concerned him?" I said, steering the conversation away from this topic as fast as was seemly.

"Of course. But he simply said there was nothing which I should worry about. That all would be well. I never doubted it until he reassured me."

"But you have no idea—"

"None. I assume it was something to do with his business affairs, because I can discover no other possible explanation. Although I saw less of him than usual."

"Why was that?"

"He was working. He would be out late. Ordinarily, he would return in the early evening, and he rarely left the house again. He preferred to eat at home, then we would read together. Sometimes he would have work to attend to, but only in his office. Sometimes he would read his papers sitting by the fire, with me next to him. In the last few weeks he would go out again, sometimes coming back late at night. But he never told me why."

"Do you know a man called Cort? Henry Cort?"

She gave no reaction, either of pleasure or anything else. "I have known Mr. Cort for more than twenty years," she replied evenly. "John also knew him for a long time."

"Who is he?"

"He is . . . I don't know how to describe him, really. He was once a journalist, although I understand he gave that up long ago. He was a correspondent for *The Times* in Paris, which is where I came to know him."

"So he was not an employee of your husband?"

"Oh, no. He has independent means. Why do you ask?"

"A name that came up," I replied. I still didn't know what FO meant. Some religious order? "Was your husband a Catholic?"

She smiled. "His mother was, but John was brought up as an Anglican. His father was a vicar. But he was not a great churchgoer."

"I see," I replied.

"Here we are," she said, opening a door on the second floor. "This was his office. And where he fell."

It was a room about eighteen feet square, the same size as the sitting room we had been in a few moments previously. And, presumably, directly above it. A simple but masculine room where the other had all the touches of a woman's hand. In this room brown dominated; the woodwork painted as mock oak, the curtains heavy velvet. A smell of tobacco hung in the air; heavy wooden filing cabinets filled one wall, and there were no paintings, only a few photographs in heavy silver frames. Family? Friends?

"All his family," she replied. "His parents, sisters and their children. He was fond of them all, but they rarely met after his mother died. She was a remarkable, if rather strange, woman. Foreign, like me. He got much of his drive from her, his kindness from his father. They all live in Shropshire, and rarely come to town."

"Would one have been close enough for him to have confessed an indiscretion?"

"I wrote and asked, but they said they knew nothing. By all means ask again, if you wish," she replied. "Now, this is his desk, and I had assumed that these documents would have been in this drawer."

I saw that the whole left-hand pillar keeping the desk up was in fact one drawer, which, when opened, revealed a metal top. It was clearly immensely heavy, but slid out on hidden rollers underneath, which bore much of the weight.

"He had this built to his own requirements," she explained. "It was the sort of thing he liked to do."

"He was a practical man?"

She laughed, thinking fondly. "No, not a bit. He was the most impractical man I have ever known. I don't think I ever saw him do anything at all with his hands, besides eat, write and light his cigar. I meant he liked solving problems to his own satisfaction. Then he would get other people to turn his ideas into reality."

I pulled at the lid on top of the strongbox; it came open easily. There were bundles of papers inside.

"Examine them if you wish," she said. "But you will find they are all deeds of our houses, and insurance policies and other domestic documents. I have looked carefully, but do so again if you want to."

"Later, perhaps. Was the drawer locked or unlocked when you first came to see what was in here?"

"Locked. And the key was in John's pocket. At the morgue."

"Is there another key?"

"I don't know."

I stood and looked at the drawer for a few minutes, hands in my pockets, thinking. That was a waste of time; no blinding flash of inspiration came to me to solve the problem and make everyone's life easier. I even considered ridiculous possibilities, and lifted the carpet to see if a sheaf of papers was underneath. Lady Ravenscliff looked on impassively.

"I have searched thoroughly," she commented.

I looked at her carefully. "I know you have," I said. And, for the first time, I really believed it. This was not a conclusion that would appeal to anyone with a fondness for tales of detection. Ask me why I concluded that she was telling me the truth, and I could give no satisfactory reason. Nothing had changed since I had walked the streets deciding that the exact opposite conclusion was the more likely. I merely wanted to believe her so much that my desire became reality. Instinct, guesswork, self-interest. Call it what you will. From that moment on I worked on the assumption that my employer was an honest and innocent woman.

She was not, however, particularly grateful for my faith. She scarcely seemed to notice it. Instead, she gestured at the window. "This is where he fell," she said quietly.

I walked over to the tall sash window in the wall opposite the desk. It was gigantic; some ten feet high as they are in buildings of this sort; stretching low and almost to the ground. The bottom of the frame was less than a foot from the floor, the top only a couple of feet from the ceiling. The two sashes were held shut by a highly polished brass clasp.

I tried to open it; it was stiff, but shifted eventually; the sash slid up only with difficulty and some noise. It was a long way to the ground, and looking out I could see that immediately underneath was a long stretch of thick, spiked, iron railings.

"How tall was your husband?"

"A few inches shorter than you," she said.

"And not athletic, I assume?"

"Not in the slightest. He was not fat, but set no great store by exercise. Shortly before he died, he was wondering about installing one of these new elevators at the back of the house so he wouldn't have to walk up and down stairs."

I smiled. "Good for him. I was just wondering how he managed to fall out of this window. If he tripped on this carpet here, and stepped forward to regain his balance"—I performed the manoeuvre myself to show what I meant—"then he should have cracked his head on the bottom sash. Certainly even the clumsiest of men should have been able to steady himself by grabbing the window frame."

She was sitting in the little plush-velvet bucket chair by the fireplace now, her hands clasped together in her lap. "I don't know," she replied sadly. "I didn't come up here until much later. I was out that evening, and did not get back until late. The police were waiting for me. They told me there had been an accident and I went directly to the hospital. He was already dead. I didn't come up here until late that day."

"And the window was open?"

"No. One of the servants said he had closed it; it was raining and the water was coming in. And he tidied up the room as he does every morning."

"And was it unusually disarranged?"

"That depends on what you mean by unusually. Once John was finished with a book or a newspaper—or anything, really—he would just drop it on the ground. I very much doubt he would have noticed even if the room was never tidied up. He lived in this house to please me, and because he thought it was the sort of house a man of his standing should live in. It isn't, of course; had we lived in such a place we would have bought something very much bigger. But he really had no taste for ostentation. We have another house in Paris, which was bought solely for my benefit. He was utterly uninterested in expensive living, although he did like good food and wine. And the sea. He always wanted to live by the sea, but had never managed it. We had planned to buy a house on the coast somewhere. The trouble was we couldn't agree where. I wanted Biarritz, he wanted Dorset. Curiously, he was a very simple man. You would have liked him, had you given him a chance."

This sentence was added on so gently I almost missed it. "You think I wouldn't have done?"

"I think you assume all rich men of business must be cruel and greedy by nature. Some are, no doubt. But in my experience they are no better or worse in general than any other class of man."

"How many people were in the house at the time of the fall?"

"No more than twelve. My husband and the servants."

"Everyone but your husband was asleep?"

"I imagine so. Although I have no doubt that some of the servants misbehave themselves when they are not watched. As long as they do their jobs, I do not interest myself in such things."

Another one of those comments which took me slightly unawares.

"Why do you ask?"

"Because, squalid little reporter with an eye for a story that I am, I still cannot rid myself of the idea that your husband did not fall. I have heard he had a terrible fear of heights. Is that correct?"

She smiled. "Yes, it was. It was what made me fall in love with him."

"I'm sorry?"

"We were walking over a bridge in Paris, and he suddenly turned pale, and grabbed hold of me. I thought he was making an advance, but in fact he was simply feeling dizzy. It was the first time I realised he had any frailties. But he needed to pretend, so he did kiss me, merely to cover up his weakness. I teased him without mercy until he confessed, and he was as shamefaced as a schoolboy."

She had such a sweet smile as she remembered this that it was almost a pity to bring her reminiscence to an end, but I did find her memories inappropriate. So I continued on remorselessly.

"So would he have walked up and down by an open window?"

"Not usually. But he did love his cigars, and he knew I hate the smell of cigar smoke. He was prepared to take grave risks, when necessary."

"Then let me ask you directly: would anyone want to murder your husband?"

"Absurd," she said promptly. "In his life he was the kindest of men. In his business he had a reputation for fairness. He had rivals, no doubt. But not enemies. He was an easygoing employer to the servants who, in any case, naturally referred to me first of all. Besides, even the most violent and detestable men generally die in their beds."

"But you know nothing of his business affairs."

"That is not entirely true. We talked a great deal. Although rarely about the details. I was not greatly interested, and he thought of me as a sort of antidote to work. He was not obsessed with his work. Methodical is a better term."

I shook my head. "I wish I could say our conversation today has helped me," I commented, "but it has made me the more confused. I do not think I am giving you very good value for money at the moment."

"You have a long way to go," she said. "I do not despair of you yet. What else confuses you?"

"The same question that has always worried me. Why are you bothering? Why do you want me to look for this child?"

"I told you; to respect my husband's wishes."

"And I am not convinced. After all, he did not respect his own wishes enough to make the task easy."

"It is all I can offer you. Have you some further unfavourable interpretation?"

"Ah . . ."

"You might as well say. You have already accused me of being a murderess, and on the whole I think I took that fairly well."

"Henderson told me that the will cannot be settled until this matter is cleared up. So you are dependent on the generosity of the executor until then."

"Oh, I see," she said. "So rather than respecting John's wishes, I am selfishly looking after my own. Is that what you are saying?"

"Well . . ."

"In that case I would hardly have hidden the papers. Besides, I did not come to this marriage a pauper. I have more than enough money, even if I receive nothing from John at all. There is no motive or reason for you at all there. Do you understand?"

"I have offended you. I apologise."

"I would rather you say these things, than think them in secret. And I suppose they are reasonable. We rich people are cruel and heartless, are we not? Not like ordinary people. Not like you."

"As I say, I apologise."

"I will tell you when I accept your apology."

She stood up. I was dismissed. Or maybe not. I did not know.

"Is there anything else?"

"No. Except—who is this other woman mentioned in his will? This Italian lady?"

"Signora Vincotti? I don't know. I have never heard the name before. I assume, as I suppose you have already done, that she was his mistress."

"Does that upset you?"

She looked gravely at me. "Of course. I am distressed he did not trust me more."

"Pardon?"

"He kept a secret from me. That wounds me. He must have known that I would not have caused a scene over such a trivial matter."

"It seems he kept more than one secret," I pointed out.

She looked at me stonily. "Any more questions?"

"Yes. To leave that amount of money to this woman suggests she was not trivial."

"That is true."

"Are you not . . . curious, at the least?"

"I suppose I am. What do you suppose I should do about it?"

"If you wish, I could visit this lady on your behalf. I understand she arrives tomorrow and will stay at the Russell Hotel in Bloomsbury."

She thought about that. "I have a better idea. I will visit her myself. You may come with me."

A vision of two jealous women rolling on the floor trying to scratch each other's eyes out floated before me. "I don't think I would recommend that."

"It is not for you to recommend anything. I will send a note this afternoon and make an appointment."

That put me in my place. I could either go with her or not; it would not make any difference to her decision. I decided to go.

"And at the same time," she said lightly, "we may discover something that will put you out of a job." Tears welled up in her eyes as she spoke, and I looked on, horrified at the thought that I might have to witness her embarrassment. She was a woman deceived, and had discovered it under the most terrible circumstances.

"I'm sorry," I said. It was not a useful remark, and she paid it no attention.

"I had no children," she said eventually. "John said he didn't mind, that it was enough to have me. That I had brought him all the happiness in the world, and he wanted no more. I am a fool to be so distressed. Of course he had the right to do as he pleased; it made no difference to our life together, and does knowing really make any difference?"

"Yes?"

She nodded. "I should have been able to do that for him. Not some other woman who was so unimportant he never even mentioned her existence. Now, if you will excuse me, I have some matters to attend to. My husband's papers are in those cabinets over there. You may look at whatever you wish. I have instructed the servants that you are to be allowed into the house at all times, whether I am here or not. You see, I have nothing to hide."

And she left. I contemplated beginning on the daunting array of filing cabinets—which, I considered, would be most likely to contain something of use—but could not face it. The interview had left me disoriented, shaking almost.

CHAPTER 11

I was feeling increasingly out of my depth. Commenting on a murder case was one thing; unravelling someone like Lady Ravenscliff was another. So I went to the Ritz, to see my little elf. It was, I gathered, where Xanthos habitually stayed when in London; I learned that he maintained permanent rooms there, at gigantic cost. "So he is some grandee, then?" I asked, slipping into reporterly mode. I was in the Lamb, just round the corner in Mason's Yard; it was where the Ritz went. I bought a round of drinks to reinforce the question. That's the good thing about hotels: servants of the variety who work for the Ravenscliffs have a sort of loyalty, and it is difficult to chisel information out of them. But people who work in hotels will tell you anything for a drink; they have no discretion at all.

"Must be" was the collective reply. But no one really knew. He came, he went. In general he was never there for more than a fortnight at a time, but always wanted his rooms ready. No women had ever been spotted, but visitors and guests aplenty. The bills, though, were paid. That they knew, but there the limitations of their trade came into operation. Xanthos was rich. He was foreign—Greek, they reckoned. What did they care how a strange little Greek came to be able to afford a suite at the Ritz? I knew salesmen, they made good murderers. Lonely people, shuffling from boardinghouse to boardinghouse, washing their shirts overnight. No family, no friends; never in the same place long enough. They were the nomads of the industrial age, always wandering, always moving on. There was, no doubt, a camaraderie, a fraternity of such people, but it did not seem much of a life to me. And they did seem to commit murder—normally squalid, dirty little murders—more often than they should have done. Or maybe they were too miserable to take the necessary steps to avoid being caught.

Mr. Xanthos was evidently a different species of salesman altogether, but the hotel people told me little in return for my money—only that he had been in London the week Ravenscliff had died, and had left shortly afterwards. That he came and went all the time, and had his mail forwarded when he was away for more than a month.

"Or if the letter says please forward," someone chipped in. "Like last autumn, when he went to Baden-Baden. To take the waters," he said in a mock-posh accent.

"Or when he went to Rome last April and that trunk arrived for him. Do you remember the trouble that caused, shipping it off? And no thanks when he got back, either. It might have been a postcard we'd sent on, for all he cared."

He was an interesting fellow, I thought, when he opened the door to his suite, and a curiously attractive one, short, dapper, unconventional, with a bright smile and quick, precise movements. Welcoming, friendly, quite unlike Bartoli.

"It is kind of you to see me," I said. We were in his fabled rooms, and very splendid they were; grand enough to intimidate someone like me, who had never even been in the public area before, let alone in one of the most expensive of the hotel's apartments. There was a huge salon ornately decorated with rich red wallpaper and gallons of gold paint, what I assumed was a bedroom and bathroom next door, and a separate dining room. While I was there, there was a constant to-ing and fro-ing of people bringing food, messages, coal and logs for the fire; even his coffee was poured for him by someone else.

"On the contrary, I am very curious about you," he replied. His eyes twinkled as he spoke, in a voice which was well modulated but overlaid with so many accents it was impossible to tell what the original might once have been. He nestled—almost snuggled—down in his armchair like someone protecting himself from a gale; I half-expected him to wrap himself up in a blanket as he spoke, or tuck his little legs underneath him.

"In that case the curiosity is mutual. If I may—"

"No," he said, "I will ask first. I invited you, and am providing the refreshments." He paused for a considerable while as he leaned forwards and poured two cups of tea. Lemon for him, milk and sugar for me. I'm a traditionalist.

"Very well. What do you want to know?"

"Just why dear Lady Ravenscliff chose you for this project? I am sure you know as well as I why that might excite some interest amongst those who knew her husband. And who, I may add, are protective of his memory."

"There I cannot really help, I'm afraid. I had never met either of them before I was offered the task. And, as you no doubt gathered from my conversation with Mr. Bartoli, I have no experience whatsoever in things financial."

"And she knew so many people who were expert . . . Do you think she wanted someone who was not employed by her husband? An independent outsider? Could that be it?"

"Why would she want that? I flatter myself that what she wanted was someone who could tell a good story, make her husband's life interesting. There are few successful novels with bankers or industrialists as the hero. Fewer still that are written by bankers or industrialists."

"That is true," he replied. "And a sad condemnation of the book-reading public it is. Perhaps you are right. Perhaps that is all it is."

"You sound doubtful. Although I thank you for being less offensive than Mr. Bartoli."

The elf waved a hand. "Oh, don't worry about him. He is just as rude to me. And everyone, in fact. It's his way. He is a very efficient man, the perfect doorkeeper for someone like John Stone. Although I imagine he is concerned about what is to become of him now. Lady Ravenscliff, I am sure, will not require his services. I assume she is the beneficiary of his will?"

Aha. I thought. So that's it. I smiled.

"I really couldn't say," I said. "I am hardly privy—"

"No, I suppose not. Still, you will have gathered that I am curious. And as you come to know more about his business you will understand why. How do you find Lady Ravenscliff?"

A question only the foreigner would ask. No Englishman would ever be so direct.

"I beg your pardon?"

"Have you fallen under her spell?"

"I'm not sure I—"

"She is a fascinating woman, I find. Beautiful, intelligent, accomplished, warm, witty."

"Yes, indeed."

"Did you know she was once one of the most famous women in France?"

"Really?"

He frowned. "Your next-door neighbours have the strange habit of the salon. Women gather male admirers around them—the best attract the leading writers, politicians, diplomats, poets, you name it. It is in the salons that the elites of France are formed. Lady Ravenscliff is said to have been a great star. It is said she even had the King—your King—in her collection. Then she married John Stone, moved to England, and has lived a life of domesticity ever since. Odd, don't you think?"

"Love?"

"Maybe so."

"You sound doubtful. Are you about to offer an explanation?"

"No," he said, "I was hoping that in the course of your researches you might. I would find the answer fascinating. It might be love, I suppose," he said with a sigh as though he found the idea disappointing.

"I cannot give an explanation for something I did not know about. As for her spell, she is indeed charming and warm, though that is tempered by her distress, which makes her fragile."

He smiled. "She is formidably intelligent, and if you think her fragile then you have very poor judgement. She married one of the wealthiest men in the world, and was his equal in all respects. Her fragility and charm are her strengths. Everything about her is a strength, or can be made so."

I stared curiously at him.

"But what are you, Mr. Braddock? Are you one of her weapons as well?"

"I believe I am an employee, there to write a life of her husband."

"No more than that?"

"No."

I got the sense he did not believe me, but he decided not to pursue it.

"You do not seem to like her very much," I observed.

"Like her?" he said, his eyes widening in surprise. "I *adore* her. All men adore her. Just as much as most women hate her. Have you seen her in the company of another woman? I have known her for—what? Years, it must be. And I know her no better, understand her no better, than the first day I met her. She is charming, radiant, lovely. But have you ever seen her using her magic, when she is hypnotising, enthralling? Then, believe me, she is frightening. It is a rare man who can resist her."

"Including her husband?"

"John?" He paused, and looked at me. "You haven't got very far if you can ask such a question. Of course he could resist her. That was his appeal. He loved her devotedly because he wanted to. And she loved him because she could not control him. As I say, they were equals. They fought like cat and dog, you know. His anger was cold, hers volcanic. 'My dear,' he would say through gritted teeth, 'your behaviour is quite unacceptable.' And she would throw a plate at him. It went on for hours. I think they actually enjoyed it. It was a central part of their marriage. Neither had power over the other, and both were used to controlling others. Can you imagine the attraction of the only person you have ever met who will not do as you wish?"

"No," I said shortly. "And at the moment it is not at the top of my list of questions."

Xanthos sighed. "A pity. The book will be the poorer for it. It contains the essence of John Stone's nature."

"I think she wants something more factual."

"That may be so," he said. "So—go ahead. Ask me your questions."

I hadn't come very well prepared, which was foolish. Normally, when I interviewed people, I made out in advance a little list of questions to give some form to the interview. This time I had nothing; so I asked randomly, snatching questions from my mind as they floated chaotically into view.

"I am struck," I began, although it had not struck me until then, "by the people I've met so far. Bartoli, an Italian. You, who I am told are Greek. Lady Ravenscliff, who is Hungarian."

"And more than that," he replied. "The head of finance, for example, is a man called Caspar Neuberger."

"German?"

"Oh, he'd be quite annoyed to be called just German," he said with a faint smile. 'I am Chewish, dear man! Chewish!' Try calling him a Prussian—he was born in Prussia—and see what sort of reaction you get. John used to refer to Caspar's military character just to see how long he would be able to control himself."

"I stand corrected. But you know what I mean."

"The corporation of mongrels and half-breeds. Yes, I do see. We are not a blue-blooded company. It is our great quality, and the reason why we have left all our competitors in the dust. John Stone had two great, remarkable qualities, which you would do well to bear in mind. One was his gift for organisation. The other was his judgment of character. He wanted people who would do a good job with the minimum of super-vision. He didn't care who they were, or where they came from. As he had no family to speak of, the board isn't stuffed with useless relations. As far as operations are concerned, Bartoli is a genius at seeing the evolution of the whole. Williams, the managing director, is a brilliant administrator but the son, I believe, of a bankrupt coal merchant. Caspar is extraordinary at finance, and I—sooner or later someone will tell you, so it might as well be me—am of mysterious but entirely unseemly origins. But it all works. John used to complain sometimes, saying it had all been organised too well, and there was nothing left for him to do. That the company no longer needed him."

"And what exactly do you do?"

"Me? Oh, I'm just the salesman. The negotiator. Nothing more than that. People want to buy, I get the best price. I am easily the most disposable of them all. But, what I do, I do well. My reputation is, alas, different. Do you want to know what it is?"

"By all means."

"I am the Angel of Death," he said softly, and looked at me in such a way that for a moment I almost believed him. Then he brightened up and continued cheerfully, "You wouldn't think it to look at me, but there we are. I am the sinister one, the worker in shadows, the man whose hidden hand is everywhere. John Stone's alter ego, who does the dirty work he could not do himself. No violence or turmoil happens anywhere on the planet without me being responsible for it somehow." He smiled sweetly at me.

"Really?"

"Not at all. I am, as I say, merely a negotiator. But it is a fine reputation, you must admit. I do not discourage it much; it makes my life seem more interesting than it is, and perhaps even gives me a small advantage in negotiations. In fact, I do little more than travel around Europe, haggling over details of contracts."

"You are not in England very much?"

"No. Sales to the Royal Navy and the army are done in a different way. I have nothing to do with it, and wouldn't be very effective anyway. The navy likes to deal with gentlemen and I, as you no doubt realise, am not a gentleman."

"The obituaries referred time and again to the organisation of the companies. What's so special about that? Aren't all companies well organised?"

Xanthos laughed. "Oh, no. You would not believe how some go about things. John Stone was remarkable: to create such an organisation, and keeping control of it was a stupendous achievement. There are other factories, all over the world. Mines, wells, ships. All perfectly choreo-graphed. And on top of that there is the money. The banks, the credit notes, the bills of exchange, the shareholdings, the loans, in many currencies and many countries. And everything has to be in the right place at the right moment, for the purpose of constructing these vast machines, some of which take nearly two years to complete. If people had any idea at all how remarkable this was, then the businessman would replace the priest and the poet and the scientist as the greatest figures of the age. But we are modest people," he said with a smile, "and do not desire fame."

"But surely, someone orders a ship, you build it, get paid for it. Isn't it straightforward?"

He sighed. "You don't understand governments, do you? Or money. No. It is not straightforward. A government orders a battleship, say. Do they pay? No. Of course not. They pay a little, the rest when it is de-livered. The greater part of the money you find yourself. That in itself is fabulously risky. Beswick's demands for capital are as great as that of many an entire country. The Government places an order, and we commit the capital. Then—they change their mind. No, Mr. Braddock, it is not simple. Not simple at all."

"I gather things are a bit difficult at the moment, is that right?"

He looked sternly at me. "A bit difficult? We have been through terrible times in the last few years. Ever since the Liberals took power, orders from the Royal Navy have all but dried up, and they are our main customer. We—and Armstrongs and Vickers and Cammell Laird—have been hard put to keep going on occasion. Fortunately, Lord Ravenscliff was more than able to see us through hard times; we are in much better shape than our competitors."

So much about Stone as a man of business. Why did everyone go on about that? Surely there must have been more to him than that?

"Did Lord Ravenscliff have close friends?"

"I have no idea."

"Surely . . ."

"He was my employer. I liked and trusted him, and I believe that regard was mutual. But that is not friendship, if you understand me. That was a different world, one which I—and no business associate—ever penetrated. I know nothing about that side of him whatsoever. Whether he associated with princes or paupers, what he liked to do when he wasn't working. Whether he had any indiscretions . . ."

"You do not know."

"I do not know. Nor have I ever been interested. And now, if you will excuse me, I have some letters to write. Still, it was pleasant to meet you. I have no doubt we will talk again."

"I'm sure I will have many questions over the coming months."

"I will gladly answer them all, if I can. As you may have discerned, I was a great admirer of John Stone."

"He had no failings?"

"John Stone never did anything without a good reason, except fall in love and die. And perhaps these stand out as exceptions merely because we do not know what the reasons were, rather than because they did not exist. Do you count that as a failing, or not?"

CHAPTER 12

Interesting. I walked out of the Ritz and up Bond Street in a reflective mood, trying to unravel what I had been told, and what I had learned. The obvious interpretation, of course, was that Mr. Xanthos truly believed I was writing a biography, in which business would loom large. He wanted to give me instruction about how to present the man. But that reference to indiscretions niggled me. Why would he have mentioned it at all?

And then there was the conspiratorial side. He was trying to draw me in, make me an insider, create feelings of loyalty, of belonging, by dropping exciting little titbits of information. And Lady Ravenscliff? A clear warning there, I thought. Don't be fooled, was the message.

But I could tease no more out of the conversation than that. Business had been tough, but everything was under control. Was that the point? To ram home the message that there was no business reason for Ravenscliff to drop out of a window, intentionally or otherwise? That I should look elsewhere if that was on my mind? But that would mean he knew I was not merely writing a biography, of course.

I hopped on a bus and relaxed. There is something about the clopping of the horses' hooves, the way the driver converses with his beast, the slight rolling of the carriage as it trundles along which has always induced a sense of peace in me—when it is not crammed with noisy, spitting passengers, at any rate. I sat upstairs, even though it was chilly, and watched through gusts of pipe smoke as the great houses of Portman Place, then the even greater establishments of Regent's Park, rolled by. I had never really considered that people actually lived in these places before; they had been as foreign to me as a palace or a prison—more so than prisons, even.

Now I was gaining entry to such places, and I watched with more interest the occasional flicker of domesticity that caught my eye. The servant sitting on a ledge, polishing the outside of a window. Another shaking a blanket to get the dust out. Some children, elaborately dressed, coming down a stairway from a great front door, accompanied by their nanny. The carts of tradesmen parked down the back alleys, so meat and fish and vegetables could be delivered through the rear entrance, unseen. I was allowed in through the front door of St. James's Square, I thought. For the first time in my life, I felt superior to those people amongst whom I had originated. Then it occurred to me that in all probability I ranked in Lady Ravenscliff's mind equally with a governess.

The splendour of Regent's Park does not last long; it is little more than a few bricks thick, an insubstantial theatre set. Behind and beyond are the drabber dwellings of Camden. To the north, though, lies an area of comfortable detached villas built for the man of enough, but not too much, property. My former editor lived in just such a tree-lined street, the houses set back from the wide avenue, private in a way the greater mansions could never be. This was the sort of thing to which I aspired in my dreams; my imagination could take me no higher, but even on three hundred and fifty a year (for seven years) it was way beyond my means. Or was it? I had never even considered the possibility, but now it dawned on me that perhaps I could live in such a place—and the reality of my change in circumstances rushed over me in a wave of pride. I imagined myself at Heal's buying fashionable furniture with a wave of my cheque-book. Engaging a servant. Marrying a desirable woman like—and here I paused, for as that piece of imagination passed through me, I saw the woman of my daydreams sitting on the sofa, looking up from her sewing and smiling as I came in, and she had the face of Lady Ravenscliff. The absurdity brought me back down to earth with a sharp and quite unpleasant crash, but I retained enough sense, at least, to smile ruefully at the tricks that the unbridled imagination can play.

The gallant cavalier who could, in his imagination, sweep the richest woman in the country off her feet, meanwhile, was hesitating outside the address of his old editor, wondering whether he dared knock on the door without arrangement. It was stupid, though, to come all that way and go away again, so after a brief hesitation I summoned enough courage to march up the little path and knock. Then announce myself to the serving girl who opened the door.

I was shown into McEwen's study and asked to wait. It was very much more my sort of place than the drab room from which Stone had controlled his empire. Big French windows opened onto the garden; fresh flowers gave a pleasant scent unspoiled by stale cigar smoke. An ancient, battered leather armchair sat on a slightly careworn carpet on which was stacked a pile of logs for the fire. It looked like a room much loved by its main occupant, and which gave back warmth and comfort in return. It was the room of a trustworthy man.

Who appeared through the door a few moments later, smiling and quite unoffended by my arrival. McEwen's familiar greeting—no longer, I thought, the greeting of editor for subordinate, of superior for employee—reassured me entirely and made me more open than I had intended to be.

"I thought you might show up at some stage," he said cheerfully, "but not quite so quickly. Have you made some great discovery you wish to tell me about? I hope it is something we can print, rather than being merely salacious. Have you discovered what is to become of us?"

"I'm afraid I have little but questions," I replied, "although I can tell you that the *Chronicle* will be in the hands of the executor until the will is settled, which may take some time."

"Yes. I thought as much. Then it goes direct to Lady Ravenscliff, I imagine?"

"Maybe. It all seems quite complicated at the moment."

McEwen was not used to employees—even former employees—being cagey with him. He frowned in displeasure, so I hurried on. "I thought you could tell me in a few seconds things it might take me days to discover on my own. I have made little progress since I saw you. Except to become more confused."

"In what areas?"

"Just about every single one. I have learned some things about his death, as you suggested I do. I have established that the companies were in good health. Unfortunately, I do not see how it assists me in any way."

"I didn't think it would," he said. "I merely wished to satisfy my own curiosity on the matter."

"Why?"

"Oh, call it the instincts of an old newspaperman, if you wish. What have you discovered?"

"Only that quite a lot of people became somewhat agitated the moment he dropped out of the window. There was a man called Cort, for example . . ."

McEwen's eyes narrowed, and he became more attentive.

"Cort?"

"Ah," I said. "You may remember him. Lady Ravenscliff said he worked as a journalist on *The Times* once. Did you know him?"

He stood up, and walked to the window, tapping his foot as he always did when thinking. Eventually he turned round and faced me.

"I'm very sorry, Braddock," he said. "I have been extremely foolish, and reckless on your behalf."

"But why? What's the matter? Who is this man?"

"Indeed. How does he come into a routine biography commissioned by a grieving widow?"

He was looking at me shrewdly, and I could see that I would get nothing out of him without giving something in advance. He was genuinely worried and I was touched by his concern. But he was a newspaperman through and through, nonetheless. Information was food and drink to him.

"It's not a biography," I said eventually. "That's not what she wants me to do. She wants me to find out the identity of Ravenscliff's child."

He raised an eyebrow. "I see. And Cort?"

"Was one of the first at the scene of his death, and I think may have suppressed the news of it for three days."

"Oh," he said softly.

"Oh what?" I was fearful. It was based on nothing, just the way he had said it—apprehensive, almost alarmed; certainly surprised, even shocked. "What's the matter? What is all this?"

"We received a request from the Government not to run the news immediately, as did every other newspaper. We agreed, as the health of

Ravenscliff's businesses is a matter of national interest. Besides, we were assured it was merely to stop an unnecessary panic on the markets. I thought there might be more to it, hence my recommendation of you, so I might have a man on the inside, so to speak, but I never realised it might be that serious." He stuffed his hands in his pockets and looked at the carpet as he did when thinking fast, then looked up at me once more. "Write to her, and say you are sorry, but this job's not for you."

"What? But it was your idea!"

"I know. But this is not idle journalism, hanging around the law courts and police stations. This is not the sort of thing you should get involved in."

"You're being melodramatic. What on earth is bothering you?"

"What do you know about Henry Cort?"

"Very little," I said firmly. "There doesn't seem to be much to know. He was a journalist; he appears to be a gentleman of leisure of moderate means. He knew Lady Ravenscliff many years ago; and he was on the scene in some capacity shortly after Ravenscliff died. There was a reference to FO, but I don't know what it means. Certainly not the Foreign Office, as he is not listed. I looked," I concluded lamely.

"Yes, well. As you say, you know very little."

"So tell me more. You clearly know something."

"Only if you promise to give due consideration to my recommendations."

"I will," I said stoutly. But I don't remember whether I meant it.

"Good. Henry Cort is possibly the most powerful man in the Empire . . ." He held up his hand, for he could see my look of incredulity. "Please. If you want me to tell you, you must not keep interrupting. I briefly came across him, as you so rightly guessed, at *The Times* about twenty years ago. Supposedly he was a journalist, but he wrote little. Yet he was sent to Paris as a correspondent even though there was one there already. No one knew where he came from, why he was given the job, except that it was said he once worked for Barings, and that his appointment was engineered by Sir Henry Wilkinson, a name which, I am sure, means nothing to you whatsoever."

"You are right. But it is not the first time that Barings has cropped up in the last week."

He waved away my diligence with impatience.

"Until he died, Sir Henry Wilkinson was the head—so they said, at least—of the Imperial Secret Service. It is said—equally without anyone really knowing—that Henry Cort is his far more efficient replacement. It is said—again without a shred of evidence or detail—that he once single-handedly prevented a catastrophe which would have brought the Empire to ruin. That he has killed men, and ordered the deaths of others."

I opened my mouth to express something, then thought better of it and shut it again.

"An enterprise which operates on the scale of the British Empire is beset by foes and dangers. We have been fending off war for several decades, and have succeeded quite well. But it is only a matter of time before our luck runs out. Who will we fight? How will we ensure the best advantage for ourselves? Who are our friends? How do we guard our diplomatic, industrial, military secrets? This—so it is said—is what occupies Henry Cort."

"You are not serious about this?"

"I am."

"You've not been reading too many yellow novels?"

"No."

"But you know this. Presumably our enemies know it."

"Presumably. But I do not know it for certain and, perhaps, neither do they. What Cort does, and how he does it, I do not know. There are stories, but nothing that I could ever pin down enough to print in a newspaper, for example. Not that I would be allowed to, even were I so unpatriotic as to consider it. Nor does it matter. What I am trying to tell you is that if Cort is involved in some way, then so is the interest of the entire Empire. And that is not something that a junior reporter of no great experience should be dabbling in."

"Perhaps he's just a family friend."

"Ravenscliff did not have family friends. Nor does Cort."

"So what is going on?"

"I have no idea. And I suggest you do not try to find out. It will do you no good. Does Cort know about you?"

"I very much doubt it. That is, I don't see how he could."

"I see. Have you noticed anyone following you?"

Now I was really getting alarmed. "You're not serious?" I was repeating myself, I know, but it seemed justifiable.

"A couple of years ago," he said, "there was a German reporter in England, a correspondent for a Berlin newspaper. He asked questions about Mr. Cort. He died a few months later. On a railway track just outside Swindon. The verdict was suicide."

"Really?"

"The moral of the story is, do not interest yourself in Mr. Cort. As you are English, he will no doubt be more indulgent towards you, as it is safe to assume you are not—or not yet—in the pay of our enemies . . ."

"Of course I'm not—"

"But you are, of course, in the pay of a woman who is, or was, a subject of the Austro-Hungarian Empire, which is in alliance with the German Empire . . ."

I gaped. I should have managed better, but I gaped. "You're making this up," I said reproachfully.

"I am merely pointing out that an excessively lucrative engagement for a spurious project might be interpreted in many different ways, some not to your advantage."

"I am certainly not going to give up £350 a year because of the fantastical notions of some civil servant," I said robustly. "If anyone wishes to ask me what I am doing I will explain fully and openly. Naturally I will. But I am doing nothing inappropriate at all. And it is my right . . ."

"Of course. But your right as an Englishman can be misunderstood, and may be held to contradict your duty. So be careful. Are you still inclined to continue with this?"

I thought hard. He was a man I trusted; until that moment I had not realised how much I trusted him. But I could not entirely discount the money. And, uppermost in my mind there floated the image of Lady Ravenscliff, sitting on the settee in her sitting room, looking so vulnerable and needy, missing her husband so greatly, and placing herself in my hands. Asking my help. Me, of all the people in London.

"I may," I said. "But not until I am sure that your warnings are correct. I do not want to place myself in danger, obviously. Nor do I wish to meddle in things which are not my concern. But I have taken on a commission, and so far I can see no real reason not to fulfil it."

He sighed, and looked frustrated and disappointed.

"I am not saying I am determined to continue. Merely that I wish to."

"I thought that might be your attitude. I am sorry for it. I think you are making a mistake."

I sat and considered. What McEwen had just said had made a deep impression. And yet, an old stubbornness was beginning to stir. Why should I be frightened off with just a word whispered in my ear? Why shouldn't I discover whatever I wanted to? I was breaking no law; in a way I was trying to discover if any had been broken. And I was being told that I should be afraid, and cautious. Englishmen should never be afraid or cautious; not of their own Government. I looked up defiantly.

"Who does Cort work for?"

"The Government."

"I mean, which bit?"

"I have no idea. The Foreign Office, the War Office, the Home Office. All or none. It is in the nature of a task like this that it is ill-defined. You will not find any piece of paper saying what it is. I doubt he is even on the rolls of the Civil Service. We finally have a formal intelligence organisation, and he is not part of that, either."

"Oh."

"He will be paid, and his expenses met, out of miscellaneous funds, untraceable to any one department of state."

"But one person cannot—"

"Oh, good heavens, there are more than Cort! All over Britain, throughout the Empire, all over Europe, there are his men, and his women, I gather, who watch our enemies and their doings. They watch troops, they watch politicians, they watch what sorts of weapons are being produced by factories. They watch ships in harbours, they watch the people watching us. I said we may eventually be at war; in truth it has already started. You've read the stories in the papers; about German spies in this country, about trained murderers waiting for the moment war breaks out to strike and cause havoc here, on the streets of London."

"Hysterical nonsense."

"Are you sure? Our enemies learn fast. They have watched the chaos a few anarchists with homemade bombs can cause. How easy it is to kill a king in Portugal, a president in France. To sow panic with a well-placed bomb in a restaurant. Do you think they do not realise what potent weapons are fear and confusion?"

Personally, I had always considered these mouthings in the news-papers to be simply a way of softening up the population so that re-pressive measures could be taken against the trade unions, and poor people who wished to strike in order to gain a living wage. It had never crossed my mind that someone like McEwen would actually take them seriously. Or that they might be true.

CHAPTER 13

The Russell Hotel in Bloomsbury was a fairly new building, having been completed only a few years previously. All terra-cotta, brick and marble, it presented a formidable appearance to the outside world, so much so that although I had walked past it on many occasions, I had never even thought of going inside. It was not for people like me, any more than the Ritz was, or drawing rooms in St. James's Square. Nor yet was it for the very wealthy. In fact, it was difficult to work out who, exactly, was meant to use it: it was too far from the West End to be convenient for the people who congregated there, and not really properly sited for those who worked in the City. And most visitors to the British Museum were not the sort who could afford its lavish prices.

That was a problem for the management, not for me. When I arrived there I simply spent my time staring at the multicoloured marble columns, the carved ceilings, the glittering chandeliers. It must, I thought, be the sort of surroundings aristocrats were used to all the time. I confess I felt rather grand; I was beginning to get a taste for this sort of living, and after only a week or so. It was slightly worrying.

"Dreadful place," Lady Ravenscliff remarked as she sat down opposite me, once she had announced herself and I had stood up to greet her. She was smiling, indeed she seemed energised by the outing. Her eyes were bright and larger than I had noticed before; she looked extraordinarily beautiful, as though she had made a special effort to intimidate the opposition. The idea of complimenting her never occurred to me.

"Don't you like it?"

"I find it somewhat ostentatious. It is designed to impress the impressionable. I suppose it does that very well."

She noticed the way I had blushed. "I'm sorry," she said. "You will find I am prone at times to be opinionated and insensitive. Please never take anything I say on such matters to be of any value at all. I was brought up with older, shabbier buildings which did not force you to admire them all the time."

"I suppose you might say I was as well," I replied. "A little ostentation I find enjoyable."

She smiled. "So it is. I stand corrected. Let us bathe in this exuberant vulgarity while we wait. Could you inform Signora Vincotti of our presence?"

I did so, while she sat immobile, a dreamy smile coming over her face. I did not know her very well, but I guessed she was calming herself before what could well be an unpleasant interview.

And, ten minutes later, Esther Vincotti descended. Let me be direct and say there was no competition possible between the two women. One alert, intelligent, beautiful, elegant; the other stout, almost square in shape, with a ruddy though amiable complexion over which she clearly took no pains at all. Never had I seen any woman less likely to be connected in some way to a vastly wealthy man. She was aged around fifty and while her clothes were not poor, she manifestly had little notion of how to dress for effect. Her hair was grey and no attempt had been made to make it look at all stylish or well groomed. Her face seemed good natured, although it bore an expression which made it clear that, if Lady Ravenscliff was anxious at the coming interview, she was thoroughly frightened.

She sat down nervously once the introductions had been made—with me acting as the go-between, as neither of the two women seemed willing to start the proceedings off and Lady Ravenscliff had (she told me) prohibited Mr. Henderson the solicitor from coming anywhere near the hotel until she had finished. Neither, however, had a look of hostility about them. Lady Ravenscliff had hardly moved a muscle, but I guessed was utterly perplexed by the idea that her husband might have dallied with such an utterly ordinary, maternal figure as this. As a result, she was hiding behind a mask of aristocratic grandeur which was both intimidating and (to me) exceptionally alluring.

"It is very good of you to come here, Your Ladyship. I am most honoured to meet you," Signora Vincotti said after a while. "And I must thank you for arranging for me to stay in this splendid hotel. It is quite beyond what I am used to."

"I do not think it is particularly good of me," she replied. "And I am afraid I must wait before I know whether I am equally honoured by meeting you. How well did you know my husband?"

Nothing like getting down to business fast, I thought. I had anticipated an interminable round of politenesses before the real subject was broached.

"I do not know him at all," replied the other woman. She spoke with something of an Italian accent, but her English was much too good for her to have been anything other than English in origin. "I am completely at a loss as to why I am here. All I know is that I received a telegram from a London solicitor telling me I had to come to London, that it was a matter of the utmost urgency. Then they sent me a railway ticket. First class. I am totally mystified and very worried. I am sure I have done nothing wrong."

This was not the reply either of us had been expecting; Lady Ravenscliff registered something like incredulity, although she managed to keep her expression under control.

"You didn't know my husband?"

"I met him when I was a child, I believe, though I do not remember it."

"Where, exactly?"

"In Venice, which is where my father lived. And where he died."

"And this was Signor Vincotti?"

"No. That is my married name, although I am a widow now. Luigi died several years ago, leaving me with four children. But my father provided for me, and I have had a good life. His name was Macintyre. He was a travelling engineer. He died in an accident when I was eight, and I was brought up by a family there."

"You are even more well-provided for now, it seems," said Lady Ravenscliff. "My husband has died, as you may know, and you are a beneficiary of his will."

Signora Vincotti looked thoroughly surprised by this. "That was very kind of him," she said. "Can you tell me why?"

I noticed she did not ask how much. I quite liked her for that.

"We were rather hoping that you might tell us."

"I'm afraid I have no idea. None."

"And you really never met him after your father died?"

"Never. Until that telegram arrived I had quite forgotten him. It was a great effort to recall him at all."

"You speak very good English for someone brought up in a foreign country," I commented.

"I was brought up by an English family. Mr. Longman was the British Consul in Venice and lived there for many years, but died when I was twenty. As I had no connections to England at all apart from him and his wife, I stayed and eventually married. My husband was a civil engineer.

With his salary, and my inheritance, we lived very well. Two of my daughters are married already. And of my two sons, one will be a lawyer, while the other intends to follow his father into engineering."

"I congratulate you," said Lady Ravenscliff. Was there something in the account of steady, modest, family life, of seeing children growing, and growing well, that she envied? Did it make her sad that she could never boast about her own children to others—oh, he's doing so well, we're so proud of him . . . ? Was she sad she could never look into the face of a child and see an echo of her husband reflected back at her?

"Do you not wish to know how much the bequest is?" I put in, as we seemed to be straying far from the point.

"I suppose I should; but I cannot see how it can be a great deal of money."

"It depends on what you consider a great deal. It is £50,000."

A total silence greeted this piece of information. Signora Vincotti grew deathly pale, almost as though she had just been told some devastating news. "There must be some mistake," she said eventually in a voice which was so quiet and so trembling it was difficult to make out.

"It seems not. I hope you will excuse our curiosity, but we are naturally interested in the reason for it. Lord Ravenscliff was an immensely wealthy man, but even by his standards this is a large sum."

I was aware I was talking like a member of the Ravenscliff entourage, like some retainer. It made me uncomfortable in some ways, but I also noted a certain smugness in my mind as I spoke.

"I cannot help you at all, I really cannot," she said, looking as though she might burst into tears at any moment.

"Was your father a rich man? Might they have been in business together?"

"I doubt it. I was always told he was very poor; quite unworldly. But not so unworldly that he did not provide for me."

"And this inheritance. It was an annuity? It comes from an insurance company? A Venetian one? Italian?"

"No, no. An English bank."

"Please do not take offence, but could you tell me how much this is for? It would help to gauge what sort of relationship your father might have had with Lord Ravenscliff."

You see—I was also beginning to think like a man of money. Never before in my life would I have considered that income flow might help determine a man's relationships, but it was now beginning to come naturally, now I realised that, for some, it was the only thing which mattered.

"I receive a cheque four times a year from Barings Bank in London for £62."

I calculated quickly, using my newfound financial sophistication. £62 a quarter was about £250 a year, which meant a capital sum of something around £6,000. Hardly in Ravenscliff's league. His bequest meant that her income had just multiplied by eight. A fortune by English standards, and I guessed a vast fortune by Venetian.

"Signora Vincotti," said Lady Ravenscliff. "I would like to ask you an even more direct question. Please do not take offence, but it is essential that I know the answer." She said it in a way which suggested she did not care one way or the other if the other woman did take offence. What was wrong with her? She really didn't have to try quite so hard to be rude.

Vincotti looked at her enquiringly.

"My husband travelled frequently to Venice. Sometimes I accompanied him, most times not. I have never really cared for Venice." She paused for a moment. "Let me put it bluntly. Was my husband the father of any of your children?"

Signora Vincotti stared in shock at the question, and I felt sure she was going to become angry, as she had every right to be. For a moment this was very nearly the case, but she was very much more intelligent than her thick-set, homely features suggested. She reached out and took Lady Ravenscliff's hand.

"Oh, I see," she said gently. "I see."

Lady Ravenscliff snatched her hand away.

"Don't be annoyed with me, I mean no insult," the Italian woman said softly. "No. There is no possibility, no possibility at all, that your husband was the father of any of my children. None. If you saw them, and saw pictures of my husband as well, you would not have to take my word for it."

"In that case, we need trespass on your time no longer," Lady Ravenscliff said, standing up immediately. "I am sure my lawyers will be in contact with you in due course. My thanks for your assistance."

And with that she walked swiftly across the hotel lobby, leaving me— feeling thoroughly embarrassed by her appalling behaviour—to make amends as best as I could by saying goodbye in a more friendly fashion, and mutter about shock and grief. None of which was true.

Then I too hurried into the noise of Russell Square and found Lady Ravenscliff waiting for me, her face dark with anger.

"Appalling woman," she said. "How dare she patronise me? If her father was as vulgar as she . . . certainly there must be a physical resemblance. She looks like a bulldog in frills."

"She conducted herself with a good deal more dignity than you did, even though she must have found the encounter very trying . . ."

"And it wasn't for me?" She turned around and confronted me for my mollifying remarks. "You think everything was calm and easy for me? That discovering your dead husband has a child, having to deal with people like that—"

"I didn't mean—"

"You are not in my employ to see both sides of the argument, Braddock."

"Mr. Braddock. And in fact I am in your employ to do precisely that. You want me to discover the truth. Not to be partisan."

"It's my money, and you are being paid. You will do as you are told."

"I will do a good and proper job, or I will not do it at all. Please decide what you want of me."

Dangerous, that. The desire, which comes upon me on occasion, to strike an attitude put me in a risky position. Of course I wanted to do a decent job; but I also wanted the money, although, after my editor's sombre remarks, I would have been quite happy to have the project brought to an end. The perfect reply (in my opinion) would have been had she told me that she wanted to pay me a huge amount of money to go away. Unfortunately, my upright, manly remarks had the opposite effect. She crumpled in front of me and began sobbing quietly, so through pure instinct I responded in a supportive and consolatory fashion, which of course made things even worse. I handed her a handkerchief, which, fortunately, was clean. Then I completely wrecked things by taking her hand and holding it firmly. She did not snatch it away.

"Let us go into the square and find a seat," I suggested. "It is a little public here on the pavement."

I led her into the middle of Russell Square and the little stall near the centre that served office workers. There I bought two cups of tea and presented her with one. I thought it was probably one of the most exotic things she had done for years, she who never did anything in public, nor anything without servants. She looked a little doubtfully at the old cracked cup.

"Don't worry," I assured her. "It's quite safe."

She sipped in silence, initially more to please me, but then with greater enthusiasm.

"I apologise for my rudeness," she said after a while. "And of course I behaved horribly to that poor woman. I will write and apologise. Please do not think badly of me. I am finding all of this so hard."

I nodded in acknowledgement. "I understand. I really do. But while we are both amiably disposed to one another, might I renew my request that you begin to tell me the truth?"

The flash in her eyes clearly demonstrated that, however much she might have been chastened, the situation was very far from permanent. I pressed on while there was still time.

"Mr. Cort," I said.

"What about him?"

"Henry Cort is in charge of government espionage. He has been described to me as the most powerful and dangerous man in the country."

"Henry?" she said. "Oh, I don't think . . ."

"You have known him for years, so you told me. I do not believe you could be unaware that there is more to him than meets the eye."

She considered for a moment. "I think you also have been less than open with me," she replied. "If I remember, I asked what your interest in Henry was, and you replied merely that someone had mentioned his name. I do not see why I should be open with you, if you dissimulate with me."

A fair point. "Very well. Let me summarise. Henry Cort visited the police within hours of your husband's death, and was quite possibly the man responsible for suppressing news of it for nearly three days. In the meantime, Barings Bank was brought in to support the price of the Rialto Investment Trust, which was your husband's financial instrument for controlling a large part of British industry."

"I know what Rialto is."

"Cort also used to work for Barings," I continued. "Barings, we now know, pays Signora Vincotti's annuity. I refuse to believe that an old friend, whom you have known for twenty years or more, would conceal all of this from you."

She smiled quietly. "Of course. You are quite correct. I didn't mention it because I did not know of his involvement when John died. Besides, Mr. Cort and I are not close."

"That means you do not like each other?"

"If you like."

"Why not?"

"That is none of your business. John necessarily had dealings with him, but I insisted that they be conducted away from me."

I brooded over this. It didn't help me at all. "Why? I mean, what dealings?"

"John made weapons, the Government bought them. Naturally they had common interests. Don't ask me more; I do not know."

"How did you meet your husband? What was he like?"

She smiled, recalling a fond memory. "He was the kindest man you could meet, the best I ever knew," she began. "That was not his reputation, perhaps, and I sense that it is not the opinion you have formed of him, but you are wrong. The man of money and power, and the man who shared my life, had little in common."

She paused and looked across the square, at all the normal, poor people strolling to and fro, or hurrying across. Some looked as though they were taking a break from the reading desks of the British Museum, others came from the shops and offices of Holborn. I even hoped—again, this was a sign to which I should have given more attention—that perhaps an old colleague from Fleet Street might appear, and see me. See me with her, in fact.

"I met him on a train," she went on, as this pleasant and dangerous fantasy flickered through my mind. "On the Orient Express."

"Is it true he had his own carriage?"

She laughed, more easily now. "No, of course not. I've told you—he was a simple man in his tastes. He had his own compartment, of course. There is no particular pleasure in sharing with total strangers unless you have to. Ostentation would have been detrimental to his business; often on these trips he liked to travel as quietly as possible so as not to be noticed."

Maybe she had really loved him; she smiled as memories flitted past, the very idea of her husband brought her pleasure, and the thought of his death caused her grief. I had anticipated a marriage of convenience and companionship at most. A rich man seeks a beautiful young woman in the same way that such people might desire a racehorse, or an expensive painting. Is that not true? And the beautiful young woman desires security and luxury. But they expect no gratification, and little affection; these (so I understood) they must find elsewhere. Perhaps this had been different.

"The thing about John, you see, is that he was quite simple in his affections as well. He thought of himself as a sophisticated man of the world, and in business matters no doubt he was. But he was not a man for gallantry, had no idea how to seduce, or flatter or be anything other than he was. I found his uncomplicated nature beguiling."

She looked at me, and smiled. "I can see I am surprising you," she said. "You think I would want an elegant man of sophistication. Handsome, athletic, worldly."

"I suppose."

"You know nothing, I'm afraid, Mr. Braddock. Nothing of me, nothing of women at all." She said it gently, as a matter of fact, but I still blushed hotly.

"Someone said that both of you met their match in the other."

She laughed. "Who on earth said that?"

"Mr. Xanthos. Do you know him?"

She nodded. "Not well. But we have met often."

"So is his opinion true?"

"I would hardly claim to be John's match. What else did he tell you?"

"Oh, that you were once one of the most influential women in France, or something like that."

Here she let out a burst of laughter, and almost choked on her tea. Her eyes sparkled with merriment as she put down her cup carefully and looked at me. "Good heavens," she said after a while. "What an extraordinary idea. How on earth did he come up with that?"

"He said you ran a salon, or something."

"And that made me the most influential woman in France?"

"Apparently."

"Well, no," she said, still smiling broadly. I think it was the first time I had seen her laugh, genuinely and without restraint. It transformed her. "No, I'm afraid not. A young girl from Hungary would stand no chance whatsoever of establishing herself like that in Paris. Not if she was respectable."

"Pardon?"

"Some of the most famous *salonnières* are—or were, I do not know what it is like now—courtesans. Very expensive ones, but still . . . I hope you do not think . . ."

"No, no. Of course not. I mean . . ." I was red in the face, blushing deeply; I could even feel the roots of my hair burning with embarrassment. She looked at me, enjoying my confusion, but then kindly looked away across the square until I recovered myself. I could see her mouth still twitching, though.

"Is Mr. Bartoli being helpful?" she asked, to change the subject.

"Mr. Bartoli does not approve of me. He has indicated he will give me as little assistance as possible."

She raised an eyebrow. "Let me deal with that" was her only reply and I realised Mr. Bartoli was not going to be happy about it.

"I asked about your husband's concerns."

"I do not know what they were. Just that he had been quite busy in the months before his death; I reproached him for it, and said that he really should be working less hard at his age, not more. But he said that this was the way of business, and if something important came up, you could not postpone it simply because you were getting old. Besides, he always maintained that working kept him young, and I think there was something in that. His mind was absolutely undiminished, and he was in no way frail."

"And this something important . . . ?"

"Tell me, Mr. Braddock, why do you ask so many questions about my husband's death?"

"I think you know perfectly well," I said. "Those papers disappeared when he died. I have two ways forward. Either to look for the child, or to look for the papers which will do the work for me. As I am naturally lazy, I think I should exhaust the latter option first of all. Besides, I don't even know when this boy—or girl—was born, or even in what country. Clearly if it was last year that requires one approach. If it was ten or twenty years ago, then it is different. Do you really have no idea at all . . . ?"

"No," she said softly and a little sadly. "None whatsoever. I really do not."

CHAPTER 14

I realise that I have said little about my own life in my account. Partly this is because I wish to tell the story of Lord Ravenscliff, but mainly because I have little enough to say. Life as a reporter involved long hours; often enough I failed even to get back to my lodgings for dinner, and I frequently had to be up and out before Mrs. Morrison had even begun to prepare breakfast. Lunch and dinner were eaten in pubs or taverns; my circle of acquaintanceship, outside my fellow lodgers and reporters, was limited. I briefly attended a reading group of worthy socialists, who would get together to discuss texts on the evils of capitalism, but I missed so many of the meetings, and so rarely had the time to read the books we were meant to be talking about, that I gradually let this drop.

I had no family nearby; my parents lived in the Midlands and I was the only member of the family to leave the town of my birth. I think I was the first of innumerable generations to stray more than ten miles from the centre of Coventry. We were not close; my wish to try my luck in London was perfectly incomprehensible to them. So it had been to me; I did not know why I wanted to leave so much. All I knew was that, if I stayed, I would end up like my father, working as a clerk in an office, or like my brothers, spending their lives in the factories and workshops of that city because they did not dare to do anything else. I do not relish adventure, but that prospect so terrified me that I was willing to swallow my fears. When I left school I worked for a year or so on the local newspaper and convinced myself that I was good at it; better still, I convinced others for long enough to get a reference. Armed with this and five pounds given to me by my father—who understood better than I why I did not wish to be like him—I caught the train to London.

It took two months and nearly all my money to get my first job, working on the social announcements page of the *Chronicle*. I later moved to football, the obituaries and after nearly two years finally had my piece of luck. The crime reporter was more of a drunk than was average, and he was entirely unconscious on the pavement outside the Duck when the first of the Marylebone murders took place. I volunteered to stand in for him, and McEwen agreed. In my desperation—such chances come very infrequently—I nearly said, "Let me go, Cox is drunk again." That would have damned me. Instead, I robustly denied all knowledge of the poor man's whereabouts, and said that I was sure he was out on a story. I would fill in until he returned.

And so I did, as he never did return. McEwen did not need me to tell tales. He knew perfectly well what Cox was working on and his patience finally snapped.

I did a good job; a very good job, dare I say it, considering my inexperience. I was told to continue until a proper replacement was found, but one never was. Eventually editorial interest faded, and I continued as acting crime reporter for another year until someone remembered that I was not supposed to be doing the job at all. Then I was promoted, given a proper position, and told to keep going.

That had been five years previously. I had dreamed of being a reporter on a London newspaper and I was one. My ambitions for life should have been satisfied. But, however splendid a job may seem when one does not have it, it rarely stands up to close acquaintanceship. I was beginning to get bored with the life, and even to find murder most foul just a little tedious. But I had not yet fixed on a new goal to fire my ambitions once more. That, quite apart from the money, was why I had taken up Lady Ravenscliff's offer with so little hesitation.

As far as the matter of Ravenscliff was concerned, I needed to look through his office with care. Perhaps the papers were there after all. Perhaps some diary or letter would provide all the information I needed, and solve the matter in a few seconds. I doubted it; his widow wasn't so helpless that she couldn't find that herself, and she had good reason to look carefully. I knew already that most of the papers were financial in nature and that I could spend days looking at them, with every possibility that I would miss the vital clue even if it was there. So I decided to recruit Franklin.

This wasn't easy, not because he wasn't willing, but because he had so little time off from work. He was at the bank from eight in the morning to seven in the evening every day, six days a week. And on Sunday he spent much of his time in church. I thought initially this was calculated; Franklin attended a church frequented by the great bankers of the City and travelled a couple of miles to do his singing and praying when he could have walked a hundred yards round the corner to St. Mary's, Chelsea. But that was attended only by shopkeepers and landladies. Eventually I realised I did him an injustice. Many people choose a church they find inspiring. Some go for ancient and beautiful buildings, some choose a church with fine music, some prefer an eloquent vicar who can deliver a good sermon. Franklin found that being enveloped in an aura of money incited religious awe in him. To sit around individuals who controlled tens of millions of pounds brought home to him the infinite possibilities of God's benevolence, and the intricacy of his Creation.

It sounds like a fundamental misunderstanding of Christianity. Eye of a needle, and all that. But it was Franklin's nature; he could do no other. Just as some people simply are incapable of loving a woman who is not beautiful, so Franklin could only think of the divine in terms of the endless flow of capital. His piety was no less for being so strange in origin, just as a man's love for a woman is no less passionate merely because it may require a decent inheritance to make it flower. He believed that the rich were better people than the poor, and that to be around them made him better as well. Wealth was both the indication of God's favour, and provided the means to carry out His wishes on earth.

Harry Franklin, you will understand, had no trouble whatsoever in reconciling God, Darwin and Mammon; indeed, each depended on the others. The survival of the fittest meant the triumph of the richest, which was part of His plan for mankind. Accumulation was divinely ordained, both a mark of God's favour and a way of earning more benevolence. True, Christ was a carpenter but, had He been living at the start of the twentieth century, Franklin was sure that the Messiah would have paid good attention to His stock levels, steadily expanded His business into the manufacture of fine furniture, while also investing in the latest methods of mass production by means of a stock market flotation to raise the additional capital. Then He would have brought in a manager to free Himself to go about His ministry.

Inevitably, I suppose, the idea of being allowed into the hallowed halls where once trod the feet of the supreme capitalist of the age gave him pause. In fact, the mere idea of Ravenscliff terrified him, and when he arrived at the house in St. James's Square on the following Sunday morning he was more nervous than I had ever seen him. He seemed to shrink as we were let in, gazed around with reverence as we walked up the stairs, tiptoed past the doors which led to the reception rooms on the first floor, and said not a word until I had firmly shut the door to Ravenscliff's study.

"I don't want to disturb your reverie," I remarked, "but can we get started?"

He nodded, and looked anxiously at the chair—the very chair—on which the divine bottom had once rested as its owner perused his books. I made him sit on it, by the desk. Just to torment him a little.

"I will read the letters, if you take care of anything with numbers on it."

"So what am I looking for?"

He had asked me this before. Several times, in fact. But so far I had avoided answering him. While I had Lady Ravenscliff's permission to use him, I was not allowed to tell him exactly what all this was about.

"I want you to look for interesting payments," I said lamely. "Nothing to do with his business interests, although you may look through that if you wish. I want to get an idea of how he spent his own money, in the hope that it will tell me what he was like. Did he buy paintings? Bet on horses? How much on wine? Did he give money to charities, or to hospitals or to friends? Did he have an expensive tailor? Bootmaker? A French chef? Paint me a financial portrait of the man. I need all the information I can get, as everyone I have talked to so far has given me nothing but generalities. I meanwhile will read through everything else, and see what there is."

Franklin found the idea of columns of money reassuring, although the thought of prying into Ravenscliff's private papers made him apprehensive. As it did me. But somewhere in those huge piles of paper might lie the little nugget that would answer all my questions. I had searched the room again the previous day and still found nothing.

So we set to work, each in our different way. I worked like a reporter: spending ten minutes reading, then jumping up and staring out the window, humming to myself. Picking up this pile, then the next, more or less at random, hoping that luck would give me something of interest. Franklin, in contrast, worked like a banker; starting at the top of the first sheet, working his way steadily down through the pile, then on to the next. Number after number, column after column, file after file. He sat still and impassively, only his eyes flickering across the tallies, his pen occasionally jotting a brief note on a pad of paper before him. He made no noise; he seemed almost to be in a dream—and a happy dream at that.

"Well?" I asked after about an hour and a half, when I could stand it no longer. "Have you found anything? I haven't."

Franklin held up a hand for quiet, and he continued reading, then jotted down another note. "What did you say?"

"I said, What have you got so far?"

"I've only just started," he began. "You can't expect . . ."

"I don't. But I want a break. Do you have any idea how bad his handwriting was? Each word is a torture. I want a diversion for a few moments so my eyes can recover."

"I'll look at them myself another time," he offered. "This stuff, in contrast, is fascinating. Absolutely fascinating. But I suspect of no earthly use to you at all."

I groaned. The worst of both worlds. Franklin was going to tell me more about stock prices.

He did. I absented myself mentally from the room after a few minutes, as he waxed lyrical about debenture stocks and dividend payouts, and operations in the market.

"Not as sound as everyone thought, you see," he concluded some time later. How long—ten minutes or an hour I could not say.

"What isn't?"

Franklin frowned. "Have you been paying attention?"

"Of course," I replied robustly. "I've been hanging on every word. I'd just like a useful summary. I'm a journalist, remember. I don't like detail."

"Very well. A summary. Ravenscliff's enterprises in England have been burning up cash. He has been sucking money out of the operation at a quite phenomenal rate for almost a year."

I stared hopefully at him. This was more my line. I could understand this. Hand in the till to pay for wine, women and song. Gambling debts. Racehorses. Jump out of the window to avoid the shame of ruin. How very disappointing. "How much?"

"About three million pounds."

I looked at him aghast. That was a lot of racehorses. "Are you sure?"

"Pretty sure. That is, I've looked back at the past seven years' accounts. They are very complicated, but he had a private set prepared every year, which summarised his total operations. I imagine no one else ever saw them. Without those, I doubt I could ever have noticed what he was up to. But these are quite clear. Do you want me to show you?" He brandished a thick folder of complicated-looking papers in my direction.

"No. Just tell me."

"Very well. If you take the amount of cash at the start of the year, add on the cash received, subtract the cost of operations and other expenses, then you get the amount of cash at the end of the year. Do you understand that?"

I nodded cautiously.

"The official accounts use one figure. These," again he waved the file in the air, "use another which is very different. All the shareholders, except for Ravenscliff, who evidently knew better, believe that the businesses have considerably more money than, in fact, they do. Three million, as I say."

"And that means?"

"That means that if anyone ever found out, then not only Rialto but all the companies it owns shares in would drop like a stone. If you'll forgive me." Franklin seemed momentarily alarmed that he could be frivolous on such a subject, even accidentally. "The companies are not bankrupt, but they are worth nowhere near as much as people think. Including these people."

I looked. It was a list of names, with figures on them. The Prime Minister, the Chancellor, the Foreign Secretary. Their opposite numbers in the Conservative party. And many other MPs, judges and bishops.

"What are these numbers?"

"Their shareholdings in Rialto. Multiply by the price. The Prime Minister in the case of a total collapse would lose nearly £11,000. The Leader of the Opposition £8,000."

"Enough reason to get Barings in to prop up the share price?"

"More than enough, I'd say."

"So what do I do about this?"

"You keep your mouth firmly closed. If you must do something, try to find out if any of the people on this list have been selling their shares. I have savings of £75, and £35 of these are in the Rialto Investment Trust. I intend to sell them first thing on Monday morning. It has taken me four years to save that much, and I don't intend to lose it. I imagine anyone else who knew about this would have the same reaction."

He looked protective as he thought of his nest egg. For my part, I had not a penny saved in the world, as yet. But I could imagine how I would feel at the prospect of losing the result of several years' parsimony.

"Where has this money gone, then?"

He shrugged. "No idea."

"There is nothing else to say? I can't imagine that such a quantity of money could just vanish."

"I quite agree. But it's not here, or at least I haven't found it. I told you I wasn't finished. And there are some files missing. I only found this one because it was in the wrong place."

"So what do I do?"

"If I were you? I'd forget I'd ever seen it. If you say so much as a word you will start a financial storm the likes of which London has not seen for decades."

I could see that he was enjoying this brush with the occult secrets of the mighty. I wasn't. I knew better than he realised what we were dealing with. He was right. I should leave this alone; forget all about it. But I *was* a reporter. I wanted to know what was going on; where that money had gone. The fact that it had nothing to do with Ravenscliff's child was irrelevant. I had completely forgotten about the little brat.

Franklin brought me back to myself. "I must go," he said. "I have to go to church."

How he could think of such a thing, when he had just discovered proof that all these people he liked to associate with in the pews were not quite what they seemed I did not know. But Franklin was not the sort who would allow one sinner to call into question his entire outlook on life. I suspected he would pray fervently that God would show him His favour by allowing him to get a good price for his Rialto Ordinaries the next morning.

I nodded. He left, but not without reminding me of his advice. "One other thing," he added as he opened the door. "File three/twenty-three. Personal disbursements. Try that. Apart from anything else, it seems that His Lordship has been supporting the International Brotherhood of Socialists for the past year."

I sat in Ravenscliff's study for the next hour in a reverie, occasionally emerging from my mood to study the notes Franklin had made. I did quite well. Not that I uncovered any significant new financial informa-tion, of course. That was quite beyond me. But I at least managed to understand it. And I discovered, by comparing handwriting, that the accounts detailing the true situation at Rialto had been prepared for Ravenscliff by Joseph Bartoli, his right-hand man. My simple solution to the problem—simply asking Bartoli what was going on—disappeared. If

Bartoli was part of some elaborate fraud, he was hardly going to open up to me.

Eventually I put down the file, and took out file three/twenty-three. It was, as Franklin had said, Ravenscliff's personal expenses, and exactly the sort of documents I should have been studying. If there were any payments for illegitimate children they should be here, buried amongst the itemised notes for clothes, shoes, household expenses, food, servants' wages and so on. The lists went back to 1900, and there were many entries which were ambiguous. I realised after a while that detailed study would yield nothing: an entire schoolroom of bastards could easily have been hidden under the heading of "miscellaneous expense" (1907: £734 17s 6d). All it established was that, by the standards of the wealthy (if, perhaps, no longer quite as wealthy as I had imagined) Ravenscliff was not at all extravagant. His greatest expense was his wife (1908: £2,234 12s 6d) and he spent more on books than he did on clothes. The payments Franklin referred to were on a separate sheet on the top of the file. Easy enough to understand, they were headed "Provisional list of payments to the International Brotherhood of Socialists." No ambiguity there. And a list of dates and amounts. This was curious. It was a lot of money; nearly £400 in the past year. Nor did it occur in the more detailed sheets of expenses underneath it. And what on earth was someone like Ravenscliff doing giving money to a group who, one assumed, were dedicated to abolishing everything he stood for? Had he had a Damascene conversion? Did that explain the sucking of money out of his own companies? I went back to his appointments diary and there, jotted down for a few days after his death, was the entry, "Xanthos—ibs."

I did not like Ravenscliff by instinct, but I was beginning to find him fascinating. A book-reading, socialist-sympathising, child-begetting capitalist fraud. Wilf Cornford at Seyd's had told me he was nothing but money; he was beginning to be very much more than that. Too much more, in fact.

"They told me you were still here," came the voice of Lady Ravenscliff from the door. I looked up. It was getting dark in the room and I glanced at the clock on the mantelpiece. Nearly eight o'clock. No wonder I felt uncomfortable. I was hungry. No more nor less than that. That was a relief.

"Working away," I said cheerfully.

"And have you discovered anything?"

"Not on the main question, no," I said, dragging my thoughts away from the disappearing millions and resolving to follow Franklin's advice. "Merely some things which revive the nosy old journalist in me."

I handed her the sheet of paper about the Brotherhood. She looked at it with a very prettily arched eyebrow, then her glance returned to me.

"Did your husband start going around calling for world revolution in his last months?" I asked. "Tell the butler over the kedgeree that property was theft, and how he should throw off his chains?"

"Not to my knowledge. He rarely said anything over breakfast. He usually read *The Times*."

"Then this is a bit of a curiosity, don't you think?"

She looked again at the piece of paper. "It is. Have you ever heard of these people?"

"No," I said, a little disingenuously. It was true, but these sorts of people had been talked about at my socialist reading group. If such an admission would have produced in her a look of alarm at my dangerous political associations, I might have mentioned it, but I suspected it would produce nothing more than contempt and even pity. Earnest men in scruffy clothes in a dingy room arguing about things they had no power to alter. Well, it was a bit like that.

"I imagine they are some sort of revolutionary group," I said lamely.

"How very odd." She tossed the paper aside, and changed the subject. "I was wondering whether you have eaten? And if not whether you would care to do so? I am not in the mood for company, but do not wish to dine alone. You would do me a great kindness if you accepted."

I looked up, my eyes caught hers and my world changed forever.

I was paralysed; literally, I could not move. Rather than simply looking at her eyes, I seemed to be peering deep into her soul. I felt as though I had been punched in the stomach. How can I put it? Lady Ravenscliff vanished from my mind to be replaced by Elizabeth; I can give no better account of the transformation in my mind. Her vulnerability and her pride were both part of it, I suppose, as were her beauty, and her voice, and the way she moved. A strand of dark-brown hair hanging down over her left eye made all the difference in the world, as did the slightest glimpse of a collarbone above the top of her dark dress.

Something happened to her as well, I believed, although I could not tell whether it was real, or simply a reflection of what was going on inside my head. I could not tell if I truly saw something, or glimpsed only what I wanted there to be. I looked away eventually, and had I been required to move just then I do not know if I would have managed to do so without trembling.

I had no idea what happened, or rather how it happened. I still do not. I was, naturally, aware that it was quite ridiculous. For me, a young man of twenty-five, to become transfixed by a woman nearly twenty years older than I, a member of the aristocracy, my employer, and a recent widow still genuinely in mourning for her husband. A woman whose annual pin money was as much as I was likely to earn in the next decade. How much more ludicrous could anything be?

Then I became aware that, although I hoped that Elizabeth had noticed nothing, she too had fallen quite silent, and was looking away from me at the fire.

"You are tired," I said, trying to be hearty but merely sounding nervous instead. "It is kind of you to invite me, but I really must see what I can discover about this matter tomorrow." I wanted to get out of that house, out of her presence as quickly as possible. It was all I could do not to bolt for the door.

She looked back at me and smiled wanly. "Very well. I will dine alone. Will you come back with your discoveries?"

"Only if there is something to tell. I do not wish to waste your time."

We rose, and I shook her hand. She did not look at me, nor I at her.

I was sweating when I got into the street although the air was cool. I felt as though I had just escaped from a furnace, or from some mortal danger. All the way home her face and her perfume and her smile, and those eyes, danced in my head and refused to obey my instructions that they should leave me alone. They were phantoms, nothing more. Again I slept badly that night.

CHAPTER 15

I will not describe the next day. Not because it wasn't interesting, but more because getting anything done was a supreme act of will when all I wanted to do was sit and stare and think thoughts I should never have allowed inside my mind. And at six o'clock, when I again entered the house, I knew the entire day had been spent killing time, waiting for the moment when I could see her again. And not wanting to, because anything which was likely to take place could only be a disappointment after the previous evening. Even though nothing whatsoever had happened then.

She received me, we talked about little of importance. There was an awkwardness in our conversation which I had not noticed before. I could not talk to her as an employee, someone doing a job for her, an expert at my task. But I dared not adopt any other tone and, in any case, was hardly experienced enough to do so.

After a particularly long pause during which the fire in the grate seemed to become of excessive importance to both of us—it was better than avoiding each other's gaze—she turned back to me once more.

"May I ask you a question?"

"Of course."

"Did you wish to kiss me last night?"

I didn't know what to say. Tell the truth? That would alter things totally; I could never stand in front of her and talk to her in a normal way again. And I did not know, still, how she would reply. As I have said, the ways of the aristocracy, and of foreigners, and of women, were a mystery to me. I did not understand her in the slightest; I could not untangle what I thought from what I wanted to think. All I knew was that the sudden shortness of breath, the racing of my heart, had returned even more powerfully than the previous evening.

"Yes," I said after a long pause. "Very much." There was another long silence. "What would you have done if I had?"

She smiled, but only very faintly. "I would have kissed you back," she said. "I am glad you did not."

My heart fell. My small experience was limited to girls who either wanted to be kissed, or did not. Not women who wanted both at the same time. But I knew what she meant.

"Your Ladyship . . ."

"I think, in the circumstances, you might call me Elizabeth," she replied, "if you wish to do so. And also I think it would be best to talk of it no more. We both know quite well that relations have changed between us. It is foolish not to recognise it, to some measure."

But how had they changed? I wanted to ask. What am I meant to do? What do you want of me?

"You must think very badly of me; I am quite shocked by myself, although not as much as I should be. I am an immoral foreigner and blood will out. That does not mean I feel free to act on my desires."

That was something, at least, although I did not know what. All sorts of explanations went through my head. This was a woman crazed by her loss who was defying fate by having such thoughts, by deliberately acting in such a fashion. Or, she was a woman who (so I assumed) had not made love to anyone for years, and was no longer in control of herself. I even considered that she might like me, that I was the only person who could offer her any sort of understanding. That I was the only person who knew anything of what she might feel. That was the most dangerous, insidious option.

"Matthew?"

She had said something. "I'm sorry," I said. "I was a little distracted."

"I said, please tell me of your discoveries."

My discoveries? I wanted to say. Who on earth gives a hoot about my discoveries? All I wanted to do was tell her how I had wanted to take her in my arms, and run my fingers through her hair, and have her look at me like that again. Lost children, fraud, failing companies, what trivial nonsense was all this in comparison?

But it was her conversation, not mine. And she had a better notion of how to be sensible than I had. Where had she learned that? How do people gain an intuitive grasp of when to stop, when to go forward in such circumstances? Is it just from age and experience?

"Oh, them," I said. "Well, there's nothing exciting there. Except for a couple of things. Did you know that the Rialto Investment Trust is having its annual meeting soon?"

"I didn't."

"Well, it is. I thought I would go along, just to get a sense of these people. From my limited experience of these things it won't be very interesting, but you never know. And you know Mrs. Vincotti told us that her father had left her some money? A certain amount which came from Barings every month?"

She nodded.

"That wasn't an annuity. It was money sent by your husband. And from what she said, it has been paid every quarter for years. The records only go back ten years, but we can assume that he was responsible for payments right back to the beginning."

She looked interested, then her face fell. "But does this help?"

"Not obviously. Mrs. Vincotti cannot be the person we are looking for. If he paid her money, he would hardly need to instruct his executors to launch a search for her. She cannot possibly be either the child or the mother of the child. I cannot explain the payments at all, except to say that they are not helpful. So I propose dropping the matter, unless something else suggests they are relevant."

"It seems John had a less straightforward life than I thought," she said. "I didn't think he had any secrets from me. Now he is dead I am discovering nothing but."

There was, of course, the greatest secret of all. All my instincts were to lay it in front of her; your husband was a cheat and a fraud. He was stealing money from his own companies on a vast scale. But how could I say that to a woman who had looked me in the eyes like that? Who had such hair? If I kept silent, it was not for the sake of the shareholders of Rialto.

"On the subject of the Brotherhood or whatever they're called," I said, hurrying along, "I've found out little. Except that it is obviously a group so small that it poses little danger to the onward march of world capitalism, and consists of people so fractious that they were thrown out of another group called the Union of Socialist Solidarity two years ago, for being disruptive. The Union of Socialist Solidarity, in turn, walked out of the International Organisation of Workers . . . well, you get the idea."

"So how many of them are there?"

"Not many. I haven't found out much."

"They don't sound very interesting either," she said calmly. "Are you sure there isn't some explanation consistent with his record as a capitalist exploiter of the masses?"

"Not that I can think of without more information."

She shook her head. "Don't concern yourself with this at the moment. It's not much money and does not seem to be relevant to your task. I think you should concentrate on that."

"I just had this vision of his long-lost son turning up as a wild-eyed revolutionist."

"In which case he would have known exactly who he was, no?"

"True."

She turned to me, and took my hand. "I need this business settled," she said softly. "It is beginning to prey on my mind. I have to start a new life, not spend my days tidying up the old one. Please help me. Promise you will concentrate on the important."

Of course I would. Anything. Once more, as she held my hand and looked at me, I wanted to reach out for her. Once more I did not. But my resistance was already becoming enfeebled.

CHAPTER 16

I did not entirely ignore her request to concentrate on the lost child, but my enquiries went nowhere over the next week or so, and slowly. I did what you do in such circumstances; paid a young man at Births and Deaths to go through the registries, week by week and month by month, to see if any child had been registered naming Ravenscliff as father. The chances of this producing anything were small. Entries are named by the child's surname, and it was more than likely that this one would not have his father's name. I made enquiries of foreign journalists in London about how to go about finding children in France, Spain, Italy and other places, and wrote letters asking for assistance. Again, this was unlikely to produce results quickly, if at all, but I was determined to do a thorough job. After a week or so of this, the only possibility left was to write to every orphanage in Europe. This I decided to put off for as long as possible.

Then I returned to my interest in Ravenscliff's money. Not least because I was beginning to find the topic of money in general quite interesting. I had been working for Lady Ravenscliff for more than a month; my bank account now had £21 in it, and every week, my income so greatly exceeded my expenses that I even took to making out little columns of numbers, calculating how much I would have this time next year, or the year after that. Having money was very much more interesting than not having it. I almost began to understand (from a lowly point of view) what made someone like Ravenscliff tick. One thing had occurred to me, and that was that the start of Ravenscliff's attempt to siphon funds out of his companies had come around the time that Seyd's had begun an investigation into Rialto and suddenly dropped it. The owner, Young Seyd, had been responsible for that decision, Wilf had said, so it was reasonable to consider him for a while.

His father had trained him up for the business, but as Wilf had said, he had no taste for it. He was clever enough to leave well enough alone, and appoint good people who knew their jobs. Then he withdrew; his only connection was to attend the quarterly board meetings, collect his dividends and put his name to all those forms which require a chairman's signature. If I have conjured up the image of the typical second-generation owner, slowly dissipating his father's accumulated wealth in a life of indulgence and idle luxury, then the image is entirely incorrect. For Young Seyd had a secret life. He was a vicar in the Church of England, to which calling he had been inclined since his earliest youth. Only the authority of a very determined father had stopped him from being ordained as young as possible, and once that authority vanished Young Seyd had taken the cloth with almost unseemly haste. It was a strange mixture, pews and pulpits on the one hand and corporatised intelligence on the other, but he seemed to reconcile the two with little difficulty. *Crockford's Clerical Directory* supplied all the information I needed to find him. Young Seyd lived in Salisbury.

"I believe I am doing God's work in both," he said with a smile once he had allowed me in—with some obvious hesitation, it must be said. "Knowing their sins will be discovered helps to keep the men of wealth honest. It means that the poor will be treated more justly. And I must say that what I learned during my apprenticeship about the weaknesses of men, and the temptations of power, has prepared me well for life in the Church."

I liked him; I had not expected to, as my opinion had been coloured in advance by Wilf's scarcely concealed disapproval. But Young Seyd—his father had now been dead for more than a decade but the name persisted—impressed me. More of an eighteenth-century vicar than a member of the newly reformed and muscular Church of England—not for him the business of evangelising workers or natives. No; Seyd was happy to let men be. If they came to him, well and good, but he did not believe he had any right to bother people unnecessarily. He christened, married and buried his parishioners; he read his books and he lived a quiet, contented life with his housekeeper, a cat and many friends.

And he kept a distant eye on the doings of his company. Which was why I had gone to Waterloo and taken a morning train to Salisbury.

Once I was in his house—a fine new villa in Manor Road, luxurious for a vicar but modest for the owner of a company—and he had some tea brought for me, I plunged straight into my tale. There seemed little point in dissimulating; to do so with such a decent man—he was perhaps in his early forties then and was just beginning to show the effects in his body of a life without want—was somehow unseemly. Also, in the train as I had watched the Wiltshire countryside pass in front of me, I had rehearsed all possible ways of broaching the subject without broaching it, if you understand me, and got nowhere. I could not discover any means of phrasing the questions which would get me the answers I wanted without being precise.

So I explained that I was writing a biography of Ravenscliff for his widow, although this was to be for private circulation only. I said that she was allowing me unparalleled access to all his papers. How some could not be found; how Wilf Cornford had mentioned the abortive investigation by Seyd's of a year or so previously . . .

At this the reverend gentleman began to look uneasy. But I continued anyway, saying that it was most important, and his wife's dearest wish, that I should have access to everything there was to know.

"It's important for my work, you understand. But it might also be important for the executors of his will, depending on what it contains, that is. These things seem to be terribly complicated."

"Yes, yes. And thank heavens they are. Otherwise Seyd's would have nothing to do at all."

"So you'll give me the report? I'm so grateful to you, and of course I will treat it in the strictest . . ."

The Reverend Seyd held up his hand. "I am afraid that I cannot do that," he said gently.

"Why not?"

"I was visited at my club in London by a man who explained that he would prefer this investigation to be discontinued."

"And just because some total stranger . . ."

"You are also a total stranger," he said. "And the first was more persuasive than you are."

"How so?"

He spread his hands in a gesture of resignation.

"And he worked for Ravenscliff?"

"I decided to do as he requested."

"But what could he possibly say to make you do that? By what right . . . ?"

Again he did not reply.

"Do you still have this report?"

He shook his head. "I gathered up all the papers and brought them all here. A fortnight later my house was burgled."

"I see," I said quietly. "And you think Ravenscliff was responsible?"

"I do not know. Certainly it would be consistent with everything I knew about him. He was a terrible man, Mr. Braddock. Utterly without principles or loyalties."

The atmosphere was so heavy it felt oppressive. Seyd had alarmed me. But I was fascinated as well. And here, sitting in front of me with his dog collar on was the first man to say something other than the standard line on Ravenscliff. Fair, decent, a wonderful husband, good employer. Kindly. A wizard with money. All that had been repeated endlessly. Finally, I had found someone with a different view—and he wasn't going to tell me why. I decided then and there I wasn't going to leave until he had.

"How far had the investigation progressed?"

"Not far. Not far enough for anyone in London to make sense of it. Not even Wilf Cornford. No one had yet put all the pieces together. Maybe they wouldn't have done, but I put them together, Mr. Braddock," he said defiantly.

"I thought you had no connection with that sort of thing?"

"Mr. Cornford has a low opinion of my expertise. That is unwarranted. I spent many years at my father's side before his death, and I learned a very great deal about the way the modern company operates. He also taught me how to read balance sheets when most young children are playing games, or struggling over their Latin irregular verbs."

"You must tell me what you found. You must."

He shook his head.

"I am who I say I am," I continued in the vague hope it would make some difference. "A reporter, a writer. I want the truth, that is all."

"Then you are an innocent. Or very brave."

"I am neither. If you won't tell me, then at least answer some questions. Did your investigations deal with Ravenscliff sucking vast sums of money out of his companies and defrauding his shareholders?"

Seyd was deathly quiet, and looked at me carefully. "Why do you say that?"

"Because he was," I said recklessly. "I discovered it. It had already started by the time you shut down your enquiry. Is that why? Is that what you discovered as well?"

Not the best way of playing, giving away your best cards with no guarantee of anything in exchange. Had Seyd been more like Ravenscliff, he would have smiled, snapped up the information and refused still to reply. Maybe he intended to, but instead he said nothing at all; he frowned, rubbed his hands together in a jerky, agitated movement, put some sugar in his tea, then, a few moments later, put some more in. Tasting the result brought him back.

"No," he said. "No, it wasn't. But it does explain why somebody wanted no investigation at that particular moment. Why was he doing this? Do you know?"

"You can't expect me to answer your questions if you don't answer mine, you know. That would be quite unfair."

"I am trying to protect you."

"So is everyone else I talk to. Very kind. But I don't want to be protected. I want to do a good job, which everyone else also seems to think I am incapable of doing."

"Pride, eh?"

"If you want. Do you know, I was recommended for this job because my editor thinks I am a poor reporter."

"Who's he?"

"McEwen, of the *Chronicle*."

He looked interested at this, but I continued. "And since then, every conversation has started: Why you? Why you? Why you? I am heartily sick of it."

"Spoken like a true twelve-year-old," he said gently.

I glared.

"But McEwen is a good man. How very curious." And he fell into a thoughtful mood, during which he poured some more tea into a clean cup.

"Do you consider yourself a patriot, Mr. Braddock? A loyal Englishman?"

"Naturally," I said, somewhat surprised. "So much so that I never think about it."

"Yes; few people do. No doubt that will change in the coming years. Mr. McEwen does think of it. He is a good man, and a trustworthy one."

"You know him?"

"Oh, yes."

The change that had come over him had been slow but distinct. Apart from the ecclesiastical garb, there was nothing of the vicar left in him. The mild, slightly slow mannerisms had been replaced by a precision which momentarily shocked me.

"The investigation concerned lines of credit," he began quietly. "That is, the means by which Ravenscliff's gigantic operations are funded. The whole structure of his cash flow, credits, the loans he makes to others to buy his products. Where the money goes. Do you understand me so far?"

"He lends people money to buy his own goods?"

"What you see with Ravenscliff's operations is the material side. The factories, the goods. But there was also another side, the banks and the finance. Money flowed into the banks, was turned into goods, which were sold, and turned back into money again. No one truly understood it but him. No one can, I think. That is the main purpose. In the last two decades, Ravenscliff devised a financial structure so complex it is all but impossible to penetrate."

"But I have read the accounts . . ."

"No. I do not know what you have seen, but you have seen only partial accounts. The profits or losses of one company mean nothing. Because they are part of a much greater whole which spreads throughout the world. Did you know that Ravenscliff controlled some six banks, in America and Europe? They were set up solely to organise financing for various deals. There are other accounts in other banks, dozens and dozens, under the control of the chief salesman, Xanthos, which exist solely to bribe foreign officials, buy presents, purchase favours."

"I've met him," I said.

"And no doubt found him a charming little fellow."

"Ah, yes, I did. Are you going to tell me something different?"

"He is a crook. He pays bribes to whoever needs them. A pimp, who supplies prostitutes to willing civil servants when required. A thief, who steals the details of other companies' bids for contracts. A fraud, who falsifies details of his products' capabilities. Whatever is necessary to win an order, Mr. Xanthos will do it. He's a trader from the bazaar, with an oriental regard for the truth. That was his value to Ravenscliff, who looked the other way, so he did not know how these orders came about. Ravenscliff took care of the big bribes. I could read it all, you know, they had a sort of signature, and I came to know the style of each of them by the end. Xanthos used several banks, mainly the Bank of Bruges in Belgium, but also one in Milan and others in Bucharest, Manchester, Lyon and Dusseldorf."

"Are you sure?"

He did not answer. "We started to unravel all this, thread by thread, but couldn't see the point of it. That was what was so puzzling. What was it all for? Why had he made everything so complicated? No one could discover it. Wilf Cornford wondered whether it was all the doing of Caspar Neuberger, the director of finance, who loves complexity for its own sake. But I wasn't satisfied, so I looked further."

"I hope you are not going to stop telling me now."

"I will tell you, if you truly wish."

"I do."

"You know what a submarine is?"

"Of course."

"Beswick Shipyard developed one of the earliest that was in any way a practical weapon. The Americans were the first, but Beswick came soon after. For the most part, they were more of a danger to their own crew than to anyone else. But Beswick got a contract from the Government to develop a new, radical design which could carry torpedoes—Beswick, as you may know, also owns the Gosport Torpedo Company and it was looking for new markets.

"The Royal Navy decided to buy some, and fund the development. The contract with the Government was that this should be entirely secret. And, above all, that there should be no sales, none at all, to foreign governments."

"Not like the torpedo, then."

"Precisely. They had learned their lesson. The navy realised, even at that early stage, that this new vessel might become a formidable weapon. Ravenscliff gave his word. Six months later he was building a dockyard for the Russians, who were then our most bitter enemies, to build submarines, torpedoes and anything else they wanted. That was the moment his finances became opaque. And the reason: to conceal any sign of treason."

I looked carefully at him. "Are you serious? You don't mean to tell me that no one noticed? When was this?"

"At the start of the 1890s. Ravenscliff built up the Russian navy to the point that it could challenge the Royal Navy in the Black Sea. All this long before Britain and Russia became allies and when it was one of our most dangerous enemies. Did anyone notice? No. Nothing could be traced back to Ravenscliff at all. The money was raised through bond issues in Paris; the companies were registered in several different countries, with the shares owned by companies set up for the purpose, their owners in turn being hidden. There was not a single thing to suggest that Ravenscliff had anything to do with these factories."

"So how did you discover it?"

"That is what we do. And, as is often the case, the weak spot was the human side of things. The expertise. You don't just build a factory, put in a bunch of illiterate peasants and start turning out complex weapons. You need people to train the workforce, to oversee things. Not many, the Russians already had many engineers. But they had little managerial expertise, and that was Ravenscliff's speciality. I found some of the people who had worked at the yard, and they all came from Beswick. Eventually, one—only one—told me the whole story."

"And then you received a visitor."

"As you say. And now you know the story as well, so you had better be careful. Ravenscliff was utterly single-minded. He is dead, but his spirit, as they say, lives on in people like Xanthos and Neuberger and Bartoli. He chose them and trained them. The company embodies his methods. It is alive, and can work without him. You might say he transferred his soul into it, so that he will live as long as his companies exist. It is the only form of immortality a man like that could expect, and more than he deserves."

"Did you ever meet him?"

Seyd shook his head. "Never. I got to know him through numbers. It is not a bad way of making an acquaintance. And safer."

"What did your numbers tell you? You see, I am having trouble. What was it all for? I'm a simple man, myself. I dream of a house and a garden and a wife. I want enough money never to have to worry. I do not want to end up in the poor house, or a pauper's grave. Ravenscliff had all that, decades ago. What did he want?"

Seyd looked thoughtfully at the carpet. "Well," he said. "Not money. I really think he had no great interest in money. That is often the case with these people. Not fame or position, either. He took the peerage with the greatest of reluctance and never sought any sort of public role. Few people had ever heard of him and he liked it like that."

"What does that leave? Power?"

"No, I don't think so. I've no doubt it pleased his vanity, but not greatly. No, I believe his motivation was pleasure."

"I beg your pardon?"

Seyd smiled. "Pleasure, Mr. Braddock. Not something usually associated with heavy industry or armaments, I know. But he seems to have approached what he did rather as an engineer approaches a problem, or an artist a picture. He took pleasure in creating something that was harmonious, integrated and balanced. He could have been an architect, I think. Or maybe he would have liked these new crosswords, where the delight lies solely in solving the puzzle. He liked taking an insuperable problem, and conquering it. I've no doubt he liked the admiration that generated, and certainly never refused any profits, but I suspect he would not have done it had he gained no delight from it. You might even call him an aesthete. The pleasure was in the mind. He set out to create the most perfect organisation the world has ever seen, and he succeeded."

"Numbers tell you that?"

"They hint. The rest is guesswork and experience."

"I think I am more confused than ever."

"Maybe so. But it is the only explanation of Ravenscliff which answers. Now, you know what I know, in an abbreviated version. What are you going to do about it?"

"Knowing him through numbers, what do mine tell you?" I summarised what the single file had contained. Seyd listened attentively, frowning in concentration as I spoke.

"So he's burning up his cash, is he? Well, I would rule out fraud, if I were you."

"Why?"

"He was too elegant a man to be fraudulent in that way. It is too crude for him."

"So?"

"He was using the money for something."

"What?"

"How should I know? You seem to have taken that task on yourself. Find out, if you want, and if you can."

The interview was over. All reporters with a little experience know when there is no more information to be extracted and I knew that I had got as much out of Young Seyd as he was able, or willing, to give. I stood up. The vicar, out of politeness, stood as well. He did not urge me to stay, to sit down again.

I walked to the door, then turned. "One question then, which you should not mind answering. The man who came to see you at your club. What was he like?"

Seyd considered, trying to find an objection, but coming up with nothing. "He was in his late forties, fair hair, thinning on top. Medium build. No moustache or beard, a large, unusually large, mouth. Entirely unremarkable. I do not know who he was, and have never seen him again."

CHAPTER 17

I got back to London at eight that evening, and went straight to the Ravenscliff residence. I had nothing particular to do there, no reason not to go home via a chop house or pub for a good night's sleep. The only reason I went to St. James's Square rather than Chelsea was because I wanted to see her. I was almost aware of it.

I did not, of course, have a key, but I had been given free run of the house and could go in and out as I pleased. I noticed a slight hesitation when the door was opened, as though the servant thought it unbecoming for a young man to turn up to a house of mourning so late in the evening. She was probably right. I asked about her mistress and was told she had already retired for the evening, which made my heart fall. I then realised there was nothing I wished to do there; but I could hardly turn on my heel and leave, so I walked up the stairs to Ravenscliff's office to make a pretence of studying his papers.

I did nothing; instead I sat in the armchair by the empty fireplace, and thought about its owner. An aesthete and an ascetic, from Seyd's description, building his complex, incomprehensible organisation in such a way that almost no one in the world could appreciate it. Perhaps that would have spoiled it. Maybe the secrecy of what he was doing was the source of the pleasure. Or not. I didn't know. I was a long way out of my depth. In a matter of days, my orderly life had been reduced to a complete mess. Not so long ago all I had to do was get up, write about crime— generally committed by simple, straightforward people—and go back to bed again.

And what was the dominant thought in my mind? The eyes of a widow nearly twice my age. Her faint smell of perfume. The way she moved. The glimpse of skin above her expensive, handmade dress. The softness of her voice. What she had said to me, what it implied. What it might lead to. What I hoped.

Awful, awful, awful. I groaned to myself as I thought about it. Truly, my £350 a year would be hard-earned if it went on like this. Ordinarily, I would have done as I had done so often before: made a list. Decided what the most important things were to get done, and then proceed single-mindedly to do them. I tried to dismiss the thoughts of Elizabeth from my mind and think once more of Lady Ravenscliff. To work out some practical means of getting this job done quickly, so I could be free to go back to the *Chronicle,* or some other paper which might have me.

But, once I did that, then the result was even more depressing. For the fact was that I had made no real progress at all. I looked blankly at the shelves of notes and files; I was sure there was something in there somewhere, but the idea of actually looking for it filled me with revulsion. I think I must have stayed there for about an hour; it was quiet and peaceful, and after a while it almost became comforting. There was a photograph of Ravenscliff on the mantelpiece; I took it out of its frame and looked at it for a long while, trying to fathom the character behind the face, before folding it and putting it in my pocket.

And eventually I was able to lever myself out of the chair and prepare to rejoin the world; to go home to sleep, and then to start afresh the next morning. It wasn't so bad. The worst that could happen would be failure. I'd still have my £350.

I was almost content as I went back down the grand staircase, walking slowly, looking at the pictures on the walls as I passed. I knew nothing of such things; they seemed perfectly pleasant decorations to me. But as I was passing the door to the sitting room, I heard a noise. Nothing exceptional, just a bump and a scrape. I knew it must be her and I hesitated; all my anxiety and irresolution flooded back.

A sensible person would have carried on down the stairs. Discipline and self-denial should have been called upon. A commonsensical realisation that the only way of returning to my mood of calm was to avoid the woman disturbing it as much as possible, keep her at arm's length, be polite and professional.

I didn't want to be or to do any of those things. I knocked, quietly and tentatively on the door, and then pressed my ear against it. Nothing. So what do you do now? I asked myself. Tiptoe away like some nervous schoolboy? That would be humiliating even if no one else knew about it. Is that how bold would-be lovers behave? Or open the door and walk in. I had a right. She had looked at me.

My heart was pounding, and I was almost breathless as I gripped the doorknob, turned and pushed. The room was dark, the curtains drawn, only a fire almost extinguished in the grate, and a candle. The expensive modern electrical lighting was not switched on. I thought I must have been mistaken, until I heard a voice, so quiet I could hardly make out the words.

"Who is it?"

It was her, but the voice sounded entirely different. Dull and without the musicality that normally made it so appealing. Slightly slurred, as though I had woken her up from a deep sleep.

"Oh, it's you," she said as I stepped into the room and the light from the landing fell on my face enough for her to recognise me. "Come and sit down. Shut the door, the light hurts my eyes."

This was not what I had expected. Going into the room, so dark I could see only shades and shadows in the candlelight, was disconcerting, even slightly frightening.

"Are you all right? You do not sound well."

She laughed softly and looked up at me. For the first time, her hair was unpinned, and fell down over her shoulders in a rich dark mass. She wore some sort of thin gown which shimmered slightly as she moved, embroidered in reds and blues. Japanese motifs, very fashionable. She was extravagantly, impossibly beautiful. I caught my breath as I looked at her for her eyes were darker than usual, the pupils wide, almost as though she was terrified of something.

"What is the matter?"

She laid her head on the back of the settee, and pushed her hair back over her ear, but said nothing; just smiled.

"Please. Tell me."

"It's nothing. A little medicine to calm my nerves. It is strong, and I haven't used it for many, many years."

"Perhaps you need a doctor for a different prescription? I could summon one very quickly if you wish."

She smiled again and looked at me with what might have been affection, or indulgence, or even sympathy.

"It is not the sort of medicine which needs a doctor, Matthew."

She pulled back the sleeve of her robe, and I could see a broad red mark around her upper arm; below it there was wound, with a trickle of dried blood coming from it. She laughed again at my incomprehension.

"Oh, my God, I have employed the most innocent man in London," she said. "You poor dear boy. You really know nothing at all."

I must have been looking horrified by this stage, so she became more serious herself. "Morphine, Matthew," she said soberly. "The great releaser, the comforter of tormented souls."

I would have been shocked, had I had the time to arrange my thoughts, but in fact I wasn't thinking anything at all at that moment. I just sat there, closer to her than I had ever been, my heart pounding.

"Do I frighten you? Or do you frighten yourself?" she asked, but not in a way which suggested she wanted a reply. "Shall I tell you what you are thinking?"

No reply from me. I was so far out of my depth I knew that the faintest wriggle might cause me to sink and drown.

"You have been thinking of me, night and day. You dream of me, of wanting to take me into your arms and kiss me. That is what you would say, were you able to say anything at all. You are silent now, but in your mind some part of you is trying to turn it to your advantage. Perhaps this is your opportunity, perhaps I would not resist if you leaned forward and took me now. But you don't want merely to kiss me, of course. You want to make love to me; you dream of me becoming your mistress. You long to see me naked in front of you, wanting only to be possessed by you. Is that not true, dearest Matthew?"

Her voice was entirely even; there was nothing in its tone or expression to suggest whether she was enticing or mocking, or both.

Perhaps she was so drugged—I could hardly imagine her talking like this had she not been—she didn't even know herself. Either way, her words and actions paralysed me. Of course, everything she said was entirely true. But there was cruelty in her saying it.

"Are you lost for words, Matthew? Do you think that if you say something, it might be the wrong thing, and ruin a moment full of such wonderful possibilities? Are you so very timid and naïve with women that you do not know what to do next?" Then she put her hand round the back of my neck and pulled my head towards her, and whispered words into my ear such as I had never heard from the mouth of a woman before, even the very lowest. Hissing, almost serpent-like, her voice became, making me feel even more like a prey being immobilised.

So I took hold of her, and began to kiss her, becoming ever more rough as she not only did not resist, but responded. Only when my hands moved down to touch her body did she stiffen, then push me away and stood up. She walked over to the fireplace and looked into the mirror a few moments.

"I must ask you to leave," she said, without even turning round.

"What?"

She gave me no answer. What had gone wrong? What had I done? I was sure I had made no terrible error. If I had been unduly forward, it was only on her provocation, and she knew it. So what had happened?

"It is late and I am tired."

"No, you're not."

"Get out."

"Elizabeth . . ."

"Get out," she screamed and wheeled round at me, her face ablaze, picking up the blue bowl from the mantelpiece. That bowl, the one she had used to humiliate me, to put me in my place. It served its purpose again, as it crashed into the wall behind me and shattered into a hundred pieces. She was terrifying. I was terrified. Then the fury drained from her face and she became calm again. It was as though I wasn't there, as if she was talking to herself. Perhaps it was the drug that was causing this whole thing. Maybe I had come under the influence of it as well, and this was all some nightmare.

"I must try and sleep tonight. I hope I can." Then she started talking in French, and I understood not one word of what she was saying. Eventually I realised she had completely forgotten about me; didn't even realise I was there. I slipped out of the room and out of the house. I was shaking.

CHAPTER 18

By the morning I felt terrible, and had convinced myself I was completely to blame. She was a widow, still in shock. I had tried to take advantage of her. I had wanted to, in any case. The drugs repelled me; I knew they existed, of course; you couldn't be a crime reporter without coming across them, but to see a woman like her so reduced was a terrible thing. It made her all the more fascinating as well.

I was more obsessed than ever. Failure is more beguiling than success; all I could think of was what might have happened, and I relived the scene in my mind again and again, each time with a different outcome. I thought of it so much, and so intently, that I half-felt I was going mad as I tossed and turned on my uncomfortable bed, hoping desperately that sleep would come and relieve me. Eventually, I got up; it was still only half past five in the morning, and there was no one else up in the house. I tiptoed out—the last thing I wanted was to come across anyone else and have to talk—and walked out. I drank some tea at a stall in the King's Road, there to serve the deliverymen on their rounds, but could not face the idea of eating anything.

At half past seven I was in St. James's Square, far too early to knock on the door, but with nothing else to do. I was determined to return and talk. But I had to wait; I walked round in circles, sometimes fast, sometimes dawdling. A passing policeman looked at me carefully. I went into St. James's Piccadilly, but the air of holiness had no effect on me at all. I looked into the shopwindows, sat in Piccadilly Circus, watching people pass by as they hurried to work. It was raining slightly and I was getting wet, but I didn't notice; I was only aware that I was damp and cold, but it might have been happening to someone else.

And eventually I decided that the time had come, and that I could properly knock on the door. It was twenty past eight.

"Good heavens, sir, whatever has happened? Has there been an accident?" It was one of the maids, a cheerful, plump girl with a country accent, who let me in. The sort who, in another life, I might have taken a shine to.

"No. Why do you ask?"

As I took off my coat, I turned slightly and caught a glimpse of myself in the mirror, and knew precisely why she asked. I looked terrible. I had not shaved, my clothes were rumpled, my shirt collar dirty. I had bags under my eyes from exhaustion and there was an unhealthy grey pallor to my skin. I looked very much as if I'd been in an accident.

I panicked. I couldn't possibly put my carefully thought-out conversation into action looking like that. I wanted to seem calm, reasonable. Man of the world. And I looked like a tramp. That was why the policeman had been looking at me in such a professional way. "I think I'd better leave . . ."

"Her Ladyship asked me to take you to the sitting room when you arrived," said the maid. "She said you were expected. Can you find your own way?"

I was being anticipated and out-thought at every step. So I was that predictable? She must have given that order before she even went to bed, so easy it was to read my mind. I felt a sudden surge of anger, but I did as I was told. I was perfectly free to leave. I could easily have said that I had changed my mind and walked out. I could easily have acted outside her plan and surprised her, regained the initiative by showing I was not so simple. But I desperately wanted to see her. I had absolutely to see her, otherwise I thought I might collapse. Certainly all the time in between would be merely wasted, an interval before I was again in the same room with her. It was the only thing that mattered.

So up I went and was brought coffee on a silver tray, with cream and sugar. And some toast, which I ate. The fire was lit and I dried myself. I tided up my clothes as best I could. Only the stubble on my chin reminded me of what I must look like.

Certainly Elizabeth did not when she came in. She shut the door, came over with her arms open and a smile on her face, and kissed me on the cheek.

"How wonderful to see you, Matthew. I am so glad you came."

Wrong-footed again. I had anticipated the capricious cruelty of the night before; had considered the possibility of coldness and distance. Even an apologetic embarrassment. I had hoped that she too had had no sleep. I did not imagine that she would act like a society lady welcoming a friend. All my preparations, my pre-formed speeches collapsed uselessly.

"Your Ladyship," I said stiffly. She looked at me with an affected air of pique and distress. She was entirely herself again. With the passing of the drug from her bloodstream, she was once again vivacious, lively, entirely in control of herself and the situation. She also looked as if she had slept well. Apparently that is one of the benefits of morphine, if it is taken carefully.

"Come and sit by me while you finish your breakfast. Are you well? You look a little haggard," she added.

I sat in the armchair, feeling myself to be behaving rudely as I did so. She was pushing me into revealing myself as petulant and immature. I didn't like that.

"You're upset," she said, this time seriously and gently. "I suppose you must be."

I remained silent.

"Will you forgive me? I know I behaved appallingly. Please believe me when I say that I intended no hurt. You are the very last person in the world I would wish to upset."

"I suppose you are going to say you don't know what came over you. That is was all the fault of the . . . of the drugs," I said stiffly.

"No. I wasn't going to say that at all," she said sadly. She did not look at me. I could not have stood that. It was too crude a weapon for her to use, however effective it would have been.

"I had hoped you would have understood," she said when it became clear I was not going to say anything at all. "But you don't."

"No."

Now she did look at me, but not in the way she had done the night before. This time her gaze seemed wholly innocent and regretful. Still I did not dare meet it.

"You poor young man," she continued. "Does it sound condescending if I say that?"

"Of course it does."

"It isn't. It is merely the truth. Shall I speak plainly, then? In an un-ladylike way? Shock you some more with the way I talk of subjects which you think I should be too refined to mention? I have seen the look on your face, you know. There is little you can hide from me, however skilled you may think yourself."

I suppose I must have glowered at her, as eventually she continued.

"At the moment you are confused and angry. You wished to make love to me; I encouraged you then capriciously changed my mind. You thought you knew what was going on inside me, but in fact you understood nothing at all. Otherwise you would realise I was trying to protect you."

"I do not need to be protected by you," I said stiffly.

"Not by me. From me," she corrected. "Look at you. One small misunderstanding and you are a wreck. You have been obsessed with me all night. You haven't slept. You look like a tramp. Do you know how easy it would be to ruin you utterly?"

"I don't think—"

"That's because you do not know what you are talking about." There was a long break as the maid came in with another tray of coffee. Elizabeth thanked the woman, and watched as the coffee was poured, talking to her as she waited. I, in contrast, said nothing at all, acutely aware that I was radiating misery from my chair. Eventually the maid left, and the door was shut. Elizabeth sipped her cup thoughtfully for a while, then put it down.

"Do you not think it strange that a widow, grieving for her recently lost husband, should behave in such a way? Or did you merely think that foreigners must be like that? Not at all proper like the English?

"I am angry, Matthew. And frightened. And last night I wished to take it out on someone. As I say, I am ashamed of myself. But not for any reason you might have imagined."

"What do you mean?"

"John died in the stupidest way imaginable. He was careless, thoughtless. His moment of absentmindedness means I have to spend the rest of my life without him. Obviously I knew that would happen eventually. He was much older than I was. But I wanted more time with him. The only person in the world I have ever truly cared for. Ever. I had a debt to repay. He fell out of a window and robbed me of my chance. I wanted to punish him, but I can't, of course. So I thought I'd pick on you."

She stopped, and I opened my mouth to reply but realised I didn't know what to say.

"It's very easy. A glance here, a suggestive movement. A provocative question. And your sleep evaporates and you take on that look of tail-wagging devotion that I detest so much. John was dead, but I could easily replace him, although not with someone half as good as he was.

"Please don't think I thought all this through, that I was simply playing with your affections. I didn't know what I was doing. And then last night I came to my senses. Only just, though. Do you really think it would have been better had I allowed you to make love to me? It would only have postponed the rejection, and made it ten times worse when it came. It was vain and cruel of me. I apologise for that without reservation. But I do not apologise for saving you from the consequences of your naïveté. You are no match for me, Matthew. Only John has ever been that."

"You have a high opinion of yourself."

"No," she said sadly. "A very low one."

"I don't understand a word you are talking about."

"I suppose you don't. One day, when you are as old as I am . . ."

"You are beautiful." The words rushed out of me; they sounded stupid.

She smiled. "Once that would have pleased me," she said. "Words like that, truly meant, were like gold to me when I was young. Now I no longer care."

"You loved him?"

"Yes," she said. "Very much."

"Why?"

She sighed and looked across the square, at all those people whose lives were nothing like her own. She seemed almost interested in them.

"He was my comfort, my friend, my warmth. The fixed point of a turning world, always there." She stopped and looked at me, almost mischievously. "I have had lovers, you know, in the past decade or so. I do hope I have managed to shock you again."

"I'm learning," I replied.

"But I have never loved anyone else. Do you understand the difference?"

"I have had neither the money or the leisure to explore such subtleties."

"Censorious. Well, perhaps you are right. But there is a big difference. I hope you discover what it is, one day. Because you will never truly love someone until you do."

She fell silent again, a look of terrible sadness on her face. "Do you believe me when I say I want you to find this child? Or do you think there is some other motive behind it?"

"I really don't know anymore."

"I do want it. When John died, it was a terrible shock. I suppose I still am in shock. I have lost him forever. But when I read the will, do you know what my reaction was? Anger? Shame? Disillusionment?"

"Maybe. All of them?"

"None of them. I was happy. There was a piece of him still alive, somewhere. I dreamed of finding this child—I imagined a ten-year-old boy sometimes, sometimes a young woman about the same age as I was when I met John. I hoped there were many children, even. Getting to know them, bringing them to live with me. Having a family in this world. Because I have nothing now. Nothing of importance, just wealth beyond the dreams of avarice. It is all John's fault, you see."

I looked puzzled.

"He taught me the pleasures of love and companionship, of trusting people and knowing them. Before that, when I was young, it was all just a game. Who you knew, how you made your way in the world. There was no time or space for real warmth. John gave me a world of affection, and I fell in love with that as much as I fell in love with him. Do you know the pleasure of doing nothing with someone, of simply sitting in the same room with them? Or of going for a walk where neither talks? He taught me that and now it is all gone. And the world is my reality again. I am frightened and alone, Matthew, more than a man like you can even imagine."

"And you never had children?"

She shook her head gently. "I fell pregnant, a year or so after we married. I was so happy, I couldn't believe it. I used to just sit and clutch myself, and cry with the joy of it. I thought my life would be complete."

"What happened?"

"It was born and they took it away from me." She shook her head. "The midwife wrapped it up, put it by the fire to keep it warm, and sat around to keep it company until it died. They didn't let me see it again. It's what they do, did you know that?"

I said nothing.

"The doctors told me that I couldn't have any more. That another pregnancy might kill me. So," she said brightly, her eyes shining, "that was my chance, you see. It took years to recover fully. John stayed with me every moment, every second, brought me back to myself. As close as I could get, anyway. I lost my dreams then and they never came back."

"I will find this child for you," I said. "If it lives."

"Do you doubt it?"

"Many children die young," I said.

There was a very long pause. She sat silently, thoughtfully, and I realised that I was back—back in her power again, if you want to put it like that.

"Tell me," I said after a while, "what do you know about the state of your husband's companies at present?"

She was not interested. "That his shareholdings are in the hands of the executor and will remain so until this is settled."

"Precisely." I took the buff folder out of the bag I had begun to carry around with me. "Look at this."

She did as instructed, but quickly, just long enough to register incomprehension.

"This indicates that a large amount of money has been removed from them. It also perhaps explains why the announcement of his death was delayed."

"How so?"

"Have you seen the list of prominent shareholders? They'd lose a fortune if shares in Rialto declined. Half the politicians in the land have bought shares."

She looked scornful. "Bought?" she said with a snort. "You don't think they *bought* them, do you?"

"How else . . ." Then I realised what she was saying.

"I know little of the details of John's business, but I know how the world works. These were gifts. Inducements. Bribes, if you want to be honest about it. They wanted rewards for giving him contracts; he obliged because he could remind them of his generosity, if necessary. And now, of course, I can do the same."

Her eyes, very briefly, flashed with excitement; then they dulled again. "I do not intend to," she said. "But you are right; it is a reason for Mr. Cort to become so interested."

"And the money?"

"That I do not know."

"Do you realise the implications of this folder?"

"Perhaps. But maybe you should tell me."

"It means that your inheritance will be very much less than you imagine. Indeed, if news of it comes out, the companies could collapse and you would be left with nothing at all."

"I see." She seemed to be taking it all very calmly. "Is your knowledge of the law as good as your knowledge of finance?"

"They are both equally feeble, as you know. In this case, I am going on what your husband's solicitor told me."

"So what should I do?"

"I don't think there is anything you can do."

"Dear me, what a time this is," she said with a smile. "You tell me one day I am about to become the richest woman in the world, and the next tell me I am to be a pauper. No one can accuse you of precision."

"There are many things I do not understand here. I will tell you them, if you wish. Then you have to take a decision. Do you want me to pursue them, or do you want me to concentrate on the original matter of the child?"

"Go ahead, then. Confuse me some more."

"Was you husband interested in spiritualism?"

She stared at me. "Spiritualism?"

"Yes. You know. Table-turning. Seances. Auras from the beyond. That sort of thing."

This finally woke her up. She threw back her head and laughed. "John? Table-turning? Of course he wasn't! He was the most practical, down-to-earth, materialistic person I have ever known. He had no interest or belief in such things. None at all. Why, he didn't even go to church."

"Then why was he attending spiritualist meetings?"

"I'm sure he was not."

"I'm sure he was. Listen." I read out some notes I had taken from his appointment book.

"Madame Boninska?" she said when I was finished.

"Otherwise known as the witch-woman. She was found murdered two days after your husband died."

I had silenced her, this time. She had nothing to say. She wanted to find it all amusing, but could not manage it.

"Why would your husband consult a medium? The obvious next question is whether there is any connection with her death. Or his?"

"Let me tell you a story," she said. "A long time ago, when I was young and beautiful, I lived in Paris. I lived a fine life, and often invited people for dinner. Friends and acquaintances. Politicians, writers, musicians. That is the origin of Xanthos's rather inflated notions of me. It amused me greatly, and when I encountered John I invited him. I wanted to show off, I suppose. Perhaps even make him jealous, although I had no notion that he was anything other than an acquaintance at the time. A pleasing man, a good companion. Someone with whom I felt comfortable.

"Anyway, he came, although not often. He didn't approve of idle conversation with artists, and gradually his scepticism made me feel it was a foolish way of spending my life as well. One evening he took me for dinner at a restaurant, with some of his business associates and some of mine. They didn't mix very well. A doctor began talking about hypnotism, which he practised on his patients, and mentioned spiritualism. Auras and emanations. He took it seriously and offered to take everyone to a séance with a medium who was then in the city. This was the time when Madame Blavatsky was causing such a stir, and there were many imitators of her around. Do you remember Blavatsky?"

"I read about her for background."

"It is of no consequence. Some of the other guests were enthusiastic about the idea, and started talking about spirituality, and the poverty of the modern age, which had taken the poetry out of men's souls. I leave you to imagine the sort of thing.

"Nothing could provoke John more. He became quite angry, and the fact that I was willing to go to this séance made him angrier still. He always held that such things were the self-indulgent foolishness of the decadent, or the miserable superstition of the peasant. Man's future lay with the roar of a blast furnace, not with the rattling of a teacup. It appalled him that grown men were willing to countenance what he considered to be obvious charlatanry. It was the first time I had seen him angry, and I thought it strange he should become so agitated over something if he thought it so absurd. Of course, it wasn't really about that at all. It was about me. What I was, what he wanted me to be. We had our first fight, then and there. It was undignified, embarrassing, and convinced me he truly loved me."

"Did you—do you—agree with him?"

"In my youth I was interested in all these things. It was a fashionable amusement, and I imagine it still is. In my case it was the same as playing

bridge. Something to amuse a company of guests, where we could all act
out our roles. Everyone acted as though they believed it, because they
thought everyone else did believe it. Not that that matters. The point is
that John had nothing but scorn for any of that sort of thing, and he was
not a man to change his mind."

"So it is not possible that, say, he might have consulted a medium in
the hope of discovering the identity of this child? Perhaps of talking to it,
if he had known it was dead?"

"John, so overcome with grief at the loss of a child he had not cared
about enough to discover, talking to shades through a charlatan? No. Not
a chance in the world."

"But he went."

"So you tell me. If you can discover why, and it does not distract you
from the main line of enquiry, then do so. Let it be another surprise to add
to the ones I am already having to deal with. Is there anything else?"

"And the morphine?"

"That is none of your business."

There was a chilly finality in her tone which brooked no objection.
She made me feel like some sort of impertinent servant, and I think I
reddened with embarrassment. She did not help me out and cover over
my mistake. Instead she instantly reverted to a formality, a businesslike
manner to indicate that I was being punished. I noticed that this was one
of her many weapons in dealing with men; she would become intimate,
friendly, imply a closeness, then pull back and revert to formality. Her
grasp of language was flawless in that regard; she could hint at intimacy
or distance, friendship or disapproval, in the mixture of tone and language
and gesture. The slightest suggestion of disapproval and I was prepared to
do anything to win back her favour. I do not think this was considered on
her part; she could not help behaving in such a way.

I wasn't completely ready to be self-effacing, though. If she could be
stiff, then so could I. "You have instructed me to forget about your
husband's payment of money to anarchists," I continued. "I suppose you
know more than I do and think this is irrelevant as well. Please say what
you want, and I will obey your wishes."

"Oh, Matthew, I'm sorry," she said beseechingly, instantly warm
again. "Please do not be angry with me, even if I am angry with you. You
are a bringer of evil tidings, you know. You cannot expect me to be happy

with what you tell me, and not feel resentful. It is not your fault my life
has become a nightmare in the past few weeks, but it has. I ask you to be
gentle with me."

"You are not gentle with me."

"I'm sorry if I have hurt you in any way. It was not my intention.
Please believe that."

I did not; but the very words, spoken gently and with warmth, made
hope fill me once more, and undid all the good work I had done in
convincing myself that our relationship was one of employer and
employee, nothing more.

"Of course I do," I said.

Reading this over, I seem like a fool. Perhaps I was; I have already
explained that Elizabeth came from a world of which I knew nothing. I
suppose it is evident that my disdain and suspicion were matched from the
beginning by an equal fascination. Her whole way of life—the money, the
servants, the clothes, the paintings, the leisure, the sheer plenty—was
intoxicating to associate with. It was impossible to separate her from those
surroundings, but I think she would have been every bit as intriguing had
she been very much poorer. She was captivating: the moods, the flashes of
anger and equal bursts of kindness; the way she moved from vulnerability
to a steely determination; the sense of humour that could give way to
sudden seriousness. Her unpredictability was hypnotic.

Even in the way she treated others, like Mrs. Vincotti. It wasn't
pleasant, but it made me sensible that she did not treat me like that. Not
often, at least. It made me feel special. I basked in it because I needed it;
it was a sensation I had never experienced before. And, when all was over,
it was something precious I took away with me. She made people—
men, let us be clear—feel better than they were, more capable, more
handsome, more worthwhile. It was not fraudulent, a technique she had
to bend others to her will so she might get what she wanted, although it
was that as well. It was, I am convinced, quite genuine, a sort of
generosity even though it was something that she used to her own
advantage.

"One last thing, then. The money."

"What about it?"

"It has obviously gone somewhere. It might be helpful to discover
where, if that can be done. My friend Franklin . . ."

"No," she said sharply. "Absolutely not. You gave me your word that you would maintain a complete discretion and you must keep to that."

"But this is a very specialised matter," I tried to explain. "Account books, high finance, that sort of thing. I know nothing about it, and it wasn't what you hired me for. If you had known you needed someone to ferret out the secrets of a balance sheet I have no doubt you would not have chosen me."

"You are an intelligent man, Matthew. And we must make the best of what is available. I do not say it would not be helpful to have expert help. Merely that you must not breathe a word of this to anyone."

Franklin, I thought to myself with a groan. Seyd. Both knew and understood even more than I did. I thought I could rely on both of them, but what if I was wrong? What if Franklin decided to show off at work? Maybe curry favour with his superiors. I think you should unload your holdings of Rialto Investment . . .

"I do not know how much Franklin grasped . . ." I said, splitting the difference between candour and dissimulation in an equitable fashion. I felt a little warm around the collar as I spoke, and she looked at me enquiringly. I hoped I was a better liar than I felt. I was sure that I could prevail on Franklin to keep quiet, after all.

"Anyone else?"

"And my editor hinted that some people consider you to be an agent for the Dual Alliance and are alarmed that much of the Empire's capacity for manufacturing weapons has fallen into your hands."

"It hasn't," she said shortly. "At present it has fallen into the hands of the executor. Where it will stay until these matters are resolved."

I looked at her curiously. "Ah," I said.

"Discover this child, Mr. Braddock," she said with a faint smile. "And the thanks of the Kaiser will be yours."

I looked at her aghast. She sighed with exasperation.

"A joke, Matthew. A joke."

"Oh. Right. Good."

CHAPTER 19

After I left Elizabeth, I went round the corner to the pub, to breathe in rancid air of normality and to order my thoughts. Please do not think that there was much chance of this. I will edit much from the account, and describe only those facts which concerned the matter of Lord Ravenscliff. In fact, they occupied my mind for only the smallest fraction of my time. The rest was taken up, almost obsessively, with my feelings for his wife. I will not dwell on them; anyone who has been in my situation will understand all too well; anyone who has not will be unable to imagine it. So I will instead pretend that, with clear head and reasoned thought, I applied myself to writing down in my little notebook the facts and the theories.

One stood out; the circumstances which led to the impossibility of finding this child meant that control of Ravenscliff's business empire had fallen semipermanently into the hands of the executor. And who was this Michael Cardano, exactly?

The more I thought about it, the more excited I got. What about Cort's intervention when Ravenscliff died? He had concealed the fact for three days, and with the time bought, had arranged for Barings Bank to intervene and prop up the share price. Had the price collapsed, the City would have wanted a full accounting, reassurance that the businesses were sound. And in such an atmosphere, it might easily have been discovered that they were not sound at all. Even worse, perhaps, regrettable information about the integrity of many senior politicians might also have been revealed. A crisis in Government, together with the collapse of the greatest manufacturer of weapons in the country: not an ideal preparation for a trial of strength against our greatest foe. It was easy to see how a man like Cort might have considered the theft of a folder of papers a small thing to avert such a calamity. And I assumed, from my limited knowledge of the subject through reading spy novels, that breaking into a house and stealing papers was simple enough.

That was one question answered to my satisfaction, although perhaps not completely. But there were many others. The big one, of course, was the money. I had not learned a great deal about finance from Franklin, but I knew that, if a large sum of money is extracted from a company, it has to go somewhere. Where did Ravenscliff's millions go? Then there were the lesser problems of the anarchists and the spiritualist. Why was Ravenscliff associating with people for whom, I assumed, he had nothing but contempt?

To that last question, I had no answer. But as I did not have the expertise even to begin tackling the first ones, I decided this would be the place to start. Someone like the witch-woman was very much in my line of business. I had covered the murder, after all. I closed my notebook, stuffed it in my pocket and drained my beer.

I still had my scribbled notes on the story, so I read them as the omnibus clattered towards Tottenham Court Road. The witch-woman had not been a particularly successful member of her trade, largely because of personality—I had not managed to get anyone to give an opinion as to the quality of her aura or the respectability of her spiritual intercessors. Although she went under the name of Madame Boninska, this was obviously a fake; all people claiming to be mediums adopted names like that and dropped heavy hints about gypsy blood and exotic lineage. It was expected; no one would ever believe that someone born in Tooting Bec would have much skill in dealing with the far-beyond. Her real name and age remained a mystery; the police doctors guessed she must have been at least in her sixties, although they freely said (off the record) that her bloated and ancient carcass was so raddled by the effects of drink that she could have been ten years younger or ten years older. Nor was her real identity ever discovered; all that was known was that she had arrived in England a few months before her death, and had previously plied her trade in parts of Germany and France, offering her services to the gullible who went to places like Baden-Baden or Vichy. They had little enough to do, were glad of the distraction, and she had made a decent living. There was a slight suspicion that she had also supplied more human intercessors for the comfort of male customers but that was never pinned down. Why she had abandoned the Continent for London was unknown.

But, abandon it she had, and had set up above a shop selling umbrellas, from which vantage point she began to make her living, giving personal appointments to solve problems, or group sessions for reasons which escaped me but seemed to be little more than light entertainment. On rare occasions she made house calls, but preferred to receive her clients in her room, which was decorated in dark colours, with aromatic candles burning all day and night and windows permanently shrouded in heavy curtains. The police investigation revealed why she did not like to perform elsewhere. She would have had to try and convince her customers without the benefit of all the little bits of trickery and stagecraft that were found stacked in the next room. The cupboards with fake doors; the bells with string, so they could tinkle mysteriously, controlled by unseen forces; the source of a mysterious purple light, which looked as though it had been bought from a theatre; the echo chambers so her assistant could make the noises of spiritual beings unseen by the rest.

The woman was a total fraud, in other words, and it was unfortunate that we reporters—who love a good tale of human foolishness—printed all this in cheerful detail before the police managed to interview her clients, as many of them refused to come forward out of simple embarrassment. If she had ever had an appointments book, it had vanished as well, as had the assistant, who, it emerged, had been a prostitute trying to improve herself.

All in all, then, a squalid business, as was her death. For she had been strangled with the velvet tie of the robe she wore when performing. The murderer had acted with force, and thoroughness; making sure of the matter by then crushing her skull with a heavy brass candlestick. There had been little struggle; the room was hardly disarranged at all. And it was unclear when the murder had taken place. There was a suggestion that the assistant, whose name was Mary, might have come back shortly afterwards—someone thought they had seen her in the street—but, if so, she had then fled rather than contact the police. Which was unfortunate, as the police never for a moment considered that she might have been responsible.

With her had gone the most valuable source of information, for she alone of the living might have known who had come that afternoon, at what time Madame Boninska had probably been killed and why. For nobody else had seen anything that day. And without her evidence there was no chance of solving the case. More alarmingly perhaps, I realised I had given Lady Ravenscliff some slightly inaccurate information: Madame Boninska had been found two days after her husband fell from his window, but the police doctors were not at all certain when she had actually been killed. The degree of uncertainty meant it could have been before Ravenscliff had dropped from the window, perhaps after. The police had concentrated their limited efforts on finding Mary, who was the only one who could enlighten them and, when they proved unsuccessful, had more or less given up. Their collective opinion was that she would turn up eventually, and they could reopen the case when she did. Until then, they had other things to worry about.

I had not been excessively diligent. Murders are rare, and it did have some of the exotic characteristics which turn a squalid death into an interesting story, but in general we follow the police lead unless there is good reason not to do so. In this case, the official reasoning seemed sound. The girl was crucial and there was not much to be done until she rematerialised. I wrote a sidebar on mediums and a piece on the fashion for the occult while I waited for some development, but could push it no further. If they couldn't find her, there wasn't much chance I could, and I did not have the leisure to try.

Now I did, and I also had a very much better reason to do so than a few column inches in the *Chronicle*. So I prepared to do all those reporterly things that I had omitted first time round.

The first thing was to talk to the neighbours. The police had already done that, and I had seen their notes one night in the pub, but I was now interested in different questions. They had asked if anyone had been seen arriving or leaving on the day of the murder. To which the answer had been no; no one in particular. But I was now interested in two days previously as well, when Ravenscliff's diary said he had an appointment. This wasn't likely to lead to much, but I wanted confirmation that he had gone there.

So I called in at the umbrella shop, as the proprietor had been the most useful of interviewees to the police, and I hoped he would prove the same for me. He was the only person, in fact, who had noticed anything at all, and had been the one who had discovered the body. It was rent day, and he had gone to collect. As the lady was too uninterested in the material things of this world to take the mundane matter of paying debts too seriously, he had refused to go away, kept on knocking and had eventually gone in. She apparently had something of a history of pretending to be out when he came to call, and she was three months in arrears.

Mr. Philpot was the sort of man who had no first name. The sort whose wife addresses him as Mr. Philpot after they have finished making love, if they ever do. He is the butt of jokes from his betters, who scorn his ilk for their respectability, and lack of imagination and utter dullness.

The very epitome of the English lower middle classes; a shopkeeper, with standards to maintain and a small place in society to defend. I liked him; I have always liked the Philpots of this world, with their honesty and trustworthiness and decency. I even like their small-mindedness, for they are content with what is theirs, and proud of the little they have. Only if that is threatened do they become testy, but what group of mankind does not? They respect their betters, and fear those below them. They go to church and reverence the King, and sweep the pavement outside their shops every morning. All they want is to be left alone, and in return they provide the nation with all of its substance and solidity. If a factory worker kills his wife, or an aristocrat fathers a child, it is scarcely remarked upon; if a Philpot does so, it is a shock. Philpots are held to higher standards than most of mankind, and on the whole they live up to them.

So, I was predisposed to like Mr. Philpot, in his neat waistcoat, with the armbands keeping the cuffs of his glistening white shirt out of harm's way. With his meticulous little moustache, and well-trimmed fingernails, and shining black shoes. And to like his shop, with its hundreds and hundreds of umbrellas, every single one of them black, with only the handles—each one pointing outwards like a row of Grenadier Guards on display—allowing just the slightest hint of flamboyance to brighten up the dark oak of the counters and floor. Philpot made me feel as though the world was in good hands. Until I met Elizabeth, I had taken it for granted that I should, eventually, marry the daughter of a Philpot, who would be as diligent in the home as her father was at work.

We talked for some time before I introduced the subject of his erstwhile tenant. It is always best to do so, if possible; to establish your credentials as a decent, upright man. I sympathised with his embarrassment, and consternation at suddenly finding his shop mentioned in the newspapers in connection with such a terrible event. The shame of the neighbours discovering that he had rented out his little flat to a charlatan and a prostitute. It might be that eventually he would live it down, but his good name had been tainted.

"And I only let her have the place out of the goodness of my heart," he protested. "I couldn't see anyone else renting her anything, and she pleaded with me not to throw her out when I discovered what she was up to. When I let her have it, I never dreamed for a moment there might be anything improper about her. She was an old woman. I felt sorry for her. I won't make that mistake again, let me tell you."

"But you knew what she did? How she made her money?"

"Eventually I found out. And I told her she'd have to leave. I wasn't going to put up with that. And she agreed, said that in a short while she'd go. She just wanted to stay until the end of the month. Then she was going to look for something much better."

"I thought you said she didn't even pay the rent on this place."

"Nor did she. But she said she had friends who would look after her. I wish they'd looked after her while she was in my flat, that's all."

"And who were these friends? Did you ever find out?"

"They didn't exist. It was just a story. She thought I was a proper fool; she'd have said anything to keep me quiet. And I did, more fool me."

"What was she like?"

"Old."

"I know that. I mean, did you like her when you first met her?"

"Why do you want to know? You come here, asking these questions, but you haven't said why. I've had enough trouble from all this . . ."

"I quite appreciate that, sir," I said. "And there is no sinister reason, I assure you. But I am helping a friend who became entangled with this woman. He is a trusting man, a bit like yourself, but very much more innocent. He fears that some of the things he said . . ."

Philpot nodded. Shame and embarrassment were things he understood all too well. "Although I think that anyone who goes to someone like that . . ."

"I quite agree. I quite agree. And so does he, now. But, you see, he lost his wife in a tragic accident, and has grieved ever since. She was all the world to him, and he never recovered. He allowed himself to think that maybe—just maybe—he might be able to have one last word with her."

"Well, she would have seen him coming, that's for sure," said Philpot, although not without sympathy. "She would have had the money out of his pocket in two seconds, and told him anything he wanted to hear in return, I've no doubt."

"Precisely," I said. "Exactly what happened. He feels deceived and angry. Until he saw the stories in the newspapers he believed he was talking to his dear departed, and contented himself that all was well with her. He felt happy for the first time in years."

"Ah, these newspapers," said Philpot, shaking his head. "They should be ashamed of themselves."

I agreed. "And now," I continued, "all he wants is that people should not know of his foolishness, so he can grieve once more without being laughed at."

That shook Philpot to the core. A good man, able to sympathise with others. To be laughed at was the worst humiliation of all. "I see, I see," he said. "Yes, of course he would want that. Well, tell me your questions."

"Well, what I'd like to know is if anyone saw him, coming and going to these—ah—séances. He is of average size, grey hair, well dressed, very distinguished-looking. Look; I have his photograph."

I took out the photograph of Ravenscliff; Philpot looked, stroked his moustache with thumb and forefinger and thought for a moment. Then he nodded. "I do remember him," he said. "He came a couple of times, as I recall. He was so much better dressed than most of the people who went up the stairs. Very handsome umbrella he had; German, with a hand-carved handle of mahogany."

Since he obviously warmed to any subject that had an umbrella in it, I continued to press, in a gentle way.

"There you are! You noticed his umbrella. And that is one of the things that he asked me to look into. You see, the last time he came, he was so overcome by what he thought were his wife's words, that he rushed out and left his umbrella behind!"

"He didn't!"

"Yes. So he asked me, if at all possible, if I could recover it. He only took it with him because Madame Boninska said it would help summon the spirits if there was something she had touched in the room."

Philpot understood immediately, and was shocked by the sacrilege. "You must go and look," he said immediately. "I insist."

"That is kind of you. I wanted to ask, but . . ."

"I understand perfectly. Poor man. Here, take these keys, and go and look for it . . ."

I went out of the shop door into the fresh air—or as fresh as the air near Tottenham Court Road ever became—and walked up the stairs in the little passage next door. The flat was oppressive, and dark and gloomy, and would have been even if a murder had not been committed there. I opened the curtains and then opened the windows as well. Everything was neat and tidy though the general appearance was thoroughly bizarre. Stuffed animals; prints on the wall of psychic events. Odd pieces of equipment and furniture. Lots of black velvet.

I wasn't interested in any of it. Immediately I started going through drawers, looking under beds and mattresses, down the sides of chairs, under furniture. Any scrap of paper, or notebook, or strongbox or photograph. Anything at all would do. An address book, old railway ticket, deed or document. There was nothing. Absolutely nothing.

Which was not right. Everybody accumulates something. Even an old bus ticket. But in this place there was not a single scrap. Which made me wonder. It had probably been the police, of course; I would have to check, but I had never come across a police investigation where they had taken everything away like that.

"Have you found it?"

"What?"

"The umbrella. Have you found it?" It was Philpot, poking his head reluctantly round the door.

"Oh. No, I'm afraid not. It's gone. I'm sorry to have been so long, but I found this room very oppressive. I think I looked everywhere twice because I couldn't keep my mind on things."

Philpot found this sensitivity unbecoming and said nothing. I followed him down the stairs and into the street. "Gloomy place," I said. "But it will be perfectly pleasant once it's cleaned up. Why not get a rag-and-bone man to come and take everything away? Open the windows for a week. Get in a painter. Everyone will forget soon enough about all this."

Philpot was grateful for the reassurance, but shook his head. "Not yet," he said. "I can't think of it yet. I'll take your advice soon enough, though."

"And no news of the girl? What was her name?"

"Mary. No. Vanished, she has. I think I was more shocked to learn what she was than anything . . ." He lowered his voice and eyes as he thought about her.

"You never knew where she came from?"

"The police asked me. 'Did she tell you where she lived?' No, she didn't. Of course, I knew where she came from, but they weren't interested. 'Facts, Mr. Philpot,' they said. 'Just keep to the facts.'"

"So how do you know?"

"The way she talked, of course. She was brought up in Shoreditch. Now, I'm not saying she lived there . . ."

CHAPTER 20

It was time to summon the runners. I went back to the newspaper offices for the first time since I had resigned, and asked at the reception
desk if the boys were about. Some of them were in Dragon Court, a
mouldy, dank little square just over the road which was surrounded by
seemingly abandoned buildings. Few of them had any glass left in the
windows; the boys had broken most of it playing football or cricket, which
is what they did when they were waiting for a job. Three of them were
there; one was hopeless, a mournful character of small intelligence and
no initiative whatsoever. Pale and pimply with an air of being underfed
and neglected. Wearing clothes two sizes too big for him. One, Derrick,
was reliable, and the cleverest grew up to become a highly successful cat
burglar.

"Listen, boys," I said. "I've got a job for you. Twice the usual rates,
and a bonus of a guinea for the one who succeeds." I had learned from
Elizabeth that if you want instant obedience with no argument, you pay,
and pay so handsomely it takes the breath away. None of these boys, I
suspected, had ever even seen a guinea before. The very idea of one made
them go quiet and reverential.

I told them what I wanted; told them the girl's name, told them she
came from Shoreditch, told them about her occupation—these were not
innocent little angels—and repeated the description I had got from the
police. About twenty years of age, with light brown hair, blue eyes and of
middling height. It wasn't much good, but at least it eliminated all the six-
foot-tall, orange-haired and red-eyed prostitutes in Shoreditch.

"Now, pay attention," I said. "This is important. If you come across
this woman, don't frighten her. Let her know that no one means her any
harm. There is no question of the police being involved in this. I might
even be able to help her, if she needs it. But I want to talk to her, and will
pay her a guinea as well. Got that?"

The urchins nodded. I told them to find me either at home or in the
pub or at the Ravenscliff house if they came up with anything. That done,
I went back to the King & Keys to find Hozwicki once more. This was a
long shot—not finding Hozwicki, as I knew he'd be there, but the
possibility of his knowing or telling me anything.

"What do you want? You haven't paid for the last bit of information I gave you."

"True enough, but I would have thought an old comrade in arms . . ." I gave up. Normally in such circumstances all you have to do is stand a round or two of drinks and all is well, but this tactic I knew wouldn't work either.

"Believe me," I said with as much sincerity as I could muster, "if I could tell you something, I would. But I don't want to put you in danger."

Hozwicki looked sceptical, but at least started paying attention. "It is all far more complicated than you can imagine. I thought I was writing a biography for a grieving widow. Now, it seems, I am being pursued by a bunch of anarchist murderers. I don't want you to get into the same position."

He looked at me. "What are you talking about?"

"The Brotherhood of Socialists. Ever heard of them?"

Hozwicki glared at me. "You think that just because I am Polish I know every revolutionary in the East End?"

"Hardly. I mean, there are so many of them, you can't know them all, can you? I just thought you might have come across the name."

"So why are they after you?"

"I don't know."

"But this has something to do with Ravenscliff?"

"I don't know."

Hozwicki rubbed the end of his nose, and thought. "Never heard of them," he said finally.

"Yes, you have."

"Yes, I have. But I'm not going to tell you anything."

"Look, Stefan—"

"If they've got a grudge against you, then steer clear of them. Or get a gun. Do you have a gun?"

"Of course I haven't."

"I'll give you the name of a man who can get one for you."

"I don't want a gun."

"Perhaps. But you may need one."

"Who are these people?"

Hozwicki's good and bad sides were wrestling for control of his conscience, which put quite a strain on him. He did not answer for some time. In fact, he didn't really answer at all. Instead, he pulled out his notebook, tore off a sheet and scribbled on it. "Here," he said. "I'm not going to help you. But go there and ask questions. That's all I'll do for you."

Written on the sheet was an address. The Anarchist Club; 165 Jubilee Street.

For those who have forgotten what London was like before the war, or who never knew, the very idea of an Anarchist Club sounds absurd. Most people are more familiar with the Reform, or the Athenaeum, and when they think of clubs, they think of leather armchairs, port and cigars, with quiet waiters padding about bearing silver platters. The idea of anarchists enjoying such surroundings cannot help but bring a smile to the lips.

And yet there was such a club, although it was closed down when the war began and never reopened. More than that, it was a popular place. The East End was a seething mass of revolution in those days; wave after wave of immigrants had swept in, bringing Jews, nationalists and revolutionaries fleeing the authorities in Russia and elsewhere. It was a cause of great tension. On the one hand, it made Britain most unpopular in those countries which preferred to have their revolutionaries either dead or in gaol, rather than freely plotting evil. On the other, the mass of men seeking work annoyed our own labourers, who found their housing taken and their wages undercut. But government after government refused to do anything. The employers liked the cheap labour and I suspect the Foreign Office enjoyed tweaking the noses of autocratic governments abroad. So the authorities reached a sort of pact with the unwelcome guests. As long as they caused no trouble in England, they could plot to visit whatever mayhem they liked on their own country. Nonetheless, the authorities kept a firm eye on what was going on, as much as they could. I had learned from the police, however, that this wasn't very much. These Letts and Poles and Pan-Slavs and Russians and whoever not only spoke a wide variety of languages, often in obscure dialects, they also seemed to change name with bewildering rapidity. Several criminals were tried in court for offences using only nicknames—the Elephant, Fatty, the Bricklayer—because the authorities had no idea who they were.

Now, the trouble with revolutionaries is, having got into the habit of opposing their own authorities, they end up opposing everything else as well. That is to say, no sooner had a party formed—to install, say, the principles of Marxist socialism, or anarchist freedom, in liberated Lithuania—than it tended to split into two on the question of what, exactly, socialism or anarchism was. Or even what Lithuania was. So the Anarchist Club was formed; fraternal loathing was suspended while members were within its portals. There you could find speeches on all manner of subjects, as long as they were intense and impractical. As I approached it that evening—I took a bus from Fleet Street to Commercial Road, then walked up Jubilee Street to my destination—I tried to imagine Lord Ravenscliff, with his silk top hat and cashmere overcoat, rubbing shoulders with such people. I almost succeeded, but eventually gave up. It was too absurd.

The club smelled, but was no worse than most pubs; it was also a good deal quieter. Chilly though, and not very clean. Anarchists did not approve of housework; that was for their women and, on the whole, there were few women dedicated enough to cook, clean, listen to the rhetoric and foment revolution all at the same time. I guessed there were about thirty men in the large room and only four women. Everybody was dowdy and poor-looking and, although some were dapper enough with waxed moustaches and strutting walks, most were subdued and moved with an air of caution. They did not give a very convincing imitation of murderous lunatics. All were foreign, I guessed many were Jews, and they seemed different from the unionists and syndicalists I had written about in my days of toil. Few had the true air of workingmen; they did not stand or move like men used to working with hand and body. They also looked very much worse fed, greyer of face.

"Can I help you?" A cautious voice, heavily accented; a small man, jacketless and collarless, stood beside me, looking at me cautiously. Not surprisingly. I was hardly dressed fashionably, but it was obvious from my healthy complexion and unpatched clothes that I was both English and not a natural member of this place.

"I was hoping to meet a friend," I said. "Stefan Hozwicki. Do you know him?"

"I do, but he isn't here," the man replied, relaxing a little. It seemed Stefan's name was a sort of passport, a guarantee of my good intentions. Which was kind of him, although mysterious. If I did not exactly slip into the background here, I couldn't imagine Hozwicki doing so either.

"You've not been here before," the man said. "My name is Josef, by the way. Welcome."

"Thank you. My name is Matthew Brad—"

He held up his hand. "We do not have second names," he said with a smile. "It is uncomradely and also there are far too many people who do not wish to give them. So Matthew will do nicely." His mouth twitched with amusement as he watched me try to look comradely.

I quite took to him. He was short, only about five foot four high, weedy and underfed, badly dressed and looked less than healthy. His hands twitched nervously all the time, as though he was trying to pull rings off his fingers, but the rest of him was totally still and calm. His eyes watched me through thick lenses, and they were kindly and a little sad.

"You have come for the talk?"

"Ah, yes. I suppose so. I'm not sure why I'm here, to tell the truth."

"Comrade Stefan no doubt has his reasons."

"I'm sure Comrade Stefan has," I said, and was quite proud of myself for suppressing the twitch of amusement. It was only because I was quite touched; Hozwicki, as I have mentioned, was not exactly the most friendly of people. He trusted no one, and liked even fewer. To tell me to come here, where he must have realised I would hear him being referred to as Comrade Stefan—thus exposing him to ridicule if not worse if I ever repeated it in the King & Keys—was a gesture. Not exactly an open offer of friendship, but probably the closest to it I or anyone else would ever get. "Who is the speaker, might I ask?"

"Ah," he said. "It is Comrade Kropotkin."

The anarchist aristocrat. The Russian revolutionary. The Anarchist Prince. All titles dreamed up by the headline writers on the *Daily Mail*, who excelled at such things. He was an odd fellow, by all accounts; a genuine Russian prince who had turned to rural collectivism and revolution. He had been imprisoned in Russia, thrown out of Switzerland, France and America, and came to rest in a comfortable part of Brighton, where he went for long walks with his dog and was perfectly sweet to the neighbours when not advocating stringing them up from the nearest lamppost.

"And what is he talking about?"

"The evils of Darwinism."

"Is it evil?"

"Comrade Kropotkin has argued in the past that Darwinism is but a reflection of capitalism because it emphasises competition and struggle over cooperation and coexistence. It justifies the exploitation of man by man, and strengthens the class ideology of the oppressors."

"Excellent. So what will be new today?"

"That we must find out. If we can understand him. There are so many people of so many different nationalities here, with so many languages, that English is the only one everybody has a chance of understanding. I don't suppose you speak Serbo-Croat?"

"Not really."

"A pity. I would have pressed you into service to give a running translation. Our Serbs are very bad at languages."

"Who else—I mean, what other languages are represented?"

Josef screwed up his eyes to think. "Well, there are Russians and Germans. Many Latvians and Lithuanians and Poles. A few Serbs. One Dane, although he comes only rarely. Many English, although for some reason few Irish, which I find strange as they are the most oppressed of all. Some Ukrainians and a few Belgians. The French tend to stay in France. And of course we have many, many people who speak only Yiddish."

"A veritable Internationale," I said, with what I hoped was a tone of approval. "And how many policemen?"

He gave me an odd look, but realised full well that I was light-heartedly broaching a serious point. "That is Serge, who hasn't arrived yet."

"You aren't tempted to throw him out?"

"Oh, no. Obviously the police are going to infiltrate, so why bother? We do nothing here that is of great interest to them. It is not as if we hold open meetings on bomb-making."

"Those are by invitation only?"

"Precisely," he said with a twinkle in his eye. "Seriously, the authorities here are stupid and coercive, but somewhat milder than their counterparts abroad. As long as we do not frighten them, they leave us alone, more or less. And nothing frightens authority more than not knowing what is going on. Then they fantasise about plots and evil, and react. So we show there is nothing to be afraid of."

"And this Serge knows you know about him?"

"The subject has never come up, but I imagine so. Do you wish to meet him? You are a journalist, I take it."

"How did you know that?"

"Because the moment you open your mouth you start asking questions. Because you clearly know nothing about anarchism and because you are a friend of Stefan, who is a journalist as well. You don't work for the *Daily Mail,* do you?"

"Certainly not," I said, almost offended.

"That is good."

"You don't mind me coming?"

"Oh, no. The more publicity the better. Comrade Kropotkin has written many articles for newspapers, here and abroad, showing the origins and nature of what we believe. He has just finished a long article for the *Encyclopaedia Britannica*. And now, if you will excuse me."

The courteous anarchist moved off towards the stage. He walked with a limp, I noticed, and he looked as though moving was painful for him. He weaved an erratic course as he went, stopping frequently to greet people, pat them on the back, talk briefly with them. One woman he bowed to in an oddly old-world fashion. She was dressed simply, with a muffler around her head, as though she had a cold, and a sprig of flowers in her hair. She briefly broke off her conversation with a large unshaven man to greet him, and half-turned to respond with an unsmiling, cold nod of the head.

"These, eh?"

"What?" I turned, to see a grim man staring at me as though I had just advocated the abolition of taxes for landowners. Powerful, intelligent, his eyes radiating annoyance at his feeble grasp of language.

He waved his arm. "Chairs. They must organise." He spoke with such a thick and indeterminate accent that it was difficult to realise his understanding of English grammar was rudimentary, as it was almost impossible to make out anything at all.

"What?" I repeated, almost panicking.

He picked up a chair, put it into my hand and propelled me roughly across the room until it was next to the one in a line, and made me put it down. Then he gestured to all the other chairs.

"Again."

"Ah. Right." He was not the sort of man who would brook any refusal. I half-expected him to whip out a revolver and shoot me on the spot if I so much as looked reluctant. So I picked up another chair, and then another, and slowly set them out, row by row.

"Good. Very good." A thunderous clap on the back and a broad smile signified my labours for the common good had met with approval. "Drink."

He thrust a bottle of beer at me, contrary to the 1892 Regulation of Drink Act, and scowled, or maybe it was a smile. Hard to tell. I smiled back, as best I could. I really didn't want a drink, but again I felt it unwise to refuse. We toasted each other, smiled again, indulged in another bout of backslapping, and then he drifted off.

"And you will be Comrade Matthew, the journalist friend of Comrade Stefan," came a cold female voice behind me. It spoke with a heavy German accent, but was both grammatical and comprehensible.

I spun round. I opened my mouth to speak. Suave and sophisticated, able to deal with any eventuality. That was the way I wanted to be, and very definitely the way I wasn't. I couldn't say a word.

"Are you here to hear the speech? It is not often we get journalists here, so I imagine you are here to see Comrade Peter." She spoke quietly, and was one of those who did not look at the person she was speaking to. Stared hard, rather, somewhere above my left shoulder, communicating a contempt which fully matched the harshness of her voice.

"Um."

"Get a good seat. He mumbles."

She tossed back her head, and swept a strand of loose hair from her eyes with one finger. I had watched her intensely; had memorised her every gesture, and that was something she did not do. It was as though she had taken on a different persona entirely. Almost as though she was a different person. I felt utterly confused. Surely it could not be so.

She was dressed in the manner of everyone else in the room; thin, old clothes, utterly unbecoming, with thick black boots. Buttoned up to the neck with a row of buttons, one of which was undone, one missing. Her face was severe and more serious, it looked as though it had been angry often. Her skin was pallid, old-looking. Weary. The smile had no warmth in it at all.

No, I decided.

"And you are?"

"Call me Jenny," she said flatly.

"Is it your real name?"

"What does that matter? With women names are ownership. Who your father was, who your husband is. We must choose our own names, you agree?"

"Absolutely. Just what I was thinking myself."

"I do not approve of frivolity."

"Sorry. Habit."

"Divest yourself of this habit." She had pronounced. She had finished. "You will find the meeting instructive if you pay proper attention."

She almost clicked her heels together, I swear, and then, very briefly, for a fraction of a fraction of a second as she turned away, I caught her eye. Grey. And I got that familiar shock, running through my system; the curdling feeling in my stomach, the outpouring of breath, the sudden speeding up of my heart.

Stefan or no Stefan, and despite the undoubted appeal of a many-houred talk from a Russian anarchist, I decided to leave and quickly. At least I managed not to run, but I made my way to the door, through the groups of people coming in the opposite direction, as quickly as I could. Josef stopped me just as I was about to regain my freedom. "You are surely not leaving?"

"I must, I'm afraid, I . . ." I tried, but failed to think of some good reason. "I've just remembered some work I have to do. Dreadfully sorry. Really looking forward to it."

"Another time, then," he said with no great interest. "As you see the doors are always open. Even to journalists."

"Thank you. That is kind, and I have found even the little I've seen interesting. Very interesting. Tell me, who is that woman over there?"

I nodded as discreetly as I could.

"Why do you want to know?"

"Oh, we talked, you see. And there are so few women here, I wondered."

"If you want to find out, you should ask her yourself. Besides, I don't know a great deal about her. She's been coming occasionally for the last six months or so. It was the first thing she did when she got off the boat."

"The boat?"

"Yes. She is German; had to leave because . . . well, that doesn't matter. But she's tough and committed. If you want to know more, ask her. But don't expect an answer."

I didn't want to push the matter too far. So I left, grateful only that Hozwicki hadn't shown up. The last thing I needed was to have to come up with another excuse.

Kropotkin arrived only about ten minutes after I left; I saw him from my vantage point across the road. It was part of the training; part of the way I had trained myself, at any rate. The ability to wait. It is a skill possessed by very few people. Most get bored after only a few minutes, they become agitated and dream up dozens of good reasons why they are wasting their time, simply to justify giving up. I had learned, not exactly to like it, but more to let my mind drift, so that time seemed to pass more quickly. It had a peaceful aspect to it. It is a small talent, I know, but it is rare and one I am quite proud of. So I found a dark corner, in an alleyway running along the side of a grocer's shop on the other side of the road, which gave a clear view but which wasn't lit up by the gaslight. I pulled my coat more firmly around my neck. And I waited. And waited. I saw Stefan hurry in, along with several others; saw a carriage draw up and a tall man with a thick bushy beard get out. That, I thought, would be Kropotkin. Let us assume ten minutes to get started; then three hours of meeting, at least. I pulled my pocket watch out of my waistcoat and peered at it. It was eight o'clock. It was going to be a long evening.

It was. Almost interminable. Even my skilled placidity in these situations was only just sufficient to get me through. My mind fixed on this Jenny. It hammered away time and again at the whole business, and I could not make head nor tail of it. I was only sure of one thing. I had been lied to, once again.

So I waited, cold, very hungry and distraught. Nine o'clock; ten o'clock; half past ten. A few people drifted out from time to time; perhaps they did not find the Prince's words satisfying. Perhaps they had heard them before. Some hung around outside talking, others walked swiftly off. None interested me.

Eventually Jenny came out. Bundled up in a coat, with a hat on her head, but there was no mistaking her. She was with a man, the one who had told me to set out the chairs. He also had a hat, pulled down over his face. His right hand was in the pocket of his overcoat.

And he touched her. Stroked her back with his left hand in an un-mistakable gesture of intimacy. And she responded, leaning her body against his. There was no mistake. I did not imagine it.

So I followed. A more hot-blooded person than I might have accosted them. "Hello, Your Ladyship, fancy seeing you here!" But I decided that knowledge was a better revenge. I would discover everything, first of all.

So I tagged behind at a good distance, just keeping them in view, ducking into the shadows whenever the man paused to tie his shoelaces, or strike a match against a wall, or when they stopped on the pavement to talk. This they did often enough to make me realise they were afraid of being followed. Nobody stops that often. But I had learned from a master. George Short had cut his teeth as a runner before becoming a reporter. He knew all the tricks of how to follow without being seen and, I suspected, knew how to pick pockets and listen in to conversations in bars and restaurants as well. When I was getting going he taught me some of his skills. "You never know when it might come in handy," he'd said. "These university graduates think it's all about a well-turned phrase. They wouldn't be able to get a story if it bit them on the leg."

His skills had never been that useful before, but now I saw their point. It is a question of getting into the rhythm of the person you are following, watching them intently until you can predict what they are going to do; moving in harmony with them, so that you are already tucked away in the shadows before they have even begun to turn. Of knowing how far back to be. Of knowing how to walk light-footedly but naturally, so that you are unsuspected even if you are seen.

I followed them for a mile or so; down Jubilee Street, along Commercial Road, up Turner Street, then into Newark Street, a row of houses, run-down and poor. They stopped outside one of them which was all in darkness, and talked. I heard nothing, but I did not need to; he wanted her to come in; that was clear. She refused, initially, and my spirits rose a little. But then she took his hand, allowed him to lead her to the door, and they vanished inside.

If I had been in a state of shocked disbelief before, it was nothing in comparison to how I felt now. I could describe my emotions for a very long time, but in fact they were very simple. I was jealous to the point of insanity. She was mine, I told myself. It was another one of her lies to add to the growing list. And such a man? Such people? Clearly, they weren't notes of her husband's payments to the Brotherhood that I had found in that folder; they were hers. He had discovered and was trying to find out what she was doing. This man was probably one of that group and she was paying him. My stomach turned over with disgust. I would expose her to the world. I would destroy her reputation so completely she would have to leave the country forever. How to do it? Hozwicki, obviously; I'd promised him a story; it would be better than he dreamed of. Then Seyd's. I'd pull her husband's companies down until their worth would fit in my back pocket in small change.

The thought calmed me. My patience slowly returned, and I became thorough. When the man emerged, I followed him until he got back to what were evidently his lodgings, then took a bus back to the West End. I went into an early-morning café—it was by now four in the morning—and borrowed some paper and an envelope from the owner. I considered a long and violent denunciation, but such things are never effective; they make the writer seem hysterical. So instead I kept it short.

> Dear Lady Ravenscliff,
> Please accept my resignation as your agent in the matter of your husband's will.
>   Yours sincerely,
>   Matthew Braddock.

I delivered it by hand to her house, then took the bus back to Chelsea. It was still only six when I slipped quietly into the house, and no one was yet up, not even Mrs. Morrison. I tiptoed up the stairs, avoiding the squeakiest of the treads, and collapsed on my bed. It was an eternity since I had slept properly, but I was afraid sleep would elude me now as well. I shouldn't have worried. I was still thinking this when my thoughts began to disintegrate and I plunged into oblivion.

CHAPTER 21

If I harboured the idea that this might be an end to it, then I could not have been more wrong. I slept until two in the afternoon, but was hardly refreshed when I finally surfaced. I did have a couple of moments' grace before the full recollection of the previous evening came back, but it was not much of a respite. I was dirty, unshaven, and my bones ached still from tiredness, so I went downstairs in search of hot water. There was no one around, which was unusual; normally at that time of day Mrs. Morrison should be in the kitchen with her half-wit of a scullery maid, arguing over how to peel carrots. So I put a large pot on the hob myself, and yawned while it heated. On the kitchen table was a telegram, addressed to me. I knew the moment I saw it who it was from, and the surge of pleasure I felt should have warned me how feeble was my resolution of only a few hours previously. I considered tearing it in two and throwing it in the bin—I don't need her; that's all over—but couldn't quite manage to be so manfully confident. What if there was something in there to show I was wrong? So I dithered while the water boiled and the kitchen filled with steam, and eventually reached a compromise. I would open it, read it and then tear it up in righteous anger.

Come immediately. Elizabeth.

The first word was enough to turn all my steely resolution a little rusty. All sorts of stories flooded into my mind. A lost twin. Devoted sisters torn asunder, and now reunited. All nonsense. It could not possibly be so. Could it? The doubt was small, but enough because I wanted it to be so. I washed and shaved and dressed in clean clothes, and by the time I was ready to face the world I was decided. I would see her. Just in case. But I would make her wait, and use the time to find out some more. It was the first time she had wanted to see me more than the other way around, and I liked the feeling too much to lose it quickly.

I went back to Fleet Street. Hozwicki wasn't in the King & Keys so I went to the *Telegraph,* walked up the stairs to the newsroom, and found him, sitting alone in a corner with a typewriter. He was the only person in the entire place to use one; everyone else wrote their stories out by hand, and I noticed he kept on getting irritated glances from others in the room every time he pressed a key. It was a woman's machine, not for men.

"I need to talk to you."

"I'm busy."

"I don't care."

I must have said it in an impressive fashion, as he stopped typing and looked up at me. "So, talk."

"Not here. I don't want your colleagues to learn about Comrade Stefan."

I hadn't meant it to come out as a threat. But that was how he took it. He stared stonily at me.

"Come outside for a walk. It will only take five minutes."

He considered for a second, then stood up and put on his coat. I could see he was angry; I imagine I would have been as well. From his point of view he had extended a hand of friendship, and I was using his gesture to blackmail him. I would have felt guilty about it, if I'd had the leisure to think straight.

"Well then? What do you want now?"

He stood on the pavement as the crowds of people parted to walk around us, and indicated he was going to go no further. We were just outside the *Telegraph*'s doors.

"I didn't mean to threaten," I said. "I had no intention of saying anything. But I have to talk, and I don't have a great deal of time."

"What happened yesterday? I heard you came, then left. Too boring for you?"

"It probably would have been, but I didn't find out. There was a woman there. She called herself Jenny. In her forties, German accent."

He nodded.

"Tell me about her."

"Why?"

"It doesn't matter."

"Not unless . . ."

"No," I interrupted. "No games. Not today. No bargains, no you-scratch-my-back nonsense. I need to know now. I must know. Who is she?"

He looked at me carefully, then nodded. "And you won't say why you want to know?"

"Not a single, solitary word. But you must tell me."

He stared at the pavement for a few seconds, then turned on his heel, and walked off, turning up Wine Office Court, past the Cheshire Cheese, where there was no one around. Eventually he stopped and turned.

"Her name is Jenny Mannheim," he said. "But that's not her real name. She arrived from Hamburg about six months ago. It appears she was involved in a murder there and had to flee the country. When she got here, she contacted some groups of exiles, but has steered clear of the Germans. She doesn't want anyone to know she is here. She's afraid of the police, or of being murdered herself in revenge. She's a very tough woman, ruthless in argument and quite capable of being ruthless in action, I imagine. Her life is the struggle. It is all she cares about, and all she talks about. She is entirely cold and deeply unpleasant. So I'm afraid I cannot tell you much more. Even what I know did not come from her. I avoid her as much as possible. And so should you, if you've any sense."

"So how do you know about her?"

"She approached these groups which—well, they don't trust many people. They're used to spies and informers and police agents trying to infiltrate them. They're careful. Naturally they wanted to make sure she was who she said."

"How did they do that?"

"Easily enough. They wrote letters to comrades in Germany. They checked she was on the boat she said she was on. They used people in the police there to see if she's done what she said. She had. She's a nasty bit of work. Even by the standards of her type."

"Quite pretty, though."

"It would be interesting to see the reaction if you said that to her face."

"She left yesterday with a man." I gave a brief description, as best as I could. It wasn't necessary.

"Jan the Builder," Hozwicki said flatly. "That's what he's called. He sometimes works on building sites. Josef pointed him out to me once, and told me to beware of him. Again, no one knows his real name. And, since you no doubt already know, yes, he is a member—probably the leader— of the Brotherhood of Socialists."

"And are they . . . ?"

Hozwicki looked at me. "Dangerous people who you do not want to know. You remember the hold-up at Marston's brewery? The armed robbery at that Cheapside jeweller's about a year ago?"

He was referring to two violent, but unsuccessful, crimes. "They were what are called expropriations, to fund the cause. Anarchism is split into two; those who think such things justifiable and necessary, and those who believe they ruin everything we are striving to achieve."

"We?"

He nodded.

"So tell me more about these people."

"Hard. It's not as if they advertise themselves. But there can't be many of them. Most are Lithuanian or Latvian, most would be executed or imprisoned if they went home. They hate Russia and all things Russian. And everyone else. They seem to have money. Presumably from robberies. More than that, I cannot tell you. I don't know. They are not interested in listening to speeches or theoretical discourses. They think that is bourgeois. They think violent action is the only true revolutionary activity. I think that if they could, they would happily murder Kropotkin as well as any other Russian."

"What is all this to you, Stefan?" I asked. I was genuinely curious. "Why are you part of all this rigmarole?"

He frowned as he turned to look at me. "I'm Jewish and I'm Polish," he said. "Why do I need to say any more? I do not wish to kill anyone, Matthew. I want to set the world free, so mankind can realise its full potential and live in harmony. An aspiration you no doubt think is foolish, naïve and absurd."

I shrugged. "As aspirations go it is not a bad one. I am merely sceptical about its chances of success."

"You are not alone. But compromise . . ." Here he turned with a smile playing over his mouth, which made quite a change. He had a pleasant smile. He really should have used it more often. "Compromise is a weapon of oppression wielded by capitalists to ensure nothing ever changes."

"Of course it is," I said heartily. "Damn good thing too."

He grinned. "And now we understand each other. I'm glad. I've always appreciated your efforts to be kind. Do not think I was unreceptive. But I grew up in a world of suspicion and it is not a habit I can abandon easily. You are a good man. For a lackey of the system."

"I will take that as a compliment," I said. "And I in turn appreciate your willingness to talk to me. I will use the information—cautiously, shall we say. And one day I will give you a proper explanation."

He nodded. "If you know what is good for you, you'll steer clear of Jan the Builder and anyone associated with him."

"We're old drinking mates," I said.

"And whatever you do, don't start making eyes at Jenny Mannheim. She'd eat you for breakfast and pick her teeth with your bones."

He nodded, and strode off to his work, leaving me pondering his last words. They had brought me back to the subject of my obsession. I had forgotten about her for the time I was talking to him. Now she came flooding back to my mind. An associate of Jan the Builder.

I had information, but no understanding. In fact, I was worse off than before. Every time I added a nugget of information to my paltry hoard, it made the rest seem the more confusing. So I now knew more about this band of anarchists; knew a small amount more about this woman I had encountered the previous day. But I still knew nothing about their connection with Ravenscliff. What was more I did not care; my obsession with Elizabeth had grown to the point that it was almost uncontrollable. I agonised over whether I would go and see her, as I had been asked to do.

I knew I would, sooner or later. I knew I would not be able to keep away. But I put up a fight. I did not embrace my fate eagerly or without resistance. Even as my feet took me down Fleet Street, past Charing Cross, up Haymarket and to Piccadilly Circus, I told myself I had not made up my mind. I could, at any moment, hop on to a bus and go home. I had free will. I would decide, in my own good time. I went through all the reasons for treating her command with the disdain it deserved, and they were overwhelming. Went through all the reasons for obeying her, and they were paltry. And still I walked on, hands in pockets, eyes looking down at the pavement, getting ever closer, with each step, to St. James's Square.

I still told myself that I had not yet made up my mind as I stood on the doorstep, and as I rang the bell. And it was true. I had decided nothing. The only decision I could take was to walk in the other direction; indecision made me sleepwalk towards her, go through the door when it was opened by the housemaid, climb up the stairs to the little sitting room where she was waiting for me. Had my heart given way then, I would not have been surprised, and might not have been ungrateful. But it did not; and I walked in to see her sitting on the settee by the fire, a book on her lap, looking at me gravely. And I felt that familiar flood of emotion coursing through my being, as I knew that I was back, exactly where I needed to be.

"Sit down, Matthew," she said softly, gesturing to the place beside her. With an immense effort of will, I sat in the armchair opposite, so I would not have to suffer her perfume, the sound of her clothes as she moved or the feeling that, with the slightest gesture, I could reach out and touch her. I was safe, immune there. She noticed, of course, and knew why I had done it: it was a gesture of weakness, not of defiance; she understood it all.

She continued to look gravely at me, but was not trying to fascinate; there was a seriousness in her glance which hinted at sympathy and understanding, although I knew all too well that I read far too much into such things, and always tried to give the best possible interpretation.

"You asked, so here I am," I said.

"I wrote because I received this distressing message from you. I thought the least I could expect was some sort of explanation."

"Do you really think you need one?"

"Of course. I was entirely perplexed by it."

I searched her face intently, trying desperately to see through to the thoughts underneath. I knew that everything depended on what I said next. Why, I do not know. I was simply certain.

"Do you ever tell the truth?"

"Do you ever do as you are told? If you remember, I told you quite plainly that you should not give any attention to the anarchists. You agreed, promised, and immediately broke your promise. I think I have more of a right to be cross than you, as your misdeed was premeditated."

"That was you, last night?" I asked, still somewhat incredulous.

"Yes. It is necessary," she said, and instantly, her voice, her expression, her face were all transformed. It was eerie and frightening, like seeing a wax puppet melt and reconstitute itself as a different character. The changes were infinitely subtle, but the effect was total. The lines of the frown around the bridge of the nose, the set of the jaw, the slightly hooded look of the eyelids, the tilt of the head and the hunched-up, wearied pose of the shoulders. Fragments of movement changed her from a society lady of aristocratic bearing into a grim, hard-living, independent revolutionary from the East End. I still could not believe it, and even worse could not see how she did it.

Then, in a twinkling of the eye, the anarchist Jenny vanished, and Elizabeth reappeared, smiling mockingly at me. "It is really not so difficult," she said. "I always had a talent for mimicry and acting. It was merely a question of studying, to get the clothes and the look and the opinions just so. And I have spoken German since birth. It is my first language."

"I suppose it would be too much to ask for an explanation—an honest, truthful one—of what you were doing there?"

She considered. "No. I think it might well be a good idea. Do you want the long version, which would indicate a willingness to forget about that unfortunate letter of yours? Or the short one?"

"The long one," I said in a tone lightly tinged with reluctance.

She rang the little silver bell on the table, and asked for refreshments, then picked up my letter and tossed it onto the fire.

"I think I told you that John was preoccupied in the last few months of his life. One of the reasons was this. He always kept a careful eye on his businesses; it was his duty, he believed, to ensure that they were run well. Obviously, he could not watch everything. For this he had managers, on whom he relied to tell him what was happening and to implement his wishes. At the same time, he would often make visits to various plants and factories, to see for himself, so he could take the temperature, as he called it. He loved these trips. You think of him, no doubt, as a financier, a man who sat far away from everything, dealing with the abstractions of capital. He wasn't like that at all. What he liked was putting it into operation, in the shipyards and the foundries and the engineering plants. He liked to see how a decision on his part could galvanise thousands of people into action. He loved his factories and, although you would no doubt not believe it, he loved the people who worked in them. The engineers, the fitters, the builders, the skilled workmen. He valued them far more than the people of his own society. Jenny the anarchist hates him; he was the worst sort of capitalist because he believed it was more than mere exploitation. He was proud of paying more than his competitors, proud of providing decent accommodation for those he employed.

"Last October, he went up to the shipyard in Northumberland and stayed for nearly a week. He often did this; every year I think he spent about ten weeks away, going round one plant or another. Sometimes there was a good reason; a huge decision on investment, problems with a contract, or something like that. Other times there was no reason at all. He simply wanted to be there, and smell the smell, as he put it. He spent as much time on the factory floor as he did in the offices, spent time talking to the men, and stood, watching. He believed you could tell the health of a company by the way it looked and felt. You didn't need to see the books."

"Did you ever go with him?"

"Not often. But then he didn't often come with me on my trips either. Each of us to our own particular universe. He was happy in his, I in mine. There were some things we could not share. And he needed to be without distractions. He would say that the factories would talk to him, and he had to listen. Sometimes, they would say one thing, the accounts another. Then he would become curious, and stay until he was satisfied. This time he came back perplexed. All had been well, he said. The yard was happy, the operations were smoothly run. They had recently finished a gigantic project to dig out a new dock which involved dredging a large part of the river itself so ships could be launched more easily. The cost of dreadnoughts is so astounding that I was always amazed by his ability to contemplate it. It didn't bother John at all. For him, large sums of money were just small sums, with more noughts on the end. Something was either a wise investment or not. Whether it was for one thousand pounds or one million did not alter the principle.

"All was well. He was satisfied. Apart from one small thing. One of the accounting clerks had been dismissed for peculation. A small amount of money, nothing more than twenty pounds, completely insignificant. But he had been a young man, full of promise, who had been earmarked by one of the managers as someone who could be trained up and given a great deal of responsibility in years to come. The manager felt to blame, that his assessment of the young man's character had been at fault. He had decided not to bring charges, but mentioned it to my husband.

"Most people in John's position, I am sure, would not have bothered about it. All companies mislay a certain amount of money; it is considered inevitable. John thought differently. He had spent years developing his organisation and wanted to achieve perfection. It did not matter to him whether it was twenty pounds or twenty thousand or even two shillings; it should not have been possible, and if twenty pounds could disappear, maybe twenty thousand could too.

"So he looked further and came to the conclusion that this was not the only time such a thing had happened, although he could not discover many details. But he found out where they were going to, an address in East London which only a small amount of investigation revealed was occupied by this man known as Jan the Builder.

"What infuriated John was that he could not discover how these payments were being authorised. The man responsible clammed up and refused to say anything at all. So he decided to tackle the problem from the other end. And that was where I came in."

"Yes," I said. We had now got to the point—the only point, if truth be known, which interested me. Embezzlement and failures in accountancy procedures were all very well, but I was still fixated on the eyes of Jenny the Red, staring icily in a meeting hall. "Why did you come in?"

"Perfectly simple. I offered, and he accepted my offer. Not willingly or readily, but I am quite persuasive. You find it all perplexing, no doubt. That is because you know nothing of me apart from what you see. You think of me as a pampered lady, used to gliding through a ball or a dinner party, but quite unfitted for real life. Too delicate and refined, shocked even at the vulgarity of a middle-class hotel. Is that correct?"

I tried to protest and say nothing of the sort but, in essence, it was an accurate summary.

"As I say, you know nothing of me. I have a long name of impeccable lineage but that covers a multitude of things. Hungarian aristocrats are not necessarily wealthy or pampered. I was neither. John could not send one of his people to get close to this group; they would have been spotted easily. These payments were coming from inside his companies, and so he felt unwilling to trust anyone connected with them. He needed someone who could be convincing, and whom he could trust. He did not for a moment think of using me.

"I decided to do it. I go to Baden for the waters every autumn—indulgent of me, I know, but I find it pleasant to talk German again—and when I was there I began to read about anarchism and Marxism and revolutionary politics—very interesting, by the way. Then I borrowed the identity of a German revolutionary whom the German police had executed in secret. An accidental fall down the stairs. It was convenient for them—and lucrative—to let it be known that she had been released and had gone into exile. Xanthos organised it for me; I suppose money changed hands in his usual fashion. I studied the clothes and the mannerisms, the way of talking. I went on to Hamburg, then travelled back on a tramp steamer to London. I arrived as Jenny the Red, brutal, uncompromising, more ardent than most men. I got to know these people and they slowly began to trust me in a way they would never have done a man, or someone English. No one John could have found would have been anywhere near as convincing."

I gaped, at her story and the pride with which she told it. It was so astounding it was ridiculous. It was all very well to lay claim to a hard and poor childhood, with nothing but a book of genealogy to burn for winter warmth, but I still did not easily credit it.

"Your husband allowed you to do this?"

"No. He expressly forbade it."

"So . . ."

"Nobody gives me orders, Mr. Braddock," she said, sounding not a little like Jenny the Red. "Certainly not John. When I proposed the idea, it was only a lighthearted suggestion. His opposition made me determined to see if it could be done. We were quite often apart; an absence of a couple of months was quite simple. I was established in my new identity well before he even discovered that I had gone against his wishes and, as I had been successful and was determined to continue whatever he said, there wasn't a great deal he could do except accept my help."

"But why did you want to?"

She shrugged. "Because."

"Because what?"

"I wanted to. Perhaps I was a little bored. I will get little sympathy from you if I say that the life I lead has its dull side."

"None at all."

"But it does, nonetheless. Most of the people I know are content to while away their lives playing bridge and going to house parties. I have little taste for such things, which is why I have to go to Paris or Italy for stimulation. John generally understood and let me come and go as I pleased. He let me do this for him, however reluctantly, because he trusted me and knew he could not stop me. I was never really able to do much to help him, beyond the things you do as a wife."

I shook my head, to try and knock all the contradictory thoughts out of it so we could get on. So, Elizabeth, Lady Ravenscliff, née Countess Elizabeth Hadik-Barkoczy von Futak uns Szala, transformed herself into Jenny the Red, revolutionary anarchist of Frankfurt. Repeat that sentence and see how easily you believe it. Then you will grasp my difficulties.

"Let us say, just for a moment, that I find all this credible," I said, "which I don't. What did you discover?"

"I discovered, in brief," she said, evidently amused, "that Jan the Builder was part of this group which called itself the International Brotherhood of Socialists, who are, in fact, little more than criminals. Fanatical, of course; they are deeply embittered about the fate of their country, which doesn't exist at the moment. But they use their anger to justify whatever they want to do, and that includes murder, robbery and extortion. They are violent, suspicious and, for the most part, not very intelligent. Only Jan is clever, but he is also the most violent of them all. He mixes his ardour with cunning and ruthlessness. He is quite a magnetic character. Women fall all over him."

"Including Jenny?"

"That is not any of your business," she said quietly. "You will have to believe whatever you think is most likely."

I blushed to the top of my ears with embarrassment. The woman had successfully thrown me into turmoil yet again. She could do it so easily, and there was nothing I could do to defend myself. I even think I must have derived some pleasure from being so tormented; certainly I put myself into that position often enough.

"What else?" I asked.

"I discovered that the money had been coming through regularly, that it was for a reason, and as long as it kept on arriving, they were content not to launch any expropriations. That is to say, they did not bother themselves with robbing jewellers' shops, or murdering people. They do, however, have a formidable stock of weapons. I have been to target practise with them on Romney Marshes."

"Pheasant?" I said hopefully.

"No. People. Not real ones, though."

"Don't sound so disappointed. Is this blackmail? Payments to stop them launching some operation against one of your husband's companies?"

"I have not yet found out. Only Jan knows and he will not say. I have tried to persuade him, but I risk his suspicion if I press too hard. That is why I still go, despite John's death. I believe I am getting close to discovering what all this is about, and having come so far, I will not give up now."

I tried, but failed, to erase from my mind all thoughts of how she might try to persuade him. And I confess here—I am deeply ashamed—that I found those thoughts irresistible, exciting, rather than disgusting as they should be. Nor did I find I could reject them as absurd as easily as I should.

"That was my contribution, and John was burrowing into the finances to figure out who was sending the money. He had not told anyone else. That was his worry."

"What do you mean?"

"He thought he had created a monster. That his companies had come to life, and were acting on their own. That they no longer responded to his orders, but followed their own instincts. That was why he told no one. He did not know who he could tell."

"I think he may have discovered what it was all about," I replied. "He was due to have a meeting with Xanthos about it. But he died instead."

"I only saw him briefly, for a few hours when he came back, and we didn't have time to talk very much. I was away for the weekend. At the

Rothschilds' at Waddesdon. Charming people. Do you know them? They were not John's bankers, but they are such congenial company. You'd like them."

She'd done it again. As fast as I settled into talking to one person, she shifted and became someone else. From the grieving widow, bored with English mores, to the critical, snobbish woman who had been so cruel to Mrs. Vincotti, to Jenny the anarchist, to the lustful woman who had driven me to a pitch of frustration, and now to the society gadabout. Do you know Natty Rothschild, darling? Such a sweet man . . . Of course I didn't know the Rothschilds, and I was sure I wouldn't find them charming at all. I felt as though I was talking to an actress who was playing several roles at the same time, all from different plays.

I glared at her; it was the best I could manage, as an explanation for the feelings behind it would have taken too long, and said too much. Besides, I'm sure she knew exactly what I was feeling.

"I think the obvious thing to do is to go to Northumberland myself and see if I can discover what he did. I will go tomorrow. It is something I can do well, and it will be pleasant to feel competent for once."

"Do you want me to come as well?" she asked.

Great fantasies swept through my mind at the very idea and, for the first time, I was ready for them. I shook my head. "No. Absolutely not."

CHAPTER 22

I went the next evening, on the night sleeper to Newcastle, leaving from King's Cross at ten-fifteen. I had never been on a sleeper before, and I found myself childishly excited by the adventure. Not only that, I went first-class; money was no object so I thought I would indulge myself. My expenses were being met, and I now had (so the bank had informed me in a handwritten letter) £36 14s 6d in my account. I was tired, which perversely spoiled the occasion; I would gladly have stayed up all night in the crisp linen sheets, listening to the rattle of the wheels and seeing the sparks from the chimney fly past the window in the darkness like a private fireworks display. It was a two-berth compartment—I was not sufficiently used to my new status to buy myself a single—and my travelling companion was a solicitor from Berwick, a middle-aged man with a wife and four children, whose father, and father's father, had been solicitors in Berwick before him. We talked over the brandy that the Great Northern provided before bedtime, served on a mahogany tray brought round by the porter, and I found his conversation soothing and congenial.

He was a happy man, was Mr. Jordan, who had created an entire universe of society in his little town on the edge of the country. On other occasions I might have found him dull, I suppose; his life of bridge and supper parties would never have suited me. But I took comfort in the fact that he liked it; and found my liking was tinged with longing. I feared for Mr. Jordan; I felt that the anarchists and the Ravenscliffs would succeed in sweeping all away, sooner or later, and the world would be the poorer for its loss. And then I slept, the sort of sleep which is entirely perfect. It was glorious and I remember thinking as I was in the deepest part of my unconsciousness that if death bore any resemblance to this, then there was nothing to fear at all.

When I woke up, the sun was shining weakly, and the porter of the night before—freshly shaved and tidy—was gently prodding me. "Morning tea, sir? Toast? Your newspaper? Hot water is on the shelf waiting for you. There's no hurry at all, sir, but if you could be up and about in an hour . . ."

My travelling companion had already gone, so I had the compartment to myself, and I made best use of it. The sleeping car had been uncoupled and pushed into a siding, where it was quiet except for the twittering of the birds and the occasional noise of a steam train passing. It was a lovely day, all the better for the fact that what I was doing there stayed out of my mind completely as I drank my tea, read the newspaper, shaved and dressed in the leisurely fashion I decided that men of means must always employ.

I tipped the porter generously then walked peacefully out of the station, and into the middle of Newcastle. The air seemed heavier; the smell of coal hung in the air in a way I had not noticed in the compartment. The buildings were black with decades of soot from the air, every single one of them, and the architecture was grim and foreboding. There was none of the bright stucco of west London, grimy though that often was, few trees, and even fewer people on the streets. Only the deliverymen and a few people on bicycles were to be seen. Newcastle was a working town, a workingman's town, and it was currently at work. I looked at the scene for a few moments, my bag in my hand, and decided there was no great rush. I was a man of business. That was why I was dressed in my best suit, my funeral and wedding suit, which I had changed into before I left. It was damnedly uncomfortable, but that served a purpose. It reminded me of my task and my role.

I behaved as I thought I should behave, and walked into the Royal Station Hotel just over the way and took a room for the night. Then spent the next hour unpacking and lying on the bed, wallowing in the opulence and comfort. I had never stayed in a hotel before. Not a proper hotel like this one. On the rare occasions I had travelled I had stayed in boarding-houses which rented rooms by the night, the sorts of place which were always cheap, sometimes clean and generally run by people like my own landlady in London. This was altogether different, and I took my time to get used to the room and to the lobby, then spied out the restaurant. It wasn't that hard, I decided. If Elizabeth could pretend to be a German anarchist, I could masquerade as a member of the professional middle classes for a few hours.

Then I was ready. I asked for a cab to be summoned, and directed it to the Beswick plant, where I was to meet Mr. Williams, the general manager. I will sketch over most of my conversations, as they were not of great significance. I had sent a telegram the day before, saying I had been retained by the executors of the Ravenscliff estate to sort out certain matters regarding the will. I let it be thought that I was a lawyer, as it would have been far too easy to discover my ignorance had I pretended to be anything else. Even with this disguise there were moments of awkwardness, as Mr. Williams knew very much more about company law than I did. He was a grim, tight little man at first sight, and did not relish his time being wasted. Only as our conversation progressed did I realise there was very much more to him. He was an interesting character, in fact, and his initial caution derived principally from the fact that he detested people like me, or rather people like I was supposed to be. Londoners. Moneymen. Lawyers. With no understanding of industry and no sympathy for it. Williams had more in common with the artisans in his yards than he had with the bankers of the City, although both gave him grief. He was an intermediary, beset on all sides.

I won him over eventually. I confessed that I knew nothing of the City whatsoever, told him of my own antecedents surrounded by the bicycle shops of the Midlands, made myself out as much as possible to be more like him than the bankers of his imagination and experience. And eventually he relaxed, and began to talk more freely. "Why are you here, exactly?"

I did my best to look a touch shamefaced. "It is completely foolish," I said. "But the law requires that the executors confirm the existence of assets in the estate. That is, if the deceased leaves a pair of cufflinks to a friend, then the executor must confirm the existence of those cufflinks. I am here merely to confirm that this shipyard exists. I take it that it does? It is not a figment of the imagination? We are not making some error here?"

Mr. Williams smiled. "It does. And, as the law is a demanding beast, I will show it to you, if you wish."

"I would like that very much," I said with enthusiasm. "I would be fascinated."

He pulled out his watch and glanced at it, then sighed like a man who can see his day being wasted and stood up. "Come along then. I normally do my rounds at lunchtime, but there is no reason why I should not vary my routine a little."

"Your rounds?" I asked as we left the office, Williams having told his clerks where he was going. "You sound like a surgeon."

"It is the same idea, in some ways," he replied. "It is important to be seen, and to take the mood of the place. We have to do more and more of that, as so many of our people now join unions."

"Does that annoy you?"

He shrugged. "If I were them, I'd join a union," he said, "even though it makes my life more complicated. But I have always done this. His Lordship thinks—thought, I should say—that it is important."

"Did you know him well?" I asked. "I never met him. He sounds an interesting man."

"He was very much more than that," Williams said, "but he will never be recognised as such. Actresses are better known than men of industry, even though the latter generate the wealth which keeps us from poverty."

"So what was so great about him?"

Williams looked at me thoughtfully, then said, "Come this way."

He took me through a doorway, along a corridor, then up a flight of stairs, then another, and another, and another. He flitted up nimbly enough, I puffed behind in the dark, wondering where we were going, until he reached another door, opened it and stepped out into the bright sunlight. "This is what was so great about him," he said as I stepped through.

It was breathtaking, a sight such as I had never seen before, never even imagined. I knew, all schoolboys knew, about British industry. How it led the world. We knew about the rise of the factory, and mass production. Of iron mills and cotton mills and railways. And daily we saw the results: Sheffield steel, railway engines from Carlisle, ships built in dozens of yards all around the country. We saw the iron girders of bridges, visited the Crystal Palace and knew all about the other marvels of the age. How such things came to be was rarely taught to people like me. They merely existed. I had only ever seen the outside of factories, and there were few enough of those in London, and certainly nothing of any great scale. Even in my hometown the biggest employer, the Starley Meteor Works, only had a couple of hundred people.

I stared in utter amazement, and with emotions verging on awe. The yard was gigantic, so big you could not see the end of it, whichever way you turned, it was simply swallowed up in the haze of sunlight through smoke. A vast mass of machinery, cranes, yards, buildings, storage areas, assembly sheds, offices, stretching out before my eyes in every direction. Plumes of thick black smoke rose from a dozen chimneys, the clanking, thudding, scraping and screeching of machinery came from different parts of the scene. It seemed chaotic, even diabolical, the way the landscape had disappeared under the hand of man, but there was also something extraordinarily beautiful in the intricacy, the blocks of brick buildings set against the tin roofs and rusting girders and the dark brown of the river, faintly in view to the east. And there was not a tree, not a bird, not even a patch of grass, anywhere to be seen. Nature had been abolished.

"This is the Beswick Shipyard," Williams said. "The creation of Lord Ravenscliff, more than anyone else. It is only one part of his interests; he reproduced factories like this across the country, and across Europe, although this is by far the biggest. What you see is not a factory, it is a sequence of factories, each one carefully linked to the other parts, and this, in turn, is linked to the other sites across the Continent. It is the most complex, elaborate structure that mankind has ever constructed."

"And you run it all?" I asked, genuinely impressed.

"I run this plant."

"How? I mean, how can one person have the slightest idea what is going on in that—chaos?"

He smiled. "That is where Ravenscliff was a genius. He developed a way of controlling all this, and not just this, but all of his factories, so that any moment you can find out what is going on, where it is happening. So that chaos, as you call it, can be tamed and the hidden patterns and movements of men, and machinery and capital and raw material, can be forced to act in a way which is efficient and effective."

"Elegant?" I suggested.

"That is not a word a businessman often uses, but yes, it is elegant, if you wish. Not many people can, or want to, understand it, but I would even say it has a sort of beauty to it, when it works well."

"And the reason for all of this is . . ."

Mr. Williams pointed, out to the east towards a dark grey shape. "Can you see that there?"

"Vaguely. What is it?"

"That is HMS *Anson*. A Dreadnought, 23,000 tons. Three million different parts are needed for that ship to do its job. Every one must work perfectly. Every one has to be conceived, designed, fabricated and assembled into its correct place so that the ship will perform properly. It must sail in the tropics and in the Arctic. It must be able to fire its guns under all conditions. It must be ready for full speed at a few hours' notice, capable of sailing for months at a time with no repairs. And all of those pieces have to be gathered together and put in place on time, and within budget. That is the point of all this. Would you like to see it?"

Williams led me down the stairs and across a cobbled road to what seemed very like a cab stand. "The plant is three miles long and two miles deep," he said as we got in the back of a horse-drawn buggy that was waiting there. "I can't waste my time walking around, so we have this system of carriages around the place. The horses are used to the noise."

And we clattered off. It was like going through a city, but a very strange city, with no shops, few people walking about, and no women. Everyone was dressed in working overalls. Instead of houses, there were warehouses, vast and windowless; blocks of offices, equally grim in appearance, and other mysterious buildings which Mr. Williams pointed out as we passed. "That's Foundry No. One," he said, "where the plate is made . . . the Gun Works, where the cannon are assembled . . ." And so we went on, the old horse clopping its way, with me in the back listening to Mr. Williams's explanations, and veering wildly between elation at what man could achieve and a certain feeling of gloom at the thought of the power of this vast organisation.

"And this," Mr. Williams said with the slightest quaver in his voice as we turned yet another corner, "is the reason for all of it."

Many people have seen a dreadnought, far out to sea, or even in dock. They are impressive, breathtaking sights, even then. But only if you see one close up, out of the water, do you get any real sense of how enormous it is, for then all that is normally concealed, the gigantic bulk of the ship that is under the waterline, becomes visible. It went up, and up and up, until I thought its very top was lost in the clouds. From end to end it was so vast that the prow could not be seen at all; it disappeared in the haze of smoke pumped out by the factory chimneys. I had no idea how advanced the building work was; it looked as though it would take years before it was ready and even then I could not easily imagine how anyone expected such a thing actually to float, let alone move.

Mr. Williams laughed when I asked. "We launch in ten days' time," he said. "From laying down the keel to final fitting out should take twelve months. We are now eight months in and making good time, I'm glad to say. Every day we run over costs us £1,100 in lost profits. Well? What do you think?"

I shook my head. I truly believe it was one of the most remarkable moments of my life, to be confronted in this way with full proof of man's audacity and invention. How anyone even dared to contemplate building such a thing was quite beyond my powers to imagine. And then I saw the people, the army of tiny figures scurrying up and down the scaffolding, shouting at the cranemen as gigantic squares of armour plate were lifted up, the riveters methodically pounding rivet after rivet through the holes already made, the supervisors and the electricians and the plumbers taking a break after their labours. Many hundreds of men, machines ranging from the huge hydraulic cranes to the smallest of screwdrivers, all working together, all apparently knowing what they were to do and when they were to do it. All to produce this beast, which had started out on its long route to the high seas in a decision taken by Ravenscliff months or years before. He spoke, and it was done; thousands of men, millions of pounds reacted to his decision, and were still following his orders, even after his death.

What did I think? Nothing; I was overcome by the scale of it all, by the power one man had created. Now, for the first time, I could see why all the descriptions of him were superlatives. Powerful, frightening, a genius, a monster. I had heard or read all of these. They were all true. Only such a person would have dared.

"I'm afraid that I cannot offer you a tour of the ship itself," Mr. Williams said, interrupting my reverie. He was pleased by my reaction, I could see. I think I must have had a look of stunned amazement on my face; my silence was very much more eloquent than anything I might have said. "It is dangerous when it is in such a state, and in fact there is little to see which would interest anyone but a specialist in naval architecture. I simply wanted you to see it up close. It is an impressive sight, don't you think?"

I nodded, but continued to gaze up and along to take in the vastness of the thing. It was dark; the hull had completely blotted out the sun, and the depths of the huge trench in the ground in which the ship was taking shape were cold, and windy and dark. I shivered.

"It does get cold. Sometimes it even starts to rain inside the dry dock, even though it is a fine enough day outside. The construction generates a lot of heat and vapour; that condenses against the sides and falls as rain. It is quite a problem sometimes. One of those little difficulties that even the most perceptive of planners cannot imagine in advance. I hope, by the way, you are convinced that this yard does actually exist now."

I nodded. "I think the executors might concede that one," I said with a vague smile. "And I must thank you for your time. It has been most generous of you."

"Not at all. As you may have noticed, I am very proud of this place. It gives me great pleasure to show it off."

"And your workers? Are they proud of it as well?"

"Oh, yes. I think so. They should be; they know they are the best in the world. And they are paid well. We cannot afford even one incompetent riveter or mechanic. They have to be paid well, and supervised very closely. When we launched *Intrepid* last year the whole city came to a halt so everyone could watch. They knew they'd done something remarkable. Come along."

We walked back to the cab, and the horse walked wearily off once more, taking a different route this time. After a few minutes, Mr. Williams asked the driver to stop. "Please forgive me," he said with a smile.

"I must just check with one of our people in here. Do come in, if you wish."

I followed him into the entrance of a block of offices, which was attached to another giant building of such size that ordinarily it alone would have made one pause for thought. But I was almost getting used to them now. Another building the size of St. Paul's. Oh, well. I wanted my lunch. Mr. Williams led the way into the warren of offices, where dozens of clerks sat at rows of oak desks, each with his piles of paper. Then through more, where men with drawing boards were working. Mr. Williams popped his head into one room, and called one of the men out.

"I have to see Mr. Ashley for a few moments. Would you be so kind as to take Mr. Braddock here to see our little arsenal?"

The young man, clearly pleased to have been chosen for such a task and to have attracted the attention of the most powerful man in the northeast, said he would be delighted. His name was Fredericks, he told me, as he led the way. He was a senior draughtsman, working on gun turrets. He had worked at Beswick for twelve years now, ever since he was fourteen. His father also worked here, in the yards. His brothers and uncles did as well.

"A family firm, then," I said, more for something to say than anything else.

"I don't suppose there's a single family in Newcastle which doesn't have someone who works in the yard," he replied. "Here we are."

He pulled open a heavy wooden door, and then followed me through. Again I was astonished, even though it took me some time to work out what I was looking at. Guns. But not ordinary guns, not like in museums, or put out for display at the Tower of London. These were more like tree trunks from some vast forest; twenty, thirty feet long, three feet thick, tapering meanly and menacingly towards the muzzle. And there were dozens and dozens of them, some long and almost elegant, other short and squat, lined up in rows on huge trestles.

"That's our biggest," Fredericks said, pointing to one of the longest, which lay in the middle of the building, shining dully from a protective layer of oil. "The 12/45 mark 10. With the breech it weighs fifty-eight tons and it can throw an 850-pound shell nearly eleven miles and land within thirty feet of the target. If the people operating it know what they're about. Which I doubt they will."

"And these are all for HMS *Anson*?"

"She'll take a dozen of them. Think of the effect of a single broadside. And these can fire once a minute. We think."

"You think? I got the impression that everyone who worked here knew. I didn't think guessing was allowed."

He looked a bit disconcerted by this. "Well, you see, it's not the guns. We know they work. It's the gun control. The hydraulics. *Anson* will have an entirely new design. The trouble is . . ."

"You can't test it in advance too easily."

He nodded. "It's what I work on. I think it will be just fine. But if it isn't . . ."

"So, what are the other ones for? If twelve go on *Anson,* there must be another couple of dozen of those great big ones here."

He shrugged. "Who knows? It's not as if they tell us. But it's the same all over the yard. There's enough guns and plate and girders to build a battle fleet out of the spare parts, with more being made. But there are no more orders."

"Who's they?"

"Scuttlebutt. Gossip. Talk in the pub. Who knows where these things come from? People are worrying about layoffs, once *Anson*'s finished."

"What about foreign orders?"

He shook his head.

"Perhaps they're being kept secret."

He laughed. "You don't know shipyards, sir. There aren't any secrets from the workers. Do you think there is anything that affects our jobs we don't know about?"

I looked thoughtfully at the vast pieces of metal lined up in that gigantic, chilly room, and shivered. It was calm in there, peaceful almost; it was impossible to connect the atmosphere with what those things were for, or what they could do.

"Tell me," I said, "perhaps you can help. I am looking for a man called James Steptoe. He works here, I believe."

Fredericks's expression changed instantly. "No," he said shortly. "He doesn't. Not anymore."

"Are you sure? I am certain . . ."

"He used to work here. He was dismissed."

"Oh? Why?"

"Theft." He turned away, and I had to grab him by the arm.

"I wish to speak to him."

"I don't. Nobody likes a thief."

"Nonetheless, I must talk to him. Ah. Here comes Mr. Williams. Perhaps he will be able to tell me . . ."

"Thirty-three Wellington Street. That's where he lives," he said hurriedly. "Please . . ."

"Not a word," I whispered back.

And then Mr. Williams came within earshot and that was the end of the conversation, but in some ways it was the most interesting part yet of my visit. A pity I hadn't had more time with the young man, who seemed serious and observant.

"I'm surprised you let me in there," I remarked as we went back to the cab. "I mean, I read in the newspapers all about spies trying to steal secrets about guns and things."

Mr. Williams laughed. "Oh, steal away, if you wish. There is nothing you have seen which is so very secret. What a gun looks like tells you nothing. It is how the metal is made, how the hydraulics work, how it is aimed. That's where the true secrets lie. And we are careful about that. Except for the gun-metal part."

"Why?"

He winked, and bent towards me conspiratorially. "Because the Germans already know."

"How come?" I asked, eager to hear a tale of espionage.

"Because they invented the process. *We* stole it from *them*." He leaned back his head and chuckled. "They're the best in the world at that, the Germans. Very advanced."

"So you have spies in Germany?"

"Oh, good heavens no. Lord Ravenscliff had shareholdings. That is very much better. He had a substantial shareholding in Krupp's, the German steel company. Not in his own name, of course; through an intermediary bank in Hamburg. They were able to obtain whatever he wanted. And Schneider in France."

I was astonished. I didn't think it worked like that at all. "But secret processes from here are not learned by the Germans by the same methods in reverse?"

Mr. Williams looked shocked. "Of course not. His Lordship was an Englishman, and a patriot."

Fair enough, I thought. On the other hand, what about that tale Seyd had told me, about building submarines for the Russians? How patriotic was that?

"So tell me, Mr. Braddock," the manager said as we headed back to the factory gate, "what did you find most impressive about Beswick? *Anson,* I imagine."

I considered. "Certainly it is a staggering sight," I said. "Quite beyond belief, really. It was worth the journey just to see it. But, oddly, I do not think that was the most impressive. I think the fact that this yard exists, and can produce such a thing more remarkable still. The idea that anyone can organise this anthill of a place is the most surprising."

I had said the right thing. Williams almost glowed at my words.

"That was Lord Ravenscliff's genius, and why the greatest compliment to his skill is to say he will not be missed. Do not misunderstand me," he said with a smile as I raised an eyebrow. "It is what he wanted. To create an organisation so perfect it could run by itself, or rather with only the managers, each of whom knows their business. I believe he succeeded."

"How so?"

"The job of any company is to make as much profit as possible. As long as that is the main aim of the managers, then there is no need to direct them. They will, collectively, take the right decisions."

"And you will soon find out whether that is the case."

We had arrived by the gate. A cab, one of several, was waiting patiently to take me back into the centre of Newcastle. Williams courteously held the door for me as I got in.

"Indeed. It will be very interesting. Have a safe journey back to London. I hope you have enjoyed yourself."

CHAPTER 23

At eight o'clock, after a rapid meal, I left once more, this time walking away from the works and into the rows of houses to the west of the city centre. Mr. James Steptoe lived somewhere in that rabbit warren. It was a dreary journey, into monotonous redbrick streets, each house exactly the same as the next, all built, I suspected, by the works and for the works. Each had a door and two windows facing the street. All the doors were green, all the windows brown. There were no trees, few patches of green, and surprisingly few pubs; I supposed that the works had intervened there as well and banned such places in order to keep its workforce sober and efficient. Or it was looking after its health, and acting responsibly. Take your pick.

But it was neat and well ordered, no doubt about that, and a few streets of newer houses showed signs of a different way of thinking. Curved porches, more fanciful roofs. Small enough, and mean enough, no doubt, but a place to live and be comfortable. There were churches and schools and shops, all laid out with thought and care. I had seen very much worse in the East End, which was a hellish, confused nightmare in comparison with this disciplined, uniform place, which, if it was a barracks, at least allowed its occupants to pretend.

The road I was looking for was off a street, and off an avenue. All were named after imperial heroes and events of the not too distant past. I wondered how many of the inhabitants noticed after a while. Did it make their hearts swell with pride that they lived in Victoria Road? Did it make them work harder, or drink less for having a house in Khartoum Place? Were they better husbands and fathers because they walked to work along Mafeking Road, then into Gordon Street? Was Mr. James Steptoe, I thought as I knocked on the door, a more respectable, patriotic Englishman for living at 33 Wellington Street?

Hard to tell. His mother, who answered the door, certainly looked respectable enough as she peered uncertainly at me. The trouble was, I could make out only a little of what she was saying; I supposed she was speaking English, but the accent was so thick she might almost have been another Serbo-Croatian anarchist. This was a problem I had not anticipated. Still, if I couldn't understand her, she seemed to understand me well enough, and invited me in, and showed me to the little parlour, kept for best. After a while James Steptoe came in, warily and cautiously; he was shaped rather like a bull, almost as broad as he was tall, with a thick neck emerging from his collarless shirt, and black hair covering his forearms where the sleeves had been rolled up. He had thick dark eyebrows, and a shadow of beard around his mouth. He looked like someone who played rugby, or worked down a mine rather than pushing pens and dockets.

I shook hands, and introduced myself.

"Are you the police?" A short sentence, gruffly spoken, but a great relief. I understood it. Mr. Steptoe was bilingual.

"Certainly not. Why should I be?"

"I'm eating," he said.

"I do apologise for disturbing you. I can either go away for a while, or wait, as you please. But I'm afraid I must talk to you this evening. I have to return to London tomorrow morning."

He studied me carefully. "Are you hungry?"

If I write out his words in normal speech, and say I could understand them, do not think that he spoke in a normal, or easily comprehensible fashion. He did not; my time with Mr. Steptoe was a triumph of concentration and much of what the rest of his family said escaped me entirely. I said I had eaten, thank you, but could easily eat some more.

He nodded at this then led me down the little corridor into the kitchen. It was a bit like being presented at a court ball; eight faces examined me intently as I came in and stood, a little sheepishly, by the little stove. I felt like an interloper, a foreigner, a threatening presence.

"Father, this is Mr. Braddock, from London. This is my mother"—the old woman smiled severely—"my sister Annie, my two brothers Jack and Arthur, Lily, my fiancée, and Uncle Bill. Jack—move. Mr. Braddock here wants your chair."

"London?" said the father, who tended to speak in one-word sentences.

"That's right," I said. "I'm here to sort out a few legal matters with regard to Lord Ravenscliff's estate. I need to discuss a few matters with your son."

"Everybody knows all about that," said he. "Don't think you have to hide anything from them. What else is there to say? I've been tried and found guilty, haven't I? Everyone knows. Or did he see the light and leave me some money?"

"I'm afraid not," I said with a grin. "And he didn't leave me any either, if that makes you feel any better."

"So?"

"Lord Ravenscliff believed that you were innocent of the accusations made against you."

This caused a stir. "He could have bloody well told me," said Steptoe junior.

"As far as I understand, he came to his conclusion about three days before he died. He had no opportunity to tell you."

There were looks all around the table, half pleased, half resentful that I should have the power to affect their lives in such a fashion.

"Now, there is a problem," I continued. "While Lord Ravenscliff may have been convinced, he did not put down in writing his reasons. So I have the task of redoing all his work. In other words, to find out what was happening. So I need from you a full account. When it is complete, Lady Ravenscliff will write to Mr. Williams at the plant, you will get your job back and, I am sure, be paid in full for the wages you have lost."

It was a handsome offer, and one which I was not entitled to make. But it did the trick nicely. From then on they were falling over themselves to tell me whatever I wanted to know.

"So, please tell me the precise circumstances of this accusation." Lawyerly, I thought.

"It was all lies," said the mother defiantly. "Jimmy'd never . . ."

"Yes, Mother, it seems we're all agreed on that," he said patiently. He thought for a while, then glanced around at his family with a slight smile, and asked his mother to make another pot of tea. As she filled the kettle from a big bowl of water near the back door and put it on the hob, he began.

"I'm a bookkeeper, you know," he said. "My dad here didn't like it, because he's a shipbuilder, a boilermaker, and didn't like the idea of me working in a suit. He reckoned I'd get grand ideas, and get above myself. But I was clever at school. I always got high marks in arithmetic and spelling, and my hand was good, copperplate when I wanted. My teacher liked me, and put in a word with the yard, and got me taken on in the offices. I began there about eight years ago, and learned the business of bookkeeping. I went on courses even, to improve myself, and did well. I was promoted, and paid more, and I didn't get above myself, I don't think."

His father scowled amiably, as though to concede the point.

"Anyway, my job was make payments out for bills that came in. Not the big ones, you understand. Miscellaneous and sundries is my department, and there's no rhyme nor reason to a lot of it. So, when I got in this bill for twenty-five pounds, I paid it, cash in an envelope, posted to the address on the docket. A couple of weeks later, all that remained was a twenty-five-pound deficit, and enough evidence that I must have been the one to have taken it; all the other pieces of paper had vanished. I was asked to explain. No one believed me, and I was fired, and told I was lucky I wasn't going to gaol.

"I was so upset I could have cried. I did, in fact. I couldn't believe it had happened to me, and even wondered whether I had made some mistake. But there couldn't have been. There were only two possible explanations—either I'd stolen the money, or the request for payment had been real. I knew I hadn't stolen anything, so that meant the dockets must have been removed. I don't make mistakes, you see. But I was in a right way; there was no chance now of ever getting another job again, not in Newcastle. Pretty soon everyone would hear something, that's the way it works. I was going to go to live with my second cousin in Liverpool, start again, and hope no one would find anything out. I was even acting as though I was guilty. Only this lot," he gestured at the people sitting round the table, who nodded, "stood by me. Not even the union would help. They didn't help thieves, they told me. Not worth their time; they had enough to do with deserving cases."

He snorted bitterly as he sipped his tea. His father looked uncomfortable.

"And then I got this short letter, asking me—ordering me, more like—to come to the Royal. No signature, nothing. I almost didn't go, but I thought—why not? I was wondering, you see, what it was about, and I had nothing else to do. So I went, and knocked on the door, and there was His Lord . . . Ravenscliff, I mean. All alone.

"I was terrified, I don't mind telling you. Just the room was frightening enough; I'd never seen the like before, even grander than the music hall, with its velvet curtains and golden furniture. And Ravenscliff . . ."

He paused to shift uncomfortably in his chair, and stirred some more sugar into his cup. "You never met him, you say? If you had I would have to say no more. He was a frightening man. Bulky, not fat, and he never moved much. Didn't have to; just looked at you, and that was enough. Didn't speak loud either; he made you listen to him. Did nothing to make you comfortable or at ease. Just told me to sit, and then looked at me, for ages. Didn't move a muscle all the while, and me getting hotter under the collar, and more and more upset.

" 'I didn't do it,' I blurted out when I could stand no more. 'And if you want to put the police on me, then go ahead . . .'

" 'Have I said anything about the police?'

" 'So why am I here?'

" 'Well, not for the police,' he said quietly. 'I could have you arrested and thrown into gaol without even leaving London, you know. You are here because I want to ask you questions.'

" 'What sort of questions?'

" 'Not why you did it. That is of no interest to me at all. How you did it does concern me, though. The controls should be proof against people like you, and they weren't. So, in return for your freedom, I want to know how you did it.'

" 'Will you, for the last time, listen to what I am saying? I didn't do anything. I did not steal anything. Not a penny. Not even half a penny.'

"That's right," his mother interrupted, nodding her head in approval. "And when he told me that, I was so proud of him . . ."

"Ravenscliff stared at me, with no expression on his face at all. I couldn't tell what he was thinking. That was frightening, you know. Normally, you say something, and you know how well it's gone down. Not with him. You couldn't tell a thing.

" 'Prove it,' he said.

" 'I can't,' I said bitterly. 'That's the trouble.' And I told him what had happened. Everything I've told you, and more. He nodded as I spoke; it was clear he knew the procedures perfectly well. Then he asked me questions.

" 'Every bill is stamped with a number, which runs in sequence. If one was removed, it should have been obvious. The same goes for payment slips.'

" 'I know,' I said. 'I can only think that it was stamped with a dupli-cate number, so that if it was removed, then there would be no gap. That would mean that someone deliberately made out a fake bill, then removed it. And not me, either.'

" 'Why not you?'

" 'Because I wouldn't have paid it myself, would I? I would have made up a bill, got hold of the stamp and numbered it with a duplicate number, and then slipped it into someone else's pile for payment. At the end of the day, after the money had been sent out, it would have been easy enough to go to the files, find the bill and remove it. Then gone to the address and picked up the money.'

" 'That is a convincing explanation, Mr. Steptoe,' he said. 'But it means you are accusing one of the people who work with you in your office.'

" 'No,' I said quickly, because I didn't want to accuse anyone. 'Lots of people come in and out all day.'

" 'I see.' Ravenscliff walked to the window and stared out of it. I was confused, a bit, but I didn't feel as though I should ask. But still, I wondered. This was a rich man, fretting about twenty-five pounds. Look after the pennies, and the pounds will look after themselves, but this seemed stupid.

"And then he told me to go. Didn't say anything more. Just dismissed me like some footman. I decided then and there to prove it. I'd been sitting at home feeling sorry for myself, but he made me mad. I wasn't going to be labelled a thief, not by him and not by anyone. I came home, and talked it over with my dad. He told me I had to try. And we talked to my cousin, another cousin, not the one in Liverpool, who works nights. He talked it over with . . ."

"Does anyone in Newcastle not know about this?" I interrupted.

He looked surprised. "I didn't tell a soul. Only my family. Of course I told them. They had a right to know. It affects them as much as it does me, you know. To have a thief in the family . . . ? But they stuck with me. Of course I told them."

"I see. I'm sorry. Go on."

"Anyway, it was all organised. I'd go in with my uncle and cousin on the night shift and go to the office. It was easy enough to get a key from one of the watchmen, who's a son-in-law of my Aunt Betty. Then I'd settle down and start going through the books, and leave with the shift when it went off in the morning."

"And?" I prompted.

"And it took ages. I went through every slip of paper, going back months, and then compared those to the shift books, showing who was on duty. Every single one. I couldn't afford to miss anything."

I nodded. I knew how he felt. I wondered if the Ravenscliffs made a habit of somehow getting total strangers to do their hard work for them. Elizabeth had done the same with me, after all.

"Eventually, I had it. Six payments, of between twenty-one and thirty-four pounds each, none with matching dockets. That told me that whoever was doing this knew how the office worked. Because anything over thirty-five has to be countersigned by the chief clerk. Whoever was doing this knew not to be too greedy."

"But you didn't find out where the money was going?"

"Not exactly."

"Not exactly?"

He held up his hand to ask for patience. "I asked second cousin Henry . . ."

I groaned.

". . . who also works in the office, to keep a look out, and eventually the chance came along. Henry couldn't take the thing, obviously, but he did copy it out, with the address for payment."

"Can you remember what the address was?"

"Of course. The one I told Lord Ravenscliff. Fifteen Newark Street, London, E."

The house I had seen Jan the Builder going into.

Steptoe had got up, and vanished. He returned a few moments later with an envelope.

I looked at the piece of paper inside. It was a bill, for £27 13s 6d, in respect of miscellaneous goods supplied. Dated 15 January 1909, with a number in the top right-hand corner, which Steptoe explained was the invoice number on the file, and which was duplicated on another, legitimate bill. At the bottom was a note: "c. pay B ham 3752." I asked what that was.

"That's another way of tracking money," he explained. "This indicates that the money was ultimately to be drawn from a bank account belonging to a different part of the organisation."

"I see. So this means . . ."

"Cash payment drawn on Bank of Hamburg account no. 3752."

I thought. So this young man had discovered that payments were being made frequently to this bunch of anarchists in London, using a loophole in Ravenscliff's pride and joy, the organisational structure he had set up over the years. It was being done by someone who understood it well, perhaps even better than Ravenscliff did.

"Who was responsible for this? Do you know?"

The young man nodded. "I do."

"And you told the company?"

"I did not."

"Why?"

"Because it's not my job to betray my workmates to the bosses. I was happy to clear my own name, but not at the cost of blackening someone else's."

All around the table nodded in agreement. I had quite forgotten they were there, but evidently what Steptoe had said had been discussed by them. This was a family decision, not his alone. So I nodded in approval as well, as though it was exactly the decision I thought he should have taken. In fact, it probably was.

"I can tell you who was behind it all, though."

I looked at him. "Well, let me take a guess, then. Obviously not one of your workmates. So, you are about to tell me it was one of the bosses themselves. Otherwise you wouldn't say a word. Correct?"

He grinned at me, in a fetchingly boyish fashion. "That's right," he said with some satisfaction. "He told me everything, once I'd figured it out. He was brought in one day, about six months ago, and told that he had to do this. Slip fake invoices into the piles and remove them afterwards. Naturally, he asked why, although he didn't expect to get a reply."

"Why not?"

"Because we're expected to do as we're told. Not understand the reasoning for it. He expected that he'd be told off, and told that he was just to do it, not wonder what it was all about. What business of his was it? Instead, he got a long explanation."

"And who was this from?"

"Mr. Xanthos, who's a boss. Very high up, he is."

"I see. Go on, then."

"Anyway, Mr. Xanthos said that people think selling things like battleships and guns is easy. It isn't, says he. You have to persuade people. And that involves things that people had best not know about. Like helping to make up their minds with little presents. Doing the necessary."

"And that's what these payments were?"

"That's what he said. Little presents to people with influence, which would bring in the orders, and guarantee jobs right along Tyneside for years. Of course, it wasn't a good idea for people to know about this. It had to be done secretly. And it had to be kept quiet if anyone found out about it."

"So this friend of yours went away, thinking he was helping the company to bend the rules a little to secure jobs. And that it was all being done with the company's approval?"

"That's right. But Xanthos had told him that no one was to know. Mr. Williams and all the others didn't want to know and wouldn't thank him for saying anything. He only told me when I asked him a question in the pub. Difficult that was; I'm not welcome in pubs anymore. Not ones used by the factory. That was a week or so before the accident."

"What accident was that?"

"Bad thing. Shouldn't have happened, poor kid. But he was going through one of the steel yards at the end of the day, and there was a slip, so it seems. A post holding the girders in place gave way, and they came tumbling down across the floor. He was in the way. Never stood a chance."

"And this was?"

"About three weeks ago. They had the funeral, and a lovely thing it was. The company paid and gave money to his mother, because he was her only support. And so they should have, but many wouldn't have. They'd have said it was his own fault, that he shouldn't have been there."

There was a moment's silence as he finished. "Are there many accidents? In the yards, I mean?"

The father shrugged. "Some, of course. It's only to be expected. Two or three a year. Mostly it's people's own fault."

"This man, the one who died, he's not going to be telling anyone else about these payments now, is he? Did he tell anyone else except you?"

Steptoe shook his head. "No. He was too frightened of losing his job. And who could he tell? I only got it out of him because he felt bad about what had happened to me."

"So if he hadn't told you, then no one would ever have been able to find out about this? And if the accident had happened only a little bit earlier . . ."

Steptoe nodded.

"Have you told anyone else? Apart from your entire family, that is?"

He grinned. "Not even them. Not all of them."

"May I suggest that you keep it that way? I do not want you to have a pile of girders falling on you as well."

The smile faded. "What do you mean?"

"The only other person to know anything about this was Lord Ravenscliff, and he fell out of a window."

I stood up, and dusted the cake crumbs from my lap. "Thank you, Mr.

Steptoe, and thank you all, ladies and gentlemen," I said, bowing to the entire table. "It was most kind of you to talk to me and feed me such excellent cake. Now, is there anything I can do for you?"

"I want my job back."

"I will talk to Lady Ravenscliff," I said, "and get her to intervene. Do not worry on that score. In the meantime, please write down your account in careful, meticulous detail, and send it to me. I will suggest to her that she offer you payment for your services. That seems only fair."

CHAPTER 24

The annual meeting of the Rialto Investment Trust was to be held on the morning after I returned at eleven. I had only been to such an event once before, and it had been deadly and interminably dull. A South African mining company, that had been, and I had been sent because the poor soul who normally attended such things was off sick. Ever since the Boer War, South African mining companies had a claim to be news, in the way that the doings of most coal mines or cotton companies were not. So I went, with strict instructions not to fall asleep. "Just spell the name of the chairman right and remember—profits for this year and last, dividend for this year and last. That's all anyone is ever interested in."

So I went and did as I was told, sitting alone—the real shareholders avoided me as though I had a strange smell and I didn't get any of the tea and biscuits either—and took down everything I was told to take down. I still maintain it wasn't my fault that I missed a share issue to raise more capital. Even had I been awake, I would not then have understood what they were talking about.

But now I considered myself almost an expert in all matters financial. Words and phrases like "scrip issue" and "debenture stock" could trip from my tongue with the same facility that "grievous bodily harm" or "assault and battery" had done only a few weeks before. And, just to be on the safe side, I persuaded Wilf Cornford to come along as an interpreter. I was there with a notebook pretending to be a reporter once more; how Wilf got in I do not know. Apart from us there were about ten other journalists—itself notable as such meetings normally only attracted one or two—and at least a hundred shareholders. This, said Wilf, was unprecedented. Something, he said, was up.

And so it was, although while it was going on it was about as thrilling as a committee meeting at a town council, all motions to amend and comments from the floor so densely wrapped up in convoluted phrases that their import was somewhat lost. The nominal chairman of the event was Mr. Cardano, the executor of Ravenscliff's will. He did a good enough job, I thought; he made a brief and entirely empty speech about Ravenscliff's great qualities and abilities—which I noted was met with suspicious silence—before passing matters over to Bartoli, who sat on his left looking studiously neutral. This gentleman then rattled through the annual accounts at such speed that he was back in his chair only a few moments later. The only bit I properly appreciated was his closing sentence—"and in view of the excellent year and good prospects for the coming year, we recommend an increase of dividend of 25 per cent, to four shillings and a penny per every one pound nominal." He sat down to a smattering of applause.

There then followed questions—although not from the journalists, who were not allowed to speak, an unnatural state which made them chatter amongst themselves to indicate their discomfort. When would the Ravenscliff estate be wound up? Very soon, promised Mr. Cardano. Could the executor reassure investors about the state of Rialto's finances? Absolutely yes: the figures were there for all to see; reassurance was surely unnecessary. And what about the companies Rialto invested in? On that he could not reply, but application must be made to those companies. However, their published accounts suggested they were all doing splendidly. And so it went on; there were votes on this, and votes on that. Hands were raised and lowered again. Cardano periodically muttered words like "Carried" or "Not carried." Wilf squiggled in his seat. And finally there was a motion to adjourn and everyone stood up.

I tried to sidle up to Cardano at the end, but he was surrounded by other members of the board almost like an emperor being shielded by a praetorian guard, and no journalist got near. Only one man approached; he got to a few feet away, and Cardano looked at him—how did I do? was clearly on his face. This man nodded, and Cardano relaxed, and left the room.

An important figure, then, but who was he? I kept him in sight as he stood, being buffeted by those making their way to the door. Not remarkable really: middle-aged; slim, short dark hair thinning on the top; of average size. A clear, open face, clean-shaven, a vague smile on a generous, well-proportioned mouth. He turned, and nodded a brief bow as a stout man, about seventy, with a round face and white toothbrush moustache looking like a retired lieutenant colonel in a county regiment tapped him on the shoulder. I could not hear the conversation, but I grasped enough. "Good to see you, Cort," said the ex-officer in a booming voice. Then they moved out of earshot. I would have loved to have heard more, but it was enough: I had a face for the name. I now knew what the mysterious Henry Cort looked like. He didn't look so frightening to me.

Then I was dragged off by Wilf, who seemed properly agitated, and said—in a quite unprecedented display of emotion—that he needed a drink. I could not imagine him drinking at all, let alone needing one, but who was I to refuse?

"Well!" he said, when we were settled into our chairs in a pub round the corner, usually frequented by Schroder's people after hours but now empty. "That was a battle to remember!"

I frowned, bemused. "What was?"

"The meeting, boy! I've never witnessed anything like it!"

"Were we both in the same room?"

He stared. "Did you not see what was going on?"

"I saw enough to make me drop off my chair with boredom, if that's what you mean."

"Oh, for heavens sake!"

"Well? What? What did I miss?"

"The ambush, man! The counterattack! The routing of the forces of dissent! Didn't you understand anything?"

I shook my head.

Wilf sighed sorrowfully. "You are really not up to this, you know."

"Just tell me," I snapped.

"Oh, very well. You noticed, I hope, that the board bought off the shareholders by bunging money at them?"

"The dividend?"

"Precisely. It was clear from the accounts that they should only really increase the payout by about 10 per cent. But they increased it by 25 per cent, and they will have to go heavily into reserves to do it. The idea, I'm sure, was to keep the shareholders quiet until the money is paid out in about six weeks' time. That dealt with some of them, and it was clever; cut the ground from under the enemy from the start. But they kept on coming."

"Did they? How?"

"What do you think all those motions and proposals and questions were about?"

"I've no idea whatsoever."

"A number of shareholders are suspicious, and others want to take control of the Trust. They banded together; there must have been meetings all over the City for the last week. I'm sure they did a deal they thought would hold. Vote in new management, then have a good look at the books. Then, perhaps, dissolve the Trust and pay out the money. I don't know. It doesn't matter, because they were defeated."

"Really?"

"Yes. They were. That Cardano is not daft; takes after his father, no doubt. But clearly there were other discussions going on as well. The 25 per cent he controls as executor, and other groups of votes, blocked every motion, and voted instead to postpone all decisions until the Ravenscliff estate is settled. Quite a lot of the shareholders were voting against their own best interests, if you ask me."

"And you are going to tell me you don't know why. I know you are."

"Precisely. But I will find out, so help me. And I can tell you who, or at least a bit of who. It was Barings, for one. I couldn't quite figure it out, but they seem to have amassed a stake of about 5 per cent. That's a guess, of course. I will be able to confirm that in a few days. I didn't know they had any. They handled the flotation but I assumed they had long since sold any shares."

"They bought some the day after Ravenscliff died," I said, feeling quite proud that I knew something Wilf did not. And gratified by his look of interest as a result.

"How do you know it was Barings?" I persisted.

"Oh, well, it was a show of strength, wasn't it? Tom Baring himself came along to cast the votes. So keep your noses out, you're wasting your time. That was the message."

"Which one was he?"

"About seventy, receding hair, the one with an orchid in his button-hole."

"The retired major talking to Cort?"

"Who's Cort?"

"Nothing. It's not important. This Tom Baring, who is he, exactly?"

"One of the Baring clan. Extraordinary man. I know what you mean about being a retired major. He looks the part. But he is one of the country's great experts on Chinese porcelain. Not that I care about that, of course."

"Of course. So he's a big cheese?"

"One of directors; it's not a family partnership anymore, of course. It's been a company ever since the disaster twenty years ago, but the family still has huge influence. The thing about Tom Baring is that he's lazy. Very good, very effective when he can be roused, but he can't be roused very often. For him to come here is a powerful message. Barings thinks this is important enough for him to abandon his porcelain, get up to London and appear. He only does that when it's really vital."

"The stuff of dinner conversations for years," I commented.

"It is. So don't be frivolous. People will be trying to figure all this out for a long time."

"So what do you think it means?"

"I have no idea. Only that, for the time being, Barings is behind Rialto and wants everyone to know. But there is obviously more to it than that. Someone was trying to launch a coup. Much of the lead was taken by a man from Anderson's . . ."

"Who were *also* buying Rialto shares shortly after Ravenscliff died," I put in. Again, Wilf looked impressed. I was rather pleased with myself.

"But who are Anderson's fronting for, eh?" he asked.

"What about the man they proposed as chairman?"

Wilf looked contemptuous. "A nothing. A face, that's all. No, my friend, it is someone else. And he won't escape me for long. You wait and see."

He drummed his fingers on the table. A strange light was glimmering in his eyes as he took an enormous swig at his glass. "Barings wishes to make it clear it is convinced there is nothing wrong with Rialto. But perhaps it is only doing this because it knows full well that there is something very wrong indeed, and it is prepared to risk losing its stake to keep it hidden. What motive could a bank have for being prepared to lose money? Eh? Tell me that."

"The prospect of losing even more money?"

He rubbed his hands together. "Ah, this will be fun."

Well, I thought, I'll let him get on with it. I didn't want to share the crown jewels of my knowledge with him. But I knew, so I thought, what it was all about. In fact, it was obvious. Any proper investigation of Rialto would throw up the fact that the accounts were fictitious, that millions had been siphoned off the underlying companies. But—and it was a fairly sizeable but—what was the point? Wasn't it just postponing the inevitable?

I wandered home, thinking I would have a quiet hour before dinner. A whole evening when I did not have to think about money or aristocrats at all. I almost felt pleasure as I turned the key in the lock of Paradise Walk, and breathed in the foul air of the entrance.

But not for long. Mrs. Morrison shot into the hall the moment she heard the door, and bore down on me with a severe, distressed look, quite unlike her normal air of amiability.

"Mr. Braddock," she began, "I am most upset. Most upset. How you could be so disrespectful, I do not know. I am very disappointed in you. I'm afraid I must ask you to leave my house."

"What?" I said in shock, pausing as I took my coat off. "What on earth is the matter?"

"I have always given my boys complete freedom, and expect them to respect this house. To invite unsuitable people is unacceptable."

"Mrs. Morrison, what are you talking about?"

"That woman."

"What woman?"

"The one in the parlour."

Lady Ravenscliff, I thought, but the surge of pleasure was quickly tempered by feelings of dismay that she should see the circumstances in which I lived. The meanness, the shabbiness. I looked around, at the brown painted wood, the dingy wallpaper, the cheap prints on the wall, at Mrs. Morrison herself, and almost blushed.

"I am sorry she came here," I said fervently. "But have no fears. She is entirely respectable. Certainly not unsuitable in any way."

"She's a trollop," she said, hesitating a moment before she used the word, and then deciding it was justified. "Don't pretend to me, Mr. Braddock. I know one when I see one, and she is. I won't have it."

I had rather expected Mrs. Morrison to be overcome with the flusters at the idea of having a real lady in the house, and my relief that Elizabeth had not got the tea and cakes routine was only matched by my dismay that she should be characterised in such a way. Had she been a trollop, she would have been far beyond my purse, even at £350 a year.

"But Mrs. Morrison, she is my employer."

Now she stared at me in blank astonishment. We had reached an impasse, with neither understanding what the other was going on about, until a noise of movement resolved the matter. The girl coming through the door of the parlour was no lady. In fact, Mrs. Morrison's characterisation seemed pretty judicious. She was about twenty, I guessed, garishly and shabbily dressed, and moved with an air of cheeky insolence mingled with caution and suspicion. Why I say that, I do not know; but that was my impression.

"Who the hell are you?" I asked incredulously.

"Well, you asked for me, didn't you?"

"No."

"I was told you'd pay me a guinea."

A guinea? For her? I wasn't that desperate. I could see why Mrs. Morrison was so angry with me. Women were the one thing she did not allow. Certainly not one like that.

"I can assure you I . . ." And then an idea came into my head. "Who said I'd pay you a guinea?"

"Jimmy."

"Who's Jimmy?"

"Never met him before. He's a kid."

Finally, I understood. "Is your name Mary?"

"Course it is."

I breathed a sigh. "Go back in there and wait for me, please."

I all but pushed her back into the parlour, shut the door, then turned to Mrs. Morrison.

"I apologise from the bottom of my heart, Mrs. Morrison. I cannot say sorry fervently enough. This woman is not what she appears, believe me. She is a very important witness, absolutely crucial to my work at the moment. I have been looking high and low for her, and I must talk to her before she takes fright and runs away. Let me do this, and I will explain fully afterwards. Please?"

She was uncertain enough to win me time, so I hurried into the room and closed the door. Mary was standing in front of the dead fire, gripping her little handbag as though it was some vital defence. I stood and looked at her. She wasn't bad looking, I realised, in an underfed, pinched sort of fashion. Many a man would . . . I drove the thought from my mind, and told her to sit down. I took over the place by the fireplace so I could look down on her.

"So you were the assistant of Madam Boninska," I said. "You know the police are after you?"

She nodded.

"Don't worry; I won't tell them. Although I should say they do not have the slightest thought that you killed her. They want you as a witness, nothing more."

"They always want more," she said. She had a dull, flat and entirely unattractive voice, which went well with the vaguely blank look in her eyes. "And they don't pay as well as you do."

"How much I pay will depend on how much you tell me," I said. "So don't get any ideas just yet. Were you there when this woman was killed? Did you see who did it?"

"No," she replied. "I didn't see anything. I was out. I came back and found her, and thought, They'll blame me for this, so I ran for it."

"Quite understandable," I commented. "But do you know who did it?"

She shook her head. "She had no enemies in the world," she said. "She was a lovely woman." She looked at me like a bird eyeing a worm. "A guinea."

I did in fact have the money in my room, but was loathe to let it go to her. Then I sighed, ran quickly up the stairs then returned and counted the money out onto the table. "Don't touch," I said as she leaned forward. "What was she like?"

"A cow," she said. "A mean, vicious cow. I hated her. I almost danced for joy when I saw her lying on the floor. She was always drunk, she smelled, and she had a way of talking to you. Made you feel like dirt. I hated her."

"Don't you have to be charming to clients in that line of business? Fortune-telling, I mean?"

"Oh, yes. For a bit. She could crawl as well as anyone when she wanted. Until she got hold of them, then she'd drop all that. When she was squeezing money out of them, there was no more of that."

"What do you mean?"

"She'd get people to these seances and get them to tell all their secrets, thinking they were talking to spirits. Then she'd say, you don't want your wife, or your partner, or your parents, to hear about that, do you . . . ?"

"Give me an example."

"One woman came, she twisted her into saying she'd had a friend. You know. She was married, you see. And the mistress got this woman's jewels, her rings, all her money off her. She killed herself, eventually, because when she was bled dry the mistress wrote a dirty little letter to the husband. I had to deliver it. She showed me the notice in the paper, she pinned it on the wall, like it was some great achievement. She was proud of it."

"And you?"

She shrugged. "What do I care?"

"More than you admit. Never mind. I want to ask you about a man who came to see her. This man."

I showed her the photograph of Ravenscliff.

"Yes, I remember him." I felt a surge of excitement rush through me at the words.

"Tell me everything. The money on the table depends on it."

"He wasn't a client," she said after thinking about it for a while. "Not for the table-turning and such. Normally she got all dressed up for that, put on her special clothes and started talking in this voice—trying to be mysterious and spooky. You know. This was different. They talked."

"Do you know what about?"

"No. But she wanted money off him."

"Did she get it?"

"Not the time I was there. He was angry about something, that I heard. 'Unless you tell me there'll be nothing for you.'"

"And you don't know what he meant?"

She shook her head.

Not very helpful. "This Madame Boninska. What do you know about her?"

"Not much. I mean, she didn't exactly tell me anything, did she? She treated me like dirt. She either looked down on everyone or tried to pull them down. You should have heard the things she said about the people who came to see her. So nice and sympathetic she was to them until she'd got her claws into them. Then they learned more about her."

"Go on."

"Don't know really. She wasn't Russian. Not a foreigner at all. But she'd been abroad for a long time. That she told me. At the Russian court, high places in Germany, so she said. They all loved Madame Boninska."

"So why did she come back to England?"

"I reckon everyone else had tumbled to her and she hadn't anywhere else to go. But she reckoned she'd hit a gold mine here. She was going to make her fortune. She was going to get her due, that's what she said. Then she did, of course. Someone killed her. And if that wasn't her due, I don't know what was."

"You have no idea . . . ?"

"I've told you—she told me nothing. I was a servant. That's all. I think I preferred the street. But I hung on just in case she was telling the truth. Just in case she was going to get hold of some money."

"There was no money in the flat when the police found the body."

She shrugged. I couldn't blame her.

"How much did you steal?" I asked quietly.

"Nothing."

She was clearly lying, so I smiled at her. "Back wages?"

"If you like."

"This gold mine. Was it anything to do with this man, do you think?"

Another shrug. I did wish she'd stop it. She managed to give the impression she couldn't care about anything in the world. Which might be true, of course. "I think so. She was excited enough after he went."

"This money you didn't steal. Was there anything else in the drawer?"

"Some papers, didn't look. Nothing important."

"Did you take those?"

"No."

They'd gone as well. I had been beaten at every turn. Every time I did something, thought of something, someone had been there before me. All I had established for my money was that Ravenscliff wasn't interested in the spirit world, but I had guessed that anyway. That this woman had known something, but I had no idea what it was. Maybe she had learned something in Russia, or in Germany. What could she possibly know that was important to a man like Ravenscliff?

"How well did they know each other? Were they friendly? Distant? Like strangers?"

"Him, you could almost see him holding his nose when he talked to her. Wouldn't shake her hand or anything like that. No; he wanted something, and then he'd never want to see her again."

"Did he get it?"

"Don't know. All I heard was her muttering to herself. 'Why? Why? Why that?' Over and over again."

"It's too much to hope that you know what she was talking about?"

She shook her head. I sighed. "Tell me," I said, very dispirited, "do you recognise any of these people?"

I showed her a picture of Lady Ravenscliff. She shook her head. Then I offered the group photograph of the Beswick board, and she looked and shrugged again.

CHAPTER 25

It turned into an eventful evening in Paradise Walk, perhaps the oddest the little house had ever known. I had just managed to persuade Mrs. Morrison that the reputation of her house really wasn't under any serious threat when the doorbell rang, a fact unprecedented and unimaginable. Respectable people do not ring the doorbell, unannounced, at eight o'clock. Respectable people do not have unexpected visitors at eight o'clock. The very sound caused consternation and excitement.

Even more the visitor. It was Wilf Cornford, who had a look of beatific pleasure on his face, except when he looked at me. Then he frowned in disapproval.

"I do believe you have not been keeping to your side of the bargain, young man," he said sternly. "I assumed that you would tell me things of importance. And I find, or at least I suspect, that you have not been."

"Why is that?"

"Because I have been talking to a sales manager from Churchill's, the machine-tool people. And he told me that Gleeson's had ordered, near eighteen months ago, three new lathes, the sort used to bore gun barrels."

"So?"

"And then I dropped into a pub in Moorgate, and talked to a broker who deals in such things, who told me quite categorically that Gleeson's had not sold off its old lathes. In fact, that the lathes it already possessed were exactly the same as the new ones."

"Is this interesting?"

"Why would Gleeson's need eight lathes? For boring guns for battleships, when it has no orders for battleships?"

"I am truly not dissimulating when I say I haven't got a clue."

"I want a little bit more information from you, if you please. What else have you found out that you haven't told me?"

I thought for a while, then decided to take the plunge. "I have discovered that a couple of million has been sucked out of Ravenscliff's companies in the past eighteen months, and that the shipyard is awash with spare parts." I described the scene as best I could. "Also that every politician in the land has shares in Rialto. And, if you want minor details, that Ravenscliff had discovered some hole in his management structure that he couldn't understand, and that the estate is tied up because of a bequest to a child who is probably dead."

Wilf leaned back and sighed with contentment. "Ah, yes," he said. "A great man, even in his fall."

"Pardon?"

"Had you told me all of this when you started, I could have put all the pieces together very much faster, you know."

"I didn't want the pieces put together at all," I said crossly. "My job was to find this child, not investigate his companies. I couldn't give a hoot about Beswick or Rialto. Anyway, what pieces have you put together?"

"Ravenscliff was a gambler. He took the biggest gamble of his life and was losing. I wonder how much longer he could have kept it going."

"Could you just tell me what you are talking about?"

"Don't you realise? He was building himself a battle fleet."

"What?"

"Obviously. He had no new orders, profits dwindling, shipbuilders everywhere are in despair. And yet he was ordering new lathes, new armour plate, the factories are bursting with parts. What do you think these are all for? How many spare guns do you think anyone needs? Three maybe. No, my friend, he was building ships. He committed five, six million pounds, and didn't stand a chance of getting it back. It was simply a question of how long he would manage to keep going before everything came crashing down. What is remarkable is that the likes of Barings are still pretending there's nothing wrong."

"You are sure that he'd lost his bet?"

"Did you not read the last Budget?"

"No."

"The Government has spent so much money on old-age pensions that there is nothing left at all. The only thing that could possibly change the situation is if a war broke out, and that doesn't seem likely at the moment."

"But Ravenscliff was a clever man."

"The cleverest."

"And he wasn't worried. If you were him, and you were in that situation, what would you do?"

"Nothing. Nothing I could do. Except jump out of a window maybe."

"Or keep going and hope for a war."

He stared at me. "That's absurd," he said. "There must be another explanation. Besides, how does it explain the shareholders' meeting?"

"I was merely repeating what you said, not advancing my own opinion, you know. What about the shareholders' meeting?"

"I have discovered who was behind the attempted *coup d'état*."

"I do very much hope you are going to tell me."

"Theodore Xanthos." He looked dreadfully smug as he said it.

"But he's just a salesman," I said scornfully.

Wilf was now the one to adopt a look of superior condescension. "Just a salesman? Xanthos is responsible for about half of Rialto's sales. Eleven million a year. For the last twelve years."

"So?"

"He gets a commission of one and three-quarter per cent. Figure it out."

I shut my eyes and tried to use my newly learned financial skills. "That's about . . . Heavens! That more than two million pounds!"

"So, not just a salesman, eh? Admittedly, he has to pay all his own bribes out of that . . ."

"Really?"

"Of course. You wouldn't want them traced back to the company, would you?"

"I suppose not." The comment, however, made me think.

"No. But even if he's been spending at the rate of £50,000 a year . . ."

"In bribes?" I said incredulously.

"Oh, yes. At least that," Wilf said airily. "It's quite normal."

I shook my head. It wasn't my idea of normal. "The point is, Xanthos often operates through a bank in Manchester, which was where the payments to Anderson's to buy the Rialto shares came from. A few favours called in, and they confirmed it. Which means that Xanthos was trying to take control of Rialto."

"How does this fit in with anything?"

Wilf was standing now and reaching for his hat. "My dear boy, I have no idea. I was hoping you could tell me that."

CHAPTER 26

I arrived to see Elizabeth the next morning. There was nobody around, so I let myself in and went up to the little sitting room to wait for her. And got a shock when I walked in. Sitting on the settee was Theodore Xanthos.

"Mr. Braddock," he said amiably as I entered. "What a pleasant surprise."

"I'm surprised to see you, as well," I replied. "Have you come to visit Lady Ravenscliff?"

"Ah, yes, but I fear we will both be disappointed. I have just been told she has gone."

"Really?"

"Yes, quite gone. To Cowes, so I am told. For the week. She and John went every year. It was one of Lord Ravenscliff's great pastimes. He loved the sea. Which I always found curious."

"Why?"

"Well, he was not one of nature's sportsmen, you know. Nor a great romantic. The lure of the elements did not burn brightly in him. We once crossed the Alps together in a train and I do not think he looked up once. All that scenery, that magnificence and grandeur, and he never once took his nose out of his book. The sea, on the other hand, had a very strange effect on him."

"In what way?"

"It hypnotised him, almost. Something about it. You English and your sea. Very peculiar. Now we Greeks are quite immune, you know, even though we were a seafaring nation while your ancestors were still grubbing around in forests."

"When did she leave?"

"Early this morning, I believe. I imagine all her bags went yesterday."

"And she comes back . . . ?"

"I don't know. Last year they spent a week there, then travelled to France for a month."

"A month?"

"Then he came back here and she went to take the waters in Germany."

"Baden-Baden."

"Yes, I believe so." He paused and looked puckish. "Aha! You are wondering how you will do without her for such a long time. I told you, you know. I tried to warn you. But she is quite irresistible."

"I wished to consult her on a matter of importance . . ."

"And so did I! So did I! But here we are, abandoned and forlorn. Ah, well. We must make the best of it. Have some of this excellent coffee. I didn't want it, but Lady Ravenscliff has her servants so well trained that the wishes of visitors are quite irrelevant."

He gestured to the tray on the table, then poured, delicately and without spilling a drop.

"How are your researches? I gather you have been to Newcastle. Were you impressed?"

I looked at him. "How did you know that?"

"Good heavens, Mr. Braddock! How can you even ask such a thing? Lady Ravenscliff begins to act in a very unusual fashion, hires someone who is quite unsuited for the task she gives him, and you expect someone like me not to be curious? Of course I have tried to find out everything I can about you. It's not as if you are very good at hiding your tracks."

"I didn't realise I was supposed to."

"Of course you didn't!"

"I found Newcastle very interesting."

"And Mr. Steptoe? Was he interesting as well? Poor man."

The shock of the question quite threw me. Naturally it did; I was perfectly unprepared for it, and in any case was hardly trained in dissimulation. It was not really necessary as a journalist. I was clever enough to know that Xanthos was trying to frighten me, clever enough to acknowledge to myself that he was succeeding, and above all, quick enough to realise that my best response was not to play on his terms. I looked enquiringly.

"Terrible accident, so I hear. Run down in the street by a horse and cart. Went right over him, broke his back. Dead, poor fellow."

He smiled sadly. I stared, horrified.

"I do wish Elizabeth was a little more generous with the cake," he said, waving at an empty platter. "I've eaten it all. I hope you don't mind. A curious way of writing a biography, when you haven't even written a letter to his family in Shropshire."

I concentrated on my coffee, trying to stop my hands from trembling. "My editor advised me that, when researching someone's life, it is best to start at the end and go back to the beginning. I always take his advice."

"Have you ever travelled, Mr. Braddock?"

"Not really."

"You must. It broadens the mind. And it is good for the health."

"And staying here isn't?"

"Violent place, London. Street crime. Innocent people attacked and murdered, just for their wallets, not even for that. It happens all the time."

"Not so very often," I said. "You forget, I was a crime reporter."

"So you were. I mention it only because I need a contract taken to Buenos Aires for signature. A trustworthy person to take it would be well paid."

"Really?"

"Seven hundred pounds. The boat leaves from Southampton in a few days' time."

"Otherwise I will meet the same fate as Mr. Steptoe?"

"A strange thing to say, but I suppose it is a risk we all face. Good heavens, is that the time? I must run." He stood up, brushed nonexistent crumbs from his jacket, straightened his tie and looked at himself in the mirror.

"Where is the bowl?"

"What bowl?"

He gestured at the mantelpiece.

"Oh, that. It got broken."

He stared at me.

"It was just a pot."

He paused, then recovered. "Of course." He took an envelope out of his pocket and placed it on the table, then left. It was addressed to me. It contained a cheque for £700, drawn on the Bank of Bruges in London, and a ticket for the *Manitoba,* sailing from Southampton in two days' time.

CHAPTER 27

It goes without saying, I imagine, that I was agitated, disturbed and very frightened. This was all so far outside my experience that I had not the slightest idea what to do. Xanthos had given me money and said that if I did not take it, he would kill me. Or have me killed. Not in so many words, but even I could grasp his meaning. Poor Mr. Steptoe was already dead. So was someone else at the works. So was Ravenscliff. And with such people dying who was I to think I was safe?

I needed time and I needed somewhere I could put aside the nagging feeling I had that I was being watched and followed. This wasn't madness on my part; I used all of George Short's skills in reverse and discovered it was true. Two people, in fact; for the first time I wondered how long they had been behind me without my even noticing. They tailed after me all the way down Piccadilly, but I led the way into my territory, not theirs, into a land where I knew every little alleyway and many of the people on the streets. Every step made me feel safer, less alone. They weren't that good, and this made me feel stronger and less helpless. I went down the Strand, carelessly, as if I had not noticed them, then into Fleet Street and into the Duck—always nearly empty at that time of day, so I could be sure I would not be surprised. I bought a drink, which I needed badly, and settled into a quiet corner. Peace. I needed that as much as a whisky.

Both in combination slowly had their effect. I calmed down, then became positively angry. How dare he? Not a sensible response, as it was obvious that he dared only too readily, but it brought me back to myself, and put to a temporary rest the quivering, frightened and somewhat shameful creature which had taken over my mind. Xanthos had threatened me, damn him. Why then? He could have said the same at any stage over the past month or so. Was it because his scheme at the shareholders' meeting had gone awry and he was planning another way of getting what he wanted? And where was Elizabeth? Had she really gone to Cowes, or was she . . . ? The thought struck horror into my mind. He was

trying to take control of Ravenscliff's companies, and she was Ravenscliff's heir . . .

Curiously, it was the thought of the little Greek sitting so calmly on
her settee which made my mind up. I would like to say it was courage, or
patriotism or chivalry or some other manly virtue which aroused me, but
it was not. It was the feeling of being supplanted, of having the image in
my mind spoiled, which fired my determination. I would be damned if I
was going to Southampton, at least to get on a boat to South America. I
was all alone; so be it. I could not go home, so I wrote a letter to McEwen
in the pub, and left it with the barman to give to him when he came in. It
set out, as fully as I could, everything I knew, and left it to him to decide
what to do about it. Then I sent a message for the runners. For five
shillings each, they agreed to follow the followers, and also make sure
they were distracted while I left the pub by the back entrance. One, I
believe, was hit in the face by a large stone, sending him to hospital. The
other had his wallet stolen, the lad involved dancing down the street,
waving it above his head and tossing the contents on the ground until the
pursuit got too close and he was obliged to show how fast he could run.

By which time I was far away, threading my way through dark alleys
and back streets down to the river. Then west, but not home; I dared not
go there. Instead I went to Whiteley's department store in Bayswater,
bought a suitcase and some clothes (what a wonderful thing it is to have
money), then to Waterloo Station and caught the 1:45 to Southampton.
By this time I felt almost comfortable in my new role. I knew what I was
doing, and why I was doing it, for the first time in weeks. I was also
completely certain that I was not being followed, as the runner I'd paid to
tag behind me signalled that all was well.

Having money and being preoccupied by a higher purpose did not
mean I was immune to the pressures of the English class system, though.
Merely being able to afford a first-class ticket does not entitle you to be in
a first-class seat, or at least does not mean you will feel comfortable there.
I endured it for half an hour, until we passed Woking, then I stood up and
marched down to the scruffier, but altogther more comfortable, depths of
second. The English Ruling Classes on holiday are terrifying, not least
because they are not on holiday; they go to Cowes (and, I imagine, to
Henley and Ascot) with the same steely determination that Grenadiers
march into enemy fire. They are on display; they are working; the only
work they do, in fact. Looking elegant, saying the right things, being with

the right people is as vital for them as getting my punctuation correct is for me, or connecting up a pipe correctly is for a plumber; except that plumbers and journalists are more forgiving. One slip, and the Ruling Class are doomed, it seems.

No wonder they talked with such a nervous twitter; no wonder they spent much of their time nervously glancing at their reflection in the window as the drab suburbs of south London drifted past. A family of five; a mother, three daughters (two of marriageable age) and a son, who would have benefited from being put into old clothes and running around the streets throwing stones through windows. Poor child; he was so well behaved it was almost unendurable to be in the same compartment as him.

Now second-class was a very different thing, and I spotted two hacks from *The Times*, feet on the seats, in a compartment filled with smoke. I felt at home and safe and secure the moment I sat down beside them, even though (in the normal course of things) they were not my sort of journalist. Gumble was a war man, so I couldn't really see what he was doing there. Jackson had been crime, but had vanished about six months ago. He seemed almost embarrassed to see me, and it took some time to discover why.

Eventually, after much questioning, he sighed, took out his notebook and handed it over for me to read.

"Whatever be her opinions as to its intrinsic joys, the woman who accepts a yachting invitation must see that she has dresses suitable for the occasion," I read. I looked up at him, and he grimaced apologetically. *"One of the new designs for Cowes is carried out in nattier blue marquisette over satin. Closely pleated in accordion fashion to give the narrow straight effect in a pleasing manner. An upturned collar of lace and tiny round-cut chemisette . . ."*

"You poor fellow!" I exclaimed and he nodded gloomily. "What on earth did you do?"

"Missed the verdict in the Osborne murder," he said. "Six months in fashion to teach me the error of my ways."

I read on. *"There was a day when serges were the only materials utilised for yachting dresses, but the weather during this week should make it possible to wear linens, tussores, shantungs and foulards . . ."*

"I don't even know what it means."

"Nor do I," he replied, taking back the notebook and stuffing it into his pocket once more. "It's all in the dressmakers' handouts. No idea what they're on about at all."

I turned to Gumble. "You're not in the doghouse as well, are you?"

"Afraid so. I was in Afghanistan, doing really well, I thought."

"But there isn't a war in Afghanistan, is there?"

"There's always a war in Afghanistan. Anyway, it's a long story. If you think Jackson's got troubles, what do you think of this?"

He also got out his notebook, and I again read. *"Their Majesties' dinner party included the Crown Prince and Crown Princess of Sweden, the Princess Victoria and Princess Victoria Patricia of Connaught, the Commander-in-Chief at Portsmouth, the Duchess of Teck and Elizabeth, Lady Ravenscliff. This morning they joined their yacht for Divine Service. The Service was conducted by Rear-Admiral Sir Colin Keppel A.D.C. In attendance were . . ."*

"Bloody hell," I said.

"I know. Two years dodging bullets in the Khyber Pass . . ."

"No. I mean Lady Ravenscliff."

"Why are you interested in her? You're right, of course. Her in mourning. She's such a fixture, I suppose they couldn't do without her. Don't know what is happening to standards. But do I care? I do not."

"You don't happen to know where she will be in Cowes?"

"Is she going? Very inappropriate. She might well be a guest on the *Victoria and Albert,* of course."

My heart sank. I thought that finding her would be simply a matter of going to her hotel and knocking on the door. But if she was half a mile out to sea, on the royal yacht, it was going to be more difficult than I had anticipated.

"Do you know," he went on, "I think you're the first person ever to be interested in this rubbish?"

I gave him back his notebook. I hadn't realised she moved in such grand circles. Who would have thought it? "So you're just going to the Isle of Wight to do this?"

"Ah! No. I hope to write something interesting about the Tsar. If I can only get something, then I win fame and favour. What about you? Didn't I hear that you'd been fired?"

"I resigned. And I am going . . . In fact, that's a bit complicated."

"Where are you staying?"

I shrugged. "No idea. I thought I'd book into a hotel . . ."

They looked at each other, then laughed. "I hope you like sleeping on park benches then," Jackson said, "if you can find one unoccupied."

"I'd not thought of that."

"You can bunk with us. We're at the George. As long as you have no revolting personal habits . . ."

"None. And thanks."

"You're welcome. You sleep on the floor and pay half the costs. We get the receipt."

Fair enough. *The Times* was more generous than other papers over expenses. The rest of the journey was almost pleasant. I was given a swift grounding in Cowes Week by my two new companions—the only thing left out was anything to do with boats, as *The Times* that year had decided not to bother sending anyone who knew about racing. Too expensive. They even offered me work as a stringer to take care of some of them— the sixty-five-foot handicap or (better still) the King's Cup. They didn't suppose I wanted to try my hand at Mrs. Godfrey Baring's *bal masqué*, did I? I declined the boats, never having been on one and not having the slightest idea how you would even tell who had won, but astonished them by accepting the ball. If Elizabeth was there, if she was still alive, it was the sort of thing she'd attend.

Cowes was crammed, and the Solent was like Piccadilly Circus on a busy Friday evening. The little ferry which took us and our luggage over from the mainland had to weave its way through hundreds of yachts—big and small, one-masted and three-masted, long and sleek and modern, old and rather run down—as well as what seemed like most of the Royal Navy lying a mile offshore for review. On shore it was even worse; the ferry was so full it looked as though it might sink at any moment, and we were hurled out onto dry land into a crowd of people—women with parasols, arm in arm, men in white ducks and blazers, holidaymakers in boaters, small children, nannies and servants. Jackson led the way to the George, a small hotel next to a printing shop, very expensive and less than luxurious. A small room with three people in it was, apparently, quite luxurious for the time of year and, even though we could scarcely all fit inside, we hoisted our bags onto the beds, then retired to the bar. Three pints of Osborne pale later, we felt quite recovered and ready for battle. I had almost forgotten why I was there. I was no longer afraid. Not for the moment, anyway.

Jackson and Gumble at least knew what they were meant to be doing;

Jackson positioned himself to take notes on what the likes of Mrs. Algernon Dunwether considered appropriate for her midafternoon wear—it seems that the wealthier women were obliged to change clothes up to six times a day, which was why houses close to the centre fetched such a premium—while Gumble wandered off to the offices of the *Cowes Gazette* to get the daily lineup of what those with titles would be up to all evening.

I, by contrast, was at a loss; I had vaguely imagined I would simply run into Lady Ravenscliff walking along the promenade, but clearly this was not going to be the case. So while I thought it over I strolled up the Esplanade to Egypt House, a large, modern pile of imitation Tudor brickwork that the Barings had taken for the week. This I stared at for a while, then looked out over the Solent to where the *Victoria and Albert* was anchored, then walked back into the town centre. I asked one of the boatmen from the royal yacht, but he hadn't got a clue who was staying on the bloody ship and who was I to ask anyway.

Frustrating, although I found that a laziness slowly crept upon me even though there was enough on my mind to make me alert and nervous. I had only ever been to the seaside properly a couple of times, Sunday trips to Southend to waste time and money. Even there—not the most elegant of places—I discovered that the motion of the sea had a decided tendency to make me sleepy and stupid; it has always had that effect on me, and still does. Perhaps I had more in common with Ravenscliff than I realised. And the beer had an effect, of course, and by the time I got back to the George—not really very far—I was as dull as it was possible to be. I forced myself to keep on walking, as I knew that if I lay down I'd fall asleep for hours, and kept on going until I hit water again, an inlet which divides Cowes in two. There is no bridge, just a strange contraption which looks like a floating wooden shed that is pulled this way and that across the water by chains, ferrying passengers from one bank to the other.

I perched myself on a bollard, watching the people—girls and boys in sailor suits, men who worked in the boatyards, women coming over, some from grand houses, others more modest, after their shopping, going home to cook dinner, or have it cooked for them. And then I woke up with a start, and pulled my hat down over my head, hunched my shoulders to avoid being noticed by the man who had walked up the ramp and turned to stare back as the wooden gates—which looked as though they had been borrowed from a farmyard—swung shut.

It was him. There was no mistake, could be none; he was dressed differently, looking now like a bank clerk on holiday, in a dark suit and starched white collar. He had shaved, oiled his hair to look the part. But he still looked like a labourer, could never really pass as English. Still had the immobile features, the lack of expression in his eyes, which glanced around cautiously every moment, rather than staring ahead stupidly as I am sure mine had been until that moment. Jan the Builder took out a cigarette and lit it as the ferry floated off into midstream, but didn't seem to notice anything strange about me.

I did my best not to look too attentive as the ferry stopped on the other side and all the passengers got off, to be replaced once more by new ones. Tried to keep my eyes on him as it came back over and at last I could get on board myself. But it was a waste of time. Ten minutes (and twopence) later, I reached the far bank and he had vanished. I walked quickly up the main road out of town, doubled back down side streets dotted with seaside villas of greater or lesser grandeur, turned left and right for more than an hour, but nothing. If the jolt in my chest when I saw him hadn't been so extreme and painful, I would have concluded it had been a mistake. But it was not. I was sure it was not.

I have read many adventure stories in my time, and many of the problems in them seem to arise from the fact that the main protagonists never think of going straight off to confide in the police when they come upon some dastardly deed. Instead, they keep their information to themselves, and all sorts of trouble results. Of course they always manfully sort everything out in the end; but often I wonder how much easier it would all have been had the authorities been kept properly informed in advance.

Besides, I had no desire to sort it all out myself, manfully or not. So I went back to town and straight to the police station. And there I realised why the strapping heroes of fiction do not spend their precious time on such activities. The authorities, on the whole, are not interested. Had I been reporting a stray dog, or the theft of an umbrella, or the loss of a pocket book, then I have no doubt that Constable Armstrong would have snapped into action as quickly as you like. Instead, he looked at me as though I was the problem, sucked his teeth thoughtfully, and frowned in a manner which suggested very strongly that he considered me to be someone who needed humouring.

"I suppose even anarchists must have holidays," he said in a jocular fashion. "Must be hard work, all that overthrowing, and all."

"This is not a joke."

"Very well. Tell me what's bothering you."

And so I did, but by the time the policeman had realised that I had only heard at secondhand that Jan the Builder was an anarchist revolutionary; didn't know his real name; only heard at secondhand that he had a gun; didn't know for certain he had one on him; only saw him at a considerable distance; had only seen him once before; and couldn't swear that he wasn't on holiday, he began to lose patience.

"We're not going to get martial law declared on the basis of that, are we, sir?" he commented.

I scowled, and stumped out.

CHAPTER 28

"What on earth do you think you're doing dressed up like that?" Jackson asked.

I looked aggrieved. It was past eight o'clock, I hadn't eaten, and I was almost ready to go.

"You asked me to do this ball, didn't you?"

He stared at me, then burst out laughing. "You're meant to report on it. Not go to it, you idiot. You don't seriously think they'll let you in, do you? You're supposed to stand by the gate and get a list of the guests as they arrive. Not trip the light fantastic with the Duchess of Devonshire."

"Oh."

I looked at myself in the mirror. I had been rather proud of my appearance. I was dressed as a fisherman, having rapidly bribed an old man in the port to let me have his oilskins and hat. To this, I had attached lots of flies and bits and bobs of the sort that fishermen use, so I thought. And I had a large wicker basket with a plaster lobster in it which I'd bought from a shop which sold tourist trinkets.

"Besides," Jackson said scornfully, "it's a *bal masqué,* not a fancy-dress party."

I stared at him; I think he heard me deflating. "There's a difference?"

"This sort of ball, the men dress as usual. The women wear masks. That's why it's called a masked ball."

"I have to go," I said. "Even if I have to break in. I have to find Lady Ravenscliff."

"Why?"

"She's . . . It doesn't matter. I need to find her."

"I doubt you'll find her at a ball. She's meant to be in mourning."

"She dined with the King."

"That's different. That is allowed, just. But a ball? It would be a scandal. It's bad enough that she came here at all. If she did."

"I mean, if everyone's masked . . . She's the sort who would slip in. Someone there will know where she is. I've got to go. Just in case."

"Not as the representative of *The Times,* you're not. It's more than my job's worth."

I must have been looking properly desperate, because he dropped the scornful jocular tone and looked at me shrewdly. "You're about the same size as Gumble. Take his clothes, then."

"Won't he need them?"

"Yes."

He opened the wardrobe door and started pulling out clothes. "You'd better hurry. He'll be very annoyed when he finds out."

So an hour later, as the evening was just tipping over into darkness, I was walking up Egypt Hill, a road that led away from the promenade and skirted the gardens of the Baring house. I had thought of trying to talk my way in, but gave up the idea; journalists can do much—get into courtrooms, police stations, people's houses—by sheer brass neck, but gatecrashing a society party, I thought, might need practise. So, drawing on the wisdom of George Short once more—never be direct if you can be devious—I kept an eye on the wall until I came across a place with a suitable tree that had branches hanging down across the stonework. Half a minute later I was in the garden, adjusting my bow tie, dusting down Gumble's suit and walking, more boldly than I felt, up to the house itself.

Nobody gave me a moment's attention. It worked perfectly; I was given a glass of champagne by a passing waiter, and strolled into the main reception room—already full of people and heady with the smell of perfume—where I leaned against a wall and watched to get my bearings and work out precisely how I should behave. Remember: such an event was as foreign to me as an Esquimaux wedding party; I needed to tread carefully. And I felt ridiculous. Evening dress was not my normal wear; I'd been more comfortable in the fisherman's oilskin. The fact that most of the women were far more ridiculous-looking than I could ever dream of being was no consolation. Why they ever consented to such absurdities, how it was considered the height of fashion, eluded me. Had they possessed the stylishness of Elizabeth Ravenscliff, they might have succeeded. But most looked like plump middle-aged Englishwomen in masks. Not for the first time, I was glad that I lived in the world of pubs and press rooms. Besides, how did society operate? Was it permissible just to go up to someone and start talking? Would I cause a scandal if I engaged some young girl in conversation?

Having achieved my aim of getting into the party, I realised that I hadn't thought too much about what I was meant to do next. I wanted to see Elizabeth, to warn her, to talk to her. But how to find her, even if she was there? All the women were in masks, and although I reckoned I could count on her to be more beautifully turned out than anyone else in the room, it was impossible to tell which one she might be. Some of the masks were tiny and did nothing to disguise the identity of the wearer, but a fair number were very large. All I could do was wander around, hoping she would notice me. If she was there, she didn't. Or maybe she was, but didn't want to acknowledge me. I was rapidly beginning to think this had been a bad idea.

"Glad you could come," said a hearty voice besides me as I retired to the wall again and tried to be as visible as possible. I had attracted the wrong person. A tall, grey-haired man with a bristling moustache and a red face—mainly from a collar two sizes two small for him, so the fat of his neck hung down over it—was standing beside me, looking vaguely hopeful. He seemed bored with the whole thing, and desperate for any reason not to have to compliment some absurdity in frills.

"Good evening, sir," I said, then remembered who he was. "I'm pleased to see you again."

Tom Baring peered at me, uncertainly, a look of vague panic passing across his face. He knew me; had met me; had forgotten who I was. Such were his thoughts, I knew. Nothing quite like embarrassment for making someone try harder.

"A meeting at Barings last year," I said vaguely. "We didn't meet properly."

"Ah, yes. I remember," he said, surprisingly convincingly in the circumstances.

"Family duties, you know . . ."

He looked a bit more interested. I had a family that had duties.

"In fact, the only interest in the meeting was the possibility that I might have been able to ask your advice. About a piece of porcelain." A fairly desperate way of winning his confidence and establishing a connection, but the best I could do. And it seemed to work. He brightened immediately.

"Oh, well. Only too glad. Ask away, please do."

"It is a dish of some sort. I was given it. It's Chinese."

"Really?"

"Well, it is meant to be," I continued with perfectly genuine vagueness. "I was given it as a present, you see, and I wouldn't trust any old dealer to tell me truthfully what it is. I'd be too easily deceived, I'm afraid. I was wondering if you could tell me of an honest one."

"No such thing," he said cheerfully. "They're all rogues and scoundrels. Now I will certainly tell you the truth. Unless it's really valuable, in which case I'll tell you it's worthless and offer to take it off your hands." He laughed heartily. "Tell me about it."

"About nine inches across. With blue foliage—bamboo and fruits, that sort of thing."

"Markings? Any stamps?"

"I believe so," I said, straining to remember.

"Hmm. Not much help. From your description it could be 1430s, or made last year and sold in any teashop. I'd have to look at it. Where did it come from?"

"I was given it. It used to be on the mantelpiece in Lady Ravenscliff's sitting room." To say she had given it to me was stretching a point, perhaps.

He raised an eyebrow. "Not the Ostrokoff bowl?"

"I think that's the one."

"Good God, man! It's one of the loveliest pieces of Ming porcelain in the world. The whole world." He looked at me with new interest and no little curiosity. "I have asked to buy it on many an occasion, but have always been turned down."

"I've been using it to eat my breakfast."

Baring gave a shudder. "My dear boy! The first time I saw it I almost fainted. He *gave* it to you? Do you have any idea what it is worth? What on earth did you do for Ravenscliff?"

"That, I'm afraid, I am not at liberty to say."

"Oh. Well, quite correct. Quite correct," he said, still quite breathless and flustered. The thought of my boiled eggs had so rattled him that he was no longer in full command of his faculties. For my part, the memory of it flying past my shoulder and smashing into the wall came flooding back to me. An extravagant gesture. I almost felt flattered.

"Well—I shouldn't. But—well, battleships."

"Oh, you mean Ravenscliff's private navy?"

I smiled, and tried to look nonchalant about the whole thing.

"I suppose you know about that?"

"Of course. I had to be brought in over moving the money around. I was very doubtful, I must say, but, as you may know, we owe Ravenscliff a great deal."

"Just so."

"What exactly do you do . . . ?"

I looked cautious. "I keep an eye on things. Quietly, if you see what I mean. Did, at least, for Lord Ravenscliff. Until he died."

"Yes, indeed. Great loss. Very awkward as well. Bad timing."

"Ah, yes."

"Damnable Government, dithering like that. Although Ravenscliff was remarkably sanguine. All will be well, he said. Don't worry. He knew exactly how to persuade them to take the plunge . . . Then he dies. Typical of the man that he foresaw even that possibility, though. When we heard I must say we rather panicked. If the shareholders found out what's been going on . . ."

"Difficult," I said sympathetically.

"Can you imagine? Telling our shareholders that the bond they thought was for a South African gold mine was in fact for a private battle fleet? I'd be picking oakum in Reading gaol by now. But at least I'd be in good company." He laughed. I joined in, perhaps a little too heartily.

"Yet here you are."

"Here I am, as you say. Thanks to Ravenscliff putting some nonsense in his will so no one can look at the books for a bit. It has bought us time. Although not much. I'm damnably worried about it."

"So is his widow, I understand," I said.

"Ah, yes. I suspect she may know more than she should. There was little Ravenscliff didn't tell her."

"How is that?"

"Well, I don't know exactly what he said, of course, but I hear that she has hired some man to find this child. Which, of course, has the effect of making its existence all the more real. The more he bumbles around, asking questions, the better it is."

Oh, God, I thought.

"Are you all right?" Baring asked.

"No," I said. "I've had a bit of a stomachache all day. Would you think me terribly rude if I excused myself?"

"I'm so sorry. By all means."

"Is Lady Ravenscliff here, by the way?"

"Of course not," he said. "She's in mourning. Not even in Cowes."

"Really? I was told she was staying on the royal yacht."

"Certainly not. I was there for tea this afternoon. No, I imagine she is still in London. I know she is no respecter of convention, but even she would not . . ."

I didn't really care one way or the other. I turned round and walked out of the ballroom, as slowly as I could manage, got to the big French windows which opened on to the garden and, when I was out of sight, broke into a run, heading for the wall where I'd come in as quickly as I could.

And there I sat, for an hour or more, half-listening to the sound of the orchestra, the occasional footfall as a couple walked past, or the men came out for a cigar, the women for some fresh air, but not really interested in any of it.

Everyone had been right. I had been chosen because of my complete unsuitability. My job really had been to confuse matters. The child did not exist, had never existed; it was a safety net, designed to protect Ravenscliff's companies should he die before this great undertaking was completed. The Government wanted battleships, but dared not order them. Barings and Ravenscliff put up the money, and gambled they would change their minds. Of course it had to be secret; the slightest whisper could bring the Government down and Ravenscliff's empire . . .

And did I care one jot? No. I had comforted her in her distress, sympathised with her loss, worked desperately to find the information she wanted, come to her with my little discoveries, been deceived by the look of gratitude in her eyes when I assured her that all would be well. And when I began to find out more than I should, Xanthos turns up to give me a good fright. Dear God, but I hated the lot of them. Let them fight it out between them.

I got up finally, stiff and cold even though the night was warm, and crawled over the wall into the freedom of the normal, ordinary, mundane world, where people tell the truth and mean what they say. Where honesty counts, and affection is real. Back into my own world, in fact, where I felt comfortable and at home. It was my own fault, really. I should have listened.

I've mentioned that I tend to sleep well, most of the time. The great gift did not desert me that night, fortunately. Even though Jackson snored abominably, and the floor was hard, I fell asleep by two o'clock, and slept as though all the world was well. In the morning I had to work to bring back the memories of the night before, but found when I did so that I was free of them. So I had been made a fool of. Used, manipulated, deceived. Not the first time, and not the last. And at least I had figured it out for myself. Even the thoughts of revenge which had flickered through my mind the night before held no more attraction. Yes, I could have told my two snoring companions everything. But I couldn't really be bothered and, besides, what good would it serve? I could destroy Ravenscliff's companies, but they would only be replaced by others just the same.

And it was a lovely, fine morning, of the sort when it was good to be alive. I even took Gumble's complaints about having stolen his clothes, and Jackson's insistence on keeping my plaster lobster as a souvenir, in good part. I was resolved to think no more of the matter. I would spend Elizabeth Ravenscliff's money, I would think no more of battleships—let alone of mediums, anarchists or any other rubbish. None of it was my business. I did not care. I would become a journalist once more, and go back to my old life, somewhat richer than I had been to begin with. What possible reason did I have to complain, anyway? I was paid well, and if it was to make a fool of myself, so be it. I was a well-paid fool, at least. And that evening, I decided, I would go to Southampton, and I would get on a boat and I would go to South America, having posted Xanthos's cheque off to my bank first of all. More money. If they wanted to give it away, why should I turn down the offer? I'd earned it.

I bought my two colleagues breakfast—a good breakfast, the best that Cowes could provide, with lashings of bacon, black pudding, eggs, fried bread, fried tomatoes, tea, toast and marmalade, the works, and then decided that, as Jackson was going on the press jaunt to the *Sandrart*, I would go with him. I now had nothing better to do. I was a free man, unemployed, my own master.

Oh, yes. The Tsar of all the Russias. Nicholas II. You would have thought, no doubt, that having such a grand gentleman in town would have caused a stir. It was not every day, after all, that the world's greatest autocrat, the last true absolute monarch in Europe, dropped into a small town off the south coast. In fact, he hadn't. He hadn't even put a foot on shore. The only evidence of his presence was the shape of the imperial yacht, the *Sandrart*, about half a mile offshore, anchored a few hundred yards from the *Victoria and Albert* and with a collection of navy gunboats posted around doing guard duty. As a sop to the journalists, who wanted something to put in their daily bulletins, there was to be a tour of the yacht. I had expected that Gumble would come along as well, but he turned his nose up at the idea. "You don't think that the Tsar is going to be on board with a lot of smelly journalists tramping all over the place, do you? Either the entire family will take refuge on the *V and A,* or they'll come on shore. And I may have fallen low in the estimation of my editors, but I am damned if I am going to spend my time looking at imperial curtains. I am going to walk up to Osborne. If he's on land, he'll be there."

So Jackson and I went; I merely curious, Jackson trying to pretend he wasn't. The main thing I discovered from the morning was that I have a tendency to seasickness in *very* small boats—we were rowed out in the yacht's cutter, which was fine until we were about a hundred yards offshore. Then it wasn't; my only consolation was that half of the press corps—well, about four of us, out of ten or so—also began smiling bravely.

Nor was it worth it; Gumble was quite correct in thinking that the imperial family would make themselves scarce; not even an imperial nanny remained on board. All we had was a bunch of Russian sailors, whose outright hostility to His Majesty's loyal press was palpable. We were escorted round the apartments at military speed; nothing was pointed out or explained, no questions were taken, no photographs allowed. All I got from the experience was a sense of wonder at how unnautical it all was—the state apartments were decorated like any house you might have found in Mayfair thirty years ago, with padded chairs, chandeliers and even a fireplace in the corner. Only the disconcerting rocking motion reminded you that you were on a boat—sorry, a yacht—at all.

And then we were put back into the cutter and rowed back to the shore. Not even a glass of vodka, but Jeremiah Hopkins did at least take his revenge by vomiting in the bottom of the boat just before we arrived back on land. "Compliments of the *Daily Mail*," he muttered as he stepped over his donation to get off. "A messy business, the freedom of the press," he added as he straightened up and walked unsteadily towards the nearest pub.

For my part, I didn't think that was the best solution to the problem of my stomach; steady land and fresh air seemed a better idea, so I decided to walk to Osborne to find Gumble; he had been correct in his judgements so far; he might be right now. I walked to the ferry, crossed over and strolled up York Avenue to the main gate. I was not alone; clearly news of some event had got around.

"The royal family and the imperial family," said one woman in tones of hushed awe when I found myself walking beside her. "They'll be coming out when they've finished their visit. They'll drive down to the Esplanade before going back on board their yachts. Isn't that wonderful and thoughtful of them?"

We walked in step, this reverential matriarch and I, strolling together like two old friends in the warm sunshine of the early afternoon. She told me—how she had found out so much information from her kitchen I do not know, she should have been a reporter—that the two royal families had crossed to Osborne's private landing stage by boat, but intended to show themselves to the town before returning. Two monarchs, two consorts and a bag of children would be on display; I could not really see the attraction of just watching people drive by, but I was clearly in a minority on that one; when we arrived there was already a crowd of a few hundred, mainly townspeople by the look of them, lining the wooded path which ran from the road to the grand entrance gate.

Gumble was there also, looking extremely displeased with the situation. His request to go inside had been flatly turned down, there would be no interview and he had to stand there like some common shop assistant, with not the slightest chance of coming up with anything worth writing about at all.

I commiserated. "But there wasn't much chance he would have said anything interesting anyway," I concluded.

"Not the point. I wanted an interview. What he might have said was irrelevant," he replied.

"You could always make it up," I suggested.

"Well, in fact, that's what got me in trouble in the first place," he said reluctantly. "I quoted Habibullah Khan on the reforms he was introducing in Afghanistan. Unfortunately, he was out of the country at the time and had just reversed them all, so he complained . . ."

"Bad luck," I said.

"Yes. So no making things up for a while. I do wish they'd get a move on. I want my lunch . . ."

I had stopped listening. I was staring over at the other line of spectators, a blur of expectant faces, all patiently waiting. Except for one, who came into sharp focus as I looked, then looked again. A poorly dressed woman, with a cheap hat pulled down over her face, clutching a handbag. I knew she had seen me. I could see that my face had registered, that she was hoping I had not seen her; she took a step back, and disappeared behind a burly man and a couple of squawking children who were waving little flags on sticks.

"Oh, my goodness," I said, and looked up and down the row of people, to see if I could catch sight of her again. Nothing. But I did see PC Armstrong, my sceptical constable of the day before.

"Still hunting anarchists, are we sir?" he said cheerfully when I walked up to him—this was a long time ago; there were no barriers or controls on people then.

"Constable . . ."

"Is he here, then?"

"Not that I've seen, but . . ."

"Well, let me know and we'll deal with him," he said complacently.

"I'm certain he is, though."

Armstrong looked sceptical but ever so slightly worried. "Why?"

"I've seen someone he knows." I pointed, and he called over another policeman on duty. Both then strolled over and began walking up and down, looking out for anyone they considered suspicious.

They had seen nothing and found no one by the time the great gates swung open, and a murmur of expectation swept through the crowd. In the distance a line of three black automobiles, Rolls-Royces, came slowly down the driveway; the canvas tops were open, so they wouldn't obscure the view. As they turned the bend, I could see that the leading car had two men in the back, resplendent in uniform; the second had two women. They were wearing hats, tied over their heads with scarves.

"Constable, stop the cars, for God's sake!" I said as I ran up to him. "Close the gate!"

Armstrong panicked. He could control the crowds as long as all was well, but wasn't capable of doing anything other than watch people, and tell himself that everything was fine. "Don't worry," he said. "Don't worry, don't worry . . ." and his lips kept moving even when he stopped speaking, as though he was reciting a prayer.

And it was too late, anyway. The big black machine was coming through the gate, slowing down so that the crowds could applaud, and see. And to allow the cars behind to catch up and make a proper procession of it. I was looking up and down the line of faces, desperate to see Elizabeth, convinced that something dreadful was about to happen. It was the way she was clutching her handbag which worried me most; all I could see in my mind was her hands, the knuckles white, as she held tightly onto that cheap canvas bag, held it up over her stomach, so she could put her hand into it . . .

The cars were now going at no more than two miles an hour, the flags were waving, the people were cheering. The King-Emperor of Great Britain and the Indias sat on the right, looking bored. The Tsar of all the Russias was by his side, gazing at the crowd with the air of someone who found all this populace slightly distasteful, and then I realised my mistake. I saw a man, a big burly man, wearing a suit like a bank clerk, step forward some ten yards away from me, his hand underneath his jacket. I shouted, and he turned to look at me, then dismissed me from his thoughts. I was ten yards from him, he was only ten yards from the car, but it was getting closer all the time, and I was just standing there, speechless and immobile.

But a man can run faster than a slow-moving car. Much faster, when he is terrified. I began to run, and the closer I got, the better I could see. I could see his hand pulling out from under his jacket, saw the black thing in it, got closer still and saw the barrel. And I saw it being lifted, and pointing just as I got close enough to leap, heard the explosion as I fell, then another one as I collapsed on the ground. And I felt the most incredible, unbelievable pain, which blotted out almost everything else, except for the one last image as I looked up from the dust and gravel, and saw Elizabeth standing over me, gun in her hand, a look of wildness in her eyes.

CHAPTER 29

I have read much nonsense over the years about being shot; the main things being firstly that it doesn't hurt, and secondly that the noise sounds more like a faint popping, rather than a loud bang. Rubbish. Firstly, the noise of the gun going off sounded like the crack of doom; I was sure my eardrums had burst. Secondly it hurt like the very devil, and from the very moment that the bullet entered my shoulder. And then it hurt more, until I lost consciousness, and hurt still more when I woke up again in hospital. In my case, at least, it was also untrue that I could remember nothing, wondered where I was and what had happened. I remembered perfectly well, thank you very much. Then I went back to sleep.

It was morning, I guessed, when I woke up again, and I stared at the ceiling, gathering my thoughts, before showing any sign that I was conscious. But I got an unpleasant surprise when I turned my head to look around. Sitting beside me, reading a newspaper, was the small, almost dainty, figure of the man I knew to be Henry Cort, a cup of tea on a small table by his side.

"Mr. Braddock," he said with the faintest of smiles. "And how are you?"

"I don't know," I said.

"Ah. Then let me tell you. You have been shot."

"I know that."

"I suppose you do. Not too seriously, I'm glad to say, although it made a nasty wound and you have lost a lot of blood. If it hadn't been for your friend Mr. Gumble, who knows something about bullet wounds from his time in Afghanistan, you would have bled to death, probably. However, the doctors tell me you will recover perfectly well, in time."

"She shot me."

"Yes. Yes, so it seems."

"What happened?"

"Why don't you read this? It's the dispatch penned by Mr. Gumble for *The Times,* and so we know it must be of the highest accuracy."

He gave me the morning paper, then summoned a nurse to help me sit up enough to be able to read it. This took a very long time, but at least it gave me an opportunity to get back to my senses. The pain helped as well—it wasn't that bad, but it reminded me I was still alive. I was given some water, and tucked into bed properly and fussed over quite charmingly. All of that took about half an hour, during which time Cort sat quite impassively, doing nothing and managing not to look bored. Then, when I was feeling tolerably human again, he once more handed me the newspaper.

" 'Feminist Outrage at Cowes,' " I read. I looked at him.

"Terrible, these women, eh?" he said.

I frowned, and read some more.

Cowes—An outrage was offered to our Royal Visitors today by a suffragist in what is regarded here as a childish and unseemly exhibition. An attempt to embarrass the people of this country by the parading of supposed grievances in front of visitors is considered another blow which women suffragists have dealt to their own cause. Miss Muriel Williamson let off firecrackers close to the Royal Party as they were leaving Osborne House, having paid their respects in the death Chamber of our late Queen, in a manner deliberately designed to alarm. The fact that it could well have been a much more serious matter gives considerable cause for concern. Miss Williamson, who we understand has only lately been released from an asylum . . .

"He should be ashamed of himself," I said weakly.

"Oh, he is," Cort said. "He really is. He took some persuading to write that."

"And why did he?"

"Because I was able to convince him that a near assassination of the Tsar on English soil would not be good for our standing in the world. And, of course, the prospect of a foreign posting, on the strong recommendation of the Foreign Office . . ."

"Why did Elizabeth shoot me?"

"Another interesting question," Cort said thoughtfully. "She says you got in the way. You hurled yourself heroically on the assassin, but not quickly enough to prevent him from bringing his gun to bear on his target. She decided it was too risky to be squeamish, so shot you both, just to be on the safe side. She killed Jan the Builder, so you may consider yourself fortunate. The question I have not yet managed to settle in my mind, though, is who is responsible for all this."

"Don't you know?" I was lying down again, staring at the ceiling, so heard his words without being able to see his face. It was curious; it was more like a conversation with myself. And as long as I talked to myself, as quietly as I liked, I found it easy enough to speak. Cort picked up his chair and moved closer to the bed.

"I was working on the assumption," he said, "that Ravenscliff had organised it in order to make the need for his battleships a little more pressing. But if so, why did his wife stop it—and in such a dramatic fashion? And so we come to you."

"Me? It has nothing to do with me at all."

"Of course not! No. I was merely hoping you might be able to shed a little light on matters."

"Why don't you ask Lady Ravenscliff?"

"Well, as she has recently shot two people, I'm not sure her word is so very reliable. Even more difficult, of course, is the fact that she claims she has been acting under the belief that I was responsible for it all."

"Why?"

"She has a long memory," he said cryptically. "It is of no importance. But there you are, you see. She thinks I was responsible, I think she was. You, on the other hand—the victim, the innocent bystander, so to speak—may be considered objective. So am I right that John Stone really was behind it all and wanted the blame to fall on the Germans?"

"Why do you think that?"

Cort shrugged. "John Stone felt betrayed. He had been persuaded to launch a private venture building battleships and was facing severe difficulties because the Government would not place the orders he had been promised. He therefore decided to organise an international crisis which would generate the orders he needed."

"Who persuaded him to build the ships?"

"A group of concerned citizens. Influential ones, I might say, who felt that the Government's naval policy was disastrously misguided."

"But the Government was elected . . . Oh, never mind." It was true. I really didn't care.

"As I was saying," he continued, "I hoped you might provide some nugget of information which would allow me . . ."

That did it. A nugget. It was all anyone expected of me. Some fragment, the significance of which I did not even realise. Only someone like Cort would understand its importance. I was too dim-witted to grasp it myself.

"It was nothing to do with Ravenscliff," I said, still quietly but deliberately so now, speaking softly to make him bend ever closer so he could hear me.

"Are you sure?"

"Yes. It looks like it was, I know. The Tsar dies, the assassins are arrested or killed, their homes are raided by the police and—surprise surprise—they find documents indicating that they had been paid by the Bank of Hamburg. An outrageous plot by the Germans, just the sort of thing you would expect of such barbarians.

"The Russians would be outraged and would declare a war of revenge. The French would follow, and the British might join in. Whatever the result, Ravenscliff would benefit. He owned shares in all the major armaments companies, and controlled many of them. He would also sell his battleships at a good price.

"But, if anyone had looked closer, they would have spotted Ravenscliff's hand behind it all. The Bank of Hamburg was his personal bank in Germany. The payments were authorised by the Beswick Shipyard. He would have come under heavy suspicion.

"Would it have made any difference? Could the Government possibly have admitted that one of their citizens had done such a thing? Or would they have buried the information?"

"Are you asking me?" Cort said. "Or is that rhetoric?"

"I'm asking."

"Publicly I imagine it would have been covered over. I can't imagine any government admitting something like that. Certainly, that would have been my recommendation. Privately, however, I think not."

"Precisely. Ever so quietly, Ravenscliff would have been removed. What would it have been? Falling under a train? A heart attack?"

Cort shrugged.

I continued. "The trouble is that Ravenscliff died before this scheme took place, and he was not behaving like someone hatching a dastardly plot to embroil the Continent in war. Far from it; he was trying desperately to find out what was going on. He had learned that there was something strange taking place inside his company; honest young men were turning into thieves; payments were being made without authorisation. But that could not happen. Everything had to be authorised. Which meant that someone, someone fairly senior, must be authorising them. But he did not know who. All he knew was that it wasn't him."

I stopped here and tried to turn, but could not. Cort lifted my head, and helped me sip some water from a glass on the little table beside the bed. He did it surprisingly gently. It made me feel safe. A dangerous feeling.

"So, instead of the usual means a man like him had of dealing with such matters, he turned to the only person he knew he could trust absolutely: his wife. She tried to find out the truth, and did so, up to a point. She established that the money was going to Jan the Builder but until the very last moment, did not know why. It was a close-run thing.

"When Ravenscliff died, there was a battle for control of Rialto. On the one hand, Barings was buying up shares—was it you who organised this?"

He nodded.

"On the other, so was someone else. Theodore Xanthos tried to take advantage of his employer's death, and was thwarted only by Barings and you. Then he tried to organise a shareholders' revolt, but was blocked again, because the estate was in limbo. Ravenscliff had tangled up his will to buy time in case of his death—something which he must have foreseen, or at least considered as a possibility.

"Xanthos also tried to distract Ravenscliff by attacking the one thing he held more dear than his companies. He lit upon the witch-woman in Germany and brought her over to England. She, I think, was attempting to blackmail Lady Ravenscliff. She told me she had had affairs; the witch-woman was the sort who would find out about them."

Cort smiled appreciatively. At least, I think that's what it was.

"Did you kill her?" I asked.

"Me?" Cort asked. "Why do you ask that?"

"You took all her papers. That was you, wasn't it?"

"That's true. I didn't want anything to fall into the hands of someone like you by accident. But there was nothing of interest. You have a very odd notion about me, Mr. Braddock. I think you must have been listening to Lady Ravenscliff too much."

"Nobody likes you very much."

"I am wounded," he said, and almost looked as though he meant it.

"Why did you threaten poor Mr. Seyd?"

He looked displeased. "Poor Mr. Seyd, as you call him, has been in the pay of Germany for years," he said. "You don't think he started investigating Rialto by chance, do you?"

I stared blankly at him.

"So who did kill her?"

He shrugged. "I have learned over the years to concentrate on essentials. I suggest you do the same." He had a quiet, gentle voice, I thought. Entirely reasonable.

"But you did steal Ravenscliff's papers?"

"I have them." He didn't seem inclined to elaborate.

"Anyway," I continued, trying to digest this, "in my opinion, this had nothing to do with Ravenscliff. He was arrogant enough not to doubt his own judgement. He could not believe any decision of his could go wrong. He was supremely confident that this gamble of his would work. There is no sign that he was worried on that score at all.

"But he was coming to grips with the one thing he feared more than anything. His companies had come alive; he had created a monster, and it was acting in its own interests, no longer taking orders. Its job was to maximise its profits; Xanthos saw a way to make them astronomically large and enrich himself at the same time. And when Ravenscliff threatened to stop it, I believe his own invention killed him. I doubt that Xanthos personally pushed him out of the window. But I am fairly certain that he was responsible for it; he threatened to kill me a few days ago. A man called Steptoe was killed by him a few days ago; another employee at Beswick died as well. I don't know if he was acting in concert with other managers. Bartoli, Jenkins, Neuberger may all be part of it, or they may have been even less aware of what was taking place than Ravenscliff himself. I don't really care. That's your job."

"And that is your understanding of what has taken place?"

"Yes. Ravenscliff was much too clever to channel money for an assassination through his own companies. He was a master of the art of hiding much larger sums. You were *meant* to trace the money. Heavens, even I managed it."

"Interesting. I had assumed Xanthos was operating on Ravenscliff's instructions. Are you sure he was not?"

"He would hardly have had to spend so much time finding out what Xanthos was doing if he already knew. And Lady Ravenscliff would have been nowhere near Cowes yesterday. I mean, in the matter of assassinations, why not let the professionals get on with it?"

He thought this one over. "In that case I think I may owe Lady Ravenscliff an apology. She must think very poorly of me. Thank you, Mr. Braddock. You have been most informative. I wish I'd talked to you earlier. You must forgive me; I assumed that you must have had some hidden role. Certainly you did seem to go out of your way to draw attention to yourself."

"I thought I was being discreet."

"Yes, well. There we must differ."

He stood up and folded his newspaper. "I do hope you recover properly, and with good speed. But I'm afraid I must leave; I have a great deal to do; giving Lady Ravenscliff her freedom, of course, being somewhere near the top of the list."

And he quietly left me alone to my thoughts, which were in some turmoil after what I had just said. I beat the mattress with my fist in frustration, so hard that my shoulder opened up again and I had to be rebandaged by the nurses, who scolded me, then gave me some nasty-tasting medicine which made me drowsy once more.

When I woke up again it was night, and she was there. Heavens but she was beautiful, so delicate, and lovely, sitting and looking out of the window so I could study her for a long time; the only time I had caught her unaware that she was being looked at. I could see what she was really like when no one else was watching.

There was nothing; she merely sat, waiting, totally immobile, with no expression on her face, no movement at all. Just perfection, no more and no less; a work of art so exquisite that it was breathtaking. I had never encountered a woman so lovely, and in all the years afterwards never met anyone who came close.

And when I moved, she turned and smiled. I felt a glow spread through me. Just to be the recipient of such warmth and concern made me feel better.

"Matthew, how are you? I've been so worried for you. I cannot apologise enough."

"I should think not," I said with an attempt at a smile. "You did shoot me."

"I have been in agonies about it. Terrible thing. Terrible. But you are still with us—and so is the Tsar."

"When did you know he was the target?"

"Not until Jan stepped forward. He'd told me to come with him, that this was important. We stayed in a boardinghouse for a night. He was unusually terse and ill-humoured. But wouldn't say anything. I tried my best, but he became threatening. So I had no choice. I just had to stay with him. I knew something was going to happen, and I began to worry about what it might be. It was only when he stepped out that I was certain and knew what I had to do. About the same time that you realised as well. I'm sorry I shot you, but you would have been no match for him. He would have murdered the Tsar, even with you hanging on to him. I couldn't take the risk."

"I quite understand," I said gallantly. "And what is a little bullet wound in comparison to a European war?"

"And I owe my freedom to you as well. Mr. Cort told me what you had said."

"Yes," I replied. "That's the bit that's puzzling me."

"Why?"

"I am normally a truthful person," I said evenly. "I've only started telling lies since I met you."

She frowned in slight dismay and confusion; just a little enough to make the bridge of her nose wrinkle attractively before she smiled again.

"I was looking at you when you shot me, you see. The expression in your eyes. I really don't think you were trying to miss me."

"Of course I was," she said a little petulantly. "I was petrified, that's all. You read far too much into my eyes."

"They are the most beautiful eyes I have ever seen. I have tried often to get you to look at me, just to have that feeling of excitement that it causes in my stomach. When I close mine, I can see them. I dream of them. I know them well."

"But why would I want to shoot you? I mean, really shoot you. You know."

"How often do you take the waters at Baden-Baden?"

She looked momentarily confused, then replied. "Every year. I go in the autumn. I have done so for many years now. Why do you ask that?"

"And Mr. Xanthos? He is an enthusiastic water-taker as well?"

"No," she said, "I'm sure he is not."

"But you were both there last autumn?"

"Yes."

"Strange that an arms salesman should go to a place like that. Unless he was visiting someone. Like you."

She raised an eyebrow. Her face, so very expressive it was, was turning cold.

"And when you were both there you came to the attention of Madame Boninska, otherwise known as the witch-woman. A nasty bit of work, who made a tidy living out of blackmail. She knew a gold mine when she saw one. She followed you back to England, and decided to try a little blackmail. How long did you pay up before you refused?"

"Matthew, you are talking such nonsense. Have these nurses been putting something into your tea?"

"Morphine, maybe?" I said, with a quite nasty tone. "Drink some. You know more about that sort of thing than I do."

That stopped her attempt at good humour, so I continued. "She wrote to your husband, who went to see her. There she gave him the details. That his beloved wife was having an affair with another man. His own employee was betraying him. Not only planning to take his company away from him, but to take his wife as well.

"Lord Ravenscliff was not a man to go down without a fight. He had already amended his will so that everything would fall into the hands of an administrator should he die. I am fairly certain that, if he had had his meeting with Xanthos the next day, Xanthos would have been dismissed. And then he would have thrown you out as well. I have heard enough to know that he was thorough and ruthless. When he acted, he moved fast and decisively. And he hated disloyalty above all.

"But you were his equal, so Xanthos told me, and he was right. You moved fast. One swift move, and he was out the window. Did you put your arms around him and tell him how much you loved him before you gave him a little push? Or was it some melodrama, opening the window and threatening to throw yourself out, until he came to stop you and made the mistake of turning his back on you?

"Before that, you had offered—what a loving gesture!—to find out what Xanthos was up to. Persuaded your husband he could trust no one else. That put you in the perfect position to relay Xanthos's instructions to Jan the Builder. You weren't doing this nonsense to find out what he was planning. The Tsar would be murdered, war would break out and Ravenscliff would get the blame—but quietly, no publicity. Xanthos would take over his companies. Then you and he would marry . . ."

She hit me, so hard that I was dizzy with the pain and my nose began to bleed profusely. And when I say hit, I don't mean some dainty slap about the face, such as an irate female might deliver. I mean punched, with her fist. And, having hit me, she hit me again, even harder. Then stood over me, eyes blazing with cold fury, teeth clenched. She stood over me, breathing hard. I really thought I was about to die.

Instead, she marched to the door, pulled it open and turned round.

"How dare you talk to me like that?" she spat. "Who do you think you are?"

I couldn't talk. I gasped through the bedsheet, which I was having to use as an impromptu bandage. The pain was so great it even over-whelmed the pain of my wound. It occurred to me that saying what I had, all alone in a room with her, had not been the cleverest thing to do. Being punched on the nose was getting off quite lightly, really. Others had not been so lucky.

"You have come to your conclusions. I will not argue against them. I told you I loved my husband. You disregard all of that. And now you are going to run to Henry Cort?"

I shook my head.

"Why not? Why not? That is what a good Englishman should do, isn't it?"

I shook my head again.

"Why not?"

"Because you're all as bad as each other. I don't want anything to do with any of you. I've had enough."

I half-expected a cold, sneering contempt, icy disdain. It wasn't there.

She gave me one last look, one of those dark hypnotic glances she did so well, and I almost failed to notice the way she turned away swiftly so I could not see her face, almost as if to hide tears. She was always a good actor.

I never saw Elizabeth again, in any of her guises. She left Cowes that day, I was told, and soon enough closed down her house in St. James's Square and crossed to the Continent, where she lived for the rest of her life. Ravenscliff's will was settled and, as he had calculated, by the time his ships were nearing completion, the Government was persuaded that they were needed. He had been right all along; the battleships were in place in August 1914, and joined the Grand Fleet at Scapa Flow, guarding the North Sea against the German threat across the water. I am sure I was not alone in thinking that the cause of the war had a certain familiar style to it.

If so, then no responsibility for events in Sarajevo attached to Theodore Xanthos. Ravenscliff's companies prospered during the war, but did so without the salesman's assistance, as he met a tragic end, falling under the wheels of an Underground train at Oxford Circus late one Friday evening a month or so after I got back from Cowes. It was, as his only obituary mentioned, singularly unfortunate, as it was probably the only time Xanthos had ever even been in an Underground station. The other managers continued in their jobs, so I assumed they had been given a clean bill of health.

When I was well enough—my landlady loved my invalid status and fed me little but beef tea and seed cake for a month—I decided to go travelling at long last. The bank in Sloane Square wrote me an almost reverential letter to say that the sum of £2,380 had been deposited in my account, and that they would be pleased—in fact they were positively salivating—to hear my instructions. They also cashed the cheque from Mr. Xanthos.

I felt I had earned every penny, so I kept it all. I travelled the world for a few years, visiting the marvels of the Empire I had read about but never dreamed I would see with my own eyes. I wrote a book of travel memoirs which was politely enough received, and was turned down for military service in 1914 on the grounds of my injury. I was briefly hurt to my patriotic heart by this, but as the news of the war rolled in, I was hard put to suppress the feeling that being shot by Lady Ravenscliff was in fact the luckiest thing that had ever happened to me. Then I went back to work as a journalist, covering campaigns in Africa and later in the Near East. Later, after my marriage and the birth of my first son, and as I had a pleasant-enough voice, I became a pioneer of radio news, a job which brought me a small measure of fame, and which was the reason I was accosted at her funeral nearly half a century later.

Thus my story; even then, at the moment I last cast eyes on that captivating woman, I knew I had only grasped part of what had transpired. I did not feel inclined to revisit the matter, though. People like Cort and the Ravenscliffs had taken up enough of my energies and nearly killed me, although I was not so foolish as to forget that the encounter had transformed my life, and for the better. I was a free man afterwards, my horizons lifted, my ambitions transformed. But the more I travelled, the more able I was to forget about them all. And I succeeded for very many years, until I was accosted at a funeral, and a large package, meticulously wrapped in brown paper, with the address of Henderson, Lansbury, Fenton, 58 The Strand, was delivered to my door.

PART TWO

June 1943

Dear Braddock,

You may be surprised to get this package—if you ever do. I apologise for the melodrama; however, having been the custodian of these documents for many years, I now have to consider what to do with them. My doctors inform me that this is now a matter of some urgency. I considered that a bonfire might be best, but could not bring myself to such an act of immolation. Thus, I pass on the responsibility to you.

I am dying, whereas our mutual acquaintance is, I understand, in rude health and has found happiness in her latter years. I do not wish to disturb that, and not merely because I continue to act faithfully on the instructions of John Stone. Accordingly, I have instructed my solicitor, Mr. Henderson (whom you may recall), not to pass this on to you until she also has died. I leave it to him to determine what course to take should she outlive you as well—as she may well do; she is, as you recall, a tough woman.

There are two bundles: one is an account of my early life— you would be astonished if you knew how many spies are authors manqué—in which she figures somewhat. I wrote it in 1900 when I returned to England after living abroad, and I could never bring myself to amend it in the light of later information.

The other contains those papers by John Stone which you so earnestly sought when you were in his wife's employ. I apologise for not having enlightened you about them, but I hope you will fully understand my reasoning when you have read them. Mine will shed light on a woman I consider to have been the most remarkable I have ever known. I hope your reading will at least go some way to modifying your opinion of her, which, I was sorry to learn, was ultimately quite unfavourable. I fully accept that your opinion of me will be even less so if you read this; I do not pretend it shows me in anything other than an unpleasant light.

Your account of the events you took part in was impeccable, except that you failed to understand how intense was the love between John Stone and his wife; this one element, however, changes everything. I fear that your prejudices then may have prevented you from taking it sufficiently seriously.

I have followed your career with great interest in recent years and taken much pleasure in hearing your reports on the radio. Only the belief that you would not have been overjoyed to hear from me has prevented me from renewing our brief acquaintance.

Yours very sincerely,
Henry Cort

Paris, 1890

———◆••◆———

CHAPTER 1

My father is the gentlest of men, but has always been subject to periodic outbursts of insanity which render him incapable of work. He did not come from a rich family, and was brought up by his aunt and uncle, but inherited somewhere along the line enough money to ensure a modest life. He trained as an architect, the idea being that he would inherit my great-uncle's business, but illness prevented consistent application to any project. Instead, he lived quietly in Dorset, where he would occasionally build an extension to a house, or oversee the rebuilding of a church roof. For much of the time he would read, or work in the garden. As I was used to his long silences and sudden refusals to answer questions, I did not think anything of behaviour which others considered decidedly queer.

My mother died when I was very young, and apart from that I never knew much about her. Only that she was beautiful, that my father had loved her. I think her death broke his heart; certainly it was about the same time that he became ill. He recovered somewhat, but my young life was periodically interrupted by sudden disappearances which (I was told) were due to Father being called away for a project. Only later did I learn that he spent these periods in a special hospital where he was slowly coaxed back to health.

I left home at eight to go to school and never really returned. My best friend—he was as miserable as I was—invited me to his home for the holidays, which was where I realised how difficult, in contrast, was my own family life. He had a father who was cheerful and playful and a mother who became the first love of my life: warm, graceful and utterly devoted to her family. They lived in a big house in Holland Park during the winter months and in a lovely Adam house in the Borders in the summer. They became my family, for Mrs. Campbell all but kidnapped me, telling my father she was quite happy to have me indefinitely. He thought it was for the best and surrendered me. He was a good man, but the responsibilities of parenthood were too much for his frail constitution. I visited him every summer, but each time he was more vague, and eventually I think he stopped recognising me altogether; certainly he stopped caring whether I came or not.

Money is not something which concerns the young; that my father's hospital bills were paid, that my school fees were settled did not excite any curiosity in my juvenile mind. It did not occur to me to wonder how this was happening. I assumed that the Campbells had taken on this responsibility as well. I loved them all the more for it, and I do believe no boy was ever more devoted to his real parents than I was to these delightful people.

Nonetheless, I repaid them poorly and was constantly in trouble. I was ill-disciplined, forever fighting, indulging in escapades which were often dangerous, and frequently illegal. I would break into the headmaster's study at night, simply for the pleasure of escaping undetected; would leave the boy's dormitory to go wandering illegally through the local town; would destroy the clothes and possessions of older boys who had bullied my friends. My schoolwork ranged from indifferent to poor and, although considered intelligent, it was clear I lacked the application ever to be a serious student.

A boy of small years must necessarily be a poor criminal; the ability to judge chances is insufficiently developed. I was finally run to ground in a housemaster's lodging—not my own housemaster, who was a decent enough man, but another who was universally disliked—apparently looting his small store of wine. In fact I was not, as I have never been a drinker. Rather I was busy trying to spike the bottles with vinegar, using a syringe of my own devising that could, I believed, introduce the contaminant without having to remove the cork. This was to be his punishment for the merciless beating which he had inflicted on a boy in my house, a somewhat diffident, frightened lad who naturally attracted the bullies to him like flies around a horse's head. I could not protect him— and felt more the injustice of the master than the suffering of the boy— but I did what I could to ensure that his misery did not go without some reply.

I should have been expelled; certainly the offence more than merited it, especially as there was some suspicion that the discovery also solved the mystery of who had locked the chapel doors and concealed the key so that the salvation of three hundred pupils was at risk until it was found four days later, punctured all the rugger balls the night before a tournament with five other schools, and committed a series of other offences against the corporate well-being. I admitted nothing, but since when did headmasters follow strictly the dictates of legal procedure?

But I was let off lightly. A thorough thrashing, detention for a term, and nothing more. A few bruises and cuts to add to the burn mark I had on my arm, received as a baby when I rashly put my hand into a fire. That was all. I did not understand it; and as the Campbells never referred to the matter, nor did I. Someone, though, was looking after me.

William Campbell's sudden death, when I was sixteen, was as great a shock as I had ever endured, and the atmosphere of despair and gloom in the house affected everyone. We—that is I and my adopted brother, Freddie—were kept completely in the dark; it was our comrades at school, as kind as young boys are, who told us that he had blown his brains out because he could not face the disgrace of ruin. With great consideration they provided the details when we did not believe them.

And it was true; Mr. Campbell was caught up in the Dunbury scandal and his fortune was destroyed. That, however, was not the worst of it; it was whispered that he had been part of a fraud to deprive other investors of massive amounts. The precise circumstances were never very clear to me; the matter was hushed up—he and others involved had been in the governing party at the time—and, in any case, I was not really old enough to understand. Young men of my type are prone to be impatient of details, and give their loyalties without regard to evidence. I remembered him as the kindest man in the world. Nothing else was of any importance to me.

It was clear that my schooldays were coming to an end, though. Mrs. Campbell assured me that the funds were there to continue to pay the fees, but I felt I could no longer impose myself on their goodness. I must begin to make my own way in the world, and so I began to consider how that way might be made. I was not denied assistance. It is one of the curiosities of the English that they are often excessively judgemental in the abstract yet match that with private kindness. The name of Campbell was hardly mentioned anymore; amongst his friends and old political comrades it was as though he had never existed. Yet for those whose lives he had ruined, there was constant sympathy and discreet help.

Mrs. Campbell herself refused to take any assistance; she remained as devoted to her husband's memory as she had been loving while he lived. She refused any offer of help that came from the opinion she was also one of her husband's victims, and took her fall with pride and defiance. She moved out of the grand house into more modest accommodation in Bayswater, where she maintained a household which ran with only two, rather than twenty, servants, and eked out a dignified, if straitened, existence for the rest of her days. I believe she had at least one offer of marriage, but refused as she did not wish to abandon the name her husband had given her. It would, she said, be the last betrayal.

I insisted that, come what may, Freddie should finish school and go to university; he was immensely talented and, more importantly, devoted to learning. My arguments prevailed; he gave up all fine notions of working to support the family, and eventually proceeded to Balliol to read Greats and become, ultimately, a Fellow of Trinity, living out his life in studious contentment, rarely straying from the narrow acreage bounded by the High Street in the south and Crick Road in the north. Eventually, his mother came to live with him and died last year, cutting an ever-stranger figure pottering around the streets dressed in the widow's weeds of twenty years ago.

For my part, I gave up the prospect of a similar trajectory with only nominal reluctance; I was not as clever as Freddie nor as disciplined, even though my love of reading was as great as his and my gift for language greater. But part of me had always hankered after something more, although I had never been able to decide what that was. I spent a few months in an architect's office, but found it uncongenial, although drawing delighted me then as it still does. I next moved to work in one of the great finance houses in the City, but discovered that while the strategy of high finance had its interest, the daily grind of counting money drove me to distraction. I might have made a splendid Baring, but as one of that family's clerks I was sorely tried.

Still, I did this for several years and gained greatly by the experience—I spent a whole year in Paris, much time in Berlin and even, on one occasion, was sent for two months to New York. At no stage did it occur to me that I was receiving remarkable treatment for a young man with no connections, unproven ability and minimal experience. I realised that most people of my sort spent their time, six days a week, in a dreary office from eight in the morning until seven at night, but I assumed it was merely good fortune on my part that I was not one of them. I was picked for one job and acquitted myself well, and so was chosen for another. And so on. The idea that any other factor was involved did not come into my thoughts.

In July 1887, though, I received a letter from a Mr. Henry Wilkinson. This was shortly after my twenty-fourth birthday. A grand man indeed, Deputy Undersecretary at the Foreign Office, a post he had occupied for some twenty years. He was not much known outside the minuscule world of diplomacy, and the name meant nothing to me, but I knew that the invitation to lunch could not be ignored. And when I requested permission from my chief to absent myself, it was given very speedily. No one seemed curious about what it was all about. Which was not really surprising, as they knew perfectly well already.

I went the following Wednesday to the Athenaeum, and met the man who was to be in effect my employer until he died, still in harness, six months ago. Many people have the idea that civil servants are sleek, well-groomed and well-bred people, suave in manner and given to murmuring incisively instead of indulging in ordinary speech like the majority of the population. Such people exist, but the Diplomatic Service in those days still found a place for the eccentric, the unusual and—in at least two cases I have met—the certifiably insane.

Henry Wilkinson did not look like a senior civil servant. He was dressed in a tweed jacket, for a start, which violated all codes of conduct for his class, his employment and his club, which would have denied entry to most members who dared commit such sacrilege. He was much given to grunting and loud exclamations. His emotions, far from being closely controlled and disciplined, overflowed all over the room, and his conversation was filled with loud laughs, groans, chuckles and sighs. He fidgeted incessantly, so much so that I came to dread sharing a meal with him, because his hands were always picking up the salt cellar and banging it on the table, or twiddling his fork around while he was listening. Or he would cross his legs, uncross them and cross them again, leaning back and forward in his chair as he spoke. He never sat still, never relaxed, even when apparently enjoying himself. He also ate virtually nothing; a meal consisted of chasing a piece of meat around the plate for a few minutes before he consented with the greatest reluctance to push a sliver of carrot or a fragment of potato into his mouth. Then, a few moments later, he would thrust the plate aside as if to say—thank heavens that's over!

He was a wiry man, with a thin, foxy face redeemed only by a most charming smile. He also had the annoying habit of almost never looking directly at you; this he kept for special occasions, and when he did, his eyes bored straight through you as though he could count the dots on the wallpaper through your head. Every now and then during our lunch, some grandee would bow discreetly at him, but he waved them all aside without even looking at them.

It was not so much a lunch, more of a viva voce examination. I was discouraged from asking any questions, and when I did, they were ignored. What was my opinion of Britain's place in the world? Who were our greatest enemies? Who our rivals? What were their advantages and weaknesses? How best to exploit their divisions? How did the health of our great industries relate to the longevity of the Empire? What proper relationship with the Continent should Britain pursue? Did I think we should continue to bolster the Ottoman Empire, or connive at its downfall? My opinion on the continued convertibility of paper specie into gold? The double metal question? The effectiveness of the Bank of England in the late crisis in the American markets? The use of financial power as a proper instrument of diplomacy?

Most of these questions, I was sure, I answered badly. I was no diplomat, reading secret briefing papers from ambassadors around the globe; most of what I knew was to be found in *The Times* every morning. Perhaps I was a little better informed on financial matters, but, as I had been pummelled by questions for a long time without making any apparent impression on him, I was beginning to be discouraged, which no doubt made my answers less satisfactory.

"You are asked by your Government to commit a crime, Mr. Cort. Do you do it or not? What factors determine your answer?"

This question came out of the blue after a response on my part to a question about whether I considered dividends of North American railway stock to be sustainable (an easy one, that: of course they weren't) and it took me so completely by surprise I hardly knew what to answer.

"It would depend on my position in relation to the Government," I said after a while. "A soldier invading a foreign country I suppose commits a crime, but is not held personally accountable. An individual with no official status might be in a less comfortable position."

"Assume you are a private individual."

"Then it depends on who is asking this of me. I assume it is a crime for the good of the country. I would have to have a very profound trust in the judgement of the person making the request. Why do you ask such a question?"

This was my second attempt, by that stage, to discover the purpose of the meeting. It was brushed aside, as the first had been.

"Your duty to your country is a matter of personal relations?" he asked, arching his eyebrows in something I took to be scorn. I was becoming a little annoyed by this stage, having endured these incessant questions for more than an hour, so that my plate lay almost as untouched as his; I thought I had been remarkably patient.

"Yes," I snapped back. "We are not talking about the country. We are talking about its representatives, only some of whom have the authority or stature to decide what is in the national good. Also I speak as one of Her Majesty's subjects, who has a right to have an opinion on such matters. Besides, I was not aware that our Government committed crimes."

I glared; he now smiled sweetly back, as though I had just said how pretty his little daughter was. (I met his family once, some years later. His daughter, slightly older than I, was the most terrifying female I ever encountered: the brains of the father, multiplied by the remarkable force of character of the mother. She was not, however, particularly pretty.)

"Goodness gracious me!" he said. "I don't believe you just said that! Of course it does. Not unless they can be avoided, of course. Let me give you an example. Suppose we learn that France, our great, civilised but entirely annoying neighbour, has advanced plans for an invasion of this country. Suppose we know how to obtain these plans. Should we do so?"

"Of course. That is a matter of war."

"No," he replied, wagging a finger in correction. "No war has been declared. We would be committing an outright theft from a nation which has done us no harm, and whose Government is currently almost cordial towards us, despite popular opinion."

"Which cordiality may turn out to be a mere deception. It is obviously legitimate to discover if someone wishes you harm. Naturally it would be permissible to steal this information."

"And if someone tries to prevent this theft? A guard or soldier? Even a member of the public? What measures could be taken against them?"

"Any that were required."

"Including killing them?"

"I very much hope that could be avoided. But if that was the only way of gaining information that might save thousands of lives, then yes."

"I see. Let us reverse the question then. Suppose a Frenchman comes to this country to steal our plans for invading France. What measures could be taken against him, should his whereabouts and intentions become known?"

"We plan to invade France?" I asked, astonished. Again, he found my response amusing.

"We should," he said with a chuckle. "It is the army's job to prepare for all such possibilities. However, I very much doubt such a plan exists. Our generals have a long tradition of being woefully unprepared, and in any case they seem to find shooting people armed only with spears quite difficult enough. Nonetheless, such plans should exist, as it is obvious that sooner or later there will be another war in Europe, and we do not know if we will be able to stand by and watch. No matter. Assume, if you can, that the generals are better prepared and more far-seeing than they are. How to react to the presence of this Frenchman on our soil?"

"Stop him."

"How?"

"By whatever means necessary."

"But he is only trying to do that which you have already declared legitimate."

"I act to save the lives of my countrymen. And would do so again in this case."

"Lives of Englishmen are more valuable than lives of Frenchmen?"

"Not in the eyes of God, perhaps, but I have no responsibility for the well-being of the French, while I am bound to the inhabitants of my country."

"So, that is two murders you have committed. Quite a bloodthirsty fellow, are you not, Mr. Cort?"

"I am nothing of the sort," I said. "I specialise in the syndication of international loans."

"So you do. So you do. And you travel widely in pursuit of your business. France, Germany, even Italy. I gather you are competent at the languages of those countries as well."

"Yes."

He smiled. "I'd like you to do me a little favour," he said, changing the subject abruptly. "When you are in Paris next week, I'd be most grateful if you could pick up a package for me. And bring it back. Would you oblige me in that matter?"

"Plans to invade England?" I asked.

"Oh, goodness me, no! We have those already; they're really quite good. No, this is something quite different. This is of no great secrecy or importance, routine correspondence, that is all; I merely want to ensure it gets here swiftly. I planned to get someone else to do it, but, alas, he had a small accident and cannot assist me."

"I'd be happy to assist," I said. "Except that I'm not going to Paris next week. I believe my employers have no plans at all to send me anywhere, at present."

He smiled sweetly. "So kind of you to come and meet me today," he said. "I have greatly enjoyed our little conversation."

I hardly knew what to make of this strange encounter, and was eager to discuss it with my chief, Mr. Hector Samson of Syndication. He, however, although normally very strict about time-keeping, never referred to my absence for so many hours and, when I raised the matter, changed the topic so swiftly I realised he did not even want to know. The only indication I had that my employers were aware of the meeting was a letter dropped on my desk late that afternoon. I was to go to Paris the following Monday to supervise the final details of the flotation of a loan for an American railway company, they of the unsustainable dividends, although naturally such misgivings were not to be communicated to the other participants. That was their problem; all Barings had to do was get rid of the stock as swiftly as possible. Anyway, it was a small matter, already settled, the centre of which was to be in London with only a small participation from one Paris bank. Barings' own correspondents in France could—and regularly did—supervise such matters, and Barings were notoriously tightfisted about extravagances like sending people on journeys. Even I could reason out what had happened.

I filled up much of my time on my recent voyage from Calcutta reading some of those stories of espionage which are so popular these days, which amused me greatly. I sometimes wonder if those few people who suspect my activities believe that I live a life of equal excitement. I am glad to say I do not. All this running around over deserts and feats of daring against sinister foreigners and secret societies makes splendid entertainment, but I do not know anyone of sense who conducts business in such a way. All governments, naturally, can call on people who are more proficient with muscle than with brain in certain circumstances. That's what armies are for. The task of discovering a rival's intentions and capabilities is, by and large, conducted in a more civilised fashion. In general, it is as dangerous and exciting as a busy day on the Baltic Exchange.

Except, that is, for my first venture into the business, which very nearly resulted in my deciding to have nothing to do with Henry Wilkinson. Hang the Empire, was my opinion, if it depends on this sort of thing.

It happened like this: I took the train to Dover as my employers directed, crossed the Channel by steamer to Calais, and arrived at the Gare du Nord at seven in the evening. I then went to my hotel in the rue Notre-Dame des Victoires. Not a grand hotel by any means; the Baring family was far too cautious with its money to allow luxury; it was why many people hankered after a job with the Rothschilds, who had a finer appreciation of their employees' comforts. But it had running water, was clean and was only a short distance from the Bourse: I have stayed in much worse. My business, such as it was, could be dealt with in half an hour the following morning, and so I had the evening to myself. Or to attend to the note that was pushed under my door ten minutes after I arrived. It contained an address, and a time. Nothing more. Fifteen, rue Poulletier. Nine o'clock.

Now, the hero of a spy story would have managed to discover the whereabouts of this address and get there with such ease it might not even be mentioned. I, on the other hand, took some forty-five minutes to acquire a map which even gave the location (shops never close in adventure stories; alas, they shut promptly at seven-thirty in reality) and then another hour to get there. Perhaps there was a tram which might have taken me, but I never discovered it. It was raining—a fine, persistent and depressing drizzle—and all the carriages were occupied. I had no umbrella, so had to walk, my hat getting sodden, my coat turning into blotting paper, into an area of Paris I had never even visited in daylight before.

This was the Ile Saint-Louis, an infested, rat-ridden tangle of criminality and sedition lying at the very heart of the city. It had once been fashionable and well-to-do, but those days had long since passed. Every building was crumbling and neglected, there was no street lighting (and, I guessed, not much progress had been made in installing modern sewage) and it was deathly quiet. The police of Paris never venture onto the island between sundown and sunrise; it becomes an independent country in the dark, answerable to no authority, and anyone who goes there must take full personal responsibility for his fate. Most of the revolutionaries and many of the anarchists and criminals who grace the pages of the popular press with their activities give their address as the Ile Saint-Louis; they inhabit great houses which once echoed to the laughter of the aristocracy and now are cut up into dozens of squalid little rooms for rent by the month, the day or the hour. It is a den of cutthroats and fugitives, perfect for people who need or wish to disappear. The address I was seeking lay right at its heart, past the raddled women standing in the alleyways; past the men with narrow faces and suspicious eyes who watch as you walk by; past the long shadows, and sudden noises of something moving behind you; past the soft laughter that you hear faintly down side alleys.

It was terrifying. I have never in my life been so petrified, and if this disappoints, then I am sorry to disabuse you still further of any notions of heroism. I did not join a banking house to get my head kicked in down some malodorous Parisian alleyway. I was cursing myself and that wretched civil servant for bringing about my presence there. I could have turned on my heel and walked out, the banks of the Seine were scarcely a hundred yards away and there at least was some gas lighting. The bridge to the Ile-de-la-Cité was another few minutes' walk. Even less if you ran in total panic, not caring for your dignity. I did not take this course. Instead, I stopped at every flicker of light coming from an open window and consulted my map, wiping the rain from my eyes, and slowly made my way forward, getting ever closer to my destination, keeping all thoughts of what on earth I might find there at the back of my mind. I have always had a stubborn streak in me; it can be a disadvantage, sometimes.

I could not decide whether I was being manfully determined or childishly stupid. I continued until I reached the door on the left that the curt instructions had mentioned. I gently pushed it with my hand. It was not locked. It was hardly on hinges at all, and was kept in place mainly by its own weight as it dragged on the floor and leaned against the door posts. Knocking seemed a little absurd in the circumstances, so I put my shoulder to it and levered it up and forwards until a gap large enough for me to slip through opened up.

The passage inside it was completely dark, and the musty smell of neglect and damp hung about it. I waited to see if my eyes could make something out but the blackness was so total that this accomplished little. Unlike the well-equipped agent of novels, I had no matches. There was no sound except for the patter of rain outside and the chuckle of the water as it ran down the street. The thing I was most aware of was my feet, which were soaking wet and icy cold. As standing feeling frightened and cold accomplished nothing, I gingerly made my way forwards, arms out like a blind man, and bumped first into a wall this way, then into another that way. Then I caught something brushing against my sleeve as I turned, and realised I had touched a banister. There was a staircase! Carefully, I put my foot on the first step, thinking to go up quietly. That was useless; the wood gave a crack like a gun going off as my full weight came upon it, so I abandoned all notion of discretion and concentrated simply on not falling, feeling my way up, step by step, until I came to a landing. There the stairs ended, and there, on the left, I felt a door. Assuming I was in the right street and the right building (about which I had no confidence whatsoever), I must have arrived at my destination. I listened carefully, but could hear nothing. I knocked; softly at first, then in frustration and annoyance, hammered on the door as loudly as I could.

I heard a low groan after my first knock and the sound of someone falling out of bed after my second, then a muttering. Next a sound like someone being sick, then urinating in a metal pot. The door opened, just a crack at first, then more widely. An oil lamp was held up, its glare preventing me from seeing who was holding it. "Come in, then," I heard. A gruff voice, speaking in a mumbling French I could barely understand.

So in I went.

I had never been in a room so filthy or so rank before, and my first instinct was to turn tail and flee. The occupant saw this reaction on my face but, instead of being offended, found it as funny as one can find anything when one is nursing a violent hangover. He was at least dressed, after a fashion, though not shaved and, I guessed, he had not shaved for days, for the grey stubble on his chin—he was a man past fifty—shone in the rays of thin light that came from the smoking lamp he put down on a rickety table.

He was short, broad and powerfully built, stooped over but with lively eyes that never rested long in one place. A deeply lined face, with a thin scar down his left cheek, which was otherwise blotchy from drink and hard living. But despite his surroundings and his gross inelegance, he had a purposeful air, almost one of confidence. All this was communicated in a few seconds and I cannot say that I realised any of this until much later. At that particular moment, the smell and the dirt was all I noticed.

"I've come from Mr. Wilkinson for a package," I said.

"You're the new boy, are you?" he said with the heavy sigh of the deeply disappointed. He had switched to English after he had examined me carefully with those eyes. I noticed that there was the faintest foreign accent to his voice. Not French, certainly, but his original language was so covered over by time and lack of use it was difficult to ascertain what it might have been. "Do you have something for me?"

"No."

"No piece of paper, no other letter?"

"No. Why?"

"Because how am I meant to believe you really do come from Mr. Wilkinson? You may be working for the French Government, which would not be good for you at all."

He said it in a quiet fashion which was deeply threatening.

"I can offer you no proof whatsoever," I replied. "And I am not sure I would, even were I able to do so."

"What's your name?"

"Cort," I replied. "Henry Cort."

"A curious name; not very English. Dutch? Flemish?"

I bridled a little at that. "I can assure you I am thoroughly English," I said stiffly. "My father's family arrived in England from the Low Countries to escape persecution, but that was nearly two hundred years ago."

"And your father is alive?"

"Yes, although he suffers from persistent ill health. My mother is dead."

I sensed a faint quickening of his interest at this, although there seemed to be nothing behind it. "And your father's occupation?"

"He is an architect when his health permits. Most of the time he is too frail to work."

"I see. And you were born in . . ."

"Eighteen sixty-three."

He leaned back in his chair and stared at the ceiling as he considered this piece of information. Then he leaned forward, grabbed my left arm, and pulled up the sleeve of my jacket. Snorted, then banged his knees with his hands and looked up.

"My apologies for the interrogation, although not for the doubts. Unless you become as suspicious as I am, you will not live long in this game."

"I do not intend to play any game," I replied. "Nor do I see how what I have just said can convince you of my honesty."

He almost smiled at this remark. "You must allow me to preserve my secrets. But Mr. Wilkinson knows what he is doing. He sent no proof of your identity because your very existence is its own proof."

He stood up. "Don't look so puzzled. It's of no significance. Have you done this before?"

I didn't understand a word he was talking about. All I knew was that even the dangers of walking alone across the Ile Saint-Louis would be preferable to staying in that dingy room a moment longer.

"I understand I am meant to collect a letter of some sort. If that is the case, please give it to me and I will be on my way."

He snorted, as though I had just said the most imbecilic thing in the world, then reached under the mattress of his bed. As he did so, I noticed a pistol jutting out from under the dirty grey pillow.

"There you are," he said. "Take it and go. Deliver it to Mr. Wilkinson as swiftly as possible. Do not stop, do not let it out of your possession for a second."

He handed it over, and I looked at it. "But it's not for him," I protested. "It is addressed to a Mr. Robbins. I know of no such man."

He stared at the ceiling, as though invoking the Lord to come and smite him.

"Yes," he said heavily. "How curious. However, fortunately, your job is not to think but to move those little legs of yours in the right direction until you have accomplished your task. If I say it is to be handed to Mr. Wilkinson, then to Mr. Wilkinson it must go. Understand? Now go away."

He turned, and lay down on the bed with a heavy sigh. The interview was at an end.

I glared at him with all the hauteur I could muster, turned and left.

My dignity was as offended by the encounter as was my sense of smell. I marched down the stairs, thankful only to be heading for the open air once more, my mind full of all the cutting remarks I might have made to put the appalling man in his place, and remind him that he was dealing with a gentleman. Not some servant, which I tried, unsuccessfully, to persuade myself was his own station in life.

I walked towards the river and safety, going more swiftly than usual because the sooner I was off that stinking island the happier I would be. My annoyance pushed all thought of danger out of my head as I walked, and my mood lightened with every step I took.

Apart from a heavy blow on the head and the sensation of falling forwards onto the pavement—stone of some sort, I noted, with weeds growing up between the cracks, one with a bedraggled purple flower on it—that was the last thing I recalled for some time. It didn't even hurt, to begin with.

CHAPTER 2

When I woke up again I felt as though my head was splitting; stars danced in my eyes, and I could feel the blood pounding through my temples. I looked around as much as I dared, considering there seemed to be a real possibility that my head might come off entirely. Mainly I saw the ceiling—from which I deduced that I was no longer in the street, but had been picked up by someone and brought into a house. What was I doing there? What had I been doing? I groaned, tried to sit up, then collapsed back again. It was the smell that made me realise where I must be.

Then I remembered. The letter. My hand rushed to my pocket and felt for the reassuring crinkle of paper. Nothing. I tried another pocket, then another, then, just to make sure, went back and tried the first once more. Nothing. It had gone.

"Oh, my God," I said as the realisation hit me. "Oh, no."

"Looking for this?"

I was lying on his bed, which smelled of dog and unwashed man. I turned my head, and saw the man I had met earlier, sitting calmly in a chair with the letter he had given me on his lap. The relief I felt was indescribable.

"Thank you, sir," I said with genuine emotion. "You rescued me from those scoundrels. Who attacked me? Did you see them? Who hit me?"

"I did," he said, still calm as ever.

"What?"

He made no effort to help me out.

"Why did you hit me?"

"To steal this letter."

"But you'd only just given it to me."

"Well noted," he said.

To be attacked in such a manner was bad enough; to be made fun of as well was well-nigh intolerable, and I decided that it was time to give this man a lesson he would not readily forget. I had spent much time at school in boxing, and felt that I could readily overcome the resistance of a man well past his prime. So I began to rise, but found that my legs were unwilling to support me; I waved my fists in his direction and even as he pushed me lazily back on to the bed with a contemptuous look on his face, I realised how utterly ridiculous I must appear.

I slumped back down, my head spinning, and groaned loudly.

"Head between your knees, until you stop feeling sick. I didn't break the skin, you're not bleeding."

Then he waited patiently until I was once more able to lift my head up and look at him.

"Right," he said. "I hit you on the head because I do not wish to die through association with an idiot. Your behaviour was not only juvenile, but also dangerous. Do you have no sense at all? You were utterly unaware I was behind you, even though I went out of my way to give you as much warning as possible. Have you learned nothing? Remembered nothing? Did you ever, even once, look round to check who was behind you? No. You strolled down a dark alley, hands in your pockets like some idiot tourist. I did hit you harder than was necessary, I am sure. I apologise for that. But I was so outraged I felt like hitting you even harder, and you should thank me for my restraint."

If my head was spinning from the blow he had inflicted on me, it was spinning even faster now as I tried to understand what on earth he was talking about.

"I was asked to come to your lodging, sir," I said stiffly, "and collect a letter. That was all. Nobody mentioned anything about playing hide and seek through the streets with a murderous lunatic."

He paused, then looked at me more soberly. "You aren't . . . Oh, my God! Who are you? What are you?"

I told him that I was a banker working for Barings. He snorted, then laughed out loud.

"In that case I owe you an apology," he said, with the air of a man who didn't really think that he owed me anything of the sort. "You must think me a very strange fellow."

"I think I could manage a better description of you than that," I said. "Come with me."

He helped me off the bed, steadied me as I almost fell over again, then guided me to the door and down the stairs.

He took me to some sort of bar. It was nearly ten o'clock. He led me over to a table in a dark corner, got me to sit, then called for brandy. I was not used, at that stage, to drinking brandy but he insisted, and after a very short while I found that my head stopped hurting, and my speech became voluble.

"So," he began once more, "I apologise. And owe you an explanation. I was under the impression that you knew what you were about. What Mr. Wilkinson is thinking of, sending me someone so unprepared, is quite beyond me. He knows how I . . ."

His trail of thought came to an end as he drank his brandy down in one go, and called for another. The place we were in was the sort of establishment I would never dream of entering, or would not have done then. I imagined that every single person in it—all were men—was some sort of cutthroat, pimp or robber. I later learned that this assessment was entirely correct.

He grunted. "My name is Jules Lefevre . . . in fact, that is not my name, but no matter. It will do. I provide certain information to His Majesty's Government which it otherwise might find difficult to obtain."

"You are French?" I asked.

"Perhaps. Now, it is important that the information I provide reaches its destination. It is also important that it does not fall into the wrong hands, it being of a confidential nature. Do you understand?"

"I believe so," I said.

"In which case, it is important that those people carrying these letters know how to keep them. You agree that this is important."

"Absolutely," I said.

"Good. So that is what Wilkinson has asked me to do with you. Teach you to look after yourself."

"Are you sure?"

"He said he was sending someone to me to finish his training, and he would identify himself by coming to ask for a package. That seems like you."

"I know, but no one has ever mentioned anything of this to me. I feel I should have been consulted . . ." I could tell I was sounding more petulant with every word I uttered, and decided to keep quiet. You could say that my future was decided solely by a desire not to appear silly to a man I scarcely knew.

"Well, you weren't. I suppose there was a good reason. Now, what I did to you just now could have been done by anyone. And your lack of attention could have had severe consequences. The only good thing to come out of it would be that you would be dead and unable to mess anything else up."

My head was still spinning, and still hurt foully, even though the brandy had steadied it a little. In compensation, my empty stomach was also beginning to add its protest at being subjected to the brandy. Lefevre was eyeing me curiously.

"You don't know what this is all about?"

"No."

His eyes narrowed, as he considered the meaning of it. Then he shook his head. "No point trying to fathom the ways of the great and the good. That's his decision and I suppose I must live with it. It seems you are to be my apprentice, so we might as well get started. Be at the Gare de l'Est tomorrow morning at eight. I will meet you in the buffet. You will not recognise me or greet me in any way. But when I move, you follow me. Do you understand?"

"I understand, but I'm not sure I agree," I replied. "What do you mean, your apprentice? And what's this about getting started? Started on what?"

"Learning how to stay alive, of course."

"I was managing quite well until I met you. And what if I don't want to be your apprentice?"

"Then you don't come. You go back to your life in the bank, and fill in ledgers for the rest of your life, or whatever you do. I don't care one way or the other. Wilkinson seems to have chosen you. Take it up with him. But don't ask any more explanation of me, because I can't give it."

He stood up. "Make up your mind by tomorrow morning. Come, or don't come."

"Just a minute," I said, a little tartly.

He looked back at me.

"What about this wretched letter?" I pointed to the envelope on the table that had given me so much grief. "You can hardly criticise me for carelessness if you are so forgetful yourself."

He looked, then shrugged. "It's only an old newspaper," he said. "It's not important. You don't think anyone's going to trust you with something important, do you?"

And he walked out, leaving me behind in that den of iniquity, which, now his protection was withdrawn, suddenly began to seem very frightening.

As discreetly as possible—which was not at all—I left as well, feeling dozens of eyes on me as I headed for the door, and the hushing of the chatter as conversations paused so people could look at me. I felt a hot flush spreading up the back of my neck, and it was all I could do to avoid bolting out of that place as fast as my legs would carry me. Pride can be a useful thing. I believe I completely hid my discomfort and my mounting fear, although the experience of the evening made me feel violently sick and my legs were still wobbling from the assault.

The night air, touched with sweet smell of sewage though it was, refreshed me considerably and, once I had leaned against a wall awhile, I began to feel much improved. It was almost midnight now and eerily quiet for the centre of a major city. I was some way from my hotel and with no alternative but to walk there. My head ached, I was starving from lack of food and felt thoroughly wretched. I was also afraid that awful man would attack me once again, so I could not even concentrate on my sense of having been ill used as I made my way to the bridge to cross over back into civilisation.

CHAPTER 3

It goes without saying that I got no sleep that night, even when I did manage to get back to my hotel. It was already two by then and I realised I would have to be up again early if I was to make my appointment for eight o'clock. It still had not occurred to me to miss it; my anxiety concentrated entirely on not being late, on not making myself out to be a fool once more. The turmoil of the evening and the fear of oversleeping did not drive away my weariness, merely the possibility of doing anything about it, and at six o'clock I found myself tiptoeing down the stairs once more and out into what would eventually be the dawn of a new day.

I took an omnibus to my destination; a sign on the front said it was going to the Gare de l'Est and I believed it, so at least I managed a short slumber in the twenty-five minutes it took to get there. This happy chance, however, meant that I arrived an hour early, and there was nothing to do except tramp the streets to try and keep warm, and sit next to the brazier in the empty waiting room as I grew more and more aware of how empty my stomach was. I was cold, hungry, bored and perplexed all at the same time and still I did not query what I was doing. Not once did I shake myself awake and consider heading straight for the bank and a normal day's work.

I did not follow instructions completely though; rather than waiting in the railway buffet, I positioned myself in a discreet place outside, as I somehow felt it would be subservient to be there first. I wished Lefevre to arrive and worry that I was not going to come, that he had failed to sway me. Then I would go in and greet him.

Alas, he did not turn up either. Slowly more people were filling the station, from trains arriving and for others leaving. I watched every single person who went into the buffet, and as there was only one entrance there was no chance of missing anyone. I was feeling ill. For the first time the full absurdity of the situation swept over me. I was working in a bank, for heaven's sake. What on earth was I doing here? I would have some coffee and some bread, then resume a normal life. Enough of this nonsense. It was going to be hard enough already to explain myself.

I stood at the counter waiting, next to a gentleman similarly consuming a rapid cup of coffee. We ignored each other, as total strangers do, until he had finished and paid.

"Come along then," he said abruptly. "Or we'll miss the train. Do you have any luggage?"

I turned to stare at him. A well-dressed man, wearing an expensive cravat and shiny top hat, immaculately brushed shoes, and a heavy grey overcoat. He bowed his head slightly in greeting as I looked. Handsome, clean shaven, about fifty years of age but with an air of strength about him. And a thin scar on his cheek. Despite his years, no one would ever consider him to be old. A faint air of eau-de-cologne hung around him as it does those who spend time and money on their appearance.

"Do you mean to say you didn't recognise me?"

It was Lefevre, now as elegant as he was scruffy before, as well manicured as he had been unshaven, as bourgeois as he had been plebeian. Only the eyes, pale and questing, and the scar seemed to remain from the person I had encountered the previous evening.

I shook my head. "Oh, my Lord," he said quietly. "This is going to be hard work."

And without any further comment, he turned and walked out onto the station forecourt. I followed, as I supposed I was meant to, getting angrier by the minute. I walked up behind him and grabbed him by the arm. He shook it off and murmured, "Not here, you idiot!" and continued walking onto platform 3, where a train stood, hissing away. Twirling his cane in a nonchalant fashion, he walked up to the first-class carriages and got in. I followed him into an empty compartment and waited while he went out to discuss his baggage with a porter. Then he came back in, shut the door, pulled down the blinds and sat opposite me.

"Don't be so angry," he said, reverting to English. "You look as though you are about to explode."

"For two pins I would get straight off this train and go to work," I said. "You are behaving in a most uncivil fashion and . . . and . . ." I knew how childish I sounded even before I had got a few words out.

"So have a good cry," Lefevre said, equably but unsympathetically. "I'm no more happy about your presence than you are, I assure you. But it seems that we must work together."

"Doing what, for heaven's sake?" I cried. "Just tell me what I am doing here, and why?"

"Do keep your voice down, please," he said wearily.

There was a sudden bustle on the station, and whistles. The train gave a shudder and, in a cloud of steam and with an abominable squeaking, it lurched forward a few inches, then a few inches more. We were under way—although where to I did not know.

Lefevre ignored me as the train drew out of the dingy, smoky station and into the light of morning. "I love trains," he said. "I always feel safe on them. I've never understood people who find them frightening or dangerous."

He fell silent, watching the streets of Paris pass slowly by until we came to the outlying fortifications and into the countryside beyond. Then he gave a slight sigh, and turned his attention to me.

"You are feeling indignant and angry, is that it?"

I nodded. "Wouldn't you be, in my situation?"

"No. At your age I had been fighting in a war for nearly two years. However, as you want all of these unpleasant emotions dissipated, and I need you to be calm and able to concentrate for the next few weeks—"

"The next few *weeks*?" I interrupted in what I fear was a squeak of alarm.

"Do try and keep quiet for a while," he said. "I will explain as best I can. Then you must decide on your course of action. When we arrive at our destination you can choose either to get on the next train back to Paris, or you can stay with me. Mr. Wilkinson evidently desires that you choose the latter option. From your performance so far I would prefer the former.

"To begin at the beginning. You have been chosen for special qualities which have not yet manifested themselves to me to become what used to be called an intelligencer, and is now rather vulgarly called a spy. Britain is alone in the world, much envied and resented for her wealth and the vastness of her Empire. Many wish to tear her down. She must be self-reliant and can count no one as her friend. She must be aware of everything, and able to sow discord amongst her enemies. That, in brief, is to be your job."

I stared at him. Surely this was some sort of bad joke?

"Silence, at last," he continued. "You are learning. If Mr. Wilkinson decides the national interest is best served by continental peace, you will endeavour—in your small but allotted way—to accomplish it. If he suddenly changes his mind and decides a war is necessary, you will try to set neighbour against neighbour. And above all you will try to discover who is thinking what and when."

"Me?"

"Good question. A very good question. You are, obviously, unsuited. But perhaps you have some qualities that might make you useful."

"And those are?"

"Money."

"I beg your pardon?"

"Money," he said wearily, looking out of the window as though he was seeing a golden age going by. "All the world is now convertible to money. Power, influence, peace and war. It used to be that the sole determinant was the number of men you could march out to meet your enemies. Now more depends on the convertibility of your currency, its reputation among the bankers. That is something I do not know and you do."

He smiled, but it was not a happy smile. "The world changed, in America, some thirty years ago. I suppose we should have seen it coming, but we did not. It was not won or lost by bravery, or skill or numbers of men, but by factories and gold. It was a war of industry against farmers, companies against cavaliers. The losers had fewer resources, less ability to produce the material of war. And those we thought our friends abandoned us for the sake of trade with the richer side."

"We?"

He ignored the question. "And what was pioneered there will be even more strongly seen here, next time."

"You think there will be a war here?"

"I am sure of it. There must be. Because you think that it will be as before and so will not care to prevent it. It will not be armies fighting next time, but economies. Vaults of gold in perpetual contest until all are exhausted. The countries of Europe will fight until they cannot afford to fight anymore."

"I think many in the City already worry about that."

"But they will be outnumbered by those who will make money from the business. The Vickers, the Krupps and the Schneiders. Men like John Stone and his weaponry. The bankers who provide the money for them, the investors who get their 15 per cent dividends. War and peace will be decided by the movement of capital."

"And how does this involve me?"

"You understand that world; I do not. I do not want to."

"You say 'our' and 'we' and refer to two different countries."

He nodded. "I am a man without a country. Not French, not British, not even American, although once I was. I work for hire and give good service."

I considered this. I was not sure I liked this man who called himself Lefevre, and I certainly did not trust him, but he had a presence which could not be lightly ignored. He could command, and it was comfortable to follow him. But I was very far from certain it was wise.

"And if someone offered more?"

"Then I would consider the offer. Men without homes must look after themselves, for they cannot surrender to the comforts of patriotism. I did that once, and will not repeat the mistake. But I am no mercenary. Part of good service is loyalty. And my masters—your masters as well, it now seems—pay me."

I leaned back in my seat and, like him, watched the landscape outside the window pass by. The train was going fast now, and the city had long since been left behind. We were in the open countryside, heading east—to Metz, so the sign in the station had said.

But if Lefevre saw worlds disappearing, I perceived a different analogy as I headed unstoppingly into the unknown. Why had I so easily acquiesced in his instructions? It was simple; I was bored, and wanted diversion. I even was prepared to risk dismissal from a job which I found wearisome. Had I really been placed on this earth to arrange discounts for South American railway lines? Was my mark on humanity to be the $3\frac{1}{8}$ per cent coupon on Leeds Water Works debenture stock? I had never dreamed of excitement as a young boy; unlike my comrades, my imagination was not full of dreams of marching at the head of (utterly devoted) men into a dangerous battle, emerging victorious through my courage and skill. But I had dreamed of something, and it is the more difficult to put aside dreams which are unformed, for they can never be exposed as mere childishness.

Lefevre, in his squalid accommodation, with his ease amongst the rascals and rogues, his metamorphosis into a gentleman seemingly at will, touched a chord in me. Do not misunderstand. I was not a reckless man, and never have been. No one, I believe, brought up in the particular circumstances of my family would ever be so foolish as to take risks unnecessarily. I knew, and from an early age, how fragile is the net which prevents the respectable from falling into the abyss. The onset of illness, a misfortune in the markets, an unfortunate accident, a foolish mistake, and all can unravel. Even though my employers paid me well enough I never spent money wildly, and nurtured my pile with care and caution. I could easily foresee a time when it might be needed.

I was, accordingly, all the more fascinated by a man like Lefevre who, whatever his natural desire to stay alive, clearly approached life in a very different fashion. Not for him the caution of respectability, the fear of poverty or the desire for comfort. He was like a member of a different species, although whether superior or inferior to mine I could not tell. My sensible self told me that my way was the more responsible, that I was fitted for the age and environment in which I lived. But part of me was drawn to the irresponsibility, the recklessness of Lefevre's way. It was a contradiction in my being and, it seemed, one which Henry Wilkinson had both spotted and decided to exploit. A man more comfortable with his choices would never have been on that train.

An odd thing, memory. I remember almost every moment of that interminable train ride—the flat countryside, the stops to pick up and set down passengers, the fields of vines and crops passing by, the smell of the carriage, the lunch in the dining car, the reluctant conversation. What followed thereafter can only be recalled with an effort. It is not that I have forgotten, but that I think of it in abstract, while my memory of the journey takes me back to that carriage as if I was still there.

And yet what passed after we left the train was far more interesting, in the usual way of reckoning. Lefevre—I will continue to call him so until a more appropriate moment—began to teach me the business of self-preservation in a far more real sense. And if I never mastered all his skills, it was because never in my wildest dreams and nightmares did I ever imagine I might need them. He took me to Nancy, then a frontier town very much closer to the German border than it wished to be. Also, as he said, a good starting point for all that we had to do.

The frontier was not that closely guarded, but the area on both sides of the border was stiff with soldiers, as it was generally anticipated that the next round of the eternal conflict between France and Germany would begin there. But when? How? Would it be a considered policy, decided on high by one side or the other, or would it be an accident, a few words spoken in haste, a riposte, fisticuffs, a few shots—and then whole armies on the march, the generals and politicians trailing behind, desperately trying to control a situation that had run on before them.

"People make the mistake of assuming far too many things about armies," Lefevre told me one evening. "They assume, for a start, that generals know what they are doing and know what is going on. They assume that orders pass down from top to bottom in a smooth and regulated fashion. And above all they assume that wars start only when people decide to start them."

"You are going to tell me that is not the case?"

"Wars begin when they are ready, when humanity needs a bloodletting. Kings and politicians and generals have little say in it. You can feel it in the air when one is brewing. There is a tension and nervousness on the face of the least soldier. They can smell it coming in a way politicians cannot. The desire to hurt and destroy spreads over a region and over the troops. And then the generals can only hope to have the vaguest notion of what they are doing."

"So what is the point of all this intelligencing?"

"To most people—those who even admit a man like myself exists—I am as you saw me the other night in Paris. Little better than a crook, a thief and maybe worse. In fact, very much worse. You are invited to become scum, the loathed of society. Only by disguising what you are will you maintain a respectable place in society. But you will also probe your way into the soul of this terrible continent. Think of the doctor. You do not go along to him and say, I am going to die next Tuesday, and hope he can do something about it. No; you present yourself, feeling a touch off-colour. And he looks at you, checks your heartbeat, takes your blood pressure, asks questions about your sleeping and your appetite. Do you have trouble climbing stairs? Are you eating? Having headaches? And from these fragments of individually meaningless information, he pieces together his conclusion: you have a heart condition. It may not stop you from dying next Tuesday, but it is some comfort to know.

"And that is your—our—job. Do not think you will ever come across a memorandum saying 'We invade next week.' What you get is a sense of nerves in the barracks, a feeling that something is happening, for soldiers are the most sensitive people on earth to a change in atmosphere. Then perhaps you notice trains being cancelled. Perhaps more smugglers get caught slipping over borders. You hear of more fights in bars in garrison towns. Of leave being cancelled. And you put it all together and conclude that someone, somewhere is about to throw the dice."

"And this is your idea, or can you demonstrate this to me?"

"Oh, I can demonstrate it. In big wars and little ones. Although I imagine you would prefer to finish your drink and have a good night's sleep before you hear me on the origins of the last war between France and the Germans. But I was there, I saw it all. And the next time will be little different."

"But in that case, I believe, the Emperor decided to go to war and everyone backed him."

"True. But why did he decide? Why then? Especially as a limited amount of study would have demonstrated that the Prussians would roll all over them. Because it was in the air. It was necessary. The gods had decreed it."

He drank down his brandy in one go and nodded ironically. "A marionette, as are we all. Your job is to report the doings of puppets to other puppets. A worthy and useful employment.

"For which you need a good night's sleep. I am going to make your life miserable tomorrow. So don't stay up writing your diary. You don't write a diary, do you?"

"No."

"That's a blessing."

CHAPTER 4

His loquacity and virtual good humour did not last long, alas. The next day began what I consider to be one of the most miserable, and extraordinary, six weeks of my life. He woke me at dawn and announced that my task for the day was to get bread from a town some five miles into the occupied part of Alsace. However, I was to accomplish this without any papers to give me free passage over the border, without any money and without any maps. Then I was told to steal the bust of Marianne from the town hall in the next city. Then to spend two nights in complete hiding, counting the number of people who crossed the border. Then to leave a package on a bridge crossing the Rhine, high up in the girders of the ironwork. Then to retrieve a file of papers from a bank, detailing the accounts of a man whose name he gave me. And we did it again, and again, and again. How to follow a man so he does not know you are there.

How to lose a man who is following you; we chased each other around different towns for days until I became almost as good at it as he was. Then he would set me to trailing an army officer selected more or less at random. Then again, with a German officer over the border. Then to burgling his house. In between these bizarre activities, he would take me into the forests with a gun, and teach me how to shoot. This was something I never became proficient at, nor ever enjoyed. I would rather be captured by an enemy than have that noise going off in my ears. Or we would spend an evening in a soldiers' bar, buying drinks and listening to their complaints and bravado. Or he would show me how to persuade someone to become an informer; a traitor to their friends and country.

This last was, in many ways, the most terrible of all the skills he made me learn. To my surprise, I was surprisingly good at them. Although I had never before considered myself a natural criminal, it appeared that I had an aptitude in that direction. Robbing a bank or town hall was not really that different from the one-boy raids I had launched at school, and I had learned young that immense walks in the far more rugged terrain in Wales or northern England—a hundred miles or more, spread over several days, camping out at night where I could—was an effective salve for the troubles of adolescence. I discovered later that the all-seeing Mr. Wilkinson knew of these activities of mine—he knew my old headmaster well—and added them all into his calculations. Schoolboy criminality, evidently, was a better qualification for his esteem than the more normal virtues associated with the civil servant.

All, bar shooting, I could do, and do well. But the evening with Virginie was different entirely. It was where Lefevre and I began to part company, and I started thinking for myself about this task which others wanted me to perform.

She was a seamstress, so Lefevre told me, of the sort that abound in the thousands throughout eastern France, eking out a small living with their hands, permanently in danger of hunger, and willing to trade all they possess for a little security. Those who are lucky find a companion, a bourgeois student perhaps, and set up house. The foolish dream of marriage, the more practical realise the liaison will be of short duration, and that eventually the respectable world will reclaim their protector. Most will then be left to fend for themselves once more, unless their former lovers can be persuaded to pay for any children that might have been produced.

Others are less fortunate and drift into a life of whoring, and the huge numbers of soldiers along the border provide ample business. Their lives are brutal and often short. It is remarkable how many remain human nonetheless; the spark of humanity is not so easily extinguished, even when there is often little to sustain it. The woman Lefevre took me to was one such. She was probably an illegitimate child who would one day generate more such as she was. She found herself in Nancy and was inevitably turning to soldiers for protection.

But she was still young and new and fresh, as the saying goes, and had ambitions above mere survival. Life burned in her and would not be easily quenched. The clarity of her vision was remarkable: she had a sophistication of thought far beyond her sex, or station or age. Listen:

"Do not think I do not understand what I am doing. I could become a flower girl, or a shop worker or labour in a factory. I might find some drunken soldier who would beat me and leave me. Or be forced to live with a man far more stupid than I am and defer to his obtuseness in exchange for security. What I do now may not prevail. I might sink to the bottom, and live out my days wheedling ever more disgusting men for a few sous. 'Hello, dearie, want a good time?' I've seen it all. It is one future that may become mine.

"But only one, and it is not inevitable, whatever the moralists tend to think and hope. I might do better. I am prepared to gamble, and if it does not work, then I will at least end my days in the gutter knowing that I have tried."

Lefevre made her a proposition. In exchange for any information she might provide, he would offer payment. Gold for betrayal; the most essential of human transactions, but he attempted to disguise it by subtle words and careful phrasing. She saw through them all immediately.

"What sort of information do you have in mind? We are in a border town full of troops. I imagine that is the sort of information you require."

"Café gossip, tales of troop movements, training. Who is up and who is down in the army."

She pursed her lips. Very well-formed lips, wide and curving, touched up by only the faintest art. "That is all very well, I imagine, but hardly vital. What country do you come from? Or work for? I will not spy for the Germans."

"We do not work for the Germans," he replied.

"Probably the English, then. Or the Russians." She considered. "I think I could manage that. Depending on the price, of course. But I think you set your sights too low."

"How is that?"

"The whole of the general staff is here. Would it not be better to have information from that quarter, rather than café chit-chat?"

Lefevre did not reply.

"You have made me a proposition, Monsieur. I will make you one. I do not want to spend my life in the company of soldiers. But to present myself to better society I need clothes, jewels, somewhere better to live."

She stopped, for what she had in mind was clear enough.

"And how much would you suggest?" Lefevre said dryly.

"About a thousand francs."

He laughed, then shook his head. "I think not, my girl. I do not have such sums at my disposal and if I gave it to you I doubt I would ever see it again. You'd be on the next train out with a different name. Do you take me for an idiot?"

I abbreviate, and my memory does not recall the exact words, but that was the essence of the conversation. It was illuminating; I considered that Lefevre had made a mistake, and that I had seen one of his limitations. He did not think broadly and was cautious in his judgement. Perhaps he was right; experience had taught him that neither men nor women were to be trusted. But I believed I had seen something he either had not glimpsed or wished to disregard.

The girl was clever. I do not mean sly, or cunning, although life had taught her much of that when it was needed. But intelligent. She saw a chance for herself. She did not, I noted, threaten—did not say she would go to the authorities and report us, which was just as well for her. She judged the situation clearly.

And even in her situation—which was poor and could easily have been squalid—she somehow rose above circumstance. She dressed well considering the quality of her clothes; she sat and talked properly. There was an animation in her eyes and expression which made one forget that she was neither particularly beautiful nor favoured in life. Even Lefevre did not address her too roughly or rudely. She had character, in sum, and I believed it was a pity to waste it.

You note I talk here entirely without reference to morality. Let me rephrase it; we were talking to a whore about how to be better at her trade and I was considering seriously that we should act in some way as her pimps. Express it in such a way and it is shocking; I was already a long way from home. Yet I did not see how her life could be made worse, or her soul even more imperilled, by the course she wished to pursue. And there might be gain all round. I put my argument to Lefevre afterwards.

He dismissed it. "A thousand francs? For a girl who charges two francs a night? Are you serious?"

"How long are we staying here?"

"Until we're finished."

I scowled. "Tell me."

"Why?"

"Because I would like to talk to that girl again."

He shook his head. "No. I forbid it."

I found her again the following evening, walking across the Place Stanislas. Even from a distance I could see the effect she had: men walking towards her would slow down as they passed; some nodded, uncertain whether she was signalling to them. Poor as she was, she was so far above the normal that there was doubt. She was not brazen or vulgar; she attracted through an appearance of vulnerability and delicacy. I briefly considered the fate that lay before her, how that delicacy would be trampled and ruined, and shuddered slightly. I had seen in her eyes the day before that she knew exactly how her future could develop.

A man began talking to her as I approached; I bristled somewhat at the indignity, and so hailed her in a louder voice than I might otherwise have used.

"Good evening, Madame, I am so sorry to have kept you waiting."

The effect was delightful; he froze with horror at the evident mistake he had just made, gave me one brief look and ran as fast as he could. Virginie looked at me coldly.

"You will have to pay for that," she said.

"I intend to. Have you eaten this evening?" It was nearly eight o'clock by then and already dark and cold.

She hadn't, so I took her to a restaurant. A moderately expensive one, deliberately chosen, as I wished to see how she would conduct herself, how much she knew about manners.

Although by far the worst-dressed woman in the place, she did not allow herself to be abashed by her obvious poverty. She behaved to the waiters with proper grace, did not allow her voice to rise as the alcohol seeped into her blood, chose her food cautiously but well, ate with delicacy. And the waiters responded; she did not flirt with them, but she made herself attractive in a distant, untouchable fashion. She got better service than I did; by the end of the meal she was getting more attention from them than anyone else in the dining room.

We were halfway through the first course when I realised I had quite forgotten who and what she was, and brusquely brought myself back to earth. "I must ask you for some information," I said. "I'm afraid I do not understand you at all, and that could be a grave impediment to any business arrangements between us."

She looked at me evenly, not perplexed, as she was already far beyond that stage. At no point so far had she asked me any questions at all, which was a good sign.

"I have been thinking about what you said yesterday," I continued. "My associate"—we had not given her any names—"is not interested in your proposal, but I see some possibilities."

Much later she told me how excited she had been by this remark; so overwhelmed that she did not know how she had prevented herself from bursting into tears. All I can say to that is that her self-control was remarkable; not a flicker of any emotion passed over her face. Had I known how well disciplined she was, I would have engaged her on the spot.

"But I need some answers from you."

"What exactly?"

"I need to know whether you will be capable of filling the role you desire for yourself. A gentle nature and pretty face will not be sufficient. You need also to be . . ."

I paused, not knowing how to phrase it.

"Good in bed?" she asked quietly.

I almost spilled my drink. "No. Absolutely not. Well, yes, of course. What I was going to say was possess a degree of breeding. An ability to manage in different social situations. To be someone who could be relied on not to make a fool of themselves. Who can elicit information discreetly, without anyone suspecting them. Basically, do the job without being exposed in any way."

She nodded.

"So far, you have behaved impeccably. Which I find extraordinary in a runaway mill girl or whatever you are."

"Were I a runaway mill girl, then you would be right," she said with a smile.

"I understood . . ."

"That is what your friend assumed, and I did not see why I should tell him my life story. It was hardly his business."

"So your story is . . . ?"

"Not one that I wish to tell you."

I frowned.

"There is no need to look like that. Just take it that I have good reasons for being what I am. As for the rest, you have seen how I stand and walk and converse and eat and drink. Have you found any fault?"

"Absolutely none."

"Do you find me grotesque, unlikely to attract the sort of men I would need to find?"

"No."

"Do you wish to discover for yourself how good I am?"

I stared, somewhat horrified, at her.

"Come along, sir. We are talking business here. I intend to go into trade selling something, with you as an investor, so to speak. It is surely wise to ensure that the goods are of high quality."

I was covered in embarrassment at this, at her calm as much as at her proposal. "I really don't think that is necessary," I muttered.

"You find me unattractive?"

"Certainly not!"

She smiled faintly. "I see. You consider yourself a gentleman."

"No," I replied. "That is becoming ever more difficult to credit. But I prefer to consider you a lady."

The smile vanished. She looked down at the table and said nothing for a while, then looked me straight in the eye. "I will remember that."

There was a long, awkward pause between us, then I coughed and tried to restart the conversation. I realised only faintly that she was now in command; the willingness to shock and surprise, the delicate display of emotion, the hint of secrecy had all so foxed me that I had allowed her to take control.

"My—ah—investment. How do you intend to spend it?"

She was as relieved as I to return to more neutral territory. "All on clothes, with a little left over for perfume. Jewellery I can rent once I have the clothes to pass as a lady. The bourgeoisie are credit-worthy."

"I know little about women's clothes, but I doubt they are less expensive in France than in London. I doubt you will get much for a thousand francs. I would hate to see the venture fail for lack of capital."

"So give me more."

"I think five thousand will be a more realistic sum," I continued. "I will arrange the money tomorrow."

"You have that much money to give away?"

"Good Lord, no! It's not my money. It's the bank's."

"The bank's?"

"A long story. But I have discretion to make some payments which do not need to be directly accounted for straightaway. And I am not giving it away. However, I will need a strict schedule of payments, otherwise questions will be asked. You will be of service to many people, but the connection must be kept discreet. I should be able to lose you in the accounts."

"And if I take the money and disappear?"

"You will not."

"How do you know?"

"Because it is your chance. The only one you will ever get and you know it. And because one day you might accidentally bump into my friend once more."

"How long are you staying here?"

"I don't know. Another few days."

"And where might I find you after that?"

I gave her the address of a corresponding bank in Paris. "You will send letters there, and I will see to the rest."

"Then there is nothing else to discuss. I will collect your money, and spend it. You will have to hope I am as honest as you believe." She stood up, and gathered her thin scarf. "I am, you know, when I can be."

I escorted her out into the cold of the night, and she slipped off into the darkness.

Lefevre was so furious with me on so many counts it is difficult to remember which loomed largest in his mind, but all his objections stemmed from his anger that I had gone against his wishes. I was there merely to learn from him, not to act independently. He raged at me for an hour, and the extent of his fury taught me much. He was a violent man, full of anger at the world, and he allowed it to cloud his judgement. He also had no understanding of people, I decided. He considered no one trustworthy, so did not try. They were to be threatened or frightened into compliance with his wishes; his methods had no greater subtlety.

To all of this I had one answer. I was not aware I was his employee, and I did not see why I should necessarily follow his orders in anything. I had not risked his money, or even Government money, but taken the risk upon myself. This was not entirely true, of course, but it sounded better. I would act as broker between the woman and the Government. If she came up with any useful information, I would sell it on, and use the money to pay off the debt. If she were caught, or proved less trustworthy than I anticipated, then no one would be able to trace it to Her Majesty's Government. Better still, I would arrange for all moneys to be paid out of the Bank of Bremen's office in Paris, so that, should suspicion fall on anyone, it would be assumed the Germans were her masters. I was rather proud of that.

He was not mollified. In fact, the realisation that I had thought the matter through made him angrier still. "You're weak, and stupid," he screamed at me, then his voice fell. "Like father, like son," he hissed.

"What does that mean?"

"Your father's a weakling, always was. Couldn't look after himself, couldn't look after you . . ."

"He's ill."

"Weak in the head. I know all about your father. Picking flowers, that's all he's ever been good for."

I hit him. It was in better circumstances than the last time I'd tried, and I didn't even have to think about it; I just lashed out and my fist smashed into his face. With most people that would have been enough, but not with Lefevre. He was much tougher than most people. I had hurt him, but not enough to stop him. He took a step back, then came at me like a steam engine, grappling with me and knocking me against the chest of drawers in the hotel room. But if he had strength and years of bitterness on his side, I had agility and weeks of bubbling resentment on mine. I twisted, rammed his head against the wall and rolled across the floor. He hurled himself on me and began pounding at my face with his fists, while I instinctively kneed him in the stomach. The mirror fell off the wall and smashed onto the floor when he hurled me bodily across the room; the bed collapsed when we fell on it, my arm tight around his throat.

He won. He simply had more stamina, could take more punishment than I could. He left me, barely conscious, gasping for breath on the floor, standing over me but also only just able to keep upright, the blood pouring from his nose. Then he kneeled down, and held a knife to my throat for a few seconds before stumbling out of the room.

"If I ever set eyes on you again, I will kill you, do you understand?"

I had no doubts that he meant it.

I did not see him again, not that night nor the next day. He simply vanished, leaving no note behind him, leaving me to pay the hotel bill and explain the destruction in the bedroom. In retrospect I accept that I was wrong. His life was more at risk than mine should anything go badly, and he had spent much of the last quarter century exercising caution and surviving. If he trusted no one it was not simply because of a fundamental ill-will in his nature, it was from bitter experience. And he was getting old; I reminded him of his failing powers, and how different his life had been from his earlier, more optimistic expectations. Had he been less closed, less distrustful, we might have established a useful cooperation based on mutual respect, if not warmth.

But then I was less understanding. We were now enemies on the same side and I was merely glad to see the back of him. His treatment of me in the previous few weeks had been monstrous, and contemptuous. He had cruelly and unnecessarily exposed me to all manner of hardships and even danger, had dismissed my successes and laughed at my failures, had been insulting in every way he could imagine, and I hated him more deeply than any man I had ever known before.

I refused to accept, even to consider, that he had been a very good teacher indeed.

CHAPTER 5

My investment was a success; over the next few months Virginie sent a steady stream of information—some useful, some not—which demonstrated that I had judged rightly. It reinforced my views of Lefevre and of myself. The system I had was this: each missive was forwarded from the Bank of Bremen to Barings, and so on to me. I read it, then passed it to

Mr. Wilkinson, who bought those he considered useful—generally no more than a few hundred francs at a time, but on one occasion mounting up to a thousand. Small sums for a government, but large for a woman making her way on the borders of a foreign country. This money I paid into the account I had opened at a third bank to work off the opening deficit and cover interest payments back to Barings. Of such small details is the world of espionage truly composed. I had no direct communications with her except when the debt was finally discharged.

But I did read her letters. In all she showed great intelligence and skill. She had an instinctive understanding of what was required, and expressed herself with dispatch. Judging by the quality of the information, I could guess that her plan to improve her standing in the world was going well. After a month, information began to come in that was supplied by a major in the cavalry, talking about exercises, and new formations that were being practised. Then came details of a new cannon, supplied by a lieutenant colonel in the artillery. And finally she achieved her goal—a whole stream of information supplied by an infatuated general of the Army of the East who had little else to do, as there was no intention of asking the army to do anything. In meticulous detail, she confirmed other evidence that France was currently determined to avoid war with Germany because of its pressing rivalry with England and a fear that it was nowhere near strong enough yet to renew the fight.

This sort of stuff was the substance of her correspondence; of far more interest, in many ways, was the human detail she added to her narrative. She could have been the Jane Austen of France, had her life developed differently. She had an instinctive understanding of the human dramas she witnessed. The rivalry of one officer with another; the ambitions of a third; the causes of another's vulgar behaviour. Money worries, thwarted desires for promotion, political aspirations. She saw and chronicled all and her little word sketches stayed with me—perhaps too much—when I later met many of the people who paraded through her letters. General Mercier, though one of the highest-ranking men in the military and a national force in politics, I could never see without remembering her description of him trying to get into his truss every morning. Dollfus the businessman's drive for wealth came (she believed) from the imperatives of a hypochondriac wife whose presence he abhorred. Some dreamed of an aristocratic wife, others had vices so hideous that they were horribly, and potentially profitably, exposed to the threat of blackmail.

Virginie saw it all, and condemned none of it. She sketched out an entire society and passed on such a vivid impression that I read her letters not only for the information they contained but also for pure enjoyment. I later learned that Mr. Wilkinson did the same, and made sure they were preserved in their entirety. Where they are now is a mystery, but the Foreign Office throws away nothing. It gives me some comfort to think that, somewhere in the bowels of that grim building, they survive, waiting to be discovered and read anew.

They came to an end after a little over nine months. I was ordered to ensure that she continued in service, but did not. Our arrangement had been honourable on both sides, and I wished it to remain so. Accordingly, I wrote to her on bank letter paper to the effect that her debt was now cancelled, the full sum of the loan having been paid off with interest, and enquiring as to her future intentions. Naturally, the bank would welcome the continued patronage of such a reliable customer.

The reply thanked the bank for its consideration, and said that, after mature reflection, she had decided to close her account. Her finances were now robust, and she no longer needed a loan facility of such a nature. Nonetheless, she remained grateful for its intervention and was pleased that the association had been so mutually profitable.

After that, I never heard from Virginie again.

That was the more cheerful side of my return to London; the less positive aspect was that I was in high disfavour with my employers, who were mightily annoyed at my disappearance. Lending me out for a few days was one thing; having me vanish for the better part of six weeks was quite another, and they saw no reason why they should pay for it. My stock had fallen so far that I was put into internal accounts for nine months, the purgatory of banking, where you sit, hour after hour, day after day, in a vast, gloomy hall, doing nothing but check columns of figures until they dance in your head and you feel like screaming out loud.

Even worse, Wilkinson saw no reason why he should put in a good word for me either, as (he said) he had not intended me to do anything other than go to Paris and come straight back again. It was all my own doing. But at least no one audited the bank before I had paid off the debit created by my loan to Virginie. It occurred to me later that, had they done so, I would have been in quite serious trouble. A brief vision flashed through my mind of standing in the dock, trying to explain to a sceptical jury that I had paid, without any authorisation, five thousand francs of Barings' money to a French prostitute. As a service to my country. Honestly, Your Honour. No, alas, I had no proof. Unfortunately my associate in France had disappeared, and the Foreign Office claimed not to know me at all.

On the other hand, it did drive home to me that removing sums of money from the most reputable bank in the world was a remarkably easy thing to accomplish. And eventually my gaol sentence in the counting house came to an end and I was restored to favour, although not to the point where I was allowed to go off to France again. Over the next year or so my knowledge of banking increased, as did my level of boredom. I even began to think fondly of cold nights sitting under a bridge over the Rhine, although the image of Lefevre scowling and shouting some sarcastic remark soon brought me back to common sense.

I hoped that I would be summoned to see Wilkinson again, but no word came, and I did not know where to find him; the Foreign Office denied having any such person in the building, and he seemed to have vanished from the face of the earth. Eventually I decided that that particular adventure was over; I suspected Lefevre had been so scathing about me that, whatever the reason Wilkinson had had for choosing me, he had changed his mind. I was unsuitable.

I had almost forgotten about the whole thing when it started all over again. Another summons, another letter, another meal.

"I hope you're not going to ask me to be your delivery boy again," I said after the preliminaries were dealt with. "I'm still paying for the last time. They haven't let me out of London for more than a year because of you."

"Oh, dear. I am sorry. But it really wasn't my fault. It's not as if I asked you to go off gallivanting around France," he said. "Mixed messages, I'm afraid."

"Maybe. But before I met you I was a banker with a fine career in prospect, and a few months later I was spending my life in miscellaneous disbursements."

"A little bored, are you?"

"Very."

"Good. Why don't you come and work for me?"

"You must be joking."

"I mean it. Your friend in Paris spoke highly of your skills, if not of your character."

"I would rather starve in the gutter," I said disgustedly. "Besides, I was not impressed by the playacting of M. Lefevre, or whatever his name is."

"Mr. Drennan."

"Pardon?"

"Mr. Arnsley Drennan. That's his name. He doesn't use it much anymore, but there is no reason why you shouldn't know it. He is an American. He came to Europe when his side lost in their war. You were saying?"

"Playacting," I repeated crossly. "Hanging around in bars, listening to tittle-tattle. A waste of time."

"You could do better?"

"Easily. Not that I'm going to. I won't have anything to do with Lefevre. Or Drennan."

"You wouldn't have to. Mr. Drennan, ah, found a more lucrative post elsewhere."

"Really? Isn't that . . ."

"Difficult, yes. I'm afraid he was most awkward about it. He knows so very much about things, you see. Unfortunately, we haven't been able to find him to talk things over."

"I can't imagine he ever found anything very useful for you anyway. I thought his antics were quite ridiculous."

"Did you?"

"Yes."

"So what would you do differently?"

And this was the moment that changed my life forever, for with a few words I then took the first steps which made the imperial intelligence system a little more coherent—I would say professional, although that would be considered an insult. I should have kept my mouth shut and walked out. I should have decided that Wilkinson was someone with whom I would not associate. But I wanted to give in. Ever since I had seen Lefevre—or Drennan—deal with Virginie I knew I could do better, and I had found the whole business exhilarating.

Besides, I had realised that Henry Wilkinson did not preside like a spider in the middle of a vast web of intelligence officers spread out across the Empire, constantly alert for dangers and opportunities, as I had assumed. Far from being all-seeing and all-competent, he was virtually blind. He had no department, no budget, no authority whatsoever. The safety of the greatest empire the world had ever known depended on a bunch of friends and acquaintances, crooks and misfits. The flow of intelligence depended on favours and requests. There was no policy, little direction and no obvious aims. It was amateurish and all but useless. They needed me, I decided with all the arrogance that a twenty-seven-year-old could muster. Far more than I needed them.

So I summarised my understanding of imperial intelligence. Wilkinson seemed quite pleased with the description.

"Yes, yes," he said cheerfully, "I think that sums up the current situation quite nicely. And if I did not inform you of all this, I'm sure you understand the reasons why perfectly well. If I cannot have the substance of proper organisation, then the appearance of one is the next best thing."

"So how does all this work?"

"As best it can," he replied. "The Government does not believe such activities to be necessary, and in any case couldn't persuade Parliament to provide money for them. Some sort of body might be set up using funds voted to the army or navy, but neither sees the need. For the last fifteen years I have been operating without any legal basis or funding whatsoever. We have people collecting information throughout the Empire, in India and Africa and in Europe, but there is no coordination at all. I have to ask to see anything they have. I cannot order them to comply or even say what they should be looking for. At the moment, for example, the Indian Army is not on speaking terms with us. I'm still not certain why. They won't answer my letters."

"So you know as well as I do that all this running around in France, collecting gossip in bars is useless."

"Not useless, no," he said judiciously. "We do the best we can, but we work despite our masters, not because of them. There is nothing unusual about that. Many Government departments feel the same. I think it might be a common condition of the civil servant. You find it all unsatisfactory?"

"I find it pathetic."

"You could do better? Considering that Government policy is unlikely to change?"

"Listen," I said. "I work for a bank. It is a commercial operation which, in effect, buys and sells money. It is all I know, it has its weaknesses, but it works. If you want information—real information, not tittle-tattle—I am convinced you have to buy it. My arrangement with Virginie was organised on a purely commercial basis, for mutual profit. That is why it worked. Information is a commodity; it is traded like any other, and there is a market for it."

"How would you go about it?"

"I would set up as a broker. Find people who wish to sell, and buy at a good price. And sell it on at a price as well."

"And that is all?"

"In essence. The difference is that such an operation would need a substantial amount of money to get it going. You get what you pay for."

"You speak like a businessman."

"And you, I'm afraid, need to think like one. I'm not thinking about the cost of a battleship, you know."

"Even small sums of money have to be accounted for. You would be surprised how well the Government likes to look after public funds. Still, perhaps something could be done. Would you do me the great favour of writing down—confidentially, of course—what your proposal is, and how you would proceed? I can then, perhaps, present it to some friends to ask their opinion."

And so I became a writer of memoranda for governments. Do I bother to draw a contrast with the flights of fancy which illuminate the pages of our novelists? Do these heroes stay up at night penning budget proposals? Laying out routes for transferring money from one bank to another? Describing methods of accounting for sums disbursed?

That is what I did. I began by describing the problem—which was to ascertain the intentions of France (although any country could have been inserted at this point), and then pointed out that we lived in an age of industry. Governments could not order armies into the field on a whim. They have to be amassed, and equipped. This takes time. I estimated that between deciding to go to war and actually doing so at least nine months was required, and that this could be monitored by watching the order books of armaments companies, the schedules of the train companies, requisitions of horses and so on. Was the Government putting in place new loan facilities with banks? Was it taking on increased powers to raise supplementary taxation? Which war was to be fought could also be estimated—was money going disproportionately to naval yards, or to the manufacturers of cannon? Technical details of how weapons worked (should such information be required) might also be better acquired by the commercial route rather than by trying to suborn officers in the armed forces. And what were the stockpiles of the opposing military forces? If they went to war, how long could they stay in the field?

Much of this information, I argued, could be bought at the right price. In addition, I realised that many politicians were susceptible to a certain amount of coercion through exposure of their finances; I also proposed that money and time should be spent on obtaining detailed information about the bribes and other inducements politicians were known to accept. This could then be used to constrain unfriendly action, or to obtain any more specific information that was required. Finally, I recommended that all the money involved be channelled through German banking houses to make it seem that it was they, not we, who were indulging in this activity.

It was, if I may say so, quite impressive. All but revolutionary in fact; however obvious all this might seem now, the application of commercial logic to what had up until then been a military and diplomatic enterprise caused some consternation. Of those who saw my note, some were outraged, others appalled and a few were intrigued. Many considered my arguments vulgar and distasteful—although most of those disapproved of any form of espionage at all.

CHAPTER 6

And some people were prepared to fund the operation. I received instructions from Mr. Wilkinson that friends would back me, and that I was to go to Paris, and that I was now to be a journalist working for *The Times*, a somewhat steep social descent after Barings. I should see the editor to find out how to do this once the man had been informed that he was to employ me. Then I was summoned to another lunch. I was expecting Mr. Wilkinson; instead I encountered John Stone for the first time.

"Your chief investor," Wilkinson said, waving at him. "Potentially. He felt that before he put money into you, he should see if you are worth the effort."

I studied him carefully as Wilkinson slid out of the room to leave us alone. He was about fifty, and quite unremarkable to look at. Clean-shaven, with thinning hair that was touched with grey, and dressed in a fashion that was proper and yet entirely anonymous. The cufflinks, I noticed, were of simple design and inexpensive; he wore no ring; he had none of the sleek prosperity about him that men like Lord Revelstoke, the Chairman of Barings, managed to exude. No whiff of cologne, no sign of hair oil, expensive or otherwise. He could have passed as—anything he wished. Certainly, he drew no attention to himself.

Physically, also, he was unremarkable. Not handsome especially, nor ugly. His eyes were attentive and held their subject with great fixity; his movements were slow and measured. Nothing hurried him, if he did not want to be hurried. His calm was one of confidence and—I would have said if the description wasn't ridiculous—contentment.

I had heard the name, but it had scarcely registered with me. Stone was not yet the force he has since become in British industry; his reputation as a sophisticated manipulator of money was growing, but not to the point where he could no longer hide his achievements. He was known as the man who had combined Gleeson's Steel and Beswick Shipyards but there was still no reason to think he was anything other than an ambitious and competent man of industry. Accordingly, although I was polite, I was not overawed by the encounter.

He surprised me, though. For the most part these industrialists are difficult people to converse with, self-made men for whom industry is everything and who judge conversation to be the stuff of the weak. They despise bankers, on the whole, for contributing nothing to society, and for acting as parasites on their endeavours. They are either overwhelmed by the likes of Wilkinson or aggressive in showing their disdain. Stone was none of these things. He was mild-mannered, almost as though I was doing him the favour. For a long time the conversation steered around anything other than the reason for the luncheon.

"So you plan to go to Paris?" he asked eventually, as though I had let slip my desire to see the sights.

"In a week or so, if all goes well."

"And Barings? They are not upset to let a man of such promise leave?"

"They seem more than ready to bear their loss with fortitude," I replied, with a touch of slight bitterness. When I told Barings of my decision, they had merely nodded, and accepted the letter of resignation. Hadn't even asked for an explanation, let alone tried to dissuade me.

"I see. You cannot blame them really. Defending the Empire is very admirable, but doing it on Barings' time is quite another. Don't judge them too harshly. Banking is not a business which has much use for individuality. Even Revelstoke thinks that initiative and daring should be his sole preserve. It is a great error on his part. Mind you, I believe he has an equally low opinion of me."

"Might I ask why?"

"Oh, he regards me as an upstart," Stone said with a faint smile, but he did not seek to convey the idea that Revelstoke was beneath contempt as a result. Rather he reported it in a manner which was entirely neutral, even as though the Chairman of Barings might have a point. "It is nothing personal, you understand. But he thinks I don't understand money."

"And you think you do?"

"I think I understand people, and Revelstoke takes too many risks. He has made a great deal of money out of it and so is emboldened to take even more. He believes he is infallible, and that will spell ruin, sooner or later. Hubris, you know, can destroy a banker as well as a Greek hero."

Now, someone criticising Lord Revelstoke, acknowledged throughout the world as one of the greatest bankers in history, made me feel a little uncomfortable.

"He is surely the greatest innovator in banking of the age," I said.

"He is the greatest gambler," Stone said sourly. "And so far he has had the greatest luck."

I tried to change the subject.

"Ah, loyalty," observed Stone. "Not a bad quality. But it is possible to be loyal and critical at the same time. They are two qualities I insist on, in fact. The sycophant is the greatest of all dangers in an organisation. I have never fired a man for disagreeing with me. I have dismissed several for agreeing when they knew better."

"On that subject, what exactly would my position be?" I asked a little crossly. "Do I run the risk of being summoned back to England because I agree with you about something?"

"I will have no say in the matter at all," he replied evenly. "You are to work for Mr. Wilkinson, not me. I merely provide the means for you to do so. As an experiment. Obviously, if Mr. Wilkinson decides the experiment is not working, or that it costs more than it is worth, then we will have to think again."

"Why are you providing the means? It is a very great deal of money."

"Not so very much," he said. "And it is money I can easily spare. I thought your approach was interesting, and amateurism annoys me wherever it occurs. I almost consider it my duty to eradicate it. And if not my duty, then my hobby."

"An expensive hobby."

He shrugged.

"So expensive I do not quite believe you."

"Call me a patriot, then."

"I know little of your companies, Mr. Stone. Such things are not my area of expertise. But I remember reading that you have supplied weapons to every single enemy our army and navy might face. Are those the actions of a patriot?"

It was an insulting remark, but deliberately made. I needed to find out what I was getting myself into.

"It is not the task of my companies to make Britain more secure, it is the duty of Britain to make my companies more secure. You have the relationship the wrong way round," he said quietly. "It is the task of a company to generate capital. That is its beginning and its end, and it is foolish and sentimental to apply morality to it, let alone patriotism."

"Morality must apply to everything. Even the making of money."

"A strange statement for a banker, if I may say so. And it is not so. Morality applies only to people. Not to animals and still less to machines."

"But you are a man," I pointed out, "you manufacture weapons of war, which you sell to all who want to buy them."

"Not quite," he said with a smile. "They must be able to afford them as well. But you are right. I do. But consider. If one of my torpedoes is fired, and hits its target, many people will die. A terrible thing. But is the torpedo to blame? It is but a machine, designed to travel from point A to point B and then detonate. If it does so, it is a good machine which fulfils its purpose. If not, it is a failure. Where is there any space for morality in that?

"And a company is also merely a machine, supplying the wants of others. Why not blame the governments who buy those torpedoes and order them to be used, or the people who vote for those governments?

"Should I stop building these weapons, and deny governments the chance to murder their citizens more cheaply and efficiently? Certainly not. I am obliged to make them. The laws of economics dictate that. If I do not, then a demand will go unsatisfied, or it may be that the money is spent on a less worthy machine, which would be an inefficient use of capital. If men do not have torpedoes, they will use cannon. If there are no cannon, they will use bows and arrows. If there are no arrows, they will use stones and if there are no stones, they will bite each other to death. I merely convert desire into its most efficient form and extract capital from the process.

"That is what companies are for. They are designed to multiply capital; what they make is irrelevant. Torpedoes, food, clothes, furniture. It is all the same. To that end they will do anything to survive and prosper. Can they make more money employing slave labour? If so, they must do so. Can they increase profits by selling things which kill others? They must do so again. What if they lay waste the landscape, ruin forests, uproot communities and poison the rivers? They are obliged to do all these things, if they can increase their profits.

"A company is a moral imbecile. It has no sense of right or wrong. Any restraints have to come from the outside, from laws and customs which forbid it from doing certain things of which we disapprove. But it is a restraint which reduces profits. Which is why all companies will strain forever to break the bounds of the law, to act unfettered in their pursuit of advantage. That is the only way they can survive because the more powerful will devour the weak. And because it is in the nature of capital, which is wild, longs to be free and chafes at each and every restriction imposed on it."

"You justify selling weapons to your country's enemies?"

"To the French, you mean?"

"Yes."

"And the Germans and the Italians and the Austrians?" he added.

"Yes. You justify that?"

"But they are not my country's enemies," he said with a faint smile. "We are not at war."

"We may well be soon."

"True enough. But with which country, do you think?"

"Does it matter?"

"No," he admitted. "I would sell them the weapons even if I knew that we would be at war with them in six months' time. It is not my job to conduct foreign policy. Such sales are not illegal and anything which is not forbidden is permissible. If the Government decided to ban sales to France, then I would comply with the law. At the moment, for example, I can see a great deal of money to be made in building shipyards for the Russian Empire. But the Government does not wish Russia to have a shipbuilding industry. I would like to supply the Tsar with our new submarines, as the Russian Government would pay handsomely for them. Again, I do not."

"There is a law against that?"

"Oh, dear no. The laws of the land are not only those on the statute book, as approved by Parliament. But I am told that my business here would suffer, and naturally I listen to such warnings. In my opinion it is a mistake. Russia will surely learn how to make battleships and submarines; all we are doing is delaying this by a few years, while also making enemies of them and denying ourselves considerable profit."

"You are very honest."

"Not at all. Only when there is no reason not to be."

I considered all this, a passionate speech delivered in an utterly dispassionate, dry manner, and tried to make sense of it. When talking of capital, Stone spoke more like a romantic poet than a businessman.

"And where do I fit into this?"

"You? You will make the Government better able to take correct decisions, if you do your job well. At the same time, you will provide a better view of the future, so that I can plan more accurately."

"Presumably you want there to be conflict."

"Oh, no. It is a matter of complete indifference to me. I merely wish to be ready for whatever occurs."

"And the safety of the country? The Empire?"

He shrugged. "If I had to judge, I would say that the Empire is inefficient and wasteful. It has no purpose and little justification. Undoubtedly the country would be better off without it, but I do not expect many people will ever agree with me. Its only justification is that India deposits its gold in the Bank of England, and that has allowed the gigantic increase in our trade with the world by strengthening the pound sterling."

I found Mr. Stone an alarming man. I had anticipated working for the Government, a patriot labouring for the public good. Not for a man like John Stone. Only towards the end of our interview did I see something else in him; puzzling, and unexpected.

"Tell me," he said as we stood to leave. "How is your father?"

"As usual, I think," I said. I felt as guilty as I was surprised; I had not made the journey to Dorset to see my father for some while, and as I have mentioned, every time I went, there seemed less point in doing so.

"I see."

"You know him?"

"We were acquainted, once. Before he became ill. I liked him. You look very much like him. But you do not have his personality. He was gentler than you. You should be careful."

"Of what?"

"Oh, I don't know. Of getting too far away from your father's nature, perhaps."

And he nodded at me, wished me well in a formal, impersonal fashion, and left.

CHAPTER 7

Having damned all others for their ineptitude and promised an entirely new way of collecting information, I found that I was left entirely without any assistance or instructions as a result. So, show us, seemed to be the general opinion and I discovered later that there were many—of the few who knew anything of this experiment—who wanted me to fail dismally.

Saying what you will do on paper is one thing; doing it is another, and I had not the slightest idea how to proceed. Getting myself to Paris was the first step, fairly obviously. After that I would have to make it up as I went along. My official employers were somewhat more useful to me; George Buckle, the editor of *The Times*, accepted my sudden irruption into his life with remarkable calm and handed me over to a junior reporter called McEwen for instruction about how to write for a newspaper, as well as practical guidance on the uses of telegraph machines for transmitting any stories I might feel like writing. The fact that *The Times* wasn't required to pay me no doubt made Buckle more easygoing about my existence.

Then I left, arriving in Paris one Wednesday morning. My luggage had already gone on ahead, and I was little encumbered by baggage. So I went straight to the offices of *The Times*—offices being a misnomer, as they were in truth little more than a single room which contained nothing that might indicate its purpose except for bundles of old French newspapers on the floor. The door was unlocked and the room was empty, but on the desk was a little note addressed to me: would I be so kind as to join the writer, Thomas Barclay, in the nearby restaurant for lunch?

I was so kind; a waiter led me over to the right table, and I joined the man who was, theoretically, my new colleague.

Thomas Barclay was in his late forties at that stage, with a fine flowing beard that was russet coloured. He had enormous ears, an oddly pointed nose and an intellectual forehead. He frowned a lot to show high seriousness, a tendency he had acquired, I suspect, through spending too much time studying German philosophy in Jena, although the effect was to make him look more confused than thoughtful.

He was, fortunately, about as serious a journalist as I was, but had been in Paris for nearly twenty years by this stage. He had written a book review in the *Spectator* in the early seventies and, as he had shown a willingness to live abroad, had been offered the job as Paris correspondent of *The Times* on this basis alone. His reports were few and far between, and always couched in such vague language that it was often impossible to ascertain what, exactly, was the subject. For Barclay, the importance of an event varied in direct proportion to the importance of the person who had given him the information, for he was a most fearful snob, and could work himself into a lather of excitement over an invitation to a prestigious salon, or dinner at a senator's private house. Their words he treated like finest gold dust, but he was so discreet he could rarely bring himself to report them without wrapping his information up in so many circumlocutions that their significance was totally lost. Besides, he had of late become the President of the British Chamber of Commerce in Paris, which post he took most seriously, thinking, rather oddly, that it was a position of the highest political and diplomatic importance, rather than a mere dining club for foreign traders.

He was delighted to see me, and not in the slightest perturbed either that no one had asked his opinion about my coming, or by my utter lack of experience. "Very few people in England have any interest in what goes on outside the Empire," he said cheerfully, "as long as it does not affect them. For the most part you can write anything you wish, and for all important events a straight translation from a reputable Paris paper will do excellently well. I wouldn't bother running around trying to get interesting stories, if I were you. No one will read them and they probably won't even get published. The only subject worth extending yourself over is a society scandal. They always go down well as they confirm the readers' opinions about the low morals of the French. Book reviews, if you don't mind, I will keep for myself. Theatre only if Bernhardt is involved."

I told him that he was welcome to keep all the book reviews. "I thought," I said tentatively, "I might write some stories about the Bourse."

He frowned. "If you wish, go ahead. I wouldn't find it very interesting myself. But it takes all sorts, of course."

"I was given a few names," I added. "It would be rude not to call on them."

"Good heavens, yes. Go ahead. Please don't think I intend to direct you in any way. As long as you write one story every fortnight, more or less, everyone will be delighted with you."

"I'll do my best," I said.

"I did one yesterday, in fact," he said. "So we're in the clear for a while. If you do the next one . . ."

I said I thought I could manage to write something in a fortnight, and he leaned back in his chair, beaming at me. "Splendid. That's taken care of. Now, where are you living?"

In fact, I was in a hotel and ended up staying there for the next year; it was the cheapest option, as I did not want the expense of a household, and it was perfectly adequate. Domesticity has never been one of my great desires in life and certainly was not then; a comfortable bed and decent food are my sole requirements, and the Hôtel des Phares—in reality, a few rooms above a bar, with an obliging landlord whose wife was happy to do my laundry and cook some food—provided both.

I will pass over my daily life, as much of it was of little interest and consisted mainly in laying down those webs of information and making those acquaintances which journalists and other seekers of information require. How this is done is fairly obvious, and consists primarily in making oneself as personable and harmless as possible, in creating a void which others seek to fill through conversation. From such gossip come hints and clues which lead, sometimes, to other things. I made my acquaintance widely for I found the French both charming and welcoming, quite unlike their reputation. I cultivated the traders of the Bourse, the playwrights of the Latin Quarter, and the politicians and diplomats and soldiers who scattered themselves at random across the city. They all, I believe, considered me somewhat dull and without any opinions of my own; it was not my role to have any.

And in August I went to Biarritz, where the new rich of the Republic went to mingle with old names and titles and keep themselves properly distant from the People, a group they admired in principle, but did not actually want to have anything to do with on a social level. It was a glorious sight to watch, for a brief while, a testament both to the wealth of the rich, and the capacity of the French to amuse themselves. All of French society that mattered squeezed itself into a stretch of coastline bordered by the Hôtel du Palais to the north, and the Hotel Métropole to the south, these two separated by a mile or so of glorious beach, and many dozen villas of exuberant and fanciful design. The town was at the peak of its prosperity then; Queen Victoria herself had come to visit the year before, the Prince of Wales showed up every year. Princess Natalie of Romania lived in exile in a handsome villa up the road; the first Russian grand dukes were putting in an appearance. The English had colonised the entire region from Pau to the Pyrenees to the coast, apparently forgetting that Aquitaine was no longer theirs.

For weeks on end, all day and all night, there was an endless round of entertainment for the well connected, and even for those who, like me, could be suspected of being well-connected. My introduction to society came through the good offices of Mr. Wilkinson, who arranged for Princess Natalie to invite me to one of her soirées. From that point, word went round swiftly that I was someone who should be known—although no one knew why. They were prepared to invite me so they could try and discover my secret. I was variously reputed to be an immensely rich banker, a bastard child of the Duke of Devonshire, a breeder of champion racehorses and a man with vast landholdings in Australia. All indicated that I was someone who should be invited to parties, and so I went, carefully ambiguous in my replies to all probing questions, and always insisting that I was really just a journalist on *The Times*. No one believed me.

The poor Princess was a drab and dreary woman, alas. A perfectly sweet temper and a kindly soul, but she had only her tragic situation and title to recommend her to the very demanding French, who expect their women to be beautiful, intelligent, elegant, charming and fascinating at all times and in all circumstances. The Princess was thoughtful, plain, serious and not given to smiling for fear of showing her bad teeth. But she was a princess, so was bound to command the respect of these devoted egalitarians.

Her reign as the most important woman in Biarritz was as insecure as her claim to the throne of Romania had been; pretenders constantly appeared to challenge her. None was more dangerous than the Countess Elizabeth Hadik-Barkoczy von Futak uns Szala, a woman of exceptional allure who was making her first trip to Biarritz that year, and who had made the town, collectively, lose its head in excitement. French society— far more than English—was remarkably good at producing such people, or at adopting them. They formed a focus for men, let other women know what they should be wearing, created gossip to fill up dinnertime conversations, and were, quite simply, admired. Some were entirely artificial creations, very little more than courtesans with terrible manners and no breeding, who burned brightly then fell to earth when boredom set in. Others—such as the Countess, according to popular report—had more substance.

To be the object of fascination is a very considerable accomplishment; it requires impeccable manners, intelligent conversation, grace and beauty. It also requires that magical quality which cannot be defined, but which is easily recognised when it is met with. Presence, in a word; an inability to be in a room without everyone knowing you are there, however quiet your entrance and discreet your behaviour. An ability to spend lavishly, but without ostentation; the best of everything whatever its price, low or high. A knowledge of how to be simple when that is better, and extravagant when that is required, and never, ever, take a false step.

Such, in sum, was this countess with the impressively long name, and beside her the poor princess from Romania wilted like a flower in a drought. Not that this concerned me, of course; I was there for an entirely different reason; the social whirl was a backdrop for my activities and I paid only very little attention to it. I heard about the leading figures of the town, but conversed with only a few of them. My main reason for being there was very specific; I needed to discover something about coal.

Equally, it was an opportunity to meet Mr. Wilkinson, who went walking every summer in the Pyrenees; he was a great expert on the flora and fauna of the region and published a book, just before he died, on wild-flowers which is now a standard text on the subject, for those who are interested in such things—which, I must confess, I am not.

But the coal was the main reason, and the justification for spending a week in the Hôtel du Palais at John Stone's expense. Britain was going through one of its periods of anxiety about the Mediterranean. It was always going through these, of course, but currently anxieties were higher than usual; the fear was that there was going to be yet another assault on Britain's position in the Near East, with the Russian Empire and the French combining to pressure our interests in the Black Sea and Egypt, and hence our communications with India through the Suez Canal. Although the Royal Navy could cope quite easily with an assault by either fleet, the fear was that the French and Russians were going to combine their efforts, and dealing with both simultaneously would be a problem. That was why, more than anything, the Government was keen to prevent Russia building a shipyard on the Black Sea and so be in a position to service a major fleet in the region. That was also why the Russians were keen to do precisely that.

So were the French thinking of sending out their fleet from Toulon? That was what I was supposed to discover. All the usual sources of information had failed; if anything was planned, word had not yet filtered down to the ranks. But it probably would not have done; I doubted anything would materialise before the following spring at the earliest, in about seven months' time. The problem was that, if Britain needed to reinforce its Mediterranean fleet, it needed to know soon, so that ships could be recalled from the West Indies, reequipped and sent out again. This also would take several months.

Hence my interest in coal. Battleships consume prodigious quantities of fuel, and keeping them at sea, ready for action, is a major logistical operation. Tens of thousands of tons of coal are required, and supplies have to be in place at coaling stations when they are needed. You cannot just send out some ships anymore; you need a lot of work in advance, for a battleship lying dead in the water, unable to move, is no use to anyone. While all navies kept reasonable quantities of coal scattered around the world, not even the Royal Navy kept that amount in place everywhere it might be needed.

Had the French navy been ordering coal in large quantities? Had they commissioned tenders from the Mediterranean merchant fleet to distribute it?

Were supplies being diverted from the Atlantic ports to the Mediterranean? If I knew the answers to these questions now, I would be able to tell the Government in London not only what the French navy would be doing next year, I could hazard a guess about French foreign policy in the near future as well.

To discover all this I ended up dining one night in August with a French naval captain and his mistress. He was a sweet man who should never have been in the military; he had not a shred of the martial about him and preferred collecting Japanese woodcuts to charging over the high seas ready to board an enemy. Family tradition and an overbearing admiral for a father had determined otherwise, however. Ordinarily, I would have spent time trying to come alongside the father, so to speak, but Captain Lucien de Koletern was quite interesting enough for me at that moment. For he was a terrible failure, poor man. His lack of ability in the business of commanding others had meant that the navy, with some acuity, had refused to allow him anywhere near anything that actually floated; instead he had been given a job in Paris, in which place he spent his time trying to avoid the disappointed frowns of his father and—more importantly—organising logistical supplies, in particular coal. For this he had some considerable talent; what he lacked in dash and flair he made up for in meticulous attention to detail and an obsessive concern with filing cards.

He was an interesting conversationalist, as well; he knew he was a bitter disappointment to his family, but was quite philosophical about it.

"I know it sounds absurd, but I really do believe that what I do is where the future of the navy really lies. Not with ships at all," he said.

"And what do you do?" I asked innocently.

"Supplies. Coal, mainly."

"But doesn't a navy need ships?"

"Not really. If you think about it, the French navy has not actually been used for anything since the Crimean War, and there is little prospect of it being used again. If the ships never left harbour, it would make no difference."

"But if that happened, you wouldn't have all that much to do," I pointed out.

"Ah," he said, waving a finger. "But ships keep their boilers going even when they are tied up. That is enough to keep me busy. Then what happens? If the fleet ever put to sea, they would suddenly decide they wanted more. Do you have any idea how much coal a fleet needs when it sets off somewhere?"

"No. Not the slightest," I said.

"About 2,000 tons per month per battleship. A fleet of, say, ten battleships, fifteen destroyers and thirty or so other ships would need about 45,000 tons a month. All of which has to be found at fairly short notice. That's why it's a nuisance."

"Difficult," I said sympathetically. "Is this making your life complicated at the moment?"

"Fortunately not," he said, and I relaxed; I was home. "There was talk that something was going to happen in the Mediterranean—exercises or some such. So I went to the Admiral and asked what was required of me. Nothing, he said. All just rumours; no more than that. In fact, he said I could run the stocks down a bit, just to punish the suppliers for hiking the price for good-quality coal last time they thought the fleet might put to sea."

"Who is your admiral?" I asked. He sounded a well-informed fellow; it might be a good idea to meet him one day. Besides, I had to check that he really knew what he was talking about.

Lucien told me, bless him, and I knew my quest had ended. The Admiral was in command of the Toulon fleet, a man with good connections to the French Foreign Office. A man with a future, who knew what he was talking about, and did not make mistakes like saying something that meant the fleet would not be ready for action when required. All that was needed now was to double-check with the price movements of wholesale anthracite on the Coal Exchange in Paris, and I would be able to report back to London. I changed the subject, and began to try and win over his mistress, who was now looking quite despairing at the tedium of the conversation. She became sulky and ill-humoured and caused several frosty moments of silence to descend on our little table. During one of these I saw Lucien gazing over at another table with a faint smile of interest.

"Maurice Rouvier, with a friend," he said with delight. The slightest emphasis on the last word made me turn to look as well. "She's a bit old for him. I gather he likes them somewhat younger."

Rouvier was the Finance Minister; I knew him by sight, although I had not yet met him. He was not widely liked. Apart from the whiff of indecency that Lucien referred to, he was also rumoured to be less than straightforward in his dealings with his fellow men. To put it another way, he was devious even by the standards of politicians; a long and successful career awaited him. His presence there was in itself testament to the importance of holidaying in the right places; Rouvier was a man of the south, Mediterranean in origin, and thus was also associated with the disregard for proprieties generally considered to be a characteristic of such people. Still, he was (it was grudgingly admitted) a man of ability: a finance minister who actually knew something of finance, which was unusual, and with a background in banking. And he had done well on the merry-go-round of French politics; he had had a turn as Prime Minister once already, and he has popped up in ministries with great regularity ever since. He had no known political opinions; indeed his only firm conviction lay in an undying opposition to income tax. Apart from that he would support anything and anyone who would further his career.

Lucien's attention, however, was not fixed on the man who temporarily held the finances of the nation in his hands, but rather on the companion opposite at a table of about six people, a willowy, tall woman with dark hair and low-cut dress which revealed exceptionally fine shoulders and a long neck set off by a single strand of some of the most gigantic diamonds I had ever seen in my life. She was young; in her early twenties, and even from a distance made the rest of the table seem drab in comparison. All those around her were men, mainly in middle age, and it was clear that all conversation was dominated by the desire to catch her attention.

I looked at her briefly, turned away, then turned to look again.

"Rude to stare," Lucien said in my ear with an amused chuckle. "Quite a picture, is she not?"

His mistress, whose name I never knew, scowled and sank lower into depressed silence. Poor thing, the contrast between the two was too great to be ignored.

"Who is she?"

"Ah, what a question! Who indeed? That is the famous Countess Elizabeth Hadik-Barkoczy von Futak uns Szala."

"Oh," I said. "That's the one, is it? I've been hearing about her."

"The sensation of the season. Conquered Paris with a speed and aplomb which the Prussian army never managed. To put it another way, she has cut a swath through polite society, broken the heart of every man who has come within a hundred metres of her, and left her rivals looking old, coarse and thoroughly shop-soiled. Every woman in the city hates her, of course."

"I'm fascinated."

"So is everyone else."

"So tell me more."

"There is a great deal of gossip and nothing of substance. She is a widow, it seems. Tragic story; newly married and husband falls off a horse and breaks his neck. Wealthy, beyond a doubt, and came to Paris because—no one knows why. She moves in the very best society, and will, no doubt, shortly marry a duke, or a politician or a banker, depending on her tastes. Does she have a lover? No one knows. She is as enveloped in mystery as—well, as you are, but (if you will forgive me for saying so) she is very much more beautiful."

"I would like to meet this woman."

Lucien snorted. "I would like to take tea with Queen Victoria," he said, "and that won't happen either. Everyone knows of her, some have been in the same room with her, few have met her."

"So what's the secret?"

He shrugged. "Who knows? She is no more beautiful than many a woman. She is said to be charming and witty. But so are many people. I do not know. She is one of those people whom others wish to be with."

"In that case," I said with a grin, "I will ask her."

And I got up from the table and walked straight across to her table. I coughed to get her attention as I bowed to the Minister and smiled as she looked at me.

"Good evening, Principessa," I said, in a discreet voice loud enough to be heard by those sitting nearby. "May I pay my compliments to the most beautiful woman in France?"

"When you discover her, you may," she said with a flash of the eye.

There I bowed, and retired, pleased with my success, and walked back to my table.

"I can't believe you did that," Lucien said with something between shock and reproof.

"She's a woman, not Pallas Athene," I replied, and returned to my meal, which now tasted very much better than it had before, and spent the rest of the evening being pleasant to his mistress, who seemed grateful for my attention.

I got back to my hotel some three hours later and there, waiting for me at the desk, was an envelope. Inside was a single piece of paper on which was written. "Tomorrow. Two p.m. Villa Fleurie."

CHAPTER 8

"I liked the *principessa* part," she said when we met. "It adds to the mystery. It is all round Biarritz already that being Hungarian is merely a subterfuge, and that I am in reality a Neapolitan princess living incognito for fear of my husband."

I shook my head. "You don't look in the slightest bit Neapolitan."

"I don't speak Hungarian either," she replied. "What do you want?"

Her brusqueness was understandable. I must have been one of the very last people in the world she wanted to meet.

Her circumstances had changed as much as her appearance, which is to say the alteration was total. She was living in an elegant new villa a few hundred yards from the Hôtel du Palais, in the midst of the most fashionable part of the town. This had been built some five years previously by a banker, who rarely used it and rented it out for a prodigious sum when he was not there. It was furnished tastefully and discreetly, and Virginie—or rather Elizabeth, as I must now call her— fitted into it as perfectly as did the handmade furniture, and hand-blown glass in the art nouveau style then coming into fashion. Neither the house, nor she, had any connection to the overblown gaudiness normally associated with the *grandes horizontales,* for whom vulgarity was part of the allure.

The same went for her behaviour, which I had briefly witnessed the previous evening. Some of her sort would try to win attention by throwing diamonds across a restaurant for the pleasure of seeing the men scrabble to find them, or to see the disdain and fury on the faces of their women at the demonstration of how easily such men could be commanded. Others talked in loud voices, or stood up to dance on their own, making a spectacle of themselves through their display. They promised gratification, but for one night only. This woman implicitly offered far more than that.

Even the way she sat was impressive. Undoubtedly she was on edge, nervous, a little frightened. How could she not be? Yet there was not a sign of it on her face, or in her posture. Her self-control was extraordinary; superhuman, almost.

"I don't want anything," I said simply. "I recognised you and could not deny myself the pleasure. That is all."

"All?"

I thought. "I suppose not. I was curious. And, I may say, deeply impressed by your achievement. I wished to congratulate you, in a way. As well as renew an acquaintance."

She allowed herself a small smile. "And what are you doing here?"

"I am a journalist, of sorts."

She raised a finely plucked eyebrow. "Of sorts? That sounds as though you are really nothing of the sort."

"No, truly. I work for *The Times*. In a few days I will be able to show you a story about the anthracite market to prove it."

"I don't believe you."

"I don't believe you are a Hungarian countess either. We both have our secret past. Which is in the past and should remain there. Although I am curious to know where you got your name. Elizabeth Hadik?"

"Barkoczy von Futak uns Szala," she completed for me.

"Quite a mouthful. You don't think something more straightforward might have been better?"

"Oh, no," she said. "The longer the name, the better it is. Besides, such a person existed, I met her mother once. She told me she had once had a daughter who would have been about my age had she lived. So I decided to bring her back to life."

"I see."

"I will do no more for you," she said suddenly.

"I haven't asked you to. Nor was I going to, tempting though the prospect is. I have no doubt that my masters, if I had any, of course, would disapprove thoroughly of my weakness. But I have never had a taste for forcing people to do things. I believe my treatment of you in the past was perfectly straightforward and honourable."

She nodded.

"Let it remain so. But I would like to know how you managed your rise to fortune since we last met. Your circumstances were somewhat different then."

She laughed, and even though there was absolutely not one jot of difference on her face, I could sense that she was relaxing. She believed me and, up to a very limited point, trusted me. Which was justifiable; as I spoke the words I meant them. But, in the back of my mind I knew that, one day, I might have to betray that trust. I did not like blackmail, but I knew enough of the world to know how well it worked. I say in my defence only that I hoped it would never be necessary.

"Would you care for some tea, Mr. Cort?"

"Thank you, Countess. That's my real name, by the way. I see no point in playing games with false ones. There, I think, we differ."

She rang a little bell on the side table, and gave the order to a servant who appeared with great speed. I very much hoped he was not the sort of servant who listened at doors.

"Don't worry," she said, reading my face well. "It is very thick wood, and neither of us have voices that carry. Besides, although Simon has waggling ears, he is both well paid and has secrets of his own that are better not exposed to public view.

"As for my little subterfuge, my own name would open no doors. A title of nobility, however spurious, does so in this republican country. One does what is necessary."

The tea arrived, with delicate china cups and a silver teapot. Very pretty, although not for the serious tea drinker. One has to make allowances. "Do you wish to sit outside?" she asked. "It is a fine day, and I have an excellent view of the sea. Then I will tell you something of my story, if you wish."

She nodded to the servant, who took the tray outside, and when all was prepared, we followed. It was delightful; the villa was halfway up a small hill which rose up from the beach, with a large and well-stocked garden, a mixture of grass and plants more used to warmer climates. There was a tall tree to provide shade, and under this we sat at a graceful metal table, looking out over the sea, which entertained with the roughness of the waves, even though it was warm and still where we were.

"Here, you see, we can be quite certain that we will not be overheard," she said as she nodded that I might pour her tea for her. "Curiously, there is not so much to tell, once you leave out details that you would find sordid and unbecoming. I will put it in your own language, just as I took your approach. I reinvested my profits, and accumulated capital, and then decided to diversify into a new area of operation. How does that sound?"

"It sounds highly commendable, even though it tells me nothing at all."

"You know the early part; I worked my way up the ladder of seniority amongst the officers in Nancy, where I made a great discovery. Which was that it was more profitable to be a man's mistress than a whore. Forgive my language. Men reward their mistresses, and married men will go to considerable lengths to keep them quiet. As they have only a limited amount of time to consort with people like me, there is much time left over. Consequently, I realised that I could be the exclusive mistress of one man on Monday, of another on Tuesday, a third on Wednesday, and so on. As long as none knew of the others, all would be well. All of my shareholders, as I call them, agreed to keep me entirely, and so I gained five times as much, the majority of my earnings being pure profit. As two were exceptionally generous, I very soon accumulated enough to consider an independent existence."

"Enough for this?"

"No. I have very little money at the moment. All my earnings I have invested once more—the jewels, the clothes, this villa, the house in Paris. I survive on a diet of debt and donations. But I no longer fear the gutter."

"I am glad for you."

She nodded.

"So you are still . . ."

"Yes?"

"How to put this? Juggling clients? How many?"

"Four. It is all that can be managed safely. And I do find I like time to myself; I reserve two or three days a week for relaxation and proper sociability. And, at present, I am on holiday. Of a sort."

"Of a sort?"

"My other great discovery is that men are much more generous to women who do not need their generosity. To put it another way, generosity is relative to a woman's social situation. You, for example, lent me five thousand francs—more than I asked for, certainly, and enough to transform my life. But would you have thought you could have bought the Countess Elizabeth Hadik-Barkoczy von Futak uns Szala for such a sum? She who is known to be worth at least a million."

"Are you really?"

"I said 'known to be.' Not that I am. Reputation is more important than reality, Mr. Cort."

"I see. And the answer to your question is no. But then, I very much doubt the idea of buying a countess would ever cross my mind."

"Then you are unlike many men, for whom the more unattainable the prize, the more they must have it."

"M. Rouvier?"

She held up a finger reprovingly. "I am happy to discuss things in general, Mr. Cort. But the particular must remain my secret."

"My apologies. If my acquaintance of last night is correct, then you are fast becoming the most unattainable woman in Paris."

"And hence the most expensive," she said with a smile. "And that takes money. Staying in this house for a month, entertaining lavishly, costs a fortune. But it also makes men more generous."

"I find it difficult to believe that each interested party is unaware of the others."

"Of course they know of each other. But each thinks he is in unique possession, while the others are merely jealous."

"I do not see how such an arrangement can endure without some mishap."

"Probably it cannot. But I believe that in another year it will not matter. I will have accumulated enough money to keep myself in comfort, and so will have no more need of such arrangements. I do not think that such a life can continue forever, and there are few things worse than a middle-aged trollop."

The words made her thoughtful, and I sensed that they had also made her uncomfortable.

"I hope you will not find me rude if I say you must leave now, Mr. Cort. I have work to do this afternoon."

I rose to my feet and stammered slightly that, naturally, I quite understood.

She smiled. "No. You misunderstand. I told you I am on holiday. I must attend the Princess Natalie. A boring and remarkably stupid woman, but I need her approval. So," she said brightly, "I must go and charm her or, at least, disguise my disdain.

"Please come and visit again," she said as I prepared to leave. "I am giving a soirée tomorrow evening here, at nine o'clock. You would be a welcome guest."

"I am flattered. But I would have thought—"

"—I would want to keep you as far away as possible? Certainly not; it is agreeable to find someone whose way of life is even more immoral than my own. Besides, I think it would be best to keep an eye on you here. And I like you."

It is strange how such a simple statement can cause an effect; from her lips, the sentence made a huge impact on me. She did not like many people, I suspected; life had taught her few were likeable and fewer still were trustworthy. Yet she offered me both. She managed to make the offer seem both generous and a privilege. Was that calculation? If so, part of the art lay in making it not seem so, but to be rather something that came from the heart.

You think me foolish, reading these words, that I could be so bemused by the wiles of a former streetwalker? Well, you are wrong, and would accept that if you had met her when she was at the peak of her powers. Not that she was gentle or vulnerable herself, however much she could appear to be so. She had learned to survive, to fight and never to give ground against a hostile world. However soft and feminine she appeared, she had a core that was as tough as steel. No one knew her, and certainly no one took advantage of her. Not twice, anyway.

She came closer to trusting me than anyone in her acquaintance. I hope I do not flatter myself by saying that I deserved it, that it was not simply because she knew my secret as well as I knew hers, although that was no doubt part of the reason. I had had the opportunity of mistreating her and had declined it. I had dealt with her fairly, and had not abused my power over her. I had treated her as her character deserved, not as her condition allowed. She was a woman of few loyalties, but when they were conferred they were boundless.

CHAPTER 9

The soirée was a great event; I could with only a touch of hyperbole say that it transformed my own position in France and (at the same time) added an important footnote to the history of the French courtesan. For much of the day I took my ease; reading the newspapers over my morning coffee, going for a walk along the beach, passing a few moments in conversation with recent acquaintances briefly encountered. And then, at lunch, I had my meeting with Wilkinson; we ate together at a restaurant in the town, and had a perfectly pleasant, though entirely useless, conversation. He went on at great length about some rare bird he had spotted in the mountains, and was so excited—apparently it had not been seen since some legendary Spanish ornithologist had recorded it in the 1850s, and Wilkinson believed that he had won undying fame in the world of bird lovers as a result—that he could talk of little else. I told him about the coal, which pleased him, but he quickly went back to his birds once he had absorbed the information. All he said was "Good, good. Very pleasing." He had no requests about anything else the Government needed to know. Apparently I was beginning to be trusted to work that out for myself.

But it was pleasant enough and it saved me a good deal of weary memorandum writing later on, so I was satisfied. I also mentioned my remarkable meeting of the previous day, for I was aching to tell someone and knew that Wilkinson was about the only person in the world it was fair to confide in. He, after all, had been partly responsible for Virginie paying off her debts and launching herself on such a meteoric career. Besides, I was proud of her, and vain about my sagacity in spotting something that Lefevre had entirely overlooked.

"In that case, I must meet her," he said gaily, and my heart sank. "A soirée, you say? Excellent, I will come with you."

"I really don't . . ."

"I have long desired to meet her; I feel as though I know her so very well."

"I very much doubt she would want to meet you."

"She does not know of our association, I hope?"

"Of course not."

"In that case, what possible objection could she have? I would like to thank her, and I think I know the best way to do it. Don't worry, Cort. I'm not going to ruin your mascot. Quite the contrary. She might at some stage prove very useful."

He would not be dissuaded, and I heartily repented of my sudden garrulousness. I should have kept absolutely silent; but the levels of discretion I was forced to maintain were quite unnatural. I am not by nature a gossip, but all men need someone to talk to. I had no one in

France, and the sudden appearance of Wilkinson made me treat him with more trust than he should have received. No harm came of it, but I had, nonetheless, made a mistake which stemmed from youth and naïveté. I never repeated it.

At nine in the evening I picked him up from his boardinghouse—one which cost less per week than mine cost per night, as he pointed out— and was at least consoled to find him properly dressed. I had feared he would arrive in tweed jacket and hiking boots, but from somewhere or other he had acquired the necessary garb and, although he was not a man who could ever look elegant, he was at least perfectly presentable.

Much to my surprise, he was a brilliant performer, for these sorts of occasions are little more than theatre. Whereas my style was to remain silent and listen, Wilkinson revealed an unsuspectedly ostentatious side to his character. He spoke French loudly and badly, with many gesticulations to make up for his grammatical eccentricities; he told anecdotes of doubtful taste to old dowagers which had them gurgling with pleasure, he leaped from topic to topic with gusto, recounted tales of horses to horsemen, birds to hunters and politics to politicians. He was, in fact, a great success; even more so when he left the party for half an hour, and returned with the Prince of Wales.

I realised later that this was the whole point; this was his thanks. I should have realised that he would have known the Prince, who had arrived only the previous day, and Wilkinson was, I am glad to say, very much more dishonest than I had been. His Highness had not been told anything about who this Countess really was. He would never have been seen in public with such a person had the faintest whiff of scandal been attached to her name, although whom he tolerated in private was, as all the world knows, a very different matter. But he came, and his arrival signalled to the whole of French society that Elizabeth was utterly, totally and completely respectable. Far more than that; she could invite the most famous man in the world to her parties and he would come. Wilkinson's *coup de théâtre* propelled her into the stratosphere of European society. Whereas before she had managed much by her own efforts, there were some who doubted her credentials. If anyone doubted her after that, it no longer mattered. It was a generous gift, as long as that was what it was.

Even in those days, and even on holiday, the arrival of a figure such as the Prince was a matter of some pomp and ceremony; ordinarily, the fact that he was coming would be talked about for days; the hostess would make sure everyone knew about it, however discreetly the news was put abroad. Guests would wait to see whether the great man would be delivered; coaches and courtiers would drift in first to build up the excitement before he made his entrance. Would the Prince come? Would he be in a good mood? What would he wear? Such was the stuff of conversation as the clocks ticked away. And there was also the equally exciting possibility that he wouldn't show up at all. In which case the standing of the hostess would collapse; the kindly would commiserate, the less kindly would scent blood and all would depend on how she dealt with such a bitter, public disappointment. Would it show? Or would she put on a brave face? All these details were noticed, and their sum total shifted the balance of power in the small but intense world of society.

So the Prince's entry to Elizabeth's soirée was absolutely sensational. There was no warning, no prior gossip or announcements, he just strolled in, greeted her like an old friend, kissed her hand, and then talked to her in a friendly, respectful manner for a full fifteen minutes before circulating around the room, as everyone else there slowly but with deliberation jockeyed for position to be next in line for a royal word. Elizabeth later told me she reckoned it had increased her value by some three-quarters of a million francs, and she probably underestimated.

It also worked wonders for my social standing as well, for after her, I received the most attention. Not much, but I became instantly a person to know, and a person who was known.

"Cort, eh? *Times*?"

"Yes, Your Highness."

"Keep it up."

"I will, sir."

"Splendid." And he gave me a huge wink, to indicate that he knew exactly who I was, but which was interpreted by all who saw it as communicating some personal intimacy.

"Charming woman," he went on, indicating Elizabeth, who was discreetly now leaving him to his business. "Very charming. Hungarian, isn't she?"

"Yes, I believe so."

"Hmm." He looked momentarily confused, as though he was mentally riffling through the *Almanach de Gotha* but was unable to find the page he sought. "Lots of people in Hungary."

"I believe so, sir."

"Well, well. It's been a pleasure."

And he strode off to take his leave, kissing Elizabeth's hand with all the fervent attention of the true connoisseur.

She was, I must say, quite brilliant, and handled the situation with perfect balance. There was no shock on her face at all, though it must have been considerable; she did not react with an unwarranted air of familiarity, nor of surprise and delight. She received him with charm, leaving it to others to make of it what they would—did she know him, or not? What was the cause of his arrival? Was she so intimate in his circle that she could regard his arrival as that of just another guest? The shock waves spread out across Biarritz the next day (Princess Natalie, who had declined the invitation in order to keep Elizabeth in her place, was hard put to keep her grief to herself), then across France and Europe over the coming weeks as the season drew to an end and the temporary inhabitants of the town dispersed to their usual countries, taking with them news of the new star.

"That was an unusual thing to do," I said to Wilkinson as we travelled back to Paris the next day. He smiled.

"The Prince does love the demimonde, and he does love beauty," he said.

"He knows . . . ?"

"Oh, good heavens no. And if he ever discovered, I would have a great deal of explaining to do. If he ever realised I had knowingly . . ."

"Then who does he think she is?"

"Lesser aristocrat, too low for inclusion in the *Almanach*. Lack of birth made up for by her radiant beauty. You told me she wasn't beautiful."

"Well, she wasn't. Not when I first met her."

"Anyway, it wasn't really my doing. He invited me to dinner, I said I was going to this soirée, and he said he wanted to meet this woman. He'd heard of her, you see, and you know what he's like. Tell her, by the way, not to get any ideas. If she goes anywhere near him, I'll put a stop to it."

I became quite indignant on her behalf. "You know quite well what I mean," he said severely. "I know perfectly well how she makes her money. It doesn't concern me, as long as she confines herself to continentals. The Prince is a man with a weakness, and he likes to visit Paris."

"Is that why . . . ?"

"It struck me that it might be a useful insurance policy. She is in our debt now, and part of the price is no scandal. Sooner or later they would have met in Paris; and he is like a child in a sweetshop when it comes to women. He really cannot resist. Certainly he would not have been able to resist her. You have no idea how much time the Embassy spends clearing up the mess from these affairs. I want to stop this one in advance. Tell her that, if you please."

"Very well."

"Besides, he is notoriously stingy. She will earn more from knowing him than from sleeping with him."

"I'll pass the message on."

CHAPTER 10

If I am spending a great deal of time digressing on the subject of this woman, rather than recounting the excitement of life as a gatherer of intelligence for the British Empire, it is for two reasons. The first is that she is relevant to my story; the second is that she was very much more interesting than my daily routine. For example, on my return to Paris I spent some considerable time putting the finishing touches to my investigation of French naval policy, and that involved a good deal of time interviewing people (in my capacity as journalist) at the Coal Exchange, and poring over daily lists of bulk coal trades. Fascinating? Exciting? Do you wish to hear more? I thought not.

In fact, I would even say that coal itself is a more interesting subject than the people who trade it. Each commodity and financial instrument attracts different sorts of people. Dealers in bonds are different from dealers in shares; those who trade in commodities are different again, and each commodity and each exchange—rubber, cotton, wool, coal, iron ore—has its own character. Coal is dull, the people who buy and sell it duller still. Their world is black, colourless and without pleasure. The brash young men who are beginning to sell oil and create a whole new market out of nothing are much more interesting; they have a touch of the desert about them, while the coal dealers have infused the gloom of the Picardy coal mines, or the Methodism of south Wales.

And two days a week I traded on my own account. Perhaps I should describe this, as it illustrates the true nature of espionage better than anything else can. I rented a dingy little office in the rue Rameau as soon as I arrived—chosen carefully so that there were several possible exits, and a clear view of the street below in both directions; I had learned from Arnsley Drennan better than ever he realised. It was bleak, uncomfortable and cheap, perfect for my needs. Then I registered myself as Julius de Bruyker, import-export broker, and under the name of that fictitious gentleman of uncertain Low Country origins, I wrote to a young man at the German Embassy who dabbled in intelligence matters. A pleasant but not particularly bright fellow, he came to see me, and I offered him information about the forthcoming British naval exercises. It was interesting, although entirely safe information, but he was delighted to get it. More information followed the next week, and the week after that, until the point came when he began to wonder what I wanted.

Nothing, I said, but any information he had acquired about French troop dispositions in North Africa I would consider a reasonable payment. Such information was of no strategic interest to the Germans, so after a short period considering the matter, they obliged.

Next, I contacted an officer at the Russian Embassy, the Austrian Embassy and in the French intelligence services and offered all of them the same information. All were keen enough, and in return from the Russians in due course I acquired information about a new French cannon, from the Austrians information about French and German diplomatic correspondence and the French gave me details of German armour plating—when complete, this information was passed on to John Stone's companies, and helped make up for some of the inadequacies of British steel manufacturing.

And so it went on; I really was a broker, taking in information and selling it on. The good thing about information is that, unlike gold, it can be duplicated. One piece of information about shipbuilding in Britain, for example, could be traded for information from half a dozen different sources, and each of these could, in turn, multiply themselves many times over. So I supplied information about the new Vickers twelve-inch gun, and got in return detailed information about the German army's new howitzer, the Austrian army's requirement for horses, the Italian Government's negotiating stance on North Africa and the French Government's real policy towards British domination of the upper Nile. Details of the German howitzer were then traded for more information. The beauty of the system was that no individual was ever asked to provide information which would damage their own country—they were asked for material which on its own was harmless until blended with information from different sources, or which affected the security of a foreign rival. Spies are bureaucrats, by and large; they have masters to satisfy and must take that into account as they go about their lives; by supplying information I made their lives easier, and so they regarded me as a useful person to do business with. Of course, the utility of the system could only last as long as I had a monopoly of the method, otherwise the same information would have started reappearing time and again.

For a very small amount of start-up capital, so to speak, I began reaping handsome returns, and do not think that the similarities between what I was doing, and what Elizabeth was doing, escaped me. We were both trading in specialised goods, exploiting weaknesses in the market to sell the same thing to many different customers simultaneously. Success depended on each customer being unaware of the existence of the others. That was the danger which faced both of us.

So, in that period when I was trying to be fascinated by the Coal Exchange, my only real entertainment was provided by Elizabeth. I was curious about her shareholders. Not for any prurient reason, I hope, but for the sake of information only. Accordingly, when I returned to Paris I had Jules, my friendly, trained foot soldier, station himself nearby to watch comings and goings.

A useful lad, this Jules. He was the son of Roger Marchant, an ex-soldier with an incurable hostility to the discipline associated with either the army or any more normal paid work, who was employed on a part-time basis by Thomas Barclay.

"As you are going to do all the energetic work, you must have Roger to help you," Barclay begged, although one look at the man—who was swaying slightly when we were introduced—forced me to say that I could not possibly deprive him of such a useful man. It was not Roger who was the main problem—although absolute reliability was not his watchword—but his wife and several children, whose demands for sustenance far outstripped the poor man's ability to provide for them. The petty-cash box of *The Times* was constantly being raided, first by Barclay and later by myself, in a desperate attempt to get the wretched woman out of the office, to which she resorted when she felt that death and starvation were only hours away. Roger was remarkably insouciant about it all. The duties of family life did not, as far as he could see, necessarily involve feeding it.

It was a flash of genius on my part to solve the problem by employing their son to be my assistant, thus guaranteeing a flow of income into the hands of the mother that could not be diverted into slaking the father's thirst, and securing for myself the services of one of the most useful people I have ever known.

I do not usually spend time discoursing on the character of sixteen-year-olds, but as young Jules is now a grand man of influence throughout France, and, as I can claim some proud responsibility for this, I feel I should divert my story awhile to give a proper account of him.

He was, as I have said, the son—the eldest son—of a poor family, the father a lazy drunkard of amiable disposition, the mother a worrying fusspot, living permanently in a haze of crisis and despair. In one small room lived parents and five children, some of whom were amongst the worst-behaved and most revolting infants I have ever encountered. That they did not all end up in gaol or worse was largely due to the efforts of Jules, who took on the burdens of parenthood which properly belonged to others. He was, in fact, an accomplished criminal by the age of twelve, expert at filching fruit or vegetables from market stalls, milk from dairies, sausages and meat from delivery vans, clothes from department stores. He was also perfecting a good line in picking pockets until I persuaded him that this was an unwise career development.

"Very risky, and for only uncertain gains," I told him severely, waving my wallet in his face. "And I understand that the penalties in France are exceptionally high for this sort of activity. You are too young to spend the next few years in prison and, on the whole, it is better to avoid spending time there at all."

He was not entirely certain how to take my remarks; I had, after all, just caught him with his hand in my pocket and had grabbed his wrist hard to make sure he did not escape. He squealed in pain as he tried to wriggle free, attracting the glances of passersby in the rue de Richelieu, along which I was walking after my luncheon. I waited until he might realise that he was not going to get free of me, and calmed down.

"Good," I said when the noise subsided. "As far as I understand these things you should never, ever work alone, but need someone operating with you to distract the attention of the person whose wallet you admire. Secondly, it is unwise to try and steal from a gentleman; they are far more violent and unpleasant than ordinary working folk, and do not hesitate to call the police. You are only a man of property if you are good at keeping hold of that property. Thirdly, like most well-dressed men, I keep very little cash in my wallet, and much more in the bank. If you want serious wealth, I suggest you address your attentions over there."

I waved behind him at the façade of the Crédit Lyonnais, just visible on the boulevard beyond.

He continued to eye me with ever more doubt, and began to shuffle uneasily from foot to foot.

"Are you hungry? You have a sort of pinched look about you. Perhaps you were stealing to buy yourself a good meal?"

"No," he said scornfully. "I mean, I am hungry, but . . ."

"In that case, young man, you must allow me to offer you a good bowl of soup and bread. The contents of this wallet were so nearly yours, I feel such proximity to triumph should not go without recompense."

He looked at me with narrowed eyes once more, but did not object when I led him—still holding on to his wrist quite firmly—up the stairs to a *bouillon* on the other side of the road.

It was still quite busy, but there was no difficulty getting a table in the corner and I sat the boy against the wall, so he could not make a run for it with any chance of getting away. I ordered him a large bowl of onion soup and bread and water, and watched with satisfaction as he ate.

"I hope all this makes you realise that I am not inclined to call the police, nor even to inform your father of your activities. Do you wish to be like him when you grow up?" I asked gently.

He looked at me with a wisdom and sadness beyond his years. "No," he replied with a touch of steel in his voice. "And I won't be."

I pondered this as he ate his soup. He was very hungry, and ate with both noise and relish; the offer of a second bowl was accepted with enthusiasm. It is remarkable how much you can find out about someone in a short time and a few words. The boy was courageous and defiant. He knew loyalty—even though its object was undeserving. He was prepared to take responsibility, to act where others might have sat and merely accepted their fate.

"Now, listen to me," I said seriously. "I have not paid to pour litres of soup into you for no reason. I have been thinking, and I have a proposal for you. Do you want to hear it?"

He nodded cautiously.

"Can you write and count adequately? I know you can read."

He nodded. "Course I can."

"Good. In which case you are well to leave school. It has nothing else to offer you. You need a proper job, which I am offering you."

He gazed at me in that same, steady fashion, not reacting at all, really. Just patient.

"As you may know, I am a journalist . . ."

"I don't like the English," he remarked, although without any personal animosity.

"Nor do you have to. In my work I need messages sent, letters delivered. I will occasionally need other tasks done. Following people, watching people without being seen. Perhaps even going into their houses and taking things."

He frowned. "You do that?"

"It's an odd job, journalism. And no, I do not. You do. Do you have any objection?"

He shook his head.

"The pay will be adequate, even generous, that is to say about a hundred francs a month. Does that suit you?"

He stared at me. I knew it was almost as much as his father earned.

"You will be punctual at all times, start work when I say and finish when I say. There will be no days off unless I say so."

He nodded.

"You agree?"

He nodded again. I held out my hand. "Then we must shake on it. Present yourself at my hotel tomorrow morning at eight."

He gripped my hand over the range of soup bowls and, for the first time, his face creased in a broad, happy grin.

CHAPTER 11

Jules did turn up the next morning, and more or less from the moment he walked through the door, he transformed my life. I only ever had to tell him once about how to do any task, or where something was to be put. Anything I requested he did speedily and well. He was never late and was as tidy as I was messy. On his own account he began teaching himself English by borrowing a copy of *David Copperfield* and a dictionary, and showed a considerable flair for the language. When there was nothing for him to do, he retired to a corner and read quietly; when there was something to do, he did it without questioning.

And so, when the question of the Countess Elizabeth Hadik-Barkoczy von Futak uns Szala's shareholders began to pique me, I naturally dispatched Jules to discover who they were. As a test of his ingenuity, I did not tell him how to go about it, but rather let him discover for himself the best way of accomplishing the task.

It took him two weeks which, on the whole, was not bad going, and at the end of that time he produced a list of four names. I was impressed; professionalism in any field is something to be admired, and in a relatively short space of time Elizabeth had captured a Russian count attached to the Embassy and a banker, both married and of stupendous wealth. In addition there was a composer of a progressive hue, who made up for his limited financial success by the possession of a very wealthy wife; while the last one was an heir, that is to say the likely inheritor of a grand fortune with no personal merit of his own. By the time Elizabeth had finished with him, the fortune was considerably smaller. And that was before she had a reputation for knowing the Prince of Wales. Shortly after she got back to Paris, the composer was replaced—she was quite ruthless in these matters—with the Finance Minister, in whose company I had met her at Biarritz and a few months after that the heir, his fortune now depleted, was also cast aside. Each one of these made her wealthy. All combined rapidly made her prodigiously so; each one, for example, took on the entirety of the rent on her house, paid for her servants and gave her generous gifts of jewellery, which she kept in a safebox, each piece labelled with the name of the giver so she would not wear the wrong piece when being visited. Four-fifths of her income, after a portion of her debts were paid off, was carefully banked.

By the time I received Jules's report, I had met three of these characters at various evenings to which she had invited me; and I must say that all of them behaved with such discretion that I would never have guessed the reasons for their presence. Each treated Elizabeth with the utmost courtesy and respect, and never gave the slightest hint of any untoward familiarity. If any suspected the role of the others, they again let no hint of it escape them, but conversed in an easy and polite manner as to any other acquaintance.

In return she was absolutely discreet, and never once caused them any embarrassment or awkwardness—although some at least would have been happy had they been known to have conquered her. Each individual was of high personal worth—I do not mean in financial terms although they obviously were that, but in terms of character. Except for Rouvier, whose position struck me as a strange lapse of taste on her part. Wherever she had learned it, Elizabeth had the art of choosing well. She gave them a sort of loyalty in addition to the other services she provided, and they responded.

She invited about a dozen people every week. All were men; if Elizabeth had a blind spot it was to have an almost total disregard for other women. Men excited in her no rivalry or jealousy; women did so often and in violent terms. I would not go so far as to say that she detested members of her own sex, but she had no high opinion of them. It must be said that many women returned this emotion in full force, instinctively disliking, suspecting or fearing her. Many would have been glad to bring her low; it was her vulnerable spot, all the more so because she was unaware of it—a surprising weakness of perception in one who in all other matters saw so clearly.

After a month or so I was promoted to the inner circle of admirers who spent every Thursday evening in her company. I was never offered, nor would I have accepted, a role as one of her shareholders. I didn't have enough money, for one thing, and besides, I rather liked things the way they were.

She ordered her evenings well. No subject was banned from discussion; all she insisted on was that conversation was conducted in the most civilised of terms. Argument she allowed as the essence of conversation, but any heat or emotion was utterly forbidden. I have seen many a man conduct a business meeting with less skill than she ran her evenings. She managed to persuade everyone who was invited that they were members of a special group, unusually insightful, witty and sagacious, and that these qualities came, in some mysterious fashion, from being in her presence. Certainly, I thought my own conversation far more sparkling on those evenings than at other times, my jokes better, my understanding of the world stage more profound, and I was far more cautious than most of the other people there.

It was also genuinely interesting and enjoyable. The routine was unvarying: a supper of excellent food accompanied by the best wine, which she spent much of the previous day choosing so that her chef could have all ready, followed by conversation which lasted until eleven-thirty, at which point our hostess would rise and tell us, quite simply, that it was time to leave. The evening would seem to be formless; sometimes we would break up into small groups and discuss different subjects, sometimes the conversation would involve all present. Elizabeth herself rarely gave her own opinion; rather she questioned, sometimes respect-fully, sometimes in fun, making her views plain by her responses to the opinions of others. Only on the subject of literature did she give her own views, and in these she demonstrated that, in French, Russian and Ger-man, she was remarkably well read. This was, you remember, when Russian Soul and Spirituality were all the rage in fashionable Europe, and everyone had to be able to quote huge chunks of *Anna Karenina* by heart. Of English Elizabeth knew all but nothing at that time.

It has been said many times both that the French are the world's most accomplished conversationalists, and that the art of conversation is dying. The former is true, and if it is also the case that it has declined since the Revolution, then the conversation of the ancien régime must have been truly splendid. I came to look forward to those evenings as the summit of my week, my evening of pleasure after a week of often unprofitable labour. In winter they would be held in the drawing room of the house she had taken in the rue Montesquieu, with dozens of candles and a fire adding a feeling of comfort to the conversation. It was a large high-ceilinged room, some fifty feet long and thirty wide. On one side was a range of windows that gave onto a glass-enclosed veranda filled with palm trees and birds; on another a wide door opened into a smaller, more intimate sitting room. All around were china, cameos and silver, the walls hung with Gobelins tapestries and paintings, mainly Italian and French. Much of this had come with the house, which she rented from the Marquis d'Alençon, who was then living in Mexico to escape the police. But she had added her own touches, and these had been chosen with care—again, where she learned discernment in such matters, and how she avoided the vulgarity of her fellows, I could not understand.

It sounds very artificial and in a way it was so; artificial in the way that an opera or symphony is different from the cacophonous blaring of a music-hall band. Some sneer at such meetings, denouncing the formality and the lack of spontaneity; they maintain that conviction is displayed best through loud voices and violent verbal assault, that politeness ensures the triumph of the commonplace. Not so. Politeness, I learned at her salon, is a demanding discipline; to convince others without recourse to the tricks of the demagogue or bully requires a high level of intelligence, especially when the audience is learned and intelligent. Courtesy elevates thought to the highest level, especially when the subject is contentious. And the salons, which were then the principal debating chambers of the French political, financial and intellectual elites, far more important than the Chambre des Deputés, always insisted on courtesy above all other qualities.

That did not mean that the conversations were bland; far from it. Frequently they were highly charged, especially where I was concerned. This was the period—one of the many periods—in which anti-English sentiment was running high in France, and many would have been more than glad to see some sort of armed conflict to vent their frustrations at England's habitual superiority. To convince me that my country was the main source of disorder in the world was a frequent aim and I was required on many occasions to justify my country to my friends—for friends they became, despite the differences between us.

Take, for example, the opinions of Jules Lepautre, Deputy for Caen, for whom England and the English (present company excepted, *cher Monsieur*) were the embodiment of all evil. We had not come to France's aid in 1870 and had positively encouraged Germany to dismember the country; had lured France into a disastrous commercial treaty with the sole purpose of wrecking its industries; had bought the Suez Canal in order to strangle France's Empire before it was even properly established; were meddling in Eastern Europe, and manoeuvring to exclude France from Egypt.

I conceded many of these points, but responded by asking: what is to be done about it? Britain and France couldn't fight a war even if they wanted to.

"Why not?"

"Because you can only have a war if both sides are fundamentally similar. Where are the two countries to fight, and with what? France, I hope, would never be foolish enough to have a naval war; a small portion of the Royal Navy would suffice to eliminate all of the French navy in a few hours. And why would Britain wish to pit its army against France's? That would be as unequal a struggle, and even if we could invade I cannot see any advantage to it. Nor can I see any likelihood of France invading

Britain. It has not succeeded in the past nine hundred years, and I see little prospect of its fortunes changing in the near future. So how is there to be a war? Much better to recognise the impossibility of it and then become friends. Ally France's army with Britain's navy and who could possibly stand against us?"

I mention this conversation—which began on a cold evening in late September 1890—not because of the wisdom of my remarks, as there was little in them, nor because they accurately reflected my views, as they did not. Rather, it was because of the intervention by Abraham Netscher, then head of the Banque de Paris et des Pays Bas and an infrequent visitor to Elizabeth's house.

"I think my two friends here are shadowboxing," he said comfortably, sipping from his glass of brandy. He was a fine man, tall and impressive in his stance, with a high-domed forehead and a piercing stare. In fact, this was because he was short-sighted and was too vain to wear his glasses in company. Accordingly he had a tendency to peer at people, and sometimes to stare a little above the right or left shoulder of the person he was addressing, a habit which was remarkably disconcerting as it gave the impression always that he was talking to someone else.

In many people such vanity would be undignified, but no one would ever have thought this of M. Netscher, once they knew him a little. He was a man of exceptional intelligence, and allied this capacity to great wisdom and immense experience, having lived through—and prospered through—several regimes and generations of politicians.

"You are both defining the notion of war far too narrowly," he remarked, "and in a fashion which, if you will forgive me for saying so, is remarkably old-fashioned for people who are so young." Netscher was somewhere near his seventieth year at this point, but still had a good decade left before his failing powers obliged him to rest.

"The marching of soldiers is usually to steal territory or money from the opponent. But in this case, as you say, neither France nor England have any such designs on the other. This is not because nations are any less greedy, I fear, but because wealth no longer lies in land or treasure. France could, perhaps, invade and annexe all of Cornwall, or Scotland and Ireland, and it would scarcely damage England in any way, except in its pride. Its power lies in its accumulated wealth, and that cannot be stolen by armies. London is the centre of the world of money. It is an empire on its own; in fact the real Empire only exists to serve the needs of London. From the incessant movement of capital comes all of England's power.

"But it is fragile, this strength. Never in the whole of humanity has so much power been generated by such a feeble instrument. The flow of capital and the generation of profit depend on confidence. The belief that the word of a London banker is his bond. On that evanescent assurance depends all industry, all trade and the very Empire itself. A determined and sensible enemy would not waste his time and gold striking at the navy or invading the colonies. He would aim to destroy the reputation of a handful of bankers in London. Then the power of England would dissolve like mist on a warm morning."

"I think such an enemy would discover that it is more resilient than you say, sir," I suggested. "Just because it is a power that cannot be touched or held, does not mean that it is not real or strong. The most enduring institution in the world is the Church, which depends on faith alone to survive, and it has survived empire after empire for nearly two thousand years. I would be quite content if the influence of the City of London lasted half as long."

"That is true," he conceded. "Though with the Pope locked in the Vatican by Italian troops, and priests being expelled from schools across Europe, and the teaching of the Church being challenged by historians and linguists and scientists across the world, I do not find that you greatly strengthen your argument. I doubt I will live long enough to see the last church close its doors forever; but you may."

The old man piqued my interest. I wondered for a moment whether he had even come that evening specifically to have that conversation with me, but eventually dismissed the notion. My secret life was unassailable, I was sure. No one connected me—the associate of aristocrats and princes, the dilettante journalist for *The Times*—with the occupant of the little office in the rue Rameau who bought and sold information from diplomats, soldiers and other spies. Nonetheless, I dwelt on his words for several days, and the more I considered them, the more I believed that his words had reflected something he had heard, or half heard.

Could such an attempt succeed? Not in the way that M. Netscher said, of course; he was exaggerating there. But it was certainly true that inflicting severe damage on the City of London would be more harmful than defeating England's army, were it ever so foolish as to join battle with any other than half-armed natives. Every week, hundreds of millions of pounds flowed through London, its banks and discount houses, clearing houses and depositories. The whole world raised its loans through the City. The decision of a banker could determine the outcome of a war, or whether that war would take place. Wars were fought on credit; cut off the credit and the army must stop dead in its tracks as surely as if it had run out of food or ammunition.

Attacking the reputation of the City could be relatively inexpensive and have no consequences if it failed. But how could it be done? I could not see it. "If it can be imagined, it can be achieved." Was anyone doing the imagining? I thought about it for several days, then realised that mere thinking would accomplish nothing. I had to do some work.

Discovering anything by examining the career of M. Netscher was fruitless, it turned out: he had been around for such a long time that he knew absolutely everyone, and heard everything. There was no simple solution there; so I had to go back over the last few years and discover who his enemies and rivals were; this also produced nothing of any great interest. Such musings came over the following days, however; and that particular evening ended without anything else of interest. I did, however, write a short report on the conversation and sent it to Wilkinson—I was a good bureaucrat already, and realised the importance of passing on responsibility for things I could do nothing about.

Thursday evening became part of my life, something I looked forward to and enjoyed, partly for the conversation, but more for Elizabeth, whose presence I came to find oddly comforting. I took pleasure in watching her in what was now her natural habitat, so to speak, the way she could conduct a gathering like a maestro, discreetly and without ever imposing herself. I watched with something close to affection as she relaxed ever more into her role, became more sure of herself, more adept at her profession. In general I quite forgot what exactly that profession was. It was impossible to think of her as anything other than that which she wished to be.

One evening, though, the salon ended differently. She had been quiet, unusually reserved all evening; her admirers appeared to feel they had been given short weight. Ordinarily, she would have risen to the challenge, drawn them out, calmed them down, flattered and reassured; this evening she seemed strained and almost ill at ease, almost as though she wished they would go away.

And eventually they all did, except for me; she signalled quietly that she wished me to remain, so I held back until we were alone, the door shut to the world outside. I wondered for a moment whether the evening was going to turn into a night of excitement, but it rapidly became clear that she had—for her—a greater intimacy in mind.

"I am afraid I feel ashamed of myself," she said, once we moved into the little salon, which she kept for herself alone. "When I said I would not help you in your work, I did not dream that I might need help. And now I do."

"I, in contrast, am delighted. How can I be of service?"

"My diaries have disappeared. And so has Simon."

"You keep a diary?" The face of Arnsley Drennan swam back into my mind at that moment, his sneering, mocking face as he congratulated me at least on not being stupid enough to keep a diary.

"It's your fault," she continued reproachfully. "I began with those letters I wrote to you from Nancy. I enjoyed writing them, and even after our association came to an end, I kept on writing them, but this time to myself only. I dare have no intimates, no real friends, no family. Only myself. And so it is to myself that I write."

"You must be very lonely."

"No," she said, "of course not. Why should I be?"

"Do you never wish for more?"

"I have never had a friend who has not betrayed me. Or whom I have not betrayed. So I do not permit it."

"I am your friend, I think."

"That merely poses the question—will you betray me? Or shall I betray you first? It will happen, you know, sooner or later. It always does."

"It is a cold world you live in."

"Which is why I must look after myself above all. I honour my promises, but must care for no one."

"I don't believe you."

She shrugged. "It is not important at the moment."

I thought it was the most important thing of all, but let it pass. "These letters to yourself, then. They contain details of all you have done? Everyone you have associated with? What are we dealing with here? How big are they?"

"Large. Two volumes, with about three hundred pages each in them."

"And they are honest?"

"A true account of my life." She smiled. "They deal with everything and everyone. In very considerable detail. It would cause severe embarrassment to many people. Frankly I do not care about that; it is no more than they deserve. But my life would be ruined as well."

"And I presume it also says a great deal about my activities in France?"

"Not that much; I didn't begin them until after our arrangement came to an end. But I think there is enough to get you into trouble. If it's any consolation, I was very warm about you."

"It isn't."

"What should I do?" she asked.

"You said Simon has disappeared. Who is he?"

"My servant. You remember? He had many troubles with the law. I employed him because—well, I thought that one day I might need such a person. He was always loyal to me."

"You found him in Nancy?"

"No. I have no contact with anyone from there. He is a Parisian."

"His loyalty to you seems to have run out. He knew about these diaries?"

"I thought not. But I suppose he did."

I tried to digest all this unwelcome news. "Well," I said eventually. "The obvious thing to do, and the easiest, is nothing. If these diaries are ever published you would be very much more famous—notorious, I should say—than you are now. I imagine they would become a great literary success."

She smiled, but only weakly. "It is not a reputation I want. Besides, far too much would not pass the censors. If that is all there was, I might see your point. It is an age where any sort of debauchery is tolerated, as long as it brings fame with it.

"But I find I like being what I am now, even if it is only an illusion. I do not want to go back."

I have rarely felt as comfortable and contented as I did sitting in that room. That may seem strange, perhaps heartless, but I must be honest on this point. It was warm, the lighting was soft, the chair I was sitting on comfortable. Elizabeth, dressed that evening in a simple costume of blue silk, was as beautiful as ever I had seen her, and her worry created a degree of intimacy between us that made even me regret my refusal of the offer she had once made and which, I knew, would never be repeated. I could easily have spent the rest of the evening, the whole night, just talking of nothing and watching the fire flicker in the grate. In my life, I think only Freddie Campbell could induce such a feeling of comfort and safety in me: of family, almost, or so I imagined, although as I never had much of a family I cannot speak with authority on the subject.

"Assuming you are correct and that this Simon stole your diaries, it will be almost impossible to find him. We will have to wait until he surfaces. Until then it would be like looking for a needle in a haystack. It is easy to disappear in Paris. There are few things more simple, in fact."

"He has already surfaced." She handed over an envelope. "This arrived today. It is the only reason I went to my bureau and checked. Otherwise I might not have noticed anything amiss until Sunday, which is when I usually write up my week."

I studied the contents carefully. It was an extract from a newspaper, a funeral notice of a Dr. Stauffer from the *Journal de Lausanne*. No date, nothing else at all. No message, no demand for money.

"What does this mean?"

She shook her head, treating the question like a fly buzzing around her, something she wanted to go away.

"It clearly means something to you."

"He was someone I knew, who was kind to me once. It is of no significance except to prove that Simon has the diaries. This was stuck into them. He is trying to frighten me. Starting with harmless information, making me nervous about what will come next. Will you help me?"

I nodded. "If I can. But you may have to pay heavily. I will not recommend you pay blackmail; that will merely encourage more demands. A one-off purchase is another thing, though. Are you ready to pay high?"

She nodded.

"Then I will try. The first thing will be to make contact. I will post someone outside your door just in case. And you must let me know immediately you hear anything else."

"Thank you, my friend." It was a word which did not often pass her lips. It sounded strange coming from her, as though she did not really know what it meant.

CHAPTER 12

The next day, I put Jules onto the task. "Time to earn your pay, my boy. You know the Countess von Futak's house?"

Jules nodded. He should; he had already spent more time than he wanted camped outside it.

"Back there again, I'm afraid. I want you to watch the gate. Someone may deliver a letter by hand; I want to know who it is. Everyone who puts anything in the letterbox—I want a full description, times, everything. And no," I said, as I could see he was about to speak. "I will not tell you why. If you are lucky it will only be for a day or so."

Jules was lucky: it took a few hours. At lunchtime another letter was delivered, and Jules followed the man who dropped it quickly in the letterbox and hurried on. The description was that of Simon, and Jules tracked him all the way up to Belleville, where he was renting a room in a hotel for itinerants. The letter, I later learned, was a demand for 10,000 francs, which was encouraging: he was getting down to business, and it seemed he was only after small change. Perhaps he did not appreciate exactly how valuable the diaries were. Or perhaps this was just the start.

Jules and I had lunch in my room, which he brought up from the kitchen. The hotel did have running water in the rooms, but not hot. The manager had kindly fitted a gas pipe and a little heater for me because I had taken the rooms for a year. On this I could brew my tea and heat up sufficient water for washing and shaving, as the sanitary arrangements were somewhat limited. That did not matter so much; lavish use of eau-de-cologne covered a multitude of sins.

"Listen," I said, as Jules set out the little table by the window. "I have another job for you. How do you feel like travelling?"

Jules brightened.

"How often have you been outside Paris?"

He thought. "Never," he said eventually.

"Never?"

"Well, I went to Versailles once, to find my father."

"And did that experience of foreign climes create a desire for more?"

"Not really."

"A pity. Because I want you to go to Lausanne. In Switzerland."

Jules gaped. I might as well have said I wanted him to go to the moon.

"It's time you saw the world a little," I said. "You can't spend your entire life in Paris. It will take you a day to get there, the same to get back and however long it takes to complete the job I want done. I will give you money for the train ticket, and board and lodging when you are there."

Jules was looking decidedly uncomfortable. He was a street urchin, even if he was one with dreams. The prospect of leaving his stamping ground, the streets and passages he knew so well, struck terror into his heart. But, brave lad that he was, he recovered swiftly. This, I could see him saying to himself, was necessary. This he had to do. I sympathised with his terror and pretended not to notice.

"When in Lausanne, I want you to find out about a man called Stauffer. I know nothing about him, except that he is dead. Start at the local paper, ask for obituaries, that sort of thing. Find out who he was. About his wife, children and relations, especially children. Any unusual stories, scandals or incidents. Anything at all, really. "

Jules nodded hesitantly. "Can I ask why?"

"No. It doesn't matter why. Think of it simply as good practise for your life as a journalist in years to come."

"What life?"

"Dear boy, you are made for it. When you leave me, as one day you no doubt will, you will have to get a proper job. You will be an excellent journalist, and I will recommend you to an editor when you are ready. You will have to start at the bottom; after that it will be up to you. What's the matter? Is there something else you want to do?"

Jules had sat down on the bed, his face white with shock. "I don't know what to say . . ." he muttered eventually.

"Well, if you don't want to do it . . ."

"Of course I do," he said, looking up urgently. "Of course I do."

"Excellent," I replied. "That's settled then. I suggest you spend your time on the train beginning to prepare yourself. Buy every single newspaper, and read them all, carefully."

The look of pleasure on his face as he bustled about, helping himself to money from the drawer to fund his journey, was worth the generosity. In fact, the idea had only just occurred to me, and I had suggested it somewhat too hastily. But it was a good one. Jules was a natural, hence his current success. And it invigorated him and made him even more diligent in my service. I was his ticket to a new life, and he was absolutely determined that it should not slip from his grasp. He went off half an hour later to find his best clothes and set off for Lausanne.

And then I put the whole matter out of my mind, to concentrate on work. "Recent Developments in the French Banking Sector." One of those wordy, ponderous articles *The Times* likes so much. I have never understood who it thinks might read them. I was following my hunch about the comments Netscher had made, and had briefly all but abandoned my other business.

Branching out into banking was difficult, as I had nothing to sell. I wrote to Wilkinson, but did not expect a reply. He never did if he could avoid it. It was somewhat dispiriting; I had a high opinion of my progress, but I had not the slightest idea whether anyone had noticed. So I contacted John Stone, the only other person in whom I could confide. I don't know why I did this; it was not my habit to go running to figures of authority when in difficulty, but I felt the need to talk the question over with someone, get an outside opinion, so to speak.

He was staying at the Hôtel du Louvre; he had a suite there more or less permanently reserved for him when he came to Paris for business. So I went to lunch with him, although not in the public dining area. I did not want it advertised that I associated with such people, for their sake as well as my own.

It was a pleasant meeting, much to my surprise, as I had not greatly taken to him on our first encounter. He told me how impressed he was by my progress, how Mr. Wilkinson was delighted, and telling everyone in Whitehall about his young prodigy, "For whom, of course, he modestly takes full credit," Stone added drily.

"It's very kind of you," I said. "I didn't know anyone paid the slightest bit of attention to what I was doing."

"Goodness, yes. You are considered quite an oracle already. Of course, there is still considerable opposition to the way you go about things, but no one argues with success overmuch. So, tell me, what can I do for you?"

"I'm not sure. I don't know whether it's anything at all. It may be just a will o' the wisp. It was a passing comment I picked up at a dinner party, at the Countess von Futak's salon . . ."

"You go to her salon?"

"Ah . . . yes. Well, not often. Sometimes. Why?"

"Oh, no matter. Go on. Your comment?"

So I told him about old Abraham Netscher, and his musings on the vulnerability of the City of London. It sounded very lame.

"I see," Stone said when I had finished. "And you think that . . ."

"Not really, not seriously. At least, it occurred to me that it would be a remarkable coup to pull off, if anyone dared try. But I have no more than that to go on."

"I know many people in banking," Stone said thoughtfully, "including Netscher, who is a fine man. But I do not suppose anyone would tell me of such a scheme, even if it existed. I will listen with more care than usual. And, if you desire, I will happily provide you with some introductions."

"That is kind of you."

He waved it aside. "Now, tell me of this Countess," he said.

"Why?"

"She is the talk of Paris; I would like to know why."

I described her as best I could, the official version, that is, and described her coup—I attributed it to her rather than to Wilkinson—in Biarritz with the Prince of Wales. I noticed I was jealous of her reputation and wanted to keep my knowledge of her entirely to myself.

"You know no more than that?" Stone said, curious for the first time in our acquaintance.

"Do you?"

"She is a Hungarian countess, who decided to travel when her husband died. I think her family disapproved of her marriage, and she was disinclined to forgive them when he died. I met her some months ago and, like you, found her quite charming."

He nodded thoughtfully. "I am giving a small dinner for friends, in four days' time," he said abruptly. "Would you care to join me? There will be a couple of people whom you might wish to know."

"That is kind."

"And would you do me the great service of escorting the Countess to the restaurant for me? I am afraid I have meetings all day and cannot be sure when they will end. Although she likes to be late, she very much disapproves of other people keeping her waiting."

"With pleasure," I said without the slightest hesitation to betray my surprise. It was not that he had invited her, nor that she had, apparently, accepted. It was the uncomfortable, almost schoolboyish bashfulness on his face which astonished me.

CHAPTER 13

Escorting a woman like Elizabeth to a dinner is something everyone really should do at least once in their lives. I had only once glimpsed her properly in her public role, in Biarritz; this was very different. I arrived with a carriage at eight, as required, having spent the afternoon preparing myself in a way which was quite unaccustomed. I was, I believe, perfectly elegant, or as elegant as I can be; dressing up formally has never been my favourite occupation and I am quite prepared to admit that I have no sense of style whatsoever. But I looked decent enough by the end, or so I thought. I seemed to have spent hours brushing my clothes and wrestling with collar studs and cravat. I even had to get the bar owner's wife to come up and help me. Eventually I could take no more; if my cravat was squint, my coat still a little dusty, so be it.

However proud I was of my appearance, my sense of personal presence dimmed to nothing when Elizabeth descended the stairs as I waited to collect her. She was breathtaking, her hair up to reveal her long, white neck, wearing a dress of such beauty that I could not understand how it might have been imagined, let alone made.

I should explain here that she was something of a revolutionary in the matter of dress; fashion she studied as assiduously as a stockbroker studies share prices, or a gambler the form of horses. She was not simply at the height of fashion; dear me no. She defined it; and in so doing created for herself an evanescent power which propelled her to a central role in the workings of society. She was one of those few, and remarkable, people whose choices told other people what they should wear and, in a particular way, determined what beauty and elegance were. She was, in other words, entirely professional and serious about her business, and made it seem natural, easy and thoughtless.

She always went for grey when she really wanted to impress, and that evening wore silver-grey silk edged with pearls—hundreds of them—cut almost obscenely low, sleeveless with long gloves in a slightly darker shade. The dress itself clung close to her body— outrageously so, considering the fashion of a mere nine months earlier— and it was darted with extraordinarily intricate embroidery. The whole was completed with a tight necklace of alternating pearls and diamonds, five strands thick, a delicate matching tiara and a painted Louis XV fan.

"Madame, you are exquisite," I said and meant every word.

"I do believe I am," she said with a smile. "Shall we go?"

And so we did, to Lapérouse on the Left Bank, a restaurant which was fashionable enough, but not the sort of place that the great courtesans of Paris normally attended. Maxim's was—and still is—the favourite haunt of such people; Lapérouse was for politicians, and literati, with a high seriousness quite at odds with the gaudy frivolity which characterised the demimonde.

"I didn't realise you knew John Stone," I said as the carriage trundled along the Champs Elysées; it was already long since dark and I could only dimly see her face, even though I was sitting only a foot away and opposite her.

"You must realise by now that I know a great many people," she said. "I met Mr. Stone on a train journey. I had taken a trip to Vienna . . ."

"To your family, no doubt?"

"Just so. In fact I was taken there by a shareholder, who then went on to the Far East. So I was alone and Mr. Stone was coming back from somewhere in the Balkans. It is a long and dull voyage, unless you are enamoured of trains, so we entertained each other. I found him very civil and gentlemanly."

I was desperate to ask, but restrained myself.

"No," she said.

"Pardon?"

"The answer to the question you are trying not to ask."

"Oh."

"I like his company, as I do yours. Of my life he knows only what I have told him, which is little. I very much hope it will stay that way."

"If it does not, it will not be my doing."

"I know that. Have you made any . . ."

"I know where Simon is living, and plan to visit him shortly," I said. "If he is reasonable—that is, if he is conventionally venal—the matter should be wrapped up soon enough."

"Thank you." She said it simply, almost proudly, but it meant much to me. Then the coach slowed and we arrived at the restaurant. Elizabeth's whole bearing changed, she transformed herself—transfigured, I might say—before my eyes. She was about to step onto her stage.

If there were any lingering insecurities still within her, she did not show them in the slightest. Nor did she let slip even a hint of the immense strain she was under because of her diaries. She was magnificent, carefree, delightful. Every single man in the room—Stone had rented one of the private dining suites—fell under her power within seconds without her having to do anything at all except breathe. She was charming, intelligent, witty, serious as required. Never coquettish—that would have been inappropriate—but always warm and thoughtful in manner. She even managed to restrain her distaste for the other women there; to them she was polite, and it only came through once that she regarded their presence as a waste of space. Why would anyone need more than one woman in the room, when she was that woman? She made the dinner party, which was vibrant, glittering as a result, instead of the rather dull dinner of businessmen it would otherwise have been. Stone was not a natural host and I could not see what the point of the occasion was as far as he was concerned. He provided a setting in which Elizabeth could shine, and she took the opportunity to do so, performing the role without a fault or false step.

I found myself sitting at the end of the table, between the wife of a banker and a senior stockbroker from Petiet, Kramstein, then one of the better-bottomed undertakings at the Bourse. The one was amusing, the other useful. Madame Kollwitz was immunised from any possibility of jealousy or envy by the fact that she was stout, about fifty-five years old and had never been beautiful. This allowed her abundant good humour and perception to come to the fore.

"And you have to talk to me, when you would rather be in orbit around the sun," she said with a twinkle in her eye once we had disposed of the usual preliminaries.

"Certainly not . . ." I began robustly.

"Oh, of course you do, who would not? She is very lovely and by all accounts quite sweet. Is that not the case?"

"I believe she is very pleasant."

"A woman whom all men love. A terrible fate for any young girl, I think. Still, I'm sure she can look after herself. Tell me, how truly besotted is Mr. Stone with her, do you know?"

"I didn't realise . . ."

"You are most unobservant for a journalist," she commented. "She has been with him to the opera twice in the past fortnight, and it is reliably reported that both of them detest the opera. Each goes to please the other. Do you think someone should tell them that they are inflicting mutual torture for no good reason?"

"I do not intend to."

"No. Still, it would be a prize, would it not? Another insult to France from our enemy, to have our most glittering jewel carried off?"

"I don't think . . ."

"Oh, look at him!" she said scornfully, brushing my doubts aside. "If you make allowances for the fact that he has not the slightest idea how to woo or seduce a woman, look at the way he is talking to her. Admittedly, he may be telling her all about profit ratios on machine-gun manufacture, but look at the way his head turns towards her, look at his eyes! And look how easily she deals with it as well; not rejecting, but not encouraging, either. Poor man. It could cost him a pretty penny before all is over."

"I beg your pardon?"

"Have you never wondered where all these diamonds come from, dear boy?"

"No," I said, with, I hope, a credible tone of surprise in my voice. "I assumed she was rich."

She looked at me pityingly.

"Well, um . . ."

Fortunately, my attention was taken over by the stockbroker on my right, whose conversation was less fascinating but more useful. We established our mutual credentials, with me stressing my current labours writing on developments in French banking, the evolution of the capital markets, the poor state of the French Bourse in comparison to vibrancy of the London stock market. He was surprised that a journalist should be so interested in such things.

"For example," I said, "French banks have never taken up the opportunities of empire. I would have thought the possibility of loans to your colonies would have stimulated immense activity in the capital markets, yet I see very little."

Monsieur Steinberg nodded. "We are risk-averse here," he said. "There have been too many disasters for people to trust the credit markets. And it is all a question of trust. Not, at the moment, something our colleagues in London have to worry about. The banks in London succeed in the most outrageous operations because people think they will succeed. They have a century's worth of trust to call on. But they do abuse that trust sometimes; it will rebound on them, and maybe sooner than they think."

"Really? Why is that?"

"Well," he said, leaning forward just a little, "there are strange stories going around, you know. About Barings."

"Dear me. What are they up to now?"

"A good question. I hear Barings may be having surprising difficulty getting takers for an Argentinian loan it is floating."

"That's not so unusual. It's part of the negotiating process, is it not? Besides, with Argentina in the state it's in . . ."

"This is a bit more serious, I think. Credit International, so I heard, is about to refuse outright to take any of the issue at all. Which is ill-mannered of them."

"What loan is this?"

"Buenos Aires Water Supply 5 per cent."

"And the reasoning?"

"Argentine Government is falling to bits, Finance Minister out on his ear, too much debt, fiscal policy in ruins. The usual sort of thing. But that has been known for some time and it has never deterred anyone before. The question is whether anyone will follow Credit International, or whether the magic of Barings will sweep all doubts away once more. But I have never heard of anyone even hesitating before."

Nor had I. Nor had I heard of a bank making public—even if discreetly—its doubts about taking part in a Barings' operation. As M. Steinberg said, it was ill-mannered. And generally, when dealing with Barings, a refusal was generally taken to indicate a weakness of the bank which refused.

"I find this fascinating," I said. "Just the sort of thing that would interest *Times* readers very much. Do you think the Chairman of Credit International would talk to me?"

M. Steinberg looked shocked at the very idea.

"There must be some way of finding out more," I said. "Will you help me? I would be greatly in your debt."

I had realised that, as a practitioner of espionage, asking for assistance is often the most effective way of going about your job. Again, tales of adventure tend to give a false picture, of deceit and subterfuge, of clever stratagems and cunning manipulations. I hope it is clear from my account so far that, in contrast, the most effective weapons in the arsenal of intelligence are money and goodwill. If you cannot buy what you want, ask for it. If you ask the right person, it produces the right response in nearly all cases of importance.

M. Steinberg, for example, was delighted to help. Why should he not be? He wanted to know what was going on as much as I did, and as long as I promised to share with him any discoveries I might make, he was more than willing to guide me in the right direction. Within a few minutes I had the name of a senior figure at Credit International, the information that he had a great weakness for horse racing and so could be found at Longchamp whenever there was a race on, as well as names in other banks which, in the past, had taken part in Barings' issues.

I had a day at the races to look forward to, and a feeling that I was at last beginning to make headway. I relaxed, and began to enjoy the dinner for its own sake, rather than for professional reasons. It was, in fact, an excellent occasion, largely because of the way Elizabeth conducted the proceedings; there was no doubt whatsoever that, although Stone was paying, it was no longer his dinner party. He was her guest, as much as I was. Not that he seemed to mind this; he was a perfectly agreeable conversationalist, if a little serious, when alone. But he shrank in company, giving short and gruff replies, incapable of addressing the whole table, but rather fixing his attention on one person at a time. I could see the effort involved in not giving his entire attention to the woman next to him; every time the conversation flagged a little, he naturally tended to look back towards her, waiting for her lead. Madame Kollwitz was right; he was more than a little taken. I did not know whether she had any vacancies, but if there was one Stone looked as though he would pay a great deal to get on the list. But did she like him enough? She was gay, amusing, friendly, warm, but she could be so even to people she detested, when required.

When the dinner finally came to its end and the party prepared to disperse, one of the guests, a doctor I had not talked to, mentioned he had been invited to an entertainment, and asked if anyone wished to come along.

"A séance," he said with a laugh. "Table-turning. Spirits. Madame Boninska. She is said to be very good."

"I will come," said Elizabeth. "Why not? Would you like to take me, Mr. Stone," she asked playfully, "so we can find out all your secrets?"

The reaction from Stone was remarkable. "No," he snapped. "And you will not go either."

Elizabeth just managed to control a look of fury that passed over her face like a storm cloud before it burst. "I beg your pardon?" There was ice in her voice; I had known her for long enough to want to signal to Stone that he would be well advised to drop the matter, and quickly. He, however, was entirely impervious to tonal subtleties and equally incapable of reading the expression on her face. Maybe he just didn't know her well enough.

"It is charlatanry, rubbish, for fools only. Any sensible person . . . I have seen what these people do to those of a weak or susceptible nature."

"And which am I? A fool or weak?" Elizabeth asked haughtily.

"If you believe in such things? Both."

"Really?"

"Yes. Don't expect me to pander to your desire for fashionable amusements."

"And what does it have to do with you?"

"You invited me, I believe."

"Mr. Cort," said the wife of the banker who had talked to me earlier, taking me by the arm and leading me away, "would you do me the great honour of accompanying me home? My husband has decided to abandon me and go back to his office. So I am quite alone and in need of an escort."

"I would be honoured," I said. Relieved was the more appropriate word, I think; I did not want to witness a fight between Stone and Elizabeth. Well, I did, of course; it was fascinating, but I realised it would be safer to be out of range. Neither, I suspected, would give way easily, and both could be unpleasant when their authority was questioned. They were behaving in a way which was unseemly, embarrassing, and Elizabeth was neither of these. Stone had penetrated to a part of her which was never, ever on public view and forced it into the open. He had exposed her, and therefore weakened her. He would not be easily forgiven. I left them as swiftly as possible—not that either was minded to notice—facing each other and, in the most polite way possible, preparing for a battle to the death.

"I thought I would extricate you," Madame Kollwitz said after we had got into her carriage and lumbered off along the Seine. "I am in fact quite capable of finding my own way home. I have done so on many occasions. But you were staring in a way which was quite impolite, you know."

"I suppose I was," I said. "I think that will be the end of it, though."

She sighed pityingly.

"What have I said now?"

"Do you think a woman like that would ever fight with someone she cared nothing for?"

"But he's . . . well, he's a lot older than she is. Besides, she's not— well, not the type to . . ."

"We shall see. Who knows? She may have met her match this time. Mr. Stone does not behave like a lapdog when he is around her. Unlike M. Rouvier, for example. I almost think it is her duty to skin him alive, although I never thought he would be quite so foolish."

"What do you mean? The Finance Minister?"

"Of course."

"Isn't he married?"

She laughed again. "Of course he's married. What I mean is that he is not rich. And rumour has it he gives her fifty thousand a month."

"What?"

"Are you really this naïve?"

"I think I must be," I said—very convincingly, I believe, for the pitying, scornful look came back to her face. "I'm sure none of it can be true."

"Well," she said, patting me on the hand, "that's very sweet of you."

"But if it was, I mean, where does he get it from? Rouvier, that is."

She shrugged. "I've no idea. Where *might* the Minister of Finance get money from? Difficult one to answer, isn't it?"

"Is there anything you don't know?"

"I know nothing about you, young man. But then, maybe you're not very interesting. Perhaps there is nothing to know."

"I don't think there is."

"Everyone in Paris has a secret, and thinks it is theirs alone. Even my husband thinks I believe him when he says he is going back to the office for an hour." She said it lightly, but turned her head to look out of the window as she spoke.

"Stick to journalism, Mr. Cort, where you never have to understand anything. Or you will find that Paris is a cruel and pitiless place. And tell that to our mysterious Countess as well. Her novelty is wearing off, and many people will take too much pleasure in seeing her fall."

I left her at the door to her apartment block, her words echoing in my ears. It was late and I had work to do the next morning. I wanted a good night's sleep.

CHAPTER 14

I took a gun with me when I went to visit Simon in Belleville. I have mentioned that I did not like them; I still do not. But at that stage I could not call on anyone to assist me in such matters, and Simon was (I recalled) a very big man. I was much more nimble and, I thought, probably more skilled, but if I do have to fight, I prefer the outcome to be beyond all doubt. On such occasions there is little virtue in only just winning.

The meeting, in fact, was quite simple; Simon was totally unskilled in subterfuge. All he had done was rent the room under an assumed name: that was the extent of his precautions. It was a simple matter to wait until I was sure he was at home, then go up the stairs and walk in. It was a dingy boardinghouse, unlit and run-down, which let out rooms to day labourers and itinerants with few questions asked. A place of hopelessness and despair, cold and depressing. Because of the time of day, it was all but deserted; only the concierge was there on the ground floor, and Simon's room was at the very top of the building, well out of earshot. I would not be disturbed.

"Good morning, Simon. I trust you are well. The Countess has been worrying about you. You really shouldn't have run off like that, you know. Not without giving her proper notice."

He stared at me in shock, too dim-witted to understand how easy it had been to find him. My sudden appearance at his door in itself was almost enough to win the battle; he was unnerved from the start and, wisely or not, decided the best response was to say nothing at all. All he could manage, however, was a look of bovine incomprehension that made him appear so stupid it was hard not to burst out laughing.

"May I sit down?" I did not wait for an answer, but occupied the only chair in the room, a rickety thing which felt very insecure. To make a small point, I took out the gun and placed it on the table. Not touching it, but making sure it was pointing in his direction.

"The Countess is concerned you were not paid your last week's wages," I said. "So she asked me to pay a visit and make sure you are well."

He briefly seemed to think that he might be off the hook, despite the gun; then even he realised that there was more to come.

"And she was concerned that you may have inadvertently taken some of her possessions. She wants them back."

"I didn't take anything." He had a low, oddly well-spoken voice; it almost sounded as though it came from a different person entirely.

"Now, Simon, we both know that is not so. I have come to take these things back. In return, I will pay you the wages you are owed."

He shrugged, his confidence returning. "I have nothing. What are you going to do? Call the police?"

I considered. "No, I think not. You know as well as I do that would be a bad idea."

"You're out of luck, then,"

"No. I will shoot you." I picked up the gun and made a show of checking it was loaded.

"Knees first, elbows second. Where do you want to start?"

I editorialise. I was not calm as I said all this; I was sweating profusely and I only just kept my voice from shaking. That may have helped; it did much, I believe, to convince him that I was serious. A nervous man with a gun is much more dangerous than a calm, reasonable one.

Simon was not overly intelligent, but he was good at calculating his position. He had nothing to gain from resisting. Only stubborn pride might have stopped him from falling in with my wishes.

"Where are those diaries?" I said.

"I don't have them."

"But you stole them?"

"She's no countess."

"Of course she isn't," I replied evenly. "She's just a whore. You don't really think that anyone will pay for that, do you? Where are they?"

"Oh, there's more. There's much more than that," he jeered at me. "There's a lot about her you don't know."

"No doubt; but I can't say it bothers me. Where are they?"

He grinned. "I told you; I don't have them."

"Who does?"

"A man. Friend of mine. A good friend. He's looking after them for me."

Oh, really! It was late; I was tired. I sighed with exasperation and picked up the gun.

"Who is he?" I repeated.

"Ten thousand," he said defiantly.

"Just to tell me where they are? You must think I'm a fool."

"It's worth that to you, Mr. Cort," he said. "I've been reading about you, as well."

That was a mistake. I picked up the gun, thought for a moment, then shot him in the leg, the way I had been taught. Simon collapsed onto the floor, gripping his thigh, and screaming; I stuffed a piece of cloth into his mouth and held him down until he stopped, avoiding the spreading pool of blood flowing across the floor as much as possible. I was now entirely calm.

"Who is he?" I said once more.

It took a long time to get it out of him, but what he eventually said made my heart sink. Arnsley Drennan was back in my life. A man calling himself Lefevre, he said. Fifties, fair hair. Thin scar on his face. He had met him in a bar, they'd talked. He'd offered to help, he'd been very persuasive . . .

I sat down on the chair again, oblivious to his moaning. This was bad news. An opportunist thief turned blackmailer like Simon was a simple problem; Arnsley Drennan was another thing entirely. A much more formidable challenge.

"Where is he?"

Again, it took a long time to get a coherent answer. "I don't know. I really don't," he moaned as I raised the gun in warning. "I told you, I met him in a bar."

It was the bar where Drennan had taken me once. It was too much to hope he still occupied the same room, but it would be worth trying. I looked at Simon, doubt in my mind. He might tell Drennan of my visit. He knew a very great deal about Elizabeth. And about me.

The building was quiet as I walked down the stairs and into the street a few minutes later. No one paid any attention to the second shot either.

I spent the rest of the day looking for Drennan, but without success. He had long since quitted the rooms where I had first met him. This was the only other thing I learned, but I was not by then at my most effective. I was in a state of shock. I think I have made it clear that I am not a man of action. I do not like violence; it offends me. What I had done terrified me, once it all sank in, even though I tried hard not to think of the scene in that dingy room, the last look on Simon's face. My lack of emotion was the most frightening of all. I had not hesitated, had not tried to find a way around the problem, had not considered other possibilities. Simon had been in the way. A problem. A threat. He was no longer. I felt no remorse, and I should have; I was not the person I had thought myself to be. I slept that night as well as if I had spent the evening dining in company, with not a care in the world.

CHAPTER 15

The next morning, as I went downstairs to the bar for a coffee and some bread, the barkeeper, who was also my landlord, handed me an envelope. I ignored it for a while, until enough coffee had been absorbed into my system to make me human once again, and only opened it when I felt sure that I would be able to read it through without my attention wandering. It was from Jules.

Dear Mr. Cort,

As you will see, I am writing this to you from Lyon, and I apologise for taking so long about the task you have given me and for spending so much of your money. I wished to see the job properly to an end. I hope you do not mind.

As you instructed, I went to Lausanne, which took a very long time, but then had difficulty finding out about Dr. Stauffer; he was in none of the directories to be found in the town library, even though these were completely up to date. I did eventually come across the name in a listing that was some four years old. I send it enclosed, and hope you do not mind that I tore it out of the library book. I know I am not meant to do that sort of thing.

I then went to the house, which is occupied by someone completely different. Dr. Stauffer died some three years ago, it seems.

It took some time before I could find out what he died of, and it appears that he hanged himself and was buried in the municipal cemetery outside the town. A woman in a flower shop told me the story. Dr. Stauffer had never recovered from the murder of his wife, she said, and eventually found life too much. The newspapers told me a little more, when I read them in the library. He died in 1887, and Madame Stauffer was murdered in 1885. According to the newspapers, she was killed by a servant called Elizabeth Lemercier. She had been taken in by the family and had been showered with every kindness. But, it seems, she had a naturally criminal temper and turned on her mistress, stabbing her to death with a knife from the kitchen. She then fled and was never seen again, but I came across a report that she had been sighted in Lyon, which is why I am now here, trying to discover the truth. I hope you do not consider I am going beyond your instructions.

I found a woman who had worked in the Stauffer family. It took some time and a lot of your money, but eventually she talked to me. I had to tell her that I was an assistant reporter on *The Times*; I added that I would be dismissed from my job if I did not produce the information you needed, as you were a horrid man and this made her more helpful. I apologise for this.

She told me the newspapers had left out quite a lot of the story to spare what little remained of Dr. Stauffer's reputation. She said the servant Lemercier had seduced the doctor, that he had given her expensive presents and that the wife had eventually found out. When Madame Stauffer confronted them, and threatened to report the girl—apparently you can be sent to gaol, or an asylum, for such behaviour here—she lashed out with the knife, and fled. The town collectively concluded that Dr. Stauffer was in the wrong to conduct such an affair in the family home (although I think what they meant was that he was wrong to have it discovered) and so concluded that he could not be invited for dinner anymore. It was this neglect which caused him, eventually, to hang himself.

The report that Lemercier had fled to Lyon was not, as far as I can tell, based on anything solid. The idea came from the fact that a citizen of Lausanne was found dead in an inexpensive hotel in the city, and because he had been a friend of the Stauffer family. I believe that the journalist who wrote the story may have exaggerated in order to make his report more interesting. However, now I am here, I can tell you that the hotel in which the man—a Mr. Franz Wichmann, who died aged forty-six—was found does seem to be a house of ill-repute. This was not part of the newspaper report.

Here I must apologise for the way in which I was forced to spend some of your money, sir. I do hope you will forgive me. But I went to this hotel all unknowing and it was not until I was inside that I began to realise what sort of place it was. By then the woman who runs it had demanded money of me, and I had paid her, thinking that I was renting a room. It was only when I was asked to choose a girl that I realised my mistake.

I looked up and grinned. Truly Jules was a very poor liar; but I had a sneaking admiration for his cheek.

Naturally, I was horrified, but I decided to disguise my shock, in order to be able to ask questions. So I told the old woman that I wished to wait, and asked to talk a bit. She took this to be a sign of nervousness—and I was really not very comfortable—and got one of the girls to join me.

I will not go into the details, if you do not mind, but we talked for some time. She was really very nice. And she remembered the death of Mr. Wichmann very well. Not surprisingly, perhaps, as the house was closed down by the police for a while, and all the people who worked there had to find their work on the streets, which they do not like very much.

The girl involved was called Virginie—none of them have second names—but she knew little else about her. They do not talk very much about their lives, it seems. Mr. Wichmann was not a regular visitor, he came once and went with one of the girls, and apparently glimpsed Virginie as he left. He was found the next morning in his room dead, with a knife wound through his heart. Virginie had vanished.

At least, this is what that girl said. The girl Virginie was never seen again, and I do not think the police looked very hard for her. She was, by all accounts, quiet and very well behaved. She associated little with her colleagues, but preferred to sit and read while waiting for a client. She was not very popular with them, as they gained the impression she considered herself better than they were.

I hope, Mr. Cort, that you do not consider that I have wasted my time and your money in finding all this out, and that you approve of my efforts. I will take the train back tomorrow morning.

I burned the letter, once I had read it carefully; I do not keep stray pieces of paper around if they are not needed. Then I sat and thought. The connection, from Elizabeth Lemercier to Virginie to Countess Elizabeth Hadik-Barkoczy von Futak uns Szala was easy for me to see. And if all of this, or enough of this, was in the diary, Elizabeth was correct to be worried. If Jules had got the story right, then she could face the guillotine.

But there was no time to do anything today, nor anything to do. I had to wait for Drennan to resurface; I was dependent on him. Still, I thought about the problem carefully as I made my way to Longchamp after lunch. I was not looking forward to it. I hate horse racing; I have never seen the point of it. Horses I like—I used to go riding quite often when I stayed with the Campbells in Scotland in my youth—and there are few finer experiences than getting up on a good horse at dawn, and riding off over the moors. The beasts have their own personalities; they really can become your friend, if you know how to deal with them. But racing around a course, with thousands of overdressed, pampered spectators shouting them on? The animals are so much more worthy than the people, who generally have little interest in the horses at all. They are there to be there, to be seen and to waste money. My day at Longchamp was not for pleasure.

I had a frantic morning gathering more information on François Hubert than M. Steinberg had been able to give me. And I was still in a state of shock over my encounter with Simon. It had deeply disturbed me; I did not see what else I could have done, but the ease with which I came to that conclusion, and acted on it, I found unsettling in the extreme. So, with François Hubert I was sloppy; I allowed myself to pay far too much for trivial information, gave away too much, because I was in a hurry and overtired.

My efforts at least produced enough to make me confident of success. M. Hubert was the head of the bonds department at Credit International; it was he who oversaw the bank's participation in loan issues, who determined what stake they would take. All very well; most large banks now have such people and they are growing in importance. That in itself was not a great deal of use. More important was the information that M. Hubert liked gambling far too much for a man in his position, and that he liked a whole succession of women more than a married man should. Put those together and you had a picture of someone deeply in debt and, naturally, you begin to wonder where the money was coming from. Such a person can be persuaded to answer questions with no great difficulty.

There was, of course, the problem of finding him. I had read my Zola and remembered well the scene in *Nana*, the description of the vast crowds, the innumerable carriages from fiacres to hay wagons, the masses, the bourgeoisie, the *gratin*, all in their different costumes with their different manners, milling about and brought together by the desire to gamble. I anticipated difficulties, saw myself pushing through the throngs, and never even glimpsing my quarry. I had considered asking Elizabeth to come with me so I could tell her about Simon at the same time as I looked, not that she would have accepted.

The idea had a certain charm; she was the Nana of her age, but very much more sophisticated and self-assured. Not for her the fate of Zola's whore, who was created solely so that her fall could be charted, to prove the cruelty of human life. Elizabeth had dedicated herself to proving the opposite, that the individual could triumph, that fate is not determined. I wished her well. And I worried about the warning given to me by Madame Kollwitz. And about those diaries. And about Drennan.

But Elizabeth hated horses, she had told me once, and disliked gambling. She did not take chances; that was her main characteristic. She was no Nana, consuming men for the sake of it, reducing them to poverty or suicide because she could. She belonged to a different generation, the age of business. She bought and sold, and built up her capital. Clear-eyed and certainly more intelligent than Zola's creation, and certainly less likely to die alone in a hotel room. Elizabeth did not intend to burn brightly and die young.

In fact, the problem of finding M. Hubert was very much smaller than I had anticipated. Zola (who can never resist the gaudy and vulgar) described one of the great events of the racing year, which attracted the multitudes. For the most part, though, Longchamp was very much more homespun; the daily events attracted only the truly dedicated, or the truly possessed. Some of the horses looked as though they would rather be living out their old age in a pleasant meadow somewhere, and at least three of the jockeys might have done better by their employers had they eaten a good deal less. All in all, the atmosphere was more like a village fête than a great racecourse; the crowd numbered a few hundred, and the bookies had turned up out of duty, rather than because of any prospect of making serious money. The great refreshment areas were all closed; the stands were empty; there was no buzz of anticipation. Indeed, the air was rather a melancholy one, the spectators knowing they were not going to be greatly excited, and realising all too well that they were there simply because they could not stay away. Nor was it even an agreeable day, with a warm sun to provide some compensation for the lack of other pleasures. Instead, the sky was low and grey, and threatened rain at any moment; the wind had a chill in it, which made me regret not having brought my thicker winter coat.

For the most part, the crowd was of the shopkeeper class, with an air of desperation to their neatness, faces which were never quite right—too pinched, too ruddy, their voices too loud or too quiet. I observed them all swiftly, and dismissed them just as fast. Only one man could possibly have been a senior employee of Credit International, and he stood alone, studying his racing card with the calm of the professional, showing no emotion or interest in what he was doing. He was utterly unremarkable; had there been a greater crowd I would have stood no chance whatsoever of finding him. I watched as he approached a bookie, paid over some money, heaved a great sigh and then retreated, though not to watch the race. His interest was abstract; it seemed as though he could spend the entire afternoon there without bothering to look at a single horse. He was obsessed with numbers, not with the sport.

I followed him as he walked away from the track, hands behind his back, with a slow purposeless gait, then walked up behind him and coughed. "Monsieur Hubert?"

He turned round to look at me, but did not smile or give any reaction. He didn't even seem curious.

"Forgive me for interrupting you," I said. "My name is Cort, from *The Times* in London. I would like to ask you some questions, if I may."

Hubert looked puzzled. "I am sure you may not," he replied. "Although I cannot think what you might want to ask."

"It is about Argentinian water."

Hubert looked very cautious at my question. "I have nothing to tell you whatsoever. It would be utterly inappropriate."

"I assure you that your name will never be mentioned—"

"That is of no significance. Please leave me in peace."

"—however, if I am unable to write this story, I might have to write another one. About Amelie Feltmann. Your debts. Things like that."

He stared at me in total shock. This, I thought, was simply too easy; the man was pathetic. He could at least put up more of a struggle. I wasn't even going to have to pay him.

"Oh, dear God," he said, with a tremble in his voice. "Who are you?"

"As I say, I work for *The Times*. I am writing an article on French banking. And I want to know everything—I mean everything—about the Argentinian bond issue. You are going to tell me."

I had expected a few moments of bargaining, at least, but instead he just crumpled up, hands shaking.

"I knew something like this would happen, sooner or later," he said. "I just knew it . . ."

"Well, you were right," I replied brutally. "It has. So just count yourself lucky that all I want is harmless information, nothing else."

He glanced around him, somewhat in the way you might if you felt your employer could be hovering nearby, watching and listening.

"Come and take a little stroll," I said. "I do not think there is anyone who will see you talking to me. And I will never reveal anything at all. Word of a journalist, if you doubt my honour."

He sighed heavily, and gave in. The surrender was complete, and I could see that he would now tell me anything I asked him. My opinion of him was not high. I would have thought better of him had he tried to run, or hit me first.

"So, let's begin. The Argentinian loan. Why is your bank not participating? Was that your decision?"

"Oh no. Not me. I am not sufficiently senior to decide a thing like that. I would never dare defy Barings on my own authority. I arrange the practicalities of taking up a subscription, I do not decide what we subscribe to."

"So? Who does decide?"

"Normally there is a committee which evaluates each issue. In this case, it was a decision taken by the Chairman alone."

"And that is unusual?"

"That is unheard of."

"How did it happen?"

He looked around, nervously, once more. "I was told to write a letter refusing to take part. And also instructed to give no reasons why this decision had been taken. Again, this is unusual. It is normally a matter of courtesy to give an explanation, even if it is informal."

"And, again, it was the Chairman who gave you these instructions?"

"Yes. He summoned me personally. I asked why, as in the past Barings' business has been very profitable. All he said was that this time no one was going to take part. Not a single institution in France was going to touch it."

"Why not?"

"Exactly what I asked. Was there something wrong with it? I asked. But no, he said there was nothing particularly wrong with it. That was why Barings was going to get such a shock. And more than Barings, he said."

"And what did he mean by that?"

"He said no more. But it puzzled me, as I can see it puzzles you. So I listened, you see, and asked questions of my colleagues at other banks. And do you know what I discovered?"

He was positively voluble now, willing to tell me things I hadn't even asked.

"I've no idea."

"It was true. All the big banks in France will refuse to take any Barings paper. Not only that, I know of two banks in Belgium, and one in Russia, which will also turn it down."

"How much is this issue?"

"In all, about five million pounds. A very great deal of money, but no more than many South American issues and with better prospects than many. Of course, you can argue that too much money has been put into Argentina, and I would sympathise with that view. Sooner or later the markets will have had enough. But if you want to reduce your liability, then this is a foolish way of going about it."

"Why so?" I knew the answer to that already, but also knew that the more he told me, the more he would tell me. He hadn't even noticed I wasn't taking any notes.

"Because we hold a substantial amount of South American bonds, and our customers have bought more off us. A failure could panic the whole sector and drive down prices across the board. We could lose a great deal of money. It would be much more sensible to sell off stock first."

"And that has not been done?"

"There has been some selling, but not enough."

If South American bonds collapsed, then French institutions would lose money, that was true. But nowhere near as much as English ones would lose. Of all the bonds sold in the past decade, since Barings discovered South America, at least half the value had been sold in England, the rest had to be spread across Europe and North America. I could not call the figures to mind, although it was obvious that it would send a shock wave through the markets. But nothing that the City could not cope with. The American railroad collapse had been just as severe, but had been surmounted without much difficulty. And the effect would run right across the Continent. Why would banks connive at conjuring up losses unnecessarily? As M. Hubert said, there were much more sensible ways of getting out of markets you feared might be nearing their peak. Bringing them down while you were still fully exposed was foolish, to say the least.

But he could tell me no more. He confined his interests to bond issues, horses and his lover. He could give no reasons, nor offer any guesses. His was not a speculative mind. I ended up quite admiring him for his little peccadilloes. It showed that he was not entirely an automaton. Somewhere in him there was a little imp, urging him to transgress and, after many years, he had given in. I hoped very much he was enjoying himself, because he was not very good at it. Sooner or later, he would be discovered and his world would crash in ruins.

"Thank you," I said when it was clear I had exhausted his knowledge. "You see, you have told me nothing that was so very dangerous. It is a small sin in comparison to your others. And will remain very much more secret than they will."

"What do you mean?" he asked, apprehensively.

"Simply that what I could find out fairly easily, then so others can. And will."

I bowed to him, and left, leaving him standing, watching me. I am glad to say—what a strange world of amorality I had come to inhabit!—that M. Hubert acted on my warning. I never got the full details, but it appears that he set about using his very considerable talents to embezzle a good deal more money over the next year. When the bank finally discovered that the accounts were not quite what they should be, M. Hubert went to Buenos Aires, and vanished forever.

I had a great deal of puzzling to do, and I think best when I am walking. So I walked back across the Bois de Boulogne to Paris, and walked still further, through the rough houses and ever-shrinking fields which were still a part of the far west of the city then, before resting in a café. There I sat, surrounded by laughter and smoke, as I pondered what M. Hubert had told me. Clearly, I would have to inform Barings. From what he had said, the bank might realize that this issue was going to be tricky, but would not yet know the full extent of the difficulties that were coming their way.

But I still could not make sense of it. These banks seemed to be acting in concert, but they were behaving like rank amateurs; almost as if they wanted to throw their money away. If, for a moment, you conceded they were not total fools (which is occasionally tempting with bankers, but rarely with the most senior ones), then there must be a reason. But what might it be? Barings issues a bond, half of which is taken up in England, leaving them with two and a half million sterling to place on foreign markets. Some of it would go, no doubt. So, assume that there is a shortfall of two million. A vast sum of money and it would cause difficulties, as Barings obviously could not cover that from its own resources. But such things had happened before, even if not quite on that scale. At the last resort there was the Bank of England, which would advance Barings the bullion from its reserves. Barings would have to pay through the nose, no doubt, but it would survive. Its reputation for canny manoeuvres would be dented, but its titanic strength would be demonstrated for all the world to see. The only result would be that everyone would have lost a great deal of money. What was the point of that?

Two large glasses of beer brought me no closer to an answer, so I resumed my walk. I enjoyed it; that part of Paris which has the Avenue de la Grande Armée running through it has become much drearier in the past decade or so. Then it was a very peculiar quarter, with great apartment blocks rising up out of nothing, with perhaps a field full of cows to provide the city with milk on one side and a mason's yard or some other small workshop on the other. Tall buildings, six floors high, snuggled up to one-storey workers' hovels which had not yet been swept away by property developers. One patch of barren land was occupied by a gypsy encampment, another by an open-air music hall, in between a fashionable, and spectacularly ugly, church, which looked forlorn and abandoned even though it was brand-new.

It was nearly six o'clock, so I had just time, if I found a cab, to get to Barings' office near the Bourse. It was a nuisance, as I didn't yet see the urgency, but I thought I might as well get it done with, otherwise my day tomorrow would be disrupted. Then I planned a trip to the public bath for a long soak, and an early night. I was exhausted. I should say that I was still in two minds about helping Barings at all; I had not quite forgiven them for their readiness to let me go. But old obligations are hard to get rid of; I thought of many of my colleagues with affection and, somewhat childishly, I thought it would be pleasant to demonstrate what they had lost.

I rattled my way to the Place de la Bourse, and walked up the stairs to the little office that Barings occupied. Again, you must remember that this was some years back; even the most powerful bank in the world felt no need to make a splash with gaudy offices, and had no need whatsoever for legions of employees to oversee their foreign business. Barings then employed ten people in Paris, of whom four were mere clerks, two were family members learning the trade with the remaining four doing all the work. These were, as was Barings' tradition, overworked and underpaid. The most underpaid and overworked, alas, hated me.

I can honestly say that no thought of Roger Felstead had passed through my mind for several years. He was a man of such diligence, stolidity and utter tedium that it was possible to forget him even when you were talking to him. He believed in order. He believed in rules. He believed in procedures. He believed in loyalty, and was sure it would be rewarded. Alas, every time he felt a reward was his due, his rightful prize had been given to me. He had wanted to go to Germany, I was sent. He had greatly desired to spend some time in New York, but it was I who got on the boat, not him. He had stayed in London, methodically learning his business, doing his duty and showing total loyalty, while I rushed around accumulating unjustified rewards.

I did not like Felstead. Felstead loathed me. On such trivial things can the fate of empires depend.

"A journalist now, aren't you?" he said, not even trying to hide the tone of superior commiseration in his voice.

"That's right," I said brightly. "Book reviews, interviews with actresses and society gossip. Great stuff."

"I was sorry to hear about you leaving," he went on, meaning the exact opposite. "There was quite a lot of talk about it."

"I'm glad to hear it. It would have been a great pity if no one had noticed."

"Were you really fired? That's what I heard. That you messed up with a contract."

"Certainly not," I said. "No. It was because I used the bank's money to set up as a pimp."

He blinked, not knowing how to take that. Then the idiot decided I was joking. "Well, come to see what you're missing? Everything seems to be running smoothly without you."

"Good. I gather you are floating a big bond issue for the Argentinians. Water company?"

He nodded. "The most ambitious ever. And I am in charge of syndicating the French participants. It's a big responsibility, I can tell you."

"How's it going?"

"Oh, pretty well. Pretty well. It'll take time to line everybody up, of course. You know the French. No discipline. No ability to take decisions. They like their pound of flesh. Make us suffer, before they do what they're told. *Pour l'honneur du pavillon,* you know." He had an odd, irritating, honking laugh, a bit like that of a goose in flight.

"So if I said that I had heard through my contacts that Credit International has decided not to have anything to do with the loan, that in fact no bank in France is going to touch any more Barings paper, that

Russian and Belgian banks are also beginning to wobble, then you will tell me that this is silly market speculation and that everything is really running smoothly?"

He blanched, and I could see from his reaction that he knew none of this. None of the banks had officially refused to participate as yet; they were saving it up as a big surprise. I wondered when that surprise was going to come.

"I certainly would," he said, although the certainty in his voice was noticeable by its absence. "Who told you this?"

"Contacts," I said. "It's what comes of spending time in society. You should try it. You think it's nonsense?"

"Absolutely. It is completely absurd. When has a Barings issue ever been snubbed? Occasionally you might get one bank scaling back on its participation. That's normal. You know that. But large numbers? They know our reputation. When has Lord Revelstoke ever put a foot wrong? Why, the man is a genius! You know all of this, and yet you give credence to a bunch of jealous gossipmongers? It's clear you were not cut out for banking, my boy, if you're given to this sort of panic."

I felt like replying that it was clear that neither was he, if he was given to that sort of imbecility. He reminded me of what I disliked about Barings, in fact: the smugness, and conviction of invincibility. Barings were the rulers of the fin de siècle. But then the Rothschilds had ruled at the beginning of the century, and were now a conservative shadow of their former selves. Did Barings think they would dominate the world forever?

"I'm glad to hear it," I replied. "So you think that I should ignore all these stories. I was thinking of writing something for *The Times* . . ."

"Oh, you mustn't do that!" he said swiftly. "That would be the grossest disloyalty. If people hear there are problems, then they will . . ."

"So there are problems?"

"I said, it's going slowly. But it's a complicated issue. A lot of money. There are bound to be difficulties."

"Has Credit International refused?"

"Certainly not."

"Has it accepted?"

"Not yet. They say they are having administrative difficulties. But they assured me I was not to worry. They will give a definite answer next Thursday morning."

Next Thursday. In six days' time. That would give two uninterrupted trading days for panic to sweep across the markets, if things worked out as I thought they might.

"Listen," I said. "I am not joking. I think a storm is brewing. You must send a telegram to London, so they can prepare."

He stared, with a particularly unappealing smile of incredulity on his face. "Warn them? Of what? Of a story heard by a journalist? You expect Lord Revelstoke to give up his weekend because of something you heard at some dowager's party?"

"It's somewhat more than that."

"It doesn't matter. No one can touch Barings. You should know that. And as for sending a telegram, I've never heard anything so absurd in my life. You stick to your actresses, Cort. Leave the serious stuff to people who know what they're about."

I shrugged. "Very well. I will do as you say. I heard this and I reported it to you. You can do as you wish with it. You are no doubt correct in your assessment. As you say, you are more experienced than I am."

"Precisely," he said with satisfaction. "And don't think that I am ungrateful for your concern. It was good of you to come in. And if you hear any other titbits in future, don't feel afraid to come and tell me, however ridiculous they are. And you must let me buy you a drink sometime, in payment for your efforts."

At that moment, the delightful image of Barings sinking with all hands and Felstead being the first to drown swam before my eyes. I wished the French well.

"Excellent idea," I said. "But not today. At the moment you would do me a greater service by letting me have a look at the Stock Exchange notices. I am trying to get something together on France's attitude to dual convertibility. So I need some basic information. *The Times* publishes it, but it would help to have it all in one place . . ."

Now he had established his superiority, Felstead was all grace. Fortunately, he did not clap me on the back as he led me to a desk before getting out the bank bulletins. Had he done so I might have spoiled it all by hitting him.

The Stock Exchange daily bulletins are the dreariest of all newspapers; the prices for dozens of government stocks, the prices of innumerable foreign stocks and utilities. The discount rates and interest rates applicable to hundreds of different instruments, in dozens of countries. News of new issues and dividend payments. By carefully considering all of these, a man of sense can make his fortune. So it is said; it was my great weakness as a banker that I never had the slightest interest in any of it. I had forced myself to understand it, but it never brought me the pleasure or satisfaction that it gave to many of my colleagues.

I tortured myself reading columns of numbers and prices and rates, hoping to find some hint of how the second stage of this adventure was going to play out. For there must be a second stage. M. Hubert was right: why do something which could scarcely hurt Barings, and could cost you a lot of money? But if banks across the Continent were indeed co-ordinating a response, something serious was taking place and it could be assumed that it was being organised by people of intelligence.

It took the better part of two hours, but then I had it. And even I was shocked. I had assumed I would find some sort of evidence of a secondary assault on Barings, but in fact it was much more serious than that. So much so that I didn't even look at the relevant figures until late; it never occurred to me it would be important.

Barings wasn't the target. They were aiming at the Bank of England itself.

The figures were clear, once I had noticed them. For the past two months, bullion had been draining out of the Bank. Money was withdrawn, new deposits were not made, or were delayed. The Bank of France, citing the need for gold to pay for a tax shortfall due to a poor harvest, had postponed depositing ten million sterling; the Bank of Russia had withdrawn fifteen million. Commercial banks which ordinarily would keep smaller but substantial quantities of gold on deposit in London had been pulling it out: £100,000 here, £200,000 there. In all—I settled down with pencil and paper and added it up going back six weeks—another seven million had been withdrawn in this way. According to my calculations, the Bank had probably less than four million in bullion in its vaults.

And next week, the most powerful bank in the world was going to get a shock which would send it reeling, causing panic throughout the London markets. When people panic, they want their money back. They want gold. And Barings would be wanting to borrow the same gold, to cover the holes in its positions. It had promised the Argentinian Water Company five million. It had to pay, and it wasn't going to have enough money. Every stock listed on the Exchange would plummet in value. Banks and their customers would panic. A queue of bankers would form at the Bank of England and it wouldn't have enough gold to satisfy demand. It would have to suspend convertibility, say it would no longer give gold for paper, and the reputation of the entire City of London would be in ruins, with Barings the first to fold. "I promise to pay the bearer on demand the sum of one pound." On demand. In gold. Except that it would be revealed as a lie. Not worth the paper it was printed on, so that paper would rapidly become worthless.

It was breathtakingly audacious. And simple. And it was going to work. "A determined enemy would not waste his time and gold striking at the navy or invading the colonies. He would aim to destroy belief in the word of a handful of bankers in London." That was what Netscher had said, and he was right. It was going to happen. And that idiot Felstead wouldn't believe me.

The beauty of the scheme was that even telling someone would merely start the panic earlier, rather than calm it down. There was not enough gold in London, and nothing could change that.

I came to the conclusion that, even though it might already be too late, I must, at least, alert Mr. Wilkinson, and for that I needed the assistance of John Stone. *The Times* could not help me, as we ordinarily sent our stories by the public telegraph, going down to the local post office and sending them off, word by word. This was not very private, and it was well known that the operators of the machines received a small stipend from the police to report anything of interest. Felstead would not help, but Stone certainly would, I thought. And I knew that his companies maintained their own private telegraph links, which might, perhaps, be intercepted but which were more likely to pass undetected.

Finding Stone, however, was not so simple. I knew that he had offices close to the Palais Royal, but these were closed—it was already so late that I went there just to be thorough, rather than with any real hope of success. I knew, also, that he stayed usually at the Hôtel du Louvre, but again he was out. It took a hefty inducement before I was allowed to go up and talk to his manservant.

"I'm afraid I do not know where Mr. Stone is, sir," said this character, his face immobile as he looked me straight in the eye.

"Yes, you do," I replied tartly. "And however commendable your lying may be under normal circumstances, it is not now. I have to see him, and as swiftly as possible. It is a matter of the highest urgency, and he will not thank you if you do not tell me where to find him."

The servant hesitated for a few seconds, then said, with the greatest reluctance, "I believe he had an appointment for tea with the Countess von Futak. But I do not know where that might be . . ."

I grinned broadly at him. "But I do. Excellent man, thank you. I will make sure he is aware of your impeccable judgement."

I didn't quite run down the stairs, but I hurried, and I certainly pushed aside an old gentleman waiting to be handed into a cab outside the main door. He scowled, I made an apologetic gesture as I leaped in and gave directions.

It took fifteen minutes to get to Elizabeth's house, and I battered on the door until I was let in and demanded to see both her and Stone. It then occurred to me that I might well be placing both of them in a position of considerable embarrassment. Elizabeth had told me that she was open to visitors only on certain days and at certain hours. For the rest she had her business to attend to. This was not an evening when she received anyone other than her shareholders. Did that mean that Stone had acquired a stake? Oddly, as I waited, I hoped very much not. But I did not have time to wonder why it mattered to me.

There was no embarrassment, fortunately. I was shown into the little salon, the one she kept for herself, rather than visitors, a charming room furnished to her tastes, not to the requirements of show. And there they were, sitting in two little chairs, side by side, just like a couple spending a few intimate moments together, talking about their day and enjoying each other's company. The difference in her struck me immediately; she was relaxed, unguarded, and completely at ease. I didn't think I had ever seen her quite like that before. Certainly she was never so when with me. Always I sensed a tension, as though she expected to have to defend herself. I felt jealous, although it did not hit me at the time.

But the moment I entered that watchfulness came back, and Stone rose to greet me and break up all impression of intimacy.

"Forgive me, both," I said. "I would not be here uninvited if it was not a matter of importance. Mr. Stone, may I have a word in private, please."

Elizabeth rose. "Stay here; I have matters to attend to upstairs. I will not disturb you."

She left the room swiftly, and Stone eyed me with a mixture of curiosity and, I could tell, no small amount of annoyance.

"As I say, I apologise. However, I need to send a telegram to Wilkinson which will not be read by anyone else. I would like to use your telegraph system."

"Well, certainly. I am happy to oblige," he said. "Do I take it you want to send it now, this very minute?"

"This very minute," I replied, "or at least as soon as possible. I do not think it can wait until tomorrow."

"And are you able to tell me what this is about? I will of course assist you in any case, but you will understand that you have excited my curiosity."

"I believe I can. In fact, I think it might be a good idea. To make sure that I am not making a fool of myself. It is about Barings."

And so I settled down and told him about the statement by Steinberg at his dinner, my meeting with Hubert at the racecourse, and the conclusions I had drawn from studying the movements of bullion out of the Bank of England.

"So you believe this is a concerted attempt against London?"

"I believe it is, although of that I have no proof. Certainly it would be a remarkable coincidence if it is not. At the moment, it doesn't matter. What does matter is that on Thursday it will become clear that the Barings bond issue has failed; people will wonder if it has enough money to cover its liabilities—correctly, as it certainly does not. There will be a run to gold, at Barings and at every other institution in the City. The Bank of England will be unable to supply the gold requested; Barings will collapse, and the Bank will have to suspend convertibility. I leave it to you to figure out the consequences."

Stone stroked his chin, and considered. "That's easy enough. Bank rates will rocket, institutions will founder, savers will be ruined, companies starved of funds, trade will be crippled. The possible effects could go on and on. Impressive."

"I beg your pardon?"

"I was talking abstractly. One cannot help but admire a fine piece of work, well executed. But, as you say, it does not matter whether this is planned or not. The question is whether anything can be done to stop it. For example, what difference will it make if Wilkinson—and through him, I presume the Bank of England, the Government and Barings— knows what is about to take place?"

"If they are prepared, they can, at least, call in all the gold they can find from the other banks. That might be enough to stop the panic growing."

Stone shook his head. "I very much doubt that. If you are correct, many foreign institutions in London will have their requests to withdraw bullion already written waiting to be delivered. To start the panic off with a vengeance. I mean, it is certainly worth a try, should the authorities so decide, but I doubt it will work. Hmm."

"What?"

"I'm sorry," he said with a faint smile. "I was just calculating my own exposure. What a pity you did not find this out yesterday. Then I could have exited the markets in time. Now, it seems, I will have to go down with everyone else; my fate tied to the demise of that fool Revelstoke. What a very great nuisance. Still, I suppose if I order my people to sell first thing on Monday morning . . ."

"But that will merely add to the panic," I said, incredulously.

Stone looked at me in surprise. "Maybe so," he said, "but I do not see why I should be ruined because of Lord Revelstoke's overweening ambition and lack of judgement."

I stared at him. I knew full well that Stone's gentle manner merely disguised the activities of one of the more ruthless of operators. But I never expected him to be quite so unpatriotic.

"Do not concern yourself," he said, as though he read my thoughts. "Self-preservation and patriotism are not entirely incompatible. I will not be ruined by this. On the other hand, I will render whatever assistance I can. I am more than aware—more than you, probably—how damaging all this might prove to be. It is not in my interest for the financial machinery of the Empire to be ruined. Quite the contrary. I depend on the markets for money, on shippers for orders, on the Government having healthy tax receipts for military commissions. And I depend on Britain's reputation to give my companies the advantage in foreign markets. For these reasons, I will help, if I can."

He stood up. "And we can begin by going to the offices and sending your telegram. I will have to come with you. Can you work a telegraph machine?"

I nodded. "I think so."

"Good. It will go to my office in London, and will then have to be delivered by hand. Do not worry yourself; Bartoli, my man there, is entirely loyal and discreet, and I will instruct him that he is to deliver it himself and speak of it to no one. He will do as he is told."

It would have to do. We walked out and called for our coats. As we were getting ready, Elizabeth came down the stairs.

"You are going?" she asked, with evident disappointment.

"I am afraid so, Countess," Stone replied. "Mr. Cort is a persuasive man, and I can deny him nothing, even at the cost of losing your company."

"But you will come back?"

"I would be delighted."

She didn't invite me, I noticed, a little annoyed at being so obviously left out. I pulled on my coat, and Stone walked out the door. Then she took hold of my arm.

"Any news?" she said quietly.

"I need to talk to you."

"Come back as soon as you can."

Stone, naturally, had his own carriage; no hire cab for him. Very comfortable, well insulated from the sounds and draughts of the outside world.

"Charming woman, the Countess," I said, for no other reason than to see how he reacted.

"She is," he replied.

"Delightful company," I added.

"She is."

"And remarkably well read."

Stone peered at me. "Do not be nosy, Mr. Cort."

"I'm sorry," I said, smiling at him. "But I consider her a friend."

"I think I might try one of these new automobiles," he said as we clopped along. "Have you ever been in one?"

I gave up, and shook my head.

"They smell, they are slow and they are unreliable," he went on. "I believe they may have a great future. It is shameful that our Government has thrown away any possibility of Britain being a leading manufacturer of them. We considered starting production—on a small scale, of course—but abandoned the idea."

"Why?"

"No market. Nor will there be until the Government allows them to go at more than four miles an hour. In France, in Italy, they already travel at twenty miles an hour. They are making huge progress and we have to sit and watch. Who wants to travel at four miles an hour when a horse will take you faster? We cannot make things that people will not buy."

"Get the law changed."

He snorted. "Not so simple. People seem to think that businesses snap their fingers, and the Government does as it is told. Unfortunately it is not like that. And the more governments have to win votes from people who do not think or understand anything at all, the worse it becomes."

"Maybe they are afraid that people will get killed."

"They are afraid voters will get killed. And so they will. But hundreds are trampled by horses every year as well, and they don't limit their speed."

He fell silent for some while as the carriage made its way along the streets of Paris.

"You may be interested to know," he said quietly after a while, "that I have asked the Countess von Futak to marry me."

"Good . . . I mean, congratulations, sir," I said with total astonishment. "Has she—?"

"She has asked for a week to consider her reply. It is a woman's privilege, I believe, and I am sure she must consider the fact that for her it would be something of a social descent. Anyway, here we are."

I imagined Elizabeth's dinner being cooked by her chef, and wondered what I was going to eat that evening. Nothing as grand, I thought. I still hadn't had the opportunity to tell her that Simon was no longer a problem for her. Nor that, in fact, her problems were now very much greater. Stone had just astonished me, but he clearly was already regretting his confidence and did not want to return to the subject. Poor man, I thought. I was certain I knew what her answer would be. At least she was being kind in pretending to consider the offer, rather than burst out laughing. But she had little to laugh about, at the moment. John Stone's offer would not last long if he knew what was in those diaries, and unless I could find Drennan, he soon would.

Stone opened the door and led the way in. And switched on the lights. Of course he had offices with electricity. He liked everything modern. Even the desks the clerks worked at were sleek and new and designed with efficiency in mind.

"Through here," he said, and led the way through one room, then through another and finally into a little cubicle containing the telegraph machine. "Don't ask me how it works, I've never used it. It's the latest machine, though, and I believe you tap on that," he pointed to a key, "and then press all sorts of buttons there," he pointed to a bank of switches and cables rising up in a vast, technological cliff above the desk, "to make it go."

"Oh, God," I said. "I don't think this is going to work very well." I had never seen a machine like it before. I had not a clue how to operate it. I pressed a button tentatively. Nothing happened. "Who normally sits here?"

Stone shrugged. "I've no idea," he said. "Aren't you meant to be able to do this sort of thing?"

"Let's abandon that idea," I said finally. But I had no other to re-place it.

Stone pursed his lips. "The only option is to write a letter, and get someone to take it. There I can help. That is, I can provide pen, paper, envelope and a trustworthy man." He looked at his watch. "Might just get the eleven o'clock train, I think. With luck you should have your letter delivered by Saturday lunchtime. If you can find someone to deliver it to."

He looked at my despondent air. "Marvels of modern technology," he said. "When I was young it still took nearly twenty-four hours to get from Paris to London."

I sighed. "No alternative, is there? Very well, then. I will write a letter."

Stone nodded. "Come back to my hotel and do it there. Xanthos will take it; you can hand it to him when you are finished."

So that is what I did; I spent the next hour in Stone's apartment at the Hôtel du Louvre, carefully crafting a letter to Wilkinson, explaining exactly what I had discovered, what I suspected, and what I thought should be done about it. I was a bit hazy about the final part as, in truth, I could not see what might be done. Even if Xanthos was as efficient as Stone said, the timing would still be tight. Finding the owners of Barings, the directors of the Bank of England, would take time. Getting them all together, deciding on some course of action . . .

Stone evidently had the same thought. He, I suspected, was writing letters as well, and I thought I knew what was in them. He wanted to hit the market with sales orders first thing Monday morning, to unload as many of his stocks as possible before anyone else suspected what might be about to happen. I couldn't blame him, of course.

"And do not lose them, Xanthos," Stone said as he handed over the letters to his secretary. "It is vital that these reach Wilkinson and Bartoli as soon as possible."

The secretary put the envelopes carefully in the inside pocket of his jacket.

"A promising young man," Stone said. "You need have no concerns. He is so eager to get on he would swim the Channel if it was necessary to do his job. A drink, Mr. Cort?" I was quite exhausted; it had been a busy day. But I accepted nonetheless.

"An interesting business," he said once the servant had served the drinks and withdrawn. "It gives a whole new meaning to the idea of modern warfare. It is fascinating to think what might be the motives of the people involved."

"They want to destroy London and the Empire."

"Oh, yes, of course. But why? From what you tell me, it seems to be the French and the Russians acting together, after a fashion. Which is curious, is it not? The only republic in Europe and the Great Despot of the East? An unlikely pair, I think."

I shrugged. "The French hate us because of the Empire, the Germans because of the war, and the Russians because of their politics. Not that it matters. My interests are more short-term. How to stop it."

"Maybe it cannot be stopped," he replied mildly. "While you were writing your letter, I was checking your figures. You are quite right. There is not enough gold, at the moment, to contain a run on the banks. Even if all the bankers were pulled together in one room, and all agreed to pool their reserves, there still would not be enough."

We sat in silence for a while, considering the dreadful possibilities that lay ahead for next week. My feeling of failure was quite overwhelming. If I had only found out about this a few days earlier—even two days would have made all the difference—then the situation would have been entirely different. But I was wasting my time with minor nonsense—trying to find out the specifications, and the purpose, of a new French cruiser then being laid down at Brest, and more particularly being diverted by the problem of Elizabeth's diaries—and failed to see what was going on. I had thought it was an abstract problem, not something real and imminent.

"I wonder though . . ." I began.

"What do you wonder?"

"Well, I told you of my conversation with Netscher, did I not? The conversation that started all this off?"

Stone nodded.

"He sounded scornful of the idea. And he is an influential man."

"A very fine one, as well," Stone added. "I have a great deal of time for him. As bankers go, he is one of the best. Although, as you realise, I do not have much time for them, on the whole."

"So what if there are others like him? Who think that this is disruptive of the smooth ordering of world trade, an unwarranted intrusion of politics into the pure and pristine world of money?"

"Go on."

"Who has the more influence? People like Netscher, or the people organising this?"

"As we don't know who is behind it . . ."

"What I mean is, are we seeing a faction fight here? Money against politics? Is this in fact a coherent policy, or a private venture? To put it another way, could this be reversed if we got to the right people?"

Stone considered. "It would depend on the price, would it not? What would the French, the Russians, want? Besides, is this your job? Should you not go to the Embassy and let them deal with it?"

I had never even considered that, but it was easy enough to dismiss it. "You know the Ambassador?"

Stone nodded.

"Do I need to say more then?"

He smiled. "Not the most effective of men, I agree. Nonetheless, I think you should keep him informed."

"I think I will go and see Netscher," I said. "It's not as if I will be divulging anything which isn't going to be common knowledge in a day or so. Besides, he might well know all about it. If he can be persuaded to help in some way . . ."

Stone stood. "It is worth a try, I suppose. As you say, it can't do much harm now. Now, if you will excuse me, I have a dinner appointment."

"Oh, I do beg your pardon!" I said. "I have taken up too much of your time."

"On the contrary; it has been most interesting. Ah . . ."

"Yes?"

"Well, you may need to contact me in the next few days. Should I not be here, then you might call at the Countess's house."

He said it quite calmly, but I could quite plainly sense the awkwardness underlying his words. Stone was not a sophisticated man of the world; he was perfectly incapable of passing off such a statement in a matter-of-fact manner, however hard he tried.

CHAPTER 16

Why do French bankers insist on living so far away? The richest had migrated out of Paris entirely, and congregated upriver in St.-Germain-en-Laye, miles away. There they had their pocket châteaux, the huge grounds, the children, and the servants, all the space they needed, apart from the further estates they kept in the country, the vineyards in Bordeaux or in Burgundy. So much easier if they had congregated in the French equivalent of Mayfair or Belgravia, as English bankers did.

When I got up the next morning, after only a couple of hours' sleep, and took the tram to St.-Germain, I had neither an appointment nor a guarantee of finding Netscher at home. I wasn't even certain I'd be able to get through the main gate to the house. But I managed, although I had to climb over a fence and wade through brambles to overcome the gate problem, then brave barking dogs, a virtual schoolroom of screaming children, three maids and a nanny—all belonging to Netscher *fils*—before I penetrated the main house, knocked and sat, looking very grumpy and feeling not unlike a travelling salesman, in the main hallway.

Netscher, however, was a gentleman; my unorthodox arrival and slightly weary appearance did not upset him one jot, even though it was Saturday. Instead, he had me shown into his office, and disappeared to make his apologies to his family. Then he returned, announcing that he had asked for breakfast to be brought.

"You do not look like someone who is capable of surviving an encounter with my grandchildren," he said with a smile.

"That is kind. And I apologise for my arrival. But I believe it is important. Do you remember the conversation we had a while back at the Countess von Futak's salon?"

"About—?"

"About the vulnerability of the City of London."

"Ah, yes. I remember it well. You seemed quite sceptical, I recall."

"Are you aware of what is happening? About to happen, I should say."

"I have heard that Barings may experience difficulties in finding subscribers to an Argentinian loan it has been proposing. Is that what you mean?"

"Yes. And you realise the consequences?"

He nodded.

"Is that what you were referring to at the salon?"

He looked at me carefully, clearly weighing what to say next. That was enough, of course, but not enough to continue the conversation.

"It certainly fits the picture I laid out."

"I am hardly divulging a great secret if I say that the Bank of England will be hard put to meet the demands that are likely to be placed on it in the coming week or so. And that the refusals and the withdrawing of bullion are too neatly bound together to be anything other than a concerted operation."

"That had occurred to me also."

"The Bank will need assistance. For its friends to rally around in time of need."

"Ah," he said, "but however well considered the Bank may be by its peers, I think you can say that England is not well looked upon in general. That is a constant in French thinking, whatever the Government, as I have no doubt you are aware. It has friends, of course but, alas, those friends have few friends themselves."

"Meaning what, exactly?"

"Well, you see, my dear sir, France is stricken. It wants revenge, but as yet has no clear notion of how to take that. It was defeated in 1870, and not just defeated but humiliated. It lost some of its most valuable provinces to Germany. It had to pay to make the invader go away. Five billion francs to pay for the cost of the Germans invading our country and stealing our land. Is it surprising that there is one thought only, in the mind of the people? Have you been to the Place de la Concorde? Seen the statues of the great cities of France? The statue of Strasbourg is permanently wreathed in black; flowers are put there daily, as on a grave. Revenge, my dear sir. We want revenge."

He stopped to make sure that I had enough to eat, then fussed and apologised for not having offered me anything to drink. The children were still playing in the garden, all bundled up against the cold, catching the weak morning sunshine. Their squeals of excitement came drifting through the closed windows.

"But how to go about it?" he went on eventually. "If we fight the German Empire alone, we will be defeated again. We have no friends, except countries like Italy or Spain, which are of no use to us. The Habsburg Empire is tied to Germany, the Russians repel us, the English oppose us at every turn throughout the world. So some people begin to mutter that this is insoluble, that there is a better way than war to regain what we have lost. Forget Germany for a while, and make common cause against England. Befriend Russia, cripple England, then turn back to the problem of Germany.

"And a second group believes that this is all fantasy, the posturings of people who do not understand the slightest thing about the way the world works, who think that the clash of nations has not changed since the days of Napoleon. Such people say that France will not be strong when it triumphs, but that it will triumph when it is strong. And a nation grows strong in peace when it can devote itself with one mind to accumulating capital and growing industries. As England has done."

"Bankers, you mean?"

"The most despised of all. It was people like the Rothschilds who conjured the five billion francs out of thin air to pay off the Kaiser in the 1870s, and yet they are reviled as manipulative Jews, fattening themselves on the labours of others. The socialists ran around Paris shouting slogans; the politicians cowered in Bordeaux; the generals made excuses; and bankers went to work evicting the enemy with an efficiency the army could never imagine. Yet who is admired, who hated?

"It is not money that corrupts politics, but politics that corrupt money. All politicians have their price, and sooner or later they come with their hand out. Do you think that a Rothschild or a Reinach or a Baring can be corrupted? In terms of morality, a banker and a beggar are similar; money matters little to them. One has it, the other does not want it. Only those who want but do not have are liable to be corrupted. That is the vast majority of mankind and nearly all the politicians I have ever met."

"And your point . . . ?"

"My point is that England's natural allies in France are, unfortunately, the most hated. Obviously, the collapse of the London credit market would be disastrous, for trade, for investment, for industry. All countries would be weakened, generations of capital accumulation would go for nought. Alas, there are many who do not see that a short-term triumph bought at the cost of long-term misery is no bargain. And any house in France which comes to the aid of its brothers in London would swiftly be condemned as an enemy. Particularly if it is Jewish."

"So you will not help?"

"I must. Barings is foolish and arrogant, yet it must not fall, however much it deserves to do so. But assistance will only be possible if the Government puts itself behind this; it cannot be through the actions of banks alone."

This was a long way out of my area of competence, and I had to work hard to keep a calm head about it.

"What would the price be?"

Netscher smiled. "A high one."

"But who are they? Are we dealing with Government policy, or not?"

"You assume governments are coherent. It is better to assume there are factions. And factions break up and recombine in different shapes. It is more a question of how to fragment the pieces and put them back together in a way better suited to your requirements. For example, if the financial interests in Paris were to approach the Bank of France and speak with one voice, say that it must come to the aid of the Bank of England, then our opinion would undoubtedly be heard. However, there are others who will argue for a more dramatic policy."

"We are talking about M. Rouvier here?"

"He is ambitious, vainglorious. He sees a great opportunity to destroy an enemy, and vaunt himself. He may be persuadable, but it would be foolish to pretend it will not be difficult."

"And what is in it for the Russians? They want to raise huge amounts of money to fund their army and their economy. How will they get it if they destroy the markets that provide it?"

"I'm afraid you will have to ask them that."

CHAPTER 17

I left him sitting down at his desk to write to colleagues and associates, to begin sounding out opinion; I did not even pause to wonder how it was that he was not surprised that a mere journalist should know, or care, so much. I was in a hurry now; I had plenty enough to do. First stop was the British Embassy, but, as I had anticipated, it was closed, and (because it was the British Embassy) no one was prepared to tell me where I might find the Ambassador. He was a man who valued his leisure, and would under no circumstances have it disturbed. I would have to wait.

Next came the Russian Embassy, which was also closed. Not completely, such places never were; I walked in, and wandered around until I found someone to ask where I might find the military attaché. The answer was forthcoming soon enough: 27 boulevard Haussmann, I was told, the second floor. It was a good half hour by foot, quicker by cab but there was none to be found, so, at three o'clock in the afternoon, I knocked on the door of Count Gurunjiev and was let in by a servant who looked as though he had just got off a horse after a long ride across the steppe.

The apartment was lavishly furnished and had a strange, almost spicy aroma quite unlike any smell you find in a house inhabited by French people. I never found out what it was, but it gave the subsequent meeting an undeniable air of foreign adventure. It was not at all unpleasant, but not the sort of aroma that fades from your mind once your nose gets used to it. I dearly wanted to know what it was, but could not find any assuredly polite way of asking.

I had never met Gurunjiev before; he did not come to Elizabeth's salon, but rather visited her separately, normally on a Tuesday afternoon. I learned later, by means which I do not wish to elaborate on, that he had always been one of her more generous supporters, although not at all the most extravagant. I had expected a strapping man of the officer class, a cross between a hero in a Tolstoy novel and an image of Alexander II on horseback, but got neither of these. Gurunjiev was good-looking enough, I suppose, but not especially tall, not particularly well built, and with no military air to him at all. Not the Cossack type, in fact. Rather, he was distinguished by a face of such abundant good nature that it was impossible to dislike him for a second; a clear forehead surrounded by dark hair, deep-set brown eyes, a straight nose and delicate, almost feminine mouth. The thought of him being intimate with Elizabeth crossed my mind for a fraction of a second, but that fragment was damaging to my purpose, so I did my best to suppress it. It was unfortunate, because he was a delightful man in every way; I could see exactly why Elizabeth considered him to be well qualified for his role. The only surprise was that she had managed not to fall properly in love with him.

"This is a most unusual visit," the Count began with a warm smile. He did not seem in the slightest bit annoyed, even though I had interrupted him at some meal. His voice was rich and civilised, his French excellent, and he gestured me to sit in the most natural way possible. "Who are you?"

"Well," I said, "I came to you because I have heard of you from the Countess von Futak."

"Any friend of the Countess is naturally someone who is welcome in my house," he said coolly. "Although I did not realise that our friendship was so well known."

"It is not, sir. I was speaking to her on a matter which has given me some concern, and she then revealed that she had made your acquaintance, considered you a friend, and told me I had to inform you of what I knew as a matter of urgency."

"I see. And one must always follow her advice. When you are done, I hope you will join me at our table. My family is always ready to welcome a new acquaintance."

You see? I am prepared to trust in your absolute discretion, because I have complete trust in hers, is what he meant. You will, no doubt, find it easy to respond with equal understanding.

"I'm afraid I have previous engagements, otherwise I would accept with great pleasure. But thank you for your kindness."

"Then begin."

"Very well. You must understand that what I am about to tell you is in the strictest confidence. I do not need to say that to a man like yourself, of course; but my superiors would consider my behaviour to be questionable, at the least, should they come to hear of it. You will have to find your own means of explaining your knowledge of what I am about to tell you."

He gestured that such a thing was entirely understandable.

"Good. I am a journalist, working for *The Times*. In addition I also do a little work for the Foreign Office of Great Britain."

"A spy?"

"I have undertaken to acquire any sort of information which might assist the well-being of Britain and its possessions. Please do not misunderstand me if I say that I am very good at it, and that in this job I also, inevitably, learn of things which concern other nations as well."

"Such as Russia?"

"When I began this job, I took over from a man called Arnsley Drennan, who subsequently found employment selling his services to the highest bidder. He is a man of the greatest violence and the smallest morals. His history has been one of war, and deceit, and killing. He is an American."

"Go on."

"I know relatively little about him. No one does. He is in his fifties and was once a soldier in the Civil War. It was there, I believe, that he began to acquire his skills as a murderer. Certainly he is an expert in his profession. He is able to slip unnoticed behind a man and slit his throat as quickly and as quietly as a mouse. His virtue for many people is that he has no allegiance and so is difficult to find, or follow."

"And what was Her Majesty's Government doing by employing such a man?"

"They no longer do so. But it may well be that they employ someone similar in his place. As do the Government of France and the Government of Russia."

He bridled noticeably at this statement, and began to deny it.

"You know quite well it is so. Six months ago a pair of Estonian nationalists drowned in the Danube. Do you really think they just fell in when they were drunk? A revolutionist was found with his throat cut last month in Rotterdam. Again, do you really think this deed was committed by an argumentative comrade? That such people are dealt with through the courts alone?"

He looked decidedly uncomfortable at this, but also I could see the glimmerings of a thrill in the way he sat. All people—all men, I should say, as I have discovered that women are by and large impervious to the charms of the occult—can be easily fascinated by such tales. They like the idea of possessing hidden knowledge. Only the very sensible truly prefer not to know. Only the saintly are truly appalled. With luck, I could exploit this weakness and go some way to solving two pressing problems at one and the same time. If I was careful and if I was lucky.

"Go on."

"His current employers are people who have no love of Russia. You are aware, I am sure, that the various revolutionist groupings have had very little success in fomenting any trouble inside Russia itself. They make a great deal of noise, but accomplish little. There are so many informers inside their ranks that they manage little before they are dis- covered. Anarchists of various sorts manage to blow up a restaurant or a bar every now and then, but there is little real point to what they do."

"Yes. I know all this."

"Good. Let me be blunt then. A group of Russian exiles have engaged the services of Mr. Drennan to effect an atrocity against Russia in France."

This statement was greeted with silence, as the Count stared at me, the atmosphere suddenly dark and serious.

"And you know this how, might I ask?"

A difficult question to answer, as I didn't know; in fact it was a tissue of lies from beginning to end.

"Russia is not the only country which keeps an eye on these people," I said airily. "And I have been keeping an eye on Mr. Drennan. That was for my own protection as he resents my existence considerably, and I did not wish to become his next victim myself."

"And this atrocity—?"

"I am afraid, sir, that I must interrupt here, and rather ruin my reput- ation. I must exchange this information, not give it."

His handsome countenance darkened.

"Don't concern yourself," I said gently. "Even if you are not able to oblige me, I will still tell you all you need to know to prevent a catas- trophe. But I would like your word that you will assist me, if you can do so. I desire no more than that."

His eyes narrowed as he considered this offer, and I could see that he was calculating possibilities. He was not, I thought, quite so direct and straightforward as his manner suggested.

"Very well," he said. "Why don't you tell me what you want, then we will see if we can do business. Please bear in mind that I have noticed you have given me no proof whatsoever of what you say."

"That will come. I hardly expect you to act on the unsubstantiated word of a total stranger. Very well, then. You have heard, I imagine, of Barings Bank?"

He looked totally astonished at the sudden change of direction, but nodded.

"In a few days' time, Barings is going to get into considerable difficulties. It has to make a payment and does not have the funds to do so. It will, as happens in these circumstances, apply to the Bank of England for assistance. News of the problems will seep out, and many people will wish to convert their funds into something more substantial than paper. Other houses will also want gold from the Bank of England's vaults."

He nodded, but cautiously. It was clear he only just understood what I was talking about. "The Bank does not have enough. One does not have to be an expert to understand the difficulties that arise when a bank does not have enough money to meet its obligations."

"I do not see—"

"In the past month the Russian state bank has withdrawn substantial amounts of the gold it habitually holds in London for safekeeping. It has withdrawn money from the Bank of England, and also from Barings itself. All for perfectly good reasons, I am sure, but if it were able to announce it was reversing this policy, then the problem would be significantly lessened. That is all I require."

I had lost him, I could see. He was a man of diplomatic balls and negotiations between grand men. He understood not one thing about how empires are really made, or how countries satisfy the needs and desires of their people. It had never occurred to him to wonder how the food on his plate got there, how it was grown, harvested, moved from place to place and merchant to merchant along the great paths of invisible money that encircle the globe, tying every man and every town to each other so efficiently that most people did not even suspect they were there. He took it for granted. And we never value what we never think about.

"You want Russia to move gold . . ."

I suppressed a groan. "No, Excellency. There is no need to move it. Simply saying that you will not move it will be more than sufficient. Belief is as good as reality, where money is concerned."

He frowned. "As you see, Mr. Cort, I know little of these things. Nor do I care about them much. An oversight on my part, no doubt. But it means that I have no idea whatsoever whether you are asking me a small favour or a gigantic one. We wish to make an exchange, but that depends on a fair price for each side. I do not know the value of what you are asking."

"Then I suggest you consult one of your people in the Embassy who does know, Excellency," I said. "But I would request that you do so swiftly. Time is of the greatest importance here."

He surprised me then. He was not at all the sort of person I had imagined. He stood immediately and called for a servant. "Prepare my clothes. I must go to the Embassy immediately. And send messengers to"—here he reeled off a list of Russian names—"and tell them to meet me there within the hour."

He turned back to me, and smiled. "I will meet my people, and attempt to understand what this is about," he said. "I may need to get hold of you, so if you would leave your address . . . ?"

I nodded.

"And I will hold you to your word, Mr. Cort. I must have that information, whether I can assist you or no."

"You will have that, and willingly," I said. "All I know at the moment is that Drennan is probably living on the Ile Saint-Louis, and that the plot involves an attack against the Russian cathedral some time next week. Please place guards around it. Twenty-four hours a day." I gave Drennan's description. "He is not a member of the Orthodox Church, cares nothing for Eastern music and has no opinion whatsoever of modern ecclesiastical architecture. If he goes there at all, it will not be for the state of his soul."

"Then you have given me a great deal to do," he said. "Diplomats must dress properly, and that takes an extraordinary amount of time."

It was a dismissal, so I thanked him, left the room and headed back home.

I had made progress, or so I thought. That is, I had contacted two powerful people in the Russian and the French camps and opened communication. The next stage was to discover their price, if indeed they were prepared to sell. I realised, however, that I had little enough to offer in exchange.

And if the price was too high? What would happen then? I paused at a café in the rue du Faubourg St.-Honoré and ordered an omelette and a glass of red wine; I had not eaten since morning and I was desperately hungry. I might as well eat and think at the same time.

Britain would be desperately weakened, of course; trade all over the world would shrink; factories would close, ships be laid up. People would lose their jobs. The Government's revenue, and its ability to pay for the Royal Navy, would fall. The colonies would then be exposed and vulnerable—India, South Africa, the Far East—and the French and Russians would move to drive home their advantage. What could we do? Except go cap in hand to the Germans, asking them to name their price. They would, no doubt, want a free hand in East Africa for a start, maybe much more than that. And would they even want to assist, sandwiched as they were between Russia to the east and France to the west?

All this for a few tons of metal. And I had made things even more complicated by introducing the business of an attempted atrocity, which I would now have to plan. What on earth was I thinking of? It was going to make my life very much more difficult. Still, I could worry about that when it was all over. Waiting and watching, not doing anything unless it is necessary; these have always been my main characteristics in the business of intelligence. It was what distinguished me from others, like Drennan, who no doubt would have blown something up first of all, as a way of catching people's attention.

And then I smiled, and ordered another glass of red wine and called for paper and an envelope.

"Dear Drennan," I wrote,

I have been engaged by a mutual friend to act in the matter of a work of fiction which you may know about. I think we must talk over the issue, and swiftly. A neutral place of meeting would be suitable. I will be at the entrance to the Orthodox Cathedral in the rue Daru on Thursday at six-thirty in the evening.

Yours,
Cort

I put it in an envelope, then travelled down to the Ile Saint-Louis and left it, addressed to M. Lefevre, at the bar. He would get it soon enough.

From there, I went back to Elizabeth; it was past nine when I arrived, but it felt like three in the morning—there had been so much going on. I was giddy with tiredness, and I think that my judgement was not what it should have been. I ought to have gone to bed for some rest, but I remembered that stricken look on her face as she held my arm, so lightly, and asked me to come back. Nothing would have kept me away. I even wondered what Stone would have thought, had he known . . .

Elizabeth roused her cook to get me some food, and was restrained about talking before I had eaten something. I was grateful for that, and made her wait, as I ate quails' eggs, a little pâté, and drank a glass of wine with great speed and little ceremony.

"Who do you go to for comfort?" she asked as I finished. "Do you have brothers, parents?"

"My father is alive, but we are not close. I have a sort of half-brother. I can tell him most things, and he relies on me similarly."

"Then you are lucky. What is he like? Is he like you?"

"No. He is hardworking and serious, and much attached to warm fires and armchairs. And you?"

"No one. Just you, at the moment."

"I'm sorry."

"Why?"

"That I'm the best you have. Listen, I don't have good news."

She composed herself, face set, a little pale.

"Simon is dead," I said. "It doesn't matter how. But he didn't have the diaries. He sold them. He told me as much."

"Who to?"

"A man called Arnsley Drennan. Otherwise known as Jules Lefevre. You met him with me in Nancy."

She nodded faintly.

"A much more dangerous character. Much smarter, and not inter-ested in money. The trouble is, I don't know where he is. I have begun to tackle the problem, and that might work. But for the next few days, at least, I cannot say what will happen. I very much doubt he is involved for gain. This will not end simply by you handing over some cash."

She cupped her hands against her face and closed her eyes. And I felt bad, sorry to disappoint her.

"I see. What might he want?"

"Me. That's my main concern. He may see your diaries as a way of getting to me. They would destroy your reputation, but they would also expose me and wreck everything I've been doing here. It would cause severe embarrassment to the British Government, and at a time when Britain can least afford it. The French, no doubt, know that there are spies here. Having it plastered all over the newspapers at the moment could be very difficult."

"I'm sorry."

"It's not your fault. But it would help if I knew how powerful a weapon these diaries are," I said. "Tell me about Dr. Stauffer."

"Is it important?"

"I think it is."

"Why?"

"I need to know everything in advance. I don't want unpleasant surprises when I pick up the newspaper one morning."

"Come and sit down," she said, and led me back into the little sitting room, lit now only by a couple of candles and the fire in the grate. It was warm and I was worried I might fall asleep. At least I was until she started talking, which she did in a soft voice, face turned to the fireplace, as if I wasn't there.

"Listen," she said. "I was put into an orphanage shortly after my mother died."

There was a long, long silence, which I did not break into. She was thinking, and she looked inexpressibly lovely, as though no cares could possibly touch her.

"So how did you become you?"

She looked puzzled by the question and thought. "Because somebody, once, was kind to me," she said simply. "So I know it is possible, however cruel the world can be."

I didn't feel able to respond to this, so I stayed silent.

"It was a terrible place. If God punishes me as I no doubt deserve, he will send me back there. It was cold and mean, and those in charge were harsh. They encouraged the children to be cruel to each other as well. I won't dwell on it because there is nothing good to say. Except that there was one woman, one of the visitors appointed by the town council to oversee it, who was not like that. She talked to me once, and I was so greatly in need that I worshipped her, just for those few words. Every time she came I watched her, how she dressed and moved, the way she bowed her head slightly when talking to others. On days when the trustees held meetings, I would get up and dress my hair carefully, and be at the gate onto the street, so that she would see me when she arrived. I hoped she would notice me, smile at me, even speak to me again.

"And one day she did. She asked me my name. I was so overcome I couldn't answer and just stared at her. So she asked, very patiently, if I was a good girl and did everything the guardians asked me. Whether I worked hard, and was quiet and obedient.

"I said that I tried.

"And what did I want to do when I grew up?

"I had no idea. I had never thought about it. So I blurted out the only thing that came to my mind. 'To get out of here, ma'am,' I said. And I could see from the look on the custodian's face that I was going to be punished for that when the time came.

"She saw it too. And understood exactly what had happened, and bent down close to my ear.

" 'Let's see what we can do, shall we?' she whispered.

"And she left me to my fate, which was terrible enough. I was nearly eleven by then, and I do not think you can imagine how cruel another woman can be to the weak and the young. It was not the bruises or the cuts, the cold water, the starvation. There are many things worse than that."

She stopped and paused, then smiled at me. "Still, they do say that the worse the misery the shorter it lasts. I do not know why they say it, because it is not true. But it did come to an end eventually, after a week or so.

"My saviour came back for me. She needed a maid, and had, in effect, bought me. In exchange for a donation, I was allowed out on licence to work in her home, doing what was needed.

"It was hard work, but like going to heaven in comparison. I was fed, clothed, the cook was kind and not too demanding. The other girls were as you might expect but not too mean to me, as by that stage I had learned how to deflect trouble and ignore all wounding comments.

"And Madame Stauffer was kind, although distant and formal. It was a French-speaking house; until then I had spoken only Swiss-German and had to learn a new language, but did so quickly. She was French herself, and had imposed the language on the household, although her husband was German. Proper German. He was a lawyer, they lived in a big house, with everything you might need—fine furniture, gardens, servants. Everything except children, for the story was that Madame Stauffer was barren, and made desolate by her failure to give her husband the children both wanted. Perhaps that was why she found a place for me, I do not know. I need say little more about her, except that she was kind to me.

"Her husband was different. I found him very frightening. He was older than she, about forty-five years old, and very quiet. He was never around very much, only in the evenings, and said little. When he came home they would eat together, and then he would go to his library, and spend the rest of the evening there reading, until bedtime. They talked little, and slept in separate rooms, but seemed to be fond enough of each other. He was always respectful and polite, considerate of her presence. More than that I did not know, or care. He spoke to the servants only rarely, and was neither a good nor bad presence in the house, for he knew nothing of its running at all.

"One day I was in his library, dusting, as I had to do every week, and found a book lying on the floor, which I picked up to put back on the table. I opened it to see what it was, in case it was some law book which should go on his desk, and saw it was a novel. Balzac, it was, *Père Goriot*. Have you read it?"

I nodded.

"It changed my life forever," she said simply. "Such things do happen, although it was very unexpected. I had never read much; it had been forbidden, apart from prayer books. They did not see why we should have to read as our task in life was to work and obey. They only taught us with reluctance. So I hardly had any idea what stories were until that moment, when I read that first sentence: '*Madame Vauquer, née de Conflans, est une vieille femme . . .*'

"I was transfixed by it, could not stop myself reading. I read as quickly as I could, skipping over the words I did not understand. I had fallen into another world and did not want to leave it. You must have felt that in your life? Everything else vanished, there was just this story, which I could not leave.

"I had to, of course; eventually the most senior maid came in and saw me, and clucked around me and scolded me terribly for my impertinence. She didn't hit me, that did not happen in that house. But I got a good talking to.

"I couldn't have cared less. If that was sin, then I was ready for hell.

All I could think about all day was how to get back into the master's library to find it again. I couldn't sleep that night. We all went to bed in the attic, all four women in one tiny room and normally the snoring didn't bother me. That night it drove me mad, and when I was sure that everyone in the house was asleep, I got out of bed, and tiptoed down the servants' staircase. It was icy cold, I remember, and I had bare feet which were numb by the time I got down to the family quarters. It didn't matter; I found the book, sat in the armchair by the fire and read.

"You have been educated, I know. Books to you are commonplace, something you take for granted. But for me such books were like a weary traveller in the desert finding an oasis. I was fascinated, excited, thrilled. I had stepped into another world, full of extraordinary things and people. I fell in love with Rastignac and saw in him the first glimmerings of my own ambition. He had nothing and wished to conquer Paris. He taught me that sweetness and kindness would serve me little. Yet he kept a goodness that could not be corroded by the world. Books taught me of friendship and loyalty, of betrayal and how to suspect others. And it taught me to dream, of worlds and people and lives that I had never thought existed."

She stopped as she recaptured, very briefly, the joy of that discovery, one of the moments in her life which would be an unalloyed treasure for the rest of her life. Whatever else had happened to her, would happen to her in the future, she had that moment of enchantment in a chair, with cold feet and a spluttering candle.

"I read almost until dawn, then made myself go back up the stairs to get some sleep. I should have been exhausted the next day, so tired I could hardly move. But I wasn't; I was exhilarated beyond imagining. It was like a first love. It *was* a first love, with Rastignac and the way we had met.

"But I now embarked on a life of crime. I could not do it every night, as even my young body could not manage to go without sleep forever, but every night I could manage I slipped down those stairs to read. I read more Balzac, everything I could discover in the library, tried Victor Hugo, Flaubert. I was so moved by the fate of poor Madame Bovary I wept for days afterwards, and felt myself in mourning.

"After a week, though, a very strange thing happened. I came down, and discovered a new book on the table. Stendhal, and a thick blanket on the chair. I was frightened, a little, but the temptation was too great, so I wrapped myself up warmly and settled down. I devoured the book as I had all the others, and wished I knew people as interesting as the Duchess of Sanseverina, or as dashing as Fabrizio. A few nights later, when I had nearly finished it, I found another one on the side table, and a glass of milk.

"And so it went on, until one night, as I stretched over to wrap myself up more comfortably, I knocked the glass over. Milk spilled over the rug, and there was a terrible noise as the glass broke on the floor. It was still early; I had begun to take more chances, and was coming down earlier and earlier. There were still people awake. I panicked, as I knew I would be thrown out of the door if I was discovered. There were footsteps coming down the corridor. And then I heard footsteps in the room itself. It was one of those rooms where there were so many books that the shelves went up to the ceiling, and a ledge had been built halfway up the wall, with a little iron staircase leading up to it. It was down this that Dr. Stauffer was now coming.

" 'Quickly,' he said in a quiet voice. 'Up the stairs, and hide behind the desk. Keep quiet.'

"In one little corner was a small desk which I had never seen used. It was always covered in piles of paper which were never moved.

"I stared at him, and he gestured at me urgently to do as I was told. With seconds to spare, I fled up the steps, and crouched down behind the papers. The evening maid, whose duty it was to close up the house for the night, knocked and came in.

" 'It's quite all right,' he said. 'I'm afraid I knocked over a glass. Please don't worry about it. It's late, and I am working.'

"The maid nodded and withdrew. The door shut, and I heard it being locked.

" 'You can come back down now. It's quite safe.'

"He had a gentle voice, not the voice of someone who was going to throw me out into the night, but nonetheless I was petrified, shivering from fright and cold.

" 'Stand by the fire and warm yourself,' he said. 'And don't be frightened. I'm not going to eat you.'

"I began to stammer out an apology, which he brushed away. 'I have been keeping an eye on you for several days,' he said with a faint smile. 'I wondered who was moving my books, but as nothing went missing, I didn't mind. Then two evenings ago I was up there, working, and I saw you come and curl up on my chair. I thought it was so charming I couldn't bring myself to disturb you. And very curious, too. Why do you spend so much time reading?'

"I did not really trust myself to answer. 'I can't stop myself,' I said eventually.

"The answer seemed to please him. 'And which of those books did you like the most?'

"I felt like saying all of them. 'The ones with Rastignac in.'

" 'Really? You don't find stories of young girls finding true love more appealing? Why do you like Rastignac?'

" 'Because he is trying to make something of himself.'

"He seemed to find this reply quite fascinating, and he came across the room, sat opposite me and stared hard at me. 'How extraordinary,' he said. 'How remarkable. Well, well . . .'

" 'I'm truly sorry, sir . . .'

" 'What for?'

" 'For my impertinence.'

" 'No, you are not. At least, I very much hope you are not. Are you?'

" 'No.'

" 'You notice that this room of mine is terribly untidy and messy? Not to say dusty?'

"I looked around, and could not see a book or ornament out of place. And as for dust, I don't think there was a single speck anywhere.

" 'I think that what I need is someone to tidy it up more often. Once the job is done, there would be no reason why that person could not fill up the remaining hours reading a book. As long as they put it back in its proper place again. Once they were finished. Can you think of anyone that might suit?'

"I could hardly believe what he was saying. 'Oh, sir . . .'

" 'Would you be so kind as to assist me, do you think?'

"I never knew that anyone could feel such happiness as I felt just then. The idea that I could spend hours a day in that room, just reading and tidying, made me want to skip and sing as I went back up the stairs. It was beyond my wildest dreams, and it was not a dream. I was given my instructions the next day by the head maid, and told to watch myself. Be quiet, be obedient. For once I intended to do just that.

"Nearly all day, every day, I spent in that library; Dr. Stauffer said he had given me the task of reorganising all the books and dusting all the shelves and making a catalogue of them. He reckoned it would take up to a year. So it would have done, had he really wanted me to do it. I was occasionally instructed to put papers in files, or find things for him, but apart from that I simply read. And talked.

"The other servants were scandalised that I should have to work so hard, and I did not enlighten them. Every day I went to the library at eight in the morning, and stayed there, reading. Part of the time I read what I wished, but I also had to read what he gave me, and he evidently decided to give me an education. My knowledge of the world came entirely from books, and bit by bit it deepened. He gave me Voltaire, and Montaigne, then Shakespeare in translation, Victor Hugo, Dumas, Chateaubriand. In German Goethe, Schiller, then other books as well, history, philosophy. He suggested Homer, Cicero, Plato. Some I understood, others not, but all fascinated me, and often in the evenings he would summon me to talk about them. What did I think of this passage, or that? Was this author correct? Why did he say such a thing? I'm sure my ideas and responses were foolish and naïve, but he didn't seem to mind, and never corrected me, or told me the right answer. This went on for months and months; it was the happiest time of my life. For the first time, I felt as though I was loved, that someone cared for me. I had never imagined that it was possible to be so happy.

"Need I say that I fell in love with him, a man in his late forties, and me a girl of fifteen, as I was by then? He was everything I needed and didn't even know existed. He was even lonelier than I was, and knew little about how to inspire warmth or friendship in his equals. So he turned to me, and sought intimacy through books and ideas. He liked having me around him. There is a joy in that, I can see, watching someone else discover the pleasures that you first learned yourself in your youth. To see someone growing and flourishing in front of you. I will have children, one day. I know I will. And I will watch them grow."

I was thoroughly confused now, for she was telling me a story of being saved, something out of those books she had devoured so avidly. A pretty little orphan, adopted by a kindly old man and given an education and love. I knew the story; she grew up with her devoted guardian and looked after him in his old age, or married some respectable, upright youth exactly like him. It was a tale of safety and contentment. Of warm emotion and fulfilment. It did not end on the streets of a small border town in winter.

She was in her own world now, and I could not interrupt. I did not want to and I was too tired; I didn't really hear her words; they just seeped into my mind as I sat next to her on the sofa. I do not think she meant to tell me this story when she started. She was asking for help, not giving a confidence. But once she started talking, she could not stop. I think I was the only person who ever heard the tale.

"He taught me other things as well," she went on. "All about prints and paintings, statues and cathedrals. Porcelain, jewellery; he was immensely cultivated, and had a small collection of art. He would sit beside me with a folder of prints and get me to look at them, describing what I saw, giving my opinions. I was never very good at it; I think he thought me rather weak in that area. But he persisted, and seemed to like being beside me. But, bit by bit, the sort of pictures he showed me changed. He began to show me prints by Boucher, of nudes, and scenes of seduction, and asked me to describe them in the greatest detail. I could hear him breathing more irregularly as I spoke and I didn't know why. Nothing had ever been said in the orphanage and the maids were all highly respectable and prim. My ignorance was total; all I knew was that a sort of playfulness came on me, and I realised that I could make him sound even more uncomfortable the more I described. His hands on her breasts. The whiteness of the skin. The hair falling down the nape of the neck.

" 'And what do you think it is about?'

" 'I don't know, sir. But I imagine she is very cold, sitting there in an open field with no clothes on like that. I hope it was painted on a warm summer's day.'

" 'But do you think she is enjoying it?'

" 'I don't know, sir.'

" 'But does this please *you*?'

"And he put his hand on my breast and began to stroke it. He was now breathing really hard, and I was frozen in confusion. I did not dislike it, but I knew enough to think I should. So I said nothing at all, but began trembling as his hands moved down my body.

"I gave him no encouragement. I did nothing. I didn't know what to do. I just sat, rigidly still, as he took my immobility for consent. Then there was a rattle on the doorknob, as one of the maids opened the door to bring in his morning coffee. He pulled his hand away quickly, and stood up. I still had only very little idea of what was going on, but I could see from his behaviour that it shouldn't be happening. That he was doing something wrong.

"The scene did not repeat itself for a very long time; on the outside, we resumed our normal way, and he was as kind and attentive as ever. But, of course, everything had changed; I had a first glimpse of my power; I knew that I could make him tremble. And I practised. With my eyes, and my gestures, and the way I sat and talked. I learned how to make him uncomfortable. I wasn't aware of what I was doing; there was no malice in me. But I think I was putting him through the tortures of hell, nevertheless. One evening, when his wife was out at the theatre, he could resist me no more.

"It hurt. It does, you know, and I cried. He was overcome with remorse, and kept stroking my hair and saying how sorry he was, and could I forgive him. I ended up comforting him, and telling him not to worry. It didn't matter. Then he went and sat on the armchair, far away from me, and looked at me in horror. I must not say anything about this to anyone. It would be our secret. Otherwise I wouldn't be allowed to come back here and read books anymore."

"So I became a whore, at the age of fifteen. I would have died rather than give up those books and if that was the necessary payment, it was one I was willing to make. I assured him I wouldn't say anything, and the tone of panic in my voice made him realise that I meant it. I was totally in his power, and he knew it.

"And that was how my education was completed. Everything went back to the way it was before; I would read, and we would talk. Except that some days, normally in the evening, I could sense a change of tone in his voice, a look in his eye. Was I paying him or was he paying me? It was an exchange. Both had something the other wanted. I did not feel wicked or sinful, although I knew I ought to, and I could not ask anyone else's opinion. Had any of the other maids known, they would have set me right immediately, I am sure. But they did not. The other thing I learned was how to be absolutely discreet. I knew enough to realise that everything that made life worthwhile depended on it.

"He was, in his way, a good man, Dr. Stauffer, but he was weak. With me he could be the gallant lover, and father, all in one, depending on his mood, and I would play whichever part he required of me.

"I was growing, and learning fast, and I came to despise the Stauffers. I should not have done so; it was not in the play he had written out in his

mind. There was no scope for me to grow and to change. But I saw how
husband and wife behaved to each other and to the outside world, and
learned that this marriage which was so enviable was pretence. It worked
well enough, I suppose, but you must remember I had been schooled by
novels; Madame Bovary was my best friend; Rastignac my real lover. The
barely concealed hatreds that kept the Stauffer marriage together began
to excite in me disdain and loathing. I would love, or I would be free. The
price for my liberty would be high; the man willing to pay it would be
extraordinary. Not like Dr. Stauffer, with his moustache, and fat belly, and
smell of cigars, and fumbling grunts as he pawed me.

"But there was also a man called Wichmann, a man I hated more
than any man I have ever known. He was sly, mendacious, cruel. A dirty
man with a dirty soul. He found out about me and Dr. Stauffer, and set a
price for his silence. The price was me, and Dr. Stauffer paid it. I was
handed over to him, when he wanted me. For all his failings, Dr. Stauffer
was a kindly man; Wichmann was not. He liked to do things, and made
me do things, which were horrible. But he taught me, as well; I learned
that I could even control a man like that, by doing more than he wanted,
and allowing him to do as he pleased. Do you want to hear what I learned
to do at his hands? I will tell you, if it pleases you. I will tell you anything
you wish to hear."

I shook my head. "I think I deserve better than that from you," I
replied reproachfully.

She shook her head. "You are an unusual man," she said.

"Perhaps."

"I couldn't stand it, eventually. So I brought it all to an end. Not
deliberately, not thought out; I didn't really know what I was doing; but
we were caught, and it was my doing. Dr. Stauffer became bolder, and I
encouraged him into taking more and more risks. One day his wife was
due to go out for a lunch, but I heard it had been cancelled, so she
decided to go for a short walk instead, and come back to eat at the house.
Dr. Stauffer did not know this, and I goaded him into wanting me. I could
do that easily by then.

"So we were surprised, in the grossest way imaginable. His wife came
in, stared, and walked out again. She was a kind but fairly stupid woman,
given to generosity to orphans, but incapable of understanding adults, or
herself. I do not think it ever crossed her mind that her preoccupation
with charities and lunches might have left a hole in her husband's life

which he would seek to fill elsewhere. A more sophisticated woman would have had a blazing row and let the matter drop. She would not. She wished to separate, and then I learned that this, for Dr. Stauffer, would be cataclysmic. He had no money of his own; the family fortune was hers, and she intended to make him realise it. I do not know the details; I was, naturally, packing my things. Dr. Stauffer dismissed me within seconds of his wife leaving the room; before I had even managed to pull my dress down. He was going to throw all the blame on me. Wiles of a temptress. Well, of course he was; I couldn't blame him.

"But it didn't work; I only gathered approximately what had happened, but I think she was not prepared to take his excuses. She was stupid, but not that stupid. That was all I knew; what happened then was not my concern anymore. I had to leave, and leave quickly. It was obvious that I would never get another position in Lausanne. So I left the city, and left Switzerland."

"You did not murder Madame Stauffer?"

"How do you know about that?"

She had not mentioned it; Jules had discovered it. She was suspicious now and on the brink of closing up on me.

"How do you know about that?"

"It was not hard," I said. "And it does not matter. You must tell me everything. Good, bad and shameful. It is not as if I am in a position to judge."

She looked coolly at me for a few more seconds, then relaxed. "I suppose you're not," she said quietly. "Very well. To answer your question, no. I would never have done that. She had been good to me. I meant her no harm at all. Do you believe me?"

I shrugged.

"Listen to the rest of my story and decide. It seems I am to lay myself bare to you, so you might as well know everything."

"Very well."

"I was penniless and without even a name; I heard about the death of Madame Stauffer and that I was being blamed. I could not call myself Elizabeth Lemercier any more. Fortunately, girls like I was then are two a penny. No one cares who they are, or what they are called. We can do without papers, or anything. So I chose a new name for myself: Virginie, as I had read my Rousseau and still dreamed of finding my Paul. There was only myself in the world to rely on. I crossed into France and the rest,

I suppose, you can guess. I had tasted enough comfort not to want to become a servant once more, but I had few abilities, and little to recommend me. Except that I knew how to attract men. I realised quite how easy in Lyon when I was walking down the street, and this man started looking at me. I ended up in a brothel, where I stayed for about six months before I had to move on.

"I was discovered. It was simple enough. Wichmann found me; I do not think he was looking, but he was the sort who would visit brothels whenever he travelled, and he travelled to Lyon. When he saw me, and recognised me, he also saw an opportunity. He said I would have to do exactly as he wanted, otherwise he would go to the police. Do you think that is enough to make me panic? It was not. By then there was nothing anyone might have asked me to do that I would not have managed, however much it might make ordinary people blanch. I would quite easily have complied with his wishes, had I had some assurance that he would keep his word. But I knew he would not. He was one of the very few people who knew me from Lausanne, and he would never let me go."

"So you killed him."

She nodded. "I did. Cold-bloodedly, and deliberately. I stabbed him in the heart, and sat and watched him die. Are you horrified?"

I thought, then, of Simon. "I don't know," I said quietly.

"I changed my clothes, packed my bag and left, locking the door behind me. By the time he was discovered I was well away from Lyon, I had cut my hair, changed the way I dressed. I changed my name, but kept Virginie. I liked it; it was my secret name, the one I had given myself."

"And Madame Stauffer?"

"I do not know. I imagine it was her husband; Wichmann all but admitted that he was still blackmailing him, but as his dalliance with me was known by that stage, there must have been something else, something serious, that he could hold over him."

"Would a man murder his wife over such a thing?"

"If the wife threatens separation and is the one who has brought the fortune to the marriage? Dr. Stauffer lived well and worked little. Many people have killed for less. Not that it matters, I think. As I freely confess to one murder, there would be no reason not to confess to another, had I committed it. I did not."

"The police did not look for you?"

"Yes, but not very hard. A foreigner found dead in a brothel is not going to be a matter of the greatest importance for them. And it is easy to escape the attention of the police, if you know how."

"Tell me."

"Firstly, do not draw attention to yourself. Change the way you dress and look and behave. It is easy to become a different person entirely, if you wish. I was very upset when you recognised me in Biarritz, you know. You are the only person to have done so. I even met General Mercier at a ball, a few months back. Even though he knew every part of my body intimately, he did not for a moment make any connection between me and the woman he knew in Nancy. How did you recognise me?"

I thought back to the moment. "I don't know, exactly. Certainly there is nothing physical that recalls what you were. All your mannerisms are now those of a countess, your voice is different, the way of walking and moving; it has all changed. I didn't recognise you at first, that I know. What can I say? I merely knew. But not so certainly that I dared introduce myself in anything but the most ambiguous fashion, in case I was wrong. It says little for your former lovers that they do not recognise you."

"That is because they were never interested in me, only in themselves. When they were with me, they thought how splendid they were to have such a beautiful woman as their companion. When they made love to me, they were aware only of what wonderful lovers they were. And, believe me, I made sure they felt that."

"All part of the service?"

She nodded. "Then and now."

I glanced down to examine my fingernails, so I did not have to look at her. "Why do you tell me this?"

"You asked. Besides, I need your help. That does not come for nothing."

I frowned. "Not everything has a price, you know."

"There are few things which do not in this life."

"A depressing way of looking at things."

"No. It is liberating, once you get used to it. And it shields you from disappointment."

I let out a huge, involuntary sigh, one of confusion and, almost, despair. She had defeated me. Every time I felt I knew her, the real woman slipped away, and put another phantom in her place. Now, there was this: cynical, cold, murderous. Vulnerable, childlike, innocent. Was this, finally, seeing into the depths of her soul and its real nature?

And then I knew. I glanced up and saw her face; it was a plastic face, an actor's face, able to show any emotion, any trait of character. But she did not see me looking and was not prepared. And I caught a glimpse of something I had seen once before, in a restaurant in Nancy, when I had called her a lady.

"You are lying to me again."

"I am not. I did not kill Madame Stauffer."

"I don't mean that. I mean, you are trying to push me away from you, to disgust me, and make me say how monstrous you are. You are trying to prove to yourself that all men are the same in the end. Why? So you can keep on living your life without changing, allowing no one near you?"

"Stop this, please."

"And why would you want to do that?" I continued remorselessly. "Let me see . . ."

"Shut up," she said, more intently now.

"Not because of me, obviously," I said. "You like me, but so what? I have been around for long enough. It must be something else. Or someone else."

"Shut up, I tell you! Just shut your mouth!" Her face was transformed; her voice was angry, furious, but her face was one of pure terror. For the first time, she looked what she was.

At that moment, I justified all her opinions about men. I was enjoying myself. I was reducing her to nothing, crying, raging, out of control—truly out of control, not with some fake passion that she sold by the yard to the highest bidder. This was the real Elizabeth, frightened, defenceless and totally alone. I had pushed through all her defences at last. I was not proud of myself, but I could not stop. I wanted to push her over the edge.

"Someone else? That must be it. Someone who does not fit into that ideal of cruelty. Who does not deserve the way you treat them, and you're frightened. Not a woman, obviously. So, a man. Oh, my God! That's it! It's obvious, really. You are in love. You have finally, really, fallen in love."

She had collapsed off the settee, and was on her knees on the floor, head in her hands, her entire body shaking with sobs as she dissolved into tears of misery and hatred. Then a wave of compassion flowed over me and I regretted what I had said. But only a little. The feeling of triumph was too strong.

"I hate you! I hate you! I hate you! I hate you!"

She attacked me, flailing at me with her fists, hitting me on the face and on my shoulders and chest. She meant it, and knew how to fight. I had to grab her by both hands to make her stop, and still she struggled to get free and renew the attack. So I bound her to me, by putting my arms around her so she could scarcely move, and then had to lie on top of her, squeezing the breath out of her body as she tried to squirm free.

"Listen to me," I said into her ear when the struggling subsided enough for me to speak. "You need to understand a few things here. I am your friend. I don't know why, but I am. You do not understand much about friendship, I know. It is time to learn. I do not judge you or criticise you. I never have. I never will. For as long as you have known me, you have hidden from me. That does not matter either. But it is time to stop. You have fallen in love with someone. Serve you right. You now know it is not merely a word in a book. Your life will change forever, and not before time. You will have to make more room for trust and generosity. And heartache and disappointment, perhaps. Don't be afraid of it. Now, can I risk letting you go without meeting the fate of Herr Wichmann?"

She sniffled, which I took to be a yes, so I cautiously let her go. She immediately came towards me again, and sobbed into my shoulder for a good ten minutes.

"I'm sorry. I have never behaved like that before."

"And I, also, am sorry you have never behaved like that before," I said with a smile. "Who is this paragon of all the manly virtues who has stolen your heart where all others have failed?"

There was a long, long pause, before she finally lifted her face, sniffled—she even managed to make that attractive—and stared at me with defiance. "Mr. Stone."

I just stopped myself from laughing. "Are you . . . I mean, really?"

"Don't laugh."

"I'm not," I said, "really I'm not," although I was. "It's just that I imagined . . . that Russian Count, now. He's a handsome, rich fellow."

"He's also married. Besides, I do not wish to live in Russia."

"But Stone is . . . you know . . ."

"Middling height, a tendency to the plump, gruff, unforthcoming and old," she replied with a watery smile.

"Yes. So . . ."

"He is the only man—apart from you—who does not look at me as a potential possession. He is kind and has asked nothing in return. He likes me, I think, and dislikes everything that others find fascinating. He is completely gauche, and uncomfortable, but seems to want nothing more than to be with me. He is not a shareholder, and never will be. I really do love him. I knew it the first time I met him. I have never known anyone like him, never felt like that for anyone else."

"Does he know about . . ."

"About me? No. Nothing. And he must not. I want to be loved. Really loved. And by him."

"Are you ashamed?"

"Of course I'm ashamed! I want to be what he thinks I am. Promise me you will never say anything? Please?"

I nodded. "I met you for the first time a few months back. I know nothing else about you at all. But I am not the problem at the moment. Drennan is."

She pulled up her legs, and wrapped her arms around them, then laid her head on her arms. She looked as she should have been, a young girl, innocent, and naïve. "I'm so tired," she said. "And I don't know what to do. I have to stay here, hoping he will come to see me. Every time the doorbell rings, I hope it is him. Every time a letter comes, I hope it will be from him. There is nothing I can do about it. For the first time in my life, I cannot do anything at all except hope."

"Classic symptoms. You should know, surely? You've read the books."

"I never thought it would be like this. It is so painful. I am more afraid than I have ever been. Always, in the past, I have been able to take control and think my way through. Now I can do nothing. And he will find out about me, I know he will. And then I will never see him again."

"Well," I said, "that is not necessarily the case. I have not walked out in outrage."

"But you, Mr. Cort, are a liar and a criminal, with the morals of the gutter."

"Oh, that's true. I had forgotten that." I took her hand, and smiled. "And we guttersnipes must stick together. So you can count on me, at least."

"And what about you?"

"What do you mean?"

"You lecture me about love, but who do you love? About friendship and trust, but who do you trust?"

I shrugged.

"Your world is as cold as mine. The only difference is that I didn't choose my world and now I want to get out of it."

"I have to go. I have a lot to do tomorrow."

"Stay with me."

I was tempted, believe me I was. But I shook my head. "I think it would be better if I had the singular honour of being the only man in the world ever to refuse you."

"Twice, now."

"So it is. Take it as a mark of my esteem."

She leaned over and kissed me very gently on the forehead, then I saw her swiftly brush a tear from her eye. "Good luck, my friend."

I kissed her on the cheek, and left. I felt utterly exhausted. I should have been preoccupied with the fate of empires and the fortunes of the mighty. Instead, the only image in my mind was of a beautiful young woman crying her eyes out.

CHAPTER 18

The next day I went as soon as it was polite to see Sir Edward Merson, Her Majesty's Ambassador to France. I was fairly certain it would be a waste of time, but I had been close to British civil servants long enough to realise that it is necessary to cover all possibilities, to stop up all routes by which blame can come and attach itself. Should everything end badly—and I thought it might well—a failure on my part to alert the British Embassy would undoubtedly become the reason why everything went wrong.

A strange morning, as it turned out, an island of tranquillity in the midst of the chaos that was surrounding me. Sir Edward was not there— it was the hunting season, and he was not a man to allow business to get between him and a quail. So I left a message, then, feeling unsure of what to do next, wandered into the nearby English church where all the English expatriates (except me) gathered as a matter of course every Sunday to listen to the Word of God and breathe in the aroma of the Home Counties. It was like stepping into a different world. The church was a perfect imitation of an English Gothic building, as reinterpreted by people like my own father in the past fifty years. I sat through the entire service, the first time I had done such a thing in many years. My father may have rebuilt the odd church, but he had only rarely gone into them for other than professional reasons. The Campbells were dutiful in their religion and took me along to St. Mary's Bayswater every Sunday, but were hardly exuberant in their religiosity. And school chapel, twenty minutes of prayer, hymn, lecture, every morning, was such a commonplace that I think most of the boys there were entirely unaware that it had any religious significance whatsoever. It was just part of the day, a moment where you could drift off in your thoughts and dream of other things.

But I found that I relaxed. The rolling sound of a good hymn badly sung is particularly evocative. The sermon had just the right blend of comic irrelevance and tedium to make it pleasurable, and the very smell of the place reminded me of England in a manner that quite took me by surprise. And to see all those men in their Sunday best, the women who had taken pains with their clothes but still looked slightly askew in comparison to their French counterparts, the rebellious children struggling to remain still, so that the whole service was punctuated by the quiet, reassuring noise of hand against trouser bottom, was strangely calming. It was a very long way from the pews to the fate of the Buenos Aires Water Supply 5 per cent, but they were intimately connected.

And finally it was all over, the last hymn sung, the collection plate full, the blessings given. A cheerful chatter broke out and the organist started showing off his command of the instrument as the congregation began to file out. I waited a few moments. The vicar was coming in the opposite direction, and stopped me.

"You looked troubled, young man."

"Oh, Reverend. You would not believe."

I nodded and walked on. What could I have said anyway? Which would have been the better one to start with? The coming attack on British finance? Or should I have said how I was trying to think of a way that a whore, whose pimp I had once been shortly after she had committed murder, could marry an English industrialist and get away with it? Or should I have mentioned how I had murdered a man in cold blood a few days previously? All, I hoped, were a little outside the experience of a Church of England cleric.

I walked out of the church feeling bemused. I had done everything I could. If the world collapsed because no one would listen it was hardly my fault now. I had—so I believed—uncovered this great plot, and passed the information on. And yet, I felt I should do more. It was pride, if you like. No one likes to be powerless. And it was patriotism, strangely enhanced by my visit to that oddly English church. For a moment—one of the few such moments of my career—I knew why I was doing my job.

And out of that came a desire to do more, to step definitively out of my role as a gatherer of information, into something different and very much more difficult. But how to go about it? I had Netscher as a means of access to the French, so I thought, and I had contacted the Russians, but the difficulty was how to persuade them to take me seriously. I had no official status whatsoever. What did I propose to do? Open negotiations on my own account? Claim to be the personal spokesman of the Empire? Why would anyone believe me? The only thing I had at the moment to claim special status was knowledge, and in a very few days, when the markets opened on Thursday morning, everybody in the world would have that knowledge. I needed more authority, and I would have to go to London to get it.

So I took the night train yet again, and arrived at Victoria on Monday morning, then drove directly to the Foreign Office to see Wilkinson. I did not sleep as the train rumbled onwards and the boat gently swung as it ploughed across the Channel. All the figures, all the facts, kept on dancing in my head as I tried to work out some way that I was wrong. That this wasn't happening. I could see no alternative, but still I could not quite believe it.

I had not the slightest idea what sort of reception my sudden, un-announced arrival would get. Would my report have even been read? Would anyone pay the slightest bit of attention to it? Would I be laughed at—"Oh, dear boy, this happens all the time. Don't worry, the Bank knows what it is doing." Or even, "Lord Revelstoke is furious that you ruined his weekend, and has demanded your instant dismissal." All such possibilities had passed through my mind, as the train and boat had brought me ever closer to London. The Foreign Office itself is not a place to inspire self-confidence. It was built to intimidate and does its job very well. Its walls and marble colonnades are designed for eternity, the product of a nation which will never fail, which will never make mistakes. The inhabitants of such a building would never allow the colossal blunder I thought I had uncovered. I must be wrong.

I almost began my meeting with Wilkinson by apologising. But when I looked at him, when he lifted his face from his desk, I could see he had not slept. He had lines of tiredness across his face, the pasty shade that only anxiety or exhaustion can produce.

"Cort," he said wearily, gesturing to my seat. "Good. I had hoped you might show up, but as you didn't mention it in your letter . . ."

"I didn't think of it until afterwards. Then I realised there was little I could do in Paris without further instructions, so . . ."

"Yes. Well, I'm glad you are here. Although, as the bearer of ill tidings, you cannot expect many others to be pleased to see you."

"Was I correct?"

"You doubted it?"

"No. But that doesn't mean I was right."

"True enough." He stood up and stretched. "At seven-thirty this morning, a French bank informed Barings by letter they would no longer trade in Argentinian or Uruguayan securities. At eight another two did so. All the indications are that no continental banks will touch them any-more. What is the significance of that?"

"Then it is beginning and will get very much worse. The price of South American securities will drop so, when Barings needs to raise serious money on Thursday, it will be able to offer little as collateral."

"So, in that respect, you are so far correct. I hope I do not see a look of pleasure at your cleverness."

"How much does it need at the moment?"

"At eleven o'clock, assuming there are no hitches, it will be given a credit for £800,000 by Glyn Mills, which is standing as proxy for the Bank of England to prevent matters becoming public. That will get it through today, I understand. Exactly how much it will need over the coming week we do not know."

"Barings has more than enough assets at the moment."

"True. And here you must remember that I know little of finance. But I understand they have also received a letter from the Russian Govern-ment, asking to withdraw bullion on deposit."

"How much?"

"A million. On top of that, you may have noticed that Argentina is in a virtual state of war. The value of Argentine bonds and securities was falling even before the French banks pulled their little surprise. All that is required is that the failure of this bond issue becomes public knowledge, and the deluge will begin."

"Which is only a matter of time."

"I presume so. The Bank has had a word with the newspaper editors here, and they will say nothing. But we cannot influence the French newspapers, who may well be already primed. Come with me, please."

He stood up, and put on his thick winter coat, which made him look suddenly small and shrunken with worry. "I have a meeting," he said. "I would like you to listen in and—if asked—give your opinion."

"You organised that quickly," I said as we walked into Whitehall, Wilkinson bundled up as though he was about to go looking for the North Pole, me less well dressed and much colder.

"My dear boy, you have no idea the chaos you have caused. I dined with the Governor of the Bank on Saturday and gave him your letter to read. He almost choked. There have been people running around like headless chickens ever since. Revelstoke was almost forcibly dragged from his bed; the Chancellor had to interrupt his shooting weekend; the Prime Minister is sulking and beginning to look menacing. Not to put too fine a point on it, Lord Salisbury sees himself as a wizard of foreign policy, and never considered for a moment that mere money might have any bearing on it whatsoever. He is managing to be alarmed and indignant simultaneously, and heads will roll unless it is sorted out quickly. Unless, of course, his rolls first."

My heart sank as the gravity of what I had started began to sink in. "Where are we going?" I asked.

"Just round the corner."

Just round the corner was Downing Street, and the house of the Chancellor. It was still quiet, even though it was past nine, and the policeman on duty, who had been there all night, paid us no attention at all as we strolled up the street past the Prime Minister's house and knocked on the door of Number 11. No one answered, so Wilkinson turned the knob and walked in.

Eventually someone did appear, though, looking annoyed at being disturbed so early, and Wilkinson announced himself. "I believe the Chancellor is waiting for us."

We were led up the stairs to a meeting room on the first floor, a surprisingly shabby place, decorated with little more than a large table, some chairs and dreary portraits of past chancellors, all of whom were striving for gravitas and gazing into eternity like statesmen rather than the politicians they were. Three men were already there: Lord Revelstoke; William Lidderdale, the Governor of the Bank; and George Goschen, the

Chancellor of the Exchequer. A secretary hovered in the background, taking notes.

I was introduced; the Governor and the Chancellor acknowledged me with a nod, Revelstoke looked as though he had no idea who I was.

"Well, let's get on," Goschen said. "Lidderdale?"

The Governor of the Bank looked up. "Well," he said. "As of this morning, we are surviving. However, it is becoming increasingly clear that this is merely a temporary respite. The full news is not yet in the market. When it is, it will sweep over the City like a tidal wave. As far as I understand it, Barings has short-term obligations of near seven million. That is what Revelstoke here has been able to discover. It is quite unbelievable. No one at present knows what its assets are; only that they are falling in value and largely illiquid. The management has been haphazard in a way which would bring any firm to grief."

I expected Revelstoke—used to plaudits and not to criticism, who took praise of his business acumen as a matter of course—to protest at this comment. The fact that he said nothing at all brought home the seriousness of the situation even more fully.

"To sum it up, unless Barings manages to borrow a very large sum of money, it will stop," Lidderdale concluded. "And it will not be able to borrow without a Government guarantee to back the loan."

"Impossible," the Chancellor interrupted. "Quite impossible, and you know it. Pledge the national credit to a private firm? One which has got itself into such a situation through incompetence? It would not survive the Commons and, in any case, public subsidy of the City of London would do as much damage as it was supposed to prevent. No. Absolutely not. The City must get itself out of this mess, and more importantly, must be seen to do so."

"Then we are lost!" Lidderdale exclaimed in a tone of melodrama not normally associated with a banker.

"I didn't say the Government would not give assistance," Goschen said tartly. "Merely that it could not be seen to be doing so. I can pledge that anything that can be done will be, of course."

"But not if it costs you anything."

"Precisely."

Lidderdale lapsed into silence and Revelstoke—who I thought might have taken leave of his senses under the pressure—continued to stare out of the window, the strange blank smile still fixed on his face. He had not said a word and did not even seem to be paying any attention to the proceedings. It appeared that he could not accept what was happening, that he had concluded he was in the middle of a nightmare and the best course was to do nothing until he woke up.

"It would have been a help," Lidderdale said, "if we had known about this in advance." Here he glared at me. "Being alerted only a few days in advance is all but useless. Aren't you paid for this?"

"No," I snapped back. "This is not what I am paid for at all. And I informed the Foreign Office of what I knew some time ago. My knowledge then was incomplete, but it gave a reasonable warning, had anyone paid attention to it."

"That was the memorandum passed on to you nearly six weeks ago," Wilkinson murmured. "You know, the one you never got around to reading."

Lidderdale glared, Revelstoke dreamed, and Goschen drummed his fingers on the table.

"Surely a rescue fund could be organised for Barings?" I asked, wondering whether it was my place to say anything at all.

"It could be," Lidderdale said, "but banks will only subscribe if they are sure that they will not need reserves to defend their own position. And they won't be able to do that unless the Bank of England can reassure them that it has the resources to maintain convertibility."

"Which is the problem."

"Precisely. At present we have scraped together reserves of twelve million in bullion. Which has been damnedly difficult, let me tell you. The Bank of France wishes to withdraw three million and has another three on deposit it could demand at any moment. That leaves us with a reliable six million. And six million of bills are drawn and expire daily. If investors panic and decide they want gold, we could run out in hours. Literally hours."

"So the Bank is the problem," Goschen said.

"No," Lidderdale snapped. "Barings is the problem."

"But Barings cannot be shored up unless people have confidence in the Bank."

"Yes, but . . ."

"Excuse me," I said. There was a sudden silence as the bickering grandees stopped and turned to me.

"Yes?"

"You are forgetting the main point," I said, "which is that this is deliberate. That certain people in France are deliberately exploiting this situation to destroy the credibility of London. Barings has played into their hands and created their opportunity, but this situation would not have arisen without a conscious policy. As things stand, there is nothing you can do. You know it. The only possible option is to surrender on the best terms you can get."

A terrible silence greeted these remarks; it was as though I had thrown a bucket of ice over the meeting.

"I beg your pardon?"

"Barings will stop unless it is saved. The banks could club together and put up enough money, but daren't. There will be a run on gold, because the French and Russians are withdrawing large amounts just for that purpose. So, at present Barings will go down, taking London's credibility and the entire funding structure of world trade with it."

The iciness persisted.

"You need more gold and you need it by Thursday morning at the very latest. And there are only two places you can get it from. The Bank of France and the Bank of Russia."

"Berlin, Vienna?" asked Wilkinson. "It is the standard policy of Britain always to ally with the opponents of those attacking us."

Here Goschen stirred. "Impossible, I think. Even if they wished to help us, which I strongly doubt, the Bank of Berlin was set up to make it impossible—illegal—for it to operate in the international market. If it was done, it would take weeks to organise. The same goes for Austria, and the Italians have so little gold that they have none to lend. Mr. Cort is correct in his judgement."

"There are then two possibilities," I went on. "Either France and Russia are determined to push this to the end, in which case there is nothing we can do. We simply have to accept our fate. Or they can be persuaded to change their minds. In which case we have to discuss what they want. And give it to them."

Goschen turned to Wilkinson. "Your area, I think. What might they want?"

Wilkinson sucked in his breath. "If this is as serious as you all seem to think, they can ask for anything. The Russians could demand a free hand in the Black Sea and in Afghanistan. The French could demand similar independence in Egypt, the Sudan, Thailand."

Goschen looked faintly sick. Lidderdale turned ashen. Revelstoke smiled sweetly.

"And all we have in return," I said, "is the Samson option. Which is to say, the certainty that, while a catastrophe might destroy us, it would also bring calamity to French banking and industry as well, and starve Russia of credit when it is in desperate need of it. I assume—in fact, I know—that there are people in France who do not want such a thing. We need to talk to them and get them on to our side swiftly. And we need to bring in the Rothschilds."

At the mere mention of the name, the atmosphere lightened. However much Barings had (temporarily, it turned out) eclipsed the Rothschilds in recent decades, their name was still magical. Their wealth, acumen, and the fervent belief that they knew and saw everything through their vast private network of informants and correspondents made them figures to be admired or reviled in equal measure. With the Rothschilds on your side anything was possible; with them as an enemy, disaster was certain.

The head of the English branch at the time was Natty Rothschild, a stout fellow who had been running affairs in this country for more than ten years. He had wide political interests, although he had never got on with Gladstone, and had demonstrated on many occasions his patriotism: it was Rothschilds, not Barings, which had stumped up the cash for Disraeli to buy the Suez Canal; Rothschilds again who intervened in the eighties to stabilise Egypt's finances, and then to float a loan from which it derived little profit. A bizarre combination of the Jewish banker and the Catholic Cardinal Manning had acted together to resolve the crippling dockers' strike in 1889. All in all, Natty Rothschild had demonstrated a solid appreciation of his duties, and how to merge these with the need for personal profit. In only two areas did emotion get in the way: Natty Rothschild hated the Russians, but he detested Barings more.

He arrived after lunch, and it was remarkable to see how even the Governor of the Bank and the Chancellor deferred to his opinions. He was not a warm fellow, although I had heard that he could be gregarious and charming in company.

Rather his manner was taciturn, with an aloofness it was hard not to see as disdainful and arrogant. Certainly poor Lord Revelstoke withered even more when he walked into the room. So he should; the battle for supremacy between the two houses was now over forever, and Barings had lost. All that remained to discover was whether Rothschild would react with magnanimity or vindictiveness.

First Goschen briefed him on the details, then Lidderdale, and then I was asked to present my interpretation. Throughout, Rothschild listened absolutely silently, stroking his closely cropped beard every now and then, but otherwise barely moving. As I finished, he poured another cup of tea and stirred methodically.

"Fascinating," he said eventually, in his thick, deep voice. "Quite fascinating. Are you quite sure of all this?"

"I am sure of the facts," I replied. "Naturally, the interpretation is my own. But it fits what has been happening in the markets this morning."

He nodded. "But at the moment the urgent problem is how to stabilise the situation here."

"Mr. Cort advocates surrender," Goschen said sourly.

I blushed. "If I am correct . . ."

"You would destroy Britain's strategic position throughout the world."

"If the stakes are so high, then surely the Government must intervene."

"I have already explained why that is impossible," Goschen said. "And why it would be counterproductive. This must be resolved within the City of London itself."

"Mr. Cort," Rothschild said, ignoring the chorus of protest from the others, "at some stage you must tell me a little more about who you are, and why you are here. For the time being, these others here seem to think you have a right to speak. Tell me—in your owns words—what you recommend."

"The City must organise a fund to rescue Barings. Or at least to get it through the next few weeks, until it can realise its assets and stop in an orderly fashion. That can only be done—you would only have the time to do that—if the Bank of France reversed its policy of withdrawing bullion from London. And if the Russians stopped pulling gold out of Barings. Better still if they signalled their intention of depositing some more. In the circumstances, the rate of interest they might demand could be high, and not payable solely in money. But at the very least we need to know their terms. May I ask if your bank has heard anything about this?"

"Nothing has been communicated to me. But that is no surprise. There are no close relations at the moment between us and the Bank of France. There are many in France who detest the Rothschilds as much as they detest the English. The question is what to do about it. As it seems the British Empire is insufficiently important for the Government to risk its own reputation, then I, like you, feel we have no alternative but to explore other possibilities."

And so it was settled. I was to return to Paris as soon as possible, with a letter to Alphonse de Rothschild and instructions to discover what, if any, price the French would accept. At the same time I was to organise a veritable insurrection amongst the moneyed elite of France, have them storming the barricades of the Banque de France, demanding calm in the markets. And I was to do this without citing the authority of the British Government in any way. This was to be a deal between bankers. It must not have anything to do with foreign policy. There would be no concessions there whatsoever.

My chances? I put them at about none. I had a matter of days to reverse what seemed to be a major move in French foreign policy, and cobble together an unprecedented alliance amongst people I did not know. Even Natty Rothschild seemed pessimistic. He walked out with Wilkinson and me, then asked if I would take a turn with him around Green Park before I headed back for Victoria.

"A thankless task, Mr. Cort," he rumbled as we walked in the direction of Green Park. It was chilly and getting dark, and there were few people around except for the occasional office worker, and governesses pushing prams. "If you succeed, no one will know; if you fail, you will undoubtedly be blamed."

"That is reassuring. Thank you."

"Which brings up the obvious question. Why do you choose to do this? It is a strange life you lead."

Evidently he knew more about me than I thought.

I shrugged. "I don't know. I wasn't a good banker . . ."

"A very inadequate answer."

"I like it, then. I like making people do things they do not wish to do, I like discovering things I am not meant to know. I think I like taking bad actions and turning them to good ends. It is so often the reverse. But I can take lies and betrayal and turn them into patriotism."

"Not the other way round?"

"Not for me, no."

"I see. I think you are going to need all your skills in the next week.

You will be trying to mix foreign policy and finance, and control them through your arts. Are you skilled enough, do you think?"

"I don't know."

"My cousin will give you all the help he can, and a great deal of advice as well. You may trust him. I ask only one thing: if you fail, let him know. I'll be damned if the house of Rothschild is going to be brought to ruin by Barings."

CHAPTER 19

I arrived back in Paris at five o'clock on Tuesday morning. I was totally exhausted. I had crossed the Channel twice in one day, had scarcely slept for two days and had been in meetings much of the rest of the time. I should, properly, have launched into action, but I could not. I did manage to get someone to take the message to Alphonse de Rothschild, sent another to M. Netscher, but that was all. I could do no more without sleep, so sleep I did. And, dare I add, I slept well; quite extraordinarily well in the circumstances.

The meeting with Rothschild and Netscher began after lunch. I very nearly disgraced myself by being late, but I arrived at the Rothschild mansion in the Eighth Arrondissement with a few minutes to spare. There were four people there: the committee for the defence, or so I came to call them in my mind. All people who wished to resolve this, if only they could do so without bringing national opprobrium down on their heads. All were fatalistic, and had a low opinion of their many colleagues, of politicians and of the people of France in general. They were fools, was the general opinion, who understood nothing of money, who had no conception of how delicate and refined were the financial structures which so efficiently delivered the comforts and necessities on which all people increasingly depended. Had it been left to politicians, said Netscher, then the bulk of mankind would still be scraping a living in the fields, dressed in rags and prone to starvation and disease. They needed to be saved from themselves.

So far, so much agreement. It was clear that all present—who

represented some of the most powerful financial institutions in France—
were prepared to put their weight behind the request that France assist
the Bank of England. But it was equally clear that none of them would do
so unless that request was going to be accepted.

"For myself," said Alphonse de Rothschild, "I am prepared to commit
half a million of gold to the general defence of the banking system; I have
already cabled my cousin to inform him that I will transfer the money to
his house today."

Netscher smiled. "That safeguards the Rothschild family, my dear
Alphonse," he observed. "It does little else."

"You cannot expect any more of me as yet," Rothschild retorted. "Not
until there is an overall agreement. Remember, if there is a run on the
banks in England, it could well trigger a panic here as well. We cannot
afford to dismantle our own defences."

"Bank of France or nothing. Is that right?" I commented.

They all nodded.

"I do not know the Governor," I said.

"M. Magnin," Netscher said. "A good man. Started as an ironmaster,
curiously enough. Still a bit of the peasant about him, but solid. He is a
man who fully appreciates the value of sound money. And he understands
how weakness in the credit markets can affect industry. That is the
trouble, in fact."

"Why?"

"Because I would have expected him to have responded already. All
his instincts, I feel sure, would be to bolster London. It is neighbourly
and it is good business. He has not done so. Which suggests he is acting
under instruction. He is not a free man, you know. The Bank of France is
not a private company like the Bank of England. Its sole shareholder is
the Government, and ultimately M. Magnin must do as he is told."

"So we are talking about Government policy here, are we?"

Netscher sighed. "I do not think so. Believe me, Mr. Cort, I am—we
all are, I am sure—trying to find out. But so far I have discovered
nothing."

Here Rothschild smiled in a superior fashion. "Fortunately, the magic
of the house of Rothschild still has some life in it," he said quietly. "In
fact, I do believe I can say what is taking place. This policy was sold to
Rouvier about six months ago. The Foreign Ministry is standing by, as it
considers it foolish not to take advantage of any weakness which Britain

might display. The trouble at Barings has been brewing for several months, and the Foreign Ministry has been quietly preparing the ground. It all developed out of the blunder by Bismarck three years ago when he denied Russia access to the Berlin credit markets. Paris took up the role, and has advanced large sums of money to the Russian Government. This, naturally, has created a bond of friendship, not to say a common interest. I would even venture to surmise that some sort of military understanding might come to pass in due course. Obviously, in that case, a weakening of Great Britain would be mutually beneficial."

"But Russia needs investment desperately. Unless it gets credit, its army is back in the seventeenth century. How can destroying the credit markets help?"

"A question so good I am afraid I cannot answer it. I have approached the Russian Embassy, but they refused to speak to me." The pained surprise was obvious. No one refused to talk to a Rothschild.

"However, they have agreed to talk to the British Government. Which in itself indicates how very much is riding on this matter. And how well prepared they are."

"But that would be Sir Edward Merson."

"I did point this out, and they have no desire to talk to Sir Edward at all, as he would not understand what was being said. No. You have to produce someone more senior and authoritative than that. I would suggest Goschen. He can make a deal and he has the authority to persuade the Prime Minister to accept."

"You expect the Chancellor of the Exchequer to grovel in public?"

"I would expect him to arrive so silently and quietly that no one is ever aware of his presence in Paris."

"To talk to . . . ?"

"The head of the Bank of France, obviously. By merest coincidence, no doubt, the deputy head of the Bank of Moscow is in Paris, visiting his relations. And Rouvier, of course. I and M. Netscher would be happy to attend as well, I am sure."

"Where?"

"Somewhere they will not be noticed."

CHAPTER 20

I had not forgotten the matter of Elizabeth and her diaries, but the rest of Tuesday and much of Wednesday morning was used up preparing. Stone's telegraph operator was back in business, so I was at least able to communicate faster, and if my own entreaties had not been enough, the state of the markets proved more persuasive. Hour by hour, the news had been getting worse. More and more people suspected some hideous crisis was in the making. Credit was drying up; suspicion was already beginning to focus on Barings, which was publicly giving assurances that nothing was amiss, while privately panicking and trying to raise as much money as possible. Members of the family pledged their houses, horses, works of art. Debts and favours were called in, assets were offered at knockdown prices, but all that did was stoke the speculation that something was going very badly wrong. Bit by bit, panic began to spread; interest rates rose, volumes in the markets began to oscillate wildly, prices followed. Time was running out. Goschen decided to come to Paris. He had no alternative.

The meeting would be in the last place anyone would ever suspect that an event of such importance would happen. When I asked, Elizabeth agreed without hesitation, and immediately went into high activity, laying in food, drink and everything else that might be needed. It was only a little different from a meeting of her salon; the topics of discussion would merely be more serious. And after many hours of labour I checked my watch. My appointment with Drennan was coming close. It was time to go.

It was a long shot, admittedly, but it was worth a try. Certainly I did not wish to risk confronting Drennan directly; I knew him too well. He had beaten me last time we met, and I had no confidence that he would not do so again. It would have been good to know exactly what he was up to, but I had concluded this was a luxury I could do without. The last thing Britain needed was an espionage scandal inflaming French public opinion against all things English just at the moment when France was being asked for assistance. Indeed, I was more and more sure the two were connected.

I arrived in the rue Daru about half an hour early, approaching from the boulevard de Courcelles and then down the rue Pierre-le-Grand, and went into an apartment block on the corner. Facing me over the road was the Alexandre Nevskii Cathedral, Eastern and entirely out of place in that strict and regimented quarter of apartment buildings, the different-sized domes and gold mosaics looking as though they had been dropped from the sky by accident. It had been built a few decades previously for the Russian community in Paris, as a sign of their presence and to give a focus for their social activities, and had proved a singular success, even though the local residents, apparently, did not entirely approve.

I climbed up the servants' staircase at the back of the lobby, all seven flights of scrubbed, cheap wood set against poorly painted walls, in contrast to the richly polished, carpeted appearance of the residents' staircase, until I reached the corridor at the top which led to the tiny cubicles that the servants slept in under the eaves. Halfway along there was a skylight, which I opened. It was noisy, but I knew there would be no one to hear, and I levered myself out onto the roof, and manoeuvred into a position where I had a clear view of the cathedral.

I kept my head low, and scanned the small square in front of the entrance with my binoculars; a faint sound of singing told me there was a service going on. A few people were hanging about, and I thought I saw what I was looking for. A man, well dressed, sitting on a bench reading a paper; another by the door looking at the order of service pinned up in a small glass case. Two more talking by a tree to the left.

My heart sank. It was all so amateurish. Drennan was too old to fall for that. A man reading a newspaper in the semidark? People idly chatting in the cold? He wouldn't go near the place. One glance and he'd take fright.

And then I saw him; he too was coming early, walking along the street bundled up, hat pulled down over his head, dressed anonymously, not scruffily, not respectable. Like a shopkeeper or clerk. Only his walk, long and loping, gave him away. He also wanted to get there first, to be able to see me before I saw him. He'd taught me that; I had anticipated him.

He took no precautions: all the methods and techniques he had so painstakingly and painfully drilled into me he didn't use. He didn't look around, didn't pause to check the landscape, did nothing. He just crossed the street, walked across the little square, began to climb the steps. I was puzzled. He was coming to see me, but he was taking no precautions, almost as though we were on the same side, as though he considered me not a threat.

The man by the order of service moved to intercept him, going close, taking him by the arm; I saw the bench man drop his newspaper and begin moving forward; the conversationalists started to spread out, one to each side, forming a circle behind his back.

Drennan turned, his hand went into his pocket. I heard nothing, it was too far away, but he fell onto his knees, looked up. The newspaper man came up close behind him, stretched out his arm to point at his head, and Drennan collapsed onto the stone steps of the cathedral.

It was done. One problem, at least, had been taken care of. I was back at Elizabeth's house, washed and changed, in time to welcome Wilkinson and Goschen when they arrived in John Stone's coach from the Gare du Nord at eight o'clock.

CHAPTER 21

It was a soirée to remember. One by one, they arrived, and I was only sorry that it had to remain entirely confidential. It would have had more of an impact on Elizabeth's reputation than the arrival of the Prince of Wales had done. Not that many streetwalkers entertain the Chancellor of the Exchequer, the British and Russian Ambassadors, the French Foreign and Finance Ministers, the Governor of the Bank of France and a smattering of Rothschilds and other bankers at one go. Not that it was a social occasion; these were men of affairs, and it was what they were good at. I might even hazard a guess and say they all enjoyed themselves. From nine in the evening to five the next morning, they huddled in corners, disappeared in pairs or groups into side rooms, shouted at each other, looked tense, angry, worried, elated, relaxed and made jokes, then began the cycle of meetings anew. Those who were not engaged gathered round Elizabeth like chickens round a hen, and she distracted them with her conversation and charm, creating an atmosphere of the possible in a way only she could manage. Her chef, the incomparable M. Favre, excelled himself, and her wine cellar impressed even M. de Rothschild. I am firmly of the opinion that the slow onset of calm she generated did more to ensure an agreement than any other factor.

For my part I had little to do, but I was given the liberty of attending the private meetings of the English delegation, and the rare occasions when the meeting, more or less by chance, became more general. It was, however, made clear that I was to offer no opinions of my own. And I rarely had the opportunity of talking to any of the Russian or French party.

Count Gurunjiev did, however, take my arm shortly after he arrived. "A word, Mr. Cort," he said quietly.

"It seems you were right," he said. "A man was shot this evening as he was about to go into the Russian cathedral. He had no papers or identification of any sort on him, but he answers your description perfectly well. And he had a loaded revolver."

"He caused no harm, I hope?"

"No. After your warning we were not prepared to take any chances. He was accosted, tried to run and was killed. We are currently persuading the police it was a murder amongst thieves, and best forgotten about. I'm sure they will agree; there have been too many of these incidents recently for them to want more publicity. What is puzzling is what he planned to do."

He went off to pay his compliments to Elizabeth, leaving me with only a deep sense of relief. All I had to do was discover where Drennan had lived, and then collect the diaries, and I had time enough for that now. The urgency had gone out of one part of my life at least.

And finally the meeting proper was under way; the English were in Elizabeth's salon, the French took over her library, the Russians were closeted in the sitting room. The dining room served as neutral territory, where all could talk freely. A ridiculous amount of time was lost in small talk, enquiries about the voyage from London, earnest entreaties that good wishes be communicated to everyone from the President to the Tsar to wives and sons and daughters. There was talk about hunting and politics as they slowly got the measure of each other, sidled towards the main subject which all knew must arise sooner or later, then backed away again.

It was necessary, all this, it set the tone, gauged emotions and nerves. Then, all of a sudden, as though some hidden decision had been taken, some sign given, Count Gurunjiev began:

"I fear Mr. Cort was trying to pull the wool over my eyes when we met the other day," he began. "I discover that what he so skilfully described as a small matter of accounting is nothing of the sort."

"And how is that?" Goschen asked.

"I do not understand finance: in that Mr. Cort was quite correct. But you make a mistake in thinking I do not understand politics, or diplomacy. His little matter of accounting seems to involve a fundamental shift in Russian foreign policy. And of French."

"I think that is an exaggeration."

Here it comes, I thought. They've been talking about it, they've agreed a joint strategy. Rouvier, I knew, had been bombarded by the Rothschilds all day, one banker after another presenting the case for intervention, for reversing the policy, and offering who knew what inducements; he was the only senior French figure who wasn't there. Delayed by the Chambre des Députés, someone said. Will be along when he can leave. No doubt those who wished to pursue the matter and go ahead had also been putting their case as well. The Count was about to give the first hint of which side had triumphed.

"I imagine the interest rate that the Bank of France would charge for lending gold to the Bank of England will be very high. Naturally, you cannot expect the Russian Government to accept a lower reward."

Better than saying there could be no deal at all. But he could still set the price so high that it would be unpayable.

"I never expected for a moment that would be the case," Goschen said a little grumpily. "Of course, your assistance would be rewarded, and acknowledged in public, if you so wish."

"Can you give me any reason why we should in any way give assistance to Great Britain?"

"From our point of view, or from yours? I can think of many."

"Really? It is in Russia's interests to weaken Britain as much as possible, surely? India, the Ottoman Empire, the Mediterranean, the Balkans. In all these areas our policies are diametrically opposed."

"That is true. But I do not think your Government believes that Afghanistan is the major problem you face at the moment."

"And what would you say that is?"

"Bismarck has gone. The treaty you had with Germany went with him. You have no allies, no friends, and you have a gigantic border facing the most powerful army in the world."

"And England will come to our aid in exchange for a few bars of gold?"

"No. No more than it will help France recover Alsace. But you, as a military man, know that the Russian army is woefully unprepared for modern war. It has no railways to ferry troops and supplies; not enough factories to produce armaments; a navy which would scarcely trouble Nelson, even if the sailors were well trained. You are a vast empire, and a military pygmy. You have the men, but lack the more important aspect of modern warfare. Which is money."

Good point, I thought, and nicely put. Goschen was revealing a combative streak I had not suspected he possessed.

"What we offer is to let the French assist you. They seem open to the proposal."

"You want to buy us with other people's money?"

"Britain's banks are supreme in the world. For the past twenty years they have made a fortune out of South America. That, as you know, has now come to an abrupt end. So they will be looking for new markets. They will crowd France out of any they choose to concentrate on. We offer the French a free hand in Russia. We will offer only a token competition for form's sake. France will be able to grow its banking sector, strengthen it in ways it could not otherwise do. And you will get all the money you desperately need.

"The point is," Goschen continued, "if there is a general financial crisis, France will not be in a position to lend you a single centime. If the banks of London are crippled, so will many French banks be. Capital will evaporate, loans vanish like morning mist. If you want a modern army or navy, then you must leave your money in Barings' vaults. What is more, you know this perfectly well."

The Russian frowned. "I have been told similar things by my advisers. The doctrine that you must strengthen your enemy in order to defeat him I find a bizarre one."

"It is nonetheless the case. I could name you at least six French banks which would be badly wounded if Barings fails. All hold Barings paper, all have loaned Russia money."

"There must be more than that. You paint me a picture of paradox, where it becomes logical for us to help our worst enemy. But, in return, our worst enemy must help us."

"Go on."

Here it comes, here comes the bill, I thought.

"You are afraid of Russian influence; you must help us increase that influence. You fear our interference in the Ottoman Empire; you must make our interference more effective. You fear we want to build a fleet to challenge you in the Black Sea, the Straits, the Mediterranean itself. You must help us build a fleet that can defeat you. That is the price, Mr. Goschen. The Russian navy needs a shipyard on the Black Sea coast, capable of building and maintaining everything that floats. The latest weapons, the best facilities. If you agree to that, then I will believe you are serious, and we can then discuss Barings."

"I'm afraid that would be impossible," Goschen replied instantly. "Even were we minded to do so, it could not be done. No government would survive such a thing; any which tried would fall within weeks, and be replaced by one who promised to oppose it absolutely."

"In that case, I fear we have difficulties," said the Count sadly. "I have tried to be reasonable—you are no doubt as aware as I that we could have asked for very much more. If such a small thing cannot be done, then I can offer no more. I, too, have people to satisfy. I cannot propose something which seems like a humiliating failure."

I pulled Wilkinson aside. "Keep him talking," I said quietly. "Whatever you do, do not let him leave. I have an idea. Just make sure he's here when I get back."

I took Elizabeth's carriage, which hurtled through the streets at the sort of speed which had pedestrians cursing me and the poor horses sweating profusely by the time we pulled up at the Hôtel du Louvre. I didn't bother with announcing myself, just ran up the stairs, all four floors, and along the corridor to Stone's suite, and hammered on the door.

"You must come. You're needed."

We were back in the carriage a few moments later, back at her house twenty minutes after that. We had been gone an hour, and the Russians were losing their tempers by the time we arrived. So, it must be said, were Goschen and Wilkinson, who felt like fools, having to make polite and meaningless conversation all that time.

"A private word, please," I said, and the Russians nodded as we trooped out.

"This is John Stone, Chancellor," I said. "I think he might be able to help."

Goschen nodded. "How?"

"Is your objection to a Russian naval base fundamental? That is to say, is the problem the base, or the consequences of people knowing about it?"

"Both. It would dramatically shift the balance of power in the Near

East. I suppose we could live with that, but the public would not wear it. We'd be massacred."

"And if no one knew?"

"How could anyone not know? Don't be absurd."

I nodded to Stone, who I now saw for the first time working as a businessman. And by heavens he was impressive. He had only had a rapid account from me, and even with that he managed to take over and dominate the meeting with extraordinary speed.

"If the Russians want a base then they have to get it from Britain, practically speaking," he said. "We are the only country which could mobilise the resources for the sort of thing they must have in mind. Enough to maintain a fleet"—here Goschen grimaced—"supplies, equipment, engineering shops. Clearly a major project. They don't have the capital, the workforce or the expertise to design, build and run it. Nor, I must say, do the French have enough spare capacity to provide it. The Germans do, but won't.

"Nor can we," he went on. "Or cannot appear to. And there would be outrage in Britain against any country—France, say—which did. Is that correct?"

Goschen nodded. "It would be tantamount to an act of war if the French built the Russians such a thing."

"Well," Stone continued thoughtfully, "it could be done. I'm sure that French banks would float the bonds to raise the money on behalf of the Russian Government; it could be a general fund for development. There would be no need to specify what it is for, if the interest rate was high enough. I could form a new construction company, registered in somewhere like Belgium, with shareholdings held in trust by banks across the Continent. As for the workforce, the crucial personnel would come from yards across Europe, directed at a distance by my companies. It would be perfectly possible to set up a structure so impenetrable that no one could ever find out who owned it. And the Russians could hail it as a triumph of Russian engineering, a sign of their industrial progress. I cannot speak about the strategic consequences, of course. That is outside my area of expertise. But if you are prepared to allow a base to be built, then it could be done without anyone knowing who was responsible."

That was a summary; the actual discussion was much longer and far more technical. Goschen was both a moneyman and a politician and wanted to know exactly what Stone was suggesting. The more he heard, the more Stone dealt with his objections, the more I could see him regaining confidence and determination.

Eventually Goschen sat back. "Any further comments?"

Wilkinson shook his head, and there was silence.

"Then I suggest we talk to the Russians once more. Mr. Stone, if you would be so good as to come with us?"

I was left out of that one. The deal was done; the French and the Russians had both got what they wanted, and the end of the crisis was in sight. All they had to do was send the telegrams to deposit money in the Bank of England and it would be over. I could still hardly believe it; Britain had got off lightly; astonishingly lightly.

"You look tired, my friend," Elizabeth said. She had come when she heard the others marching down the corridor.

"I'm afraid you've been a guest in your own house this evening."

"Yes, and my chef might resign tomorrow. The amount these people eat and drink is astonishing. It all seems quite good-tempered, though."

"I think they've been thoroughly enjoying themselves," I said. "It's what they love more than anything. I don't think it would suit me at all." I yawned. "Lord, but I'm tired. I'll sleep well tonight."

There was a ring at the doorbell, and a few moments later a footman came in with a card on a tray.

"Please show M. Rouvier into the sitting room," she said, then turned back to me. "That is where the French are?"

"Just in time to hear what has been agreed. Good."

"I gather you visited Count Gurunjiev a few days ago."

"Yes. And I apologise for mentioning your name. I did it very discreetly, though. I gave no hint at all of knowing anything about you, other than saying I was your friend."

"Thank you. But please don't do it again."

"I promise."

Fateful words. A few moments later the door opened and Goschen and Wilkinson came in, followed by Stone and Rothschild, who looked worried.

"Problem?" I asked.

"M. Rouvier is apparently shouting at the Governor of the Bank of France, telling him he had no right to agree to anything without his approval. And that he does not give his approval. To put it another way, he won't take the deal. And if the French won't the Russians won't either. Come, gentlemen, let us go and talk this over."

They trooped out again, leaving me with Stone and Elizabeth. He went and sat opposite her, and smiled gently.

"Well, this is a problem," he said.

"You mean you didn't foresee it?"

"What do you mean?"

I shook my head and frowned, thinking furiously. A whole host of little details, previously unconnected, seemingly random, seeming to be sticking themselves together into new and troubling patterns. And then, there it was. Undeniable.

"This is all you, isn't it?" I said. "From the start."

"I don't think I understand."

"When did you come up with this scheme? To create a crisis, and force a solution that allowed you to do as you wanted?"

He smiled. "You overestimate me, Mr. Cort. That does not happen often. I'm not used to it. What do you mean, my scheme?"

"The first time I met you you mentioned that the Government had forbidden you from working for the Russians. Now you will be able to do so with their blessing and appear a selfless patriot at the same time. The banks to organise all this, they will be the same as the ones leading the assault on London. Credit International, Banque de Bruges. This whole business could not possibly have taken place without you knowing about it long in advance."

Stone, who had been examining a Chinese bowl on the mantelpiece, turned around.

"I haven't broken it yet, you see," she said. "And I have given it a place of honour."

"I am flattered," he said with a gentle smile.

Stone put it carefully back in its place, then stood back anxiously to make sure it wasn't about to crash to the floor.

"I'm sorry, Mr. Cort. You were saying?"

"The Russians and the French could have destroyed London, but they are settling for a shipyard and a few bond issues. And, by pure coincidence, the owner of Britain's biggest arms company is in a hotel down the road, ready to oblige. And you came up with this staggeringly complex scheme in the time it took to take a cab from the Louvre to here.

How could anybody think of something that complicated in a matter of minutes?"

"I'm very good at my job."

"Not that good. Not without thinking it out in advance."

"I did not create this situation," he said quietly. "Barings was going to fail anyway; that has been obvious for months. I merely made sure that I benefited. And that my country benefits as well."

"What do you care about your country?"

"It may surprise you if I say I care a great deal. The Russians were going to get a shipyard; it was merely a matter of who built it and profited from it. They will be bound ever tighter to France, and that will make Germany . . ."

I held up my hand. "That was Wilkinson's argument as well. Does this come from him as well? Was this his doing? A Civil Service plot to rewrite Britain's foreign policy against the wishes of the Government and the electorate?"

"You sound very pompous for such a young man. We merely agree on certain matters. And you will discover there are many people who will be well satisfied how things have turned out," he said.

"Goschen?"

"No. Not him. Nor the Prime Minister. But this is how Britain governs itself, and how its Empire prospers. And how governments take decisions the electorate does not wish to know about. Business needs to be protected from politicians. I could say that the country does as well."

"And you make a lot of money out of it?"

"I do. That is my job."

"But how did you get the French to agree? The Russians?"

"Everybody benefits, you know, and the Russians do like their bribes. Count Gurunjiev required prodigious amounts of money. Of course, he also has a fine triumph to take back with him to St. Petersburg."

I came very close then to saying what the Count had done with Stone's money, but stopped myself.

"And me? I didn't even need bribing."

"No. But you played your part very well. Do not think that your skills and intelligence are not appreciated. There is little point continuing this, you know."

"I like to get things clear. The Government had to be panicked into realising that this was a plot that had its price, rather than the random chaos of the market. And I did that. I was essential for that. It had to be noticed in time. So you got me to do it. With just a little hint here and there from people like Netscher to point me in the right direction. So I would work out what was going on, frighten the life out of the Government . . ."

Stone nodded. "You deserve everybody's thanks."

But I wasn't finished yet. There was something else as well. It niggled me. "So that's the Russians. The French are a different matter. How did you plan to control them? The banks could be bought off with the promise of a free run at Russia, but what's going on now? What about Rouvier?"

I paused and looked at him and finally understood. "Oh, my God. It's out of control, isn't it? Rouvier isn't part of the plan. And he's about to wreck everything."

"It does seem that M. Rouvier is acting unreasonably at the moment," Stone said quietly.

"You assumed that Rouvier would do what the banks and the Governor of the Bank of France told him."

"What they told him was in the best interests of the country. Yes. And it is. Anyone but an idiot could see that."

"Unfortunately he's an idiot."

"It does seem that he dreams of some grand personal triumph."

"He blocks the Bank of France, the Russians will follow suit and the deal is off. Do you have any idea what you have done?"

"Not all gambles pay off, unfortunately."

"Is that all you can say?"

He shrugged perfectly calmly.

I couldn't believe it. It was his calm, emotionless way of confronting what was happening that bowled me over. Mingled with that was my fury at what he had done to me. That was a weakness, I know. But he had deceived and manipulated me from beginning to end. Was that even why Wilkinson had sent me to Paris? Was that in his mind even then? Did he plan this so very far in advance?

I did not get the chance to ask. The door opened, and Rouvier came in, already wearing his winter coat and carrying his hat and gloves.

"Dear Countess, I come to take my leave of you, and to thank you once again for your hospitality," he said as she rose from the sofa to have her hand kissed. "Alas, I wish the conversation had been as agreeable this evening as is customary in your house."

"I am sorry you were disappointed, Minister," she replied. "Can I not persuade you to stay a little longer?"

Rouvier had a look of such self-satisfaction that it was almost intolerable. "It is very late, and I think everything that can be said, has been. More importantly, I believe I will have a busy day tomorrow. A very busy day."

"One moment, Minister," I said. I still did not know precisely what I was going to say but I knew that the moment he was out the door all was lost.

"Mr. . . . ?"

"Cort, sir. Henry Cort. I work for *The Times* newspaper."

He looked puzzled by that, as well he might. "What could you possibly say of interest to me?"

I was completely without emotion. The fury at Stone was so intense that I didn't even notice it; it was suffusing my being so much that it was all I was. I had a choice, and I took it fully aware of what I was doing. I can offer no excuse and no explanation which would not be false. I wanted to beat Stone, and hurt him. I wanted to show I could retrieve a situation when he had failed. Whatever the price, whatever was necessary to do it. And there was only one way. May God forgive me, I did not hesitate.

"Minister, you are a politician. You have been Prime Minister once, you may very well have the honour of that great position once more. I wish you well; I do not wish anything to stand in your way. Public spirit is a fine thing, and you have demonstrated over the years that you are a highly competent administrator."

"Thank you, young man," replied Rouvier, with a look of amused surprise on his face.

"Unfortunately, I will ensure that your career comes to an end unless you consider what I have to say. The Bank of France and most of the banking community of Paris desire to stave off a dreadful crisis which will plunge the whole of Europe into a terrible slump. The Bank cannot do so unless you give it permission. You will give that permission."

"And why should I do that?" he asked in mocking astonishment.

"You want something else?"

"The evacuation of Egypt, the withdrawal of the Royal Navy from the waters off Siam, and a free hand in the Lebanon. I am afraid bankers have poor vision, and think only of money. I can see further than they. I am saving them from their small-mindedness."

"That will not be possible."

"In that case, we have no more to talk about."

"I'm afraid we do," I said. "We must also talk about the Countess von Futak."

Elizabeth froze. She did not move, but I could see her eyes widening, and she took up that position—unnoticeably to anyone who did not know her as well as I did—that signified tension, watchfulness. Fear. Stone did not react at all. Not yet.

Rouvier smiled. "Ah, dear Elizabeth. I do hope you are not going to threaten to expose me. I really do not think that it would do my career any harm at all. Only the puritanical English could think of such a thing. In France we—"

"Yes, yes. I know all about that. Having conquered the Countess von Futak would indeed be a fine thing. But having paid for her out of Government funds is another matter. She is a very expensive woman, as Count Gurunjiev and many others will tell you. You didn't think you were the only person she was skinning, do you? Surely not, a man of the world like you? You must have realised you were only one of heavens knows how many people she—what's the word—entertains?"

He shot her a look of growing alarm. Stone still did nothing, but stood, hands in pockets, looking at Elizabeth, as he listened to my words, unable to take his eyes off her. I wanted to see the disgust and the revulsion spread into his face. He had everything. I was damned if he was going to have her as well.

Rouvier shrugged dismissively. "A small scandal which will be forgotten if I become known as the man who restored France to pre-eminence."

"She's not a countess, of course. You've been spending fifty thousand a month on a common streetwalker from Nancy. Didn't you realise? What you paid ten thousand a night for, any soldier on the eastern frontier who wanted her has had for a franc. She is also a murderer, wanted for the cold-blooded slaughter of a client in Lyon."

He was pale now, but still undecided. Elizabeth was sitting with her hands in her lap, quite unmoving, her self-control still total. Except that I could feel the numbness spreading through her, the chill of despair as she heard her life, her reputation dissolving as someone she trusted— perhaps the only person she had dared to trust—tore her life to shreds. It was a numbness that was in me, as well.

"Do you know of a man called Drumont?" I said quietly.

He stared at me.

"He is a journalist; a detestable man. Twisted, violent, hateful. I must say I cannot even be in the same room as him without feeling sick. But he has extraordinary ability. He hates all Republicans, all politicians. The delight he will get from grinding you into the dust will be very great. Destroying people is more than duty for him. It is a pleasure. Can you imagine the headlines? How he will enjoy himself? How your enemies will delight in hounding you from office? France may triumph, Minister. But you will not taste any of the fruits of victory. M. Drumont will see to that."

"There is nothing that can be discovered," he said airily. "Do you think I gave her receipts?"

"She keeps a diary," I said wearily. "It is very detailed, in every respect. And she was a foreign spy. I can prove that also. I have details of payments made to her by the German military via the Bank of Hamburg. She passed on pillow talk for whatever price she could get. You will soon be able to read about it yourself. In his paper. In a couple of days, I imagine."

"What do you want?"

"Three million sterling. In gold bullion. To be deposited with the Bank of England immediately. You may, if you wish, make an announce-ment via the Bank about international responsibilities, how France has decided to act to guarantee the stability of the money markets. Say what-ever you wish to gain the maximum advantage from the situation. But the money will be deposited or the diaries will be published."

"You are asking the impossible."

"I think not. A word to the Governor of the Bank of France next door is all that is needed."

"You cannot possibly think I will reverse myself like that? Even to save my own skin? My reputation—"

"—will be enhanced. You will have pulled off a masterstroke. Enhancing France's international standing with one small gesture and at no cost at all."

"It can't be done."

"It can be. So, what is your decision, Minister? Ridicule and possible prosecution for corruption, or a quiet but powerful reputation as the most skilful Treasury Minister the Republic has ever had?"

"I need time to reflect."

"You don't have time. You will go next door to your colleagues and agree to the deal they have so carefully worked out. You will go now."

He was calculating fast, not even able to look at Elizabeth, then threw down his hat and gloves and strode out of the room. I thought I had won, but wasn't sure. That was not what was on my mind in any case. I did not really care. I wanted to beat Stone, that was all, show him I was as clever as he, and take away from him something he wanted at the same time. And I didn't care how I did it.

Elizabeth sat, looking suddenly so tired, so reduced, trembling at what I had done, but unable to show any other emotion. She was in shock at the speed and ease with which I had torn her world to shreds, and trampled it into the dust. Because I had not hesitated, not tried to spare her in any way. She was merely a weapon in negotiations which I had used without hesitation. Her worst enemy had never betrayed her on such a scale. She couldn't even look at me, could not raise her eyes to look at Stone, standing still by the fireplace.

Eventually she lifted her head, but to Stone, not me. "I imagine you will want to leave now, Mr. Stone," she said so quietly I could only just hear her. "You realise, I am sure, that everything Mr. Cort said is true."

Stone put his face in his hands and breathed deeply. I was no longer in the room for them. I didn't exist. I stood up. Neither of them noticed. When I got to the door I turned.

"One more thing."

"Go away, Cort," he said wearily. "Leave this house."

"I will. But I need to say this. Elizabeth, I am sorry. I did what I had to. But at least I have taken care of Drennan for you. He is dead. I will recover the diaries and deliver them to you, unread."

And here Stone whirled round. "What?"

"It is not something that concerns you, Mr. Stone."

"I think it is. You say Drennan is dead?"

I frowned in puzzlement. "You know him?"

"What happened?"

"He was shot this afternoon."

Stone turned pale. "Oh, my God. What have you done? You killed him?"

"I didn't kill him. The Russians did. It was part of the deal you wanted. Part of the price. It made them trust me enough to listen to me. Why?"

"You told me your servant had robbed you," he said to her, ignoring me. "You didn't say what had been taken. I assumed it was some jewellery. I asked Drennan if he could help, I've known him for years. It was to be a surprise, to show you . . ."

He looked at me in total disbelief. "You killed him?" he repeated.

"Just trying to make the world safe for business," I said. "It's what everybody wanted."

I left, leaving the final part unsaid, the bit about why Stone seemed almost relieved when I had tackled Rouvier. Almost as though he was glad he did not have to. I couldn't put the pieces together. I am still not sure. Besides, it was nearly three in the morning. I was tired. Perhaps I was imagining things.

It really was over. Rouvier concluded that a small guaranteed triumph was a better bet than a bigger prize that might be torn from his grasp. Three hours later the cables started going out to newspapers and agencies that the Bank of France and the Bank of Russia, in a spirit of international solidarity and to ensure the smooth operation of markets, had agreed to deposit extra gold at the Bank of England. It turned the tide; Barings collapsed and the family was all but ruined, but it resurfaced in a new guise soon enough, although it was only ever a shadow of its former self. The markets recovered from their nasty fright and settled down to normal business after a month or so. The City's reputation was damaged, the prestige of France and Russia climbed, but London's position remained unchallenged and the beginnings of a mutual understanding began to emerge. Russia and France signed a secret alliance, and French money began pouring in to build up the Russian economy and army. London banks, often enough, didn't even compete.

John Stone got to work. The construction of the port of Nicolaieff on the Black Sea produced only token and ineffectual protest from Britain, surprising considering that such a thing might ordinarily have been enough to start a war. It proved that Russia was not as backward as everyone had thought, considering that it was able to mobilise the resources and technology to construct such a vast enterprise without outside help.

And in the spring of 1891, John Stone married the Countess Elizabeth Hadik-Barkoczy von Futak uns Szala at St. Oswald's Church in Malpas, Shropshire. I was not invited to the wedding. I scarcely came across them for years although, now I have finally returned to England because of Mr. Wilkinson's death, we inevitably meet occasionally. We are formal and polite.

We never talk about his wife.

PART THREE

Venice, 1867

CHAPTER 1

I was not intended by family, education or natural instinct for a life of, or in, industry. I still know surprisingly little about it, even though my companies own some forty factories across Europe and the Empire. I have little real idea how the best steel is smelted and have no more notion of how a submarine works. My skill lies in comprehending the nature of people and the evolution of money. The dance of capital, the harmony of a balance sheet, and the way these abstractions interact with people, their characters and desires, either as individuals or in a mass. Understand that one is the other, that they are two separate ways of expressing the same thing, and you understand the whole nature of business.

A few months ago I read a book by Karl Marx on capital. Elizabeth gave it to me, with a smile on her face. A strange experience, as the author's awe exceeds even my own. He is the first to understand the complexity of capital and its subtlety. His account is that of a lover describing his beloved, but after describing her beauty and the sensuality of her power, he turns away from her embrace and insists that his love should be destroyed. He could gaze clearly into the nature of capital, but not into his own character. Desire is written in every line and paragraph of his book, but he does not see it.

In my case, I surrendered to the excitement that came over me when I glimpsed the extraordinary process by which food turned into labour into goods into capital. It was akin to a vision, a moment of epiphany, all the more surprising because it was so unexpected. It was a strange process, this metamorphosis of a curate's son into a businessman, and deserves some description, not least because it involved events now completely unknown.

I am considered a secretive man, although I do not see myself in this fashion. I do not guard my privacy with any unusual jealousy, but feel no need for all the world to know my affairs. Only one thing have I hidden which is of any importance. This account will, I hope, explain some elements of my life and may give the information needed for fulfilling the requirements of my will. It is an aide-memoire, and I put down here all the details I can remember while I conduct my search for a definitive answer.

I write sitting in my office in St. James's Square, and all is quiet. Downstairs, my Elizabeth is curled up in front of the fire, reading a book, as she usually does in the evening before going to bed. I can imagine her yawning, her face illuminated by the firelight, entirely beautiful and calm. As there is no one there, she will be wearing her reading glasses. When she hears me coming down the stairs, she will whip them off and hide them; it is her vanity. I would tell her it means nothing to me, but having to use them so annoys her that I do not wish to trespass on her little secret. For the rest, she is at peace; I have given her that, and it is the best and most worthwhile thing I have ever done, worth more to me than all the factories and money I have accumulated over the years. I will not have it disturbed. But I must settle this other business once and for all; it has been gnawing at me for some time, and I am no longer young enough to afford any delay. I will find the truth, and will settle my mind. I do not fear that it will disturb Elizabeth greatly, as likely as not, the story ended long ago. I wish to know; that is all.

I will write as my researches progress; I have begun my enquiries, they will bear fruit sooner or later. I am, I am sorry to say, unused to not getting what I want. In that lies my reputation for arrogance and I suppose it is probably deserved. It is necessary; a humble businessman is about as much use as an arrogant priest and if you are not by nature self-confident, then you must appear so, or you will fail. It is not a quality that will ever be sung about by poets, but like all the darkness within us, such characteristics—shame, guilt, despair, hypocrisy—have their uses.

This pensiveness is foolish, I know. It began simply because of the death of William Cort; he asked me to come and see him in his wasting state and I went, travelling down to Dorset, where he had lived for the past forty years. A mournful meeting, but he was resigned to his end and not unhappy. Life had been a burden to him and he was looking forward to being rid of it. He gave me his message; it weighed on him. I made some remark, changed the subject as quickly as possible. Then I dismissed it from my mind. But it would not go. The thought came back to me, nestling in the back of my mind, ambushing me at the strangest of moments.

And when I was sitting with Tom Baring, trying to come up with an insurance policy to safeguard my companies in case of accident, the thought came into my mind once more. It would be an appropriate denigration, I thought, to tame my unease by using it so cynically. A block on opening the books so that the great hole in the finances is not revealed to shareholders—not watertight, nothing can be, but enough to enable an ingenious solicitor to tie everything up in knots for as long as is necessary.

My beloved shareholders would be alarmed and panic if all was open. But then shareholders are sheep, which is why they invest in little bits of paper, rather than in something real. Why they whinge and moan if something goes wrong but would never test their own mettle against the markets. Why they congratulate themselves on their acumen if their bits of paper rise in value due to the labour of others. It is the great unspoken passion of all businessmen: they may battle against their workers, criticise bungling governments, try their hardest to bankrupt and ruin their competitors, but they all, invariably, have some respect—if only small—for each of these. But shareholders disgust them, and if they could find a way of ruining them all, they would do so with pleasure and satisfaction. Managers of public companies are like slaves, as much as the workers they in turn employ. They may serve their masters well, be obsequious and conscientious, but deep in their hearts there is loathing. I feel it in myself, and I see it in others. I can detect it in Theodore Xanthos, as resentment and greed take hold of him. He will test himself against me sooner or later. I have expected it for years.

At the moment, I have committed my entire fortune to one extraordinary operation, to build battleships which no one has ordered, for a government which has not enough courage to tell the truth, to safeguard a people which does not want to pay for them. I have calculated that they will change their minds and I am prepared to back my judgement. And if they don't, I can ruin them all. They are corrupt, greedy, little men, and their grasping nature gives me the power to bend them to my will, should they thwart me. It is exciting, what business should be when it rises above

mere production and strives for grandeur. Naturally, the shareholders
would take fright if they knew what I was doing—although I have long
believed that people who are not prepared to risk their money should not
be allowed to keep it.

So I would protect myself from my shareholders with my niggling
concern. Turn it to my advantage. Show it who was the master. I visited
Henderson, had a sentence put into my will: "£250,000 to my child, whom
I have never acknowledged . . ." The sum had to be big, so that it would
affect all the other legacies, make it impossible to wind up the estate.
Unacknowledged because nonexistent.

I did not even mention it to Elizabeth, whom I tell most things,
because I never considered it would be necessary. Dying has never been
something which has struck me as even a remote possibility. That is for
others. Even visiting Cort at his last did not make me think that, sooner
or later, I would become like him. All I felt when I looked at him on his
bed, so thin and weak, hardly able even to speak, was a distant interest.
Concern, a little sadness for him, but no identification with his plight.
No; in due course the provision would become redundant, the will would
be recast. That would be the end of the matter.

Writing down the words did not make me the master of the thought,
though. Instead, I found I had given it life. It preyed on me even more.
Old memories came back, jumbled and confused, some all too real, some
no doubt imaginary. It distracted me, and I hate distractions. I have never
sat and waited for a problem to resolve itself on its own. I issued my
instructions, began enquiries, and started to jot down these notes, to
order the past, sort out what was real and what was not.

The source of my concern lay in Venice—then and now, the city in
Europe which has the least interest in anything industrial or commercial,
despite the fact that its wealth was built on trade every bit as much as its
buildings rest on wooden piles driven deep into the mud of the lagoons.
Like a grand English family fallen on hard times, it has turned its back on
commerce, preferring genteel decay to a vigorous restoration of its
fortunes. At the time I visited it, I almost admired the old lady (if ever a
city could be so described, Venice in the late 1860s merited such a title)
for her refusal to compromise with the modern world.

I was there on a tour, my first and only holiday until Elizabeth began
her futile attempts to convert me to the pleasures of idleness. I had had a
certain good fortune a year or so before; my uncle had died, childless and

unmarried and, rather than leave his small fortune to my father, whom he utterly despised, he left it to me. Certainly this showed a desire on his part to sow dissent in our family, as my father lived only on a small stipend, and my sisters he pretended did not exist. Not a penny to them, and the entire amount of £4,426 to me, with strict instructions that I was in no way to distribute, give or otherwise alienate any part of the said sum to any other member of my family. Nasty of him, and had my father been less gentle than he was, Uncle Tobias might have had his way and begun a family feud. Possession in this fashion gave me no pleasure, so I resolved to dispose of the money in a way which would have the old man rolling in his grave, gnashing his teeth in rage.

Why did he despise my father so much? That story, like that of so many family disputes, went back a long way. My father had married poorly. Scandalously poorly, in fact, for he had married a woman of no family or wealth. She was, even worse, the daughter of people who had arrived on these shores from somewhere in Spain only a few decades before, and had even been born in Argentina herself. She was (to my eyes) fabulously exotic and (to Uncle Tobias's) totally unacceptable. How he knew this I do not know, as they never met. He refused ever to come anywhere near her. A pity as (old rogue that he was) he could not have failed to be charmed by her.

But she was not English; of that there was no doubt, and to the end of her life spoke with a noticeably foreign accent—although of such a mixture it was impossible to discern what it was. This made her all the more charming to those who liked her, all the more repugnant to those who did not. I am quite well aware that the memory of her predisposed me to Elizabeth when we met.

She also communicated to me a tendency to be different. Because of her, I have never fitted in quite comfortably to this country of mine, much as I love it. I could, I suppose, have become totally conventional in response, but some of the fiery defiance of the mother transferred itself to the child, and I instead did the opposite. I have, in my life, followed my own course, wherever it might lead. And thus have been able to grasp opportunities others have not even noticed.

When I received Uncle Tobias's money, I realised that the usual options available to a young man of small fortune were not open to me. Wine, women and gambling would not do, because Uncle Tobias had dissipated a far greater fortune on such things in his youth, and would have thoroughly approved of my recklessness. It would have meant the triumph of his side of the family. Donating the money to a worthy cause was also out because, although he loathed my father's gentle brand of Christianity, he was a resolute high Tory himself and would have held that, at least, the money was helping to keep the lower classes in their place.

Then, one day in London, lunching with a friend, I hit on the perfect solution. If there was one thing Uncle Tobias hated more than the common people, it was the commercial ones. The traders, the industrialists, the factory owners, the bankers, the upstart new orders, the Jews, with their crassness and breathtaking wealth. Ruining the country with their gaudy vulgarity, their contempt for everything that was proper and decent and ordered. And now taking over the country in politics as in money. It was his defeat at the 1862 election by a Liberal factory owner (if only of gloves) that finished him off. England was ruined, all that was good in the country had been destroyed; there was no point in continuing.

Six months later he expired in the midst of sexual congress with the parlourmaid on a billiard table at the age of seventy-nine, at which point it was discovered that his fortune, net of debts, was very much less than anyone anticipated, and that I was the sole beneficiary.

After a certain amount of thought, I gave all the money to precisely one of these upstarts so they could continue the labour of reducing Uncle Tobias's England to rack and ruin. In brief, a highly speculative and utterly hopeless early venture in imperial mining that was being run by an associate of my mother's family who was not only Jewish but had a reputation for highly doubtful honesty. In this, popular report was only part accurate. Joseph Cardano (whom I knew ever better for a quarter of a century until his death in 1894) was indeed Jewish, but he was also perhaps the most honest person I have ever met. Had I known this about him at the time, of course, I would never have entrusted Uncle Tobias's money to him.

At this point I thought the matter was taken care of and resumed my life as it had been before. Then, at the beginning of 1867, I received a letter from Mr. Cardano, informing me of certain important developments concerning my investment. It had, quite literally, struck gold, and Uncle Tobias's legacy was now worth many times what it had been. I was, in fact, tolerably wealthy and, as most of my money was earned (in a fashion) by myself, I felt quite free to give a sum equivalent to the legacy to my parents and to my sisters, thus causing, I hope, Uncle Tobias's mortal remains to give a few more spins in their coffin.

In the meantime I had turned my thoughts to dissipation, but found it did not suit me overmuch. My parents had brought me up too well and, besides, my head was ill-suited to it. I found the life of pleasure-seeking frivolity too dull to endure. I visited Joseph Cardano once more, this time to place my money in the most advantageous but safe fashion, and prepared to leave England for a tour of the Continent, in the hope that this would provide inspiration for some suitable way of filling in my days.

By that stage I had spent considerable time, with his assistance and often enough in his offices, studying money and its infinite variety. I had started with *The Times,* but found the daily reports of stock prices and interest rates of insufficient interest. So I became something of an apprentice to Mr. Cardano, in whose company I discovered the great secret that multiplying money is remarkably easy, once you have some to begin with. The first five thousand is the most difficult, the second less so, and so on. As Uncle Tobias had got me over the difficult stage, there was little to stop me. The only thing I have never understood is how others are blind to this obvious fact. Although, I suppose, I must be grateful that they are.

On the whole, I stick firm to the conclusions I formed then. The Stock Exchange is merely an elaborate means for the wealthy to extract money from the less well off. It is not those who buy and sell shares who prosper; it is those who insert themselves in between the two sides who grow rich. Once I realised this, and (tutored by Mr. Cardano) grasped the poetry of capital formation, of share issuance and flotation, of how to make capital be in two, three or four places simultaneously so that all profit accrues to you, and the losses to someone else—only then did my interest begin to be aroused. Even so, I found this all too abstract. It has never been my desire to amass money; I find possession a dull business. Rather, I had the desire to do something with it. In England, commerce is divided strictly into three parts: the world of money, the world of industry and the world of trade. While I was at Mr. Cardano's side, I began to ponder how vast fortunes might be made by blending those three worlds into one.

I should also mention that I was married by that stage. My wife was good and kind. We did not love each other and we never had, but she did her duty, and I mine, and I held firmly to the belief that this was all that was required. I can say that nothing I did harmed her, and so, were I to be strictly rational, I would say that my behaviour was unobjectionable to all but the religious moralist. But I am aware that religious moralists can make a good case, and I accept that my behaviour fell short.

We married when I was twenty and she eighteen; she died six years later of pneumonia, shortly after my return from my travels. I cannot even remember why I chose her, except that I accepted that I should. My mother disapproved, although she did not say so. Perhaps she was offended that I married someone with a nature so very different from hers—quiet, docile, polite, dutiful, obedient. She would have approved very much more of Elizabeth, had they ever met. But then I thought Mary was everything a wife should be. So she was; she was not, alas, everything a woman could be. After only a short while I could find little to say to her, and found little in what she said interesting; but I did not expect anything else, and I do not believe I ever made her aware of this. I spent more time with my fellows, less at home. I lived two lives and treated my home as little more than a place to sleep. My wife accepted this and was not discontented.

She did not wish to accompany me when I decided to travel around Europe; the idea of leaving her home, or London, or England, filled her with dismay. She begged me not to go and, when she saw I was displeased, urged me to go on my own. And so, eventually I did, although my attempts to persuade her of the joys and pleasures we would have together were quite genuine. I do not believe she missed me in the slightest; her daily routine was slightly disrupted, to be sure, but my place in it was so small she easily adjusted. During the eight months I was away we corresponded once a fortnight, and neither of us said anything which was more than formal, considerate and polite. We got along perfectly well, and I considered myself happily married.

CHAPTER 2

I was not a very good tourist. Travelling alone I found wearisome, and when solitude is broken only by statue after statue, painting after painting, the joy of contemplating the great masterpieces of the human spirit begins to dissipate quite quickly. I was not one of those hermit-like creatures who needs no man besides Mr. Baedeker for company. Although I do not need to be surrounded by others in order to feel alive, I do need some conversation and distraction. Otherwise all becomes too much like study; pleasure becomes duty and—dare I say it—one church begins very rapidly to look pretty much like another. In this way I passed down one side of Italy, and back up the other again, travelling by train when I could, and by coach and horse when I had to. I enjoyed it, although my memories have little to do with the great walled cities or the many acres of canvas I viewed, noted and sketched in those few months. I cannot remember a single painting, although I do remember trying hard to be deeply impressed by them at the time.

Venice was different, not least because on my first day there I made the acquaintance of William Cort, whose sad life has intersected with mine, on and off, ever since. I came in from Florence on one of those wretched trains which arrive at somewhere close to dawn. I had had little sleep during the night but it was too late to go to bed, especially as I was wide awake by the time my trunk had been recovered, loaded onto a boat and taken off to the Hotel Europa, where I had booked a room. I should say that at this stage the city had made next to no impression on me, not least because the weather was (unusually for September) grey and drab. It had canals. Well and good; I had heard about those, and Birmingham has canals as well. But the sense of wonder and amazement which one is meant to feel did not come to me. All I wanted was somewhere to eat a little breakfast.

Venice is—or was then—decidedly short on such places. It was not long since the Austrian occupation had ended, and the city had finally become a part of the new Italy. Hope for a new dawn was in the air, no doubt, but the effects of more than half a century of occupation and neglect were manifest. It was a dull place, which had still not thrown off the simmering resentments of the past. Many had befriended the Austrians, and were shunned for it; others had become too close to revolutionaries, and had suffered for it. Society had been disrupted, many of the best had left, others had become impoverished. Trade had dwindled, the legendary riches of the past were mere memory. This was the place I had dutifully come to visit, thinking more of the images of Canaletto than of the present reality.

I wandered off in quite the wrong direction and passed by those few eating places I saw, too befuddled to make up my mind and enter. So I walked on, turning this way and that, but not a shop or coffee house or restaurant or taverna was there now to be seen. Few people, either. It seemed to be a ghost town.

Eventually I rounded a corner and came across a perplexing sight in a small but pretty enough square. By an old wooden door some twenty feet high, in an ancient, ivy-covered wall, I saw a young man, well dressed in a dark suit and with a hat in his hand. He was rhythmically and with some force bashing his head on the door, occasionally producing an almost musical staccato sound by slapping his hand on it as well. At the same time I heard an incantation that came from his lips:

"Damnit, damnit, damnit, damnit."

An Englishman.

I stopped and looked at him from a distance, trying to figure out a reasonable explanation for his behaviour, rejecting the idea of an escaped lunatic as being both too easy and insufficiently interesting.

After a while, and when he reached some sort of internal resolution, simply resting his head on the door and sighing deeply, all passion spent, I ventured to speak.

"Are you all right? Can I be of any assistance?"

He looked round at me, his head still resting on the wood of the door.

"Are you a plumber?" he asked.

"No."

"A bricklayer?"

"Alas."

"Do you have any knowledge at all of carpentry, or stone masonry?"

"All subjects that have passed me by. To think that I wasted my time at school on Virgil, when I could have been preparing myself for a life of gainful labour."

"You're useless to me, then." He sighed once more, turned round, then slid down the door to sit disconsolately on the ground. Then he glanced up.

"The builders haven't shown up," he said. "Again. We're two months behind schedule, autumn's come on and the roof's come off. They're impossible. A nightmare. Time is a concept they simply do not understand."

"This is your house?"

"Palazzo. And no, it's not. I'm an architect. Of sorts. I'm supervising its restoration. I had a choice. This or building a prison in Sunderland. I thought this would be more fun. Wrong, wrong and wrong again. Have you ever felt suicidal?"

A chatty fellow, but I did wish he wasn't sitting on the ground like that. I didn't feel like joining him in the dirt, and it was awkward talking down onto the top of his head. He had fair, sandy hair which already showed signs of thinning on top. A small man, slightly built, but neat of movement and quite engaging in his manner, with a broad mouth and easy, open smile.

"How long have you been waiting?"

"About an hour. Don't know why I bother. They're not going to show up today. I might as well go home."

"If you could tell me of somewhere to eat, I would be delighted to offer you breakfast, if that would help to ease the pain."

He jumped up instantly and held out his hand. "My dear fellow, I take it all back about your being useless. Come along. William Cort by the way, that's my name. Call me William. Call me Cort. Call me whatever you want."

And he shot off, left down a dark alley, right at the end, across a small square, moving as fast as a ferret. I had barely time to introduce myself before he started talking again. "Trouble is, I'm stuck here until the place is finished, and at the rate we're going, I might well die of old age before I see England again. I don't reckon they had any idea what sort of condition the place was in when they bought it."

"They?" I asked, panting a little in my effort to keep up.

"The Albemarles. You know? Albemarle and Crombie?"

I nodded. Had he asked I could have told him the magnitude of the bank's capital, the names and connections of all the directors. It was not a serious challenger to houses like Rothschild or Barings, but it had a reputation as a good solid family bank of the old-fashioned variety. Entirely wrongly, as it turned out; it stopped in '82, and the family was ruined.

"Bought this place without even looking at it and sent me off to do what was necessary. Lord only knows what they want it for, but the client is always right. My uncle wants to build their country house, y'see, so he couldn't displease them and say it wasn't a job for us. Besides, it was supposedly good for me. My first solo job. It's enough to make me want to go into the Church."

"I don't recommend it," I replied. "I think you need more patience than you have shown so far."

"Probably. Doesn't matter anyway. I'm going to die here. I know it."

"So you are an incurable optimist as well as an architect. I suppose the two go together."

He didn't answer, but turned into a dank and unwelcoming doorway which I would never have guessed was some sort of public eating place. Inside there were just two tables, one bench to sit on, and no people at all.

"Elegant," I commented.

He smiled. "And by far the best eating place around this quarter," he said. "I take it you've not been here long?"

"A few hours."

"Well, then, you will soon discover that the magnificence of the city conceals the utter degradation of the inhabitants. There are few restaurants, and those are poor and hideously expensive. The wine generally tastes like vinegar, the people are lazy and the accommodations horribly overpriced and uncomfortable. I long for a good piece of roast beef sometimes."

"Venice seems to have won a place in your heart, then."

He laughed. "It has. No, I mean it. I can complain about it for hours, list all its faults in relentless detail, grumble incessantly about every facet of life here. But, as you notice, I have come to love the place."

"Why?"

"Ah, it is magic." His eyes lit up with something of a twinkle. "That's all I can say. I think it is probably something to do with the light. Which you have not yet witnessed, so there is no point in trying to persuade you. In a short while—tomorrow maybe, when the weather picks up, maybe this evening—you will see."

"Maybe so. But in the meantime, I'd like some breakfast."

"Ah, yes. I'll see what I can do." And he disappeared into a back room, from which there came, after a while, the sound of banging pots and shouting.

"All sorted," he said cheerfully when he returned. "But they were quite reluctant to serve us. You have to plead with them. Luckily, I come here quite often, and so do the builders. When they show up."

The thought put him into a mood of melancholy again.

"Do they often do this to you?" I asked.

"Oh, goodness, yes. I will have a meeting with the foreman one evening, he will look me in the eye and swear blind they will all be there at eight sharp the next morning. We will shake hands and that will be the last I see of any of them for a week. And when I complain the reaction is generally astonishment that I should expect anyone to show up on St. Sylvia's day, or the morning of a regatta, or something like that. You get used to it after a while."

"You don't seem very used to it this morning."

"No. Today is special, not least because there is no roof on the place, and I have an engineer coming to advise on strengthening the walls. That sort of thing isn't an area I know much about, I'm afraid. I can design buildings, but what exactly keeps them up is quite beyond me."

The coffee and bread arrived, both equally grey and unappetising. I looked at them doubtfully. "Not one of the great culinary capitals, Venice," Mr. Cort commented, dipping bread in cup with enthusiasm. "You can get decent food, but you have to look hard and pay high. They probably have fresh bread out there somewhere, but they don't think highly enough of me yet to let me have any. They keep it for their own."

He swallowed a lump of bread, then waved his hand. "Enough. What are you doing here? Passing through? Staying awhile?"

"I am without plans," I said airily. "I go hither and thither as I wish."

"Lucky man."

"For a while, anyway. I was thinking of staying here for a few weeks, at least. But I cannot say you are the best salesman for the city. Ten minutes of you and any reasonable man would pack his bags and head for the railway station."

He laughed. "You will find we like to keep the place to ourselves."

"We?"

"The ragbag of drifters, idlers and adventurers who wash up in this place. There are few foreigners in Venice, you will notice. The railway and the end of the occupation is beginning to change that, but as there are few places for visitors to stay when they get here, there is a limit to how many people will ever come."

An interesting comment, which I placed in the back of my mind for the future. As I wandered the streets over the next few weeks, I realised that Cort was right. There was an immense market for decent accommodation of the sort that would shield the traveller from the beastliness of Venetian life. The French, I knew, were well ahead in this area, constructing gigantic palaces in the centre of cities which offer every luxury to travellers prepared to pay well to avoid any real contact with the place they were visiting. Fed by the railways, organised by Thomas Cook, any hotel placed at the end of a line in an appealing destination could hardly fail to prosper.

Even at that stage, I turned down in my mind the idea of involving myself with Mr. Cort in any commercial way. I learned early that liking someone, trusting someone and employing someone are three very different things. Mr. Cort was going to stay firmly in the first category. I have always had the tendency to pick people up from all manner of places; my fortune and my judgement are one and the same. Being agreeable and being of use are not necessarily incompatible, but they not identical either.

Cort was an amiable man, intelligent and amusing. Honest and decent, as well. But to give him any position of authority would have been foolish. He was too prone to despair, too easily discouraged. He could not even control a dozen or so recalcitrant workmen. He had some desire to be successful, but it did not burn so strongly in him that he was prepared to overcome his character to achieve it. He desired peace more; alas, he achieved little of either.

Nonetheless, we passed a pleasant half hour together, and I found his company charming. He was a good raconteur, and a mine of information about the city, so much so that I invited him to dinner that evening, an offer he accepted until he remembered that it was Wednesday.

"Wednesday?"

"Dottore Marangoni's at home, in the café."

"At home in a café?"

He laughed. "Venetians do not often entertain in their home. In six months I have scarcely passed the front door of a Venetian's abode. When they do entertain, most do so in public. Tonight is Marangoni's entertainment. Why not come? I will happily introduce you to my limited acquaintance, such as it is."

I accepted, and Cort looked guiltily at his watch. "Goodness, I shall be late," he said, jumping up from his seat. "Macintyre will be furious. Come and meet him. I expect you will hate each other on sight."

He shouted a farewell through the door, jammed his hat on his head and headed off. I followed, saying, "Why should I not like him? Or he me? I consider myself quite amiable normally."

"You are a human being," Cort replied. "And thus to be detested. If you were made of steel, were you something that could be honed to perfection on a mechanical lathe, were your movements capable of accurate measurement to one-thousandth of an inch, then Macintyre might approve of you. Otherwise, I'm afraid not. He hates all of humanity, except for his daughter, whom he built himself out of gunmetal and ball bearings."

"Yet he is assisting you?"

"Simply because there is a problem to be solved. He offered; I would never have asked even though he is the only person I know of here who is qualified to assist. Oh, Lord. He's there already."

We had turned the corner into the little street which contained the palazzo's entrance, and outside the heavy wooden doors which some forty-five minutes ago had been battered by Cort's frustrated head stood a man with a ferocious scowl on his red face.

Certainly "friendly" was not a word that sprang to mind. He had immensely broad shoulders, so wide that he barely fitted into his suit; he stood with legs apart, heavily-booted feet planted like trees in the mud. Hands thrust deeply into his pockets. He stamped a foot in frustration, turned and battered on the door with his fist before he saw us. "Cort! Open this door! D'ye think I've no better things to do today?"

Cort sighed nervously as we approached. "Good of you to show up," Macintyre continued acidly. "So kind of you to plan an amusement for me this morning. To fill my idle hours."

"Sorry, sorry," Cort muttered. "The workers didn't show up again, you see."

"And that has something to do with me?"

"No. Sorry. May I introduce Mr. Stone? I have newly made his acquaintance."

I held out a hand. Macintyre ignored it, gave me a cursory nod and renewed his assault on poor Cort, who stood there wanly.

"I'm conducting an important test this morning. And I postponed it, just to assist you. I would have thought the very least you could do would be . . ."

"Stop complaining," I interjected suddenly, "or the rest of your morning will be lost as well."

Very rude of me, but not half as offensive as Macintyre was being. I calculated that he simply liked bullying people when he was in a foul mood, and that matching him, rude for rude, was the best way of dealing with the situation. Poor Cort was too cowed to do much to protect himself, and that was his choice, but I did not see why I had to endure it as well.

Macintyre's flow of eloquence dried up immediately. His mouth snapped shut and he turned his gaze—remarkably blue eyes, I noted, clear and large—on me. There was a heavy pause, and then he let out a loud "Pfah!" and thrust his hands back into his pockets again. "Very well," he grumbled. "Let us get on."

Everything about him suggested a man of strength and character. Certainly he was uncouth, but England owns an excessive supply of the well-bred and polite. Macintyre was a man to get things done, and they are much harder to find. He was not one to waste time on flattery, or to cover over awkward situations with a finely turned phrase. A man to avoid at a soirée, but invaluable in a battle—or a factory.

Cort, meanwhile, had fished out a huge key from his pocket and had unlocked the great and ancient door, pushing it open by leaning his whole frame against it. It gave way with a screech that sounded like the dead in torment, and Macintyre and I followed him in.

As in many Venetian palazzi (so I discovered), the entranceway gave onto a small courtyard; this was where the domestic business of the place had been conducted. On the other façade, giving directly onto the rio di Cannaregio, was all the architectural finery to impress the passerby. What that looked like I did not as yet know. But the sight from the courtyard was terrifying. I could just see that it was a building, of a sort, although it looked as though it had been hit by several cannon shells. Rubble lay all around, piles of brick and stone, lumps of wood. A rickety frame of wood had been erected around the structure, presumably to allow the workmen access, but it hardly looked capable of supporting the weight of more than one or two at a time. Half a dozen cats eyed us suspiciously from atop a pile of wood; that was the only sign of life.

Cort surveyed the mess sadly, I looked astonished, Macintyre paid it no attention whatsoever. He marched straight over to the scaffolding, scooping up a ladder as he went, and began climbing. Cort reluctantly followed, and I watched from the ground.

Macintyre was remarkably agile and fearless, some sixty or seventy feet in the air, skipping over crumbling masonry, occasionally bending down or kicking a lump of brickwork with his boot, sending fragments cascading down to the ground. I was about to go up and join them when he returned back to earth, looking only a little less grumpy than when he started. Cort followed a few moments later, somewhat more gingerly.

"Well?" asked Cort.

"Knock it down."

"What?"

"The whole thing. Flatten it. Start again. Never seen such rubbish in my life. I'm surprised it's still standing."

Cort looked alarmed. "I'm commissioned to restore it, not demolish it," he said. "The owners bought a sixteenth-century palazzo, and that is what they want when I am finished."

"They're idiots, then."

"Maybe so. But the customer is always right."

Macintyre snorted. "The customer is never right. Ignore them, give them what they need, not what they think they want."

"Nobody *needs* a palazzo in Venice," Cort said a little pettishly, "and when I am well-enough established, I might take your advice. For the moment, I have one client only and cannot afford to lose him by demolishing his house."

"Wait then. And it will fall down anyway. Or if you prefer I could come back this evening." He paused and surveyed the scene carefully. "One small charge, in that corner where the two central load-bearing walls meet"—he pointed—"and there would be nothing left in the morning at all. Then you could show what sort of architect you really are."

Cort blanched at the idea, then looked at him carefully. "I never realised you had a sense of humour."

"I don't. It's the most sensible course of action," Macintyre said gruffly, as though offended at the very idea of whimsy. "But if you are resolved to waste your clients' money for them . . ."

"I am quite determined."

"Then what you need is a supporting framework of girders. Three by six should do it. Inches, I mean. Tapering to two and a half by four on the upper floors. Perhaps less; I'll have to do the calculations. Extending up the back and side walls to form a framework inside the structure. That will take the weight of the roof, not the walls, which are too weak to support it. You'll have to build down to dissipate the weight under the level of the foundations . . ."

He paused and looked thoughtful. "I suppose it does have foundations?"

Cort shook his head. "Doubt it," he replied. "For the most part these buildings rest on wooden piles and mud. That's why the walls are so thin. If they were too heavy they'd sink."

Macintyre pursed his lips and rocked forwards and backwards in thought. He was enjoying himself, I observed. "In that case, you'll need to sink some, but at an angle to the vertical, to take the weight of the girders and roof and spread it outwards. Otherwise you'll just push the walls out instead. What you need, y'see, is an internal frame, so that the walls can be little more than a curtain covering the real business."

"Will it be strong enough?"

"Of course it will be strong enough. I could balance a battleship on top of a properly strutted framework."

"That won't be necessary."

Macintyre grunted once more and drifted off into his own train of thought, muttering periodically as he whipped a pad of paper from his pocket and began jotting down hieroglyphics.

"Look," he said eventually, thrusting the notes under Cort's nose. "What do you think?"

The architect studied it carefully, desperate to understand what the older man was proposing. Eventually his face cleared and he smiled. "That's very clever," he said appreciatively. "You want me to build another building inside the existing one."

"Precisely. Lightweight, efficient and fifty times as strong. You won't knock down the old one, but you do get to build a new one. Best of both worlds."

"Expensive?"

"Iron's not expensive, even here. Sottini's in Mestre will supply it. Putting it up won't be cheap. And you won't be able to rely on the half-wits you employ at the moment. Best get rid of them and find a new team. Again, I can make suggestions, if you wish . . ."

Cort's look of gratitude was overwhelming. Macintyre pretended not to notice. "Thought I'd suggest it. That's the trouble with architects. Know everything about the right sort of Gothic window, nothing about load-bearing walls. Pathetic. Good day to you."

And he marched off, not responding to our farewells.

"Goodness," I said. "Something of a force of nature there."

Cort wasn't listening. He was glancing up at the crumbling walls, and back down to the notes Macintyre had thrust into his hand before leaving. Back and forth went his eyes, which narrowed as he calculated.

"This is clever," he said. "Really clever. It'll be cheaper, stronger and quicker. In principle. Oh dear."

"What?"

"I wish I could claim it was my own idea. That would really make my uncle take notice of me."

I noted the remark, the wistfulness of it. "In my experience," I commented, "it is finding the best advice and using it which counts. Not coming up with the ideas yourself."

"Not in architecture," he replied. "Or with my uncle." He sighed. "I just hope Macintyre can keep his mind on it. Once he's solved a problem in his head he tends to lose interest. Besides, he does tend to drink a little."

He was rapidly adopting the air of someone who wanted to be left alone, although what he had to do was unclear. Not wanting to impose myself any further, I thanked him for his company, and the unusual introduction to Venice he had afforded. After requesting directions I left him standing in the rubble and made my way back to my hotel.

CHAPTER 3

I slept for many hours, a dreamless sleep, although it was far from my habit to be so idle during the day. I put my head on my pillow at around ten in the morning and did not awake until early evening, which annoyed me greatly. I had missed an entire day, and now faced a bad night's sleep into the bargain.

I forgot completely Cort's invitation to join him and his friends for dinner, which didn't matter too much. I had neglected to discover where the event was to take place and, in any case, had no desire that evening for company. Rather, I wanted to view the place I had travelled so far to visit, for I had as yet seen little except the railway station, a few streets and a pile of rubble pretending to be a house.

So I walked. And was captivated, as never before or since in my life.

I am not, by nature, a romantic person—considering my small reputation in the world it is surprising I even bother to say this. I do not skip a heartbeat over a sunset, however striking it may be; rather I see the light of a star refracting in particular ways through the atmosphere and giving off predictable, if pleasing, light effects. Cities have even less impact. They are machines for generating money; that is their entire function. Created for the exchange of goods and labour, they either work or do not work well. London was, and still is, the most perfect city the world has ever seen, efficient and directed to this one aim, not diverting unnecessary energy or resources into public finery as Paris does. Even London, though, may soon surrender its crown to one even more single-minded and ruthless in its pursuit of wealth, if my impressions of New York are accurate.

Venice, in contrast, is without purpose. There is no exchange of goods there, no generation of capital. What remains is a shell of a past manufactory which has long since become obsolete. It too was created by trade; it is nothing more than capital petrified. But the capital had fled, leaving only a corpse whose soul has departed. It should have been abandoned, left to rot into picturesque ruin, as the Venetians themselves abandoned Torcello, cathedral and all, once they had no further use for it.

So I believe, and I have argued my case with many a sentimentalist who waxes eloquent about the glories of the past, and how human life has degenerated under the impact of the modern age. Nonsense. We are living at the highest point human civilisation has ever reached, and it is people like me who are responsible for it.

Yet I still have my Venice problem. Everything I say about it is true, and yet that first evening I walked without a break for food or drink or rest for near seven hours, forgetting my map, not caring where I was or what I was looking at. I was hypnotised, overwhelmed. Nor did I understand why. It was not what most people find attractive, the vistas and palaces, churches and works of art. These I appreciate well enough, but not to the point of passion. I would talk of the spirit of the place, although to do so would risk seeming foolish and, as I have indicated, the most obvious examples of its spirit were degenerate and corrupt. Nor was it the light, as for much of the time I marched in darkness, nor the sound, as it is the quietest habitation I have ever visited. The average English village of a few hundred people is a noisier place. I cannot offer a convincing explanation of my own, although when I told Elizabeth of my reaction she suggested that it was because I did not wish to resist its charms; that, having been disappointed by Florence and Naples and all the other places I visited, I wished to be seduced, that I fell not for what it was but what I needed it to be, at that particular moment. And that having generated such feelings in me, it became associated with that feeling forever after. I had tried to be dissipated and failed, tried to be an aesthete and failed, and now I was attempting no project at all, and succeeding beyond my expectations. It is as good an explanation as any other, although had I given her a more detailed account, she might have come up with a different interpretation.

I ended back near the Campo San Stin, which contained Cort's palazzo, and there had a most unusual experience. I had what I took to be an hallucination, brought on by tiredness and irregular food. I am minded to mention it—at some risk of arousing amusement in any who might read this—because it has a bearing on the rest of my stay in the city.

I hope it is clear already that I am not of an hysterical disposition; I am not susceptible to delusions, and have never had any time for the mystical or supernatural. Even in this particular case, I was sure, both before and after, that I was witnessing only a phantasm. Nonetheless I could not fault it; could not discover any proof that it was merely an illusion playing out before me.

In brief, it was this: at (I believe) somewhere after midnight, I was on a bridge over what I later discovered to be the rio di Cannaregio. It was handsome enough; the canal curving away to my left, the looming shapes of the buildings rising up and reflected on the still surface of the water. It was very dark, as there was no lighting at all, not even from the windows of the houses which, for the most part, were shuttered. I stopped to admire the scene, and to consider, yet again, whether I was going in the right direction to get back to my hotel—which, in fact, I was not. As I wondered I stared idly back towards the Grand Canal, leaning on the iron balustrade.

Then I heard a noise, a sound of laughter, and sensed at the same time an immensely powerful feeling of not being alone. I turned around swiftly (Venice is an exceptionally safe city, but I did not know that at the time) and saw a most peculiar sight. There was a torch burning in a socket on the wall of a palazzo some thirty yards away from me, although I swear it had not been there before. And underneath, there was a small boat, which contained one man standing amidships, and singing. I could not see clearly in the flickering light, but he seemed short, wiry and almost ethereal, as though you could see the stucco of the building through his dress coat and breeches. His song was not one I had ever heard before, but it sounded, at one and the same time, like a lullaby, a lament and a love song, delivered in a soft but slightly reedy voice. Extraordinarily beautiful and affecting, although circumstance perhaps made it seem more so than it was.

I did not know to whom he was singing; one window, I now noticed, was unshuttered and slightly open, but there was no light within, and no figure to be discerned. The only human being in sight was this man, who was dressed in a manner more suited to the eighteenth century than to the present age. I saw this without any sense of it being unusual or strange. All I knew was that I desperately wanted to know what the song was, who was the singer, and whether the woman being so serenaded—surely that was what was taking place—was receptive to his song. Who was she? Was she young and beautiful? She must be, to produce such a wistful sadness in the man's voice.

I moved to get a better view, making enough noise to carry over the water. The man stopped singing—not abruptly, but rather as though he had finished his tune—and turned to look at me, making the slightest of bows in my direction. My first impression of age was correct; he had no beauty. His features were not horrible, but they were terribly old. He seemed as old as the city itself.

I watched, immobile, as he settled down in the boat, picked up the oars and began to row away from me, and then the spell broke. I walked, then ran after him, over the bridge, and left, up an alleyway which ran parallel to the canal, hoping to overtake him—he was not rowing very fast—and get a better look. After a hundred feet or so, another turn took me down to a small jetty, and I ran there, and began looking up and down. There was nothing. The boat had vanished. And as I stood there, wondering where he had gone, I heard faint laughter echoing over the water.

I was shaken by this, by my own reaction as much as anything, and turned round to retrace my steps. When I got back to the bridge, the windows of the palace were now firmly shuttered, and looked as though they had not been opened for years.

There was nothing else to do but to leave, and make my way back to my hotel, which I reached (after many false turns) about an hour later. I slept, finally, at about four in the morning, and slumbered until ten. But it was not an easy sleep. The atmosphere of that place had suffused my mind, and like some childish and irritating tune that lodges itself and will not be shaken out, the images of those few moments repeated themselves in my head all night.

CHAPTER 4

Why do I write this? I have spent many an hour, many an evening, at these notes now. It has no real purpose, and I am not used to doing anything without a purpose. Only Elizabeth can manage to make me waste time, although with her nothing is a waste. It is worth any sort of nonsense or frivolity to make her happy, see her smile, to have her turn and say—thank you for putting up with that. For her I even learned to dance, although never well; but I am content to behave like an elephant to see her graceful, to feel her body move as I hold her in my arms. I am not even aware of others. I can honestly say that not once have I thought of how others might admire her and envy me, although surely they do.

But my happiness with her has been different from the sort I found in Venice. We have never experienced together the sort of irresponsible carelessness that I tasted that one time. Inevitably, I am sure; when I met her I was too old to make a fool of myself in the way that only the young can manage, and her life had been too hard, too much of a struggle, ever to be carefree. No; we have made something very different; a world that is safe and warm. We have done grand things, exciting things, pleasurable things together, but never foolish ones. Such things are not truly in my nature, and she knows too well the dangers of them.

Although perhaps a side of her misses the excitement, the need to live on her wits. She gave something up when she married me, in a way that I did not. I still have the pleasure of taking risks; she put aside a part of her character and it may have been a greater loss than either I, or she, realised. Perhaps that is why she is now disobeying me. I refused absolutely her suggestion that she help me track down where this money was going to, identify the people being paid through these strange disbursements in Newcastle. She pointed out that I could hardly use anyone from inside the company itself. I said no. Absurd idea; and so it was, for the wife of a man like myself. But not for the woman she had been, whom I thought was long since dead. She went ahead anyway, took herself off to Germany and returned to live off her wits, disguising herself as someone else, returning to a way of life I thought was gone forever.

I was so angry, so furious when she told me, that I completely lost control of myself. And, as often happened when her iron will collided with my equally strong determination, we fought. Why should she not help me? She was my wife. Did I really know anyone who could do it better? Could I think of any better way?

All of which was irrelevant. What troubled me most was the light in her eyes as she confronted me; the light of excitement, of adventure. That old side of her, the one I had always feared, the one which could not possibly be satisfied with the company of an old man. She has never given me the slightest cause to distrust her. She has had the occasional lover, I have no doubt. But she has never hurt me. They were nothing more than passing amusements, moments of distraction. This was different; it appealed to her sense of danger and her need for real excitement. She said it was for me, but it was for herself as much.

Giving way was one of the most difficult things I have ever done, and one of the best. I quelled my jealousy, subdued my fears, and let her do as she wished. I let her help me, although our life together has been built on my helping her. But it was hard; I knew, could distantly feel, the pleasure she had in acting thus because I also had once been free to do anything I wanted, without having to look forward more than a day or backwards more than an hour. And that is why I write about Venice, because by seeing how much I remember those days, I can judge better how powerfully her own past draws her now.

I was sombre and ill-humoured when I finally descended for breakfast after my bizarre night with my apparition, only to discover a great reluctance on the part of the hotel to supply me with anything to eat at all. Eventually they condescended to provide some watery coffee and stale bread, the sight of which reminded me that I had eaten nothing of substance for nearly a day and a half. That, in itself, went a long way towards explaining my bad mood and headache and also the delusional nonsense of a few hours previously. I needed a purpose and had none, so decided I might as well take care of business, registering myself with the British Consul and picking up any mail that he might be holding for me.

That at least was easy enough. Francis Longman lived in a small apartment with an office attached a few streets away from San Marco, and welcomed me in with enthusiasm. He was a short, fat man, with a squeaky voice which gave him an air of perpetual excitement. His chins wobbled dramatically every time he became agitated and, as I learned over the coming weeks, he was agitated quite frequently and on the least pretext. His abode did not embody the gravity I expected of one of Her Majesty's diplomatic representatives, being dark and disordered and covered in books and papers. His situation seemed somewhat sad and, while I was gratified to be received with such warmth, I did find it somewhat peculiar.

"My dear sir!" he exclaimed. "Come in, come in!"

I thought initially that he must be mistaking me for someone else, but no: Longman was merely bored to tears, and had little enough to do. As he told me at some length, once I had signed the book to confirm my presence and cast myself officially under both his and the Government of Her Britannic Majesty's care while in the city.

"Nothing to do here, you see," he explained once I had been settled down—quite against my will—into an elaborately carved chair in his office. "It's virtually the life of a recluse."

I enquired about his duties. "None, to speak of," he said. "And a salary commensurate with the responsibility. I keep a fatherly eye on British subjects here and once a quarter compile a report on economic activity for the Board of Trade. But there are few enough visitors and little enough trade."

"A useful task," I said drily.

"Indeed. Venice is not as interesting as it was."

"I've noticed. How many people are there here? British people, that is?"

"Never more than a hundred. At the moment"—he paused to glance at his register—"I have sixty-three on the books. Most of those are merely passing through; only about twenty have been here more than a couple of months. And that's including women and children."

"I met a Mr. William Cort yesterday," I ventured. "And a Mr. Macintyre, whom I found quite interesting."

Longman chuckled. "Ah, yes. Macintyre is one of our more difficult residents. Northern bluffness, you know. He can be quite overbearing on occasion. Cort, on the other hand, is a very gentle fellow. You must meet his wife; she is in the kitchen talking with Mrs. Longman at the moment. I will introduce you before you leave."

I didn't really want to meet her, but nodded politely. "And Cort?"

"Mr. Cort, yes. He's been here about four months now. From the way he talks, he'll be around for another decade at least. He comes from a good family in Suffolk, I believe, although both his parents died when he was young, and he was brought up by his uncle. Spellman, the architect, you know?"

I shook my head. I did not know.

"He is being trained to take over his uncle's practise, as there are no direct heirs. But I fear it is not a good idea."

I prompted, as required.

"No business sense at all. It may be his designs are all very well, but the workmen here run rings round him. I found him crying—can you believe it?—*crying*, a week or so back. They bully him terribly, and he does not possess the strength of character to impose himself. Not entirely his fault, of course. He is much too young to take on such a task. But it's ruining him, poor boy. His wife even asked Marangoni about him, she was so worried."

"Marangoni? Is he the physician of choice among exiles?"

"Not precisely, but he is willing to lend such expertise as he has and he speaks good English. Delightful man. Delightful. You must meet him. About the only Italian whose society is tolerable. He is an alienist, sent by the Government to reorganise the asylum. He is from Milan and so is in exile, like all of us. Anyway, Mrs. Cort asked him about her husband's state of mind."

"And?"

Longman sighed. "Alas, no one could understand the answer. These doctors do talk in a peculiar fashion. Nonetheless, it accomplished one purpose. Marangoni is alerted, and Cort is being watched, to make sure no harm comes to him."

"I'm surprised there are so few people in Venice. English people, I mean."

Longman shrugged. "Not so surprising, really. It is ferociously expensive, as you will soon enough discover. And terribly unhealthy. The miasmas arising from the canals are poisonous, and sap the vitality. Few people wish to stay for long. The sensible go to Turin."

"And you have been here . . . ?"

"Far too long." He smiled sadly. "I don't suppose I shall ever leave now."

There was a note in his voice of disappointment, of hopes frustrated, of someone who had expected more from life.

"Now, tell me about yourself, sir." Here he hesitated. "You *are* English, I take it?"

"You doubt it?"

"No, no. Not at all. But every now and then some fraud and charlatan does try to hurl himself on our good offices, you know."

I do not, I suppose, look like an Englishman. I inherited far more of my mother's looks than my father's and that side of my ancestry is very much more obvious. It is another of the things that have always set me aside from my countrymen; the difference is always noticed, even if unconsciously. Others have always been slightly suspicious of me.

I had already sized up Mr. Longman as an incorrigible gossip, and had the distinct feeling that everything I told him would not only be noted, but also relayed to any interested party in due course. Such people can oil the wheels of society, but too great an interest in the doings of others, I find, is often accompanied by a degree of malice which is dangerous. So I replied in as brief a fashion as was commensurate with good manners.

"Then you are rich! Must be!" he cried.

"Far from it."

"That depends on your point of reference. It may be that three hundred yards from Threadneedle Street you are a pauper among your fellows. But here you will be rich. Few people here have any money. Especially among the Venetians; it is why society is so drab. But one can live a rich life with little money, do you not agree?"

"Of course," I replied.

"You should be careful, though. It is dangerous to have a reputation for wealth. You will be amazed by how many people wish to borrow money from you, or forget their wallets when you dine with them."

"Then it would be better if they do not develop a false impression," I replied, with a slight tone of warning in my voice. I could not tell if he took the hint.

I prepared to leave, and Longman bustled around me to show me to the door. "Mrs. Cort!" he called. "You must meet another resident before he goes. He has already met your husband and has only been here a few hours."

I turned to present myself to the woman, and got the shock of my life when the door to the little salon opened. Louise Cort was beautiful. In her early thirties, a few years older than I was, with beautiful skin and eyes, and a delightful, rounded figure. About as different from her husband as could be imagined. She looked directly at me, and I felt a soft stirring as my eyes met hers. She never looked at Longman, barely acknowledged his existence as she shook my hand.

I bowed to her, and she nodded. I expressed my pleasure in meeting her, and she did not reply. I said I hoped to meet her again.

"And my husband," she said with the faintest tone of mockery in her voice.

"Naturally," I said.

CHAPTER 5

I had a dream that night, which I remembered. This was so strange that it unsettled me for days. Not that I had a dream, but that I should remember it, that it should come back to me. Indeed, it has come back to me ever since. Sometimes, for no reason that I can think of, this insubstantial fragment of memory will well up in my mind. Not very often, only perhaps once every couple of years, although more often of late. It is so very perplexing; great events that I have witnessed, taken part in—momentous events, I should say—I can scarcely recall at all. But a fevered imagining of no reality and less importance still stays with me, the images as fresh as if they were brand-new.

I was standing by an open window and could feel the wind blowing over my skin. It was dark outside, and I felt the terror of indecision. I did not know what to do. About what, I do not know; that was part of the dream. The indecision was independent of all cause. Then I heard a footfall behind me, and a soft voice. "I told you," it said. Then I felt the pressure of a hand on my back, pushing.

And that was the dream. Nothing more. What was it about? I do not know. Why was it so vivid it stuck in my mind? There is no answer to that, either. And nothing to be done about it; dreams have no reason or explanation or meaning. The strange thing is that from then on I began to have a vague fear of heights—nothing too extreme, I did not become one of those poor souls who feel faint if they are more than a few feet off the ground, or who clutch at the railings halfway up the Eiffel Tower and become dizzy. No; I merely developed a tendency to feel uncomfortable, wary, whenever I was, say, on a balcony, or by an open window. It was a very annoying weakness which I tried not to indulge; the more so because it was so obviously foolish. But I could never shake it off and ended up by simply ensuring I was never in a position to make it appear.

The incident was all of a piece with how my life developed over the next few weeks; I became increasingly introspective. My life slowed down markedly; the urge to move on, which had afflicted me wherever I had been so far, quite left me. I still do not know why; I think it was the hypnotic effect of the sun on the water, such a constant feature of life in Venice, that slowly befuddled my mind and sapped my will. It is hard to think of normal life when it is so easy to watch the twinkling reflections of sunlight instead. Remarkably easy to spend a few seconds, then minutes, then even longer, studying without thought or conscious awareness the effect of light and shade on a wall of peeling stucco, or listen to the mixtures of sounds—people, waves, birds—that make Venice the strangest city in the world. A week went past, then two, then more, and I would only occasionally stir myself to do anything.

In retrospect, it is all very clear; I was uncertain of myself. I wished to do something grand in my life and had prepared myself well for it. But the days of apprenticeship under Cardano were at an end. He had no more to teach me, and I was now faced with a choice. I could, very easily, make more than enough money to keep me and mine in perfect comfort. It is, as I have said, not hard. But what was the point of that? Such a way of life did no more than fill out the space between cradle and grave. Agreeable and with its own little satisfactions, no doubt, but ultimately purposeless. I did not want power or wealth for themselves, and I did not in the slightest desire fame. But I wanted, on my death, to be able to expire feeling that my existence had made the world a different place. Preferably a better one, but even that, at the time, was not uppermost in my mind; I have never had any great desire to abolish poverty or save fallen women. I am, and always have been, deeply suspicious of those who do wish to do these things. They normally cause more harm than good and, in my experience, their desire for power, to control others, is very much greater than that of any businessman.

When I began to weary of my own company, I decided to take up Longman's invitation, made as I was leaving, to join him at dinner. I did not quite grasp what sort of an occasion this would be, but in effect Longman had been offering to induct me into his particular group of English exiles, for the men all ate together almost every night. This is common in Venice, where there is really only one meal a day, eaten in the evening. Breakfast consists of little more than bread and coffee, lunch of a bowl of broth bought from a cookshop, and so, come dinnertime, the entire population is both exceptionally hungry and, often, quite ill-tempered. Usually people eat in the same place every evening, and then go on to the same café, also every evening. There is a unchanging rhythm to Venetian life which all foreigners eventually adopt, if they stay long enough. There are advantages to being a regular customer: you tend to get better food, always get served more swiftly and, most importantly, the owner will set aside a table for you so you are not disappointed and have to go away hungry.

Longman and his group ate at Paolino's; not as grand as the establishments in the Piazza San Marco, which already earned their living mainly from visitors, as they had previously from the Austrian soldiers occupying the city. With its simple wooden chairs, cheap cutlery and roughly painted walls, Paolino's was for the poorer bracket of the respectable ranks, and Longman's friends were all of this type. I could dine in style, or I could dine in company; that was the choice that the city presented to me. I liked—have always liked—to eat well, but as there was no refined cooking in the city, or none that I had yet heard of, then I was prepared to compromise. Besides, there is a comradely sense among the genteelly impoverished which is often lacking among the wealthy; it was not a great sacrifice.

When I greeted the Consul, there were only two others sitting at a table prepared for six or more; periodically others drifted in as the evening wore on. There was, in fact, a group of ten or more who came there, but not every night; each evening there was a different combination, some of whom liked each other, others who plainly did not. Cort was one of those present that night, and he greeted me warmly; a quiet, softly spoken American was the other. This man spoke with the gentle, drawling tones of the South of his country, a strange accent and quite foreign until you got used to it. It is a way of speaking well-suited to a dry and lazy-sounding humour, which Mr. Arnsley Drennan possessed in fine degree.

He was rugged in appearance, and a few years older than I was, and spoke little until he was ready. When he did, he could be an entertaining conversationalist, delivering pithy observations in a voice which sounded as though he was half asleep, feigning a lack of interest in his own words that added greatly to the delivery. He was decidedly difficult to figure out; even Mr. Longman, far more adept than I was, had failed to breach his walls of discretion and discover much about him. This, of course, added an air of mystery to his person which made him all the more cultivated by others.

"And is your wife to join us later?" I asked Longman.

"Oh, good heavens, no," he replied. "She is at home. If you look around, you will see there are no women here. You will find few in any dining place, except for those in San Marco's. Mrs. Cort also eats at home."

"They must find that a little tedious," I remarked.

Longman nodded. "Perhaps. But what is to be done?"

Now I might have remarked that he could have eaten at home himself, or that perhaps the company of his wife might be preferable to that of friends, but I did not, and at the time it never occurred to me. A man must eat, and a man must have friends, or what of humanity is left in us? Longman's dilemma I found as insoluble as he did, but nevertheless my thoughts strayed briefly to consider how much his wife must pine for company. Then they paused briefly on the thought of Cort's wife in a similar purdah. They did not, however, then move on to considering how my own wife was faring without me.

"Where do you live, Mr. Drennan? Do you have a lonely wife tending the hearth for you?"

It was a lighthearted question, but did not receive an equally facetious reply. "I am a widower," he said softly. "My wife died some years back."

"I am sorry for you," I said, genuinely contrite at my faux pas.

"And I live on the Giudecca, some half hour's walk from here."

"Mr. Drennan has found the only inexpensive lodging in Venice," Longman remarked.

"It is one room only, with no water and no maidservant," he said with a smile. "I live like most Venetians."

"You are a long way from home, then," I observed.

He regarded me intently. "That I am, sir."

He did not seem to find this line of conversation at all interesting, so he switched his gaze to the window and left matters to Longman, who was the impresario of dinner-table conversation.

"Do you intend to continue living in a hotel throughout your stay, Mr. Stone?"

"Unless something better offers itself, yes. I would happily move somewhere more commodious and less annoying, but on the other hand I do not intend to spend my time here house-hunting."

Longman clapped his hands in joy at being so useful. "Then there is a perfect solution!" he cried. "You must take rooms with the Marchesa d'Arpagno!"

"Must I?"

"Yes, yes. A delightful woman, desperately in need of cash, with a vast, tumbling-down palazzo begging for occupants. She would never be so coarse as to solicit lodgers, but I can tell she would not be displeased with an enquiry. It would be central and charming. I will happily send a letter around for you, if you like the idea."

Why not? I thought. I had no plans to stay long, and no plans to leave either. I should have realised this haziness of intention was indicative of a strange state of mind, but no such thought occurred to me. I did not find the cost of the hotel onerous, but the discrepancy between how much you paid and what you got for it I found offensive. So I said, "It would be interesting to look. Who is this lady?"

I noticed that the other two did not look so delighted at the mention of her name, but had no chance to pursue the subject as Macintyre the engineer was stumping over towards the table.

He was clearly in something of a social bind as he wished to dine with the company, but manifestly found it quite unreasonable to admit the fact. He resolved the matter by looking exceptionally ill-humoured and growling his greetings in a manner which escaped being impolite only by a whisker. The effect of his sitting down was to stifle all conversation for several minutes. Longman looked faintly displeased, Cort somewhat frightened. Only Drennan nodded in greeting and appeared unperturbed by his appearance.

"Food arrived yet?" Macintyre said after we had sat in uncomfortable silence for a while. He snapped his fingers at the waiter to call for wine and downed two glasses, one after the other, in swift succession. "What is it this evening?"

"Fish," Cort said.

Macintyre laughed. "Of course it's fish. It's fish every bloody night. What sort of fish?"

Cort shrugged. "Does it matter?"

"I suppose not. It all tastes the same to me anyway." He scowled ferociously at Cort as he pulled a roll of paper from under his coat.

"There you are. I had my draughtsman do it up properly. Did the costings myself. As I said, Sottini has the proper lengths in stock; good Sheffield bars, won't let you down. I've set him up to give you a fair price. Get in touch with him quickly, though, otherwise he'll forget. Don't give him more than twenty-seven shillings a length. But I think you will have a problem with the foundations. I looked again; the central pillar is buried deep down and must be taken out, if this is to work. It will be expensive."

"How expensive?"

"Very. You will have to support the entire building, then remove it, to give space to put in the new structure. Best thing to do, frankly, would be to blow it out."

"What? Are you mad?"

"No, no. It's a very simple. Not dangerous at all, if you know what you're doing. A very small charge placed low down, just to knock a few of the bigger stones out of the place. Then the entire pillar will come down, leaving the rest of the building standing—if you have buttressed it properly."

"I'll think about it," Cort said uncertainly.

"It's the only way of doing it. I've got the explosives in my workshop. When you see that I'm right, let me know." Then Macintyre turned to me, a refilled glass in his hand. "And you. What are you doing here?"

Certainly, no one could accuse Macintyre of an excessive courtesy. His flat, northern accent—I placed him as a native of Lancashire, despite the Scottish name—added to the general impression of rudeness, something which, as Longman noted, northerners deliberately accentuate.

"Merely a traveller, from London, where I have lived much of my life," I replied.

"And your profession? If you have one."

There was a hint of hostility in his tone. I looked like a gentleman, I suppose, and it appeared Mr. Macintyre did not like gentlemen.

"I suppose you might call me a man of business. If you wish to know whether I live off the money of my family, and idle my days away on the labour of others then the answer is that I do not. Although, I freely admit, I would do so happily if the opportunity came my way."

"You don't look English."

"My mother is of Spanish origin," I said evenly. "My father, on the other hand, is a vicar of impeccable Englishness."

"So you're a mongrel."

"I suppose you could say that."

"Hmm."

"Now, now, Macintyre," said Longman jovially. "None of your bluntness, if you please. Not until Mr. Stone is used to you. I was just recommending the Marchesa to him as a potential landlady. What do you think?"

Macintyre's reaction was peculiar. It was a remark of no importance, so I thought, designed merely to divert the conversation into safer waters. But it accomplished the exact opposite. Macintyre snorted. "Bloody madwoman," he said. "And you'd be mad to go anywhere near her."

"What was that about?" I asked Drennan later, once Macintyre had wolfed down his food, tossed his napkin on the table and left again. All in all, he was there for less than fifteen minutes; he was not a man to waste time on inessentials.

"I have no idea," he replied. "It seems Macintyre does not like the lady."

"He tried to get rooms there once. She wouldn't have him and he was offended," Cort said.

"That explains it," Longman said cheerfully. "I wondered how he might have come across her. Not through me, at any rate. I didn't think he took enough time off to sleep. He works on that machine of his from dawn to dusk."

"Machine?" I asked. "What machine is this?"

"Nobody knows," said Drennan with a smile. "It is Macintyre's secret obsession. He has, so he says, been working on it for years, and has poured his entire fortune into it."

"He has a fortune?"

"Not anymore. He is—or was, until he settled here a few years back—a travelling engineer. Hiring himself to the highest bidder. A shipyard in France, railway project in Turin, a bridge in Switzerland. A very skilled man."

"Personally, I prefer the life of the mind, of study and reflection. And, as you may have noticed, he is not best suited for getting on with others. He never stays anywhere long," Longman commented.

"Is he married?"

"His wife died in childbirth, poor man. So he is left with a daughter, who is about eight. A most unfeminine creature," Longman continued, even though I had asked for no elaboration. "Utterly uneducated, with the looks of her father. He can just about get away with it, but what is almost tolerable in a man . . ."

He did not finish. He had successfully painted a picture of what was to come: a lonely old spinster, fending for herself, cut off from any good or proper company. He shook his head slowly to indicate his distress.

"I think she's a sweet kid," Drennan said. "Nice smile. Not much to smile about, though."

And so the conversation proceeded. It improved in tone and temper once the effects of Macintyre faded, and Cort, to my surprise, proved the most entertaining. He was, perhaps, the person most like myself in temperament if not in character, and I found his wit congenial. I had known many like him at school; he blossomed under my appreciation and was in a rare good humour by the time the meal was finished and the small party began to break up. Longman and Drennan decided to head to Florian's for brandy, Cort and I declined the idea, and were left standing by the doorway as the others disappeared.

I turned to thank him for his company, and as I did so, a most remarkable change came over him. He grew tense and pale, his jaw clenched tightly in distress, and he gripped me by the elbow as we shook hands in farewell. He seemed to be looking aghast at something behind me, so I turned round swiftly to see what had so grabbed his attention.

There was nothing. The street which contained the restaurant was dark but entirely empty. At the end a broader street crossed over it, and this was lit by the faint flicker of torch flame, but that, too was deserted.

"Cort? What is it?" I asked.

"It's him. He's there again."

I looked at him blankly, but Cort did not respond. He continued staring, as though frightened out of his wits.

I touched him gently on the arm to stir him; he did not react immediately, but eventually his eyes moved away from the blank point they were staring at, and he looked at me. He seemed dazed and confused.

"Whatever is the matter?" I asked, feeling a quite genuine concern as much as a very real curiosity. My mind went back to what Longman had said about Cort having a breakdown from the strain of his task at the palazzo. Was this a manifestation of his troubles? I had little enough experience of such things.

"I do beg your pardon," he said eventually in a faltering voice. "Quite absurd of me. Please forget it. I must go now."

"Certainly not," I replied. "I have no idea what is distressing you, but I could not possibly leave you alone just yet. Come! I will walk with you. It is no trouble, and I feel like a stroll in any case. If you do not wish to talk, we will pace the streets together in solemn silence and enjoy the night air. Have no fear that I wish to pry into your affairs. Although I do, of course."

He smiled at that, and allowed me to lead him towards the alley's end. Then he pointed to the left, away from San Marco, and indicated that we should head in that direction. He said nothing for a long while. We had passed the Rialto before he groaned loudly and scratched his head furiously with both hands. "You must forgive that performance," he said with an effort to return to normal. "I must have seemed absurd."

"Not at all," I replied in what I hoped was a reassuring manner, "but you did alarm me. Do you wish to tell me what it was that so distressed you?"

"I would, were I not afraid that Longman would hear of it. He is a terrible gossip, and I do not wish to become an object of ridicule."

"Have no fear of that," I replied. "I would not tell Mr. Longman anything of importance. Should you come to know me better you will realise that any confidence consigned to my care is perfectly safe."

Which was true. A natural tendency on my part had been confirmed by my experiences in the City, where knowledge is all. Exclusive possession of a fact is worth far more than money. Money you can borrow; knowledge has a higher price. Say (for example) that you hear a company has struck gold in South Africa. It is easy enough to borrow some money to buy shares in it before they rise, and make a profit. All the money in the world will not help you if you do not discover this fact before everyone else. I have never in my life traded without advance knowledge, and I do not know of anyone with sense who has done so either.

"Well, then. I would like to relate my experiences, if you are prepared to listen, and also promise to stop me should you find my story ridiculous or dull."

"I promise."

He took a deep breath and began.

"I mentioned that I was sent here by my uncle, to fulfil a contract with the Albemarle family. I arrived some five months ago with my family, and took up operations as best I could. It has not been easy, and would have strained even a native speaker with more experience than I possess. The house is in far worse shape than I was led to believe, the workforce is erratic, and finding the right materials difficult and expensive. My wife did not want to come, and is deeply unhappy, poor woman.

"You might not believe it from what you have seen, but I have made progress, although every advance is matched by some setback. Everything is way behind schedule and far above the budget, of course, but that is because the family had no conception whatsoever of the task they had taken on.

"That is not what is giving me such concern, although I am quite prepared to countenance the idea that the strain makes me more susceptible. I have always been of a nervous disposition. I do not imagine for a moment that someone like you—who seem very sound and sensible—let alone a man like Macintyre, would be subject to the torments I have endured in the past few weeks.

"In brief, I have become the victim of hallucinations of the most terrible kind. Except that I cannot fully accept that this is what they are. They are too real to be fictitious, yet too bizarre to be real.

"I should tell you that I am an orphan; my mother died giving birth to me, and my father shortly thereafter. That is why I was brought up by my mother's sister, and her husband, the architect. My mother died in Venice. They had been travelling Europe on an extended honeymoon and stopped here for a few months while they prepared for my birth.

"I lived; she died. There is nothing else to add, except to say that my father was heartbroken. I was sent back to England to my aunt and he continued his travels to recover. Alas, he caught a fever in Paris while on the verge of returning to England, and died as well. I was two years old at the time. I remember nothing of either of them, and know only what I have been told.

"Please do not think I am talking off the point when I mention this. I was perfectly healthy in mind and body until I came here. I was brought up properly and well; I am not certain I was suited by nature to be an architect, but I may in time turn out to be perfectly competent. There is nothing in my past at all to foreshadow what has been happening to me here, the place of my mother's death.

"It all began when I was walking along a street, going to a mason's yard, as I recall, and I saw an old man walking towards me. There was nothing about him to excite any interest, and yet I found myself looking at him in the way you do when you see something that fascinates, yet know you should not look. You look away and find your eyes straying back again, and again.

"As he drew near he bowed, and then we passed, each going on his separate way. I turned round to look at him again, and he was gone."

"That was it?" I asked in some surprise, as he seemed to think that nothing more needed to be said.

"The first time, yes. As your tone suggests, there was nothing to cause any concern; indeed, it was not even clear why I should have noticed him. Nonetheless, it disturbed me, and I found my mind going back to the moment. Then it happened again.

"I was walking along the Riva this time. It was midafternoon, and the loafers and wastrels were all there, sitting on the ground, cluttering up the steps of the bridges, idling away the hours as is the custom. I was in a hurry; I had an appointment and I was late. I was walking up the steps of a bridge and looked up, and there he was again. I slowed down, just a little, when I saw him, and he reached inside his coat, pulled out a watch and looked at it. Then he smiled at me as if to say, You're late.

"I hurried past, feeling almost stung by the implied reproach and determinedly kept on my way. This time I didn't look back. He knew I was late, you see. He knows about me. He must be watching me, finding out about me."

"But you know nothing about him?"

"No."

"And this person you were going to visit. He couldn't have said something? Did you ask?"

"Impossible," he said shortly.

"Describe this man to me."

We were walking slowly, and as far as I was concerned, aimlessly. I assumed that Cort knew where he was going. Certainly he turned left and right as though he was following some course, rather than wandering lost in thought as he talked. Walking the silent, deserted streets, our footfalls echoing between the buildings, accompanied by the lap of water and the occasional reflection of moonlight in the canals when the clouds cleared, created a strange and wonderful atmosphere that Cort's tale enhanced rather than dissipated.

"He was quite short, dressed in an old-fashioned manner, slightly stooped. There was nothing particularly remarkable about his gait, although he can travel quickly and silently when he wishes. It is his face that grabs the attention. Old, but nothing in it weakened or enfeebled. Tell me he is as old as the city and I would believe you. It is the face of generations, paper pale, tired beyond belief, and filled with sadness. See it, and you must keep looking at it. Dottore Marangoni practises hypnotism on his patients sometimes. He believes that the personality of the operator is more important than any technique; that what he does is an imposition of his will on the subject. That is what I felt like: that this man was trying to take over my mind."

I let his words evaporate in the night air for a while as I considered whether Cort was being melodramatic, deliberately trying to create some sort of impression for his own ends. Certainly my inclination was to believe that I was hearing a manifestation of the breakdown that Longman considered imminent. But I was aware of my own vision shortly after I arrived in the city; of the old man and the serenade. That, also, had wrought a strange effect on me. Either we were both mad, or neither of us was, and I held firm to a belief in my own sanity.

"That seems a grand claim to make on the basis of two momentary encounters, when you didn't even speak," I said in a reasonable tone.

"They weren't the only ones," he answered, anxious to allay my suspicions. "Over the next few weeks I saw him more and more often. He is following me. Everywhere I go."

His voice was becoming more high-pitched and hysterical, so I endeavoured to calm him.

"He offers you no injury? Does not threaten you? From your description he could do no harm even if he wanted."

"No. In that respect he does me no harm."

"Has he ever spoken to you?"

"Once. Once only. I saw him in a crowd last week as I was walking home from work. He was coming towards me and nodded in greeting as I approached. I could take it no more, so I tried to grab him by the arm to stop him. But I could not. I reached out for his arm, but it was as though it wasn't there. Almost as if my hand passed right through him. He kept on walking, and I called out to him, 'Who are you?'

"He stopped, and turned round, and answered in English, as I had spoken to him. 'I am Venice,' he said. That was all. Then he hurried off again and in a few seconds was lost to sight."

"He was Italian?"

"He spoke in Venetian. But you see? He is following me, for some purpose of his own. Why else would he say such a thing? Who can he be? Why is he doing this to me? I feel I am going mad, Mr. Stone."

The panic was back, rising higher in his voice. I gripped his arm tightly, trying to inflict pain on him to bring him back to his senses before he lost control. I dared not say that I considered it more likely that this encounter was yet another hallucination, that he should seek medical advice before it turned into a full hysteria. But neither did I mention my own vision; I do not know why. I think that I was slightly revolted by his show of weakness. I saw myself as a man of strength and rationality, and wished to keep my distance.

"Calm, my friend, calm," I said gently, still gripping tightly. Slowly he relaxed, and obeyed. Then I realised he was shaking with sobs, as his efforts at self-control, at manly dignity, crumbled. I could say nothing; I was deeply embarrassed by the spectacle. It was undignified, we were in a public place and I hardly knew the man. My better self said that Cort must be in dreadful straits to so unburden himself to me; the rest of me wished fervently he had not.

"I am most dreadfully sorry," he said eventually when he regained control of himself. "This has been a nightmare, and I do not know where to turn."

"And what does your wife think?"

"Oh, I don't want to bother Louise," he said hesitantly. "Poor thing, she has so much to concern herself with, what with Henry being so small. Besides . . ."

He didn't finish, but lapsed into a moody silence instead.

"Forgive me for asking," I said as delicately as I could. "But are you certain this man is real?"

"You think I am imagining it?" He was not angry at my question.

"Believe me, I have considered it. Am I going mad? Is this man a figment of my imagination? Of course, I wonder. I almost hope he is; then at least I could go to Marangoni and he could do . . . whatever such people do with the insane. But his feet make a distinct sound on the pavements. He speaks and smiles. He smells, a very distinct smell, like an old cupboard that hasn't been opened for years, slightly damp, musty."

"But you failed to touch him, you said."

He nodded. "But I felt his breath on me as he spoke. He was as real to me as you are now."

He gripped my arm as if to reassure himself on that point.

"I do not know what to say," I answered. "If this man exists, we must accost him and make him answer questions. If not . . ."

"Then I am insane."

"There you go beyond my knowledge. I am a practical man. I will assume for the time being that you are not about to foam at the mouth."

He laughed for the first time since dinner. "That is good of you," he said. "And can I rely on you . . ."

"Not to say a word to anyone? I give you my word. I assume you have said nothing of this to anyone else?"

"Who could I tell?"

We had reached his lodging, a grim, tumbledown place in what I later learned had been the Ghetto, where the Jews of Venice had been corralled by the city until Napoleon liberated them. Whatever good that new freedom might have done the Jews, it had little benefited that part of town, which was as malodorous and depressing as any grim industrial town of England. Worse, I should say, for the buildings were rank and collapsing, a positive rabbit warren of tiny little rooms where once thousands had been crammed in, exposed to every unhealthy miasma that huge numbers and unsanitary conditions might create. Cort lived here because it was cheap; I could well imagine it. I would have insisted on hefty payment even to enter his building. It seems that his uncle (though dutiful in the matter of his upbringing and training) was known for a certain parsimony that came from the belief that pleasure was offensive to God. Cort was therefore kept on a tight leash, and had barely enough to house his family as well as live and eat, although their conditions were poor. His lodging was a necessary economy to put aside some small surplus for diversion.

He saw my look as we stopped by his doorway. "I do not live in luxury," he said apologetically. "But my neighbours are good people, and even poorer than I. In contrast to them I am *nobilissimi*."

It would not have served me. But his remarks reminded me that I had engaged to visit Longman's Marchesa. I asked Cort about her. "A charming woman," he said. "By all means go; she is worth meeting. Louise knows her and speaks highly of her; they have become quite close."

He gave me the address and then shook my hand. "My apologies for the display, and my thanks for the company," he said.

I told him to think nothing of it, and turned to walk back to the hotel. Cort and his troubles were wafted away on the night air almost before he was out of sight.

CHAPTER 6

By six the next evening I was established in my new accommodation, the Palazzo Bollani on the rio di San Trovaso in Dorsoduro, and the property of the Marchesa d'Arpagno. I had sent my card at ten that morning and was instantly ushered in to see her. In my mind's eye I had seen an old lady, decorously dressed with the signs of departed beauty all about her. A little stout, perhaps, but in diminished circumstances, dreaming perpetually of the glitter of youth. A pleasing, if melancholy, vision, which lasted until the moment I entered the salon.

She was quite ugly, but strikingly so. In her late forties, I guessed from the fine lines that could just be seen beneath the thick powder around her eyes and mouth; tall and imperial in manner, with a long nose, black hair which was plainly dyed hanging down her back in a thick plait. She was wearing a dress with an overskirt in white satin trimmed with green, which was far too fashionable for one of her age. Around her neck was a necklace of emeralds that drew attention to her extraordinary eyes, which were of exactly the same hue. On her bony fingers were several excessively large rings, and she wore a perfume so strong and overpowering that even now, more than forty years later, I can still smell it.

It is not often that I am lost for words, but the contrast between expectation and reality in this case was so strong that I couldn't find anything to say at all.

"I hope you do not mind speaking in French," said the lady as she approached. "My English is terrible, and I imagine that your Venetian is worse. Unless you prefer German."

She had a harsh voice, and the slight smile she gave as she spoke was grotesque in its girlishness. I replied that I could manage French, and quietly thanked my mother for having had the wisdom, all those years ago, to engage a French governess for me and my siblings. They could not afford much at the time and, with governesses, you get what you pay for—in this case a lazy, coarse wretch. But she spoke French and, once inside our home, was dislodged only with difficulty. She stayed long enough to teach me the language, although far too much of its nether reaches and not very much of its higher flights. Only with Elizabeth did I ever properly master it; she is one of those annoying people who pick up languages quickly, by merely listening. I have to study hard, but Elizabeth has always preferred French to English. So study I did, to please her.

The Marchesa sat down, indicating that I could do the same, offered coffee, and fell silent, looking at me with a faint smile.

"I understand from Mr. Longman that you occasionally consider allowing people to stay in your house," I began a little hesitatingly. That was why I was there, and the subject would have to come up sooner or later.

"That is true. Maria will take you to see the rooms a little later, if I decide I can bear to have you under my roof."

"Ah."

"I do not do this for money, you understand."

"Quite, quite."

"But I find it interesting to have people around me. The Venetians are such bores, they drive me to distraction."

"You are not Venetian yourself?"

"No."

She offered no more information and, much as I would have liked to, I felt unable to continue the questioning.

She was not an easy conversationalist. Rather, she was one of those who command through silence, contributing little, but looking with a faint smile that affected her mouth more than her eyes, summoning the other on to fill the void.

So I told her of my journey around Italy, my current stay in the Hotel Europa, my decision to stay and my desire for slightly more comfortable accommodation.

"I see. You leave out much in your account, I think."

I was astonished by the remark. "I don't believe so."

No response to that one either. I sipped my coffee, and she sat quietly, watching me.

"And how do you find Venice, Mr. Stone?"

I replied that I found it perfectly agreeable, so far, although I had seen little.

"And you have done as everyone does here, and hired a gondola to think sad thoughts in?"

"Not yet."

"You surprise me. Are you not disappointed in love? Recovering from a broken heart? That is why people come here, for the most part. They find the city a perfect place to indulge in self-pity."

A sudden sharpness in her tone, all the more strange for being so unexpected. I looked at her curiously, but could see nothing in her face. She had said it as a matter of fact, an observation only, perhaps.

"Not in my case, madam," I replied. "I am perfectly unencumbered." If she desired to make me ill at ease and put me on the defensive, then she was succeeding. I was not used to such conversations. She saw that and was enjoying my discomfort, which made me fight back.

"Then you are here to have your heart broken. You will become like the others."

"What others?"

"Those who cannot leave. There are many here. The city traps the weak and never lets them go. Be careful if you stay here for long."

I shook my head. I had no idea what she was talking about.

"Foreigners, especially from northern countries, make a mistake when they come here. They do not take Venice seriously. They come from their lands full of machinery and money, and feel pity for it. They think it is a harmless relic of the past, once glorious, now beyond hope. They walk and admire, but never rid themselves of a feeling of contempt and superiority. You are the masters now, no?"

Again, I said nothing.

"And Venice waits, bides its time. Most come, and see, and go away again. But the weak are its prey. It sucks the life out of them, bit by bit.

Robs them of their will, their autonomy. They stay, they stay a little longer and then they cannot even imagine leaving. Their life has had its purpose removed, they become mere shadows, walking the streets, eating at the same place every day, walking the same routes every day, for what reason they cannot recall. This is a dangerous place, Mr. Stone; it is cursed. Beware of it. It is alive, and its spirit feeds on the weak and unwary."

"I think it unlikely that this is to be my fate."

She laughed softly. A beguiling laugh, but disturbing in the context of her words, which had nothing humorous about them. "Perhaps not. But you came for a few days, and now you are taking an apartment for a longer stay. I sense you are searching for something, Mr. Stone, although I do not know what it is. Nor do you, I think. But be careful: you will only find sadness here. I feel that in you; you thrive in adversity. You think yourself strong, but your weakest place is your heart. One day it will destroy you. You know that, do you not?"

This melodrama completely reduced me to silence. Obviously she was trying to fascinate me, put me off balance, and, if you wish, dominate the conversation by the bizarre nature of her words. And, equally obviously, she was succeeding. I felt an air of foreboding descend over me, and realised it was the same feeling I had experienced the day before. The feeling of sadness as I walked the streets, the sense of the inexplicable I had had that first night watching the palazzo, these were all part of the same sentiment that she had expressed in words. The desire to taste the recklessness of extreme emotions, throw off the usual cautious, careful way of life I had developed for myself. That was why I had left England, was it not? Why I had roamed Italy for three months, in search of precisely that? But had not yet found it. I caught myself, at that very moment, thinking of my brief introduction to Mrs. Cort, the way her eyes had met mine.

It was mere absurdity, a combination of the light and the tiredness, the strangeness of the surroundings, the water. Quite soothing and relaxing in its way, all the more so because it was so foreign to my normal life. I looked up at the Marchesa and smiled. Almost grinned. It was a challenge to her. Silently countering that I was not be fooled by her words, try as she might. I was a tougher nut than a man like Cort.

She smiled back, accepting the challenge, and clapped her hands.

"Maria!" she called out. "Please show Mr. Stone the apartment."

"So you can bear to have me in your house? I am flattered," I said.

"You should be. But you have the aura of an honest man, a good man," she replied seriously.

"I beg your pardon?"

"Your aura. It radiates around you, revealing the nature of the spirit which animates the machinery of your body. Yours is gentle, blue and yellow. You are divided in spirit, between the desire for peace and for adventure. For power and for tranquillity. You desire much, but I feel that you have a sense of fairness. You are divided between the masculine and the feminine, but in you the attributes are wrongly apportioned. It is your feminine which is adventurous, the masculine which desires peace. You will have trouble reconciling these, Mr. Stone, but they make you interesting."

She gave the distinct impression that she wanted me in her house so she could study me, like some grotesque entomologist, but she none-theless had described the battle between my fiery mother and my peaceable father remarkably well. Disconcertingly so, and she saw that I was impressed despite the fact that she was talking nonsense.

The business of packing was delayed by an encounter I had in the hotel on my return. As I walked into the lobby and asked for my key, I noticed a small man get up from his chair, and come towards me.

"My dear Stone!" this person said in a thick Italian accent as he grabbed me by the hand and pulled me round to face him. "I hardly expected it to be true! Remarkable! I'm so pleased to see you!"

I looked at him blankly for a moment, then it dawned on me who he was. I believe I mentioned that, several years previously, I had tried my hand at dissipation. I am not ashamed of this period of my life, I believe it is inevitable in young men whose energies are not wasted by manual labour, and, as I say, I found that the pleasures of such a life faded quickly and have never returned. I have not spent my older years wondering what it would have been like to have done certain things, nor did I have any temptation in middle age to try and recapture my youth and thus make myself into a laughingstock.

During that period, I made the acquaintance of a group of young men: some were the useless sprigs of nobility well on their way to illness and early death from excess (thus weakening a class of society and fending off the likelihood of revolution, for why trouble to overthrow people who are doing such a good job of rendering themselves powerless?); some were simple idlers spending an inheritance pretending to be poets or painters; and a couple were medical students, who had a wildness of such severity that I would hesitate ever to place myself under their care. One of these, however, is now a personal physician to His Majesty, which goes to show that even the greatest sinners are capable of redemption. Of the others, one became a high court judge and one shot himself in the aftermath of the Dunbury scandal, a foolishly conceived scheme to dun the public by proposing vast profits from a railway built across a two-hundred-mile swamp in Russia. My friend, a man for whom I continued to have affection to the end, went vastly into debt to buy shares in the hope of recovering a dire financial situation, and was ruined.

The man who now greeted me was one of the medical students. I never paid him much attention and never even knew his name—something foreign, I knew, but everyone always called him Joe, a nickname more insulting than friendly, for it assumed an informality more suited to a pet or native bearer than an equal.

Joe—or Dottore Giuseppe Marangoni, as he was now called—had changed over the past few years, that was clear. Previously he had had the sort of personality that could lead you to overlook him entirely; one of those who waited to be spoken to, and appeared grateful to be included in any conversation. Only his eyes suggested there might be something more to him, for he was always watching, always interested. For what purpose never seemed clear.

And this was the person now beaming at me and shaking my hand, leading me to a table in the corner for a chat. It is disconcerting to encounter someone once known but not seen for several years. At that stage the shock was limited, but still real. Now it is positively a heartache to meet a person I have not seen for thirty or forty years, to see the thinning hair, the stoop, the lines when you expect (no matter how much your realise it cannot be so) the person to look exactly as they did when last seen. And to realise they are as shocked by your appearance as you by theirs.

As we had swapped country, so we also exchanged roles; my surprise at Marangoni's sudden reappearance in my life was so great that I said little. He, in contrast, never stopped talking. We remembered things very differently; he talked of the good fellowship of his days in London, the fine friends he had made, asked about the members of that little group of apprentice rakes—which information I could not provide, as, apart from

Campbell, I had cast them off as I had abandoned that way of life, and I have never cared for gossip in any case. Then he began to surprise me.

"I wish I'd liked London more," he said. "It is such a dull place."

"In comparison with Venice?"

He groaned. "Ah, no. Professionally Venice is interesting, but hardly glittering, alas. No, in comparison to a place like Paris, for example. The English—do forgive me, my friend—are so respectable."

I was half-minded to be insulted by this, but looked enquiringly instead.

"Take my fellow medical students, for example. In Paris, they live together, and eat together, and all have their shopgirls for mistresses and housekeepers until they qualify or find someone suitable to marry. Their life is their own. In London everyone lives with a landlady, eats every evening some hideous meal she has cooked and goes to church on Sunday. Riotous living consists of getting drunk, and little else."

"I'm sorry you were disappointed."

"I wasn't there to enjoy myself; merely to learn and observe. Which I did, with great profit."

"To learn and observe what?"

"Medicine, as you know. Particularly the science of alienism. I am a doctor of the mind and so it is my business to study people in all their variety. I learned much there, although less than I did in Paris. The group you were attached to was full of instruction."

I was, as may be imagined, a little offended by this remark; the idea that all the time we were ignoring him, treating him as some insignificant little foreigner, he was, in fact watching and assessing us. A bit like the Marchesa, only more scientific, I hoped. He saw my discomfort and laughed.

"Do not be perturbed. You were the least interesting person there."

"I do not find that reassuring."

"But who knows what lurks beneath the surface? I joke. You were by far the most normal of my companions. The others, mind you, were quite fascinating in their many different ways." He mentioned one man. "Clear degenerate tendencies, with a pronounced swelling indicating distorted cranial lobes. Certainly a tendency to insanity, erratic judgement and a pronounced attraction to violence."

"He has just become a Queen's Counsel," I commented dryly.

"Proves my point, does it not?"

I said nothing. (A few weeks ago, as I write, I discovered my erstwhile acquaintance has been confined to an asylum after a murderous attack on his wife of thirty years. The matter has been kept quiet lest the idea of a complete lunatic in charge of criminal cases—as a judge he became notorious for his infliction of the death penalty—lessens the awful majesty of the law in the public's mind.)

"Alas, I rarely have the opportunity to deal with such intricate cases now," he said almost wistfully. I was not hugely interested, but asked him of his progress since we had last met. It appeared that Marangoni, his studies in Paris ended, had returned to Milan, where he had briefly worked in an asylum, trying to introduce the best French practises. He had done so well (this was his account, not mine) that he had then been transferred to the Veneto, to embody there the new ideas that unification with Italy represented. He was the emissary of the State, sent to organise the asylums of the city and to corral, bully, persuade and intimidate the insane back to health, using the most up-to-date methods. He was not overoptimistic about his prospects, although gratified by the salary his new employment provided.

"And, lest you think I am being rude about England, I must assure you that in comparison with Venice, it was like being in paradise. Here the insane are still in the hands of the priests, who intone their mumbo-jumbo over them, and pray they will get better and beat them when their prayers are not answered. So you see, I have a big job on my hands. I must fight the insane and the Church simultaneously."

"Which is worse?"

He waved his hand. "Do you know, sometimes I can't tell them apart. Degenerates," he said, as he sipped his drink. "Little to be done for them except identify, isolate and eliminate. The city is inbred, generation after generation has never even left the lagoon. What you see as a city of unparalleled beauty and untold richness is, in fact, a festering, seeping sore of mental illness. A people weakened and debilitated, incapable of fending for themselves. You have read the history of the city, no doubt, about how it finally fell to Napoleon. It was not Napoleon who conquered this city; it was the steady eating away of the population by degeneration, which stripped it of all ability to resist."

"And you recommend what, exactly?"

"Oh, if I had my way, I'd ship everyone out."

"Everyone? You mean the whole city?" I asked slightly incredulously.

He nodded. "If there is a house with plague in it, you don't adopt half measures, do you? That is what Venice is; a plague city, spreading corruption to all who are in contact with it. We are at last trying to build a nation here in Italy, we need a forceful, healthy population that will multiply and meet the challenges of modern life. We cannot take the risk of having a place like this undermining all our efforts, sapping our vitality with contaminated stock."

He smiled as he saw my surprise at his remarks. "I say that so forcefully because I know no one is going to listen to me. No one has the will to take the necessary measures. So, instead, I do what I can and must, case by case."

"I hate to challenge the opinion of a scientist, but I have seen many idlers in London and Paris. And noted no tendency here to violence."

He nodded sagely. "There are degenerates everywhere. Particularly in Europe, which is crumbling. Do you know, one eminent doctor has estimated that up to a third of the entire population might be afflicted?"

"And you would like to get rid of all of them?"

"Not possible," he replied, clearly suggesting he would like nothing better. "What I am trying to do is identify them. If they could be stopped from breeding, for example, then eventually the problem would diminish on its own. As for the violence, don't be fooled. Their natural lassitude makes them seem passive enough, but when something snaps they behave like beasts. What is more, the city attracts more such people, every day they arrive, and find the place congenial. There is a man called Cort, for example—"

"I have met Mr. Cort," I said, no doubt a little stiffly. "I found him very pleasant."

Marangoni smiled in a slightly superior fashion. "That is why there are alienists," he said. "To spot things the untrained eye cannot perceive. Mr. Cort is a man on the edge, and could topple over into the ravine of madness at any moment. He should never have been sent here. But that's you English all over. He was sent here to toughen him up, I believe the saying is. It may well do the exact opposite, and finish him off. He is having hallucinations, you know. He thinks there is a man following him. And not just any man, oh, dear me, no. He is being followed by the city itself."

"How do you know that?"

"Ah." Marangoni smiled, touching his nose. "There is little secret here, as you will discover."

"You would consider him insane?"

"Cort, or the spectral Venetian?"

"Both."

"If the Venetian exists at all, then both, naturally. Thinking yourself immortal is not unusual, of course, and persuading yourself that you are someone else is common enough. I have encountered Napoleon on many occasions, as well as princes and children of popes, all snatched away at infancy. Persuading yourself you are a *city* is most odd. I have never encountered such a thing. I rather hope he does exist. I would love to meet him."

"And Cort?"

"A hypersensitive young man, in my opinion. He is picking up the unhealthiness of the city, but instead of responding in a rational manner, he embodies it in his fantasies. This Venetian is the degenerate city which killed his mother and it exerts an unhealthy fascination for him. He should leave immediately. I have told him this, but he refuses to listen. He says it would be cowardly, that he has a job to do here. But it will cost him his sanity, if he is not careful. Especially if he continues to keep his wife with him."

Marangoni was no gentleman. It was bad enough, surely, for a doctor to discuss a man who was a patient in such terms, but to cast aspersions on Mrs. Cort as well I found deeply offensive. I think he saw the look on my face.

"Oh, you chivalrous English," he said, with a very faint air of contempt. "Very well, I should not have said that. But Mrs. Cort I find to be—"

"That is no doubt because you do not appreciate refinement and character in women," I said, "being used only to Italians."

Still the wretched man did not take offence. "That may be so; certainly they are very different in manner. Though not so different in nature. You have met the lady? I think you must have."

"I found her charming."

"So she is. So she is. Well, I stand corrected. You no doubt know her better than I, a mere Italian, ever could."

I found his conversation somewhat alarming. I am used now to capitalists such as myself being detested for their pitiless fixity of purpose, their ruthlessness at the exploitation of others. Perhaps we are so, but I must say that I have never encountered a capitalist half as pitiless as one of those doctors of the mind. Should they ever be allowed to put their ideas into practise, they would be fearsome. The conviction that their method makes them unchallengeable, that their conclusions are always correct, leads them to lay claim to a remarkable authority over others. Capitalists want the money of their customers, the bodies of the workers. Psychiatrists want their souls.

Fortunately Marangoni was tiring of the subject as well as I, and out of politeness turned to questioning me about my trip. "You have met some people already, I believe. It was Mr. Longman who mentioned you to me."

"A few," I said. "And I am about to move to new accommodation, in the palazzo of the Marchesa d'Arpagno."

"Oh ho!" he said with a smile. "Then you must be a special person. She is fussy in her choice. What did you say or do to win her over?"

"It's my aura, apparently. Or the size of my wallet."

Marangoni laughed. "Oh, yes. I'd forgotten. The Marchesa is a seer."

I looked at him.

"Really, she is. The spirits positively queue up to chat to her. It must be like bedlam in her sitting room sometimes. She has the Gift. The Eye. That certain spiritual something which means she is—totally crazy."

"Another one? You alarm me."

"Oh, she's harmless enough. Remarkably so. Naturally, I scented a customer when I first came across her. But I was disappointed. You will note that apart from a few matter-of-fact comments, she is entirely normal."

"And that means . . ."

"Clearly she is insane. It is only a matter of time before the madness bursts forth and becomes more explicit. At the moment, though, she is quite normal in her behaviour. Apart from the spirits, of course. You will, I imagine, be summoned to take part in a séance at some stage. Everyone is. But you won't have any excuse for not attending. So you'll have to go. Do you believe in spirits? Ghosts? Auras? Things that go bump in the night or under the table?"

"I don't think so," I said.

"A shame. But she won't mind. If you express your doubts, all she does is smile at you in a pitying manner. Blind fools, who do not see the obvious even when it is in front of their very eyes. It is your loss, not hers, if you cut yourself off from the pleasures of the astral planes and the higher wisdom they offer."

"A bit like alienists, then," I said with some relief.

"Exactly like alienists," he agreed jovially. "What is more, the Marchesa doesn't talk like some charlatan. This is what makes her so fascinating. Her madness is entirely logical and reasonable. So much so that she is very convincing. Mrs. Cort seems to have fallen under her spell, for example. I use the word 'spell' metaphorically, you understand."

"Do you believe all women are insane? You must know some who are not so?"

Marangoni considered the question, then shook his head. "Taking all things as equal, no. All women are insane at one level or another. It is merely a question of when—or if—the insanity will manifest itself."

"So if I come across a woman who is entirely normal and balanced . . ."

"Then she merely has not yet manifested the signs of madness. The longer she remains in a state of apparent normality, the more violent is the underlying insanity. I have wards full of them. Clearly, some women hide the symptoms all their lives, and the insanity never rises to the surface. But it is always latent."

"So being sane is a proof of insanity? In women, I mean?"

"I fear so, alas. But I am not dogmatic on the subject, unlike some of my colleagues. Tell me," he continued, abruptly changing the subject, "is money still your main occupation in life?"

"Why do you say that?"

He shrugged. "It was always obvious that you were never going to be one of the poor of this world," he replied with a smile. "You were always too watchful. If I said 'calculating' you would take it as an insult, which I do not intend. So let us say too aware, and too intelligent."

"Yes. Let us say that then. I do have some financial interests."

"Which you are not pursuing here?"

"No."

"I see." He smiled again, which I found annoying. There is something acutely irritating about men whose expressions depict a sort of omni-science, who pretend to be able to read the minds of others. "I never thought of you as a man for holidays."

"It is time to think again then. Although you are right, in general. My inactivity does weigh on me a little."

"But you are staying here."

I nodded. "Perhaps there are other things to do in Venice than look at buildings."

"Such as?"

I shrugged. I was beginning to find him irritating. "Build them?"

"I see you are not minded to say more," he said after he had considered my face for a few moments. "You leave me to work it out for myself."

"Precisely."

"Very well. Give me a week, and a few meals together, and we will see. If I guess your purpose, you buy me a meal. If I fail, I buy you one."

"Agreed," I said with a faint smile. "And if you will excuse me, I must see to my packing. The Marchesa expects me by six."

"Willingly. I must go as well. I have a new patient who was brought in this morning."

"Interesting?"

He sighed. "Not in the slightest."

CHAPTER 7

Until I made that response to Marangoni about building, I had not thought at all seriously about the vague ideas that had passed through my mind. It was only because of this chance conversation that it became a fixed purpose; a small project that might give me occupation, and end the purposeless wandering that I was beginning to find disturbing.

To that end, I needed to find an appropriate site. A preferred option would have been to buy some ground in the centre of the city and demolish all the buildings to make way for a modern and efficient structure. I soon learned, however, that such a proposal was unlikely to come to anything. Permission had to be gained from the council for any work of that nature, and the local government had the instinct to oppose anything which smacked of the modern. Permission to demolish half a dozen palaces on the Grand Canal (however magnificent the result) was unlikely and, in any case, the initial cost of purchasing the site would have been prohibitive.

Nonetheless, I hired a gondola for the next morning and instructed the rower to go wherever he wished. It was a pleasant enough pastime, idling along broad canals and narrow ones, watching the water carriers fill the wells, the faggot vendors selling wood, all the business of the city carried out in the strange way that must evolve in a city drowned in water. Listening to the echoes of voices against tall narrow buildings, made slightly sharper and more diffuse by the effect of the water, began to bring back to me the mood of odd peacefulness that had overcome me my first evening, and which was so opposite to my supposed purpose.

In brief, I indulged in all sorts of fantastical notions. This happened time and again during my stay. My wonder was, not that the citizens of Venice were now so idle, but rather that they had once been sufficiently energetic to raise themselves from the lagoon, and turn their wooden huts on mudflats into the great metropolis that had once ruled the Mediterranean. Had the Venetians of old been more like me in mood then, they would still be paddling about in silt up to their knees.

I write as I remember, and give some sense of my mood that fine September morning, as the gondola slowly turned a corner, and I saw Mrs. Cort walking along the side of the canal we had now entered. It was easy to recognise her; she looked and walked in a way which meant she could only be English—more upright, and with more bearing than Venetian women, who do not discipline their bodies into deportment.

On top of that, she was dressed in the same manner as when I had met her, eschewing a top coat in honour of the fine weather, and wearing only a hat to guard her fine white skin from the sun. I called out to her and gestured to the gondolier to pull over to the side, where there were some landing steps.

"I have been to the pharmacist for some cough medicine," she said once we had exchanged greetings. It did not matter what she said. I noticed that her eyes were bright and met mine when we spoke. She stood closer to me than I would have expected from a woman I hardly knew.

"And is this your son?" I asked, gesturing at an infant in the arms of a stocky peasant woman standing a few feet away. The child looked sick and was whimpering. The other woman—a nurse or nanny of some sort—rocked it gently in her arms and sang a crooning song in its ears.

"Yes. That is Henry," she said, scarcely giving him a glance. "He is very like his father."

The conversation faltered. I was pleased to see her, but had nothing to say. That easy talk which passes between men, or couples of long acquaintance, was not possible. Neither of us wanted to go on our way, but neither could think how to prolong the interview.

"And you are seeing the sights?" she said eventually.

"After a fashion, although I do believe I have been down this canal three times already. Or perhaps not; they all begin to look the same after a while."

She laughed lightly. "I can see you have not benefited from Mr. Longman's expertise," she said. "Otherwise you would know that that house on the corner," she gestured behind me, and I turned to look at a nondescript pile that looked long deserted, "was once the home of the lady with the skull."

She smiled at me as I looked again. "Do you want to hear the story as he told it to me?"

"By all means."

"I do not know when it happened," she said. "Most stories in Venice have no date to them. But, a long time ago, a man was walking down an alley a short way from here. He was thinking of the woman he was about to marry, and his happy thoughts were disturbed by a beggar, asking for money. He was angry, and kicked the man for his insolence, and caught him on the head with his boot. The beggar rolled over into the canal, struck dead, and the young man ran off.

"The wedding day came and eventually the bride and groom were alone in their bedchamber. There was knock on the door. The man, cursing, opened it and saw a horrible apparition. A corpse, flesh dropping from its bones. Eyes staring from their sockets. Teeth protruding where the flesh had been eaten away by fish.

"The man screamed, as you might expect.

" 'Who are you? What do you want?' the man cried.

" 'I am the beggar you killed. I want burial,' the apparition replied.

"Again the man ignored the request. He slammed the door, and bolted it. When he had recovered enough he went back upstairs to the bedchamber.

"But when he walked in the room, he turned pale and fainted.

" 'What is the matter, my love?' cried the wife.

"She got up, and began to walk towards him. But as she passed a mirror, she turned to look at herself.

"Her face was white and skull-like, the hair torn out, the eyes staring from their sockets, the teeth protruding where the fish had eaten away the flesh."

She was talking ever more softly, and I found myself moving closer to her as she told this hideous, fascinating fairy story. When she ended, I was close enough to feel her breath on my face. She looked openly and frankly at me.

"And the moral of the story is, never be unkind to beggars," I said.

"No," she replied softly. "The moral is, do not marry a man who is cruel and heartless."

I came to myself and stepped back. What had just taken place? I did not know, but it was as though a charge of energy had surged through me; I was in a state of shock. Not the story, but the teller, and the manner of the telling.

It was the way her eyes fixed on me that caused the true shock, so far beyond what was correct, and to which I responded. Or didn't; I initiated it, perhaps. Perhaps she responded to me.

"Now I feel dissatisfied to travel so ignorantly," I said.

"Perhaps you need a guide."

"Perhaps I do."

"You should ask my husband," she said, and registered the disappointment in my face. "I'm sure he would allow me to show you the sights of the city."

Again those eyes.

"Do I need to ask his permission?"

"No," she said with a touch of contempt in her voice.

"I do not wish to trouble you. I'm sure you are very busy."

"I could spare you some time, I'm sure. I would enjoy it. My husband is always telling me I should do more out of the house. He knows there is little of my own here, not that he does anything except apologise."

I could not get the encounter out of my mind, then or later. It grew in me, like my feeling for the city itself, without me even noticing. But I was aware that what I saw and did was blending with my thoughts, almost to the point of not being able to tell one from the other. Although I wished to clear my head, I also wished the strange state to continue. It was luxurious to surrender to the least impulse, to allow any thought to pass through my head, to abandon that careful discipline I had steadily cultivated. To be other than myself, in fact.

I needed company for distraction, but I also wished to discover more about Louise Cort. What was her history, her nature? Why had she talked to me in such a fashion? What sort of person was she?

I had only met her on two occasions by this point, and only for a few minutes in all. Not enough to explain her place in my thoughts; certainly no other woman—and by then I had met many more charming, more beautiful, more notable in all respects—had such a rapid effect on me. For the most part I had forgotten them the moment they had passed from my sight.

I found my way to the restaurant a few days later as I again needed company to fill my hours; the Marchesa was perfectly happy to provide food, at an extravagant extra cost, but her cook was dreadful and she insisted on dining in state in the old dining room. Just her and me, at opposite ends of a very long table. Conversation was difficult, to say the least, and the predominant sound was of clinking cutlery and the noise she made as she ate, for she had false teeth which did not fit very well and which needed to be sucked back into place after every bite.

She would also, at least once every mealtime, get a dreamy look on her face, which I soon enough learned was the sign of a imminent visitation from the Other Side. On top of that there was no gas lighting; the only illumination after dusk came from candles, and the great multi-coloured chandelier in my sitting room—though large enough to hold several dozen candles—had not, I thought, been lit since long before the extinction of the Serenissima. It was blackened with use, and covered with dust from disuse. It was dark and impossible to read after dinner.

Strangely, the person I most looked forward to meeting again was Macintyre. I found him curious, and my interest was heightened by the desire to discover what, exactly, a Lancashire engineer was doing in a city so far away from any industry. So I engaged him in conversation, ignoring Cort and Drennan, who were the only other people there that evening.

It was not easy, as conversation was a skill Macintyre had not mastered. Either he did not reply at all, or answered in monosyllables, and as he ate, he drank, which made his words difficult to understand. All my attempts to indicate an interest, to ask careful questions, met with grunts or noncommittal replies.

Eventually I lost patience with him. "What are you doing in this city?" I asked, bluntly and quite rudely.

Macintyre looked at me, and gave a faint smile. "That's better," he said. "If you want to know something, ask. Can't stand these manners, skirting round things all the time."

"I didn't wish to be rude."

"What's rude about curiosity? About things or people? If you want to know something, ask. If I don't want to say, I'll tell you straight out. Why should I find that rude?"

He pulled a pipe from his pocket, disregarding the fact that no one else had finished their meal, filled it swiftly and lit it, blowing thick clouds of pungent, choking smoke into the air like a steam train preparing for a long journey. Then he pushed his plate away and put both elbows on the table.

"So how did you end up here?"

"By chance. I work for hire, shipyards, mainly. I served my apprenticeship with Laird's in Liverpool."

"Doing?"

"Everything. Eventually I worked with a little group of people designing different sorts of propellers. By the time I left I was in charge of the entire design office."

He said this with pride, almost defiance. He must have been used to expressions of blank indifference from the sort of people he encountered in Venice, who considered designing a propeller as an accomplishment of no significance whatsoever.

I wished to ask more. Laird's was an impressive company; its ships set the standards for others to match. But he was already standing up. "That's too long a story for tonight," he said gruffly. "If you're interested, I might tell you. Come to my workshop sometime, if you've a mind to hear it. But I must go and see to my daughter."

"I would like that very much," I replied. "Perhaps I could take you for lunch."

"No restaurants where I work," he said, but he was easier in his speech now; the roughness of resentment had eased off him. His final parting was almost civil.

"Well, you are the privileged one," Drennan drawled as we both stood to put on our coats after the meal. The days were still lovely, but the evening air was now getting steadily cooler. "What have you done to win his favour? No one has ever been allowed in that workshop of his."

"Maybe I just showed interest? Or perhaps I was just as rude as he, and he was drawn to a kindred spirit."

Drennan laughed, a pleasant laugh, easy and warm. "Maybe so."

Nor should I have been surprised by Macintyre's workshop, when I arrived there the next day, somewhat late due to the difficulty of finding its location. The part of Venice where he had settled was not only unfashionable amongst the Venetians, I am prepared to wager that not one tourist in a thousand has ever ventured into it.

He had rented a workshop in the boatyards around San Nicolo da Tolentino, a quarter in which all pretensions to elegance fade away to nothing. This is not the poorest part of the city, but it is one of the roughest. Many of the inhabitants, I am told, have never wandered even as far as San Marco, and live in their quarter as though it is a world of its own, entirely independent of the rest of humanity. I gather (though my own lack of skill prevented verification) that they even speak in a way which is distinctly different from their fellow citizens, and that the forces of law and order rarely penetrate, and then only with some trepidation.

Their business is boats; not the grand seafaring vessels which were once the pride of Venice, and which were constructed on the other side of the city, but the vast numbers of small craft on which the entire lagoon depends. Need has produced whole species of boats and in a manner which would have satisfied Darwin: specialised to the point where they can do one thing, and one thing only, dependent absolutely on their conditions of existence for their survival, vulnerable to changes which can wipe out an entire class of construction. Some prosper, some fail; thus it is in life, in business and in Venetian shipping as well.

The galley has gone, vanquished by the sailing ship, just as the sailing ship is inevitably falling victim to the superiority of the steamer. Many have vanished even in my lifetime, but their names live on. The gondola, but also the gondolino, the fregatta, the felucca, the trabaccolo, the costanza, all of these still survive, but their days doubtless are numbered. Their passing will be a loss only to the aesthetic sense of those who do not have to operate them, for how much better is a steamer at nearly all things!

Macintyre worked and lived amongst the sounds and smells of timber and pitch, and was as alien in his operations as he was in his nature and nationality. For he was a man of iron and steel; in his domain the screech of metal replaced the softer sounds of wood being worked. Lathes had displaced saws, finely calibrated instrumentation had seen off the rule of thumb, calculation had vanquished the accumulated experience of the generations.

He was not waiting for me. He never waited for anyone. He always had something to do and used every moment to get on with it. I never knew a man so unable to be at rest. Even when forced to sit still, his fingers would drum on the table, his foot would tap on the floor, he would grimace and make odd noises. How anyone had ever consented to live with him was one of life's little mysteries.

And books? I do not believe he had read a single book except for a technical manual since he left school. He could see no point in them. Poetry and prose he found in the juxtaposition of metal, the flow of oil and the subtle interaction of carefully designed component parts. They were his art and his history, his religion, even.

When I arrived he was as still as he ever became, lost in a temporary reverie as he contemplated a large metal tube lying on the bench before him. It was about fifteen feet long, rounded at one end, with a host of smaller tubes coming from the rear which spoiled the neatness of the whole by disintegrating into a formless, tangled mass. At the end of all this was a metal stanchion to which was attached—even I could recognise it—a propeller of shiny brass, about a foot in diameter.

I didn't feel like disturbing him; he was so obviously at peace, almost a smile on his usually dour face. The years which normally showed through in frowns and lines had fallen away and he seemed boyish in complexion. He was a man who took delight in reducing complexity to order. In his mind the tangled mass of pipes and wires made sense, with each part having its allotted task and with no surplus or waste. It had its own elegance: not the learned, scholarly elegance of architecture, to be sure; this was stripped of the past. A new order, if you wish, justified only by itself and its purpose.

In that tangle of brass and steel, whatever it was, lay the reason for his contempt for Venice, for people like Cort. He felt he could do better. He did not feel the need to live in old buildings and worship dead artists, imitating and preserving. He felt he could surpass them all. This stumpy Lancastrian was a revolutionary in his way.

It disturbed me, for some reason. Perhaps an echo of my upbringing came back to me then, those many hours spent in church or being lectured by my father and others. Some of it sticks, it cannot fail. Man is justified by faith and submission. Macintyre would have none of it and was putting his disagreement into solid form. Man was justified by his ingenuity, and his machines only by whether they performed their allotted tasks.

Not that I thought or felt any of that; I was simply aware that I could not share his absorption, that I was an observer, aware of myself standing there, looking at the concentration of others. But even before I could pin that feeling down, he gave a sigh of contentment, turned and saw me.

Instantly the dour northerner returned to life, the joyful boy banished.

"You're late. Can't abide people being late. And what are you looking at?" he scowled. I could have taken offence at his lack of civility, but I had seen into him, glimpsed his secret. He could offend me no more. I liked him.

"I was admiring your . . . ah"—I gestured at the contraption on the worktable—"your plumbing."

He peered at me intently. "Plumbing, d'you call it, you scoundrel?"

"It is surely a means of heating water for a gentleman's bathroom," I continued in an even tone.

It was so easy to reduce him to a state of apoplexy but it was unfair to do so. He turned bright red and spluttered incoherently, until he realised I was making fun of him. Then he calmed himself and smiled, but it was an effort.

"Tell me what it is then," I continued. "You will have to, because I can make neither head nor tail of it."

"Maybe," he said. "Maybe I will."

I could barely hear him. The noise in the workshop was considerable, and came from the three people who seemed to be his assistants. All, I could see from their dress, were Italians, all young, all of them concentrating hard on their tasks. Except for the girl, who was obviously his daughter. She was about eight, I would imagine, and was going to be the same shape in female form as her father. Broad of shoulder with a square face and strong jaw. Her fair, short hair was curly, and could have been an advantage had it been tended in any way at all, but as it was it resembled an overgrown bramble patch. She was dressed, also, in a way utterly unbecoming: a man's oversized sweater almost disguised the fact that she was a girl at all. But her face was open, her glance intelligent, and she seemed like a pleasant creature, although the frown as she concentrated on the job of producing some technical drawing in the corner took away most of the small prettiness she possessed.

Macintyre seemed to ignore her completely; it was only as our interview continued that I realised his glance stole away, every few minutes, to that corner of the room where she sat lost in concentration. This was the man's weakness, the only person he loved.

"Come and look around," he said abruptly when he noticed me looking at her, and led me across the open space to where most of the machinery was installed.

I find it astonishing that any man can regard fine machinery without admiration. The machines our age has produced can induce an awe in me that is as powerful as the impulse to religion in other men. Again, perhaps this is a legacy from my upbringing, with a natural piety diverted and deformed into other channels. But I find I look on such things rather in the way a medieval peasant must have looked on the looming mass of a cathedral, stunned into reverence without comprehension.

In these great halls of production there are marvels to behold. Go to the great ironworks of Sheffield and see the forges, or the new steel presses that have sprung up around Birmingham, see the gigantic monsters that can crush and bend many tons of metal in one swipe of a press, machines so vast that it would seem arrogant even to have dreamed of them. Or to the vast turbine halls that turn water into steam and then electricity in rooms so big clouds can form in their upper levels.

And, in all of these, look at the men who work there. Are the floors clean, the men well dressed and proud of their appearance? Do they work with willingness, is there a sense of purpose in their eyes? Do the employers seek out the best, or the cheapest? Five minutes is enough to tell me if an enterprise will rise or fall, prosper or diminish. It is all in the eyes of labour.

Macintyre's operation was on a much smaller scale, but the principles were the same. And the signs were good. Although ramshackle on the outside, inside the shed was spotless. All the tools were neatly ordered, the floors swept, the benches well organised. The brass on the instruments gleamed, the steel was well oiled. Each machine was cared for and well situated. It had all been thought through. And those he employed went about their business with a quiet resolve, talking rarely and then quietly. They knew what they were doing.

"I found them," he said when I asked, "here and there. Giacomo over there was supposed to be a boatbuilder, but his father died and he could find no master. I noticed him carving a piece of driftwood to sell to passersby. He had such fine control of his hands I knew he was intelligent. He made himself indispensable inside a week. He can set up a machine faster and more accurately than any man I have come across. If he had the technical knowledge to go with his skill, he would be formidable."

He gestured to another. "Luigi is another. He has more training; I found him in an artist's studio being trained as a restorer. He has no talent for painting, so he had not much of a career ahead of him. His talent is for drawing, he is an immensely skilled draughtsman, and can take my sketches and turn them into plans. He and Giacomo can then turn them into precise settings on the machinery."

"And that one?"

"Ah, Signor Bartoli. A man of all tasks. He is the general, all-purpose worker. He helps one or the other of the two and knows how to follow his instructions perfectly. If something needs doing, he will do it, faster and better than you hoped."

"You are more fortunate than Mr. Cort in your choice of labour, then."

"I am a better judge of men, more like. And more able to command them. When I see Mr. Cort at work, I feel like grabbing him by the neck and giving him a good shake."

He snorted in disgust, in a way which spoke volumes. Macintyre was thinking what he would have accomplished if he had had the advantages of Cort's birth and opportunities. There are many such men in our industries; I have made it my business to find them and give them their chance.

"Yet you assisted him the other week?"

"Oh, that. That was nothing. It took no time at all, and I was getting heartily sick of listening to his despair. At least he has decided to take my advice. He is even prepared to contemplate blowing the column out with explosives. There may be a man of sense in there after all. His trouble is that he has been trained to do things the way they are done, not the way they should be done."

"Are you going to tell me what that great thing is over there?" I called out to him. He had wandered over to Luigi, and was discussing some

problem, my presence perfectly forgotten. A strange way of talking he
had, as well. A sort of pidgin English with smatterings of Italian thrown
in. It was the lingua franca of the workshop, where conversations were
conducted half in words, half in gestures and mime. All the technical
words were in English, not surprisingly perhaps as none of the three
Italians knew any of them before they came to Macintyre, and he did not
know the Italian equivalents, even when they existed. The grammar was
Italian, and the rest was a mixture of the two, with a lot of grunting
thrown in to fill up space.

I had to wait for an answer; whatever the problem was it took some
sorting and ended with Macintyre on his knees before the machine—
some sort of drill, as far as I could discern—like a penitent at prayer,
slowly twisting knobs to make fine adjustments, measuring distances
with calipers, repeating the operation several times before an outburst of
grunting suggested the problem was resolved.

"What was that?" he asked when he returned to my side.

"Your plumbing."

"Ha!" He turned and led the way back to the lone machine lying
clamped on a solitary workbench. "What do you think it is?"

I looked carefully at the machine before me. It was a thing of some
elegance, essentially a steel tube with wing-like projections along its
length, tapering at the back and ending with a small three-winged
propeller in shiny brass. At the other end, it stopped abruptly and opened
to the air, but a little way away was a continuation which obviously bolted
on to the end to give a rounded shape.

"It obviously is designed to go through the water," I said. I walked
around and peered into the nose of the machine. It was empty. "And this
clearly holds something. Most of its length is taken up with machinery,
which I take to be the engine, although there is no funnel, and no boiler.
This empty piece must hold the cargo." I shook my head. "It looks a bit
like a very big shell with a propeller attached."

Macintyre laughed. "Very good! Very good! A shell with a propeller.
That is precisely what it is. A torpedo, to be precise."

I was puzzled. A torpedo, I knew, was a long pole pushed from the
front of a ship to impale an opponent, then explode. Hardly useful in the
days of ironclads and ten-inch guns.

"Of course," he continued, "I merely borrow the word as I could think of nothing better. This is an automobile torpedo. A charge of explosive there," he pointed at the nose, "and an engine capable of propelling it in a straight line there. Aim it at the opposing ship, set it off and that's that."

"So the front will be full of gunpowder."

"Oh, no. Gunpowder is too susceptible to damp. And something which goes underneath the surface of the water is liable to get wet, however well it is made. So I will use guncotton. And, of course, I can make it myself; one part cotton wool in fifteen parts of sulphuric and nitric acids. Then you wash it, dry it. Look."

He gestured to a series of boxes in the corner that rested on top of several vats.

"That's the guncotton?"

"Yes. Over the past few months I've made several hundredweight of the stuff."

"Isn't it dangerous to have it lying around?"

"No, no. It's quite safe, if it's prepared properly. If it's not cleaned and dried as it should be, then it can easily go off all on its own. But this is perfectly safe. To make it explode, it will have to be compressed, then set off with a detonator made of mercuric fulminate. At the moment you could jump up and down on it all day and come to no harm. That's the dangerous stuff over there." He pointed to another corner.

"What's that?"

"Gunpowder. I bought it before I realised it wouldn't do. It's useless now; I'm going to use it on Cort's pillar, if he can make up his mind what he wants."

"So the explosive is in the front, it hits the ship and—bang."

"Bang. Precisely," he said approvingly.

"What size bang? I mean, how much explosive will you need to sink a battleship?"

"That will be determined by experiments."

"You're going to fire off torpedoes at passing battleships until one sinks?"

"I don't think that will be necessary," he said, with the air of one who would have loved nothing more. "Detonating explosives against plates of armour will do."

"I'm almost disappointed," I said. "But isn't a gun more reliable? Less chance of something going wrong, and less chance of the other ship getting out of the way? And cheaper?"

"Possibly so, but to send a shell of equivalent power on its way you need a gun weighing some sixty tons. And for that you need a very large ship. Which has to be armour-plated, and carry a large crew. With a few of these, a corvette of three hundred tons and a crew of sixty will be a match for the largest battleship in the world."

"The Royal Navy will thank you for that, I'm sure," I said ironically.

Macintyre laughed. "They won't. This will neutralise every navy in the world! No one will dare send their capital ships to sea, for fear of losing them. War will come to an end."

I found his optimism touching, if misplaced. "That would kill off demand for your invention, would it not? How many of these could you sell?"

"I have no idea."

I did. If it worked, and he could persuade one navy to buy them, then he would sell them to every navy in the world. Admirals are as discerning as housewives in a department store. They must have what everyone else is having.

"Does it work?"

"Of course. At least, it will work, when one or two problems are ironed out."

"Such as?"

"It has to go in a straight line, as I say. That is quite straightforward. But it also has to propel itself at a constant depth, not rising and falling. Through the water, not over the top of it."

"Why?"

"Because ships are plated above the waterline, but not so heavily below it. Shells burst when they hit the water, so there is rarely direct damage under sea level, and so little need to protect the hulls so far down."

"How much does it cost to make these?"

"I've no idea."

"And how much will you try to sell them for?"

"I haven't thought about that."

"Where would you manufacture them? You could hardly do it here."

"I don't know."

"How much have you spent on developing it so far?"

All of a sudden the boyish look of enthusiasm which had animated his face since he began talking about his machine faded. He looked his age and more so, careworn and anxious.

"Everything I have, or had. And more."

"You are in debt?" He professed to like direct questions. Normally I do not, except where money is concerned. There I desire absolute and unambiguous precision.

He nodded.

"How much?"

"Three hundred pounds. I think."

"At what rate of interest?"

"I don't know."

I was appalled. However skilled Macintyre was as an engineer, he was no businessman. In that department he was as naïve as a newborn babe. And someone, I could tell, was taking advantage of that.

I do not object to such practises. Macintyre was an adult and far from stupid. He had entered into an agreement fully conscious of what he was doing. If he did so, that was his fault, not the fault of the person who was so exploiting his unworldly nature. It turned out, so he told me, that he had needed money, both to pay the wages of his men, and to buy the material necessary for his great machine, and had assumed he would be able to pay it off with a job he had taken on designing the metalwork for a new bridge to be thrown across the Grand Canal. But that project had collapsed, so no payment was forthcoming, and the debts had mounted up.

"I arrived in Venice with enough money, so I thought, to live indefinitely. But this machine has been more difficult than I could ever have imagined. The problems to be solved! You cannot believe it. Building the case and ensuring it is watertight, designing the engine, the detonator, coming up with an entirely new device to regulate depth. It takes time and money. More money than I have."

"So you are heavily in debt, with no assets to draw on, paying what I imagine is a high rate of interest. How long before you are unable to continue?"

"Not long. My creditors are pressing. They are insisting that the torpedo be tried out and quickly, otherwise they will call in their debts."

"Can you do that?"

"I'm going to give a demonstration soon. If it works, I will be allowed to borrow more. But it is too early; much too early."

He did not continue, and had no need to.

"I think you need a bookkeeper as much as you do a draughtsman or a machinist," I said. "Money is as important a component as steel."

He shrugged, plainly uninterested. "They're thieves," he said. "They'd steal my invention and leave me with nothing unless I was careful."

"I hate to say it, but you are not being careful."

"Oh, everything will be just fine next week. When the test is done."

"Are you sure?"

He looked weary. "Any sort of calculation in engineering I can do. But show me a contract, or a page of accounts . . ."

"With me, it is the precise opposite. Listen. If you wish, I could look through that side of things, see what the situation is precisely, and tell you—in words even an engineer could understand—how you stand at the moment. Only if you wish. I do not want to interfere in any way."

I was very reluctant to make this offer, as it is generally unwise to give financial advice unbidden. But the look of hopelessness on his face as he talked of his debts was beguiling. And my mind was racing. An entirely new class of weapon could be formidably profitable—witness Mr. Maxim's rapid-fire gun, which, from small beginnings, rapidly became more or less obligatory equipment for every army in the world.

And the beauty of Macintyre's machine was that it was so wasteful. Unlike a cannon, which was (so to speak) a fixed investment, with the cost of employment quite low—only the amount needed to buy the shell and the gunpowder—the torpedo could be employed once only. Once sent on its way, the whole thing would have to be replaced. The potential for replacement orders was considerable and (if I knew my sailors) in a conflict they would fire them off like rockets on Guy Fawkes night.

Regular orders from an organisation with bottomless pockets. The prospect was enticing. Not least because I was fairly certain that Macintyre's aim, of eliminating war by making destruction certain, was as unlikely as it was noble. No weapon has ever made war less likely; they merely end wars more quickly by killing people at higher speeds. Until the mind of man invents something capable of killing everyone, that will not change.

But it seemed that the chances of Macintyre ever succeeding with his device were small to nonexistent. He barely had the resources to finish one, so what chance had he of producing them in bulk? Who would provide the capital to fit out a factory, hire a workforce? Who would run it, ensure that the machines were properly made, sold and delivered? Macintyre had no idea of any of this, nor did he even know how to find those who did.

The whole situation was full of possibilities. If the machine worked.

CHAPTER 8

He did not buy me lunch, or even share a meal with me, but I was quite content as I walked back to my apartment, taking diversions here and there, so that it was early evening by the time I finally returned. It had been a most interesting day, and my spirits were further buoyed by three messages that awaited my return. One from the Marchesa, saying that I should dine with her the following week, as she had a delightful entertainment for me; the next from Mr. Macintyre, containing a bundle of papers and a curt note, saying that here were his accounts, if I wished to look at them. And the last was from Mrs. Cort, saying that her husband had given his permission for her to guide me around the city. We could begin tomorrow, if I wished.

My stay in Venice was settling down to being remarkably enjoyable, and no small part of it was due to the surroundings. The quiet of the place has a wonderful appeal if you are receptive to it, the more so because it is so unnoticed. The effect of the light also really cannot be put into words. It is not the peace of an English Sunday, for example, when the quiet is almost total but there is always the knowledge of what came before and what will come the next day. There is always the faintest haze in Venice, suggesting to the mind that the moment will continue forever, that there never will be a tomorrow. It is hard to occupy yourself with the concerns of the world, for concerns are always about what will happen in the future, and in Venice the future will never come, and the past will never disappear. I find that I have only a small recollection of buildings and scenery from that time; I have no strong memories of views or vistas. I had reached a stage where I hardly noticed any of it; some of the greatest works of art and architecture made no conscious impression on me at all. The effect, however, was total and overwhelming. It was like being in a different world, where everything fitted together. An old woman sitting on a step, a palace, a waiter setting out tables, washing on a line, boats crossing the lagoon, islands hazy in the morning mist, seagulls in the sky, all of these were part of this whole, relating perfectly to each other and to my mood, which moved rapidly from dream to purposeful activity seamlessly.

I became a Venetian that afternoon, walking to a spot on the Riva with a book. I had intended to view something, but I do not even remember what, as I never got there. I sat down on the steps of a bridge, and watched the boats go by. A pretty girl was selling pears fresh from the tree. I wanted one, but had no money on me. But they were so luscious, so fat and juicy-looking, some bruised already and oozing sweet sticky liquid in the basket. And eventually, I leaned over, and took one, biting into it before she even noticed what I had done. Then she turned, and I shook my head. I couldn't help it, my glance said. The girl, dark-haired and bright-eyed, smiled at my pleasure, then laughed and offered me another. Take, take, she said. Take what you want. And I did; I took another, bowing in acknowledgement, and not feeling in the slightest bit embarrassed about offering nothing in return. She waved her hand anyway. Don't worry, you will pay later, was the sense of her smile. Everything is paid for, eventually.

That evening, I settled down to read Mr. Macintyre's accounts. Some may consider this a dull way of spending time, even an anticlimax after a day such as I had just enjoyed. I know that it is an unusual pleasure and that account books are a byword for spiritless, mechanical drabness, but that is said by those who do not understand them. In truth, a set of accounts can be as full of drama and passion as any novel. A whole year, more than that, of human endeavour is abbreviated, compressed down into a page of hieroglyphics. Add understanding, and the story bursts forth, rather as dried fruit expands when water is added to it.

Macintyre's accounts were a particular challenge because they were so sloppy, and did not conform to any rules of accountancy that I had ever come across. What Italians consider expenditure or income is very different. For some items there seemed to be no fixed definitions at all; had they been deliberately designed to confuse, then they could not have been better constructed.

But eventually I teased out their secrets. Macintyre had run out of money about a year previously, and had had to prepare approximate accounts of the previous few years' endeavours to back his application for a loan. These showed that he had started with £1,300; and he had spent it at about £500 a year. Since taking the loan, he had spent a further £300, which, with accumulated (and unpaid) interest, meant he was now £427 in debt. That is, he was paying interest at about 37 per cent a year, which was quite enough to sink any project.

Most of the money had gone on machinery (part of which was recoverable if necessary), wages and materials for building his machine. His net position was in fact not as bad as it looked at first sight—if all the machinery had been sold at a reasonable price, he would be able to pay off most of his debts. But not all; he would be left with nothing at all for his efforts, except for his invention.

At this point, we entered the land of fantasy. Macintyre had essayed a guess about bringing his torpedo into production, but it was so devoid of any common sense or knowledge that it was almost laughable. I swiftly enough made my own calculations. Purchase of a suitable premises would cost around £700, the necessary machine tools about £6,000, a workforce of about forty to begin with would mean running costs of about £7,000 a year, which would have to be borne out of initial investment as it was unlikely to produce any revenue for at least that time. Plus the cost of material, which would be about £30 for each machine. Say another £3,000 for the first year. A required initial investment, therefore of £16,700 before a single torpedo was carried onto its first ship, or the first request for payment sent out.

And Macintyre could not even manage a debt of £300 without sinking into near bankruptcy. What was worse, he had been obliged to offer security for the loan and had nothing to give. Instead, he had in effect handed over the patent. Not outright for cash, but merely for permission to borrow. Possibly the most foolish, thoughtless bargain any man has ever made. He no longer owned his own invention.

This part of the paperwork took me some time to get through, as it involved a considerable amount of legal jargon with which I was unfamiliar. Besides, I could not initially believe it, even when I had managed to make it out. But it was all too true. If the torpedo failed, Macintyre would suffer, as his debt would be called in. If it succeeded, he would not benefit, as the machine was not his.

I could only conclude that he did not care: that he was so unworldly that all he wanted was to perfect his invention, to show the world his ability. Macintyre did not want to manufacture his torpedo or make money out of it. Once it was finished, he would probably lose interest. Judging by how he had talked about ending war, it was quite possible he would be almost pleased not to have anything more to do with it. He wanted to show it could be done. That was all.

But why? Why so obsessed, why so careless? Here the limitations of accounts come into play. They can tell of the movements of men, of their money, but rarely give much of an insight into their motives—although Macintyre's fanaticism was written into every column of payments. He bought the best of everything: the highest quality steel; the most expensive German precision instruments. Materials he had imported from Sweden or England, when I was sure perfectly reasonable local substitutes were available at a fraction of the price he had paid. Bills were settled promptly when he had the money. He could not be bothered with the minor savings a delay of a week or a month might bring.

I sat on a chair on my balcony, looking down at the quiet of the canal below, dreaming peacefully. I was calculating fast, something I can do without the need for actual thought. Numbers, money, take shape in my head, and flow into new forms without the need to consider it at all actively. A woman was slowly propelling a barge down the canal, talking loudly to a little girl perched in the front of the boat. They were cheerful, even though it was the end of what had probably been for them a day of long labour. She was in no hurry; would give the oar a twitch, enough to make the boat spurt forward, then rest as it slid along and almost stopped, before twitching it again. By the time she had rounded the corner halfway down, into a tiny side canal I had not noticed before, I had the entire plan laid out in my head.

Macintyre needed to be rescued from himself. In effect, his foolishness had done me a great favour. I would have never even considered trying to wrest control of his invention from him, of forcing my assistance on him against his will or without his knowledge. But it was no longer his; he had sold it. And I had no qualms about taking on his bankers. They were opponents for whom one needed to feel little sympathy, if I could triumph over them.

Cardano would help, I felt sure. He would be able to back a private loan, so that I would retain absolute control and be able to pay off the debt when profits began to rise. I knew exactly the man who could help me set up the enterprise, could put me in touch with land agents to find a site. I would put in six—perhaps five—thousand of my own money, depending on the terms that Cardano could get. A limited company to protect myself. By carefully not paying any bills unless forced to do so, it would be a simple matter to make the suppliers in effect pay for the loan itself. They would get their money eventually, or we would all sink with the torpedo.

I found it all very relaxing, although I knew I would have to revisit my figures the next day, to see whether they were still realistic, or whether I had constructed too optimistic an outlook—underestimated costs, over-estimated possible revenues. And I would wander down to the foreign library near San Marco, to see what, if any, information could be had on the world's navies.

I emerged from the library the next day feeling even more cheerful. The main navies of the world were the Royal Navy (everyone knew that) with the French next. After these two came Austria, Italy, the United States, Russia. After them a few South American countries had ideas and ambition, as did Japan. All in all, the world could boast, if that is the right word, some 700 capital ships, 1,400 medium-sized vessels which could be used for fighting, and another 4,000 used for coastal protection and so on. Say fifteen torpedoes for the first category, five for the second, one for the third. A possible world market of more than twenty thousand torpedoes, and I reckoned I could charge £300 each. Possible revenues of more than six million pounds. Assume only half of the potential was turned into orders over a period of ten years, and replacement orders of 1/20th part of the total per year. That would suggest recurrent orders of about a thousand a year, and revenue when properly under way of more than £300,000. Possible profits per year of about £100,000, for an initial investment of £5,000. Assuming the business would be valued at fifteen years' purchase, then that would create an enterprise of about one and a half million pounds.

Navies would order, if it worked. But would it? Macintyre was confident, and I was sure his acumen as an engineer was greater than his skill as a businessman, but even so obsession—and he was surely a man obsessed—leads to cloudy judgement.

Then there was the issue of wresting control from his creditors who, I was sure, had a better notion of his machine's financial potential than he did. They would not give it up for a paltry sum, and I did not wish to pay high. The whole point of the game is to get a bargain. Anyone can pay a full price.

How was this to be done? First, know your opponent, and here, much to my surprise, my landlady proved to be a fount of useful information. Ambrosian, the head of the bank that had made the loan, was, she told me, highly respected as a man who had stayed in Venice during the Austrian occupation, but who had refused to have many dealings with Vienna. He had done most of his business with Venetians, and forged contacts with banking families in Italy, France—anywhere but Austria. Like most patriotic citizens, he had refused all invitations to official functions, refused to go to the theatre or opera, refused to sit in a café where an Austrian was sitting and (so it was said) subsidised forbidden groups of nationalists to annoy the foreign oppressors. He was something of a hero; whether he was any good as a banker was another matter entirely. Such information as I could gather from newspapers suggested a well-bottomed, but somewhat unimaginative, operation, which was good. Such people do not like risks. But newspapers are often wrong.

I did wish communications were better. I had sent off a letter to Cardano shortly after I arrived, and had mentioned Macintyre and also Cort, but had received no reply—even going by express mail, it would take a week for a letter to arrive in London, a week for the reply to come back. Better than it had been only a few years previously, no doubt, but in London I could have found all the information I needed in a morning. Now the telegraph crisscrosses the world, telephones are becoming common, and people take instantaneous communication for granted. They should try to imagine a world where a letter—to California, or Australia or India—could take up to a month, even at speed.

CHAPTER 9

The next day was a dream of such perfection that I have never approached the like again. It was, of course, all illusion, but I like to think of it still in isolation from what came after, as a moment of bliss, one of those days when one is no longer oneself, but becomes bigger, and better, able to overcome the normal preoccupations of life and breathe more freely.

Should anyone read this who knows me only from my reputation, I have no doubt that this narrative of idleness and dreaminess will occasion nothing but incredulity. If business and romance do not mix, how very much more incompatible are finance and passion? One requires a personality that is purely cold and rational, the other must give way to the impetuous. Such feelings cannot coexist in the same individual.

To which I must reply that anyone who thinks this knows nothing of money. Finance is every bit as much an art as painting or music. It is very similar to musical performance, for while much does depend on skill—a musician who cannot play is not a musician; a financier who cannot understand a balance sheet will soon be a beggar—skill can only take you so far. Beyond that point lies poetry. Many find this difficult to believe, but it is true. Some people are so much in tune with the markets that they do not need to manipulate a stock price or break a law to profit. They can feel the ebbs and flows of capital in the way a horse rider understands his steed, and can make it obey him without use of whip or stirrup.

Money is merely another term for people, a representation of their desires and personalities. If you do not understand one, you cannot hope to understand the other. Take the matter of giving an inducement to win a contract. This is frowned on, called bribery and in some cases is even considered criminal. But it is an area in which rational calculation and emotional empathy are the most perfectly fused. It is an art form; a Russian expects an envelope full of money; an English civil servant would be outraged at the idea, but is no less corrupt or greedy. He desires employment for his nephew—which is often a more generous gift. It is diplomacy carried over to the world of affairs, and both require delicacy and judgement. I acknowledge no equal in the art—not even Mr. Xanthos, for he is too cynical, too ready to hold the person he persuades in contempt. As I write, I have before me a sheet of paper listing the shares in my companies owned by some of the greatest politicians in England. I arranged it all some six years ago as a precaution and have never asked for anything in return. Nor will I; but these people will, in due course, do what is necessary in their own interests, and mine. Not that anyone else knows of this; it is why my managers are becoming nervous and are unable to understand my calm belief that all will be well. They fear I have lost my touch.

My Venice that day was a city full of tremulous anticipation. I wished to spend the day with Mrs. Cort even more than I wished to travel in a gondola around the canals. We met by a landing stage not far from the Rialto, where gondola, gondolier, and a hamper of food already awaited. It was eight in the morning, and brilliantly clear. Warm already, with the promise of more to come. The city itself was sparkling and Mrs. Cort—I hope I do not give away too much if at this point I begin to call her Louise—was standing waiting for me, and smiled as I approached, a smile of such warmth and promise that my heart skipped a beat.

Gondolas are not a place for any sort of intimate conversation, although we sat side by side rather than opposite each other. The boats are arranged (for those who do not know) with the gondolier standing at the back, so he had a clear view, not only of the waters ahead, but also of his passengers. They miss nothing, and a flimsy construction over our heads provided only limited privacy. A brushing of hand against hand; the faint pressure of bodies touching in the cramped confines of the hull. It was almost unbearable and I could sense she was under a similar pressure. I could feel the tension within her, longing for some outlet.

And so the morning passed in delicious frustration, the conversation edging towards intimacy, then pulling back before moving closer once more.

"How long have you lived in Venice?" I asked, this being an example of a conversation that proceeded in fits and starts, punctuated by long silences as we were both calmed by the soft splashing of the water against the side of the boat.

"About five months," she replied.

"You met Mr. Cort in England?"

"Yes. In London. Where I was working. As a governess."

She said this with a slight defiance, as if to see whether my attitude to her would change as a result of learning of her situation.

"How did you come to that position?"

"My father died when I was young, leaving my mother to look after us, two boys and two girls. I was the eldest. When I was fourteen my mother fell ill. So I had to work. Eventually, I was engaged by a family in Chelsea, not rich by many standards, but well enough off to afford me. I cared for their two children until I left to marry. They were delightful children. I miss them still."

"True love?"

"No. He desired a wife to look after him and I craved the certainty of marriage. It was an arrangement suitable to us both."

She sighed and broke off to look over the lagoon towards the Lido, which was slowly coming closer. I did not wish to intrude, so asked no further, but I understood all too well that she lived in a loveless marriage, deprived of that affection that all human beings must have. It is the situation of many, perhaps it is the normal circumstance of most, and she did not complain of a contract freely entered into. But it is not in our nature to remember how much worse things might have been; we only dream of the better that slips through our fingers.

"And he brought you here."

"Yes. But I find this dreary conversation for such a day. Tell me about yourself instead. You must have had a more interesting life than I have so far enjoyed."

"I doubt that. What can I say?"

"Are you married?"

"Yes."

"Happily?"

Which is the moment I stepped closer to the edge. Yes, happily. My adored wife. I miss her so much. Words acting like an impregnable fortress, able to keep her out, me inside, both separated forever. I said nothing, and she understood my meaning.

"But your wife is not here. Why is that?"

"She does not like to travel."

"Does she have a name?"

She was probing, teasing me. Betrayal mounted on betrayal as I turned aside and did not answer once more, then turned back and met her eyes as they looked calmly straight into mine, communicating endlessly, whole volumes about us both.

"And what do you do?"

"I spend my time investing money for gain. It takes up much of my life."

She looked curious. "I understand nothing about money," she said.

"This is not the time to start learning," I said. "I find it fascinating and can discuss it for hours, but I also think there must be other topics to talk about when one is in a gondola on a fine morning in the company of a beautiful woman."

She smiled faintly and looked away. I wondered how long it had been since anyone had spoken thus to her, if anyone ever had.

"I like that," she said softly.

There then followed the longest silence of the day; our closeness had already grown too great to require words. Instead we both sat quietly, watching the flat strip of land growing closer, I so aware of her it was almost painful.

The Lido has changed greatly since then; now the hotels I once imagined in my mind's eye have sprung up along its length. Then it was all but deserted; the main road was little more than a track that led out of the tiny settlement on the city side of the strip; within a few hundred yards all habitation ceased, and there were instead only cows and a few sheep occupying an island near fifteen miles long and a mile wide.

At the time I was somewhat disappointed; I had anticipated a voyage in the inner lagoon, seeing the sights I thought every visitor should see— Murano, Torcello and all of those. I had not yet seen much even of the main city, let alone its outlying regions, so coming to a place which was virtually deserted, and which had no features of note, was not what I desired at all.

"Why have you brought me here?" I asked, somewhat petulantly.

"Wait and see," she said. "I love this place. It is the only place where you can be alone. Come."

She directed the gondolier to pick up the hamper of food and carry it over the island to the other side. She later told me she had discovered this spot many weeks before, and had kept it secret from everyone, treasuring it as a place she alone in the world knew about. To show it to me was the greatest compliment.

The other side was not far; although a mile or more wide at its tip, the Lido narrows down along its length until it is only a few hundred yards across. It is not one island; rather it is a whole string of them, artificially joined over the centuries to form a barrier protecting the city from the Adriatic. It was all but deserted, offering nothing to the population except uncertain weather in winter and a place to walk in summer.

And to swim; I had learned to swim as a boy when I stayed for the summers at the house of a relative in Hampshire. This family possessed a large garden with a fine pond, surrounded by reeds. Once you waded through them, you had the finest swimming place imaginable, with clear fresh water that warmed pleasantly in the sun. There my cousins had taught me to swim and, although I was not expert, I had learned also to love the feel of water. To see the rolling waves of the Adriatic basking in the sunshine of late summer gave me one thought only, which was to wade into the water as quickly as possible.

Again, the thought occurred to me; I had been sent to school at a boarding establishment in Brighton until I was thirteen, and had seen the bathing houses and the women ponderously wading into the icy water— for their health, I imagine, as it is difficult to see how it could have been for their pleasure—dressed in voluminous costumes so heavy they could not possibly have swum without sinking. I remembered also the habitually leaden skies, and the chill that hit you as you emerged from the water dripping wet, only to be frozen by the frigid winds of an English summer.

And here was something close to paradise on earth. Men now go to the South Seas to search for such an unspoiled landscape; back in 1867 it could be found much closer to home, only a short boat ride from San Marco.

"It's beautiful," I said as we walked down a little path that led to a copse of trees.

She smiled. "Listen," she said, pausing for a moment and holding up a finger. I listened.

"What?"

"Nothing," she replied. "Nothing at all. There is only the sound of the sea and the birds. That is why I like it."

We had arrived at her special place, a clearing inside the copse surrounded on three sides by thick foliage that prevented any passerby from seeing us, and open on the other to the sea, like the most glorious theatre set in the world. It was dark and cool in the shade, and I spread out our blanket on the ground, while Louise opened the hamper and took out the simple food she had prepared—a cold chicken, some bread, and a bottle of water.

"How do you like the architecture of Palladio?" she asked coyly as we finished our meal—which, for all its simplicity, was delicious.

"I like it very much. Or would do, no doubt, if I had seen any. Why?"

"Because that is what you are admiring at the moment."

"Really?"

"Yes. Mr. Cort gave me permission spend the day showing you the city. I believe he felt that it was improper for me to be alone with you otherwise. In the middle of Venice there could be little scandal."

"And you disobeyed his orders."

She nodded. "Are you shocked?"

"Dreadfully."

And then I leaned over and kissed her. Very clumsily, even aggressively, but I could stand the tension no more. I was well aware that she might pull back, that the moment might be ruined by my behaviour, but I did not care. I was a Venetian; I could take what I wanted. I had to know and had to show my intentions, however dishonourable and however much I might risk losing her esteem had I made a mistake. It was appalling behaviour, to try and take advantage of a married woman in an isolated spot when she had trusted me. I can only say that I was overtaken by a sort of madness, the impetuousity that comes from being in a foreign land where the usual demands of behaviour are relaxed, combined with the special magic of a place which encourages emotional display normally kept hidden from view.

She did not pull back. Instead, she responded to my advance with a ferocity that encouraged still more from me, and we lay back on the ground, bodies entwined, groans being the only communication between us apart from the eloquent conversation of our bodies.

How it happened I do not know; I cannot recall whose initiative it was, but I felt her hands exploring my body so firmly that I was roused to a pitch of excitement greater than anything I had ever experienced before, and I scrabbled vainly at her clothes—oh, the clothes of that period, like medieval castles they were, designed to repel all assault— until she pulled back.

Again I was surprised, for I expected her to come to her senses then, and realise the peril of her situation, but she did not. All she said was, "Not like that," and slowly began unbuttoning her blouse, then her skirts, until she was revealed to me in all her beauty, and lay back on the blanket, and held out her arms for me, an expression of desperation and longing on her face.

It was not good, that first time, perhaps it never is between two people so uncertain of each other, so unknowing of the other's needs and desires, but she cried out, almost in pain, towards the end and I could feel the tension seeping from her body as it ebbed slowly from mine.

Then we lay together, I slowly caressing her belly, still unable truly to believe that such a thing had happened. What was this woman? What sort of person gives herself up in such a fashion? But again I did not care. I had had such thoughts before, with others, and in each case the result had been a sort of disgust, a separation of lust from respect and an inability to reconcile the two feelings. There was no such difficulty now; I was merely content, blissful, and desired nothing more than to hold her close forever. I felt whole for the first time in my life.

But as I turned to look on her face, I saw tears trickling slowly down her cheek and was startled into sitting up.

"Oh my dear, I am so sorry, so very sorry," I said genuinely, convinced that she had, at last, realised the folly of her actions.

She laughed through her tears, and shook her head. "No, I am not crying for that," she said.

"What then?"

She said nothing, but reached across and found her blouse, which she put, without any underclothes, across her shoulders.

"Tell me," I insisted.

"I don't know if I can," she said. "It is not easy to say it."

"Try."

She looked out to sea for a long while, gathering her thoughts.

"I was twenty-seven when I married Mr. Cort," she began softly. "An old maid. I had all but given up thought of marrying, and believed I would have to make shift as best I could on my own. Then he appeared and proposed. I accepted, even though I knew there would never be any love between us. He made me no promises, nor I him. He wanted a housekeeper; he has no notion of love or romance. Besides, I was giving nothing up, and I thought we would make do together. I would have children, and they would provide affection enough.

"I learned soon enough that was simply a dream as well. He cannot . . . do what you do."

"What do you mean?"

"We do not have the intimacy of the sort that is usual between man and wife," she continued stiffly. "Nor has he any interest in women in that way. I thought to begin with it was just the shyness of a habitual bachelor, but I soon realised that it was more than that. No! I must say no more!"

"As you wish, but do not keep silent for my sake."

I could see what she meant by this being difficult; it was hard to listen to. But once she had started she could not stop; it was as though all her words had been blocked in her for years and took the first opportunity to come bursting out into the open, to the first sympathetic listener. I said nothing at all, merely listening cemented our intimacy and drew our lives closer together, made us lovers in the soul as well as the body.

"He has other tastes. Terrible, perverted, disgusting ones. He did his duty, and we had our son, but that was all. When I discovered . . . what he was, I could no longer go near him. I will not have him touch me, if I have the choice. Do you understand?"

I nodded, but only hesitantly.

"That is why he likes Venice. There is opportunity, for people like him. You think of him as a mild, gentle man, do you not? Foolish, in-effectual but good-natured."

"I suppose that is my general impression, yes."

"You do not know him. You do not know what he is like."

"I find this all difficult to believe."

"I know. Much of the time he is as you know him. But then the madness comes on him and he changes. He is violent, cruel. Do you want me to tell you the things he does? The things he makes me do, when I don't run away, or lock myself in a room so he cannot come to me, him and the people he finds? He likes pain, you see. It excites him. It is the only thing which does. He is not manly in the world and he takes his revenge on me."

I shook my head. "Don't tell me."

I reached out and took her had, horrified by what she was saying. How could anyone treat such a woman—any woman—in the fashion she hinted at? It was beyond all understanding.

"You do not seem like someone who has been so abused," I said.

"I do not have bruises or cuts, at the moment," she said. "Do you doubt me? Wait a little and soon enough I will have marks to satisfy you."

"I did not mean that," I replied quickly. "I meant that you do not have the air of a woman mistreated. Neglected, unloved, perhaps."

"I have grown used to it," she said. "It was not always so. In the beginning I rebelled, but how could I do so successfully? I have no money of my own, no position, he is my husband. If I ran away, where would I run? He would find me again, or I would starve. I tried, once, but I was discovered before I could leave.

"So I have learned. I think to myself that perhaps not all men are like

that. I tell myself that it will pass. Once the madness passes, he is
perfectly agreeable for weeks before it starts again. He has allowed me to
show you around; is that the decision of a monster? The man you have
met, is he cruel and violent? No. To the outside world he is meek and
mild. Only I know the truth of what he is like. But who would ever believe
me? If I said anything it is I who would be called mad, not him."

Here she broke down completely, her head in her hands, sobbing
silently. She could not go on, and even turned her back on me when I
tried to comfort her. I insisted, and eventually she gave way, throwing
herself into my arms and crying without restraint.

I could not yet see my course of action; all I knew was that I would
eventually have one. "You must leave," I said. "Leave Venice and your
husband."

"I cannot," she said scornfully. "How could I do such a thing? Where
would I go?"

"I could . . ."

"No!" she said, really frightened now. "No, you must say nothing. Do
nothing. You must promise me."

"But I must do something."

"You must not! Do you think of yourself as a knight in shining armour,
rescuing the damsel in distress? We do not live in an age when such
things happen. He has rights. I am his property. What would happen? He
would deny it all, of course. He would say I was inventing things. He
would get someone like Marangoni to say that I was a habitual liar, that I
was mad. Do you think that if I told the truth, said that he beats me to
become excited . . ."

She broke off, horrified at what she had said, that she had let out
more than she wished about her hellish existence.

"Please," she said, pleading with me, "please do not take matters into
your own hands. Do not intervene. There is nothing you can do for me.
Except to love me a little, show me that there are men who are not
monsters, that there is more to love than pain and tears."

I shook my head in confusion. "What do you want?"

"I need to think, to clear my head. Meeting you was—I cannot
describe it. The moment I saw you I felt something I have never known
before. I do not ask you for help; there is nothing you can do for me. I ask
you simply for your presence, a little. That is more soothing and
comforting than anything you can say or do."

"You ask for too little."

"I ask for more than any person has ever given me," she replied, stroking my cheek. "And if I asked for more, I might not get it."

"You doubt me?"

She did not reply, but threw herself on me once more. "No more words," she said. "Not for a while."

She was ferocious; it was as though, having unburdened herself to me, shown me her secrets, she had no need left of any modesty or caution. She was violent with me, just as others had been violent in their hatred of her; it was her defence, I thought, to respond to her tormentors in such a way. Afterwards she lay once more on the ground, stretched out with a total lack of caution or care.

"I wish I could die now," she said as she ran her fingers through my hair. "Do you not agree? To end your life in this place, with the sound of the sea and the trees, the light twinkling through the branches. Will you kill me? It would make me happy, you know. Please, kill me now. I would like to die at your hands."

I laughed, but her face was serious. "Then I would never see you again, or talk to you or hold you," I said. "And I am a selfish man. Now I have you, I will not let you go so easily, whatever your wishes."

"Oh, if only I had known men such as you existed! I might have made different choices."

"Listen," I said, beginning to pull on my clothes. Time was passing far quicker than I wished, and one of us had to remember the outside world continued to exist. "How do you wish to proceed now? I need hardly say that I want to repeat this afternoon. Do you want that also? If you do not, then tell me now because I could not stand to be repulsed."

"What would you do if I refused you?"

"I would leave, and quickly. There is no vital reason to stay here."

"Do not leave. I really would die if you did."

"So, what do we do now? We cannot come all the way to the Lido every afternoon. And we cannot meet either in your lodging or mine."

"I have had no experience in arranging secret meetings with a lover," she said, and I could hear in her voice a faint tremor of excitement, as though the very idea was bringing her spirits back to life.

"Nor I," I replied truthfully. "But I believe it is usual in such circumstances to rent a room, generally in some poor part of the city. It would not be elegant, and would offer few conveniences except privacy.

Such things are normally for women of low quality, though, and I would hesitate . . ."

"No! Let us do that! That is what I am. Nothing more than that, and I will be that for you with pleasure."

I looked closely at her. She was serious.

It was settled, and in the most businesslike terms. There was no need for delicacy of language, for in our acts we had already passed beyond the point of dissimulation. Secrecy was of the essence. I would acquire a room for our meetings. We would be conspicuous to some, no doubt, but not to anyone who might care. As long as we were safe from the prying eyes of other foreigners, we could be safe. The Venetians see all and say nothing.

And so we made our way back, as the evening light was beginning to settle over the city. The gondolier rowed methodically, making us feel safe by his knowing silence. We sat together, side by side, until we were close in, and said not a word to each other. The evening shadows were our conversation, the softness of the light and the calm of the water were our emotions made tangible. Venice is quiet in comparison to most cities, yet it seemed noisy and raucous to my ears as we came in to land. The people walked too fast, had too many reasons for what they did and said, unlike me, as I no longer had any reason or desire to do anything.

I touched her only as I helped her out of the gondola, and our eyes met briefly before the collusion and dissimulation that was to be our life from now on intervened. It was an electric moment, as we both realised how much we were now bound to each other, conspirators together, living a secret life of lies and deceit.

I consider myself a moral man, who upholds the laws of God and man as best as he is able. I was married and, in all the time since I wed my wife, I had never deceived or betrayed her in any way. I hold to my contracts and keep my word. I considered that Louise had been absolved from whatever vows she had sworn by the treatment she had received. She had said too much, and regretted her words, but I now had some idea of the hellish life she endured with her husband. No one owes loyalty to such a person.

I had no such excuse and I try to make none. Except to say that excitement is a drug, and Venice is a treacherous place, which sucks people down. I wanted her, and for the first time in my life all the arguments and reasons which would have stopped me were of no effect. I didn't even consider what I was doing; did not feel guilty for a single moment. All objections I brushed aside. Venice had taken hold of me, and I had rushed into its embrace as willingly as I had rushed into hers.

The rest of the world would not have viewed it with such indulgence, of course; I had seduced another man's wife, and what had begun in hot blood I intended to continue in a spirit of calculation. The life of deception started that moment. "I must thank you, Mrs. Cort, for your assistance today. I trust you did not find it too dull."

"On the contrary," she replied. "And if you wish me to accompany you again, then please do not hesitate to say so. I am sure Mr. Cort will not object."

And then we bade each other farewell in a stiff and formal fashion, and I turned to leave, my heart pounding with excitement.

My liaison demanded secrecy, and what better way of ensuring that than to act entirely normally? I might have wandered the streets, soaking up the atmosphere of the place which was already coiling itself around my being. Venice is the most dangerous place on earth, or was then, until the tourists came and swamped the air of threat, which existed in its very stones, with the futile frivolity of the sightseer, and converted the inhabitants into supplicants of the transient.

"Why so moody?" Such might have been the question had any acquaintance encountered me, and it was far too soon to run such risks. So I resolved to shut off that part of my thoughts and switch my attention to other things. There was a part of me—an ever-diminishing, weakening part, it is true—which fought against the seductions of the city, although only halfheartedly.

I walked to the offices of the Banca di Santo Spirito and left my card for Signor Ambrosian. I wished to meet a man who knew about the city— knew how it worked, that is, rather than knew about its buildings, which is always the easiest thing to discover, and who also knew about Macintyre. I have always found it strange that people are willing to travel to a place, and devote some considerable energy to doing so, yet leave with not the slightest knowledge or interest in the lives of the inhabitants.

An old friend of mine travelled through the Balkans a few years ago and spent months in those countries, yet came back knowledgeable only about landscapes and the architecture of Orthodox monasteries. How was capital accumulated? How were the cities run? Was the system of taxation efficient or no? What levels of literacy and discipline could you count on amongst the population? What, in other words, about the stuff of their lives? Not only did he have no knowledge of these things, he had no interest in them, seeming to think that monasteries merely pop out of the ground like mushrooms without any application of either money or labour, and that cities are simply wished into existence for no reason other than to delight the eye of the visitor.

The same applies to Venice, but on a grander scale. What were these people doing living in the middle of the sea like that? Why, in their days of greatness, did they not migrate to the land? How, now that those days of grandeur were past, did they intend to adapt themselves to a new world? Signor Ambrosian seemed the best fitted to answer such questions. No one else I had yet met was likely to do so.

I wrote a note on the back of my calling card, asking him to send a message to my accommodation, and then returned there for a rest before dinner. I was hungry; the day had been long, and the food not plentiful, and the excitement had worked up a fine appetite in me. I was looking forward to dinner and my own company, for I resolved that that evening I would eat alone. It was natural, even necessary, to place myself in the way of English society, but I was not, that evening, willing to converse with the likes of Longman in a fashion of easy conviviality—and I knew that such a manner was utterly vital if my deception was to be successful. Besides, I was not yet ready to meet Cort again.

For the next few days a certain watchful peace descended on me. All thoughts of leaving and moving on to new sights and places fell away so softly I did not even realise they had departed. I could not even keep myself fixed on reality through business, as I received a letter from Signor Ambrosian's secretary to say the banker was away for a few days, but that he would be happy to make my acquaintance on his return.

I was in love; for the first time in my life, so I thought. When I had taken her, I had abandoned all my caution and any doubts; she was irresistible, and I did not want to resist. Her vulnerability, which hid so well a terrible animality, fascinated me. I could see nothing but perfection. I wanted her more than anything else in my entire life. I was not a passionate man in my habits, not romantic in my behaviour: I imagine this is obvious already. I had disciplined myself carefully and thoroughly, but nature will out; Venice, and Louise Cort, broke the dam, and a torrent of emotion burst through. The more I possessed her, the more I was prepared to lose myself in that glorious, unmatched feeling and prove it through recklessness.

I thought I was in love because I knew so little. I thought I loved my wife, but Louise showed me that was mere affection, with not even much respect to solidify it. And then I thought I loved Louise, not realising it was simply passion, untrammelled by knowledge. Only when I came to Elizabeth did I finally understand, and by then I was getting old; it was almost too late. She saved me from a dry and empty life. I had looked for someone perfect, but did not realise until then that this was not the point. Only when you can know someone's every fault, failing and weakness and not care do you truly know what love is. Elizabeth certainly has her failings; every single one of them makes me smile with affection, or feel sad for her sufferings. I have known her now for nearly two decades, and every day I know her better, love her more. She is my love and more than that.

But then Louise Cort, the image and remembrance of her, filled my days and my mind, and tinted the city I daily grew to know ever better. I became lover and saviour; my pride and vanity grew as my association with her contrasted my nature all the more powerfully with that of Cort. The practical matters were easily disposed of; there was a man who worked at the hotel I had initially stayed in, Signor Fanzano, who spoke English and who had struck me as a robust, commonsensical fellow, worldly and discreet.

"I have a certain requirement for accommodation," I said, when I discovered him near the kitchens of the hotel. "I need some rooms that are comfortable but private."

He did not ask what I wanted such a thing for, merely applied himself to the matter. "Do I take it you do not wish anyone to know you have these rooms?" he asked.

"Yes. That is the main necessity."

"So not in the centre. Not in San Marco. But, presumably, not too far away either."

"Precisely."

"Do you have any particular price in mind?"

"None."

"And how long would you need this for."

"I do not know. I will happily pay for three months to begin with. They must be furnished and clean."

He nodded. "Leave it to me, Mr. Stone. I will send a message when I have come up with something."

Two days later I received a message to apply to a Signora Murtano in a small street close to San Giovanni è Paolo, near the Fondamenta Nuova. She turned out to be one of Fanzano's relations (although everyone in Venice seems to be a relation of everyone else) with a sitting room and bedroom to rent in a dingy house which had fallen far from its days of glory, if it had ever had any. But it had a fireplace (wood extra, as usual), a separate entrance and only the cruellest luck might have caused me to encounter anyone I knew as I was entering or leaving. The price was exorbitant, not least because I had decided to give Fanzano a handsome reward both for his dispatch and for his discretion. It was a good bargain, as it turned out: it acquired the loyalty of a man who served me well for the next three decades, but nonetheless, I felt at the time that the price of love in Venice was steep.

Still, it was done, and the day after I had made the arrangement, I arranged for Louise to accompany me on another tour of the city. We visited San Giovanni together, and then I showed her my find.

She knew exactly what I intended as we approached the front door, and I was afraid that the practicality of it might affect her sensibilities. And so it did, but only to make her more wild and passionate.

"Don't open the shutters," she said, as I moved to let some light into the rooms so she could see it better. We spent the next two hours exploring a new land far more exotic than a mere city of brick and marble could ever be, even if it does float in the ocean like some fading flower.

She was the most exciting woman I had known. She brought out a recklessness in me that I had never believed existed. Only very occasionally did things go awry between us, then and every time thereafter that she could steal away for an afternoon, an hour, even on one occasion a fumbling, desperate encounter of less than fifteen minutes when she tore at me as her husband waited below. That excited me, thinking of her returning to her duties as a wife, clothes immaculately in order, face calm and showing no sign of the way I had only a few moments before pushed her against the wall and pulled up her dress to make her cry out with pleasure. He could not do that. I half-wanted him to know.

Once she pulled away as I was reaching for her, I grabbed her arm and she turned angrily away, but not before I caught sight of a red weal across her upper arm.

"What's that? How did that happen?"

She shook her head and would not answer.

"Tell me," I insisted.

"My husband," she said quietly. "He thought I had misbehaved."

"Does he suspect that . . ."

"Oh no! He is too stupid. I had not done anything amiss. It does not matter. He gets the desire to hurt, that is all."

"That is all?" I replied hotly. "All? What did he do to you? Tell me."

Again a shake of the head. "I cannot tell you."

"Why not?"

There was a long pause. "Because I am afraid that you might wish to do the same."

CHAPTER 10

And so it went on; we found time to meet more and more often, sometimes every day; she became expert at slipping away unnoticed. We talked little; she became sad when we did, and in any case we had little enough to say. Then I did not think that mattered.

I had forgotten the Marchesa's salon, and groaned with disappointment when I remembered it. Nonetheless, I did my duty, and presented myself on the following Friday evening at seven. I was bathed, as well as is possible in a house with no running water and no easy means of heating what there was, shaved, changed, and felt moderately satisfied with my appearance.

I imagined an evening such as one might encounter in London or Paris; alas, it was very different—remarkably dull for the first part, deeply disturbing for the second. A soirée in Venice is a dreary, weary affair, with about as much joy in it as a Scottish funeral and a good deal less to drink. The spirit of Carnevale has so deserted the city that it requires real effort to remember that it was once famed for its dissolution and carefree addiction to pleasure. That pleasure is now well watered, and joy rationed as though in short supply.

I attended few such events in my time in the city and when I left them I felt I had been there for hours, though my pocket watch said it

was less than half an hour on each occasion. You enter, are presented with
a dry biscuit and a very little wine. Then you sit in a respectful circle
around your hostess until decorum says it is time to leave. I freely admit
I understood little of the conversation, as even the elevated talk in dialect,
but the seriousness of the faces, the lack of laughter, the ponderousness
of the speech all indicated I was missing little.

And it was cold, always. Even if a small fire burned bravely away in a
far corner, its feeble heat did little but tantalise. The women were allowed
to tuck earthenware pots of hot ashes about their persons to give some
minimal warmth, but such things were not allowed to men, who had to
freeze and try to forget the slow progress of icy numbness up the fingers
and arms. Decline had expelled merriment, which belongs to greatness;
the feebler Venice had become, the more humourless were its inhabitants. They were in mourning, perhaps.

The Marchesa was Venetian by marriage only, but had embraced
dullness with the enthusiasm of a convert. She dressed for the occasion
in black with acres of lace and a headdress which almost completely
covered her face, then sat on the settee, quietly greeting those who
arrived, conversing briefly with them and, as far as I could tell, waiting
pointedly until they got up, bowed and left.

At least I was being introduced to Venetian society, although I later
learned that the most respectable had long since refused to enter her
door, and she had equally long ago ceased to invite them. There had been
something of a scandal—the Marchesa, as I have mentioned, was not
Venetian and, even worse, was penniless when she married her husband.

Which was done against the wishes of his family, and that was the
source of the scandal. Especially as the good gentleman—many years her
senior—had died not long after without successfully providing an heir.
This was such a complete failure of responsibility that the Marchesa was
held to be somehow to blame, because someone had to be at fault for
such a lapse in a family which, however impecunious of late, had
successfully negotiated disease, war and ill fortune to survive in an
unbroken line for seven centuries.

Now it was all over; a great name was on the verge of extinction—
already was extinct, in the opinion of many. Bad fortune attends all
families eventually; England itself sees regular snuffings out of great
names; for my part I care not one jot, nor would I if they all disappeared,

although I grant the utility of aristocracy in holding land, for unless that is stable the country cannot be. But, for the most part, three generations is more than enough to complete the ruin of any line. One generation to make the fortune, a second to enjoy it, and a third to dissipate it. In my case, of course—unless my current quest produces an answer I do not expect—not even that is allotted to me. I have no heir. It is something we could not do. All wish to leave something behind them and the vast organisation I have created is not enough. I would have liked a child; as I buried my father, so he should have buried me, and looked after Elizabeth when I was dead. It is our only chance of any immortality, for I do not delude myself that my creations will outlive me for long; the life of companies is very much shorter than the life of families.

That, in truth, was the greatest sadness of our lives together; we were so close. Elizabeth was transformed by joy when she told me she was to have a baby, and tasted true, uncomplicated happiness for the first time. But it was snatched away in the most horrible fashion imaginable. The child was a monster. I can say it now, although for years I banished all thought of him. He had to die; would have anyway. She never saw it, never knew what had really happened, but the sorrow was overwhelming for her. We buried him, and mourned—for him and for what might have been. It was not her fault; of course it wasn't. But she took it on herself, thought that her life had somehow been responsible, that the degradation she had known had suffused her being to such an extent that even the product of her body was corrupted. I thought for a while she might never recover, worried she might go back to those terrible drugs that she had once used so readily when strain and nervousness overtook her. Her life had been hard and dangerous; the syringe of liquid made her forget just enough to keep going.

She came through, of course; she is so very brave. But there were no more children. The doctors said another pregnancy might kill her. I think she would have embraced such a death gladly. She is more precious than all the heirs, all the children in the world. Let everything turn to dust, blow away on the winds! But let me have her by my side until the end. If she left me, I would die myself.

"I do hope you enjoyed my little evening," the Marchesa said when all was, at last, over.

"It was charming, madam," I replied. "Most interesting."

She laughed, the first lighthearted sound to have filled the room all evening. "It was terrible, you mean," she said. "You English are so polite you are ridiculous."

I smiled in an uncertain fashion.

"Yet you behaved yourself, and made a good impression. I thank you for that. You have solidified the reputation of your country as a place of seriousness and dignity, by sitting and saying nothing for such a long time. You may even receive an invitation to some evenings from one or two of my guests."

She noticed the look of dismay which passed over my face.

"Don't worry; on that they are easy enough. They will be quite happy if you do not go."

She stood up and let her dress fall about her. I got up as well.

"And now," she said, "we may begin on the more interesting part of the evening."

My spirits lifted at the very idea.

"We will eat first of all, and then . . ."

"Then what?"

"Ah, for that you must wait and see. But there will be people you know, so you will not be lonely. Have you encountered Mrs. Cort, for example?"

I trust that I did not give myself away, but in some ways she was excessively perceptive. I said I had met Mrs. Cort.

"Poor woman."

"Why do you say that?"

"It is not hard to see that she is unhappy," she said softly. "We have become friends, in a fashion, and she has told me much of her life. The cruel way she was treated by employers in England, the failings of her husband . . ." She put a painted nail to a painted lip to indicate the need for discretion. "She is drawn to the Beyond."

I could have said that, in my experience, her interest in more earthly matters was rather more notable, and that I had no need to be told about discretion, but said nothing.

"But then, this life has little to offer her," she continued.

"She has a husband and a child."

She shook her head in a melodramatic fashion. "If you knew what I know . . ." she said. "But I must not gossip. Let us go in and welcome the guests."

She allowed me to take her arm, and we finally left the cold, draughty salon. I did feel slightly aggrieved that what I had taken to be Louise's confidences to me she had also divulged to the Marchesa, but accepted that desperation does make women tell each other secrets. I put it out of my mind, and felt my mood improving with every step towards the dining room; merely moving began to unfreeze my flesh, although feeling her so close was a little uncomfortable. She wore her usual overpowering perfume and pressed herself against my arm in a manner which was perhaps more intimate than her age made respectable.

In the dining room the candles were lit, and a fire blazed to take off the evening chill—it was warm outside but the houses are so permanently damp they are never truly comfortable at night—and food was waiting to be served. We ate, and as we ate others entered. Marangoni, first of all, then Mr. and Mrs. Cort, and my heart leapt as I saw her, and we exchanged a brief glance of complicity. She held my gaze for only a fraction of a second; no one could have seen it, but it was enough. I wish to be with you, now, she told me, as plainly as anything could. Not with him. I greeted Cort as ordinarily as I could, but my feelings towards him had changed utterly. As much as possible I had taken to avoiding those places where I was likely to run into him; I did not trust myself not to betray some hint of my contempt, as I could not now think of him without remembering Louise's description of what he was truly like. He noticed, I am sure, and was bemused by it, as well he might be, and the temptation to explain welled up in me. For her sake only I controlled myself and made polite conversation for a few moments, although his replies were vague and slow.

Macintyre was not there, of course. He was too solid a man to consider attending such an event, even had he not been offended by the Marchesa's rejection of his wish for rooms that might have made his daughter more comfortable. Longman and Drennan made up the party, so we were seven in all by the time the meal was done—not a Venetian amongst us, I noted.

Then the Marchesa began to talk, all about auras and journeys, souls and spirits, This Side and the Other Side. The room was darkened, the atmosphere became more tense, even though not a single guest was anything other than sceptical about the entire business. Except perhaps Louise, who seemed quite nervous. About Cort I could not tell; he seemed almost drunk, unresponsive to what was going on all around him.

We were going to have to pay for our meal with a visit to the Other Side. It was absurd, of course, but in comparison to a more orthodox Venetian at home, it was positively enticing. Certainly it was different, and I was interested to see how it might be done. What stagecraft was to be deployed, how convincing it would all seem. To begin with, it was hard to stop laughing; I noticed that even Drennan—not a man to give way to raucous amusement—was working hard to prevent his mouth twitching into a grin. The Marchesa adopted an ethereal tone of voice and waved her arms around so the folds of her sleeves billowed out. "Is anybody there? Do you wish to communicate with anyone in this room?" She put her hands to her forehead to indicate concentration; stared wild-eyed at the ceiling to hint at the awesome nature of what was happening; sighed heavily to show spiritual disappointment; groaned softly to prove how hard she was having to work. "Be not afraid, O spirits! Come and deliver thy message." In fact, it was very like a parody of a spiritualist meeting, and hard to avoid giving the table a kick, just to see how she would react.

But then the atmosphere changed. "A message for the American amongst us?" she moaned quietly. "Yes, speak!" And we all looked at Drennan, who seemed not best pleased to be singled out in this fashion.

"Do you know someone called Rose? It is a message from someone called Rose," she intoned, oddly businesslike now, talking in a normal voice which was much more frightening than the obviously fake ethereal tone she had employed up to now. "She wishes to talk to you. She says she loves you still."

This was when the amused air of the audience truly vanished, and utter silence descended. For we were all aware that Drennan's face had turned ashen, and he had stiffened in his chair as though he had received a terrible shock. But we said nothing. "She says she forgives you."

"Really? What for?" Longman asked, his plummy voice—quizzical and normal—sounding entirely out of place and almost shocking. Alas, the spirit was talking to itself, not indulging in a conversation. We got no answer to his question. Whether or not it made any sense to Drennan was unclear; his face was frozen and he was gripping the arms of his chair so tightly that his knuckles had turned white.

"Ah! She is gone!" the Marchesa said. "She cannot stay."

Then a long sigh and theatricality took over once more. We had another five minutes of little smiles, and frowns and "Ohs! and "Ahs!" Then more of the "Come to me, O spirits!" nonsense, before she got down to business again. This time it was Cort who was being contacted, and I knew the moment she began that this was going to cause trouble. Drennan was tough, unemotional, sensible. But even he had been rattled. How Cort—so much more fragile—would react was fairly predictable. He was already looking pale, his gaze glassy, had complained of a headache during the meal, had eaten little. He did, however, drink prodigious quantities of water.

The Marchesa spun it out as well, the spirits coming and going, starting to speak then hesitating, having to be cajoled into giving their message. The buildup of tension was remarkably well done, and it was all too evident that Cort, now bolt upright and sweating, was succumbing to a bad case of nerves.

"Is there someone called William here?" she asked, which did not impress me overmuch, as she knew perfectly well that there was. "There is someone here who wishes to talk to him."

Cort, looking pale, but trying to maintain an expression of manly scepticism, put up his hand.

"Her name is Annabelle," said the Marchesa, reverting to her usual voice. "She is in great distress."

Cort did not reply, but the Marchesa took silence as assent. "It is one who loves you," she said. "She is sad and distressed. She says you know full well what she means."

Cort, again, said nothing, but was breathing heavily, sweating profusely. Then the Marchesa began speaking in voices, a girlish squeak that was quite terrifying to hear even for me. The effect on Cort was indescribable. "William, you are cruel. You dishonour your name. Stop, or he will take your soul. I am the one who gave my life, that you might live."

A savage cry came from Cort's throat at this statement, and he screamed, pushing over his chair and backing, wild-eyed, to the wall. The noise brought the Marchesa from her reverie, and she stared around in confusion—very convincingly, I must say. I do not think she was faking; she clearly did go into some sort of trance. Even I, sceptic though I was, was prepared to grant her this.

Then she focused on the scene her words had created, peering with alarm at the mayhem she had let loose. Cort, hard against the wall, sobbing and moaning; chairs tumbled over the floor as he had struck out at imagined apparitions; Drennan, the only one of us to maintain some self-possession, moving to pick up the candelabrum that had tumbled onto the floor and which threatened to burn the place down; Louise leaping back from the table and standing stock-still, staring at her husband.

"Cort, my dear fellow . . ." Longman began, advancing towards him.

Cort stared in terror at him, rushed to a side table where the sweetmeats and brandies had been placed, and grabbed a sharp knife used for peeling fruit. "Get away from me! Get away! Leave me alone!" The tears flowed down his cheeks as he spoke, but underneath them there was anger as well.

Even though he had certainly never used a knife for such a purpose before, he looked dangerous to me and I was quite prepared to follow his instructions. Longman was made of braver—or more foolish—stuff. Even though Drennan called out a warning, he advanced on the young man, hands held out.

"Calm yourself, dear boy," he said in a kindly fashion. "There's nothing . . ."

He did not finish. Cort backed away towards his wife and began lashing out violently; it was obvious from his expression that he was not feinting. Louise fell back just in time, a long red scratch showing through her sleeve of her green dress. She fell to her knees with a piercing cry, gripping her wounded arm.

"Dear God!" "Stop him!" "Are you mad?" All these conventional phrases burst from people's lips as Cort turned, threw the knife on the floor, and ran for the door, just as Drennan hurled himself forward and brought him to the ground. There was no struggle; Cort made no resistance, but broke down completely, sobbing on the floor as all around looked on at the scene, horrified, appalled, disgusted, embarrassed, according to their temperaments.

Then people reverted to type. Longman started moaning as though he had been stabbed, not Louise; Marangoni became medical and started to treat her, examining her wound with remarkable gentleness. The Marchesa collapsed in a fit of vapours, and Drennan, reassured that the violence had gone out of the man, coaxed Cort to his feet and over to a chair. Only I—not victim, not healer, not a hunter—had no natural role to adopt. I went to Louise to assist, but was pushed back by Marangoni, and I noticed an interested, knowing look on his face as he did so. So I pretended; surveyed the scene, escorted the Marchesa to a chair, and poured her—and myself—a large brandy. Louise was still kneeling on the ground, trembling with fear and shock. But her eyes puzzled me; they were wide, but not with the horror and fear of what had just happened.

The wound was not severe; the knife had penetrated flesh, but the damage was more dramatic than real. Marangoni swiftly bound it up with a napkin, and sat her down with a brandy as well. His pronouncement that she would live—it was obvious, but it is always good to have an expert opinion—lightened the atmosphere considerably. Then he turned his attention to Cort, who had collapsed and was sitting on the floor by the wall, hunched up, his arms around his legs, his head on his knees. I felt, at that moment, total loathing for him.

"He needs to be sedated," he said, "and he needs to sleep. Then we can see what is to be done with him. I assume no one wishes to involve the authorities?"

There was a chorus agreeing that this would be bad idea. Marangoni looked almost satisfied, as though his predictions about Cort had come spectacularly true. But at least he knew what to do, could propose some course of action. He was, suddenly, a commanding presence and I realised for the first time why he was in a position of authority. He was good at it.

He gave his orders. Cort would be taken to his hospital for the night; Drennan would accompany him there, to make sure there were no further problems. In the morning he would begin a proper examination.

"And Mrs. Cort? Someone must escort her home."

"Of course you must not! You must stay with us, my dear Mrs. Cort," Longman said kindly.

"Or here. I have more room," the Marchesa interrupted, seemingly a little annoyed at Longman's offer.

Louise nodded. "Thank you," she whispered. "You are all very kind . . ."

Everybody was attempting to comfort her. Only Marangoni said nothing, but watched her carefully; I could see his eyes flickering to me as well. That annoyed me. Even at a moment like that, all he could do was diagnose, watch and interpret.

"And your son?" he said eventually.

Louise looked at him, and hesitated for a moment. "He is at home with the nurse. No harm will come to him," she said.

And so it was arranged; Longman offered to come back if any further assistance was needed and took his leave. I also made my excuses and retired to my rooms.

An hour later Louise came to me. I was waiting for her. By the time she slipped away at dawn I had told her I would never leave her, that I wanted her forever. That I loved her, would protect her.

CHAPTER 11

I met Signor Ambrosian on his return; the meeting was arranged swiftly, and I waited on him at his bank, close to the Piazza San Marco. Not at all like the palaces of London, where Rothschilds and Barings hold court to Europe and the world. The Banco di Santo Spirito (quite a charming name, I thought, implying that all this usury was to serve God the better rather than to enrich a few families) could not be compared to one of the great houses of London. Nonetheless, it showed ambition in the way it had cleaned out a Renaissance palace, and refitted it in the dark wood and heavy veined marble that was the necessary indicator of solidity in every serious financial centre.

Ambrosian matched his building. Venetians, of all Italians, are the most difficult to read; they do not show their emotions easily. Life is a serious business for them and many have a natural melancholy which makes social intercourse quite difficult. Ambrosian was very reserved; perfectly polite, but with no openness or welcome about him. He was a handsome man, immaculately dressed with a shock of silver grey hair which was matched by a grey necktie and (a foreign touch) large pearl cufflinks, and a vase of silvery flowers on his desk. He was a fine fellow, a shrewd businessman, more than ready to exploit the gullibility of others, as was only proper for a man in his position. I hoped very much that he would be quite merciless in his dealings with me. A great deal depended on it.

I expressed my pleasure in meeting him, and explained my current circumstances. "I have identified several possibilities for investment in Venice, and wish to consult you as to their practicality," I said, once the preliminaries were disposed of. These were the usual sort of thing, questions and answers so that he could determine whether I was someone to take seriously. The name of Joseph Cardano served me well here. He was known amongst financiers throughout much of Europe, even if only by name or reputation. But not outside that circle. The fact that I realised mentioning his name meant something was enough to make Ambrosian accept I was a man of purpose. He slowly became more attentive, more careful in his speech. He was too vain to think he was talking to an equal, but intelligent enough to realise that some consideration was required. That, at present, was exactly as I desired. His triumph at exploiting me would be all the greater, and thus less easy to resist.

For the next hour we discussed the possibility of building a grand hotel in Venice; I laid out my ideas, he explained all the difficulties. Of finding the right land, of getting the workforce, the managers, of raising the necessary capital at the appropriate price for such a venture—who, after all, wanted to come to Venice?

To each problem I proposed an answer. Build on the Lido, not in the centre of Venice. Bring in all the architects, engineers and surveyors from France and England, if necessary. Make use of my skills—I exaggerated a little here—and Cardano's contacts to form a company that could raise the money in London. I had thought it all through; my answers were considered and thorough.

"And why do you need me, then?" he asked with a smile.

"Because it couldn't be done without you," I said, entirely truthfully. "The money must flow into Venice, and payments must be made here. It would need established banking facilities. I have been here long enough to suspect that dealing with the authorities is a quagmire. Suitable land cannot be found without local knowledge and influence, and I have discovered that you are the most highly regarded man of finance in the region."

He acknowledged my discernment. He was genuinely interested; interested enough to start questioning what, precisely, there was of profit in this project for him. That, I pointed out, rather depended on how much money his bank was prepared to put in. This was going to be expensive and the profits would be several years down the road.

"Ah, you English," he said. "You do like to think on a grand scale, do you not? Now we Venetians would naturally think of several dozen small establishments, each one to be erected when the previous one was paid off. It is an interesting idea. Even more interesting is why you don't worry that I might go ahead without you. You need me, but do I need you?"

"Build something on this scale, without being able to raise capital in

London? Find the skilled workforce scattered across Europe? Persuade companies like Cook's to run excursions to Venice and stay in your hotel?"

"True enough. If you can do all of these things. I have learned that the English promise more than they deliver, sometimes."

"For example?"

"We have lent a substantial amount of money to an Englishman," he said. "Who, like you, promised wonderful things. But so far has delivered none of them."

"I have met Mr. Macintyre," I said, "if that is who you refer to."

"He is a scoundrel and a rogue."

"Really? I find him to be very straightforward."

"Far from it. We learned—this was only after he took our money—that the only reason he is in Venice is because he would be thrown into gaol should he ever have the temerity to return to England."

"You astound me." And that was a genuine statement; I found it momentarily difficult to believe we could be talking about the same person. I would have wagered a very considerable amount of money that Macintyre was entirely honest.

"It seems that he embezzled a very substantial sum from his employers, and absconded with it. It is only the fact that he owes us money which stops us from sending him packing."

"Are you sure of this?"

"Quite sure. Naturally, once we learned of it, we declined to advance him any more and I now have grave doubts whether we will ever see our money returned. So you see, a proposal from an unknown Englishman . . ."

"I quite understand. Naturally, any collaboration between us would require total trust, but I am confident I would be able to satisfy your concerns with no difficulty. And, as it is a matter of patriotic pride, I will willingly offer to provide assistance over the matter of Mr. Macintyre. How much does he owe you?"

"I believe about five hundred pounds sterling."

Interesting, I thought to myself. I knew quite well he had put in considerably less than that. This was very hopeful.

"Very imaginative, I must say," I continued. "Few people would have been prepared to take such a risk."

He waved a hand. "If his machine works, then it has obvious

possibilities. If it doesn't, of course, then that is different. And the constant delays and excuses make me concerned. Consequently . . ."

". . . another proposal from another Englishman does not fill your heart with gladness."

He smiled.

"In that case," I continued, "I will make a down payment to acquire your trust. Let me buy Mr. Macintyre's debt from you. Pay it off on his behalf. Should we come to a later agreement on this project for a hotel we will be able, I am sure, to adjust the matter then. I cannot have you thinking that all the English are scoundrels. Even if some undoubtedly are. If you wish, I will reach an agreement now."

Ambrosian was much too cautious a man to accept. He looked almost shocked. Well, not quite, but he did have the air of someone who is being taken for a simpleton. He did not object to me trying, of course, and he knew perfectly well that I knew he would not accept the offer.

"I can see no reason to sell what may turn out to be a fine stream of future profits," he said reproachfully. "Particularly as my investment gives me complete rights to the machine."

"Well, I cannot blame you," I said with a smile to indicate I understood perfectly well. "None the less, my interest remains. Should you change your mind . . ."

I left, feeling very thoughtful. My offer to acquire Macintyre's debt had had the desired effect, I thought; Ambrosian was prepared to take me seriously. It would have been a different matter had he suddenly accepted the proposal. The last thing I wanted was to spend money on a machine that might well be useless. If that was the case, he could keep it. But if it did work, he would keep it. Should the trials be a success, he would certainly refuse to put in any more money, call in the debt and take full possession of the patent. Macintyre would have nothing more to do with it, except, perhaps, as an employee, a declared bankrupt who would have to work for whatever pittance he was paid.

A pity the machine wasn't a complete disaster, I thought. That would not be good for Macintyre, but at least he would have the pleasure of realising that Ambrosian had lost his money as well. Small compensation, and I didn't think it would give him much joy. Only financiers think like that. But . . .

It made me think, though, and as I walked across the Piazza San Marco, I ran through all the possibilities in my mind.

I stopped, and smiled happily at a group of urchins throwing stones at a washing line, seeing if they could knock a sparrow off it. That was it, of course. The only problem was how to organise it.

CHAPTER 12

Anyone reading this might be surprised that I was not more concerned at Ambrosian's assertion that Macintyre was some sort of crook. Often enough such characteristics are something of an impediment to good business. But not always, and not if the scoundrel is in no position to do you harm. I had not the slightest intention of giving Macintyre any money in a manner I could not control. He could not abscond with what he did not have. Besides, such people can be useful, if they are working for you, rather than against you. The past life of Xanthos, for example, is not something I would wish to know too much about—although when he came knocking at my door I did discover that it would be unwise ever to send him anywhere controlled by the Sultan, as it would be a long time before he would be let out of gaol. But now his devious skills are employed to my advantage, and he has been a good and loyal employee, up until recently.

So Ambrosian's beliefs about Macintyre did not worry me much. But it would be wrong to say I was not intrigued, and I was impatient that my dear friend Cardano, to whom I had written some time previously, had not yet replied. Until he did, there was very little I could do. I could find old newspapers in Venice, some basic reference books, but little more; the sort of information I required could only be found in the dining rooms and boardrooms of the City of London, and then it would be available only to those who knew how to ask.

So I had to wait, and become a proper tourist for once, and indulge my ever-growing passion. Four more days, in fact, before the letter finally reached me—wonderful days, spent in the autumnal warmth, and often enough with Louise, for the more rendezvous I had with her the more I wanted. After the events at the Marchesa's salon, we threw off all caution and discretion. I began buying her presents, we walked together in the city, were seen together. It made me proud and uncomfortable at the same time—I once had to tell her to be more discreet with her husband.

"I will leave him now, because of you. Now I know what it is really to love someone, I cannot stay anymore. We can be together forever, then," she said, turning to look me in the eyes. "We can be like this forever. Just you and me."

"What about your son?"

She made a gesture of disgust. "He can have him. He is not my child; I merely bore him. There is nothing of me in him at all. He will be like his father; weak, useless."

"He's only four." She had spoken with a harshness I had never heard in her before. There was real cruelty in her words and they disturbed me.

I must have reacted, for she instantly changed. "Oh, I love him, of course I do. But I am no good for him. I don't understand him."

Then she put her arms around me once more, and changed the subject totally for an hour. But I left our rooms with an uneasy feeling that afternoon; it faded soon enough, but did not disappear entirely.

It also changed the way we were together; Louise did not refer to leaving her husband again, but more and more often the conversation came round to her desire to be with me. I could understand why her life was hellish, and why she so desperately sought a means of escaping. When I considered the weals and cuts, Cort's behaviour at the séance, his hallucinations, the indignities and humiliations she endured when no one was there to see, it was hardly surprising she clung to me.

And I was besotted with her. So why did I not leap at the chance to capture her forever? It could have been done. A separation of some sort from my wife was possible, messy and unpleasant though it might be. But Louise and Venice were linked too closely together. Love and city were intermingled; I could not imagine one without the other, and I think my hesitations and doubts were linked to my sluggish awareness of my growing immobility. The Marchesa was right; Venice was like an octopus, which slowly and stealthily entangled the unwary in its tentacles until it was too late. Longman would never leave; Cort might not either; in other Englishmen I met in that period I learned to recognise the slightly vacant look of the entranced, the people hypnotised by the light, who had lost their willpower, voluntarily given it up, like the followers of Odysseus on the island of the lotos-eaters.

They did not enter a state of bliss by so doing; Venice does not offer happiness in exchange for servitude. The opposite, rather: melancholy and sadness are its gifts; it allows the sufferers to be all too aware of their lassitude and inability to leave. It taunts them with their weakness, but still will not let them go.

Some were immune; Drennan seemed unaffected, for example. Nor did it have any effect on Macintyre, because he scarcely knew where he was. For him Venice was merely the place where his workshop was; he had sacrificed his will to his machinery already; there was nothing for the city to take.

And some were driven into madness. Cort deteriorated rapidly after his explosion at the séance; I saw little enough of him, indeed I tried to avoid him, but could not but notice how he looked more haggard by the day, heard reports that he was receiving visitations from his phantom more often. He worked obsessively, but got nothing done; until then he had actually been making progress. Macintyre's internal buttressing was all but complete. But now most of his workforce abandoned him as his behaviour became so erratic they did not want to come near him. So he worked alone, furiously making drawings that no one would execute, ordering materials that lay in the courtyard untouched until he sent them back and began an argument with the supplier.

"Is Cort insane?" I asked Marangoni. I fully anticipated his reply, and was astonished by what he in fact said.

"Well, do you know," the doctor replied in his heavy accent, putting the tips of his fingers together to look more professional, "I do not think he is. Unbalanced, certainly. But I do not think he is insane. His mother's name was Annabelle," he said, in total breach of the normal notions of discretion. "She died when he was born, and he worships her memory. The idea that she was displeased with him shook him to the core. He told me this a couple of days ago."

"You're still seeing him?"

"Oh, yes. It is vital considering his state of mind. He was in the hospital for the better part of a week, and I thought it a good idea to get him to come for a regular chat. He finds it peaceful just to sit in the sun looking at the lagoon, undisturbed. He goes away calm and contented. Normally. Sometimes we find him a bed here. We have a guesthouse, you know. A strange arrangement, but the monks were very hospitable, and for some reason we keep up the tradition."

"Have you worked out what happened at the séance? Do you think the Marchesa did it deliberately?"

"I'm sure she is entirely genuine in her beliefs," he said with an indulgent smile at the foolishness of women unaccustomed to the rigours of the scientific method. "The trouble is she is in many ways a very stupid woman. She will hear something then forget it entirely. She has a very poor memory. But it remains in her mind, and when it pops up again, she believes it is a spirit which has told her. I'm sure she was told that Cort's mother's name was Annabelle, but forgot it. Then it came back to her."

"You seem to think he will recover."

Marangoni shrugged. "That depends on what you mean by recovery, of course. If all matters which might disturb him were removed, I dare say he would soldier on. The trouble is that this is unlikely. He should return to England immediately. If he stays here, then perhaps not."

"But is he safe? His behaviour—"

"—is the behaviour of a madman. I grant you that. But does that mean he is insane? I have already told you how many people—women especially—are mad while showing none of the symptoms of madness. So we must equally consider the possibility that someone who behaves as though he were mad might, in fact, not be." He smiled.

I stared, quite uncomprehendingly, at him.

"Perhaps his behaviour is a perfectly reasonable response to his current situation," Marangoni suggested quietly. I knew exactly what he meant.

"He stabbed his wife with a knife. Are you telling me she deserved it?"

"Oh no. I very much doubt anyone deserves to be stabbed. He may—at that particular moment—have considered she deserved it; that by striking at her, he was warding off the torments he was experiencing. Of course, this was heightened by the drugs."

"What?"

"Oh, you people!" he said with exasperation. "You really notice nothing, do you? Did you not see the glassy eyes, the sweating, the slurred expressions, the way his movements became more uncontrolled and exaggerated?"

"I thought he'd been drinking."

"He drank nothing but water. Opium, my dear Stone. Classic symptoms."

"Cort is an opium addict?"

"Dear me, no. But he had undoubtedly consumed some of the drug shortly before he arrived. It is easy enough to come by. You can buy it in most pharmacies."

"He told you this?"

"No. He denied it absolutely. Nevertheless, he was certainly under its influence."

"So, he's lying. Perhaps he is ashamed."

"Perhaps he was unaware of it," Marangoni said absently. "Not that it matters. He will get no more of it while he is in my care."

"What do you think of Marangoni?" I asked when I next saw Louise.

"Ugh, disgusting," was her reply. "Do you know, he tried to seduce me, that dirty little man? I was so ashamed, I have never told a soul. But you I can tell. I know you will not hold it against me. Just don't listen to anything he says about me; I'm sure it would be nasty and cruel."

"Of course not," I said. "Why should I, when I seduced you myself?"

"But with you I wanted to be seduced," she said. "I would sacrifice anything for you. I even accept," she said, her voice trembling, "that you will sacrifice nothing for me."

"But you know . . ."

"It doesn't matter," she said with a sigh, looking away from me. "I will be your mistress and one day you will leave me. It is enough."

"Don't say that."

"But it's true. You know it is. And when you do leave me, I will kill myself."

She said it seriously, and looked steadily at me as she spoke.

"Why would I want to live without you? To spend the rest of my life with a disgusting husband and a snivelling child, to be tormented day and night by them? If only I could be free of them! All I have that is worthwhile is you."

"That cannot be true."

"Oh, believe that, then," she said, turning away. "Believe that, then you will be able to leave me with a clear conscience. I do not wish you to suffer as well. You do not love me, I know. Not really."

"But I do."

Then prove it. She did not say these words; she did not need to.

CHAPTER 13

Two days after this encounter, Cardano's letter—his first letter, I should say—arrived, and the last piece of my plan took place. His news explained much; after the normal sort of chatter about the markets, he got onto the subject of Mr. Macintyre. Here his information was surprising. I had asked whether anything was known about Macintyre's reputation. This was not the sort of thing that a man like Cardano would know, but it was easy enough to discover. I thought I would hear merely that Macintyre was a decent, competent, well-respected engineer of skill. Until my interview with Ambrosian I had expected nothing more.

Cardano's letter was very much more informative than that, however.

Fortunately, the annual meeting of Laird's took place yesterday afternoon, and I went to it; I have some shares in the company (so do you, if you recall). Normally these meetings are worse than useless, but it is good to show one's face occasionally. I asked Mr. Joseph Benson, the general manager, about your Mr. Macintyre and got a most surprising response. He looked rather shocked, and disturbed that I should mention the name. Why was I asking? What had I heard? He was very worried indeed.

I found this perplexing, of course, and kept at him until he was sufficiently reassured to tell me the entire tale—one which you had best keep to yourself.

Macintyre was extraordinarily able, and remarkably pig-headed, it seems. He would never listen to advice, constantly having disputes with anyone who disagreed with him, and was, all in all, well-nigh impossible to work with. It seems he was always coming up with novel ideas, and would work on them in the company's time, using the material and resources which should have been used for something else.

That is beside the point, which is that he was a man who could turn his hand to any engineering problem. If there was anything which defeated all others, Macintyre would be called in, and would find the solution. He was, in other words, both impossible and indispensable at the same time. I do not know if

you remember the *Alabama*? It was a Laird's ship which ended
up in Confederate hands. As it caused a great deal of damage to
Northern shipping, the Yankees were extremely angry about it,
and are still trying to blame Laird's and the British Government.
Laird's maintain it was nothing to do with them; they sold the
ship in good faith, and could hardly have guessed it was going to
be fitted out with weapons by the owners, then sold to the
Confederates . . .

   Except that the man who fitted the ship out was your Mr.
Macintyre, who was—until he vanished from the face of the
earth—living proof of Laird's complicity. Or should I say
duplicity? It doesn't matter. In order to avoid recriminations, he
was given a large amount of money and told to make himself
scarce. When asked, Laird's now say officially that he disappeared a few years ago and stole money before he left. They are
as angry at him as anyone else, and in public demand his arrest
and return . . .

I found all this fascinating, and at least it explained how the story of dis-
honesty had come to hang over Macintyre's reputation. The story of the
Alabama is little known now, but it had a certain currency in its day; a
wooden-hulled, thousand-ton barque, commissioned by the Confederacy
in 1861. The Unionists heard of the purchase and tried to stop it. Laird's
was caught between its customer and the wishes—however reluctant—
of the British Government to maintain a strict neutrality in the terrible
Civil War.

   Strict, but in my opinion, foolish, for the refusal of Britain to allow its
industry to supply both sides led to the Americans supplying themselves,
and thus building up the industries which now challenge our own. A
more enlightened policy would have supplied both evenhandedly, thus
draining the United States of gold, and shackling their industry; with a
little wisdom and ruthlessness Britain could readily have reestablished its
predominant interest on that continent, and been ready to congratulate
whichever side emerged victorious.

   But the moralists triumphed, and from that triumph will come,
eventually, the eclipse of Britain's industrial might. Be that as it may,
Laird's (which was in need of commissions) found a way around the
problem by using some other company as a go-between. How could we

prevent our client reequipping the vessel and selling it on? they asked when the matter was raised in Parliament. We build ships, we do not oversee their use as well.

A clever move but one which the victorious Unionists would not accept; they began to pursue Britain for liability for losses caused by the ship, and only settled the matter sometime after I returned to England from Venice. The Government and the insurance companies eventually paid out some four million pounds—for by the time she was caught off France in 1864, the *Alabama* had sunk a fearsome amount of Unionist shipping. But in 1867 the Americans (a people prone to extravagance in both speech and action) were insisting that anything less than two thousand million pounds compensation would be an insult to their national pride, and threatening all manner of reprisals if they didn't get it.

I was thrust into Macintyre's company once more a few days after I received this interesting sideline on his past life, when he invited me to come along for the first real test of his torpedo. I was highly honoured; no other Englishperson was even told this great moment in his life was taking place, but I had suggested that he try it out secretly first of all, rather than with the bankers there. What if you try it and there is some small hitch? That could ruin everything, I suggested. Best to have a test run away from prying eyes. If all goes well, then you can repeat the experiment in front of the bankers. It was good advice, and he realised it. The date was set, and I was—rather shyly—invited. I was touched by the gesture.

So, one cold morning a few days later, I found myself on a wooden barge, wrapped up warmly against the mist which hung over the lagoon like a depressing shroud. We were far away from land, to the north of the city, with a couple of his workmen for company. The barge owner had been told he was not wanted, and the previous evening the torpedo had been loaded in secret onto the deck and covered with tarpaulins.

It was a sailing barge, and there was a flurry of anxiety that there wasn't going to be enough wind, but eventually, at half past four in the morning, the bargee declared that we could go, and we set off—very slowly indeed, the boat creeping along at such a pace that an hour later we were still just off the Salute. By six we were in the dead waters north of Murano, where the lagoon was shallow and few boats, only those with the most shallow of draughts, ever ventured. It was a magical experience in a way: to sit in the prow of the vessel smoking a cigar as the sun rose, and wild ducks flew low over the marshes, seeing Torcello in the distance with its great ruined tower, and far away the occasional sail—red or yellow—of one of the sailing ships that endlessly crisscrossed the lagoon.

Macintyre was not the best company, continually fussing over his invention, unscrewing panels and peering inside with an old oil lamp held over him by Bartoli so he could see what he was doing. Adding a little oil here, tightening a bolt there, tapping an instrument and grumbling under his breath.

"Nearly ready?" I asked when I had seen enough of birds and got up to walk back to the middle of the ship.

He grunted.

"I will take that to mean 'No, it needs to be stripped down and rebuilt entirely,'" I said. "Macintyre, the damned thing is either going to work, or not. Bung it in the water and see what happens."

Macintyre glowered at me.

"But it's true," I protested. "I've been watching you. You aren't doing anything important. You're not making any real changes. It's as ready as it will ever be."

Bartoli nodded behind him, and lifted his eyes to heaven in despair. Then Macintyre sagged as he accepted that, finally, he could do no more; that it was time to risk his machine in the water. More than that: to risk his life, for everything that made him what he was he had embedded into the metalwork of his torpedo. If it failed, he failed.

"How does it move, anyway?" I asked. "I see no funnel or anything."

There was nothing quite like a stupid remark to rouse him. Immediately, he straightened up and stared at me with withering contempt. "Funnel?" he snarled. "Funnel? You think I've put a boiler and a stack of coal in it? Or maybe you think I should have put a mast and a sail on as well?"

"I was only asking," I said. "It has a propeller. What makes it turn?"

"Air," he replied. "Compressed air. There's a reservoir with air at three hundred and seventy pounds per square inch pressure. Just here." He tapped the middle of the torpedo. "There are two eccentric cylinders with a sliding vane to divide the volume into two parts. In this fashion the air pressure causes direct rotation of the outer cylinder; this is coupled directly to the propeller, you see. That way, it can travel underwater, and can be ready for launch at all times, at a moment's notice."

"If it works," I added.

"Of course it will work," he said scornfully. "I've had it running dozens of times in the workshop. It will work without fail."

"So? Show me," I said. "Chuck it over the side and show me."

Macintyre straightened up. "Very well. Watch this." He summoned Bartoli and the others, and they began to put ropes round the body of the torpedo, which was then rolled carefully to the side of the boat, and lowered gently into the water. The ropes were then removed, and the torpedo floated, three-quarters submerged, occasionally bumping softly against the side of the boat. Only a single, very thin, piece of rope held it close by, attached to a small pin at the rear. That, it seemed, was the firing mechanism.

Macintyre began rubbing his chin with anxiety. "No," he said. "It's not right. I think I'd better take it out and check it over again. Just to make sure . . ."

Bartoli began to shake his head in frustration. "Signor Macintyre, there is nothing left to check. Everything is just fine."

"No. Just to be on the safe side. It will only take an hour or . . ."

Then I decided to intervene. "If I may be of assistance . . ." I said.

Macintyre turned to look at me. I grabbed the thin piece of rope in his hand and gave a sharp tug.

"What the hell do you think you're doing?" he screamed in shock. But it was too late. With a quiet ping, the pin popped out of the torpedo, which immediately gave off a whirring, gurgling noise as the propeller began to spin at high speed.

"Whoops," I said. "Sorry. Oh, look, off it goes."

True enough. The torpedo accelerated at an impressive speed in a straight line at a slight angle to the boat.

"Damned interfering fool," Macintyre muttered as he pulled out his watch and started staring at the torpedo as it grew smaller and smaller in the water. "My God, it works! It really works. Look at it go!"

It was true. Macintyre told me later (he spent much of the trip home poring over a piece of paper, working out his calculations) that his torpedo accelerated to a speed of about seven knots within a minute, that it travelled with only a 5 per cent deviation from a perfectly straight line, and that it was capable of going at least fourteen hundred yards before running out of power.

At least? Yes. I had been a little hasty in my desire to force Macintyre to get on with the business of testing. I should have made sure there was nothing in the way first of all.

"Oh, my God," Bartoli said as he looked out, appalled. The torpedo, still clearly visible, was now at maximum speed, all five hundred pounds of it, travelling a few inches underwater, heading straight for a felucca, one of the little vessels used often enough for fishing, or transporting food around the lagoon. The crew could be seen quite clearly, sitting in the stern by the rudder, or leaning on the side, admiring the view as the sail billowed in the light wind.

A peaceful scene; one that painters travelled many hundreds of miles to capture on canvas, to sell to romantically inclined northerners desperate for a bit of Venice on their walls.

"Look out!" Macintyre screamed in horror, and we all joined in, jumping up and down and waving. The sailors on the felucca looked up, grinned, and waved back. Crazy foreigners. Still, a pleasant morning, why not be friendly?

"How much gunpowder is in that thing?" I asked as I jumped up and down.

"None. I put fifty-four pounds of clay in the head instead. And it won't use gunpowder. It will use guncotton."

"Yes, you told me."

"Well, remember it. Anyway, I can't afford to waste it."

"That's lucky."

The felucca kept going, the torpedo as well; it was going to be a close-run thing. Another quarter of a knot and the boat would pass over the torpedo's course entirely and it would miss. All would be well, if only the boat would go faster or the torpedo would slow down.

Neither obliged. It could have been worse, so I assured Macintyre later. Had the torpedo hit amidships, then something of that weight and that speed would undoubtedly have stove a hole right through the thin planking, and it would have been hard to pretend that a fourteen-foot steel tube wedged in their boat was nothing to do with us.

But we were lucky. The boat was almost out of the torpedo's path; almost but not quite. Macintyre's invention clipped the end of it; even at a distance of four hundred yards, we heard the cracking, breaking sound as the rudder gave way, and the boat lurched under the impact. The sails lost the wind and began flapping wildly, and the crew, a moment ago waving cheerfully and idling their time away, launched into stunned action, trying to bring their vessel back under control and work out what on earth had happened. The torpedo, meanwhile, went silently on its way, and it was clear no one on the felucca had seen it.

Bartoli was brilliant, I must say. Naturally, we steered towards the stricken boat, and he had a quick word with the crew. "Never seen anything like that before," Bartoli called in Venetian. "Amazing."

"What was it? What happened?"

"A shark," he replied sagely. "Really big one, travelling fast. I saw it clearly. It must have clipped the end of your boat, bitten the rudder off. Never seen a beast like that in the lagoon before."

The crew was delighted; this was much better than rotten wood or some ordinary accident. They would dine out on this for weeks. Bartoli, after expressing surprise that they hadn't noticed the fin sticking out of the water, offered assistance, which made Macintyre fretful. He wanted to go and get his torpedo back; he had no real idea what its range was, and it could be anywhere by now. It was his most treasured possession, and he did not want it to fall into the hands of some spy or rival, for he was convinced that all the governments and companies of the world were desperately trying to steal his secrets.

He need not have worried; Bartoli was too skilled for that. He knew quite well that no Venetian sailor would submit to being towed ig-nominiously into harbour by a bunch of foreigners. They were duly grateful, but turned the offer down. Then they rigged up a makeshift rudder from an oar, poking over the back rather as on a gondola, and after half an hour of enjoyable conversation, they set off again.

We all—and Macintyre in particular—breathed a sigh of relief when the felucca disappeared into the early morning mist; then we turned to the business of recovering his invention. I thought that the time had come to apologise.

"I think I had better find some way of compensating those sailors as well," I ended. "I imagine repairing that rudder will cost something."

But no apologies were really necessary; Macintyre was transformed. From the anxiety-ridden fusspot of an hour or so ago, he was like a man who had just been told he had inherited a fortune. He positively beamed at me, his eyes sparkling with excitement.

"Did you see it?" he exclaimed. "Did you see it? Straight as an arrow.

It works, Stone! It works! Exactly as I said. If there'd only been some explosives in the nose I could have blown that boat to kingdom come. I could have sunk a battleship."

"It would have been difficult to blame that on a shark," I pointed out. But Macintyre waved my objections aside and ran up to the prow of the boat with a pair of field glasses.

We searched for about an hour for, although Macintyre was convinced it had gone as straight as an arrow, in fact it had a tendency to veer to the left a little. Not by much, but over several hundred yards, this made quite a difference. Also it had settled low in the water, only just visible on the surface, and that also made the search more difficult.

But we tracked it down eventually, embedded in a mudbank in water too shallow for us to approach in the boat.

"Now what do we do?" I asked as we gazed at it, some twenty yards away from us off our starboard bow, not daring to go any closer lest our boat also got wedged in the mud.

We spent half an hour throwing a hook tied to a rope towards it, hoping to hook the thing and then drag it towards us, but with no luck whatsoever. There was no point waiting for the tide to change, as there was none.

"Can anyone swim?" I asked.

A general shaking of heads, which I found extraordinary. It didn't surprise me that Macintyre couldn't, but I was amazed that none of his employees—brought up surrounded by water as they were—could either. I wondered how many Venetians drowned every year if this was normal amongst them.

"Why?"

"Well," I said, now suddenly reluctant, "I thought—just an idea, you know—that one of us could try to swim over to it. The water might be deep enough."

"If you got stuck in the mud you'd never get out again," Bartoli said. I didn't like that "you."

"Good point," I said.

But Macintyre thought my untimely death would be a worthwhile price to pay. "Take two ropes," he said. "One for the torpedo and another for you. Then we could pull both out. You can swim, can't you?"

"Me?" I said, wondering whether my father would have considered lying justifiable in these particular circumstances. On the whole he disapproved strongly of the practise. "Well, a little."

"Excellent," Macintyre said, his worries all over. "And I am deeply grateful to you, my dear sir. Deeply grateful. Although as it's your fault that the torpedo is there in the first place . . ."

Point taken. Very reluctantly I began to take off my clothes and peered over the side. I would have to let myself into the water very slowly, for fear of sinking down and becoming embedded in mud before I even started. It was cold and the water looked even colder.

Bartoli tied two ropes around my waist and grinned at me. "Don't worry," he said. "We will not leave you there."

And then I lowered myself gently into the water. It was even colder than I had feared, and I began shivering immediately. But, nothing to be done now; using a gentle breast stroke, I set off for the torpedo, trying to keep my legs as high in the water as possible.

The only danger came when I got close to the torpedo and had to stop. Then the water was only about three feet deep and my feet had slid across the mud several times; as I manoeuvred into position, I had to push down and I felt them slip into the mud properly. When I tried to hang on to the torpedo and drag them out, I realised they were stuck hard.

"I can't move," I shouted to the boat.

"Tie the rope onto the torpedo! Stop pushing it further into the mud," Macintyre shouted back.

"What about me?"

"We'll pull you out afterwards."

Well, thank you, I thought bitterly. Still, he was right. That was what I was there for. I was so cold now that I could barely untie the knot, let alone push the rope through the propeller casing and tie it securely. My teeth were chattering uncontrollably by the time I was finally done.

"Excellent," Macintyre shouted. "Pull away."

It took some effort by the people on the boat, but eventually the torpedo began to move, and once the suction was broken it slipped rapidly past me and into deeper water. Macintyre was all but dancing up and down in joy.

"Now get me out of here!" I shouted.

"Oh, very well," came the reply, and I felt the rope tighten around my chest as they began to tug. Nothing happened. I moved a few inches, but the moment the pressure was relaxed, I sank back down even deeper than before. I was now getting frightened.

"Don't stop!" I shouted. "I'm going lower. Get me out of here!"

Nothing happened. I glanced round and saw Macintyre staring at me and stroking his chin. Then he talked to Bartoli. For a fraction of a second I was convinced he was going to abandon me there.

But no. Although what he planned was nearly worse. As he explained afterwards, the suction from the mud was too strong for them. All they were doing was pulling the boat itself into danger. They needed more power.

I saw Bartoli pulling up the sails, and Macintyre pulling up the anchor, and one of his men manning the oar to turn the ship. I realised with horror what they had in mind. They were setting sail, and were going to use the full power of the boat and the wind to try and dislodge me.

"You'll pull me apart!" I yelled. "Don't do that."

But Macintyre just waved cheerfully. The boat began to move, and I felt the rope tighten once more, until it was as taut as a bowstring and the pressure on my chest, the rubbing of the rough cord, unbearably painful. It was all I could do not to scream. I certainly remember thinking that if I was still in one piece at the end of this experiment I would thump Macintyre on the nose.

It got more and more painful; I could feel my body stretching as the mud refused to let me go, and that seemed to go on forever. Then, with the most disgusting slurping sound, it gave me up; my legs and feet were belched out of the mud in a huge cloud of foul-smelling water, and I floated free, trailing behind the boat as it headed towards Venice.

It took another five minutes to haul me in, and by then I could not move; I was shivering so badly I couldn't control my arms or legs; my chest had the beginnings of a bright red weal across it, my spine felt as though it was several inches longer than it had been, and my legs still smelled unspeakably foul.

And Macintyre paid me not the slightest bit of attention. Instead, he was busily clucking over his lump of iron while Bartoli wrapped me in a blanket, and brought me some grappa. I drank it from the bottle, then rolled over in the blanket until I began to recover.

"It's fine," Macintyre said, as though certain that his torpedo would be uppermost in my mind. "No damage at all. Although the cowling bent from the way you attached the rope to it."

I ignored him. He didn't notice.

"But no matter. That can be hammered out. Apart from that, it is in perfect condition. All I have to do now is clean it, dry it and make a few minor adjustments and it will be ready for the big test next week."

"May I say that I would not have cared had the damnable thing sunk to the bottom of the lagoon, never to be seen again?"

Macintyre looked at me in astonishment. "But, my dear Stone," he cried, "just look at you! I am so sorry, I haven't thanked you enough. What you did just now was generous. Generous and a mark of true kindness. Thank you, from the bottom of my heart."

I was somewhat mollified by this, but only somewhat. I kept on drinking the grappa, and slowly felt some warmth creep back into my body. Everyone made a fuss over me, said how wonderful I had been. That helped. If one is to behave selflessly and courageously it is pleasing to have it recognised. I wrapped myself in blankets and encomiums all the way home, and lay there dreaming of Louise by my side. I even felt almost content by the time the boat finally docked just by the workship three hours later. But I did not help unload the torpedo. I had had enough. I left them to it, Macintyre shouting, everyone else working, and walked back to my lodgings. There I demanded a bath with limitless hot water immediately, and would not take no for an answer. I had to wait another hour before it was prepared, by which time everyone in the house had been told that the idiot Englishman had fallen into the lagoon. Well, what do you expect from foreigners?

CHAPTER 14

The next morning, a note was delivered to my room, from Marangoni, of all people. "I stand corrected," he wrote, and I could almost see the smile on his face as I read. "It seems that Mr. Cort's Venetian really does exist. Come and meet him, if you wish; he is a fascinating creature."

I had as leisurely a breakfast as Venetian habits allow and decided that, as I had nothing better to do that morning, I would take up the invitation and go to San Servolo. The island lies between San Marco and the Lido, a handsome-enough place from a distance; you would never

know that it was an asylum for the insane—certainly it is very unlike the
grim prisons which England was then throwing up all over the country to
incarcerate the lunatics which all societies produce in abundance.
Marangoni hated the place, and would have preferred a modern,
scientific establishment, but I think his real objection stemmed from his
determination to detach his profession from any taint of religiosity.
Otherwise, the old Benedictine monastery would have been a beautiful
place to spend his time. Apart from the inmates: there is something about
madness which casts a pall on the loveliest of buildings; the clouds always
seem to hover above such places, no matter how brightly the sun shines.
And, of course, no one spends much money on lunatics; they get the
leftovers, after the more astute and agile have taken what they want. San
Servolo was in a pitiable state, crumbling, overgrown and depressing. The
sort of place you wish to get away from; the sort of place that might easily
send even a perfectly healthy person insane.

Marangoni had colonised the best part for himself, the abbot's
lodgings were now his office, with remarkable painted ceilings, and large
windows that opened onto the lagoon. It was a room that could make you
see the virtues of a contemplative life, though not those of a custodian of
the insane. Marangoni was a thief in someone else's property and looked
it. He would never exude the necessary style to seem as though he
belonged there. He was a bureaucrat in a dark suit: the room hated him,
and he hated it back.

"Pleasant enough now, but you should be here in January," he said
when I admired the frescoes. "The cold gets into your bones. Damp; no
amount of fires make any difference at all. I have learned to write with
gloves on. When November comes I start dreaming of applying for jobs in
Sicily."

"But then you would fry in summer."

"True enough. And there is work that needs to be done here."

"Tell me about this man."

He smiled. "He was arrested by the police a few days ago, and was
passed on to me yesterday."

"What had he done?"

"Nothing, really, but he was stopped for questioning and asked for his
name. He was then arrested for insulting a policeman by making frivolous
remarks."

"What sort?"

"He insisted, and keeps on insisting, that his name is Gian Giacamo Casanova."

I snorted. Marangoni looked serious as he read from his police report.

"He was born, so he says, in Venice in 1725, which makes him now—what?—one hundred and forty-two years old. A good age. I must say he is in a very good state, considering. Personally, I would have guessed him to be no more than seventy. Possibly nearer sixty."

"I see. And you told him that you did not believe this?"

"Certainly not. That is not a very sensible procedure. If you do that, then the patient insists, and you get into a childish game. Am. Aren't. Am. Aren't. Ten times am. A hundred times aren't. You know the sort of thing. Besides, the trick is to win their confidence, and that can't be done if they feel you do not believe them. What you have to do is institute a healthy regime—proper food, cold showers, exercise—and make them feel regulated and safe. And while that is going on, you listen to them, and pick out holes and contradictions in their stories. Eventually, you present those to them and ask them to explain. With luck, that breaks down their belief."

"With luck? How often does it work?"

"Sometimes. But it can only be effective with those who are rationally insane. Raving lunatics, or those subject to catatonia, require other methods."

"And Signor—Casanova?"

"Perfectly coherent. In fact, it will be a pleasure to treat him. I am looking forward to it. He is an excellent storyteller, highly entertaining and, so far, I have not spotted a single flaw in what he has said. He has given us no clues at all about who he really is."

"Apart from telling you his age and name."

"Apart from that. But if you grant that, then everything else so far follows perfectly logically."

"Have you asked him about Cort?"

He shook his head. "Not yet. You may do so, if you wish. If you want to meet him."

"Have you asked Cort about him?"

"No. He is too delicate at the moment; but clearly he will benefit from knowing that his hallucinations are nothing of the sort."

"This man is not dangerous?"

"Not in the slightest. A charming old fellow. And he couldn't hurt you even if he wanted to. He is quite frail."

"Does he speak anything but Venetian?"

"Oh, yes. Casanova was quite a linguist, and still is, if I may put it like that. He speaks perfect Italian, good French and English."

"Then I will meet him. I don't know why I want to. But it will be a curious experience."

"I will take you to him myself. But, please, do not say anything to suggest you do not believe him. That is most important."

He led me out into the courtyard, and past a group of buildings that contained the inmates. "This is for the nonviolent ones," he said as we strolled in the warmth. "The more difficult characters we keep in the block you can see over there. Alas, they get much less generous treatment; we don't have the money to do much for hopeless cases. There's no point, either. We can merely stop them harming themselves and others. In here."

It was quite a pleasant surprise; I had imagined something like a Piranesi print, or Hogarth at his most despondent, but the room was light and airy, simply furnished and comfortable. Only the shadow of a large cross on the wall, where a crucifix had once hung, hinted at the building's previous purpose. There was one solitary person in it.

Signor Casanova—there was no other name to give him and in fact Marangoni never did find out who he was—was sitting in a corner, by a large window that looked out towards the Lido. He was reading a book, his head bowed, but was undoubtedly the man I had seen singing on the canal on my first night in Venice. Only the clothes were different; the hospital had taken away his old-fashioned costume, and clothed him in its drab, colourless uniform. It diminished him, that garb, made him seem less of a person. Certainly less disconcerting.

"Signor Casanova," Marangoni called. "A visitor for you."

"Please be seated, sir," he said, as though about to offer me a drink in his salon. "As you see, I am well able to pass some time with you."

"I'm glad of that," I replied, as courteously as he. Already I had entered a sort of dream world; only later did it seem strange that I talked with such respect to a man who was insane, penniless, without even a name of his own. He set the tone of the conversation; I followed him.

He waited for me to begin, smiling benignly at me as I sat down opposite him. "And how are you?" I asked.

"Very well, considering my circumstances," he replied. "I do not like being locked up, but it is hardly the first time. I was locked in the Doge's dungeons once and I escaped from there. I have no doubt I will leave here soon enough as well."

"Really? And this was?"

"In 1756," he said. "I was accused of occult knowledge and of spying. A strange combination, I thought. But then authorities have never liked things to be hidden from them. The only good knowledge is that which they, not other people, possess." He smiled sweetly at me.

"And were you guilty?"

"Oh, good heavens, yes! Of course. I had many contacts with foreigners, some of them in the highest positions. And my explorations into the world of the occult were well advanced, even then. It is why I am here now."

"I beg your pardon?"

"I am over one hundred and forty years old. And, as you see, still in remarkably good health. I only wish that I had finished my studies earlier; then I might have presented myself as a younger man. But still, all creatures prefer some sort of life to none at all. Nobody wishes to die. Do you?"

A strange remark, half statement, half query. "Why do you ask that?"

"Because you will. But you are still too young to realise it. One day, you will wake up and you will know. Then the rest of your life will be merely preparing for that moment. And you will spend your time trying to rectify your mistakes. The mistakes you are making now."

"What mistakes are those?"

He smiled elliptically. "The mistakes that will kill you, of course. I do not need to tell you what those are. You know them well enough yourself."

"I'm quite sure I do not."

He shrugged, uninterested.

"Why do you follow Mr. Cort?"

"Who is Mr. Cort?" he asked, puzzled.

"You know very well, I think. The young English architect. The palazzo."

"Oh, him. I do not follow him. He summons me. And is a very great nuisance, I must say. I do have better things to do than dance attendance on him."

"That is ridiculous," I said, a little angrily. "Of course he doesn't summon you."

"But he does," Casanova replied calmly. "He really does. He is a man with many conflicts. He wishes to know about this city, and impose himself on it. He wishes to be here and away. He loves a woman who is cruel and heartless, and who dreams of his ruin. All these things call me to him, as they called his mother to me when she lay on her deathbed. I know about love and cruelty, you see, in all their forms. And I am Venice. He wants to know me. And his desire summons me to him."

I could scarcely restrain myself from reacting to this nonsense, which he spoke so calmly. Casanova—you see, I call him that—sighed a little.

"I know about women, you know," he said. "Their natures. I can peer into their souls, see what lies beneath the professions of love, the lies, the demure sweetness. No other man in history has studied them as I have. I can see her thoughts. She thinks of hunting or being hunted. There is no kindness in her, and she sees only herself, never others."

"Be quiet," I ordered. "I order you to keep silent. You are mad."

"It is of no moment to me whether you believe me or not, you know," he said. "You will find out for yourself soon enough. I did not ask you to come here. My explorations into the occult caused me to drink in the soul of Venice, to become the city. Her spirit has extended my life. As long as Venice exists, so shall I, wandering her streets, remembering her glory. We will die together, she and I. And I see everything that happens here, even in small rooms rented for a month, or in a copse on the Lido."

"You are not wandering the streets now," I said with some savage satisfaction, deeply disturbed and shocked by what he was saying.

"No. For the time being I rest. And why should I wish to escape?" He smiled, and looked around him with amusement flickering on his face. "The good doctor, it seems, is fully wedded to the best notions of gentleness for his poor inmates. I am fed well, and have to do little in return for my board and lodging, save allow myself to be measured and photographed, and to answer questions about my life. Which I have not yet decided how to do."

"What does that mean?"

"They are most interesting questions," he continued by way of explanation. "They are trying to discover contradictions, impossibilities in what I say. It is excellent fun, for they go off to read my memoirs, then come back to quiz me about them. But I wrote them! Of course I know the answers better than they do. Every truth and every little fib I put in. The question is, do I tell the truth, or do I give them what they want? They so greatly desire to prove I am insane, and not who I am, that I am dreadfully sorry to disappoint them. Perhaps I should drop a few hints and contradictions into my conversation so they can conclude I am someone else entirely? It would make them so happy and grateful, and I have always desired to please. What do you think?"

"I think you should tell the truth at all times."

"Pish, sir, you are a bore. I suppose you say your prayers every night, and ask God to make you virtuous. And you are a hypocrite. You lie all the time, except you do not even realise you are doing it. Goodness! This is a dull time to be living."

He leaned forward, so that his face was close to mine.

"What are you in your dreams, when no one is there? What do you do in this city, which you have persuaded yourself is just a dream? How many people are you lying to now?"

I glared at him, and he chuckled. "You forget, my friend, that I am in your dreams as well."

"I don't know what you mean," I said stiffly. I found that I could not answer him properly.

"Standing by a window? You don't understand it. Why didn't you turn and ask me? I could have answered, you know. I was there, you know I was. I could have told you everything."

"How do you know about that?"

"I told you, I see everything."

"That was just a dream."

He shook his head. "There are no such things as dreams. Do you want to know more? Ask, if you wish. I can save you, but you must ask. Otherwise you will cause terrible hurt to others."

"No," I said, abruptly enough for my fear to shine through all too obviously.

He nodded his head and smiled gently. "You may change your mind," he replied softly. "And thanks to the good doctor, you will know where to find me, for the time being. But you must hurry; I will not be here for long."

I rose and left without another word. He, meanwhile, sat on his little chair and picked up a book. When I closed the door I leaned with my back against it and closed my eyes.

"Not in a talking mood? Or did you think better of it?" It was Marangoni, standing exactly where I had left him.

"What? No; we talked for a long time."

"But you have only been in there a minute or two."

I stared at him.

He pointed at the clock. It was two minutes past three. I had been in that room for slightly more than a minute.

CHAPTER 15

That evening I had my first proper conversation with Arnsley Drennan. I had talked to him before, of course, but never alone, and he never said very much. He was a strange man; he seemed to need no one, but would frequently dine with us. Perhaps even his self-sufficiency needed a rest, on occasion. He was the obvious choice for me at that moment; I needed quite badly to talk to someone normal, rational and calm, who could point out that my afternoon with Signor Casanova had been all complete nonsense. Drennan, who gave off an air of solid good sense, could be relied on not to gossip about it afterwards.

I hadn't planned a conversation with him; it came about by chance, as he and I were the only two people to show up for dinner that night. Longman had one of his rare reports to write as Consul; Cort, fortunately, hardly ever came nowadays; Macintyre and Marangoni were also absent. We ate our fish—Macintyre was correct there, it always was fish and I was starting to get a little tired of it—more or less in silence, then he suggested a coffee down the road in more salubrious surroundings.

"Have you seen Cort recently?" I asked. "I haven't seen him for some time . . ."

"I ran into him yesterday, poor man. He's in a bad way; he really should go back to England. It would be quite easy for him to do so. But I am afraid he is quite obsessed now. He sees it as a matter of honour to finish this job of his."

Then bit by bit, as we drank more brandy, I told him about Signor Casanova. He was interested; or at least, I think he was. Drennan was one of those men whose expression never changed very much. But he listened quietly and attentively.

"I can't say I know much about madness," he said. "I have come across men driven mad by fear, or by horror, but that is a different sort of insanity."

"How so?"

"Modern warfare," he said. "As you may have guessed already, I was a soldier. I saw many things I did not wish to see, and which will be hard to forget."

"You fought for the Confederates?"

"Yes. And we lost." He shrugged to dismiss the subject from his mind.

"So you are an exile? A strange place to choose, if I may say so."

He glanced at me, then smiled slightly. "So it would be, if that was why I was here. Well," he continued, "maybe I should tell you. Why not? It is all history now. Have you heard of the *Alabama*?"

I looked at him. "The warship? Of course I've heard of it. . . . Does this have anything to do with Macintyre?"

It was his turn to look surprised. "How do you know that?"

"I made enquiries."

"I'm impressed. Truly I am. What else do you know about Mr. Macintyre?"

"That he is not wanted back in England at the moment."

He stared at me in astonishment, the first time I had ever seen any sort of strong emotion pass on his face. I felt quite pleased with myself.

"And who else knows of this?"

"In Venice, you mean? No one. Signor Ambrosian of the Banca di Santo Spirito seems to think he is here because he stole a lot of money. Why do you ask?"

"Because it is my job to protect him."

"From whom?"

"Yankee lawyers, mainly. He is the living proof of Laird's culpability. Great Britain maintains that the conversion of the *Alabama* was entirely out of its control. Everyone knows this is a fiction, but it will hold as long as there is no proof. Macintyre is that proof, and there are many people who would dearly like a conversation with him. And, I suspect, would pay high for the opportunity. He was paid off and told to lie low until the matter was settled. And I was hired to make sure that he does. Which is why I am here."

"Who hired you?"

"Well, that I cannot say. Your Government, Laird's, Lloyd's of London.

Should this lawsuit go badly it would cost a great deal in money and reputation. So as I was out of a job at the time . . ."

"What do you mean?"

He shrugged. "I have no country, and do not wish to live amongst my conquerors. And I am—or was—a soldier. What should I do? Herd cows in Texas for the rest of my life? No; when all was lost, I came to England to seek work. This is what I found. It is not the best of jobs, but it will do for the moment."

"I see. You are a most interesting man, Mr. Drennan."

"No. But I have had an interesting life. If you can call it that."

"And Macintyre cannot go back to England?"

"Not until this is settled. I wanted him to go to Greece, change his name, but this is as far as he would travel."

"You can be assured that I—and my friend in London—will be absolutely discreet on the subject."

"Thank you."

"And he doesn't want to leave Venice?"

"Not yet."

"And if he decides to go back to England?"

"Then it will be my job to stop him."

"How?"

Drennan shrugged. "I will worry about that when it happens. At the moment, he seems perfectly happy here. Which is a pleasant change from the Corts."

"A disturbed man," I observed.

"Yes. But if I was married to a woman like that, so would I be."

"I beg your pardon?" It was offensive, gratuitously so. But I looked at him and he stared evenly back. He knew exactly what he was saying; was saying it deliberately.

"I went on a boat ride with her; she invited me. We went to the Lido, although I wanted to tour the inner lagoon. I found her behaviour unfortunate."

"Did you?"

"I did. And now it is time for me to leave. As you know, I have a half-hour walk back to my lodging. Good evening to you."

When I left him I walked over to Macintyre's workshop; I could have got there much faster had I hurried, but I had much to think about. Drennan had very carefully given me a warning. From someone like Longman or Marangoni, I would have dismissed it out of hand as the remarks of a vulgarian, but Drennan I took seriously. He was not a man to gossip or to invent stories. What he said could not possibly be true, I was sure of that, but I wondered what his reasoning was. There was no obvious answer. But there were other questions now welling up in my mind as well.

I found Bartoli alone in the workshed, and greeted him. We talked for a while, and I expressed an entirely false disappointment that Macintyre wasn't there.

"He's gone to feed his daughter," Bartoli said, speaking English in a thick accent.

"You speak well," I replied. "When did you learn?"

"Here and there," he said. "I lived in England for a while, and then met Mr. Macintyre in Toulon. I learned much from him."

"It is unusual, isn't it? To travel like that? Why did you do it?"

He shrugged. "I wanted to learn," he said. "And there is not much chance of that here."

"You are Venetian?"

"No," he said scornfully. "I come from Padua. I hate it here."

"Why is that?"

"They are lazy. All they want to do is live, and die."

He spoke in short, sharp sentences; he said what he wanted to, then stopped. There was no ornament about his words, which was refreshing although slightly disconcerting.

"Is this second test going to work as well as the first?" I asked abruptly.

"Of course. Why do you ask?"

"Because Mr. Macintyre has asked me to look at his books. The money. And they are in a bad state. I am worried for him."

He nodded. "I, also," he said. "Very worried. He is a good man. A fine engineer. But he is not very sensible. You know what I mean?"

"I do. And he is in a very dangerous position. You too, I suppose, as your job depends on this."

He shrugged. "There are other jobs. But I want Mr. Macintyre to be successful. He would die of disappointment. It will be a success. It will work as well at the next test as it did at the first. I am sure of it."

"That's unfortunate," I said quietly.

Bartoli looked at me. "Why do you say that?"

I took a deep breath. "I will tell you," I said. "But you must give me your word you will say nothing to anyone else."

"I do."

"Good. Then listen carefully. Mr. Macintyre has borrowed money foolishly. If this machine of his fails next week, then he will get no more. He will be bankrupt. He will not be able to continue his work here. You understand?"

"I know this."

"But it will be even worse if it succeeds. He sold the patent for the machine as part of the loan agreement. I don't know if he was aware of what he was doing, but that is the truth. He is busy trying to build something which no longer belongs to him. If the machine works, he will not see a penny of profit. Do you understand?"

Bartoli nodded slowly.

"If the machine fails, it will be unfortunate. If it succeeds, it will be a disaster."

Bartoli shook his head. "Ah, Mr. Stone, what foolishness this is! We must help him. Poor man, he is too innocent for such people."

"I agree. Unfortunately, he is also too straightforward to get out of this mess. He would never stoop to anything underhand or deceitful, however justified it may be."

Bartoli looked quizzically at me. "What do you mean?"

"The situation can be retrieved," I said quietly.

"How?"

"I am prepared to pay off his loans and buy the patent. But if the test succeeds there is not a chance they will wish to sell. Mr. Macintyre's only hope is that it fail. Then I can approach the creditors and safeguard his invention. But, I repeat, only if the test fails, and I imagine Mr. Macintyre is determined it should succeed. He is a proud and foolish man."

Bartoli nodded, evidently thinking hard. "Are you sure of all this?"

I nodded.

"The question is how to save him."

"That's simple," I said bluntly.

"How?"

"The torpedo must fail the test."

Bartoli looked at me in total silence.

"I am going to visit the bankers tomorrow about another matter. I will repeat my offer to buy his debts, but make it seem that I know nothing of the test. They will refuse to sell, of course. But if it fails, they will contact me swiftly, hoping to get their money back from a foolish Englishman who does not know he is buying a heap of scrap metal."

"And you will look after Mr. Macintyre? Do you promise me that?"

"I could hardly build the machines myself. I know nothing about engineering. He will make the machines, I will look after the money. He might not choose such a solution, but I'm afraid he must be saved from himself."

Bartoli nodded. "I must get back to work," he said quietly.

I left him. I had won, I thought. But only time would tell.

The procedure was exactly the same as the previous week; except that this time, the torpedo was handled as though it was made of the purest and most expensive porcelain. It was important that I was nowhere around, but I went down to the workshop to see the preliminaries from a distance, and to assure myself that all the arrangements were made.

There was no need to have done so; Bartoli nodded at me as I approached, as if to say—don't worry; all will be well. So I retreated rapidly when I saw Ambrosian and two others—presumably people from the bank—walk up and view the scene for themselves. As the boat pulled away from the side of the canal, I could see Macintyre, in a high state of excitement, stroking the sleek side of the torpedo lovingly, pointing at this part or that. Very faintly I heard his voice, unusually animated, as he described in great detail how his torpedo worked, what it would do, its revolutionary potential. I knew that, once in such a mood, he could probably carry on without a break for hours, and I rather pitied the Venetians' ears.

Then they were gone, and there was nothing for me to do except go to my rendezvous with Louise, which I had fixed for eleven o'clock that morning. I was in a state of some nervous excitement myself, and she picked up my mood; we said hardly a word for the next hour, but devoured each other as though it was to be our last meal. At the end we lay on the bed intertwined, until I remembered Macintyre.

"Don't go," she said. "Stay with me."

"Very important business," I said. "I need to go and see Macintyre. It's a big day. But tell me, before I go, tell me some news."

She shook her head. "There is nothing good I can say that will please you."

"Why? What's the matter?"

"It is my husband. He is worse and worse. Even more violent than you, but not to give me pleasure, as you do."

"He doesn't seem like that at all."

"Do you doubt me? Think I am a liar?"

"Of course not. I was only saying . . ."

"You've seen the marks, the wounds? If he broke my leg, blackened my eye, would you feel happier? It's only a matter of time, you know. I'm sure you'll be satisfied eventually."

"That is not what I meant."

"You do not know him," she said, furious now. "I am afraid, terribly afraid what he might do when one of his attacks comes on him. If only I could run away somewhere! But that will never be. I know that now. There will be no escape for me."

I sat down on the bed once more and took her in my arms. She nestled her head against my neck, and stroked my hair. "Just being with you gives me courage," she said softly. "But it fades when you're not there. I dream of being with you all the time, you know. The moment I met you I knew you were all I wanted; all I ever wanted in the world. But you don't feel the same for me, I know."

"I do," I replied. "I do."

"Then we must be!" she cried, looking me in the eyes. "Somehow, we must be! It is our fate, I know it. Please tell me you will do this! Tell me now!"

"I cannot. You know I cannot."

"You will not."

"You will leave your husband, your life . . . ?"

"It is no life," she said scornfully. "What sort of life is it, do you think, living in a hovel with a screaming child and a man like that? What sort of life is that, in comparison to what we could have together, just you and me, alone?"

"It is easy to suggest when you are here, in Venice, away from the judgment of society," I said. "You might think you had made a poor bargain once you returned to England."

"You are thinking of yourself," she said bitterly. "You are happy to meet me here, in this little room, as long as no one knows. But I am not worth a single disapproving glance from society. You take everything you want, and I give it. I am happy to give it; I would die for you. Very well; I will be only your whore, to give you your pleasure as you want, when you want. That is enough for me; it gives me the only pleasure I have in the world. I want nothing you will not give me."

She fell silent and I said nothing.

"Tell me you will take me from him, forever. Tell me now."

Another long silence, then I said, "No."

I remember it well; there was a total silence, broken only by the sound of people, faintly heard, pushing barrows in the street below. She had been lying on the bed, I next to her. Suddenly there was a distance between us; she curled away, and I sat up, and the gap became immense and unbridgeable.

"You are like the others," she said, softly but coldly. "You want to get rid of me, you've found your excuses. I've felt it growing in you; I've been expecting it, just wondering what reasons you were going to give yourself. Why not just say it directly? Why pretend it is for my good?"

"What others? Drennan, for example?" I asked, still remarkably calm. She laughed.

"Why are you laughing?"

She shrugged.

"Did you give your husband opium the night of the séance? Prepare the Marchesa by giving her information you knew would come out in her trance?"

A little smile of satisfaction, but no answer.

I expected some story I could believe, something that reassured me and made me think I had been foolish ever to doubt her. But she gave me nothing.

"You want to leave me," she said. "I know you do. Why not just say so? Holiday over, so back to your little wife in England?"

She stopped, looked at me for a second, then said, coyly and softly: "Don't you think she deserves to know how you've been spending your time?"

"What did you say?"

"Dear Mrs. Stone, I was your husband's mistress until he became bored with me. He seduced me on a beach while you were sitting at home. I'm . . ."

"Be quiet!"

"You don't really think you can leave me here and go back to England as if this never happened? Do you really think that? I will never leave you. I will follow you to your dying day. Are you ashamed? I'm not. I don't care who knows about you, or what they think of me."

"I said, enough!"

"Why? Whatever's the matter? Are you upset? Oh!" she said in mock sympathy, "you feel deceived! How sad! I'd forgotten. You're the only one who can deceive people, and tell lies."

"I think I should leave. It would be better if I did not see you again."

"For you, perhaps. Not for me."

I walked to the door and she began to pull on her clothes.

"Do you know what I'm going to do now?" she said with a smile.

"What?"

"I think it's time William knew the truth about everything, don't you? I'm looking forward to telling him about the time we made love while he was waiting outside. How you particularly enjoyed that. It might finish him off for good, don't you think? And once I'm free of the boy as well, it will be your turn." She looked at me with such a glance that I felt a shiver run down my spine.

"You will do nothing at all."

"And you are going to stop me . . . how exactly?"

I was silent.

"How much?"

She was the one who said it, not me. It was a mistake, a complete miscalculation. She brought everything back into an area I could understand. Until then she had been in charge, I merely responding.

"And what does that mean?"

"A word to my husband, a letter to your wife. How much?"

"And what do you suggest?"

"I think that £100 would be about right."

"A hundred pounds?"

"A year."

And then I laughed out loud. "Do you know, until you said that, a little bit of me still felt sorry for you? Do you really think I am going to keep you for the rest of your life? I have done nothing you have not done yourself. I owe you no more than you owe me. Let me tell you how much your silence is worth. Nothing. Not a penny. You will do nothing, and I will give you nothing in return. That is fair payment on both sides.

Otherwise you will regret having threatened me. More than anything, you will regret that."

She smiled. "We shall see."

I was shaking when I left, walking fast and trying to get away from that accursed room as quickly as possible. The change, from complicity to antagonism, love to hatred, had been so swift, so unforeseen, that I was trembling with shock. How could it have happened? How could I have been so mistaken? How could I have made such a terrible error? How did I not see more clearly, I, who prided myself on my judgement? It was a lesson for the future, but at that moment I was simply too stunned to think clearly.

What stuck most forcibly in my mind was her lack of emotion. Had she raged and screamed, behaved like some monster or hysteric, had she attacked me, or fallen on the floor sobbing, it would have been more understandable. But she behaved like a man of affairs; she'd done her best, it hadn't worked, it was time to cut her losses. She behaved like me, in fact; and it was I who was shocked, trembling, overcome with emotion. Only her clumsy attempt at blackmail had saved me. Had she said nothing at all, I might well have offered her something, but I have never liked to be threatened. That changed everything.

But I remembered the look in her eyes, her threats. Was she capable of carrying them out? I thought she was. In fact, I was certain of it. That did not bother me personally. At the most it would cause a temporary embarrassment—tiresome, no doubt, but nothing that could not be shrugged off soon enough. I had no fear of anything she might do to me.

Cort was another matter; and there I did not know what to do. I had justified my behaviour with the thought that his mistreatment of her had been so monstrous that his punishment was deserved. I had now seen another, dark side of her, one I did not wish to be close to. But those marks, those weals and bruises, had been real. Merely because I now recoiled from Louise did not mean I felt so much more sympathetic to her husband. Perhaps they deserved each other?

So I did nothing, and constructed good reasons for my passivity. I did not excuse myself, though; please do not think that. I did not blame anyone, say that it was the influence of Venice or of strange madmen, or the light or the sea which had forced me to behave in such a reckless fashion. It was I, and I alone, who was responsible, and I was very lucky

to have escaped so lightly. Had it not been for the hints and warnings of
Marangoni and Drennan—and of Signor Casanova, whose words had,
perhaps, the greatest effect of all—I could easily have been swept away
by the elation of passion, sworn to love her forever, taken her for my own.
Had I done so, I would have lived with my error, which soon enough
would have become clear, of that I was sure.

It took a long time to calm myself, walking through the back streets,
staring out over the lagoon, all sights which once pleased me, and I now
began to find humiliating. I was waking up from my reverie fast. It was
time to move; I wanted to leave Venice quickly. My dream world with
Louise—what I had thought she was, at least—and of Venice were the
same thing, and it was time to shake free of both. Neither had any more
power over my mind. This decision came over me quickly and unconsciously. From a state where I was not even considering the question a
short while previously, I began to think of packing my bags, making
arrangements to travel. It was time to be off.

Bartoli found me in a quiet, determined mood when he walked into
the café where we had agreed to meet, and it took an effort on my part to
pay proper attention to his story. But it did me good to do so; the more we
talked, the more Louise faded from my mind, became a problem to be
contained and managed, nothing more. He also needed attention, for
he was having very severe second thoughts about what he had just
done. Macintyre was distraught, half-crazed with disappointment, incon-
solable.

As he told it, all had been as before; the boat had sailed slowly out to
the northern part of the lagoon, where they could be fairly sure there
would be no prying eyes. The torpedo had been prepared and lowered
over the side once more. The only difference this time was that
Macintyre had very carefully removed a pin from the front end of the
torpedo and held it up for all to see.

"The safety pin," he had announced. "The torpedo is now armed,
with fifty-four pounds of guncotton ready to explode the moment this
projecting bolt is depressed by impact. The sort of impact you would get
if it hit the side of a ship."

Macintyre had tugged gently on a rope to line it up with the outline
of an old hulk, a fishing boat that had run ashore many years before and
been abandoned. He thought it would be a nice demonstration of his
invention's power if this could be reduced to matchwood. When all was

ready he took a deep breath, and pulled out the pin, which allowed the air from the pressurised tank to flow down the pipes into the small turbine which turned the propeller.

This is where Bartoli's interventions came into play. At first, all went well; the propeller whirred, the machine began to move. But it quickly became apparent that, instead of heading in a dead straight line towards the hulk, it was veering very sharply off to the right, and only at about two miles an hour, rising and falling in the water like a demented porpoise. Already, the bankers were exchanging glances, and Macintyre was looking distressed.

Worse was to come. For it became obvious—something Bartoli had not intended at all—that the machine was describing an erratic circle in the water, so that its course would bring it back, more or less, to where it had started. That it was going to hit the boat, with that much-advertised fifty-four pounds of guncotton ready to explode on impact.

Something like panic had set in, everyone trying to figure out where the machine would hit and get as far away from it as possible. Only Macintyre stood there, immediately above the likely spot, as it lurched towards them.

Then, the motor stopped. Instead of the supposed fourteen hundred yards range, it gurgled to a halt after little more than three hundred, which was just as well, as another five yards and it would have blown the boat, and all in it, to kingdom come. There was a moment's silence, then, with a loud and apologetic burp, it sank.

Fortunately, they were in a fairly deep part of the lagoon, as the torpedo went down headfirst and exploded the moment it touched the bottom. I had never witnessed such a thing, but apparently fifty-four pounds of explosive makes a tremendous bang. It must do, if it is enough to sink a battleship. There was a muffled roar, an eruption of water some forty feet high, a small tidal wave which almost turned the boat over, and everyone got soaked. The demonstration had come to its spectacular conclusion.

Macintyre's backers were unimpressed, to say the least. They had seen the machine fail completely, they had been soaked and frightened out of their wits. The journey back to Venice took place in total silence.

I looked at Bartoli as he finished. "What did you do to it?" I asked.

"Very little, really," he replied, in a tone which did little to disguise his feelings of guilt. "Just a turn of a screw here and a mismatched connection there. A bit of weighting to put the gyroscope out. Little things, of the sort Macintyre wouldn't notice."

"He certainly won't now," I said, "as it's in little pieces. What about the bankers?"

He shrugged. "They didn't say a word. Not even goodbye. They just marched off the boat when it docked and walked away. Macintyre tried to talk to them, say it worked fine, really. But they didn't want to hear his excuses. Listen, I have to go back to him. He is really upset and he's drinking. He could do something very foolish if he's not watched. Are you sure we did the right thing?"

"Absolutely sure," I said robustly. "I fully expect a letter from Ambrosian very soon. In their view, the only way to recover their money will be to persuade me to buy the debt before I realise that the machine is useless. News spreads fast in this city, so they will have to move quickly or it will be too late. If I hear something, I will let you know immediately. Meanwhile, go and find Macintyre, tell him not to despair, that all will be well. Tell him whatever you want, but cheer him up."

I was right. When I returned home, there was a letter awaiting me. In the florid, formal Italian normal for such letters, it informed the illustrious signore—me—that my proposal concerning the Macintyre project had now been put to the board, and had been decided upon favourably. If I wished to pursue the matter, then I should indicate that I wished to purchase the credit note.

There was also a handwritten note from Ambrosian accompanying this formal missive. He had worked hard on this matter on my behalf, he said, and had only persuaded the board to agree because one member was away. He was due to return tomorrow and would undoubtedly try to overturn the decision when he heard about it. If at all possible, then I should come and conclude the deal as quickly as possible, otherwise it would be too late.

I loved the audacity of the man, the smooth and reasonable way he managed to tell such enormous lies. A fine fellow indeed—astute, calculating, ruthless, mendacious; it cheered me up considerably.

I hurried back to the bank as swiftly as I could, then dallied a little, in order to make him a little more nervous. At six-twenty in the evening, just ten minutes before it was about to close, I presented myself and asked to see Signor Ambrosian.

You may think that I should have attended to other matters. Perhaps

I should have gone myself to tell Macintyre what was happening; should have gone to see Cort. I agree. I should have done both of these. And if I did not, it was not because I did not consider both of them. But I believed Bartoli could take care of Macintyre and as for Cort—what can I say? I was not yet ready to face him.

"I am so glad we can reach agreement on this matter," I said once I had sat down and accepted the offer of a glass of cold wine.

"As am I," he replied with a warm smile. "Although, as I said in my letter, it was not easy to accomplish. But I felt that really we did not want to get involved in the business of setting up factories. However excellent Mr. Macintyre's machine, any profits that might accrue become greatly postponed. And we Venetians no longer do this sort of thing; we prefer to leave it to the more enterprising English, and pursue lesser, short-term profits ourselves. It is no doubt why England has an empire and Venice has lost hers."

"That may be so. Certainly I think you do not have a ready supply of the necessary engineers, managers and skilled workers that would allow you to set up such an establishment here. Such people can be found more easily in England."

"You will manufacture there?"

"I think so. The most obvious customer is the Royal Navy. If it will buy, every other navy in the world will have to follow suit. And it is a patriotic organisation. They will not buy foreign wares if they can avoid it."

"In that case, I will watch your progress with the greatest interest," he said. "Now, perhaps we might get the business dealt with? Then I would be very happy to invite you to dinner."

"That is kind," I replied. "But I feel I should go and find Mr. Macintyre, and tell him the news. I was just about to go and see him this afternoon, in fact, when your letter arrived."

Ambrosian ordered a sheaf of papers on his desk, turned them round and proffered them to me. "Then you will no doubt have a great deal to discuss when you see him. Perhaps you wish to read this? I am assuming you can read Italian? If not, I will gladly call someone in to translate."

I said I could manage, and spent twenty minutes sipping my wine, and struggling through to make sure there was nothing untoward. The language was legal, but essentially clear, and why should there be any hidden catches? It was a deed of sale drawn up in a hurry, and the object was to get rid of a useless property as quickly and cleanly and as absolutely as possible.

"Yes," I said eventually. "Now, about the price . . ."

"I would have thought . . ." he began with a slight frown.

"I am evidently to buy £500 of debt. Now we have to agree at what price I shall acquire it."

Ambrosian positively beamed at me, and reached for the bottle of wine, pouring two more glasses before settling back in his seat. This, of course, was exactly what he wanted; nothing is more suspicious than someone prepared to pay a full price. Besides, where was the enjoyment in such a miserable, straightforward transaction?

"In view of the long-term risks, and the inevitable requirement to raise a large amount of additional capital, without which this machine is no use at all, to you or anyone else, I thought a small discount might be in order. To reflect the savings to your bank of divesting itself of this loan."

"But you yourself have said how much potential it has."

"And so it has. But at the moment it is without value. You do not wish to go further with it, and I suspect there is no one else in the world who would be prepared to buy it at any price. It is a question of discovering a fair rate for relieving your bank of an unwelcome burden . . ."

And off we went, for an hour of pure entertainment, which both of us appreciated and which I in particular needed. Here deception was open and understood, emotion under control. It was an antidote to my troubles and concerns. I suggested that a 50 per cent discount would be the very least I could possibly accept. He expressed surprise that I did not consider a price over and above the nominal sum, to reflect the risks that the bank had already absorbed. I countered that those risks were more than covered by interest payments already received . . .

But, all the way through, I knew he was thinking that the moment I talked to Macintyre, the value of his loan would go down to nothing immediately. Either he reached agreement with me soon, or he lost his entire investment. I gave him an extra £33 and we settled. For £283, I bought the sole and complete rights to the most important new weapon seen for a century.

It was a simpler world then: a gentleman's word—especially an English gentleman's word—was as good as gold, quite literally. For payment, I wrote out a brief note to my bankers in London, asking that £283 be paid into credit of the Banco di Santo Spirito's correspondent in the City. And that was payment made, for even if I turned out to be a charlatan, with not enough money in the bank to cover the amount, Coutts would have felt obliged to pay, and Ambrosian knew this quite well—although I had no doubt that he had already made enquiries about me. He placed all the documents into a large, thick folder, sealed it with a massive seal using prodigious quantities of wax, and handed it over to me, shaking my hand.

"My congratulations, dear sir," he said with a smile. "And may I say how greatly I admire your trust in your fellow countryman? I would not so readily take such a risk on something without knowing whether it would fulfil its inventor's promises."

"Oh, goodness, I've done that," I said as I paused at the door. "It worked splendidly last week. I gather it didn't perform so well today, but that is a matter easily fixed. No, I have no doubt the torpedo has a great future before it."

I bowed graciously, restrained myself from smiling in triumph, and left. To his credit, his face showed no anger at all; indeed, I think I even saw just a little twitch of appreciation.

CHAPTER 16

I thought it was time to put Macintyre out of his misery, and tell him that his future was assured, or as assured as I could make it. I had refined my calculations over the past few days, and what I planned was well within my financial capabilities, although I had no doubt I would have to call on friends such as Mr. Cardano for some support at various stages. I was excited; more excited than I had ever been, and it was a welcome distraction from Louise. The more I thought of torpedoes, of banks and factories, the less I thought about her.

My vision was becoming clearer by the minute. It was all very well passing my time as I had done in the past few years, but the buying and selling of shares and bonds is a secondhand operation, removed from the real source of wealth generation. And the prospect of organising an enterprise fascinated me. I did not, I should make it clear, intend to become the manager myself; I knew my limitations and the day-to-day operation of a factory would quickly have wearied me. But setting up the way the managers worked within an elegant, balanced, efficient structure of my own devising—this suffused me with pleasurable anticipation, made me look forward, not back. My eyes turned to England and stopped being dazzled by Adriatic light.

I was in a hurry now. This beautiful, ridiculous old relic was not where things got done, was not where money was made. It was a distraction only, a pause, a place where time was wasted, lives ruined. I needed to inform Macintyre, get the workshop packed up into crates, and the whole lot transported back to England. Somewhere on the south coast, I thought, near to water, which was obviously necessary for testing, not too far away from the great naval bases, close enough to a supply of skilled labour. And where land was cheap enough so that a large enough site could be acquired with ease.

So I was in a confident mood, although that did not last long; when I arrived once more at Macintyre's workshop it was dark and abandoned; I called out, rapped on the doors, listened for any sound, but there was nothing at all. Nor was he to be found in the little rooms that he and his daughter called home, a scruffy, decrepit building a few hundred yards away. Only the girl was there, all alone.

"Where is your father?"

She shook her head.

"Don't you know?"

"No. He's out. I don't know where."

"How long have you been here on your own?"

"All day." She said it defiantly, as though it was the most normal thing in the world.

"I need to find him quickly. I have some good news for him. Will you tell him? It's important. I have very good news for him."

She hesitated, and looked at me suspiciously. Some inward tussle was going on inside her tousled head.

"You do know where he is, don't you?"

She nodded.

"Inside?"

She nodded again.

"Please let me in. I won't say you told me." She frowned seriously, bit her lip, then stepped aside. The little sitting room and kitchen were filthy and smelled of old cooking and unwashed clothes. Dark and dingy, the furniture broken down. Poor child, I thought, to be brought up like that. She said nothing more, but simply looked at me seriously, disapproval on her face.

"Macintyre!" I called out. "Where are you? It's Stone. I need to talk to you."

There was a thump from the next room, as though something had fallen heavily onto the floor. And eventually Macintyre appeared. He was drunk; dead drunk, redder of face than usual, clothes awry, stumbling and leaning against the door to keep upright.

"Celebrating your good fortune?"

He didn't even manage to scowl.

"Are you able to talk?"

"Course I am," he said, and slowly walked to the table, and sat down heavily. "What do you want?"

"I've been talking to Bartoli. I've heard about the test. Is that the reason you are like this?"

He didn't answer. So I laid it out to him, simply and clearly, stopping and checking that he understood what I was saying. "So, you see," I concluded, "all is well. You are delivered from the hands of the Italian bankers, the torpedo is safe and, I would guess in about nine months, we will be in a position to begin production. All we have to do is get everything back to England."

I'd gone into too much detail. Somewhere along the way I had lost him. He stared at me, head low on his shoulders looking like a confused, dim-witted bullock. I could see his mouth moving as he tried to follow what I was saying. I don't know what he got from my little speech, but he didn't seem grateful.

"You did this behind my back?"

"My dear Macintyre," I cried in surprise and with some annoyance, "I would have told you, truly I would. But I was meeting Signor Ambrosian over quite a separate issue and the topic of your machine came up. I mentioned that I would greatly like to invest in it, and he turned me down point-blank. Out of the question, he told me. I did not mention it, because there was nothing to mention.

"And then, only this afternoon, I received a letter saying that he'd changed his mind. But that I had to make up my mind as swiftly as possible. I had to take a decision then and there, otherwise all would have been lost."

"You've stolen my invention from me."

"I've not stolen it from you. Because of your foolishness it wasn't yours anyway."

"Let me buy it back, then. If you're a man of honour. It's mine, you know it is. As long as I'm alive it will be mine."

"You don't have any money."

"I'll get some."

I shook my head. "No, you won't." I did not, fortunately, have to deal with what I would have done if he had been able to find some.

"And whose business will it be?" he asked sullenly. "What if I want to enter into partnership with someone else? What if I do not wish to have anything to do with you?"

"Then you will be free to do so," I said evenly, "if you can raise the money to buy back your patent. Then find a partner willing to work with you. And raise the money to finance production. But could you really think of someone better to work with? You are hopeless with money and you know it. Leave that to me."

"But you never told me." He had fixed on this; it was the one point which had penetrated the alcoholic haze and lodged in his mind.

"Well, I apologise for that, if it offends you. But do see reason. I am not forcing you to do anything. You can stay here in debt if you really want to. Except that the debt will be to me, not to Ambrosian. Do you have any objections to entering into a partnership with me?"

"Yes."

"What are they?"

"I don't want to."

"Why not?"

"Because you've cheated me."

It was hard to keep patience with him. Why he wasn't dancing up and down for joy was quite beyond me. Why could he not see how much this was to his advantage?

"Listen, Macintyre," I said, firmly and calmly, trying to impose myself on him. "You are drunk. In a moment I will leave you alone. When you are sober we can talk again. But bear this in mind before you drink yourself into an even greater stupor. I am in a position to put thousands of pounds behind this machine of yours. You will have the finest workshop in the world at your disposal. Your machine will be perfected and manufactured, without you having to bother with anything at all. All that I am offering you. If you think not consulting you is such a betrayal that you wish to turn my offer down, then you may do so. I do not need you. I can manufacture the torpedo without your help, and will do so, if necessary."

He let out a bellow of rage and charged at me, but was too drunk to cause me any harm. I stepped aside, and he fell heavily to the floor. His daughter ran into the room, shooting me a look of such concern and worry as I had never before seen on such a young face. I hesitated, feeling that at the very least I should assist her, even if I was not so very well disposed to the father at that moment, but she made it clear I was not wanted. She took her father's head in her arms, and began stroking it gently, reassuring him like a mother does an infant. Macintyre caught my eye. Go away, was what he meant. Leave me in peace. I did.

Not entirely though; I sent a message round to Longman, asking if his wife could do me the great favour of calling on the engineer to check all was well. I was not wanted, but that did not mean the child could cope on her own, and Mrs. Longman was a competent woman, the sort who could reassure a frightened child and coax a drunken, bitter man into resting. So I thought, at any rate.

And then I went back to my apartment, and slept. I was in a thoroughly bad mood; what should have been a day of triumph had turned out to be anything but, and I was furious that it had been ruined. I know: Macintyre was proud, he was disappointed, he was humiliated. He was an independent man, and I had taken that away from him, was presenting him with a fait accompli. Of course he was angry. I understood all that. But what did he want? Ruin? He would come round and accept that he was lucky to have me look after his interests, or he could drink himself to death. Those were the only real alternatives open to him. As I lay in bed, I couldn't really care which one he might choose.

I suppose I had wanted gratitude, thanks, a look of relief. That was naïve of me. You rarely get thanks in business for saving people from themselves.

CHAPTER 17

There was much to do the next day, and it started badly. Awaiting me, along with my morning coffee, were two letters. One was a long, tear-stained and emotional letter from Louise which gave me pause. She apologised wholeheartedly, blamed herself, begged for a second chance to explain everything. She was ashamed of what she had said. It was only her love for me, her fear of losing me, which had made her act the way she had. She had been happy for the first time in her life. She implored me to meet her and talk to her, if only so we could say farewell as friends. Could I bring myself? If so, she would be waiting at Cort's palazzo at eleven. She didn't want to go to our apartment anymore; she couldn't face it. But the palazzo would be empty. We could talk there.

I almost crumpled the letter up and threw it into the fireplace, dismissing it and the writer from my mind. But my better side won out. I did owe her that, at least, otherwise everything would be tarnished by a few last, bitter words. I had no intention of revising my decision, but it would be mean and cruel not to give in to her request. She deserved that. I would go. And that would be the end of it.

Thus my decision, until I picked up the second letter. It was from Cardano.

"My dear Stone," the letter began,

> After my letter about Macintyre, I write again with some more information, trivial no doubt, but as I have managed to find out no more for you, this is the only additional news I can provide.
>
> A day or so after the Laird's meeting, I dined with John Delane, the editor of *The Times,* and was sitting next to Mrs. Jane Nevison, a charming lady and the wife of one of his correspondents. A very pleasant woman who, as is usual, valiantly tried to pretend some interest in matters financial to keep the conversation going. I, in turn, cast around for something to say which might engage her interest.
>
> So I began to tell her about your sojourn in Venice—she had mentioned wishing to visit the city—and your impressions of the place. I mentioned that some people were actually buying

property there, and referred to the Albemarles and your friend whom they had employed to restore it. I had hardly got started, however, when her face darkened, and her voice became quite icy.

Did she know this Mr. Cort? I asked when I saw her reaction. I added that you had a positive impression of the man. She said she did not, but had once employed the woman whom he married. It was quite a story and I pass it on to you unadorned. When she was engaged as a governess, Miss Louise Charlton, she said, had seemed meek and obedient, kindly and thoughtful to their two children. They admired her for her fortitude, as her previous employer had abused her terribly; she even showed them red weals on her forearm made with a rope, which he had inflicted when she said she was leaving the post.

What happened, however, is that very slowly a contented household descended into malevolent backbiting. Wife and husband fought because this woman dropped remarks about what one had said about the other. The children, previously devoted to each other, began to be jealous. They could not understand this, until it became clear that their devoted governess had been telling one child that her parents did not love her, and preferred the other. She was also terribly cruel to them, but in a way which for a long time passed unnoticed. The boy was frightened of the dark and enclosed places, so he would be punished by being locked in a cupboard for hours if he displeased her; the girl was mocked, told she was ugly, that no one would ever love her. The children were terrified, and did not dare say anything to their parents. The parents, meanwhile, were worried that the children would be upset if they lost the governess they loved so much.

It all ended, apparently, because she began to make eyes at one of Nevison's young colleagues, and started telling him how cruel and abusive were her employers. How they beat her, half starved her . . . This was a mistake, as the young man was devoted to the family, and told them what she was saying. Then everything came out, and she was dismissed immediately. But she had lasted in the job for nearly a year, and it apparently took some time for them all to recover from the experience. The last

they heard was that she had ensnared this man Cort. How she
managed that Mrs. Nevison did not know, although she
suspected that elaborate tales of their brutality had some
influence on the matter. She said that, in her opinion, Cort
would regret his foolishness very rapidly.

A pity he had not written this earlier, I thought. I remember that my mood
was one of calm, of relief, even. I dismissed her from my mind forever,
folded the letters carefully and ate my breakfast, thinking instead of
Macintyre and his torpedo. When I was done, I prepared to go to his
workshop, where I fully intended to spend the entire day.

Then there was a knock on the door, and Longman walked in.

"You got my message?" I asked.

"Yes, I did. Mrs. Longman spent the night there, and was happy to
help. The poor girl. She is a very sweet child, really, and devoted to her
father. It's a great shame."

"And has Macintyre sobered up?"

"Yes, and gone to keep an appointment with Cort. How he managed
it considering how drunk he was I don't know. He must have the
constitution of an elephant. He wouldn't be stopped. He said he had
promised, that he kept his word even if others didn't. That's partly what
I've come to see you about, in fact. I'm afraid I've just had a very
distressing interview with Mr. Cort."

"Why?"

"I came across him this morning. Cort, that is. And he was in a very
bad way. He looked quite murderous, I've never seen him looking so
angry. He was really very offensive. I asked him how he was, you know
how you do . . ."

"Yes, yes," I said. "Please get on. I am a little preoccupied this
morning."

"Oh, indeed. Indeed. Well, you see, he snapped at me and told me to
leave him alone. He knew all about me, and I was lucky he didn't hit me,
there in the street. He was shouting, you know. Made quite a scene."

"What was it about?"

"I have no idea. I was too insulted to ask. I became very angry and
walked away, and he just stood in the middle of the street, screaming
abuse at my back. That I was a nasty, malevolent gossip, and much worse.
I can tell you, I was shocked by his behaviour."

He looked it too; merely recalling the incident made him shake and grow pale.

"He didn't even give a hint what he was talking about?"

"No. But he was particularly rude about you."

"Oh."

"He said that if he ever cast eyes on you again, he was going to kill you. So I thought I'd better warn you."

"Well, I'm sure he didn't mean it."

"I very much hope not. But he looked perfectly capable of it. We know he can be violent, and if you'd seen the look on his face . . ."

She'd done it, I knew it. She'd told him. It was all too easy to imagine how much she'd enjoyed it. I felt an overwhelming tide of guilt sweep over me at the thought of that poor, tormented man, and how I had not only increased his anguish, but enjoyed doing so, seen myself almost as meting out deserved punishment. I had been Louise's instrument, but I had become like her also. The realisation made me grow cold and numb; I tried to shake it off with a gratuitous, insulting concern for the man I had so wounded.

"You didn't try to stop him? Reason with him?"

"Of course I did! But he was completely deranged. If you'd seen him . . ."

"So you have said."

"He frightened me quite a bit, I don't mind telling you."

"Well, what do we do? I think we need to call on Dr. Marangoni again."

"I've done that! Of course, that was the first thing that came into my mind. I told him to meet us at the palazzo. I'm fairly certain that's where Cort was going."

"Really?"

"Yes. Perhaps we should go there as well. Will you accompany me? I also sent a message to Drennan. He's the sort who's good in a crisis. I think Cort might need to be restrained, stopped from doing himself harm."

And we left, as quickly as possible once I had prepared myself. I took a stout walking stick with me, I think because Longman had alarmed me with the thought of a murderous Cort. We walked through the rabbit warren of streets and passageways; I wish I could say we ran, but Longman was quite incapable of it. I was glad he was with me, even though his barely concealed pleasure at the possibility of some sort of scene irritated me. He had lived in Venice for years, and knew every street; for about the first time in my stay, I arrived at my destination without getting lost. Two workmen were standing outside the gate, which was closed. Drennan was also there, pushing against the door. He looked slightly concerned, which was alarming. Drennan never looked concerned about anything.

"What's going on?"

"I don't know. Apparently a few days ago Cort had asked Macintyre to come and help him knock down some pillar. Macintyre showed up about an hour ago and went inside. Some sort of argument started and Cort began screaming at him. Then he pushed all the workmen out and locked the doors."

"What was it about?"

"They didn't really understand it. But apparently Cort said something about people wanting to take his building as well."

"As well?"

Drennan shrugged. "Look."

He pointed at one of Cort's workmen, who had a reddening, swelling eye and a look of fury on his face.

"That was Cort?" I asked incredulously.

"So it appears. Macintyre went into the building, and Cort became quite deranged. Started screaming at the men, pushing them, and when one protested, he hit him. Then he picked up a sledgehammer and ran at them with it. Calling them all thieves and traitors. So they retreated, not surprisingly. But they're worried. They're good people, and they like him, even though they think he's a bit mad."

"Macintyre can look after himself, though," Longman said uncertainly.

"Maybe. But can Cort?" Drennan replied.

"Perhaps we should try shouting over the wall," Longman suggested.

And so we did, but it was no use. The entrance to the building was many yards back across the courtyard, the wall was high, the door thick. Had either Macintyre or Cort been outside, they would have heard. But not if they were inside.

Drennan and I looked at each other. "What do you think?"

Drennan shrugged. "I don't imagine anything really bad can happen.

I can't imagine Cort really picking a fight with Macintyre. He's half his size."

"There's several boxes of explosives in there, though," one of the men said. "The big Englishman brought them two days ago. We were told they were dangerous, and weren't allowed to go near them."

Then Drennan took charge. He talked to the men, and one of them turned and left. The other gestured for us both to follow him.

"He's got a boat. We can row round to the front of the palace on the canal, and see if we can get in through the main door. It's probably locked, though."

"What's the other one doing?"

"I sent him to get Marangoni to hurry up."

We walked down the alleyway to the canal, and in a few moments the little boat came along, rowed by one of the workmen, who looked remarkably placid, considering how agitated we were. He was a good rower and a taciturn one. He gestured to us to get in, then he rowed us, swiftly and silently, along a tiny inlet and then out into the canal which went past the main entrance of the palazzo.

I recognised it immediately; it was the building the old man had sung below; I could see the window, the place where the torch had flickered; I looked back and saw the bridge that I had been standing on. Under normal circumstances, I would have been impressed. Seen from water level, it seemed huge, four storeys high with complex Gothic windows on the main floor, neglected and imposing even in its decrepit state. Covered with stucco which had once been painted a rich red, but was now blotchy and with weeds growing out of the crevices in the brickwork. It loomed over you like some vast, polychrome monolith. The main door was large and covered in a heavy iron grille which, although rusting, was more than strong enough to keep us out. It would need specialist tools or an expert locksmith to open it.

Drennan pointed at a small hole in the side of the building, only about five feet high, the place where, once, supplies had been brought in. It was a dark, forbidding place, only just higher than our heads as we sat in the boat. The rower obediently dipped his oars into the water once more and propelled us towards it.

The ceiling of the corridor which ran along the left side of the house was dank and slimy, and the darkness was total until our eyes adjusted.

But we soon enough made out a little landing stage, over to the right. Beyond it there seemed to be the faintest outline of a door. We slipped and stumbled our way out of the boat, and onto the slimy stone, Drennan in the lead and me following. He got to the door first and fumbled for a latch. A clunking, scratching sound told me he'd found it. Then I heard him grunt, and the crack of old wood as he put his shoulder against the door and pushed.

A splinter of light. Dark by normal standards, but almost blinding to our eyes. And a great relief as well. We were in. Drennan led the way through, and I came after him, bumping into his back when he stopped to listen. It was all completely quiet. Not a sound could be heard, not even the water lapping against the landing behind us.

"Cort!" I shouted. "Macintyre? Where are you?"

No reply. Drennan started moving again, his feet on the stone floor making no noise at all, and I became preoccupied with the loud clatter of my boots as I followed. Drennan seemed to know what he was doing; he walked a few steps, then stopped, his head cocked, to listen. Then he walked a few more. After one longer pause, he turned to me and pointed. We crept quietly up a short stone staircase, into a huge room, which must have been about the same size as the great reception rooms on the floors above. There we came across a terrible sight.

Macintyre was lying on the ground, one arm above his head, blood trickling from a wound in the back of his skull. Not serious, perhaps; there was not much blood, but the blood had been enough to knock him unconscious. Cort was sitting on a rickety wooden chair beside him, a flame in one hand, chin resting on the other. In between was a column of masonry reaching perhaps fifteen feet into the air. And around it were half a dozen packages, with a long string coming out of the side, curled round into neat circles and lying on the floor.

"Cort," I called. "What the hell is going on here?"

He turned and looked at me. "Ah, Stone," he said in an entirely normal voice. "About time too. I've been waiting for you."

"What are you doing?"

He said nothing.

"What happened to Macintyre?"

"He tried to take over. Said I didn't know what I was doing. I've had enough of his patronising attitudes."

"Will you come outside? I think we should have a talk."

"I've nothing to say to you, Stone. I never want to talk to you again. I know what's been going on. Louise told me. How could you? How could you do that to such a sweet, kind woman?"

"Do what?"

"I know everything. You thought she'd be too ashamed to tell me. And she was, almost; she was in tears, crying her eyes out as she told me what you'd done to her."

"What are you talking about?"

"She showed me the bruises, the marks of the rope. Everything. Told me what you'd done to her. I should kill you for it. You're a monster. A beast even to think of doing something like that to a woman . . ."

"She's been telling you lies . . ."

"She said you would say that. But she told me about you, Stone. How you attacked her, raped her. The poor defenceless, sweet woman! And it's all my fault! If only I hadn't brought her here, been able to give her the sort of life she wanted. But it will be all right. I'll look after her now. I love her so much. From the moment I saw her, I loved her. I must look after her."

"Cort, don't be absurd," I said. "This is nonsense. She told me the same things about you. She's a liar, Cort. She says these things."

"Oh, Mr. Drennan!" Cort said, frighteningly conversational again. Drennan had been moving softly around the column as I talked. "Please stand where I can see you. Otherwise I will put this match into the gunpowder here. It will only take a moment to ignite it. Would you be so kind as to stand next to Mr. Stone?"

Drennan did as he was told.

"Listen, Cort," I said urgently and as calmly as I could manage. "It's not true, do you understand? It's not true. She does that to herself. I know she does. I've got proof, back at my rooms. Do you want to see it? No one has been beating her, whipping her, anything. She's been saying things like that for years. It's all invented."

"Who would invent a thing like that?" he snarled, reverting to his furious, demented state in an instant. "Are you saying my wife is a liar? Haven't you done enough already?"

"Look at me."

He did, suddenly, but only briefly, obedient. His eyes were glassy, wide open. And dark, as they had been on the night of the Marchesa's séance.

"Cort, you've taken opium."

"Of course I haven't."

"She gives it to you. What did she give you to drink or eat?"

"You're lying. I can always tell when someone is lying. He was lying too," he said, gesturing at the still immobile Macintyre. "He said he was only trying to help. 'Only trying to help. Only trying to help,'" he said in a high-pitched childish mimicry which bore no resemblance at all to the way Macintyre spoke.

"So you hit him."

He nodded.

"And these explosives," I continued, trying to keep his mind focused on the conversation, "who set those up?"

"Macintyre did. He brought them over a few days ago. Once they're prepared, the rest is quite straightforward; I just added the rest of the boxes, the ones he didn't use. I don't need help. I can do this job on my own. Wait and see."

"But Cort, you've used all of it. Far too much," Drennan said in alarm. "Listen, I know about explosives. There's enough there to blow up half of Venice."

"No, no. Just enough to bring down that column. Look, I'll show you."

His face cleared, and he smiled. And he leaned forward and lit the fuse, which began sputtering.

"Macintyre told me the fuse would last for about ninety seconds. Don't come any closer, mind. I can still set off the whole thing. I'll stay here to make sure it doesn't go out. Don't worry. I'll be quite safe. Macintyre will help."

"I'm not going without Macintyre. And you," Drennan said. I could hear that even he was now very worried.

"No." Cort moved nearer to the explosives, the flame now perilously close.

"What's the point of you killing yourself? How can you look after her if you die as well?"

"I'll be fine. Don't worry about me. I know what I'm doing. Then I'll take care of Stone."

I looked at Drennan. I didn't know what to do; I rather hoped he did. He'd been a soldier, hadn't he? I could see him looking carefully, his eyes darting from Cort to Macintyre to the explosives. Back again. Measuring, calculating. And I could see that he was giving up. We were about four yards away; too far a distance to grab Cort and bring him to the ground before he saw what we were doing. He only had to move his hand a couple of inches.

"About a minute left, I would guess," Cort said thoughtfully.

"Let us take Macintyre, just in case."

"Oh, no. He has to supervise. He insisted on it. He said he wouldn't trust me to pull a cork out of a bottle."

Drennan took hold of my arm. "Come on," he said quietly. "We have to get out of here."

"We can't. We have to do something."

"What do you suggest?"

"Macintyre is going to die."

"And so is Cort. And we will too unless you start moving."

I wish I had been more heroic. I wish I could have seen an opportunity to dash forward and grab Cort's arm. I wish I could have thought of something to say to bring Cort to his senses, or at least distract him for a moment and give Drennan a chance. I wish many things now, and that is enough to indicate that I managed none of them. Drennan had to drag me out, not because of my determination to stay, but because I had frozen, could not move. He dragged me to the door—about thirty-five seconds left—then pushed me down the steps. Only when I fell on the slippery floor did I come alive again, and the panic swept over me. I got up, stumbled—I remember it all—and then ran into the darkness, heedless of where I was going. Just following the sound of Drennan's feet.

We got back to the boat, Drennan screaming at the man we had left behind. Twenty seconds. Fell into it so hard that it almost capsized, the American reaching out at the same time to pull the painter loose and push the boat away from the side. Fifteen seconds. Began to row furiously, seeing the light of the day outside come closer and closer. Ten seconds. Got halfway into the normality of the canal outside, the boats laden with fruit, clothes, wood. People calling to each other, some singing. Five seconds. Then we were clear, but still heading across the canal, Drennan shouting like some lunatic at the other boats, telling them to get out of the way, keep their heads down. Two seconds. And I looked back and up, and saw Cort standing by the window, the one I had once seen open as an old man had sung below it. He rested his elbow on the sill, his chin on his hand. He looked content.

There was a tremendous explosion, followed by another and another as other charges ignited around the column. Masonry and plaster and roof tiles began flying through the air and the inside of the building was suddenly lit up by a bright red-and-orange light. Something like a tidal wave swept outwards across the canal; our boat capsized, and so did many others which were on our side of the palazzo. Fruit and vegetables and washing and people were flung into the water, and when I rose gasping to the surface and looked back, I could see that the entire roof and upper storeys of the building had vanished, the thin walls had collapsed like paper, falling inwards with a deafening noise, a huge cloud of dust rising above the scene, pushed upwards by the blast.

Drennan and I managed to get to our boat, which had spun round so completely it was now the right way up again, half full of water but floating. Then the masonry, flung into the air by the explosion, began crashing down into the canal like some bombardment. Enormous fountains of water erupted randomly; one boat was sunk by a piece of what looked like a chimney; windows were smashed and brickwork stoved in. People were screaming, running, lying on the ground with their heads in their hands. Our oarsman had swum for the far side, and I saw him dragging himself out of the water, pale-faced but apparently unharmed. Then I looked around. The water was littered with debris and people thrown out of the boats; men and women alike were panicking and were being rescued; I grabbed a woman who was sinking and got her to hang on to the side of our boat. Drennan and I tried to push her into it, but she was too fat, her clothes too heavy with water, and she started screaming and hitting us instead, so we stopped and began pushing her to the side. A crowd was gathering by the edge of the canal, some were jumping in to assist, others were just looking, open-mouthed at the catastrophe before them.

We said nothing; we were too out of breath, too much in shock, to say a word, but our boat eventually drifted close to the far side of the canal, and Drennan started kicking with his feet to finish the job. I helped, then we pulled ourselves round until we were within reach of outstretched arms, waiting to pull us out, and drop us on the warm stone, where we lay, panting furiously from terror and exhaustion.

Drennan recovered much faster than I, standing up shakily, and accepting a thick blanket to wrap around his shoulders. I took longer but eventually stood, my legs shaking so much I almost sank back to the ground again.

At least it didn't look as though any passersby had been hurt; they had been given a nasty shock and a soaking, that was the extent of it. But I knew there was no hope for the other two. Nothing could have survived that; anyone inside must surely have died.

Then Drennan touched my arm and pointed. A body was being dragged from the water, and people were shouting for assistance. It was Cort. He was mortally pale, and blood had soaked the sleeve of his black coat and matted his hair, but he seemed to be alive—at least those around him seemed to think so as they were shouting for a doctor to come as quickly as possible, laying him with touching gentleness on the ground, holding his hand.

"He must have been blown through the window," Drennan said softly.

"And Macintyre, you think?"

"No hope there. None." He said no more, but I knew he must be right. The engineer had been lying only about two feet from the main explosive charge. That alone, quite apart from the falling masonry and fire, would have killed him instantly.

"We will be questioned by the authorities," Drennan said quietly. "We need to decide what we will say."

"The truth, I imagine."

But Drennan nodded at Cort. "And what about him?"

I looked at Cort's poor white face and felt suddenly sick. I knelt back on the ground, and leaned my forehead on the stone, trying desperately to control the violent heaving of my stomach. I failed.

Drennan dragged me upright again and shook me violently. "Pull yourself together," he hissed in my ear. "We have to get away from here before the authorities arrive. We can go and talk to them later when we know what we're doing. Follow me quickly."

No one paid much attention to us as we disappeared into a little side alley, then hurried off. I took Drennan back to the Marchesa's, where I ordered hot water from the maidservant, and insisted that it be brought immediately. Faster than immediately. Then we went to my rooms, stripped off and wrapped ourselves in towels to wait. Neither of us said a word; I slumped in a chair, conscious only of the smell of rank mud that was in my nose and my hair and all over my body. Drennan paced up and down impatiently but was no more capable of speech than I. I poured two large tumblers of Italian brandy—harsh, unpleasant stuff but strong and effective, and we drank that instead. Then another, until the water arrived, and was poured into the tin bath by the servants.

Then we were done and dressed, Drennan looking slightly baggy in a borrowed suit, for he was smaller than I.

"Listen, Drennan, I have to tell you something."

"Go ahead."

"I do not think that what we witnessed today was Cort murdering Macintyre."

"No?"

"I believe we witnessed Louise Cort trying to murder her husband."

I sat down and told him, very meticulously and honestly, everything that had happened. He showed no surprise, indeed gave no reaction at all. I ended by handing him the letters which had been delivered that morning. He looked at them, and gave them back.

"I see. So you are afraid . . ."

"No. I am not afraid of her at the moment. I am afraid for the boy. The last time I spoke to her she said all she had to do was to free herself of her husband and the boy, then she would deal with me. I didn't take her seriously then, but now it worries me."

Drennan stood up. "Do you want me to go to his lodging and see?"

"If you're up to it, I would be very grateful. More grateful than I can say. I do not think my going would help."

"I think that is right."

He left, and I sent word for the Marchesa, to ask for a few moments of her time.

She heard me out impassively, then sighed sadly. "That poor man, of course I knew such a thing would happen. His aura . . ."

"Just stop this rubbish about spirits and auras," I snapped. "We haven't got time. Cort has killed a man. He might be insane, but if so, it was your ridiculous séance that set him off. How is that going to look when it gets round this city, eh?"

The spirits retreated whence they came as the Marchesa realised her peril. Scandal has killed as many people as knives and bullets.

"If it was just your reputation, then I wouldn't care too much. But Macintyre had a daughter. Cort has a son. And there is Cort as well, who is now likely to spend the rest of his life in an insane asylum, if he is lucky."

"Well, he must be packed off to England immediately," she said breezily. "As for the dreadful accident which claimed the life of poor Mr. Macintyre . . ."

"It wasn't an accident."

"The dreadful accident," she repeated. "Which happens when people play with explosives . . ."

"You cannot possibly think anyone will believe . . ."

"I think people believe the simplest explanation." She stood up. "I must talk to Signor Ambrosian. He is a friend, and is powerful enough to tell the police how to proceed."

"I don't want—"

"What you want is of no importance, Mr. Stone. You do not know this city, nor how it works. I do. And it sounds to me as if you have caused enough trouble already. You will leave it to me to arrange matters as I see fit. Go and rest, and do nothing until I get back."

I was left alone for the rest of the afternoon, until well in the evening. It was dark before the Marchesa got back. Under any other circumstances, I would have been taken aback by her sudden transformation from ethereal spiritualist to political manipulator, but nothing could surprise me anymore that day. Marangoni was with her. Cort was fine, he said. "He's some burns, cuts, bruises and a broken collarbone, but that's all. He was extraordinarily lucky.

"Physically, that is," he continued. "As for his mental state—well, that is another matter. I'm afraid he has had a total breakdown. Not unexpected, but unfortunate, nonetheless. Well, we shall see how he is in a few days' time. Luckily, he is in hospital, so he won't bump into his wife . . ."

"What do you mean?"

"She was brought to me a few hours ago. I am beginning to resent being used as a convenient way of hushing up English scandals, you know."

"Why?"

"For having set fire to her apartment block. With her child still in it. When they realised there was a blaze, all the occupants fled into the street in panic but no one thought to check Cort's apartment. Drennan did, when he arrived, and he was nearly too late. He kicked in the door—very bravely, I must say, as the fire was a bad one—scooped up the infant and ran down the stairs with it. The child has a burn on his left arm, and Drennan has a bad cut on his cheek from flying glass. Apart from that they are both fine. But many people's apartments and possessions have been destroyed. It's a bad mess."

At that moment I felt more grateful to Drennan than I could express. He had saved me, as well.

"What makes you think she started it?"

"She was seen doing it," he said, "and she was later found at the railway station about to board a train to Switzerland. She had all her money, clothes, jewellery and passport with her. Everything but her child and her husband, in fact. And her reaction when she was told her son had been saved from a fire was not that of a loving mother. When I also told her that both her husband and you had had a narrow escape her response was so violent she had to be restrained."

"So what happens to her?"

"That is out of my hands, of course. It will depend on what the authorities think appropriate."

"They will regard it as a terrible misfortune," the Marchesa said firmly.

"Will they?"

"Yes. You are a lucky man, Mr. Stone," she continued, turning her attention to me. "You have friends with influence. Signor Ambrosian was most concerned about your mishap and will interest himself in the matter. The explosion was indeed an accident, apparently caused by the carelessness of Mr. Macintyre. As for Mrs. Cort, she must be dealt with in a manner which causes no embarrassment."

"And that's it?"

"Well, there is, of course, the question of Mr. Macintyre's daughter, and Cort's son. There, I don't know. I suppose we must ask Mr. Longman what is to be done. That is his job."

St. James's Square,
London
15 March 1909

10 p.m.

Dear Cort,

You will find with this letter a bundle of papers which I wish
you to keep entirely confidential. It will explain my current
actions, as you, above all men, need to know. In the package you
will find all the relevant documents concerning the battleships,
and guidance as to how you should proceed over the coming
months. You will also find a memoir which, to my mind, is of
greater significance.

You will see from those pages how my rise to success began,
and it will also tell you of my involvement with your mother,
many long years ago. You will finally know the circumstances of
your father's breakdown and why you were abandoned. It was
my doing; your mother was a terrible woman, I say this frankly. I
have little sympathy for her. But if she was mad, then it was I
who drew out that madness, and turned it from petty cruelty
into something much more dangerous. Marangoni used to say
that the madness of the degenerate was latent, and needed
merely the right circumstances to awaken it. Perhaps so;
perhaps such fury builds up over the generations until it bursts
out like some festering sore. Perhaps I was merely the trigger,
not the underlying cause. I do not know. I do not excuse myself
with such arguments. Her punishment was harsh, but at the
time I regarded it as a relief, a satisfactory solution to a problem
which allowed me to forget all about it. I do not claim that I was
better than she. Merely more fortunate.

Your father broke down completely after these events, and never properly recovered. He was always of an excessively sensitive temper, and the duties placed on him in Venice were too great. He was an easy target for someone like Louise, who not only tormented him but enjoyed his suffering. Drennan accompanied him back to England, and I ensured that he never wanted for anything in the financial way. It was little enough to do. He was a kind, gentle man, who deserved better. I also made the necessary arrangements to allow Mr. and Mrs. Longman to look after Esther Macintyre, and continued paying her an allowance when she married.

I did this because I knew that, although my title to Macintyre's torpedo was perfectly legal, I had in reality all but stolen it by subterfuge. It was far more valuable than the sum I paid for it, and a more honest person would have admitted this fact and made greater amends. In my ambition, I did not make any such admission and I clung to a belief in my integrity, in the laws of business, instead. It is now time to give that illusion up. I have made provision for Signora Vincotti in my will, but I do not wish her to know the reason behind it.

Now I must proceed to more important matters, that is the other provision in my will, which I told you was merely to block undue inquisitiveness in case I died. That was not its origin, which lay more with a last conversation with your father just before he died. It was very important for him to see me that one last time, I do not know why. There was, I'm glad to say, no trace of the old bitterness in him, even though he was more than justified in hating me. Louise had told him she was going to have my child. She had told him this in their last conversation when her cruelty and taunting sent him mad with despair. It was her special way of goading him, a way to prove his weakness and failure, to demonstrate how completely I had taken her from him.

I did not take it seriously. She was a habitual liar, and prepared to say whatever she felt would have the greatest effect. But once he had told me, I could not let it rest. I began making enquiries.

It took a considerable time to get the asylum in Venice to respond, and I had to apply considerable pressure to break through the walls of confidentiality which surround such places. It would have been easy had Marangoni still been alive, but he died in 1889, at the age of only forty-eight. His files live on, however. He did as he was told, although with some resentment; Louise was declared insane, incarcerated without a hearing or charge, by administrative fiat. A simple solution to an awkward problem. As the Marchesa said, I had influential people on my side. Louise did not.

She was never released while he was alive, and was kept perpetually in that wing given over to the dangerous, the raving and the incurable. Such people are allowed no hearings and no appeal, and it sent her truly insane. But when he died, she won her freedom. She apparently gave no more sign of being dangerous, and the hospital was overcrowded. She never tried to contact me; I think she knew quite well what my response would have been had she done so.

Instead, she became a medium, Madame Boninska, and adopted what she remembered from the Marchesa as her only way of making a living. She travelled the Continent performing tricks of the far beyond, eking out a penurious living duping the foolish, mixing this in with a little blackmail and emotional torture. She was good at that. It was, if you like, her natural calling.

But there had been a child; for once she had told your father the truth, even though she did so out of cruelty and a desire to hurt. It was taken from her at birth, as is usual. She was never allowed to touch it or see it. Marangoni took care of everything. He knew her by then. He knew what she was capable of, and what being the child of such a creature might mean. It was tainted by bad blood, degenerate. The wrong circumstances could bring that out in the next generation and begin the cycle again. Only an entirely safe environment might counteract the tendency. Even then, I imagine, he was not hopeful.

So the child was hidden from its mother in the forests of

bureaucracy with no name and no identity, no birth certificate, nothing. And he destroyed all records of where it had gone. Adopted? By a family, one in a town nearby? The records were silent, I was told. His successors told me the truth; I could sense it from their letter; they did not have to deny me knowledge, and did not have to lie. They simply did not know.

But Louise looked. This was clear from the record; she had left the asylum and the notes had recorded her intentions. Not you; she never once asked about you in the twenty-three years she spent in that place. In her eyes, you were your father's child, not hers. But the other one, the one she gave birth to in the asylum, that one she wanted to find; that one was hers, she knew it; felt it in her blood.

As I had never heard from her again, I assumed she had not succeeded, or that the child was dead. But I found I wanted to know about this infant, my child, and she was the one person who might be able to tell me something. I became almost obsessive in a way that business never affected me. You know me there well enough; the greatest problems, the biggest projects, are things I take in my stride. Even disaster and failure make me lose no sleep.

This did; I became preoccupied, it played on my mind. Elizabeth saw it and worried, but I was too ashamed to tell her what concerned me. I know all about her life and what it was like, but she has never done a cruel thing. I did not want to acknowledge how much better a person she was than I.

So, all in secret, when I should have been concentrating on other things, I looked for Louise Cort, as my one chance of finding the truth. Eventually I got a lead from Germany, and instructed Xanthos to go and make sure it was really her; I would not go myself. The idea of seeing her once more frightened me. What did he say to her? What did she reply? I do not know; I have not seen him since; he always finds a reason to be out of the country, plotting away and thinking I am unaware of his ambitions.

But, whatever passed between them, it brought her to London and produced several whingeing letters asking for money. Threatening, hinting, but empty. She knew I wanted

something, that was all. She did not know what. A few days ago,
I went to see her, and again this afternoon.

She never knew the significance of what she told me. Any
feeling of sympathy or remorse for her evaporated on meeting
her again. She has spread nothing but cruelty in this world and
now she is my end as well. She will have her final triumph.
Mine is that she will never know what it was.

Oh, she was foul; rank, wheedling, disgusting. I could
hardly bear to talk to her; could not sit down in the same room.
"Why don't we talk over old times? You loved me once."

No; I didn't. I never did. Any more than she ever loved me.
She never knew the meaning of the word and, until I met
Elizabeth, neither did I. We deserved each other, I have no
doubt, but neither your father nor Macintyre deserved either of
us. They were better men than that.

She was too addled in her brain to know what I was asking;
could not put the pieces together. All she wanted was money;
she could have had it all, if she had given me a different answer.
She got the money, much good would it do her. Oh, her lovely
little child, so cruelly snatched from her mother's arms. But a
mother's love is insatiable, she tracked it down, almost, had
found the woman who had taken it away, persuaded her to talk.
Such a long way they had sent it, so she would never suspect.
She outwitted them, she was clever. But fate was cruel, she was
defeated again. It had gone by the time she got there, walked
out. It was working nearby, she went to see. The child had fled.
Oh, she looked, certainly she looked, a child in trouble needs a
mother's love. But not a sign or a trace was there ever again.

And there were only a few more questions left to ask. I
didn't expect the answers to be anything but banal,
uninteresting, a tidying up. I was perfectly calm, almost relaxed.
Just a bit of unfinished business before I could leave. I almost
didn't bother to ask at all.

Was it a boy or a girl?

A girl.

Where was this?

Lausanne.

What was the name of the family?

Stauffer.
And her name?
Elizabeth.

I was wrong. I thought that I had left Venice behind me when I
travelled back to England with Macintyre's machinery, but it has
been with me all my life. I have now made my preparations;
swiftly and inadequately, no doubt, but they will serve. I must
carry out my plans before I weaken, and I have a change of
heart. I am a coward physically, I know myself well. It will not
be easy to take the necessary steps, all too easy to find some
reason for changing my mind. But I must not weaken. This is
the only entirely satisfactory end. Many people will be
inconvenienced because of what I am about to do, but I do not
care. Elizabeth would suffer if I acted differently, and that I
could not bear.

I cannot remain with her. I cannot ever see her again, for
fear that I would confess the terrible truth that I learned this
afternoon. I cannot even say goodbye, nothing must suggest
anything other than an accident. She would work to find out the
truth. She is a very intelligent, determined woman, as you know.
Despite my efforts to protect her, she might succeed.

You must know this, Cort. You owe me nothing; had I acted
differently, your father might, perhaps, have held on to his frail
health long enough to be a proper parent. I do not apologise for
using you in the matter of Barings in Paris and I imagine you do
not expect such an apology. These things happen in politics and
in business. My only mistake there was assuming you were
sufficiently worldly-wise to expect it. Equally, I do not think that
watching you over the years pays off my debt to you in any way.
Had things been otherwise, you would not have needed me.

But you do owe a debt to Elizabeth. You took it on in Paris
when you were willing to sacrifice her for the sake of some gold.
You were her friend, she trusted you, and you betrayed her to
vent your anger at me. I did not understand it at the time, but I
fear the cruelty of your mother lives on in you. You enjoyed what
you did that night too much; I saw it in your eyes, and I know
that you have tried to justify yourself since by thinking that I,

too, was prepared to do the same, if necessary. That I had
Drennan acquire her diaries that I might use them myself. You
were wrong. Even then I would have allowed the entire Empire
to crumble to protect her. And you killed the man who saved
you from the flames.

The bill you incurred then is outstanding, and I am calling it
in. It is your only chance of throwing off forever that terrible
inheritance which lies within you. You must hide or destroy this
memoir of mine, ensure Louise Cort never grasps the truth, and
watch over your half-sister for the rest of your life, enduring her
hatred of you, never saying a word. Your father is part of you as
well; you will comply with my wishes.

I love Elizabeth more than anything else in my life. I would
gladly and willingly have given up every last penny I possessed
for her. She could have asked anything, and I would have done
it. She is my love. To see her sleep, to see her smile, to see the
way she rests her head on her hand as she sits reading on the
settee. That is all I have ever needed. This is my wife, and for
every moment of the past twenty years I have loved her as a
wife. She is the best person I have ever known; how that is I do
not understand. Perhaps the cruelty and malice of her parents
cancelled each other out, and by some miracle produced a
woman who has neither. I do not know. All I know is that I
would have laid down my life for her. Now I will.

My sins, the sins of Venice, have defiled the one person I
have loved, the woman I should have protected and nurtured. I
am married to my own daughter, the child I should have held in
my arms and loved as a father. Whom I should have brought up,
cherished, seen married, seen holding children in her arms.
Instead, I consigned her to a cruel childhood, and then a
terrible fate. I saw with my own eyes what I had done when I
was confronted with the hideous product of our union, but I did
not recognise it as such until now. It is too great to bear. I can
no longer live with her, and I cannot live without her.

As long as she knows nothing, she will miss me and regret
my passing, and will be able to build a new life, a happy one.
Her husband, who was getting on in years, tripped on a carpet
and fell from a window. Sad; he was a loving husband, but he

never liked heights. She will mourn and, I hope, forget. She is young enough to remarry, and will be wealthy beyond care. I had wished to grow old with her—older, I should say—and that is no longer possible. She will instead carry a fond memory of me, rather than the repelled loathing that she must feel if she knew the truth.

She has done nothing wrong in her entire life, except love me. You thought I did not know of her past. I knew nearly everything; but I could find out nothing about her origins. Her story began at that orphanage in Lausanne. There was no trace of the identity of her mother, or her father, no notion where she had been born or even when. I looked, but came up with nothing. She was an orphan and what did it matter who or what her parents were? I loved her too much to be bothered by her way of life, so why should matters so far beyond her control be of any importance? Why should I have connected her with the ravings of a monster in Venice years before, cajoling a man with a tale to bend him to her will?

In a few moments I will open the window that has been waiting for me for near half a century. I do not fear it. That old Venetian has been patient, and will wait a few moments longer. All those things of which I was so proud, which gave me such satisfaction, have fled from my mind as if they had never happened. All those businesses, those tangled connections of money, will unravel when I am dead. I leave it to you to salvage what you can, if you wish. In a few short years, everything I have done will fade and be forgotten, as I will be and deserve to be.

Very well. Let it be so.

WITH THANKS TO

Charlotte Bannister-Parker, Felicity Bryan, Véronique Cardi, Dan Franklin, Julie Grau, Kalypso Nikolaides, Lyndal Roper, Nick Stargardt, Karina Stern, Lucinda Stevens, Françoise Triffaux and, more than anyone and as usual, Ruth Harris.

ABOUT THE AUTHOR

IAIN PEARS was born in 1955. Educated at Wadham College, Oxford, he has worked as a journalist, an art historian, and a television consultant in England, France, Italy, and the United States. He is the author of the international best-seller *An Instance of the Fingerpost, The Dream of Scipio,* a series of highly praised detective novels, a book of art history, an opera libretto, and countless articles on artistic, financial, and historical subjects. He lives in Oxford, England.